READER'S DIGEST
SELECT EDITIONS

READER'S DIGEST
SELECT EDITIONS

www.readersdigest.co.uk

The Reader's Digest Association Limited
11 Westferry Circus Canary Wharf London E14 4HE

For information as to ownership of copyright in the material of this book, and acknowledgments, see last page.

Printed in Germany
ISBN 978 0 276 44285 8

SELECTED AND CONDENSED
BY READER'S DIGEST

THE READER'S DIGEST ASSOCIATION LIMITED, LONDON

CONTENTS

A scientist is found dead on the Mulholland Overlook in downtown Los Angeles, and forensic tests show that he had access to radioactive material. The authorities suspect terrorist involvement, so an LA Police Department team, headed by veteran investigator Harry Bosch, is thrown into a race against time to try to work out exactly what's going on before the city comes under possible attack. A fine new novel from one of the very best of today's crime writers.

It's 2003, and during the Iraq War a priceless treasure—an ancient clay tablet inscribed with cuneiform writing—is looted from the National Museum of Antiquities in Baghdad. The thief, a teenage boy, runs off into the night and the tablet is sold and soon forgotten. Years later, however, when Israeli-Palestinian peace talks are at a critical stage, the missing artefact—and the instructions it bears—turn out to be of crucial relevance to all sides. Gripping action drama from a rising star.

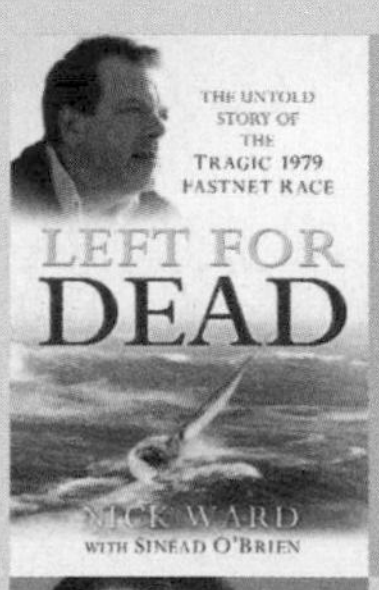

LEFT FOR DEAD

NICK WARD WITH SINÉAD O'BRIEN

331

There are not many true stories of dramatic events at sea that are as well told or as nail-bitingly tense as this one. From boyhood, Nick Ward dreamed of taking part in the yachting world's presitigious Fastnet Race, so when he was invited to join the team on *Grimalkin* in 1979 he was thrilled. But just hours into the race a force 12 storm hit, bringing terrible chaos and plunging *Grimalkin*'s six-man crew into radio silence and a desperate fight for survival.

When Cynthia Archer was a teenager, she woke up one morning to find that her parents and brother had vanished, leaving no note or clue as to where they'd gone. Twenty-five years later, she is still trying to make sense of it all when strange things start happening to her and her family.

Is she losing her mind, as some people think? Or is she on the verge of discovering what really took place all those years ago? There's a twist in the tail of this captivating story of long-buried secrets and obsessive love.

NO TIME FOR GOODBYE

LINWOOD BARCLAY

441

THE OVERLOOK

MICHAEL CONNELLY

When Detective Harry Bosch of the Los Angeles Police Department is called out to his first homicide in months, it has all the signs of being a tough one. For a start, he has a new young partner who objects to his maverick ways; worse, the FBI are determined to muscle in on his case. But by far his biggest headache is the uncompromising Special Agent Rachel Walling . . .

ONE

The call came at midnight. Harry Bosch was awake and sitting in the living room in the dark. He liked to think that he was doing this because it allowed him to hear the saxophone better. By masking one of the senses, he accentuated another.

But deep down, he knew the truth. He was waiting.

The call was from Larry Gandle, his supervisor in Homicide Special. It was Bosch's first call-out in the new job. And it was what he had been waiting for.

'Harry, you up?'

'I'm up.'

'Who's that you got playing?'

'Frank Morgan, live at the Jazz Standard in New York. That's George Cables you're hearing now on piano.'

'Good stuff. I hate to take you away from it.'

Bosch used the remote to turn the music off.

'What's the call, Lieutenant?'

'Hollywood want you and Iggy to come out and take over a case. They've already caught three today and can't handle a fourth. This one also looks like it might become a hobby. It looks like an execution.'

The Los Angeles Police Department had seventeen geographic divisions, each with its own station and detective bureau, including a homicide squad. But the divisional squads were the first line and couldn't get bogged down on long-running cases. When a murder came with any political, celebrity or media attachment, it was usually shuttled down to Homicide Special, which operated out of RHD—the Robbery-Homicide Division—in Parker Center. Any case that appeared to be particularly difficult and time-consuming—that would invariably stay active, like a hobby—would also be an immediate candidate for Homicide Special. This was one of those.

'Where is it?' Bosch asked.

'Up on that overlook above the Mulholland Dam. You know the place?'

'Yeah, I've been up there.' Bosch got up and walked to the dining-room table. He opened a drawer designed for silverware and took out a pen and a small notebook. On the first page of the notebook, he wrote down the date and the location of the murder scene. 'Any other details I should know?'

'Not a lot,' Gandle replied. 'Like I said, it was described to me as an execution. Two in the back of the head. Somebody took this guy up there and blew his brains out all over that pretty view.'

Bosch let this register a moment before asking the next question. 'Do they know who the dead guy is?'

'The divisionals are working on it. Maybe they'll have something by the time you get over there. It's practically in your neighbourhood, right?'

'Not too far.'

Gandle gave Bosch more specifics on the location of the crime scene and asked if Harry would make the next call out to his partner. Bosch said he would take care of it.

'OK, Harry, get up there and see what's what, then call me and let me know. Just wake me up. Everybody else does.'

Bosch thought it was just like a supervisor to complain about getting woken up to a person he would routinely wake up over the course of their relationship.

'You got it,' Bosch said.

He hung up and immediately called Ignacio Ferras, his new partner. They were still feeling their way. Ferras was more than twenty years younger and from another culture. The bonding would happen, Bosch was sure, but it would come slowly. It always did.

Ferras was awakened by Bosch's call but became alert quickly and seemed eager to respond, which was good. The only problem was that he lived all the way out in Diamond Bar, which would put his ETA at the crime scene at least an hour off. Bosch had talked to him about it the first day they had been assigned as partners, but Ferras wasn't interested in moving. He had a family support system in Diamond Bar and wanted to keep it.

Bosch knew that he would get there well ahead of Ferras, and that would mean handling any divisional friction on his own. Taking a case away from the divisional squad was always a delicate thing. It was a decision usually made by supervisors, not by the homicide detectives on the scene. No homicide detective worth the gold trim on his badge would ever want to give away a case. That just wasn't part of the mission.

'See you there, Ignacio,' Bosch said.

'Harry, I told you. Call me Iggy. Everybody does.'

Bosch said nothing. He didn't want to call him Iggy. He didn't think it was a name that matched the weight of the assignment and mission. He wished that his partner would come to that realisation and then stop asking him.

Bosch thought of something and added an instruction, telling Ferras to swing by Parker Center on his way in and pick up the city car they were assigned. It would add minutes to his arrival time, but Bosch planned to drive his own car to the scene, and he knew he was low on gas.

'OK, see you there,' Bosch said, leaving names out.

He hung up and grabbed his coat out of the closet by the front door. As he put his arms into it, he glanced at himself in the mirror on the inside of the door. At fifty-six years old, he was trim and fit and could even stand to add a few pounds, while other detectives his age were getting round in the middle. The grey had not yet chased all of the brown out of his hair, but it was getting close to victory. His dark eyes were clear and bright and ready for the challenge awaiting him at the overlook.

He reached across his body with his left hand to pull the gun out of the holster on his right hip. It was a Kimber Ultra Carry. He quickly checked the magazine and the action and then returned the weapon to its holster.

He was ready. He opened the door.

The lieutenant had not known a lot about the case, but he had been right about one thing: the crime scene was not far from Bosch's home. He dropped down to Cahuenga and then took Barham across the 101 Freeway. From there it was a quick run up Lake Hollywood Drive to a neighbourhood of homes clustered on the hills surrounding the reservoir and the Mulholland Dam. They were expensive homes.

Bosch worked his way round the fenced reservoir, stopping only for a moment when he came upon a coyote in the road. The animal's eyes caught the headlights and glowed brightly, almost daring him to do something. It was in no hurry to get out of the way. Then it turned and sauntered across the road. It reminded Bosch of his days on patrol, when he saw the same challenge in the eyes of most of the young men he encountered on the street.

After passing the reservoir, he took Tahoe Drive further up into the hills and then connected with the eastern terminus of Mulholland Drive. There was an unofficial overlook of the city here. It was posted with NO PARKING and OVERLOOK CLOSED AT DARK signs. But these were routinely ignored at all hours of the day and night.

Bosch pulled in behind the grouping of official vehicles—the forensics van and the coroner's wagon, as well as several marked and unmarked police cars. An outer perimeter of yellow police tape surrounded the crime scene, and inside this was a silver Porsche Carrera with its hood open. It had been sectioned off by more yellow tape, and this told Bosch that it was most likely the victim's car.

He parked and got out. A patrol officer assigned to the outer perimeter took down his name and badge number and allowed him under the yellow tape. He approached the crime scene. Portable lights had been erected on either side of the body, which was in the centre of a clearing that looked down upon the city. Forensics techs and coroner's people were working on and around the body, and a tech with a video camera was documenting the scene.

'Harry, over here.'

Bosch turned and saw Detective Jerry Edgar leaning against the hood of an unmarked detective cruiser, a cup of coffee in his hand. Edgar pushed himself off the car as Bosch came over.

Jerry Edgar had been his partner once, back when Bosch had worked in Hollywood Division. Back then Bosch was a team leader on the homicide squad. Now Edgar was in that position.

'Been waiting on somebody from RHD,' Edgar said. 'Didn't know it would be you, man. You working this solo?'

'No. My partner's on the way.'

'Your new partner, right? I haven't heard from you since that mess over in Echo Park last year.'

'Yeah. So what do you have here?'

Bosch didn't want to talk about Echo Park with Edgar—or with anyone, as a matter of fact. He wanted to stay focused on the case at hand. It was his first call-out since his transfer to Homicide Special. He knew there'd be a lot of people watching his moves. Some of them would be hoping he'd fail.

Edgar turned so that Bosch could see what was spread out on the trunk of the car. Bosch took out glasses and put them on as he leaned in close to look. There wasn't a lot of light but he could see an array of evidence bags.

The bags separately contained items taken from the body, including a wallet, a key ring and a clip-on name tag. There was also a money clip with a thick fold of currency, and a BlackBerry that was still on, its green light flashing and ready to transmit calls its owner would never make or receive.

'The coroner's guy just gave me all of this,' Edgar said. 'They should be done with the body in about ten minutes.'

Bosch picked up the bag containing the ID tag and angled it towards the light. It said SAINT AGATHA'S CLINIC FOR WOMEN. On it was a photograph of a man with dark hair and dark eyes, identified as Dr Stanley Kent. Bosch noticed that the ID tag was also a swipe key that could open locked doors.

'Why don't you run down what you've got, Jerry?' Bosch said.

'Happy to,' Edgar said. 'The stiff was found about an hour ago. As you can see from the signs out on the street, there's no parking up here and no loitering after dark. Hollywood always has a patrol swing by here a few times a night to chase looky-loos away. Keeps the rich locals up here happy. I am told that house over there is Madonna's. Or it was.'

He pointed to a sprawling mansion about a hundred yards from the clearing. The moonlight silhouetted a tower rising from the structure, which was on a promontory that afforded a magnificent, sweeping view of the city below. Bosch imagined the pop star up in the tower looking down on the city that lay at her command.

'The patrol car swings around about eleven and sees the Porsche with the hood open,' Edgar continued. 'Engine's in the back of those Porsches. It means the trunk was open.'

'Got it.'

'The patrol car pulls up. They don't see anybody in or around the Porsche, so the two officers get out. One of them walks out into the clearing and finds our guy. He's face down and has two in the back of the head. An execution, clean and simple.'

Bosch nodded at the ID tag in the evidence bag. 'And this is the guy, Stanley Kent?'

'Looks that way. The tag and the wallet both say he's Stanley Kent, forty-two years old, from just around the corner on Arrowhead Drive. We ran the plate on the Porsche and it comes back to a business called K and K Medical Physicists. I ran Kent through the box, and he came up pretty clean. He's got a few speeding tickets on the Porsche, but that's it.'

Bosch nodded as he registered all the information.

'You're going to get no grief from me, taking over this case, Harry,' Edgar said. 'I got one partner in court this month and I left my other one at the first scene we caught today—a three-bagger, with a fourth victim on life support at Queen of Angels.'

Bosch remembered that Hollywood ran its homicide squad in three-man teams instead of the traditional partnerships.

'Any chance the three-bagger is connected to this?'

'No. That's a straight gang shoot-'em-up,' Edgar said. 'I think this thing is a whole different ball game and I'm happy for you to take it.'

'Good,' Bosch said. 'I'll cut you loose as soon as I can. Anybody look in the car yet?'

'Not really. Waiting on you.'

'OK. Anybody go to the victim's house on Arrowhead?'

'No on that, too.'

'Anybody knock on any doors?'

'Not yet. We were working the scene first.'

Edgar obviously had decided early that the case would be passed to RHD. It bothered Bosch that nothing had been done, but at the same time he knew it would be his and Ferras's to work fresh from the start, and that wasn't a bad thing. There was a long history in the department of cases getting damaged or bungled while in transition from divisional to downtown detective teams.

Bosch looked at the lighted clearing and counted a total of five men working on or near the body for the forensics and coroner's teams.

'Well, since you're working the crime scene first, did anybody look for foot impressions around the body before you let the techs approach?' He couldn't keep the tone of annoyance out of his voice.

'Harry,' Edgar said, his tone now showing annoyance with Bosch's annoyance, 'a couple hundred people stand around on this overlook every day. We coulda been looking at footprints till Christmas if we'd wanted to take the time. I didn't think we did. We had a body lying out here in a public place and needed to get to it. Besides, it looks like a professional hit. That means the shoes, the gun, the car—everything's already long gone by now.'

Bosch nodded. He wanted to dismiss this and move on. 'OK,' he said evenly, 'then I guess you're clear.'

Edgar nodded and Bosch thought he might be embarrassed. 'Like I said, Harry, I didn't expect it to be you.'

Meaning he would not have dogged it for Harry, only for somebody else from RHD.

'Sure,' Bosch said. 'I understand.'

After Edgar left, Bosch went to his car and got the Maglite out of the trunk. He walked to the Porsche, put on gloves and opened the driver-side door. He leaned in and looked around. On the passenger seat was a briefcase. It was unlocked, and when he popped the snaps it opened to reveal several files, a calculator and various pads, pens and papers. He closed it and left it in its place. Its position on the seat told him that the victim had probably arrived at the overlook by himself. He had met his killer here. He had not brought his killer with him. This, Bosch thought, might be significant.

He opened the glove box next, and several more clip-on IDs like the one found on the body fell to the floor. He picked them up one by one and saw that each access badge had been issued by a different local hospital. But the swipe cards all bore the same name and photo: Stanley Kent.

On the back of several of the tags were handwritten notations. Bosch looked at these for a long moment. Most were numbers with the letters *L* or *R* at the end, and he concluded that they were lock combinations.

Inside the glove box he found even more IDs and access key cards. As far as he could tell, the dead man—if he was Stanley Kent—had clearance access to just about every hospital in Los Angeles County, and the combinations to security locks at most of them. Bosch briefly considered that the IDs and key cards might be counterfeits used in some sort of hospital scam.

He returned everything to the glove box and closed it. Then he looked under and between the seats and found nothing of interest. He backed out of the car and went to the open trunk.

The trunk was small and empty. But, in the beam of his flashlight, he noted four indentations in the carpet lining the bottom. It was clear that something square and heavy with four legs or wheels had been carried in the trunk. Because the trunk was found in the open position, it was likely that the object—whatever it was—had been taken during the killing.

'Detective?'

Bosch turned and put the beam of his light into the face of a patrolman. It was the officer who had taken his name and badge number at the perimeter. He lowered the light. 'What is it?'

'There's an FBI agent here. And she's asking permission to enter the crime scene.'

'Where is she?'

The officer led the way back to the yellow tape. As Bosch got close, he saw a woman standing next to the open door of a car. She was alone, and she wasn't smiling. Bosch felt the thud of uneasy recognition hit his chest.

'Hello, Harry,' she said when she saw him.

'Hello, Rachel,' he said.

TWO

It had been almost six months since he had seen Special Agent Rachel Walling of the Federal Bureau of Investigation. As he approached her at the tape, Bosch was sure that not a day had gone by in that time when he hadn't thought about her. He had never imagined, however, that they would be reunited—if they ever were reunited—in the middle of the night at a murder scene. She was dressed in jeans, an Oxford shirt and a dark blue blazer. Her dark hair was unkempt but she still looked beautiful. She obviously had been called in from home, just as Bosch had. She wasn't smiling, and Bosch was reminded of how badly things had ended the last time.

'Look,' he said, 'I know I've been ignoring you, but you didn't have to go to all the trouble of tracking me down at a crime scene just to—'

'It's not really a time for humour,' she said, cutting him off. 'If this is what I think it might be.'

They had last had contact on the Echo Park case. He had found her at the time working for a shadowy FBI unit called Tactical Intelligence. She had never explained what exactly the unit did, and Bosch had never pushed it, since it wasn't important to the Echo Park investigation. He had reached out to her because of her past tenure as a profiler—and their past personal history. The Echo Park case had gone sideways, and so had any chance for another romance. As Bosch looked at her now, he knew she was all business, and he had a feeling he was about to find out what the Tactical Intelligence Unit was all about.

'What is it you think it might be?' he asked.

'I'll tell you when I can tell you. Can I please see the scene?'

Reluctantly, Bosch lifted the crime-scene tape and returned her perfunctory attitude with his standard sarcasm. 'Come on in, then, Agent Walling,' he said. 'Why don't you just make yourself at home?'

She stepped under and stopped, at least respecting his right to lead her to his crime scene. 'I actually might be able to help you here,' she said. 'If I can see the body, I might be able to make a formal identification for you.' She held up a file that she had been carrying at her side.

'This way, then,' Bosch said.

He led her to the clearing, where the victim was cast in the sterilising fluorescent light from the mobile units. The dead man was lying on the orange dirt about five feet from the drop-off at the edge of the overlook. Beyond the body and over the edge, the moonlight reflected off the reservoir below. Past the dam the city spread out in a blanket of a million lights.

Bosch put out his arm to stop Walling at the edge of the light circle. The victim had been rolled over by the medical examiner and was now face up. There were abrasions on the dead man's face and forehead, but Bosch thought he could recognise the man in the photos on the hospital tags in the glove box. Stanley Kent. His shirt was open, exposing a hairless chest of pale white skin. There was an incision mark on one side of the torso where the medical examiner had pushed a temperature probe into the liver.

'Evening, Harry,' said Joe Felton, the medical examiner. 'Or I guess I should say, good morning. Who's your friend there? I thought they teamed you with Iggy Ferras.'

'I am with Ferras,' Bosch responded. 'This is Special Agent Walling from the FBI's Tactical Intelligence Unit.'

'Tactical Intelligence? What will they think of next?'

'I think it's one of those Homeland-Security-type operations. You know, don't ask, don't tell, that sort of thing. She says she might be able to confirm an ID for us.'

Walling gave Bosch a look that told him he was being juvenile.

'All right if we come in, Doc?' Bosch asked.

'Sure, Harry, we're pretty much squared away here.'

Bosch started to step forward, but Walling moved quickly in front of him and walked into the harsh light. Without hesitation, she took a position over the body. She opened the file and took out an eight-by-ten face shot. She bent down and held it next to the dead man's face. Bosch stepped in close at her side to make a comparison himself.

'It's him,' she said. 'Stanley Kent.'

Bosch nodded his agreement, then offered his hand to her so that she could step back over the body. She ignored it and did it without help.

Bosch looked down at Felton, who was squatting next to the body. 'So, Doc, you want to tell us what we've got here?' He stooped down on the other side of the body to get a better look.

'We've got a man who was brought here or came here for whatever reason and was made to get down on his knees.' Felton pointed to the victim's trousers. There were smudges of orange dirt on both knees. 'Then somebody shot him twice in the back of the head and he went down face first. The facial injuries you see came when he hit the ground. He was already dead by then.'

Bosch nodded.

'No exit wounds,' Felton added. 'Probably something small, like a twenty-two, with the ricochet effect inside the skull. Very efficient.'

Bosch realised now that Lieutenant Gandle had been speaking figuratively when he mentioned that the victim's brains had been blown across the view from the overlook. He would have to remember Gandle's tendency towards hyperbole in the future.

'Time of death?' he asked Felton.

'Going by the liver temp, I'd say four or five hours,' the medical examiner replied. 'Eight o'clock, give or take.'

That last part troubled Bosch. He knew that by eight it would have been dark and all the sunset worshippers would have been long gone. But the two shots would have echoed from the overlook and into the nearby houses. Yet no one had called the police§ and the body wasn't found until a patrol car happened by three hours later.

'I know what you're thinking,' Felton said. 'What about the sound? There is a possible explanation. Guys, let's roll him back over.'

Bosch stood up and stepped out of the way while Felton and one of his assistants turned the body over. Bosch glanced at Walling and for a moment their eyes locked, until she looked back down at the body.

Turning the body had exposed the bullet entry wounds in the back of the head. The victim's black hair was matted with blood. The back of his white shirt was spattered with a fine spray of a brown substance that immediately drew Bosch's attention.

'That's not blood, is it?'

'No, it's not,' Felton said. 'I think we'll find out from the lab that it's good old Coca-Cola syrup. The residue you might find in the bottom of an empty bottle or can.'

Before Bosch could respond, Walling did. 'An improvised silencer,' she said. 'You tape an empty plastic litre Coke bottle to the muzzle of the weapon, and the sound of the shot is significantly reduced as sound waves are projected into the bottle rather than the open air. If the bottle had a residue of Coke in it, the liquid would be spattered onto the target.'

Felton looked at Bosch and nodded approvingly. 'Where'd you get her, Harry? She's a keeper.'

Bosch looked at Walling. He, too, was impressed.

'Internet,' she said.

Bosch nodded, though he didn't believe her.

'And there's one other thing you should note,' Felton said. He reached across the body to point at the hand on Bosch's side. 'We have one of these on each hand.'

Bosch stooped down again. Felton was pointing to a red plastic ring on the middle finger. Bosch looked at it and then checked the other hand. There was a matching red ring. On the inside of each hand, the ring had a white facing that looked like some sort of tape.

'What are they?' Bosch asked.

'I don't know yet,' Felton said. 'But I think—'

'I do,' Walling said.

Bosch looked up at her. He nodded. Of course she knew.

'They're called TLD rings,' Walling said. 'Stands for thermal luminescent dosimetry. It's an early-warning device. It reads radiation exposure.'

The news brought an eerie silence to the gathering.

'And I'll give you a tip,' Walling continued. 'When they are turned inward like that, with the TLD screen on the inside of the hand, that usually means the wearer handles radioactive materials.'

Bosch stood up. 'OK, everybody,' he ordered. 'Back away from the body. Everybody just back away.'

The crime-scene techs, the coroner's people and Bosch all started moving away. But Walling didn't move. She raised her hands like she was calling for a congregation's attention in church.

'Hold on,' she said. 'Nobody has to back away. It's cool. It's safe.'

Everybody paused, but nobody moved back to their original positions.

'If there was an exposure threat here, then the TLD screens on the rings would be black,' she said. 'That's the early warning. But they haven't turned black, so we're safe. Additionally, I have this.' She pulled back her jacket to reveal a small black box clipped to her belt like a pager. 'Radiation monitor,' she explained. 'If we had a problem, believe me, this thing would be screaming bloody murder and I'd be running at the front of the pack. But we don't. Everything is cool here, OK?'

The people at the crime scene started to return to their positions. Harry Bosch moved in close to Walling and took her by an elbow.

'Can we talk over here for a minute?'

They moved out of the clearing towards the kerb at Mulholland. Bosch was agitated. He didn't want to lose control of the crime scene, and this sort of information threatened to do just that.

'What are you doing here, Rachel?' he asked. 'What's going on?'

'Just like you, I got a call in the middle of the night. I was told to roll out. I assure you that I am here to help.'

'Then start by telling me exactly what you are doing here and who sent you out. That would help me a lot.'

Walling looked around and then back at Bosch. She pointed out beyond the yellow tape. 'Can we?'

Bosch held out his hand, telling her to lead the way. They went under the tape and out into the street. When he judged that they were out of earshot of everyone else at the crime scene, Bosch stopped and looked at her.

'OK, this is far enough,' he said. 'What is going on here?'

She locked eyes with him again. 'Listen, what I tell you here has to remain confidential,' she said. 'For now.'

'Look, Rachel, I don't have time for—'

'Stanley Kent is on a list. When you or one of your colleagues ran his name on the National Crime Index Computer tonight, a flag went up in Washington, DC, and a call went out to me at Tactical.'

'What, was he a terrorist?'

'No. He was a medical physicist. And as far as I know, a law-abiding citizen.'

'Then what's with the radiation rings and the FBI showing up in the middle of the night? What list was Stanley Kent on?'

Walling ignored the question. 'Let me ask you something, Harry. Has anyone checked on this man's home or wife yet?'

'Not yet. We were working the crime scene first. I plan to—'

'Then I think we need to do that right now,' she said in an urgent tone. 'You can ask your questions along the way. Get the guy's keys in case we need to go in. And I'll go get my car.'

Walling started to move away, but Bosch caught her by the arm.

'I'm driving,' he said.

He pointed towards his Mustang and left her there. He headed to the patrol car, where the evidence bags were still spread on the trunk. As he made his way, he regretted having already cut Edgar loose from the scene.

Bosch signalled the watch sergeant over. 'Listen, I have to leave the scene to check on the victim's house. I shouldn't be gone long, and Detective Ferras should be here any minute. Just maintain the scene until one of us gets here.'

'You got it.'

Bosch pulled out his cellphone and called his partner.

'Where are you?'

'I just cleared Parker Center. I'm twenty minutes away.'

Bosch explained that he was leaving the scene and that Ferras needed to hurry. He disconnected, grabbed the evidence bag containing the key ring from the cruiser's trunk and shoved it into his coat pocket.

As he got to his car, he saw Walling already in the passenger seat. She was finishing a call and closing her cellphone.

'Who was that?' Bosch asked after getting in. 'The president?'

'My partner,' she replied. 'I told him to meet me at the house. Where's your partner?'

'He's coming.'

Bosch started the car. As soon as they pulled out he began asking questions.

'If Stanley Kent wasn't a terrorist, what list was he on?'

'As a medical physicist, he had direct access to radioactive materials. That put him on a list.'

Bosch thought of all the hospital name tags he had found in the dead man's Porsche. 'Access where? In the hospitals?'

'Exactly. That's where it's kept. These are materials primarily used in the treatment of cancer.'

Bosch nodded. 'OK. So what am I missing here? Lay it out for me.'

'Stanley Kent had direct access to materials that some people in the world would like to get their hands on. Materials that could be very, very valuable to these people. But not in the treatment of cancer.'

'Terrorists.'

'Exactly.'

'Are you saying that this guy could just waltz into a hospital and get this stuff? Aren't there regulations?'

'There are always regulations, Harry. But just having them is not always enough. Repetition, routine—these are the cracks in any security system. We used to leave the cockpit doors on commercial airlines unlocked. Now we don't. It takes an event of life-altering consequences to change procedures and strengthen precautions. Do you understand what I'm saying?'

Bosch thought of the notations on the back of some of the ID cards in the victim's Porsche. Could Stanley Kent have been so lax about the security of these materials that he wrote access combinations on the back of his ID cards? The answer was probably yes.

'I understand,' he told Walling.

'So if you were going to circumvent an existing security system, who would you go to?' she asked.

He nodded. 'Somebody with intimate knowledge of that security system.'

'Exactly.'

Bosch turned onto Arrowhead Drive and started looking at address numbers on the kerb. 'So you're saying this could be an event of life-altering consequences?'

'No, I'm not saying that. Not yet.'

'Did you know Kent?'

Bosch looked at Walling as he asked, and she looked surprised by the question. It had been a long shot, but he threw it out there for the reaction. Walling turned from him and looked out her window before answering. Bosch knew the move. A classic tell. He knew she would now lie to him.

'No, I never met the man.'

Bosch pulled into the next driveway and stopped the car.

'What are you doing?' she asked.

'This is it. It's Kent's house.'

They were in front of a house that had no lights on inside or out. It looked like no one lived there.

'No, it isn't,' Walling said. 'His house is down another block—'

She stopped when she realised that Bosch had smoked her out. Bosch stared at her for a moment in the dark car before speaking.

'You want to level with me now or do you want to get out of the car?'

'Look, Harry, I told you. There are things I can't—'

'Get out of the car, Agent Walling. I'll handle this myself.'

'Look, you have to under—'

'This is a homicide. *My* homicide. Get out of the car.'

She didn't move. 'I can make one phone call and you'd be removed from this investigation before you got back to the scene,' she said.

'Then do it. I'd rather be kicked to the kerb right now than be a mushroom for the feds. Isn't that one of the Bureau's slogans? Keep the locals in the dark and bury them in cow shit? Well, not me, not tonight, and not on my own case.'

He started to reach across her lap to open her door. Walling pushed him back and raised her hands in surrender.

'All right, all right,' she said. 'What is it you want to know?'

'I want the truth this time. All of it.'

BOSCH TURNED in his seat to look directly at Walling. He was not going to move the car until she started talking.

'You obviously knew who Stanley Kent was and where he lived,' he said. 'You lied to me. Now, was he a terrorist or not?'

'I told you no, and that is the truth. He was a citizen. He was a physicist. He was on a watch list because he handled radioactive sources that could be used—in the wrong hands—to harm members of the public.'

'What are you talking about? How would this happen?'

'Through exposure. And that could take many different forms. Individual assault—remember the Russian who was dosed with polonium in London? That was a specific target attack, though there were additional victims. The material Kent had access to could also be used on a larger scale—a mall, a subway, whatever. It all depends on the quantity and the delivery device.'

'Delivery device? Are you talking about a bomb? Somebody could make a dirty bomb with the stuff he handled?'

'In some applications, yes.'

'I thought that was an urban legend, that there's never actually been a dirty bomb.'

'The official designation is IED—improvised explosive device. And put it this way, it's only an urban legend until precisely the moment that the first one is detonated.'

Bosch nodded and got back on track. He gestured to the house in front of them. 'How did you know this isn't the Kent house?'

Walling rubbed her forehead as though she were tired of his annoying questions and had a headache. 'Because I have been to his house before. OK? Early last year my partner and I came to Kent's house and briefed him and his wife on the potential dangers of his profession. We did a security check on their home and told them to take precautions. We had been asked to do it by the Department of Homeland Security. OK?'

'Yeah, OK. And was that routine for the Tactical Intelligence Unit and the Department of Homeland Security, or was that because there had been a threat to him?'

'Not a threat specifically aimed at him, no. Look, we're wasting—'

'Then to who? A threat to who?'

Walling adjusted her position in the seat and let her breath out in exasperation. 'There wasn't a threat to anyone specifically. We were simply taking precautions. Sixteen months ago someone entered a cancer clinic in Greensboro, North Carolina, circumvented security measures and removed twenty-two small tubes of a radioisotope called caesium one thirty-seven. The legitimate medical use of this material in that setting was in the treatment of gynaecological cancer. We don't know who got in there or why, but the material was taken. When news of the theft went out on the wire, somebody in the Joint Terrorism Task Force here in LA thought it would be a good idea to assess the security of these materials in local hospitals and to warn those who have access to and handle the stuff to take precautions and to be alert. Can we *please* go now?'

'And that was you.'

'*Yes*. You got it. It was the federal trickle-down theory at work. It fell to me and my partner to go out and talk to people like Stanley Kent. We met him and his wife at their house so we could do a security check of the place, and at the same time we told him that he should start watching his back. That's why I was the one who got the call when his name came up on the flag.'

Bosch dropped the transmission into reverse and quickly pulled out of the driveway. 'Why didn't you just tell me this up front?'

In the street, the car jerked forward as Bosch threw it into drive.

'Because nobody got killed in Greensboro,' Walling said defiantly. 'This whole thing could be something different. I was told to approach with caution and discretion. I'm sorry I lied to you.'

'It's a little late for that, Rachel. Did your people get the caesium back in Greensboro?'

'No, not yet. The word is that it was sold on the black market. The material itself is quite valuable on a monetary basis, even if used in the proper medical context. That's why we are not sure what we've got here. That's why I was sent.'

In ten more seconds, they were at the correct block of Arrowhead Drive and Bosch started looking at address numbers again.

Walling directed him. 'That one up on the left, I think. With the black shutters. It's hard to tell in the dark.'

Bosch pulled in and chunked the transmission into park. He jumped out and headed to the front door. The house was dark. Not even the light over the door was lit. But, as Bosch approached the front door, he saw that it had been left ajar.

'It's open,' he said.

He and Walling drew their weapons. Bosch placed his hand on the door and slowly pushed it open. With guns up, they entered the dark and quiet house. Bosch quickly swept the wall with his hand until he found a light switch.

The lights came on, revealing a living room that was neat but empty, with no sign of trouble.

'Mrs Kent?' Walling called out loudly. Then to Bosch in a lower voice, she said, 'There's just his wife, no children.'

Walling called out once more, but the house remained silent. There was a hallway to the right and Bosch moved towards it. He found another light switch and illuminated a passageway with four closed doors and an alcove.

The alcove was a home office, which was empty. He saw a blue reflection on the window, cast by a computer screen. They passed the alcove and went door by door, clearing what looked like a guest bedroom and then a home gym, with cardio machines and with workout mats hanging on the wall. The third door was to a guest bathroom. The fourth led to the master bedroom.

They entered the master, and Bosch once more flicked up a wall switch. They found Mrs Kent.

She was on the bed naked, gagged and hog-tied with her hands behind her back. Her eyes were closed. Walling rushed to the bed to see if she was alive while Bosch moved through the bedroom to clear the bathroom and a walk-in closet. There was no one.

When he got back to the bed he saw that Walling had removed the gag and used a pocketknife to slice through the black plastic snap ties that had been used to bind the woman's wrists and ankles together behind her back.

Walling was pulling the bedspread over the woman's naked body. There was a distinct odour of urine.

'Is she alive?' Bosch asked.

'She's alive. I think she's just passed out.'

Walling started rubbing the woman's wrists and hands. They had turned dark and almost purple from lack of blood circulation.

'Get help,' she told him.

Annoyed with himself for not reacting until ordered, Bosch pulled out his phone and walked out into the hallway while he called the central communications centre to get paramedics rolling.

'Ten minutes,' he said, after hanging up and returning to the bedroom.

Bosch felt a wave of excitement go through him. They now had a live witness. The woman on the bed would be able to tell them at least something about what had happened. He knew that it would be vitally important to get her talking as soon as possible.

There was a loud groan as she regained consciousness.

'Mrs Kent, it's OK,' Walling said. 'You're safe now.'

The woman tensed and her eyes widened when she saw the two strangers in front of her.

Walling held up her credentials. 'FBI, Mrs Kent. Do you remember me?'

'What? What is . . .? Where's my husband?'

She started to get up, then realised she was naked beneath the bed covers and tried to pull them tightly round herself. Her fingers were apparently still numb and couldn't find purchase. Walling helped her.

'Where is Stanley?' the woman asked.

Walling knelt beside the bed. She looked up at Bosch as if seeking direction on how to handle the question.

'Mrs Kent, your husband is not here,' he said. 'I am Detective Bosch with the LAPD, and this is Agent Walling with the FBI. We're trying to find out what happened to your husband.'

The woman looked up at Bosch and then at Walling, and her eyes held on the federal agent. 'I remember you,' she said. 'You came to the house to warn us. Is that what is happening? Do the men who were here have Stanley?'

Walling leaned in close and spoke in a calming voice. 'Mrs Kent, we . . . It's Alicia, right? Alicia, we need for you to calm down a little bit so that we can talk and possibly help you. Would you like to get dressed?'

Alicia Kent nodded.

'OK. We'll give you some space here,' Walling said. 'You get dressed, and we'll wait for you in the living room. First, let me ask, have you been injured in any way?'

The woman shook her head.

'Are you sure . . .' Walling didn't finish, as though she were intimidated by her own question.

Bosch wasn't. He knew they needed to know precisely what had happened here. 'Mrs Kent, were you sexually assaulted here tonight?'

The woman shook her head again. 'They made me take off my clothes. That was all they did.'

Bosch studied her eyes, hoping to read them and be able to tell if she was telling a lie.

'OK,' Walling said, interrupting the moment. 'We'll leave you to get dressed. When the paramedics arrive, we will still want them to check you for injuries.'

'I'll be fine,' Alicia Kent said. 'What happened to my husband?'

'We're not sure,' Bosch said. 'You get dressed and come out to the living room, then we'll tell you what we know.'

Clutching the bedspread round herself, she tentatively stood up from the bed. Bosch saw the stain on the mattress and knew that Alicia Kent had either been so scared during her ordeal that she had urinated or the wait for rescue had been too long.

She took one step towards the closet and appeared to be falling over. Bosch moved in and grabbed her before she fell.

'Are you all right?'

'I'm fine. I think I'm just a little dizzy. What time is it?'

Bosch looked at the digital clock on the right-hand bedside table, but its screen was blank. He turned his right wrist without letting go of her and looked at his watch. 'It's almost one in the morning.'

Her body seemed to tighten in his grasp. 'Oh my God!' she cried. 'It's been hours. Where is Stanley?'

Bosch moved his hands to her shoulders and helped her stand up straight. 'You get dressed and we'll talk about it,' he said.

She walked unsteadily to the closet and opened the door. A full-length mirror was attached to the outside of the door. Her opening it swung Bosch's reflection back at him. In the moment, he thought that maybe he saw something new in his eyes. A look of discomfort, perhaps even a fear of the unknown. It was understandable, he decided. He had worked a thousand murder cases in his time, but never one that had taken him in the direction he was now travelling. Maybe fear was appropriate.

Alicia Kent took a white towelling robe off a hook inside the closet and carried it with her to the bathroom. She left the closet door open and Bosch had to look away from his own reflection.

Walling headed out of the bedroom and Bosch followed.

'What do you think?" she asked as she moved down the hall.

'I think we're lucky to have a witness,' Bosch replied. 'She'll be able to tell us what happened.'

'Hopefully.'

Bosch decided to make another survey of the house while waiting for Alicia Kent to get dressed. This time he checked the back yard and the garage, as well as every room again. He found nothing amiss, though he did note that the two-car garage was empty. If the Kents had another car in addition to the Porsche, then it wasn't on the premises.

After the walk-through he stood in the back yard, looking up at the Hollywood sign as he called central communications again to ask that a second forensics team be dispatched to process the Kent house. He also checked on the ETA of the paramedics coming to examine Alicia Kent and was told that they were still five minutes away. This was ten minutes after he had been told that they were ten minutes away.

Next, he called Lieutenant Gandle, waking him at his home. His supervisor listened quietly as Bosch updated him. The federal involvement and the rising possibility of a terrorism angle to the investigation gave Gandle pause.

'Well,' he said when Bosch was finished, 'it looks like I will have to wake some people up.'

He meant he was going to have to send word up the department ladder of the case and its larger dimensions. The last thing an RHD lieutenant would want would be to get called into the office of the chief of police in the morning and asked why he hadn't alerted command staff earlier. Bosch knew that Gandle would now act to protect himself as well as to seek direction from above. This was fine with Bosch and expected. But it gave him pause as well. The LAPD had its own Office of Homeland Security. It was commanded by a man most people in the department viewed as a loose cannon who was unqualified and unsuited for the job.

'Is one of those wake-ups going to Captain Hadley?' Bosch asked.

Captain Don Hadley was the twin brother of James Hadley, who happened to be a member of the Police Commission, the politically appointed panel with LAPD oversight and the authority to appoint and retain the chief of police. Less than a year after James Hadley was placed on the commission by mayoral appointment and with the approval of the city council, his twin brother jumped from being second in command of the Valley Traffic Division to being commander of the newly formed Office of Homeland Security. This was seen at the time as a political move by the then chief of police, who was desperately trying to keep his job. It didn't work. He was fired and a new chief appointed. But in the transition, Hadley kept his job commanding the OHS.

The mission of the OHS was to interface with federal agencies and maintain a flow of intelligence data. In the last six years, Los Angeles had been targeted by terrorists at least two times that were known. In each incident, the LAPD found out about the threat after it had been foiled by the feds. This was embarrassing to the department, and the OHS had been formed so that the LAPD could make intelligence inroads and know what the feds knew about its own back yard.

The problem was that in practice it was largely suspected that the LAPD remained shut out by the feds. And in order to hide this failing and to justify his position and unit, Captain Hadley had taken to holding grandstanding press conferences and showing up with his black-clad OHS unit at any crime scene where there was a remote possibility of terrorist involvement. An overturned tanker truck on the Hollywood Freeway brought the OHS out in force until it was determined that the tanker was carrying milk. A shooting of a rabbi at a temple in Westwood brought the same response, until the incident was determined to have been the product of a love triangle.

And so it went. After about the fourth misfire, the commander of the OHS was baptised with a new name among the rank and file. Captain Don Hadley became known as Captain Done Badly. But he remained in his post, thanks to the thin veil of politics that hung over his appointment. The last Bosch had heard about Hadley through the department grapevine was that he had put his entire squad back into the academy for training in urban assault tactics.

'I don't know about Hadley,' Gandle said in response to Bosch. 'He'll probably be looped in. I'll start with my captain and he'll make the call on who gets the word from there. But that's not your concern, Harry. You do your job and don't worry about Hadley. The people you have to watch your back with are the feds. Remember, with the feds it's always time to worry when they start telling you just what you want to hear.'

'Got it,' Bosch said. The advice followed a time-honoured LAPD tradition of distrusting the FBI. And, of course, it was a tradition honoured for just as long by the FBI in terms of distrusting the LAPD right back. It was the reason the OHS was born.

When Bosch came back into the house, he found Walling on her cellphone and a man he had never seen before standing in the living room. He was tall, mid-forties, and he exuded that undeniable FBI confidence Bosch had seen many times before.

The man put out his hand. 'You must be Detective Bosch,' he said. 'Jack Brenner. Rachel's my partner.'

Bosch shook his hand. The way he said Rachel was his partner was a small thing, but it told Bosch a lot. There was something proprietary about it. Brenner was telling him that the senior partner was now on the job.

'So you two have met.'

Bosch turned. Walling was off the phone now.

'Sorry,' she said. 'I was filling in the special agent in charge. He's decided to devote all of Tactical to this. He's running out three teams to start hitting the hospitals to see if Kent has been in any of the hot labs today.'

'The hot lab is where they keep the radioactive stuff?' Bosch asked.

'Yes. Kent had access to just about all of them in the county. We have to figure out if he was inside any of them today.'

Bosch knew that he could probably narrow the search down to one medical facility. Saint Agatha's Clinic for Women. Kent was wearing an ID tag from the hospital when he was murdered. Walling and Brenner didn't know that, and Bosch decided not to tell them yet. He wanted to hold on to what might be the one piece of inside information he still had.

'What about the LAPD?' he asked instead.

'The LAPD?' Brenner said, jumping on the question ahead of Walling. 'You mean, what about you, Bosch? Is that what you're asking?'

'Yeah, that's right. Where do I stand in this?'

Brenner spread his hands in a gesture of openness. 'Don't worry, you're in. You're with us all the way.'

'Good,' Bosch said. 'That's just what I wanted to hear.'

He looked at Walling for confirmation of her partner's statement, but she looked away.

THREE

When Alicia Kent finally came out of the master bedroom, she had brushed her hair and washed her face but had put on only the white robe. Bosch now saw how attractive she was. Small and dark and exotic-looking in some way. He guessed that taking her husband's name had hidden a bloodline from somewhere far away. Her black hair had a luminescent quality to it. It framed an olive face that was beautiful and sorrowful at the same time.

She noticed Brenner, and he nodded and introduced himself. Alicia Kent seemed so dazed by what was happening that she showed no recognition of Brenner in the way that she had remembered Walling. Brenner directed her to the couch and told her to sit down.

'Where is my husband?' she demanded, this time with a voice that was stronger and calmer than before. 'I want to know what is going on.'

Walling sat down next to her, ready to console if necessary. Brenner took a chair near the fireplace. Bosch remained standing. He never liked to be sitting down all cosy when he delivered this sort of news.

'Mrs Kent,' Bosch said, taking the lead in a proprietary effort to keep his hold of the case. 'I am a homicide detective. I am here because earlier tonight we found the body of a man we believe to be your husband. I am very sorry to tell you this.'

Her head dropped forward as she received the news, then her hands came up and covered her face. A shudder went through her body and the sound of a helpless moan came from behind her hands. Then she started to cry, deep sobs that shook her shoulders so much that she had to lower her hands to hold the robe from coming open. Walling reached over and put a hand on the back of her neck.

Brenner offered to get her a glass of water and she nodded. While he was gone, Bosch studied the woman and saw the tears streaking her cheeks. It was dirty work, telling someone that their loved one was dead. He had done it hundreds of times, but it wasn't something you ever got used to or even good at. It had also been done to him. When his own mother was murdered more than forty years before, he got the news from a cop just after climbing out of a swimming pool at a youth hall. His response was to jump back in and try to never come back up.

Brenner delivered the water, and the brand-new widow drank half of it down. Before anyone could ask a question there was a knock on the door, and Bosch stepped over and let in two paramedics carrying big equipment boxes. While they came forward to assess the woman's physical condition, Bosch signalled Walling and Brenner into the kitchen, where they could confer in whispers.

'So how do you want to handle her?' Bosch asked.

Brenner spread his hands wide again, as though he was open to suggestions. It appeared to be his signature gesture. 'I think you keep the lead. We'll step in when needed. If you don't like that, we could—'

'No, that's good. I'll keep the lead.'

He looked at Walling, waiting for an objection, but she was fine with it too. He turned to leave the kitchen but Brenner stopped him.

'Bosch, I want to be up front with you,' Brenner said.

Bosch turned back. 'Meaning?'

'Meaning I had you checked out. The word is, you—'

'What do you mean you checked me out? You asked questions about me?'

'I needed to know who we're working with. All I knew about you prior to this is what I'd heard about Echo Park. I wanted—'

'If you have any questions, you can ask me.'

Brenner raised his hands, palms out. 'Fair enough.'

Bosch left the kitchen and stood in the living room, waiting for the paramedics to finish with Alicia Kent. One of the medical men was taking a blood-pressure reading. Bandages had been placed on her neck and one wrist, apparently covering wounds that he hadn't noticed.

His phone buzzed and Bosch went back into the kitchen to take the call. He noticed that Walling and Brenner were gone, apparently having slipped into another part of the house. It made Bosch anxious. He didn't know what they were looking for or up to.

The call was from his partner. Ferras had finally made it to the crime scene.

'Is the body still there?' Bosch asked.

'No. The ME just cleared the scene,' Ferras said. 'I think Forensics is finishing up too.'

Bosch updated him on the direction the case appeared to be going, telling him about the federal involvement and the potentially dangerous materials that Stanley Kent had had access to. He then directed him to start knocking on doors and looking for witnesses who might have seen or heard something. He knew it was a long shot, because no one had called 911 after the shooting.

'Should I do that now, Harry? It's the middle of the night and people are sleep—'

'Yes, Ignacio, you should do it now.'

Bosch wasn't worried about waking people up. It was always better to find witnesses sooner rather than later.

When Bosch came out of the kitchen, the paramedics had packed up and were leaving. They told Bosch that Alicia Kent was physically fine, with minor wounds and abrasions. They said they had given her a pill to help calm her and a tube of cream to apply to the chafe marks on her wrists and ankles.

Walling was sitting on the couch next to her again and Brenner was back in his seat by the fireplace. Bosch sat down on the chair directly across the glass coffee table from Alicia Kent.

'Mrs Kent,' he began, 'we are very sorry for your loss and the trauma you have been through. But it is very urgent that we move quickly with the investigation. In a perfect world, we would wait until you were ready to talk to us. But it's not a perfect world. You know that better than we do now. We need to ask you questions about what happened here tonight.'

She folded her arms across her chest and nodded.

'Then let's get started,' Bosch said. 'Can you tell us what happened?'

'Two men,' she responded tearfully. 'I never saw them. I mean their faces. I never saw their faces. There was a knock at the door and I answered. There was no one there. Then, when I started to close the door, they jumped out. They had on masks and hoods—like a sweatshirt with a hood. They pushed their way in and grabbed me. They had a knife and one of them grabbed me and held it against my throat. He told me he would cut my throat if I didn't do exactly what he told me to do.' She lightly touched the bandage on her neck.

'Do you remember what time this was?' Bosch asked.

'It was almost six o'clock,' she said. 'It had been dark for a while and I was about to start dinner. Stanley comes home most nights at seven. Unless he's working down in the South County or up in the desert.'

The reminder of her husband's habits brought a new rush of tears. Bosch tried to keep Alicia Kent on point by moving to the next question. He thought he already detected a slowing down of her speech. The pill the paramedics gave her was taking effect.

'What did the men do, Mrs Kent?' he asked.

'They took me to the bedroom. They made me sit down on the bed and take off all my clothes. Then one of them started to ask me questions. I was scared. I guess I got hysterical and he slapped me and yelled at me. He told me to calm down and answer his questions.'

'What did he ask you?'

'I can't remember everything. I was so scared.'

'Try, Mrs Kent. It's important.'

'He asked me if we had a gun and he asked me where the—'

'Wait a minute, Mrs Kent,' Bosch said. 'Let's go one at a time. He asked you if you had a gun. What did you tell him?'

'I was scared. I said yes, we had a gun. He asked where it was and I told him it was in the drawer by the bed on my husband's side. It was the gun we got after you warned us about the dangers Stan faced with his job.'

She said this last part while looking directly at Walling.

'Weren't you afraid that they would kill you with it?' Bosch asked. 'Why did you tell them where the gun was?'

Alicia Kent looked down at her hands. 'I was sitting there naked. I was already sure they were going to rape me and kill me. I guess I thought it didn't matter any more.'

Bosch nodded slowly as if he understood. 'What else did they ask you, Mrs Kent?'

'They wanted to know where the keys to the car were. I told them. I told them everything they wanted to know.'

'Is that your car they were talking about?'

'Yes, my car. In the garage. I keep the keys on the kitchen counter.'

'I checked the garage. It's empty.'

'I heard the garage door—after they were here. They must have taken the car.'

Brenner abruptly stood up. 'We need to get this out,' he interjected. 'Can you tell us what kind of car it is and the licence plate number?'

'It's a Chrysler 300. I can't remember the number. I could look it up in our insurance file.'

Brenner held up his hands to stop her from getting up. 'Not necessary. I'll be able to get it. I'll call it in right away.'

He got up to go to the kitchen to make the call without disturbing the interview. Bosch went back to his questions.

'What else did they ask you, Mrs Kent?'

'They wanted our camera. The camera that worked with my husband's computer. I told them Stanley had a camera in his desk. Whenever I answered a question, one man—the one who asked them—would translate to the other, and then that man left the room. I guess he went to get the camera.'

Walling stood up and headed for the hallway leading to the bedrooms.

'Rachel, don't touch anything,' Bosch said. 'I have a crime-scene team coming.'

Walling waved him off as she disappeared down the hall.

Brenner then came back into the room and nodded to Bosch. 'The BOLO's out,' he said.

Alicia Kent asked what a BOLO was.

'It means "be on the lookout",' Bosch explained. 'They'll be looking for your car. What happened next, Mrs Kent?'

She grew tearful again as she answered. 'They . . . They tied me in that awful way and gagged me with one of my husband's neckties. Then after the one came back with the camera, the other took a picture of me like that.'

Bosch noted the look of burning humiliation on her face.

'He took a photograph?'

'Yes, that's all. Then they both left the room. The one who spoke English bent down and whispered that my husband would come to rescue me. Then he left.'

That brought a long space of silence before Bosch continued.

'After they left the bedroom, did they leave the house right away?'

The woman shook her head. 'I heard them talking for a little while, then I heard the garage door. It rumbles in the house like an earthquake. I felt it twice—it opened and closed. After that, I thought they were gone.'

Brenner cut in. 'When I was in the kitchen, I think I heard you say that one of the men translated for the other. Do you know what language they were speaking?'

Bosch was annoyed with Brenner for jumping in. He had intended to ask about the language the intruders used but was carefully covering one aspect of the interview at a time. He had found that it worked best with traumatised victims.

'I'm not sure. The one who spoke in English had an accent but I don't know where it was from. I think Middle Eastern. I think when they spoke to each other it was Arabic or something. It was foreign, very guttural. But I don't know the different languages.'

Brenner nodded as if her answer was confirming something.

'Do you remember anything else about what the men asked you or said in English?' Bosch asked.

'No, that's all.'

'You said they wore masks. What kind of masks?'

She thought for a moment before answering. 'The pullover kind. Like you see robbers put on in movies or people wear for skiing.'

'A woollen ski mask?'

She nodded. 'Yes, exactly.'

'OK. Were they the kind with one hole for both eyes, or was there a separate hole for each eye?'

'Um, separate, I think. Yes, separate.'

'Was there an opening for the mouth?'

'Uh . . . yes, there was. I remember watching the man's mouth when he spoke in the other language.'

'That's good, Mrs Kent. You're being very helpful. What haven't I asked you?'

'I don't understand.'

'What detail do you remember that I haven't asked you for?'

She thought about it and then shook her head. 'I don't know. I think I've told you everything I can remember.'

Bosch wasn't convinced. He began to go through the story with her again, coming at the same information from new angles. It was a tried-and-true interview technique for eliciting new details and it did not fail him. The most interesting bit of new information to emerge in the second telling was that the man who spoke English also asked her what the password was to her email account.

'Why would he want that?' Bosch asked.

'I don't know,' she said. 'I didn't ask. I just gave them what they wanted.'

When the forensics team arrived, Bosch called for a break in the questioning. He walked the tech team back to the master bedroom so they could start there. Then he stepped into a corner of the room and called his partner. Ferras reported that he had found nobody so far who had seen or heard anything on the overlook. Bosch told him that when he wanted a break from knocking on doors he should check into Stanley Kent's ownership of a gun. They needed to find the make and model. It was looking like his own gun was probably the weapon he was killed with.

As Bosch closed the phone, Walling called to him from the home office. Harry found her and Brenner standing behind the desk and staring at a computer screen.

'Look at this,' Walling said.

'I told you,' he said, 'you shouldn't be touching anything yet.'

'We don't have the luxury of time,' Brenner said. 'Look at this.'

Bosch came round the desk to look at the computer.

'Her email account was left open,' Walling said. 'I went into the "sent mail" file. This was sent to her husband's email at six-twenty-one last night.'

The email subject line said HOME EMERGENCY: READ IMMEDIATELY!

Embedded in the body of the email was a photograph of Alicia Kent, naked and hog-tied on the bed. The impact of the photo would be obvious to anyone, not just a husband.

Below the photograph was a message:

> We have your wife. Retrieve for us all caesium sources available to you. Bring them in safe containment to the Mulholland overlook near your home by eight o'clock. We will be watching you. If you tell anyone or make a call, we will know. The consequence will be your wife being raped, tortured and left in to many pieces to count. Use all precautions while handling sources. Do not be late or we will kill her.

Bosch read the message twice and believed he felt the same terror Stanley Kent must have felt.

'"We will be watching . . . we will know . . . we will kill her",' Walling said. 'No contractions. The "too" in "too many pieces" is spelt wrong. I don't think this was written by someone whose original language is English.'

As she said it, Bosch saw it and knew that she was right.

'They send the message right from here,' Brenner said. 'The husband gets it at the office or on his PDA. Did he have a PDA?'

Bosch had no expertise in this area. He hesitated.

'A personal digital assistant,' Walling prompted. 'You know, like a Palm Pilot or a phone with all the gadgets.'

Bosch nodded. 'I think so,' he said. 'There was a BlackBerry cellphone recovered. It looks like it has a mini-keyboard.'

'That works,' Brenner said. 'So no matter where he is, he gets this message and can probably view the photo, too.'

All three of them were quiet while the impact registered. Finally Bosch spoke, feeling guilty now about holding back earlier.

'I just remembered something. There was an ID tag on the body. From Saint Aggy's up in the Valley.'

Brenner's eyes took on a sharpness. 'You just remembered a key piece of information like that?' he asked angrily.

'That's right. I for—'

'It doesn't matter now,' Walling interjected. 'Saint Aggy's is a women's cancer clinic. Caesium is used almost exclusively for treating cervical and uterine cancer.'

Bosch nodded. 'Then we better get going,' he said.

SAINT AGATHA'S CLINIC for Women was in Sylmar at the north end of the San Fernando Valley. Because it was the dead of night, they were making good time on the 170 Freeway. Bosch was behind the wheel of his Mustang, one eye on the fuel needle. He knew he was going to need gas before coming back down into the city. It was him and Brenner in the car. Brenner had decided that Walling should stay behind with Alicia Kent to continue questioning her. Walling didn't seem happy about the assignment, but Brenner, asserting his seniority, didn't give her room to debate it.

Brenner spent most of the drive taking and making a series of cell calls to and from superiors and fellow agents. It was clear to Bosch from the side of things that he was able to hear that the big federal machine was gearing up for battle. A greater alarm had now been sounded. The email sent to Stanley Kent had brought things into better focus, and what was once a federal curiosity had now gone completely off the scale.

When Brenner finally closed the phone, he turned slightly in his seat and looked over at Bosch. 'I've got a RAT team heading to Saint Aggy's,' he said. 'They'll go into the materials safe to check it out.'

'A rat team?'

'Radiological-attack team.'

'What's their ETA?'

'Didn't ask, but they might beat us. They've got a chopper.'

Bosch was impressed. It meant that there had been a rapid-response team on duty somewhere in the middle of the night. He thought about how he had been awake and waiting for the call-out that night. The members of the radiological-attack team must wait for the call they hope never comes. He remembered what he had heard about the LAPD's own OHS unit taking training in urban assault tactics. He wondered if Captain Hadley had a RAT team, too.

'They're going full field on this,' Brenner said. 'The Department of Homeland Security is overseeing from DC. This morning at nine there will be meetings on both coasts to bring everybody together on it.'

'Who is everybody?'

'There's a protocol. We'll bring in Homeland, the JTTF, everybody. It'll be alphabet soup. The NRC, the DOE, RAP . . . Who knows, before we get this contained we might even have FEMA setting up a tent. It's going to be federal pandemonium.'

Bosch didn't know what all the acronyms stood for, but he didn't need to. They all spelt out *feds* to him.

'Who will be running the show?'

'Everybody and nobody. Like I said, pandemonium. If we open up that safe at Saint Aggy's and the caesium is gone, then our best shot at tracking it and getting it back will be to do it before all hell breaks loose at nine and we get micromanaged to death from Washington.'

Bosch nodded. He thought maybe he had misjudged Brenner. The agent seemed to want to get things done, not wallow in the bureaucratic mire.

'And what's the LAPD status going to be?'

'I already told you, the LAPD remains in. Nothing changes on that. You remain in, Harry. My guess is that bridges are already being built between our people and your people. I know the LAPD has its own Homeland Security office. I'm sure they will be brought in. We're obviously going to need all hands on deck with this.'

Bosch glanced over at him. Brenner looked serious.

'Have you worked with our OHS before?' Bosch asked.

'On occasion. We shared some intelligence on a few things.'

Bosch nodded but felt that Brenner was either being disingenuous or was completely naive about the gulf between the locals and the feds. But he noted that he had been called by his first name and wondered if that was one of the bridges being built.

'You said you checked me out. Who did you check with?'

'Harry, we're working well here. Why stir it up?'

'Who'd you check me out with?'

'Look, all I'm going to tell you is that I asked Agent Walling who the

LAPD point man was and she gave me your name. I made a few calls while driving in. I was told you were a very capable detective. That you had more than thirty years, that a few years back you retired, didn't like it too much and came back to the job to work cold cases. Things went sideways in Echo Park—a little thing you dragged Agent Walling into. You were off the job a few months while that was, uh, cleared up, and now you're back and assigned to Homicide Special.'

'What else?'

'Harr—'

'What else?'

'OK. The word I got is that you can be difficult to get along with, especially when it comes to working with the federal government. But I have to say, so far I don't see any of that at all.'

Bosch figured that most of this information had come from Rachel—he remembered seeing her on the phone and her saying it was her partner. He was disappointed that she had said such things about him, if she had. And he knew that Brenner was probably holding back most of it. The truth was that he'd had so many run-ins with the feds—going back well before he ever met Rachel Walling—that they probably had a file on him as thick as a murder book.

After a minute or so of silence, Bosch decided to change direction and spoke again. 'Tell me about caesium,' he said.

'It's a by-product. The fission of uranium and plutonium creates caesium. When Chernobyl hit meltdown, caesium was the stuff that was dispersed into the air. It comes in powder or a silver-grey metal. When they conducted nuke tests in the South Pacific—'

'I don't mean the science. I don't care about the science. Tell me about what we are dealing with here.'

Brenner thought for a moment. 'OK,' he said. 'The stuff we're talking about comes in pieces about the size of a pencil eraser. It's contained in a sealed stainless-steel tube about the size of a forty-five-calibre bullet cartridge. When used in the treatment of a gynaecological cancer, it's placed inside the woman's uterus for a calculated amount of time and irradiates the targeted area. It is supposed to be very effective in quick doses. And it's the job of a guy like Stanley Kent to make that calculus—to run the physics down and determine how long a dose is called for. He would then go and get the caesium out of the hospital's hot safe and deliver it to the oncologist in the operating room. The system is set up so that the doctor administering the treatment actually handles the stuff as little as possible. Because the surgeon can't wear any protection while performing a procedure, he's got to limit his exposure, you know what I mean?'

Bosch nodded. 'Do these tubes protect whoever handles them?'

'No. The only thing that knocks down the gamma rays from caesium is lead. The safe they keep the tubes in is lined with lead. The device they transport them in is made of lead.'

'So how bad is this stuff going to be if it gets out in the world?'

Brenner gave it some thought before answering. 'Out in the world, it is all about quantity, delivery and location,' he said. 'Those are the variables. Caesium has a thirty-year half-life, so the radiation danger diminishes by half every thirty years. If you set off a good amount of this stuff in an enclosed environment—like maybe a subway station or an office building—then that place could be shut down for three hundred years.'

Bosch was stunned as he registered this. 'What about people?' he asked.

'Also depends on dispersal and containment. A high-intensity exposure could kill you within a few hours. But if it's dispersed by an IED in a subway station, then my guess is that the immediate casualties would be very low. But a body count is not what this would be about. It's the fear factor that would be important to these people. You set something off like this domestically and what's important is the wave of fear it sends through the country. A place like Los Angeles? It would never be the same again.'

Bosch just nodded. There was nothing else to say.

AT SAINT AGGY'S, they entered through the main lobby and asked the receptionist for the chief of security. They were told that he worked days but that she would locate the night-shift security supervisor. While they waited they heard the helicopter land on the front lawn of the medical centre and soon the four-member radiological team came in, each man wearing a radiation suit and carrying a face guard. The leader of the group—it said KYLE REID on his nameplate—carried a handheld radiation monitor.

Finally, after two prompts to the woman at the front desk, a man who looked like he had been rousted from a bed in a spare patient room greeted them in the lobby. He said his name was Ed Romo and he couldn't seem to take his eyes off the hazmat suits worn by the lab team. Brenner badged Romo and took charge. Bosch didn't object. He knew that they were now on turf where the federal agent would be best suited to walk point and maintain investigative velocity.

'We need to go to the hot lab and check the materials inventory,' Brenner said. 'We also need to see any records or key-card data that will show us who has been in and out of there in the last twenty-four hours.'

Romo didn't move. He paused as if groping for understanding. 'What's this about?' he finally asked.

Brenner took a step closer to him. 'I just told you what it's about,' he said. 'We need to get into the hot lab in oncology. If you can't get us in there, then find somebody who can. Now.'

'I gotta make a call first,' Romo said.

'Good. Make it. I'll give you two minutes and then we're going to run you over.' The whole time he was making the threat Brenner was smiling and nodding.

Romo took out a cellphone and stepped away from the group to make the call.

Brenner looked at Bosch with a sardonic smile. 'Last year I did a security survey here. They had a key lock on the lab and the safe and that was it. They upgraded after that. But you build a better mousetrap and the mice just get smarter.'

Ten minutes later, Bosch, Brenner, Romo and the rest of the lab team stepped out of the elevator into the medical clinic's basement. Romo's boss was on his way in but Brenner was not waiting. Romo used a key card to gain entrance to the oncology lab.

The lab was deserted. Brenner found an inventory sheet and a lab log on an entrance desk and started reading. There was a small video monitor on the desk that showed a camera view of a safe.

'He was here,' Brenner said.

'When?' Bosch asked.

'Seven o'clock, according to this.'

Kyle Reid pointed to the monitor. 'Does that record?' he asked Romo. 'Can we see what Kent did when he was in there?'

Romo looked at the monitor as though it were the first time he had ever seen it. 'Um, no, it's just a monitor,' he finally said. 'Whoever's on the desk is supposed to watch what's taken out of the safe.'

Romo pointed to the far end of the lab, where there was a large steel door. The trefoil warning symbol for radioactive materials was posted on it at eye level, along with a sign: CAUTION! RADIATION HAZARD. PROTECTIVE EQUIPMENT MUST BE WORN.

Bosch noticed that the door had a push-button combination lock as well as a magnetic key-card swipe slot.

'It says here that he took one source of caesium,' Brenner said as he continued to study the log. 'One tube. He was taking the source over to Burbank Medical Center for a procedure there. It says that there were thirty-one pieces of caesium left in inventory.'

'Is that all you need, then?' Romo asked.

'No,' Brenner said. 'We have to physically inspect the inventory. We'll need to enter the safe room and open the safe. What's the combination?'

'I don't have it,' Romo said.

'Who does?'

'The physicists. The head of the lab. The chief of security.'

'Get the chief on the speaker.'

Brenner pointed to the phone on the desk. Romo sat down and tapped in a number from memory. It was answered immediately.

'This is Richard Romo.' The chief of security was in his car.

Ed Romo leaned forward to the phone and looked as though he was embarrassed by the revelation of the obvious nepotism at play. 'Uh, yeah, Dad, this is Ed. The man from the FB—'

'Mr Romo?' Brenner cut in. 'This is Special Agent John Brenner of the FBI. I believe we met and spoke about security issues a year ago. How far away are you, sir?'

'Twenty to twenty-five minutes. I remember—'

'That's too far, sir. We need to open the hot-lab safe right now to determine its contents.'

'You can't open that without hospital approval. I don't care who—'

'Mr Romo, we have reason to believe the contents of the safe were turned over to people without the interests or safety of the American people in mind. We need to open the safe so that we know exactly what is here and what is missing. And we can't wait twenty to twenty-five minutes to do it. I have properly identified myself to your *son*, and I have a radiation team in the lab right now. We have to *move*, sir. Now, how do we open the safe?'

There was silence from the speakerphone for a few moments. Then Richard Romo relented.

'Ed, I take it you are calling from the desk in the lab?'

'Yeah.'

'OK, unlock it and open the bottom-left drawer.'

Ed Romo rolled his chair back and studied the desk. There was a key lock on the upper-left drawer that apparently unlocked all three drawers.

'Which key?' he asked.

'Hold on.' Over the speakerphone there was the sound of a key ring being jingled. 'Try fourteen fourteen.'

Ed Romo pulled a key ring off his belt and went through the keys until he found one stamped with the number 1414. He then inserted it into the lock on the desk drawer and turned it. He pulled open the bottom drawer.

'Got it.'

'OK, there's a binder in the drawer. Open it up and look for the page with the combination lists for the safe room. It's changed week to week.'

Holding the binder in his hands, Romo started to open it at an angle that would allow only him to see the contents. Brenner took it from him roughly. He opened it on the desk and started leafing through pages of safety protocols.

'Where is it?' he said impatiently to the speakerphone.

'It should be in the final section. It will be clearly marked as hot-lab combinations. There's one catch, though. We use the previous week. The combination for the current week is wrong. Use last week's combo.'

Brenner found the page and drew his finger down the listing until he found the combination for the previous week. 'OK, got it. What about the safe inside?'

'You will use the key card again and another combination. That one I know. It doesn't change. It is six-six-six.'

'Original.' Brenner held his hand out to Ed Romo. 'Give me your key card.'

Romo complied, and Brenner then handed the card to Reid.

'The door combo is five-six-one-eight-four, and you heard the rest.'

Reid turned and pointed to one of the others in hazmat suits. 'It'll be tight in there. Just Miller and I go in.'

The leader and his chosen second snapped on their face guards and used the key card and combination to open the safe-room door. Miller carried the radiation monitor and they entered the safe room, pulling the door closed behind them.

'You know, people go in there all the time and they don't wear space suits,' Ed Romo said.

'I'm happy for them,' Brenner said. 'This situation is a little different, don't you think? We don't know what may or may not have been let loose in that environment.'

'I was just saying,' Romo said defensively.

'Then do me a favour and don't say anything. Let us do our job.'

Bosch watched on the monitor and soon saw a glitch in the security system. The camera was mounted overhead, but as soon as Reid bent down to type the combination into the materials safe, he blocked the camera's view of what he was doing. Bosch knew that even if someone had watched Kent when he went into the safe at 7 p.m. the evening before, he could easily have hidden what he was taking.

Less than a minute after going into the safe room, the two men in hazmat suits stepped out. Brenner stood up. The men unsnapped their face guards and Reid looked at Brenner. He shook his head.

'The safe's empty,' he said.

Brenner pulled his phone from his pocket. But before he could punch in a number, Reid stepped forward, holding out a piece of paper torn from a spiral notebook.

'This was all that was left,' he said.

Bosch looked over Brenner's shoulder at the note. It was scribbled in ink and difficult to decipher. Brenner read it out loud.

'*I am being watched. If I don't do this, they'll kill my wife. Thirty-two sources, caesium. God forgive me. No choice.*'

FOUR

Bosch and the federal agents stood silently. There was an almost palpable sense of dread hanging in the air. They had just confirmed that Stanley Kent took thirty-two capsules of caesium from the safe and then most likely turned them over to persons unknown. Those persons had then executed him up on the Mulholland overlook.

'Thirty-two capsules of caesium,' Bosch said. 'How much damage could that do?'

Brenner looked at him sombrely. 'We would have to ask the science people, but my guess is that it could get the job done,' he said. 'If somebody out there wants to send a message, it would be heard loud and clear.'

Bosch suddenly thought of something that didn't fit. 'Wait a minute,' he said. 'Stanley Kent's radiation rings showed no exposure. How could he have taken all the caesium out of here and not lit up those warning devices like a Christmas tree?'

Brenner shook his head dismissively. 'He obviously used a pig.'

'A what?'

'The pig is what they call the transfer device. It basically looks like a lead mop bucket on wheels. With a secured top, of course. It's heavy and built low to the ground—like a pig. So they call it a pig.'

'And he could just waltz right in and out of here with something like that?'

Brenner pointed at the clipboard on the desk. 'Interhospital transfers of radioactive sources for cancer treatment are not unusual,' he said. 'He signed out one source but then took them all. That's what was unusual, but who was going to open up the pig and check?'

Bosch thought about the indentations he had seen in the floor of the Porsche's trunk. Something heavy had been carried in the car and was then removed. Now Bosch knew what it was and it was one more indication of the worst-case scenario.

He shook his head and Brenner clearly thought it was because he was making a judgment about security in the lab.

'Let me tell you something,' the agent said. 'Before we came in last year and revamped their security, anybody wearing a doctor's white coat could have walked right in here and taken whatever he wanted out of the safe.'

'I wasn't making a comment on security. I was—'

'I have to make a call,' Brenner said.

He moved away from the others and pulled out his cellphone. Bosch decided to make his own call. He pulled out his phone, found a corner for privacy and called his partner.

'Ignacio, it's me. I'm just checking in.'

'Call me Iggy, Harry. What's happening with you?'

'Nothing good. Kent emptied the safe. All the caesium is gone.'

'Are you kidding me? That's the stuff you said could be used to make a dirty bomb?'

'That's the stuff. Are you still at the scene?'

'Yeah, and listen, I've got a kid here who might've been a witness.'

'What do you mean, "might've been"? Who is it, a neighbour?'

'No. It's sort of a screwy story. You know that house that was supposedly Madonna's?'

'Yeah.'

'Yeah, well, she used to own it but doesn't any more. I go up there to knock on the door, and the guy who lives there now says he didn't see or hear anything— I'm getting the same thing at every door I knock on. So anyway, I'm leaving when I spot this guy hiding behind these big potted trees in the courtyard. I draw down on him and call back-up, you know, thinking maybe he's our shooter from the overlook. But turns out it's a kid—twenty years old and just off the bus from Canada—and he thinks Madonna's still living in the house. He's got a star map that still lists her as living there and he's trying to see her or something—like a stalker. He climbed over a wall to get into the courtyard.'

'Did he see the shooting?'

'He claims he didn't see or hear anything, but I don't know, Harry. I'm thinking he might've been stalking Madonna's place when the thing went down on the overlook. He then hides and tries to wait it out. Only I find him first.'

Bosch was missing something in the story. 'Why would he hide? Why wouldn't he just get the hell out of there? We didn't find the body till three hours after the shooting.'

'Yeah, I know. That part doesn't make sense. Maybe he was just scared or thought that if he was seen in the vicinity of the body he might get tagged as a suspect or something.'

Bosch nodded. It was a possibility. 'You holding him on the trespass?'

'Yeah. I talked to the guy who bought the place from Madonna and he'll work with us. He'll press charges if we need him to. So don't worry. We can hold him and work him with it.'

'Good. Take him downtown, put him in a room and warm him up. And Ignacio, don't tell anybody about the caesium.'

'You got it, Harry.'

Bosch closed the phone before Ferras could tell him to call him Iggy again. He listened to the end of Brenner's conversation. It was obvious he wasn't talking to Walling. His manner was deferential. He was talking to a boss.

'According to the log here, seven o'clock,' he said. 'That puts the transfer at the overlook at around eight, so we're talking about a six-and-a-half-hour lead at this point.'

Brenner listened some and then started to speak several times but was repeatedly cut off by the person on the other end of the line.

'Yes, sir,' he finally said. 'We're on our way back in now.'

He closed the phone and looked at Bosch. 'I'm going back in on the chopper. I have to lead a teleconference debriefing with Washington. I'd take you with me, but I think you'd be better off on the ground, chasing the case. I'll have someone pick up my car later.'

'No problem.'

'Did your partner come up with a witness? Is that what I heard?'

Bosch had to wonder how Brenner had picked that up while conducting his own phone conversation.

'Maybe, but it sounds like a long shot. I'm going downtown to see about that right now.'

Brenner nodded solemnly, then handed Bosch a business card. 'If you get anything, give me a call. Anything at all, call.'

Bosch took the card and put it in his pocket. He and the agents then left the lab and a few minutes later he watched the federal chopper take off into the black sky. He got into his car and pulled out of the clinic's parking lot. Before hitting the freeway, he gassed up at a station on San Fernando Road.

Traffic heading south into the centre of the city was light and he cruised at a steady eighty. The driving helped Bosch smooth out his thoughts. He realised the case was shifting. The feds, at least, were chasing the missing caesium instead of the killers. There was a subtle difference there that Bosch thought was important. He knew that he needed to keep his focus on the overlook and not lose sight of the fact that this was a murder investigation.

'Find the killers, you find the caesium,' he said out loud.

When he got downtown, he took the Los Angeles Street exit and parked in the front lot at police headquarters. At this hour, nobody would care that he wasn't a VIP or a member of command staff.

Parker Center was on its last legs. For nearly a decade a new police headquarters had been approved for construction but there had been repeated budgetary and political delays. In the meantime, little had been done to keep the current headquarters from sliding into decrepitude. Now the new building was under way but it was an estimated four years from completion. Many who worked in Parker Center wondered if it could last that long.

The RHD squad room on the third floor was deserted when Bosch got there. He opened his cellphone and called his partner.

'Where are you?'

'Hey, Harry. I'm at SID. I'm getting what I can so I can start putting the murder book together. Are you in the office?'

'I just got here. Where'd you put the wit?'

'I've got him cooking in room two. You want to start with him?'

'Might be good to hit him with somebody he hasn't seen before. Somebody older.'

It was a delicate suggestion. The potential witness was Ferras's find. Bosch wouldn't move in on him without his partner's at least tacit approval. But the situation dictated that someone with Bosch's experience would be better conducting such an important interview.

'Have at him, Harry. When I get back, I'll watch in the media room. If you need me to come in, just give me the signal.'

'Right.'

'I made fresh coffee in the captain's office if you want it.'

'Good. I need it. But first tell me about the witness.'

'His name is Jesse Mitford. From Halifax. He's kind of a drifter. He told me he hitchhiked down here and has been staying in shelters and sometimes up in the hills—when it's warm enough. That's about it.'

'Maybe he was going to sleep up there in Madonna's courtyard. That's why he didn't split.'

'I didn't think about that, Harry. You might be right.'

Bosch ended the call, got his coffee mug out of his desk drawer and headed to the RHD captain's office. There was an anteroom where the secretary's desk was located, as well as a table with a coffeemaker. The smell of fresh-brewed coffee hit Bosch as he entered, and that alone almost gave him the caffeine charge he needed. He poured a cup, dropped a buck in the basket, then headed back to his desk.

The squad room was designed with long rows of facing desks so that partners sat across from each other. The design afforded no personal or professional privacy. Since Bosch and Ferras were the newest additions to the squad, their desk tandem was located at the end of a line in a windowless corner, where the air circulation was bad and they would be furthest from the exit in the case of an emergency, like an earthquake.

Bosch's work space was neat and clean, just as he had left it. He noticed a backpack and a plastic evidence bag on his partner's desk across from him. He reached over and grabbed the backpack first. He opened it and found that it contained mostly clothing and other personal items belonging to the potential witness. There was a book called *The Stand* by Stephen King and a bag with toothpaste and a toothbrush in it. It all amounted to the meagre belongings of a meagre existence.

He returned the backpack and reached across for the evidence bag next. It contained a small amount of US currency, a set of keys, a thin wallet and a Canadian passport. It also contained a folded 'Homes of the Stars' map, the kind sold on street corners all around Hollywood. Bosch unfolded it and located the overlook off Mulholland Drive above Lake Hollywood. Just to the left of the location there was a black star with the number 23 in it. It had been circled with an ink pen. He checked the map's index and star number 23 said: 'Madonna's Hollywood Home'.

The map had obviously not been updated and Bosch suspected that few of the star locations were accurate. This explained why Mitford had been stalking a house where Madonna no longer lived.

Bosch refolded the map, put all the property back into the evidence bag and returned it to his partner's desk. He then got a legal pad and a rights waiver out of a drawer and stood up to go to interview room 2, which was in a hallway off the back of the squad room.

Jesse Mitford looked younger than his years. He had curly dark hair and ivory-white skin. He had a stubble of chin hair that looked like it might have taken him his whole life to grow. He had silver rings piercing one nostril and one eyebrow. He looked alert and scared. He was seated at a small table in the small interview room. The room smelt of body odour. Mitford was sweating, which of course was the objective. Bosch had checked the thermostat in the hallway before coming in. Ferras had set the temperature in the room to eighty-two.

'Jesse, how are you doing?' Bosch asked as he took the empty seat across from him.

'Uh, not so good. It's hot in here.'

'Really?'

'Are you my lawyer?'

'No, Jesse, I'm your detective. My name's Harry Bosch. I'm a homicide detective and I'm working the overlook case.'

Bosch put both his legal pad and his coffee mug down on the table. He noticed that Mitford still had handcuffs on. It was a nice touch by Ferras to keep the kid confused, scared and worried.

'I told the Mexican detective I didn't want to talk any more. I want a lawyer.'

Bosch nodded. 'He's Cuban American, Jesse,' he said. 'And you don't get a lawyer. Lawyers are for US citizens only.'

This was a lie, but Bosch was banking on the twenty-year-old not knowing this.

'You're in trouble, kid,' he continued. 'It's one thing to be stalking an old girlfriend or boyfriend. It's something else with a celebrity. This is a celebrity town, Jesse, and we take care of our own. I don't know what you've got up there in Canada, but the penalties here for what you were doing tonight are pretty stiff.'

Mitford shook his head. 'But I was told that Madonna doesn't even live there any more. So I wasn't really stalking her. It would just be trespassing.'

Now Bosch shook his head. 'It's about intent, Jesse. You thought she might be there. You had a map that said she *was* there. You even circled the spot. As far as the law goes, that constitutes stalking a celebrity.'

'Then why do they sell maps to stars' homes?'

'And why do bars have parking lots when drunk driving is illegal? We're not going to play that game, Jesse. The point is, there's nothing on the map that says anything about it being OK to jump over a wall and trespass, you know what I mean?'

Mitford dropped his eyes to his manacled wrists and nodded sadly.

'Tell you what, though,' Bosch said. 'You can cheer up, because things aren't as bad as they seem. You've got stalking and trespassing charges here, but I think we can probably get this all fixed up and taken care of if you agree to cooperate with me.'

Mitford leaned forward. 'But like I told that Mexi—that Cuban detective, I didn't see anything.'

Bosch waited a long moment before responding.

'I don't care what you told him. You're dealing with me now, son. And I think you're holding back on me.'

'No, I'm not. I swear to God.'

He held his hands open and as wide as the cuffs allowed in a pleading gesture. But Bosch wasn't buying it. He decided to go right at him.

'Let me tell you something, Jesse. My partner is good and he's going places in the department. But right now he's a baby. He's been a detective for about as long as you've been growing that peach fuzz on your chin. Me,

I've been around, and that means I've been around a lot of liars. And Jesse, I can tell. You're lying to me, and nobody lies to me.'

'No! I—'

'And so what you've got here is about thirty seconds to start talking to me or I'm just going to take you down and book you into county lockup. I'm sure there's going to be somebody waiting in there who will have a guy like you singing "O Canada" into the mike before sunup.'

Mitford stared down at his hands on the table. Bosch waited, and twenty seconds slowly went by. Finally, the detective stood up.

'OK, Jesse, stand up. We're going.'

'Wait, wait, wait!'

'For what? I said, stand up! Let's go. This is a murder investigation and I'm not wasting time on—'

'All right, all right, I'll tell you. I saw the whole thing, OK?'

Bosch studied him for a moment. 'You're talking about the overlook? You saw the shooting on the overlook?'

'I saw everything, man.'

Bosch pulled his chair out and sat back down.

BOSCH STOPPED Jesse Mitford from speaking until he had signed a rights waiver. It didn't matter that he was now considered a witness to the murder on the Mulholland overlook. Whatever it was that he witnessed, he saw because he was in the act of committing his own crime—trespassing and stalking. Bosch had to make sure there were no mistakes on the case. No fruit-of-the-poison-tree appeal. No blowback. The stakes were high, the feds were classic second-guessers and he knew he had to do this right.

'OK, Jesse,' he said when the waiver form was signed. 'You're going to tell me what you saw and heard up on the overlook. If you are truthful and helpful, I'm going to drop all charges and let you walk out of here a free man.'

Technically, Bosch was overstating his hand. He had no authority to drop charges or make deals with criminal suspects. But he didn't need it in this case, because Mitford had not yet been formally charged with anything. Therein lay Bosch's leverage. It came down to semantics. What Bosch was really offering was to not proceed with charging Mitford in exchange for the Canadian's cooperation.

'I understand,' Mitford said.

'Remember, only the truth. Only what you saw and heard. Nothing else.'

'I understand.'

'Hold up your hands.'

Mitford raised his wrists and Bosch used his own key to remove his partner's handcuffs. Mitford immediately began to rub them to get the circulation going again. It reminded Bosch of seeing Rachel rub Alicia Kent's wrists earlier.

'Feel better?' he asked.

'Yeah, good,' Mitford replied.

'OK, let's start from the top. Tell me where you came from, where you were going, and what you saw up on the overlook.'

Mitford nodded, then took Bosch through a twenty-minute story that began on Hollywood Boulevard with the purchase of the star map from a kerbside vendor and his long trek on foot up into the hills. His journey had taken nearly three hours and he told Bosch that by the time he got up to Mulholland Drive it was getting dark and he was tired. The house where the map said Madonna lived was dark inside. No one appeared to be home. Disappointed, he decided to wait and see if the pop singer would arrive home later. He found a spot behind some bushes where he could rest against the exterior of the wall that surrounded the home. Mitford said he fell asleep there until something woke him up.

'What woke you up?' Bosch asked.

'Voices. I heard voices.'

'What was said?'

'I don't know. It was just what woke me up.'

'How far were you from the overlook?'

'I don't know. Like fifty metres, I think. I was pretty far away.'

'What was said after you were awake and could hear?'

'Nothing. They stopped.'

'All right, then what did you see when you woke up?'

'I saw three cars parked by the clearing. One was a Porsche and the other two were bigger. I don't know the kind.'

'Did you see the men on the overlook?'

'No, I didn't see anybody. It was too dark out there. But then I heard a voice again and it was coming from over there. In the dark. It was like a yell. Right at the moment I looked, there were two quick flashes and shots. Like muffled shots. I could see somebody in the clearing on his knees. You know, in the flash of light. But it was so quick that was all I saw.'

Bosch nodded. 'This is good, Jesse. You're doing good. Let's just go over this part again so we have it right. You were asleep and then voices woke you up and you saw the three cars, right?'

'Yes.'

'OK, good. Then you heard a voice again and you looked towards the overlook. Just then the shots were fired. Is that right?'

'Right.'

Bosch nodded. But he knew that Mitford might simply be telling him what he wanted to hear. He had to test the kid to check that wasn't happening.

'Now, you said that in the flash from the gun, you saw the victim drop to his knees. Is that right?'

'No. I think he was on his knees already. It was so fast I wouldn't have seen him drop to his knees, like you said. I think he was already kneeling.'

Bosch nodded. Mitford had passed the first test.

'OK, good point. Now let's talk about what you heard. You said you heard somebody yell right before the shots, right?'

'Right.'

'OK. What did that person yell?'

Mitford thought for a moment, then shook his head. 'I'm not sure.'

'OK, that's all right. We don't want to say anything we're not sure about. Let's try an exercise and see if that helps. Close your eyes.'

'What?'

'Just close your eyes,' Bosch said soothingly. 'Think about what you saw. Try to bring up the visual memory and the audio will follow. You're looking at the three cars and then a voice pulls your attention towards the overlook. What did the voice say?'

Mitford closed his eyes. Bosch waited.

'I'm not sure,' the young man finally said. 'I can't get it all. I think he was saying something about Allah and then he shot the guy.'

Bosch held perfectly still for a moment before responding. 'Allah? You mean the Arabic word *Allah*?'

'I'm not sure. I think so.'

'What else did you hear?'

'Nothing else. The shots cut it off, you know? He started yelling about Allah and then the shots drowned the rest out.'

'You mean like "*Allah Akbar*". Is that what he yelled?'

'I don't know. I just heard the Allah part.'

'Could you tell if he had an accent?'

'An accent? I couldn't tell. I only heard the one word.'

Bosch thought about this for a few moments. He remembered what he had read about the cockpit recordings from the 9/11 attacks. The terrorists called out "*Allah Akbar*"—God is greatest—at the last moment. Did one of Stanley Kent's killers do the same?

Again, he knew he had to be careful. Much of the investigation could hinge on the one word Mitford thought he had heard.

'Jesse, what did Detective Ferras tell you about this case before he put you in this room?'

The witness shrugged. 'He didn't tell me anything, really.'

'He didn't tell you what we think we're looking at here or what direction the case may be going?'

'No, none of that.'

Bosch looked at him for a few moments. 'OK, Jesse,' he finally said. 'What happened next?'

'After the shots, somebody ran from the clearing to the cars. There was a streetlight out there and I saw him. He got into one of the cars and he backed it up close to the Porsche. Then he popped the trunk and got out. The Porsche's trunk was already open.'

'Where was the other man while he did this?'

Mitford looked confused. 'I guess he was dead.'

'No. I mean the second bad guy. There were two bad guys and one victim, Jesse. Three cars, remember?'

'I only saw one bad guy,' Mitford said. 'The shooter. Somebody else stayed in the car that was behind the Porsche. He never got out.'

'He just stayed in that other car the whole time?'

'That's right. In fact, right after the shooting that car made a U-turn and drove away.'

Bosch thought about this for a moment. What Mitford had described indicated a real division of labour between the two suspects. This mirrored the description of events that Alicia Kent had given earlier: one man questioning her and then translating and giving orders to the second. Bosch assumed it was the English speaker who had remained in the car.

'OK,' he finally said, 'go back to the story, Jesse. Right after the shooting, one guy drives away while the other backs up closer to the Porsche and pops the trunk. Then what happened?'

'He got out and took something from the Porsche and put it in the other car's trunk. It was really heavy and he had a hard time with it. It looked like it had handles on the sides because of the way he was holding it.'

Bosch knew that he was describing the pig used to transport radioactive materials. 'Then what?'

'He just got back in the car and drove off. He left the Porsche's trunk open.'

'And you saw nobody else?'

'Nobody else. I swear.'

'Describe the man you did see.'

'I can't really describe him. He was wearing a sweatshirt with the hood up. I never really saw his face or anything. I think that under the hood he was wearing a ski mask, too.'

'Why do you think that?'

Mitford shrugged again. 'I don't know. It just seemed that way to me. I might be wrong.'

'Was he big? Was he small?'

'I think he was average. Maybe a little short.'

'What did he look like?' Bosch had to try again. It was important. 'White, black, Middle Eastern?'

'I couldn't tell. He had the hood and the mask and I was so far away.'

'Think about the hands, Jesse. You said there were handles on the thing he transferred from one car to the other. Could you see his hands? What colour were his hands?'

Mitford thought for a moment and his eyes brightened. 'No. He wore gloves. I remember the gloves because they were those real big kind, like the guys wear who work on the trains back in Halifax. Heavy-duty with the big cuffs so they don't get burned.'

Bosch nodded. He had been fishing for one thing but got something else. Protective gloves. He wondered if they were gloves specifically designed for handling radioactive material.

Bosch paused there. Sometimes the silences are the most uneasy moments for a witness. They start to fill in the blanks.

But Mitford said nothing. After a long moment, Bosch continued.

'OK, we had two cars up there besides the Porsche. Describe the car that backed up to the Porsche.'

'I can't, really. I know what Porsches look like but I couldn't tell about the other cars. Both were a lot bigger, with four doors.'

'The one in front of the Porsche, was it a sedan?'

'I don't know the brand.'

'No, a sedan is a type of car not a brand. Four doors, trunk—like a police car.'

'Yes, like that.'

Bosch thought about Alicia Kent's description of her missing car.

'Do you know what a Chrysler 300 looks like?'

'No.'

'What colour was the car you saw?'

'I don't know for sure, but it was dark. Black or dark blue.'

'What about the other car? The one behind the Porsche.'

'Same thing. A dark sedan. It was different from the one in front—maybe a little bit smaller.'

Bosch nodded. He considered things for a moment. Mitford's story matched up with information provided by Alicia Kent. The two intruders to the Kent house had to have had transportation to get there. One would have taken the original vehicle, while the other took Alicia Kent's Chrysler to transport the caesium. It seemed like the obvious thing.

His thoughts prompted a new question for Mitford. 'Which way did the second car go when he drove off?'

'He also made a U-turn and drove down the hill.'

'What did you do then?'

'Me? Nothing. I just stayed where I was.'

'Why?'

'I was scared. I was pretty sure I'd just seen some guy get murdered.'

'You didn't go check on him to see if he was alive and needed help?'

Mitford looked away and shook his head. 'No. I was afraid. I'm sorry.'

'It's OK, Jesse. You don't have to worry about that. He was already dead. He was dead before he hit the ground. But what I'm curious about is why you stayed in hiding for so long. Why didn't you go down the hill? Why didn't you call nine-one-one?'

Mitford raised his hands and dropped them on the table. 'I don't know. I was afraid, I guess. I followed the map up the hill, so that was the only way I knew back. I would have had to walk right by there and I thought, What if the cops come while I'm walking right there? I could get blamed. And I thought, If it was like the Mafia or something that did it and they found out I had seen everything, then I'd be killed or something.'

Bosch nodded. 'I think you watch too much American TV up there in Canada. Don't worry. We'll take care of you. How old are you, Jesse?'

'Twenty.'

'So what were you doing at Madonna's house? Isn't she a little old for you?'

'No. It wasn't like that. It was for my mother.'

'You were stalking her for your mother?'

'I'm not a stalker. I just wanted to get my mother her autograph or see if she had a picture or something I could have. I wanted to send something back to my mom. You know, just to show her I'm OK. I thought if I told her I had met Madonna, then I wouldn't feel like such a . . . you know. I grew up listening to Madonna because my mom listens to her stuff. I just thought it would be kind of cool to send her something. Her birthday's coming up and I didn't have anything.'

'Why'd you come to LA, Jesse?'

'I don't know. It just seemed like the place to go. I was hoping I could get in a band or something.'

Bosch thought Mitford had adopted the pose of the wandering troubadour, but there had been no guitar or other mobile instrument with his backpack in the squad room.

'Are you a musician or a singer?'

'I play the guitar but I had to pawn it a few days ago. I'll get it back.'

'Where are you staying?'

'I don't really have a place right now. I was going to sleep up in the hills last night. I guess it's the real answer to why I didn't leave after I saw what happened to that guy up there. I really didn't have any place to go.'

Bosch understood. Jesse Mitford was no different from a thousand others who got off the bus every month or thumbed it into town. More dreams than plans or currency. More hope than cunning, skill or intelligence. Not all of those who fail to make it stalk those who do. But the one thing they all share is that desperate edge. And some never lose it, even after their names are put up in lights and they buy houses on top of the hills.

'Let's take a break here, Jesse,' Bosch said. 'I need to make a few phone calls and then we'll probably need to go over it all again. You cool with that? I'll also see about maybe getting you a hotel room or something.'

Mitford nodded and Bosch left him there.

In the hallway, Bosch switched on the air conditioning in the interview room and set it at sixty-four. It would soon cool off in the room and instead of sweating Mitford would start to get cold—though coming from Canada, maybe not. After he chilled for a while, Bosch would take another run at him and see if anything new came out. He checked his watch. It was almost 5 a.m., and the case meeting that the feds were organising was not for another four hours. There was time for a second round with Mitford.

Out in the squad room, Bosch found Ignacio Ferras working at his desk, typing on his laptop. Bosch noticed that Mitford's property had been replaced on the desk by other evidence bags and file folders. It was everything from SID that the case had spawned so far on the two crime scenes.

'Harry, sorry I didn't get back in there to watch,' Ferras said. 'Anything new from the kid?'

'We're getting there. I'm just taking a break.'

Ferras was thirty years old and had an athlete's body. On his desk was the trophy awarded him for being his academy class's top achiever in physical conditioning and testing. He was also handsome, with mocha skin and short-cropped hair. He had piercing green eyes.

Bosch stepped over to his own desk to use the phone. He was going to wake up Lieutenant Gandle one more time to give him another update.

'You track the vic's gun yet?' he asked Ferras.

'Yeah. I got it off the ATF computer. He bought a twenty-two-calibre belly gun six months ago. Smith and Wesson.'

Bosch nodded. 'A twenty-two fits. No exit wounds.'

'Bullets check in but they don't check out.'

Ferras delivered the line like a television commercial huckster and laughed at his own joke. Bosch thought about what was lying beneath the humour. Stanley Kent had been warned that his profession made him vulnerable. His response was to purchase a gun for protection.

And now Bosch was betting that the gun he'd bought had been used against him, had been used to kill him by a terrorist who called out the name of Allah as he pulled the trigger. What a world it was, Bosch thought, when someone could draw the courage to pull the trigger on another man by calling out to his God.

'Not a good way to go,' Ferras said.

Bosch looked across the two desks at him. 'Let me tell you something,' he said. 'You know what you find out on this job?'

'No, what?'

'That there are no good ways to go.'

FIVE

Bosch went to the captain's office to refill his coffee mug. When he reached into his pocket for another buck for the basket, he came out with Brenner's card. It reminded him of Brenner's request to be updated on the possibility of a witness. But Bosch had just finished updating Lieutenant Gandle on what the young Canadian said he had seen and heard at the overlook and together they had decided to keep Mitford under wraps for the time being. Until at least the 9 a.m. meeting, when it would be time to put up or shut up. If the feds were going to keep the LAPD involved, it would become clear at that meeting. Then it would be quid pro quo time. Bosch would share the witness's story in exchange for a share of the investigation.

Meantime, Gandle said he would send another update through the department's chain of command. With the latest revelation about the word *Allah* cropping up in the investigation, it was incumbent upon him to make sure the growing gravity of the case was communicated upwards.

With his mug full, Bosch went back to his desk and started going through the evidence collected from the murder scene and the house where Alicia Kent had been held. He removed Stanley Kent's personal belongings from the evidence bags and started examining them. At this stage, they had been processed by Forensics and it was OK to handle them.

The first item was the physicist's BlackBerry. Bosch was not adept in a digital world. He had mastered his own cellphone, but it was a basic model that made and received calls, stored numbers in a directory and did nothing else—as far as he knew. This meant that he was quite lost as he tried to manipulate the higher-evolution device.

'Harry, you need help with that?'

Bosch looked up and saw Ferras smiling at him. Bosch was embarrassed by his lack of technological skill but not to the point where he wouldn't accept help. That would turn his personal flaw into something worse.

'You know how to work this?'

'Sure.'

'It has email, right?'

'It should.'

Bosch handed the phone across both of their desks. 'About six o'clock yesterday, Kent was sent an email that was marked urgent from his wife. It had the photo in it of her tied up on their bed. I want you to find it and see if there is a way you can somehow print it out with the photo. I want to look at the photo again, but bigger than on that little screen.'

As Bosch spoke, Ferras had already been working the BlackBerry. 'No problem,' he said. 'What I can do is forward the email to my own email account here. Then I'll open it up and print it out.'

Ferras started using his thumbs to type on the phone's tiny keyboard. It looked like some sort of child's toy to Bosch. He didn't understand why people were always typing feverishly on their phones. He was sure it was some sort of warning, a sign of the decline of civilisation, but he couldn't put his finger on the right explanation for what he felt. The digital world was always billed as a great advancement but he remained sceptical.

'OK, I found it and sent it,' Ferras said. 'It'll probably come through in a couple minutes. What else?'

'Does that show what calls he made and what calls came in?'

Ferras manipulated the controls on the phone. 'How far back do you want to go?' he asked.

'For now, how about going back till about noon yesterday.'

'OK, I'm on the screen. You want me to show you how to use this thing, or do you want me to just give you the numbers?'

Bosch got up and came round the row of desks so he could look over his partner's shoulder at the phone's small screen. 'Just give me an overview for now. If you tried to teach me we'd be here for ever.'

Ferras smiled. 'Well, if he made or received a call to or from a number that was in his address book, it's listed by the name in the address book.'

'Got it.'

'It shows a lot of calls to and from the office and various hospitals all through the afternoon. Three calls are marked "Barry". I'm assuming that was his partner. I looked up the state corporate records online, and K and K Medical Physicists is owned by Kent and someone named Barry Kelber.'

'Yeah,' Bosch said. 'That reminds me that we have to talk to the partner first thing this morning.'

He leaned across Ferras's desk to reach the notepad on his own desk. He wrote down the name *Barry Kelber* while Ferras continued to scroll through the cellphone's call log.

'Now, here we are after six, and he starts alternately calling his home and his wife's cellphone. I get the feeling that these weren't answered, because he's got ten calls logged in three minutes. And these were all made after he received that urgent email from his wife's account.'

Bosch saw the picture beginning to fill in a little bit. Kent had a routine day on the job, then got the email from his wife's account. He saw the photo attached and started calling home. She didn't answer, which only alarmed him further. Finally, he went out and did what the email instructed him to do. But for all his efforts and following of orders, they still killed him.

'So what went wrong?' he asked out loud.

'What do you mean, Harry?'

'Up at the overlook. I still don't understand why they killed him. He did what they wanted. He turned over the stuff. What went wrong?'

'I don't know. Maybe he saw one of their faces.'

'The witness says the shooter was wearing a mask.'

'Well, then maybe nothing went wrong. Maybe the plan was to kill him all along. They made that silencer, remember? And the way the guy yells out "Allah" doesn't make it sound like something went wrong. Makes it sound like part of a plan.'

Bosch nodded. 'Then if that was the plan why kill him and not her? Why leave a witness?'

'I don't know, Harry. But don't those hard-core Muslims have a rule about hurting women? Like it keeps them out of nirvana or heaven or whatever they call it?'

Bosch didn't answer the question, because he didn't know about the cultural practices his partner had crudely referred to. But the question underlined for him how out of his element he was on the case. He was used to chasing killers motivated by greed or lust or any one of the big seven sins. Religious extremism wasn't often on the list.

Ferras put the BlackBerry down and turned back to his computer. Like many detectives, he preferred to use his own laptop because the computers provided by the department were old and slow and most of them carried more viruses than a Hollywood Boulevard hooker.

He saved what he had been working on and opened up his email screen. The email forwarded from Kent's account was there. Ferras opened it and whistled when he saw the embedded photograph of Alicia Kent naked and tied up on the bed.

'Yeah, that would do it,' he said.

Meaning that he understood why Kent had turned over the caesium. Ferras had been married for less than a year and had a baby on the way. Bosch was just starting to get to know his young partner, but knew already that he was deeply in love with his wife. Under the glass top of his desk, Ferras had a collage of photos of his bride. Under the glass on his side of the workstation, Bosch had photos of murder victims whose killers he was still looking for.

'Make me a print-out of that,' Bosch said. 'Blow it up if you can. And keep playing with that phone. See what else you can find.' He went back to his side of the workstation and sat down. Ferras enlarged and printed out the email and photo on a colour printer at the back of the squad room. He went over and retrieved it, then brought it to Bosch.

Bosch already had his reading glasses on, but from a desk drawer he pulled a rectangular magnifying glass he'd bought when he noticed that his prescription was no longer strong enough for close-up work. He never used the magnifying glass when the squad room was crowded with detectives. He didn't want to give the others something to ridicule him with.

He put the print-out on his desk and leaned over it with the magnifier. He studied the bindings that held the woman's limbs behind her torso. The intruders had used six snap ties, placing one loop round each wrist and ankle, then one to link the ankles, and the last one to link the wrist loops to the loop connecting the ankles.

It seemed like an overly complicated way to bind the woman's extremities. It was not the way Bosch would have done it if he were trying to quickly hog-tie a perhaps struggling woman. He would have used fewer bindings and made the work easier and quicker.

He wasn't sure what this meant, or if it meant anything at all. Perhaps Alicia Kent hadn't struggled at all and, in return for her cooperation, her captors used the extra links in order to make the time she was left bound on the bed less difficult. It seemed to Bosch that the way she had been bound meant that her arms and legs were not pulled behind her as far as they could have been.

Still, remembering the bruising on Alicia Kent's wrists, he realised that no matter what, the time she had spent hog-tied naked on the bed had not been easy. He decided that he needed to talk with her again and go over what had happened in more detail.

Nothing else came to mind during his study of the photograph. When he was finished, he put the magnifier aside and started skimming through the forensics reports from the murder scene. Nothing grabbed his attention there either and he quickly moved on to the reports and evidence from the Kent house. Because he and Brenner had quickly left the house for Saint Agatha's, Bosch had not been there when the SID techs searched for evidence left behind by the intruders. He was anxious to see what, if anything, had been found.

But there was only one evidence bag, and it contained the black plastic snap ties that had been used to bind Alicia Kent's wrists and ankles and that Rachel Walling had cut in order to free her.

'Wait a minute,' Bosch said, holding up the clear plastic bag. 'Is this the only evidence they bagged at the Kent house?'

Ferras looked up. 'It's the only bag they gave me. Did you check the evidence log? It should be in there. Maybe they're still processing some stuff.'

Every item removed from a crime scene by the technicians was always entered on the forensic evidence log. It helped track the chain of evidence.

Bosch looked through the documents Ferras had obtained until he found the log. He noticed that it included several items removed by technicians from the Kent house, most of them tiny hair and fibre specimens. There was no telling if any of the specimens was related to the suspects, but in all his years working cases, Bosch had yet to come across the immaculate crime scene. A crime always leaves its mark—no matter how small—on the environment. There is always a transfer. It is just a matter of finding it.

On the list, each snap tie had been individually entered, and these were followed by numerous hair and fibre specimens extracted from locations ranging from the master bedroom carpet to the sink trap in the guest bathroom. The mouse pad from the office computer was on the list, as well as a Nikon camera lens cap, which had been found beneath the bed in the master bedroom. The last entry on the list was the most interesting to Bosch. The evidence was simply described as a cigarette ash.

Bosch could not think what value as evidence a cigarette ash could be.

'Is anybody still up there in SID from the Kent house search?' he asked.

'There was a half-hour ago,' Ferras answered. 'Buzz Yates and the latents woman whose name I always forget.'

Bosch picked up the phone and called the SID office.

'Scientific Investigation Division, Yates.'

'Buzz, just the guy I wanted to talk to.'

'Who's this?'

'Harry Bosch. On the search of the Kent house, tell me about this cigarette ash you collected.'

'Oh, yeah. The FBI agent who was there asked me to collect it.'

'Where was it?'

'She found it on top of the toilet cistern in the guest bedroom. Like somebody had put their smoke down while they took a leak and then forgot about it. It burned all the way through and then out.'

'So it was just ashes when she found it?'

'Right. A grey caterpillar. But she wanted us to collect it for her. She said their lab might be able to do something with—'

'Wait a minute, Buzz. You gave her the evidence?'

'Well, sort of. Yeah. She—'

'What do you mean, "sort of"? You either did or you didn't. Did you give Agent Walling the cigarette ashes you collected from my crime scene?'

'Yes,' Yates conceded. 'But not without a lot of discussion and assurances, Harry. She said the Bureau's science lab could analyse the ashes and determine the type of tobacco, which would then allow them to determine country of origin. We can't do anything like that, Harry. We can't even touch that. She said it would be important to the investigation because they might be dealing with terrorists from outside the country. So I went along with it. She told me that she worked an arson case once where they found a single ash from the cigarette that lit the fire. They were able to tell what brand and that tied it to a specific suspect.'

'And you believed her?'

'Well . . . yeah, I believed her.'

'So you gave her my evidence,' Bosch said in a resigned tone.

'Harry, it's not *your* evidence. We all work and play on the same team, don't we?'

'Yeah, Buzz, we do.'

Bosch hung up the phone and cursed. Ferras asked him what was wrong, but Bosch waved the question away.

'Just typical Bureau bull.'

'Harry, did you get any sleep at all before the call-out?'

Bosch looked across the desks at his partner. He knew exactly where Ferras was headed with that question.

'No,' Bosch answered. 'But lack of sleep has nothing to do with my frustration with the FBI. I've been doing this for more years than you've been alive. I know how to handle sleep deprivation.' He held up his mug of coffee. 'Cheers,' he said.

'It's still not good, partner,' Ferras responded. 'Your ass is going to be dragging in a while.'

'Don't worry about me.'

'OK, Harry.'

Bosch went back to thoughts about the cigarette ash. 'What about photos?' he asked Ferras. 'Did you pick up photos from the Kent house?'

'Yeah. They're here somewhere.' Ferras looked through the files on his desk, came up with the folder containing the photos and passed it across.

Bosch found three shots from the guest bathroom. A full shot, an angled shot of the toilet that showed the line of ash on the cistern lid, and a close-up of the grey caterpillar, as Buzz Yates had called it.

He spread the three shots out and used his magnifier once again to study them. In the close-up shot of the ash, the photographer had put a six-inch ruler down on the cistern lid to give the shot scale. The ash was nearly two inches long, almost a full cigarette.

'See anything yet, Sherlock?' Ferras asked.

Bosch looked up at him. His partner was smiling. Bosch didn't smile back, deciding that now he couldn't even use the magnifying glass in front of his own partner without getting ripped.

'Not yet, Watson,' he said.

He thought that might keep Ferras quiet. Nobody wanted to be Watson.

He studied the shot of the toilet and noted that the seat had been left up. The indication was that a male had used the bathroom to urinate. The cigarette ash would further indicate that it had been one of the two intruders. Bosch looked at the wall above the toilet. There was a small framed photograph of a winter scene in New York or somewhere else in the East.

The photo prompted Bosch to remember a case he had closed a year ago while he was in the Open-Unsolved Unit. He picked up the phone and called SID again. When Yates answered, Bosch asked for the person who had checked the Kent house for latent fingerprints.

'Hold on,' Yates said.

Apparently still annoyed with Bosch from the earlier phone call, Yates took his time getting the latents tech to the phone. Bosch ended up holding for about four minutes, using his glass to go over the photos from the Kent house the whole time.

'This is Wittig,' a voice finally said.

Bosch knew her from prior cases. 'Andrea, it's Harry Bosch. I want to ask you about the Kent house. Did you laser the guest bathroom?'

'Where they found the ash and the seat was up? Yes, I did that.'

'Anything?'

'No, nothing. It was wiped.'

'How about the wall up above the toilet?'

'Yes, I checked there, too. There was nothing.'

'That's all I wanted to know. Thanks, Andrea.'

Bosch hung up and looked at the photo of the ash. Something about it bugged him but he wasn't sure what.

'Harry, what were you asking about the wall over the toilet?'

Bosch looked at Ferras. Part of the reason the young detective was partnered with Bosch was so that the experienced detective could mentor the inexperienced detective. Bosch decided to put the Sherlock Holmes crack aside and tell him the story.

'About thirty years ago there was a case in Wilshire. This woman and her dog found drowned in her bathtub. The whole place had been wiped clean, but the lid was left up on the toilet. That told them they were looking for a man. The toilet had been wiped but on the wall up behind it they found a palm print. The guy had taken a leak and leaned on the wall while doing it. By measuring the height of the palm, they were able to figure out the guy's height. They also knew he was left-handed.'

'How?'

'Because the print on the wall was a right palm. They figured a guy holds his tool with his preferred hand while taking a leak.'

Ferras nodded in agreement. 'So they matched the palm to a suspect?'

'Yeah, but only after thirty years. We cleared it last year in Open-Unsolved. Not a lot of palms in the data banks back then. My partner and I came across the case and sent the palm through the box. We got a hit. We traced the guy and went out to the desert to get him. He pulled a gun and killed himself before we could make the arrest.'

'Wow. So you didn't get a chance to talk to him?'

'Not really. But we were sure it was him. And I sort of took his killing himself in front of us as an admission of guilt.'

'No, yeah, of course. I just mean I would've liked to talk to the guy and ask him why he killed the dog, that's all.'

Bosch stared at his partner for a moment. 'I think if we had talked, we'd have been more interested in why he killed the woman.'

'Yeah, I know. I was just wondering, why the dog, you know?'

'I think he thought the dog might be able to identify him. Like the dog knew him and would react in his presence. He didn't want to risk it.'

Ferras nodded like he accepted the explanation. Bosch had just made it up. The question about the dog had never come up during the investigation.

Ferras went back to his work and Bosch leaned back in his chair and considered things about the case at hand. At the moment, it was a jumble of thoughts and questions. Once again, most prominent in his mind was the basic question of why Stanley Kent was killed. Alicia Kent had said that the two men who held her captive had worn ski masks. Jesse Mitford had said that he thought the man he saw kill Kent on the overlook was wearing a ski mask. To Bosch this begged the questions: why shoot Stanley Kent if he couldn't even identify you, and why wear the mask if the plan all along was to kill him? He supposed that wearing the mask could have been a ploy to falsely reassure Kent and to make him cooperative. But that conclusion didn't feel right to him either.

Once more he put the questions aside, deciding that he didn't have enough information yet to go at them properly. He drank some coffee and got ready to take another shot at Jesse Mitford in the interview room. But first he pulled out his phone. He still had Rachel Walling's number from the Echo Park case. He had decided never to delete it.

He pushed the button and called the number, preparing for it to have been disconnected by her. The number was still good, but when he heard her voice it was a recording telling him to leave a message after the beep.

'It's Harry Bosch,' he said. 'I need to talk to you about things and I want my cigarette ashes back. That crime scene was mine.'

He hung up. He knew the message would annoy her, maybe even make her mad. He knew that he was inextricably heading towards a confrontation with Rachel and the Bureau that probably wasn't necessary and could easily be avoided.

But Bosch couldn't bring himself to roll over. Not even for Rachel and the memory of what they once had. Not even for the hope of a future with her that he still carried like a number in a cellphone's heart.

SIX

Bosch and Ferras stepped out of the front door of the Mark Twain Hotel and surveyed the morning. The light was just beginning to enter the sky. The marine layer was coming in grey and thick and was deepening the shadows in the streets. It made it look like a city of ghosts and that was fine with Bosch. It matched his outlook.

'You think he'll stay put?' Ferras asked.

Bosch shrugged. 'He's got no place else to go.'

They had just checked their witness into the hotel under the alias Stephen King. Jesse Mitford had turned into a valuable asset. Though he had not been able to provide a description of the man who shot Stanley Kent and took the caesium, Mitford had been able to give them a clear understanding of what had transpired at the overlook. He would also be useful if the investigation ever led to an arrest and trial. A prosecutor could use his story as the narrative of the crime, a way to connect the dots for the jury.

After Bosch had consulted with Lieutenant Gandle, it was decided that they shouldn't lose track of the young drifter. Gandle approved a hotel voucher that would keep Mitford in the Mark Twain for four days. By then things would be clearer in regard to which way the case was going to go.

Bosch and Ferras got into the Crown Victoria that Ferras had earlier checked out of the car shed, and headed down Wilcox to Sunset. Bosch was behind the wheel. At the light, he got out his cellphone. He hadn't heard back from Rachel Walling, so he called the number her partner had given him. Brenner answered right away.

Bosch proceeded cautiously. 'Just checking in,' he said. 'We still on for the meeting at nine?' Bosch wanted to make sure he was still part of the investigation before updating Brenner on anything.

'Uh, yes . . . yes, we're still on, but it's been pushed back. I think it's ten now. We'll let you know.'

The answer didn't make it sound like the meeting with the locals was a done deal. He decided to press Brenner. 'Where will it be? At Tactical?'

Bosch knew from working with Walling before that the Tactical Unit was off campus in a secret location. He wanted to see if Brenner would slip.

'No, in the federal building downtown. Fourteenth floor. Just ask for the TIU meeting. How helpful was the witness?'

Bosch decided to hold his cards close until he had a better idea of his standing. 'He saw the shooting from a distance. Then he saw the transfer. He said one man did it all, killed Stanley Kent and then moved the pig from the Porsche to the back of another vehicle. The other guy waited in another car and just watched.'

'You get any plates from him?'

'No, no plates. Mrs Kent's car was probably the one used to make the transfer. That way there would be no caesium trace in their own car.'

'What about the suspect he did see?'

'Like I said, he couldn't ID him. He was still wearing a ski mask. Other than that, nada.'

'Too bad,' Brenner said. 'What did you do with him?'

'The kid? We just dropped him off.'

'Where's he live?'

'Halifax, Canada.'

'Bosch, you know what I mean.'

Bosch noticed the change in tone. That and the use of his last name. He didn't think Brenner was casually asking about Mitford's exact location.

'He's got no local address,' he replied. 'He's a drifter. We just dropped him off at the Denny's on Sunset. That's where he wanted to go. We gave him a twenty to cover breakfast.'

Bosch felt Ferras staring at him as he lied.

'Can you hold a second, Harry?' Brenner said. 'I've got another call coming in here. It might be Washington.'

Back to first names, Bosch noted.

'Sure, Jack.' He heard the line go to music and looked over at Ferras.

His partner started to speak. 'Why'd you tell him we—?'

Bosch held a finger to his lips. 'Just hold it a second.'

Half a minute went by. The light changed and Bosch turned onto Sunset. Then Brenner came back on the line.

'Harry? Sorry about that. That was Washington. As you can imagine, they're all over this thing.'

Bosch decided to draw things out into the open. 'What's new on your end?'

'Not a lot. Homeland is sending a fleet of choppers with equipment that can track a radiation trail. They'll start up at the overlook and try to pick up a signature specific to caesium. But the reality is, it's got to come out of the pig before they'll pick up a signal. Meantime, we're organising the status meeting so that we can make sure everybody's on the same page.'

'That's all the big G has accomplished?'

'We're just getting organised. I told you how it would be. Alphabet soup.'

'Right. You called it pandemonium. The feds are good at that.'

'No, I'm not sure I said that. But there's always a learning curve. I think after the meeting we'll be hitting this thing on all cylinders.'

Bosch now knew for sure that things had changed. Brenner's defensive response told him the conversation was either being taped or overheard.

'It's still a few hours till the meeting,' Brenner said. 'What's your next move, Harry?'

Bosch hesitated, but not for long. 'My next move is to go back up to the house and talk to Mrs Kent again. I have some follow-up. Then we'll go over to the south tower at Cedars. Kent's office is there and we need to see it and to talk to his partner.'

There was no response. Bosch was coming up on the Denny's on Sunset. He pulled into the lot and parked. Through the windows he could see that the twenty-four-hour restaurant was largely deserted.

'You still there, Jack?'

'Uh, yeah, Harry. I should tell you that it probably won't be necessary, you going back to the house and then by Kent's office.'

Bosch shook his head. I knew it, he thought.

'You've already scooped everybody up, haven't you?'

'Wasn't my call. Anyway, from what I hear, the office was clean and we have Kent's partner in here being questioned right now. We brought Mrs Kent in as kind of a precautionary thing. We're still talking to her, too.'

Bosch killed the car's engine and thought about how to respond. 'Then maybe my partner and I should head downtown to TIU,' he finally said. 'This is still a homicide investigation. And last I heard, I was still working it.'

There was a long thread of silence before Brenner responded.

'Look, Detective, the case is taking on larger dimensions. You've been invited to the status meeting. You and your partner. And at that time you'll be updated on what Mr Kelber has had to say and a few other things. If Mr Kelber is still here with us, I'll do my best to get you in to speak with him. And with Mrs Kent, too. But to be clear, the priority here is not the homicide. The priority is finding the caesium and we're now almost ten hours behind.'

Bosch nodded. 'I have a feeling that if you find the killer you find the caesium,' he said.

'That may be so,' Brenner responded. 'But the experience is that this material is moved very quickly. Hand to hand. It takes an investigation with a lot of velocity. That's what we're engaged in now. Building velocity. We don't want to be slowed down.'

'By the local yokels.'

'You know what I mean.'

'Sure. I'll see you at ten, Agent Brenner.'

Bosch closed his phone and got out. As he and his partner crossed the lot, Ferras barraged him with questions.

'Why did you lie to him about the wit, Harry? What's going on? What are we doing here?'

Bosch held his hands up in a calming motion. 'Hold on, Ignacio. Let's sit down and have some coffee and maybe something to eat and I'll tell you what is going on.'

They almost had their pick of the place. Bosch went to a booth in a corner that would allow them a clear view of the front door. The waitress came over quickly. She was an old battle-axe, with her steel-grey hair in a tight bun. Working graveyard at a Denny's in Hollywood had leached the life out of her eyes.

'Harry, it's been a long time,' she said.

'Hey, Peggy. I guess it's been a while since I've had to chase a case through the night.'

'Well, welcome back. What can I get you and your much younger partner?'

Bosch ignored the dig. He ordered coffee, toast and eggs. Ferras ordered an egg-white omelette and a latte. When the waitress smirked and told him that neither could be accomplished, he settled for scrambled eggs and regular coffee. As soon as the waitress left them alone, Bosch answered Ferras's questions.

'We're being cut out,' he said. 'That's what's going on here.'

'Are you sure? How do you know?'

'Because they've already scooped up our victim's wife and partner, and I can guarantee you they are not going to let us talk to them.'

'Harry, did they say that? Did they tell you that we couldn't talk to them? There's a lot at stake here, and I think you're being a little paranoid. You're jumping to—'

'Am I? Well, wait and see, partner. Watch and learn.'

'We're still going to the meeting at nine, aren't we?'

'Supposedly. Except now it's at ten. And it will probably be a dog and pony show just for us. They're not going to tell us anything. They're going to sweet-talk us and brush us aside. "Thanks a lot, fellas, we'll take it from here." Well, fuck that. This is a homicide and nobody, not even the FBI, brushes me off a case.'

'Have a little faith, Harry.'

'I have faith in myself. That's it. I've been on this road before. I know where it goes. On the one hand, who cares? Let them run with the case. But on the other hand, I care. I can't trust them to do it right. They want the caesium; I want the bastards who terrorised Stanley Kent for two hours then forced him onto his knees and put two slugs in the back of his head.'

'This is national security, Harry. This is different. There's a greater good here. You know, the good of the order.'

It sounded to Bosch like Ferras was quoting from an academy textbook or the code of some secret society. He didn't care. He had his own code.

'The good of the order starts with that guy lying dead on the overlook. If we forget about him, then we can forget about everything else.'

Ferras had picked up the salt shaker and was nervously manipulating it in his hand, spilling salt on the table. 'Nobody's forgetting, Harry. It's about priorities. I'm sure that when things shake out during the meeting they will share any information relating to the homicide.'

Bosch grew frustrated. 'Don't you get it? There will be no meeting. They put that out there so we would stay in line until nine and now ten, all the while thinking we're still part of the team. But then we'll show up there and they'll delay it again and again until they finally trot out with some organisational chart that's supposed to make us feel like we're part of everything when the reality is we're part of nothing and they've run out the back door.'

Ferras nodded as though he was taking the advice to heart. But then he spoke from somewhere else. 'I still don't think we should have lied to them about the witness. He might be very valuable to them. Something he told us might fit with something they know about already. What's the harm in telling them where he is?'

Bosch emphatically shook his head. 'No way. Not yet. The wit is ours and we don't give him up. We trade him for access and information or we keep him for ourselves.'

The waitress brought their plates and looked from the salt spilt on the table to Ferras and then Bosch. 'I know he's young, Harry, but can't you teach him some manners?'

'I'm trying, Peggy. But these young people don't want to learn.'

'I hear you.'

She left the table and Bosch immediately dug into his food, holding a fork in one hand and a piece of toast in the other. He was starved and had a feeling they'd be on the move soon. When they would next have time for a meal was anybody's guess.

He was halfway through his eggs when he saw four men in dark suits walk in with unmistakable federal purpose in their strides. Wordlessly, they split into twos and started walking through the restaurant.

There were less than a dozen diners in the place, most of them strippers and their boyfriend pimps heading home from four-o'clock clubs. Bosch calmly continued to eat and watched the men in suits stop at each table, show credentials and ask for IDs. Ferras was too busy splashing hot sauce on his eggs to notice what was happening. Bosch got his attention and nodded towards the agents.

Most of the people scattered among the tables were too tired or buzzed to do anything but comply with the demands to show identification. One young woman with a Z shaved into the side of her head started giving one pair of agents some lip, but she was a woman and they were looking for a man, so they ignored her and waited patiently for her boyfriend with the matching Z to show some ID.

Finally, a pair of agents came to the table in the corner. Their creds identified them as FBI agents Ronald Lundy and John Parkyn. They ignored Bosch because he was too old and asked Ferras for his ID.

'Who are you looking for?' Bosch asked.

'That's government business, sir. We just need to check IDs.'

Ferras opened his badge wallet. On one side it had his photo and police ID, and on the other side his detective's badge. It seemed to freeze the two agents.

'It's funny,' Bosch said. 'If you're looking at IDs, that means you have a name. But I never gave Agent Brenner the witness's name. Makes me wonder. You guys over there in Tactical Intelligence don't happen to have a bug in our computer or maybe our squad room, do you?'

Lundy, the one obviously in charge of the pick-up detail, looked squarely at Bosch. 'And you are?' he asked.

'You want to see my ID, too? I haven't passed for a twenty-year-old in a long time but I'll take it as a compliment.'

He pulled out his badge wallet and handed it to Lundy. The agent opened it and examined the contents very closely. He took his time.

'Hieronymus Bosch,' he said, reading the name on the ID. 'Wasn't there some sick creep of a painter named that?'

Bosch smiled back at him. 'Some people consider the painter a master of the Renaissance period,' he said.

Lundy dropped the badge wallet on Bosch's plate. Bosch hadn't finished his eggs yet, but luckily the yolks were overcooked.

'I don't know what the game is here, Bosch. Where's Jesse Mitford?'

Bosch picked up his badge wallet and used his napkin to clean egg off it. He looked back up at Lundy. 'Who's Jesse Mitford?'

Lundy leaned down and put both hands on the table. 'You know damn well who he is and we need to take him in.'

Bosch nodded as though he understood the situation perfectly. 'We can talk about Mitford and everything else at the meeting at ten. Right after I interview Kent's partner and his wife.'

Lundy smiled in a way that carried no friendliness or humour. 'You know something, pal? You're going to need a Renaissance period yourself when this is all over.'

Bosch smiled again. 'See you at the meeting, Agent Lundy.'

THE SUN WAS STILL below the ridge line but dawn had a full grip on the sky. In daylight, the Mulholland overlook showed no sign of the violence of the night before. Even the debris usually left behind at a crime scene—rubber gloves, coffee cups and yellow tape—had somehow been cleaned up or maybe had blown away. It was as if Stanley Kent had not been shot to death, his body never left on the promontory with the jetliner view of the city below. Bosch never got over how quickly the city seemed to heal itself—at least outwardly—and move on.

He kicked at the soft orange ground. He made a decision and headed back towards the car. Ferras watched him go.

'What are you going to do?' Ferras asked.

'I'm going in. If you're coming, get in the car.'

Ferras hesitated, then trotted after Bosch. They got back in the Crown Vic and drove over to Arrowhead Drive. Bosch knew that the feds had

Alicia Kent but he still had the key ring from her husband's Porsche.

The fed car they had spotted when they drove by ten minutes earlier was still parked in front of the Kent house. Bosch pulled into the driveway, got out and headed with purpose to the front door. He ignored the car in the street, even when he heard its door open. He managed to find the right key and get it into the lock before they were hit with a voice from behind.

'FBI. Hold it right there.'

Bosch put his hand on the knob.

'Do not open that door.'

Bosch turned and looked at the man approaching on the front walkway. He knew that whoever was assigned to watch the house would be the lowest man on the Tactical Intelligence totem pole, a screwup or an agent with baggage. He knew he could use this to his advantage.

'LAPD Homicide Special,' he said. 'We're just going to finish up in here.'

'No, you're not,' the agent said. 'The Bureau has taken over jurisdiction and will be handling everything from here on.'

'Sorry, man, I didn't get the memo,' Bosch said. He turned back to the door.

'Do not open that door,' the agent said again. 'This is a national security investigation. You can check with your superiors.'

Bosch shook his head. 'You may have superiors. I have supervisors.'

'Whatever. You're not going into that house.'

'Harry,' Ferras said. 'Maybe we—'

Bosch waved a hand and cut him off. He turned back to the agent. 'Let me see some ID,' he said.

The agent put an exasperated look on his face and dug out his creds. He flipped them open and held them out. Bosch was ready. He grabbed the agent by the wrist and pivoted. The agent's body came forward and past him, and Bosch used a forearm to press him face first against the door. He pulled his hand—still clutching his credentials—behind his back.

The agent started struggling and protesting but it was too late. Bosch leaned his shoulder into him to keep him against the door and slipped his free hand under the man's jacket. He jerked the handcuffs off the agent's belt and started cuffing him up.

'Harry, what are you doing?' Ferras yelled.

'I told you. Nobody's pushing us aside.'

Once he had the agent's wrists cuffed behind him, he grabbed the credentials out of his hand. He opened them and checked the name. Clifford

Maxwell. Bosch turned him round and shoved the creds into the side pocket of his jacket.

'Your career is over,' Maxwell said calmly.

'Tell me about it,' Bosch said.

Maxwell looked at Ferras. 'You go along with this and you're in the toilet, too,' he said. 'You better think about it.'

'Shut up, Cliff,' Bosch said. 'The only one who's going to be in the toilet is you when you go back to Tactical and tell them how you let two of the local yokels get the drop on you.'

That shut him up. Bosch opened the door and walked the agent in. He pushed him down into a chair in the living room.

'Have a seat,' he said. 'And shut the fuck up.'

He reached down and opened Maxwell's jacket so he could see where he carried his weapon. His gun was in a pancake holster under his left arm. He would not be able to reach it with his wrists cuffed behind his back. Bosch frisked the agent's legs to make sure he wasn't carrying a throw-down. Satisfied, he stepped back.

'Relax now,' he said. 'We won't be long.'

Bosch started down the hallway, signalling his partner to follow him. 'You start in the office and I'll start in the bedroom,' he instructed. 'We're looking for anything and everything. We'll know it when we see it. Check the computer. Anything unusual, I want to know about it.'

'Harry.'

Bosch stopped in the hallway and looked at Ferras. He could tell that his young partner was running scared.

'We shouldn't be doing it this way,' Ferras said.

'How should we be doing it, Ignacio? Do you mean we should be going through channels? Have our boss talk to his boss, grab a latte and wait for permission to do our job?'

'I understand the need for speed,' Ferras said. 'But do you think he's going to let this go? He's going to have our badges, Harry, and I don't mind going down in the line of duty, but not for what we just did.'

Bosch admired Ferras for saying 'we', and that gave him the patience to calmly step back and put a hand on his partner's shoulder. He lowered his voice so Maxwell would not hear him.

'Listen to me, Ignacio. Not one thing is going to happen to you because of this. I've been around a little longer than you and I know how the Bureau works. Hell, my ex-wife is ex-Bureau, OK? And the one thing I know better than anything is that the number one FBI priority is not to be embarrassed. So when we are done here and we cut that guy loose, he's not going to tell a single soul what we did or that we were even here. Why do you think they had him sitting on the house? Because he's working off an embarrassment—either to himself or the Bureau. And he's not going to do or say a thing that brings him any more heat.'

Bosch paused to allow Ferras to respond. He didn't.

'So let's just move quickly here and check out the house,' Bosch continued. 'When I was here this morning, it was all about the widow and dealing with her, and then we had to run out the door to Saint Aggy's. I want to take my time but be quick, you know what I mean? I want to see the place in daylight and grind the case down for a while. This is how I like to work. You'd be surprised what you come up with sometimes. The thing to remember is that there's always a transfer. Those two killers left their mark somewhere in this house and I think everybody else missed it. Let's go find it.'

Ferras nodded. 'OK, Harry.'

'Good. I'll start in the bedroom. You check the office.'

Bosch moved down the hallway and was almost to the bedroom when Ferras called his name again. Bosch turned and went back to the office alcove. His partner was behind the desk.

'Where's the computer?' Ferras asked.

Bosch shook his head in frustration. 'It was on the desk. They took it.'

'The FBI?'

'Who else? It wasn't on the SID log, only the mouse pad. Just look around, go through the desk. See what else you can find.'

Bosch went down the hall to the master bedroom. It appeared to be undisturbed since he had last seen it. There was still a slight odour of urine.

He walked over to the night table on the left side of the bed. He saw black fingerprint powder dusted across the knobs on the two drawers. On top of the table was a framed photograph of Stanley and Alicia Kent. The couple was standing next to a rosebush in full bloom. Alicia was smiling broadly, as if she were standing proudly next to her own child. Bosch could tell that the rosebush was hers, and in the background he could see others just like it. Further up the hillside were the first three letters of the Hollywood sign and he realised the photo was taken in the back yard of the house.

Bosch slid open the table's drawers one by one. They were full of personal items belonging to Stanley. Various reading glasses, books and prescription bottles. The lower drawer was empty and Bosch remembered that it was where Stanley had kept his gun.

Bosch closed the drawers and stepped into the corner of the room. He was looking for a new angle, a fresh take on the crime scene. He realised that he needed the crime-scene photos and he had left the file in the car.

He walked down the hallway towards the front door. When he got to the living room, he saw Maxwell lying on the floor in front of the chair he had been placed in. He had managed to move his handcuffed wrists down over his hips. His knees were bent up with his wrists cuffed behind them. He looked up at Bosch with a red and sweating face.

'I'm stuck,' Maxwell said. 'Help me out.'

Bosch almost laughed. 'In a minute.'

He walked out to the car, where he retrieved the file containing the crime-scene reports and photos. He had put the copy of the emailed photo of Alicia Kent in there as well.

As he walked back into the house, Maxwell called to him. 'Come on, help me out, man.'

Bosch ignored him. He walked down the hallway and glanced into the home office as he passed. Ferras was going through the drawers of the desk.

In the bedroom, Bosch got the email photo out and put the file down on the bed. He held the photo up so he could compare it to the room. He then went to the mirrored closet door and opened it at an angle that matched the photograph. He noticed in the photo the white towelling robe draped over a lounge chair in the corner of the room. He stepped into the closet and looked for the robe, found it and put it in the same position on the lounge chair.

Bosch moved to the position from which he believed the email photo had been taken. He scanned the room, hoping something would poke through and speak to him. He noticed the dead clock on the bedside table and checked it against the email photo. The clock was dead in the photo, too.

He walked over to the table and looked behind it. The clock was unplugged. He crouched down and plugged it back in. The digital screen started flashing 12:00 in red numerals. The clock worked. It just needed to be set.

Bosch thought about this and knew it would be something to ask Alicia Kent about. He assumed the men who were in the house had unplugged the clock. The question was why. Perhaps they didn't want Alicia Kent to know how much or how little time had gone by while she waited tied up on the bed.

Moving to the bed, Bosch opened the file and took out the crime-scene photographs. He studied these and noticed that the closet door was open at a slightly different angle from the one in the email photo and that the robe was gone, obviously because Alicia Kent had put it on after her rescue. He stepped over to the closet, matched the door's angle to the one in the crime-scene photograph, then stepped back and scanned the room.

Nothing broke through. The transfer still eluded him. He felt discomfort in his gut. He felt as though he was missing something. Something that was right there in the room with him.

He left the bedroom and made his way down the hall towards the kitchen, stopping in each room and checking closets and drawers and finding nothing suspicious. In the workout room he noticed a rectangular discoloration on the wall next to the hooks where rubber workout mats hung. There were slight tape marks indicating that a poster had been taped to the wall.

When Bosch got to the living room, Maxwell was still on the floor, red-faced and sweating from struggling. He now had one leg through the loop created by his cuffed wrists, but he apparently couldn't get the other through in order to bring his hands to the front of his body. He was lying on the tiled floor with his wrists bound between his legs.

'We're almost out of here, Agent Maxwell,' Bosch said.

Maxwell didn't respond.

In the kitchen, Bosch went to the back door and stepped out onto a rear patio and garden. Seeing the yard in daylight changed his perspective. It was on an incline and he counted four rows of rosebushes going up the embankment. Some were in bloom and some weren't. Some relied on support sticks that carried markers identifying the different kinds of roses. He studied a few of these, then returned to the house.

After locking the door behind him, he crossed the kitchen and opened another door, which he knew led to the two-car garage. A bank of cabinets stretched along the back wall of the garage. One by one he opened them and surveyed the contents. There were mostly tools for gardening and household chores, and several bags of fertiliser and soil nutrients for growing roses.

There was a wheeled trash can in the garage. Bosch opened it and saw one plastic trash bag in it. He pulled it out, loosened the pull strap and found that it contained what appeared to be only basic kitchen trash. On top was a cluster of paper towels that were stained purple. It looked like someone had cleaned up a spill. He held one of the towels up and smelt grape juice on it.

After replacing the trash in the container, Bosch returned to the kitchen. He checked the cabinets and the walk-in pantry and studied the groceries and supplies. Then he went to the guest bathroom in the hall and looked at the spot where the cigarette ash had been collected. On the white porcelain cistern top there was a brown discoloration almost the length of a cigarette.

Bosch stared at the mark, curious. It had been seven years since he had smoked, but he didn't remember ever leaving a cigarette to burn like that. If he had finished it, he would have thrown it into the toilet and flushed it away. It was clear that this cigarette had been forgotten.

With his search complete, he stepped back into the living room and called to his partner. 'Ignacio, you ready? We're leaving.'

Maxwell was still on the floor but looked tired from his struggle and resigned to his predicament. 'Come on, damn it!' he cried out. 'Uncuff me!'

Bosch stepped close to him. 'Where's your key?'

'Coat pocket. Left side.'

Bosch bent over and pulled a set of keys out of the agent's pocket. He found the cuff key, grabbed the chain between the two cuffs and pulled up so he could work the key in. He wasn't gentle about it.

'Now be nice if I do this,' he said.

'Nice? I'm going to kick your fucking ass.'

Bosch let go of the chain. Maxwell's wrists fell to the floor.

'What are you doing?' Maxwell yelled. 'Undo me!'

'Here's a tip, Cliff. Next time you threaten to kick my ass, you might want to wait until after I've cut you loose.'

He straightened up and tossed the keys onto the floor on the other side of the room. 'Uncuff yourself.'

Bosch headed to the front door. Ferras was already going through it. As Bosch was pulling it closed he looked back at Maxwell sprawled on the floor. The red-faced agent sputtered one last threat in Bosch's direction.

'This isn't over, asshole.'

Bosch closed the door.

When he got to the car, he glanced over the roof at his partner. Ferras looked as mortified as some of the suspects who had ridden in the back seat.

'Cheer up,' Bosch said.

As he got in, he had a vision of the FBI agent crawling in his nice suit across the living-room floor to the keys.

Bosch smiled.

SEVEN

On the way back down the hill to the freeway Ferras was silent, and Bosch knew he had to be thinking about the jeopardy his young and promising career had been placed in because of his old and reckless partner's actions. Bosch tried to draw him out of it.

'Well, that was a bust,' he said. 'I got nada. Find anything in the office?'

'Nothing much. I showed you, the computer was gone.' There was a sullen tone in his voice.

'What about the desk?' Bosch asked.

'The desk was mostly empty. One drawer had tax returns. Another had a copy of a trust. Their house, an investment property in Laguna, insurance policies, everything like that is held in a trust.'

'Got it. How much the guy make last year?'

'A quarter million take-home. He also owns fifty-one per cent of the company.'

'The wife make anything?'

'No income. Doesn't work.'

Bosch grew quiet as he contemplated things. When they got down off the mountain, he decided not to get on the freeway. Instead, he took Cahuenga to Franklin and turned east. Ferras quickly noticed the detour.

'What's going on? I thought we were going downtown.'

'We're going to Los Feliz first.'

'What's in Los Feliz?'

'The Donut Hole on Vermont.'

'We just ate an hour ago.'

Bosch checked his watch. It was almost eight and he hoped he wasn't too late. 'I'm not going for the doughnuts.'

Ferras cursed and shook his head. 'You're going to talk to the Man? Are you kidding?'

'Unless I missed him already. If you're worried about it, you can stay in the car.'

'You're jumping about five links in the chain, you know. Lieutenant Gandle is going to have our asses for this.'

'He'll have *my* ass. You stay in the car. It'll be like you weren't even there.'

'Except what one partner does, the other always gets equal blame for. That's how it works. That's why they call them *partners*, Harry.'

'Look, I'll take care of it. There's no time to go through proper channels. The chief should know what is what and I'm going to tell him. He'll probably end up thanking us for the heads-up.'

The partners drove the rest of the way in silence.

The Los Angeles Police Department was one of the most insular bureaucracies in the world. It had survived for more than a century by rarely looking outwards for ideas, answers or leaders. A few years earlier, the city council had decided that, after years of scandal and community upset, it required leadership from outside the department. The outsider who was brought in to run the show was viewed with tremendous curiosity, not to mention scepticism. His movements and habits were documented and all the data dumped into an informal police pipeline that connected the department's 10,000 officers like the blood vessels in a closed fist. The intelligence was passed around in roll calls and locker rooms, text messages, emails and phone calls, at cop bars and back-yard barbecues. It meant that street officers in South LA knew what Hollywood premiere the new chief had attended the night before. Vice officers in the Valley knew where he took his dress uniforms to be pressed, and the gang detail in Venice knew what supermarket his wife liked to shop at.

It also meant that Detective Harry Bosch and his partner Ignacio Ferras knew what doughnut shop the chief stopped at for coffee every morning on his way into Parker Center.

At 8 a.m. Bosch pulled into the parking lot of the Donut Hole, but saw no sign of the chief's unmarked car.

Bosch killed the engine and looked over at his partner. 'You staying?'

Ferras nodded without looking at Bosch.

'Suit yourself,' Bosch said.

'Listen, Harry, no offence, but this isn't working. You don't want a partner. You want a gofer and somebody who doesn't question anything you do. I'm going to talk to the lieutenant about hooking me up with someone else.'

Bosch looked at him and composed his thoughts. 'Ignacio, it's our first case together. Don't you think you should give it some time? That's all Gandle's going to tell you. He's going to tell you that you don't want to start out in RHD with a reputation as a guy who cuts and runs on his partner.'

'I'm not cutting and running. It's just not working right.'

'Ignacio, you're making a mistake.'

'No, I think it would be best. For both of us.'

Bosch stared at him for a long moment before turning to the door. 'Like I said, suit yourself.'

He got out and headed towards the doughnut shop. He was disappointed by Ferras's reaction but knew he should cut him some slack. The guy had a kid on the way and needed to play it safe. Bosch was not one to ever play it safe and it had lost him more than a partner in the past. He would take another shot at changing the young man's mind once the case settled down.

Inside the shop, Bosch waited in line behind two people and then ordered a black coffee from the East Asian man behind the counter. The man turned to a brewer on the back wall and filled a cup. When he turned back round, Bosch had his badge out.

'Has the chief been in yet?'

The man hesitated. He had no idea about the intelligence pipeline and was unsure about responding. He knew he could lose a high-profile customer if he spoke out of turn.

'It's all right,' Bosch said. 'I'm supposed to meet him here. I'm late.' Bosch tried to smile as though he were in trouble.

'He not here yet,' the counterman said.

Relieved that he hadn't missed him, Bosch paid for the coffee and went to an empty table in the corner. It was mostly a take-out operation at this time of morning. People grabbing fuel on their way into work. For ten minutes Bosch watched a cross-section of the city's culture step up to the counter, all united by the addiction to caffeine and sugar.

Finally, he saw a black Lincoln Town Car pull in. The chief was in the front passenger seat. Both he and the driver got out. Both scanned their surroundings and headed towards the doughnut shop. Bosch knew that the driver was an officer and served as a bodyguard as well.

There was no line at the counter when they came in.

'Hiyou, Chief,' the counterman said.

'Good morning, Mr Ming,' the chief responded. 'I'll have the usual.'

Bosch stood up and approached. The bodyguard, who was standing behind the chief, turned and squared himself in Bosch's direction. Bosch stopped.

'Chief, can I buy you a cup of coffee?' Bosch asked.

The chief turned and did a double take when he recognised Bosch. For a moment Bosch saw a frown move across the man's face—he was still dealing with some of the fallout from the Echo Park case—but it quickly disappeared into impassivity.

'Detective Bosch,' he said. 'You're not here to give me bad news, are you?'

'More like a heads-up, sir.'

The chief turned away to accept a cup of coffee and a small bag from Ming. 'Have a seat,' he said. 'I have about five minutes, and I'll pay for my own coffee.'

Bosch went back to the same table while the chief paid for his coffee and doughnuts. He sat down and waited while the chief took his purchases to another counter and put cream and sweetener into his coffee.

Bosch believed that the chief had been good for the department. He had made a few missteps politically, and some questionable choices in command staff assignments, but had largely been responsible for raising the morale of the rank and file. Crime stats were even down, which to Bosch meant there was a good possibility that actual crime was down as well—he viewed crime statistics with suspicion.

But all of that aside, Bosch liked the chief for one overarching reason. Two years earlier he had given Bosch his job back. Bosch had retired and gone private. It didn't take him long to realise that it was a mistake, and, when he did, the new chief welcomed him back. It made Bosch loyal, and that was one reason he was forcing the meeting at the doughnut shop.

The chief sat down across from him. 'You're lucky, Detective. Most days I'd have been here and gone an hour ago. But I worked late last night hitting crime-watch meetings in three parts of the city.'

Rather than open his doughnut bag and reach in, the chief tore it down the middle so he could spread it and eat his two doughnuts off it. He had a powdered sugar and a chocolate-glazed.

'Here's the most dangerous killer in the city,' he said, as he raised the chocolate-glazed doughnut and took a bite.

Bosch nodded. 'You're probably right.' He smiled uneasily and tried an icebreaker. 'How's my old partner doing, Chief?'

His old partner was Kiz Rider, who had just come back to work after recovering from gunshot wounds. She had transferred out of Robbery-Homicide to the chief's office, where she had worked once before.

'Kiz? Kiz is good. She does fine work for me. I think she's in the right spot. Are you in the right spot, Detective?'

Bosch looked at the chief and wondered if he might already be questioning his jumping the chain of command. Before he could work up an answer, the chief asked another question.

'Are you here about the Mulholland overlook case?'

Bosch nodded. He assumed that the word had gone up the pipe from Lieutenant Gandle and that the chief had been briefed about the case.

'I know it's got federal interest. Captain Hadley called me this morning. He said there is a terrorism angle.'

Bosch was surprised to learn that Captain Done Badly and the OHS were already in the picture.

'What's Captain Hadley doing?' he asked. 'He hasn't called me.'

'The usual. Checking our own intelligence, trying to open lines with the feds.'

Bosch nodded.

'So what can you tell me, Detective? Why did you come here?'

Bosch gave him a fuller run-down on the case, accenting the federal involvement and what was looking like an effort to shut the LAPD out of its own investigation. Bosch acknowledged that the missing caesium was a priority and true cause for the feds to throw their weight around. But he said the case was a homicide, and that cut the LAPD in. He went over the evidence he had collected and laid out some of his theories.

The chief had consumed both doughnuts by the time Bosch was finished. He wiped his mouth with a napkin and then checked his watch before responding. They were well past the five minutes he had initially offered.

'What aren't you telling me?' he asked.

Bosch shrugged. 'Not much. I had a little dustup at the victim's house with an agent, but I don't think anything will come of it.'

'Why isn't your partner in here? Why is he waiting in the car?'

Bosch understood. The chief had seen Ferras when he scanned the lot upon his arrival.

'We're having a little disagreement on how to proceed. He's a good kid, but he wants to roll over for the feds a little too easy.'

'And of course we don't do that in the LAPD.'

'Not in my time, Chief.'

'Did your partner think it was appropriate to ignore the department's chain of command by coming directly to me with this?' The chief's voice had taken on a stern tone.

Bosch dropped his eyes to the table. 'As a matter of fact he wasn't happy about it, Chief. It wasn't his idea. It was mine. I just didn't think there was enough time to—'

'Doesn't matter what you thought. It's what you did. So if I were you I would keep this meeting to yourself, and I will as well. Don't ever do it this way again, Detective. Are we clear on that?'

'Yes, clear.'

The chief glanced towards the glass display case where the doughnuts were lined up on trays. 'And by the way, how did you know I would be here?'

Bosch shrugged. 'I don't remember. I just sort of knew.'

It then occurred to him that the chief might be thinking that Bosch's source was his old partner.

'It wasn't Kiz, if that's what you mean, Chief,' he said quickly. 'It's just something that gets known, you know? Word gets around the department.'

The chief nodded. 'It's too bad,' he said. 'I liked this place. Convenient, good doughnuts and Mr Ming takes care of me. What a shame.'

Bosch realised that the chief would now have to change his routine. It did not serve him well if it was known where he could be found and when.

'Sorry, sir,' Bosch said. 'But if I might make a recommendation. There's a place in the Farmer's Market called Bob's Coffee and Doughnuts. It's a bit out of the way for you, but the coffee and doughnuts would be worth it.'

The police chief nodded thoughtfully. 'I'll keep it in mind. Now, what is it you want from me, Detective Bosch?'

The chief obviously wanted to get down to business.

'I need access to Alicia Kent and her husband's partner, a guy named Kelber,' Bosch replied. 'The feds have them both and I think my window of access closed about five hours ago.' He paused. 'That's why I'm here, Chief. I need access. I figure you can get it for me.'

The chief nodded. 'I can make some calls, raise some hell, and probably open the window. As I said before, we have Captain Hadley's unit on this already and perhaps he can open up the channels of communication. We've been kept out of the loop on these things in the past. I can raise the flag.'

To Bosch it sounded like the chief was going to go to bat for him.

'You know what reflux is, Detective?'

'Reflux?'

'It's a condition where all the bile backs up into your throat. It burns, Detective.'

'Oh.'

'What I'm telling you is that if I make these moves and I get that window open for you, I don't want any reflux. You understand me?'

'I understand.'

The chief wiped his mouth again and put the napkin down on his torn bag. He then crumpled it all into a ball, careful not to spill any powdered sugar on his black suit.

'I'll make the calls, but it's going to be tough. You don't see the political angle here, do you, Bosch?'

Bosch looked at him. 'Sir?'

'The bigger picture, Detective. You see this as a homicide investigation. It's actually much more than that. You have to understand that it serves the federal government extremely well with this thing on the overlook being part of a terrorism plot. A bona fide domestic threat would go a long way towards deflecting public attention and easing the pressure in other areas. The war's gone to shit; the election was a disaster. You've got the Middle East, the price of a gallon of gasoline, and a lame-duck president's approval ratings. The list goes on and on, and there would be an opportunity here for redemption. A chance to make up for past mistakes. A chance to shift public attention and opinion.'

Bosch nodded. 'Are you saying that they might try to keep this thing going, maybe even exaggerate the threat?'

'I'm not saying anything, Detective. I'm just trying to broaden your perspective. A case like this, you have to be aware of the political landscape. You can't be running around like a bull in a china shop—which in the past has been your specialty.'

Bosch nodded again.

The chief stood up, ready to go. 'Think about it and be careful,' he said. 'Remember, no reflux. No blowback.'

'Yes, sir.'

BOSCH DIDN'T SPEAK until they were out of the parking lot. He decided that the Hollywood Freeway would be overrun by the morning commute and Sunset was the fastest way downtown.

Ferras made it only two blocks before asking what had happened in the doughnut shop.

'Don't worry, Ignacio. We both still have our jobs.'

'Then, what happened?'

'He said you were right. I shouldn't have jumped command. But he said he would make some calls and try to open things up with the feds.'

'Then I guess we'll see.'

'Yeah, we'll see.'

They drove in silence for a while until Bosch brought up his partner's plan to ask for a new assignment.

'You still going to talk to the lieutenant?'

Ferras paused before answering. He was clearly uncomfortable with the question. 'I don't know, Harry. I still think it would be best. Best for both of us. Maybe you work best with female partners.'

Bosch almost laughed. Ferras didn't know Kiz Rider, his last partner. She never went along to get along with Harry. Like Ferras, she objected every time Bosch went alpha dog on her. He was about to set Ferras straight when his cellphone started buzzing. He pulled it out of his pocket. It was Lieutenant Gandle.

'Harry, where are you?'

His voice was louder than usual and more urgent. He was excited about something and Bosch wondered if he had already heard about the Donut Hole meeting. Had the chief betrayed him?

'I'm on Sunset. We're heading in.'

'Did you pass Silver Lake yet?'

'Not yet.'

'Good. Head up to Silver Lake. Go to the rec centre at the bottom of the reservoir. The Kent car's been located. Hadley and his people are already out there setting up the CP. They've requested the investigators on scene.'

'Hadley? Why's he there? Why is there a command post?'

'Hadley's office got the tip and checked it out before deciding to clue us in. The car is parked in front of a house belonging to a person of interest. They want you on the scene.'

'"Person of interest"? What's that mean?'

'A suspected terrorist sympathiser. I don't have all the details. Just get there, Harry. Call me and let me know what's happening.'

'All right. We're on the way.'

Bosch closed the phone and tried to pick up speed, but the traffic was too thick for him to get anywhere. He filled Ferras in on what little he knew from the phone call.

'What about the FBI?' Ferras asked. 'Do they know?'

'I didn't ask.'

'What about the meeting at ten?'

'I guess we'll worry about that at ten.'

In ten minutes they finally got to Silver Lake Boulevard and Bosch turned north. This part of the city took its name from the Silver Lake Reservoir, which sat in the middle of a largely middle-class neighbourhood of bungalows and postwar homes.

As they approached the recreation centre, Bosch saw two shiny black SUVs that he recognised as the signature vehicles of the OHS. Apparently, he thought, there was never much trouble getting funding for a unit that supposedly hunted terrorists. There were two patrol cars and a city sanitation truck as well. Bosch parked behind one of the patrol cars.

As he and Ferras got out, they saw a group of ten men in black fatigues—also distinctive to the OHS—gathered round the fold-down rear gate of one of the SUVs. Bosch approached them and Ferras trailed a couple of steps behind. Their presence was immediately noticed, and the crowd parted and there was Captain Don Hadley sitting on the gate. Bosch had never met him but had seen him often enough on television. He was a large, red-faced man with sandy hair. He was about forty years old and looked like he had been in the gym working out for half of them.

'Bosch?' Hadley asked. 'Ferras?'

'I'm Bosch. This is Ferras.'

'Fellas, good to have you here. I think we're going to tie your case up for you in a bow in short order. We're just waiting on one of my guys to bring the warrant and then we go in.'

He stood up and signalled to one of his men. Hadley had a definite air of confidence about him.

'Perez, check on that warrant, will you? I'm tired of waiting. Then check the OP and see what's happening up there.' He then turned back to Bosch and Ferras. 'Walk with me, men.'

Hadley headed away from the group and Bosch and Ferras followed. He led them to the back of the sanitation truck, where he adopted a command pose, putting his foot up on the back end of the truck. Bosch noticed that the captain carried his sidearm in a leg holster strapped round his thick right thigh. Like an Old West gunslinger, except he was carrying a semiautomatic. He was chewing gum and not trying to hide it.

Bosch had heard many stories about Hadley. He now had the feeling that he was about to become part of one.

'I wanted you men to be here for this,' Hadley said. 'We've located your Chrysler 300 two and a half blocks from here. The plate matches the BOLO, and I eyeballed the vehicle myself. It's the car we've been looking for.'

That part was good, Bosch, thought. What's the rest?

'The vehicle is parked in front of a home owned by a man named Ramin Samir,' Hadley continued. 'He's a guy we've been keeping our eye on for a few years. A real person of interest to us.'

The name was familiar to Bosch but he couldn't place it at first.

'Why is he of interest, Captain?' he asked.

'Mr Samir is a known supporter of religious organisations that want to hurt Americans and damage our interests. What's worse is, he teaches our young people to hate their own country.'

That last part jogged Bosch's memory and he put things together. He could not recall which Middle Eastern country Ramin Samir was from, but Bosch remembered that he was a former visiting professor of international politics at the University of Southern California who had gained widespread notice for espousing anti-American sentiment in the classroom and in the media. He had been making media ripples before the 9/11 domestic terrorist attacks. Afterwards, the ripples became a wave. He openly postulated that the attacks were warranted because of US intrusion and aggression all around the globe. He was able to parlay the attention this brought him into a position as the media go-to guy for the ever-ready anti-American sound bite. He denigrated US policies towards Israel, objected to the military action in Afghanistan and called the war in Iraq nothing more than an oil grab.

This role gave Samir a good few years of guest shots on the cable-news debate programmes, where everybody tends to yell at one another. Meanwhile, he used his soapbox and celebrity status to help start and fund a number of organisations, on and off campus, which were quickly accused of being connected to terrorist groups. But while Samir was often investigated, he was never charged with any crime. He was, however, fired by USC on a technicality—he had not stated that his opinions were his own, and not those of the school, when he wrote an op-ed piece for the *Los Angeles Times* that suggested the Iraq war was an American-planned genocide of Muslims.

Samir's fifteen minutes ran their course. He was eventually discounted in the media as a narcissist who made outlandish statements in order to draw attention to himself rather than to comment thoughtfully on the issues of the day. His star waned and he dropped from public sight. But all the rhetoric aside, the fact that Samir was never charged with a crime during a period when the climate in the United States was hot with fear of the unknown, and the desire for vengeance, always indicated to Bosch that there was nothing there. If there had been fire behind the smoke, then Ramin Samir would be in a prison cell or behind a fence at Guantánamo Bay. But here he was, living in Silver Lake, and Bosch was sceptical of Captain Hadley's claims.

'I remember this guy,' he said. 'He was just a talker, Captain. There was never any solid link between Samir and—'

Hadley held up a finger like a teacher demanding silence. 'Never a solid link *established*,' he corrected. 'But that doesn't mean anything. This guy raises money for the Palestinian Jihad and other Muslim causes.'

'The Palestinian Jihad?' Bosch asked. 'What is that? And what Muslim causes? Are you saying Muslim causes can't be legit?'

'Look, all I'm saying is that this is a bad dude and he's got a car that was used in a murder and zesium heist sitting right in front of his house.'

'Caesium,' Ferras said. 'It was caesium that was stolen.'

Not used to being corrected, Hadley narrowed his eyes and stared at Ferras for a moment before speaking. 'Whatever. It's not going to make much difference what you call it, son, if he dumps it into the reservoir across the street or is in that house putting it in a bomb while we're sitting here waiting on a warrant.'

'The FBI said nothing about it being a waterborne threat,' Bosch said.

Hadley shook his head. 'Doesn't matter. Bottom line is that it's a threat. I'm sure the FBI said that. Well, the Bureau can talk about it. We're going to *do* something about it.'

Bosch stepped back, trying to draw some fresh air into the discussion. This was moving too quickly.

'So you're going to go in?' he asked.

Hadley was working his jaw in quick, powerful bites of the gum. He seemed not to notice the strong odour of garbage emanating from the back of the truck. 'You're damn right we're going to go in,' he said. 'Just as soon as that warrant gets here.'

'You got a judge to sign a warrant that's based on a stolen car being parked in front of the house?' Bosch asked.

Hadley signalled to one of his men. 'Bring the bags, Perez,' he called.

Then to Bosch he said, 'No, that's not all we got. Today's trash day, Detective. I sent the garbage truck up the street and a couple of my men emptied the two cans that were in front of Samir's house. Perfectly legal, as you know. And lookee at what we got.'

Perez hustled over with the plastic evidence bags and handed them to Hadley. 'Captain, I checked the OP,' he said. 'Still quiet up there.'

'Thank you, Perez.'

Hadley took the bags and turned back to Bosch and Ferras. Perez went back to the SUV.

'Our observation post is a guy in a tree,' Hadley said with a smile. 'He'll let us know if anybody makes a move up there before we're ready.'

He handed Bosch the bags. Two of them contained black woollen ski masks. The third contained a slip of paper with a hand-drawn map on it. Bosch looked closely at it. It was a series of crisscrossing lines with two of them marked as Arrowhead and Mulholland. The map was a fairly accurate rendering of the neighbourhood where Stanley Kent had lived and died.

Bosch handed the bags back and shook his head. 'Captain, I think you should hold up.'

'Hold up? We're not holding up. If this guy and his pals contaminate the reservoir with that poison, do you think the people of this city are going to accept that we held up to make sure we dotted every "i" and crossed every "t"? As far as I'm concerned, we've got the leader of a terrorist cell operating out of that house and we're going to go in and shut it down. What's your problem with that, Detective Bosch?'

'It's too easy, that's my problem. It's not about us dotting every "i", because that's what the killers already did. This was a carefully planned crime, Captain. They wouldn't have just left the car in front of the house or put this stuff in the trash cans. Think about it.'

Bosch held there and watched Hadley work it over for a few moments.

The captain then shook his head. 'Maybe the car wasn't left there,' he said. 'Maybe they still plan to use it as part of the delivery. There are a lot of variables, Bosch. We're still going in. We laid it all out to the judge and he said we have probable cause. That's good enough for me.'

Bosch refused to give up. 'Where did the tip come from, Captain? How did you find the car?'

'One of my sources,' Hadley said. 'We've been building an intelligence network in this city for almost four years. Today it's paying off.'

'Are you telling me that you know who the source is, or did it come in anonymously?'

Hadley waved his hands in a dismissive manner. 'Doesn't matter. The info was good. That's the car up there. There's no doubt about that.'

Bosch knew by Hadley's sidestepping that the tip was anonymous, the hallmark of a set-up.

'Captain, I urge you to stand down,' he said. 'There is something not right about this. It's too simple and this wasn't a simple plan. It's some sort of misdirection, and we need to figure—'

'We're not standing down, Detective. Lives could hang in the balance.'

Bosch shook his head. He wasn't going to get through to Hadley. The man believed he was poised at the edge of some sort of victory that would redeem every mistake he had ever made.

'Where's the FBI?' Bosch asked. 'Shouldn't they be—?'

'We don't need the FBI,' Hadley said, getting in Bosch's face. 'We have the training, the equipment and the skills. We're going to take care of what's in our own back yard ourselves.' He gestured to the ground as if the place where he stood was the last battlefield between the Bureau and the LAPD.

'What about the chief? Does he know? I was just—' Bosch stopped, remembering the chief's admonishment about keeping their meeting at the Donut Hole to themselves.

'You were just what?' Hadley asked.

'I just want to know if he knows and approves.'

'The chief has given me full authority to run my unit. Do you call the chief every time you go out and make an arrest?'

He turned and marched imperiously back to his men, leaving Bosch and Ferras to watch him go.

'Uh-oh,' Ferras said.

'Yeah,' Bosch said.

Bosch stepped away from the back of the foul-smelling sanitation truck and pulled out his phone. He scrolled through his directory to Rachel Walling's name. He had just pressed the CALL button when Hadley was there in his face again. Bosch hadn't heard him coming.

'Detective! Who are you calling?'

Bosch didn't hesitate. 'My lieutenant. He told me to update him after we got here.'

'No cellular or radio transmissions. They could be monitoring.'

'They who?'

'Give me the phone.'

'Captain?'

'Give me the phone or I will have it taken from you. We're not going to compromise this operation.'

Bosch closed the phone without ending the call. If he was lucky, Walling would answer the call and be listening. She might be able to put it together and get the warning. The Bureau might even be able to triangulate the cell transmission and get to Silver Lake before things went completely wrong.

He handed the phone to Hadley, who turned to Ferras.

'Your phone, Detective.'

'Sir, my wife is eight months pregnant and I need—'

'Your phone, Detective. You are either with us or against us.'

Hadley held his hand out, and Ferras reluctantly took his phone from his belt and gave it to him. Then Hadley marched over to one of the SUVs, opened the passenger door and put the two phones into the glove box. He slammed the compartment shut with authority and looked back at Bosch and Ferras as if challenging them to try to retrieve their phones.

The captain's attention was distracted when a third black SUV pulled into the lot. The driver gave the captain a thumbs-up. Hadley then pointed a finger into the air and started a twirling motion.

'All right, everybody,' he called out. 'We have the warrant and you know the plan. Perez, call air support and get us the eye in the sky. The rest of you warriors, mount up! We're going in.'

Bosch watched with growing dread as the members of the OHS chambered rounds in their weapons and put on helmets with face shields. Two of the men began putting on space suits, as they had been designated the radiation-containment team.

'This is crazy,' Ferras said in a whisper.

Bosch said nothing. He was thinking back to his time in Vietnam. It was there that he'd learned that men of rank often fought battles with enemies that were inside.

He and Ferras rode in the back seat of Captain Hadley's SUV. Perez drove and Hadley rode shotgun, wearing a radio headset so he could command the operation. The vehicle's radio speaker was on loud and set to the operation's back-channel frequency—one that would not be found listed in any public directories.

They were third in line in the entourage of black SUVs. Half a block from the target house, Perez braked to let the other two vehicles move in as planned.

Bosch leaned forward between the front seats so he could see better through the windshield. Each of the other SUVs had four men riding on runners on either side. The vehicles picked up speed and then turned sharply towards the Samir house. One went down the driveway of the small Craftsman-style bungalow towards the rear yard, while the other jumped the kerb and crossed the front lawn. One of the OHS men lost his grip when the heavy vehicle impacted the kerb, and he went tumbling across the lawn.

The others leapt from the runners and moved towards the front door. Bosch assumed that the same thing was happening at the back door. He didn't agree with the plan but admired its precision. There was a loud popping sound when the front door was breached with an explosive device. Almost immediately there was another, from the rear.

'All right, move up,' Hadley commanded Perez.

As they drove up, the radio came alive with reports from inside the house.

'We're inside!'

'We're in the back!'

'Front room clear! We—'

The voice was cut off by the sound of automatic gunfire.

'Shots fired!'

'We've got—'

'Shots fired!'

Bosch heard more gunfire, but not over the radio. They were now close enough for him to hear it live. Perez jammed the SUV into park at an angle crossing the street in front of the house. All four doors opened at once as they jumped out, leaving the doors open behind them and the radio blaring.

'All clear! All clear!'

'One suspect down. We need medical for one suspect down. We need medical!'

It was all over in less than twenty seconds.

Bosch ran across the lawn behind Hadley and Perez. Ferras was to his left side. They entered through the front door with weapons out and up. Immediately they were met by one of Hadley's men. Above the right pocket of his fatigue shirt was the name Peck.

'We're clear! We're clear!'

Bosch dropped his weapon to his side but he didn't holster it. He looked around. It was a sparsely furnished living room. He smelt gunpowder and saw blue smoke hanging in the air

'What have we got?' Hadley demanded.

'One down, one in custody,' Peck said. 'Back here.'

They followed Peck down a short hallway to a room with woven-grass mats on the floor. A man Bosch recognised as Ramin Samir was lying on his back, blood from two chest wounds flowing over a cream-coloured robe onto the floor and one of the mats. A young woman in a matching robe was lying face down and whimpering, her hands cuffed behind her back.

Bosch saw a revolver on the floor by the open drawer of a small cabinet with lit votive candles on top of it. The gun was about eighteen inches from where Samir was lying.

'He went for the gun and we took him down,' Peck said.

Bosch looked down at Samir. He wasn't conscious and his chest was rising and falling in a broken rhythm.

'He's circling the drain,' Hadley said. 'What have we found?'

'So far, no materials,' Peck said. 'We're bringing in the equipment now.'

'All right. Let's get the car checked,' Hadley ordered. 'And get her out of here.'

While two OHS men raised the crying woman up and carried her out of the room like a battering ram, Hadley headed back out of the house to the kerb, where the Chrysler 300 awaited. Bosch and Ferras followed.

They looked into the car but didn't touch it. Bosch noticed that it was unlocked. He bent down to look in through the passenger-side windows.

'Keys are in it,' he said. He pulled a pair of latex gloves from his coat pocket, stretched them and put them on.

'Let's get a reading on it first, Bosch,' Hadley said.

The captain signalled one of his men, who was carrying over a radiation monitor. The man swept the device over the car and picked up only a few low pops by the trunk.

'We could have something right here,' Hadley said.

'I doubt it,' Bosch said. 'It's not here.' He opened the driver-side door and leaned in.

'Bosch, wait—'

Bosch pushed the trunk button before Hadley could finish. He heard the pneumatic pop and the catch came open. He backed out of the car and walked to the rear. The trunk was empty, but Bosch saw the same four indentations he had seen earlier, in the trunk of Stanley Kent's Porsche.

'It's gone,' Hadley said, looking into the trunk. 'They must've already made the transfer.'

'Yeah. Long before the car was brought here.' Bosch looked Hadley squarely in the eyes. 'This was a misdirection, Captain. I told you that.'

Hadley moved towards Bosch so he could speak without his whole crew hearing him. But he was intercepted by Peck.

'Captain?'

'*What?*' Hadley barked.

'The suspect went code seven.'

'Then call off the paramedics and call the coroner.'

'Yes, sir. The house is clear. No materials, and the monitors are picking up no signature.'

Hadley glanced at Bosch, then quickly looked back at Peck. 'Tell them to check the place again,' he ordered. 'He went for a gun. He had to have been hiding something. Tear the place apart if you have to. Especially that room—it looks like a meeting place for terrorists.'

'It's a prayer room,' Bosch said. 'And maybe the guy went for the gun because he was scared shitless when people came busting through the doors.'

Peck hadn't moved. He was listening to Bosch.

'Go!' Hadley ordered. 'The material was in a lead container. Just because you got no reading doesn't mean it's not in there!'

Peck hustled back to the house and Hadley turned his stare to Bosch.

'We need Forensics to process the car,' Bosch said. 'And I don't have a phone to make the call.'

'Go get your phone and make the call.'

Bosch went back to the SUV. He watched as the woman who had been in the house was placed in the back of the SUV parked on the lawn. She was still crying, and Bosch assumed the tears wouldn't stop any time soon. For Samir now, herself later.

As he leaned through the door of Hadley's SUV, he realised that the vehicle was still running. He turned off the engine, then opened the glove compartment and took out the two phones. He opened and checked his to see if the call to Rachel Walling was still connected. It wasn't, and he didn't know if the call had gone through in the first place.

When he straightened up and turned from the door, Hadley was standing there. They were away from the others and no one would hear them.

'Bosch, if you try to make trouble for this unit, I will make trouble for you. You understand?'

Bosch studied him for a moment before responding. 'Sure, Captain. I'm glad you're thinking about the unit.'

'I have connections that go all the way up and right out of this department. I can hurt you.'

'Thanks for the advice.'

Bosch started to walk away from him but then stopped. He wanted to say something but hesitated.

'What?' Hadley said. 'Say it.'

'I was just thinking about a captain I once worked for. This was a long time ago and in another place. He kept making all the wrong moves, which kept costing people their lives. Good people. So eventually it had to stop. That captain ended up getting fragged in the latrine by some of his own men.'

Bosch walked away but Hadley stopped him.

'What's that supposed to mean? Is that a threat?'

'No, it's a story.'

'And you're calling that guy in there "good" people? Let me tell you, a guy like that stood up and cheered when the planes hit the buildings.'

Bosch kept walking as he answered. 'I don't know what kind of people he was, Captain. I just know he wasn't part of this and he was set up, just like you. If you figure out who it was who tipped you to the car, let me know. It might help us.'

Bosch walked over to Ferras and gave him back his phone. He told his partner to remain on the scene to supervise the forensic analysis of the Chrysler 300.

'Where are you going, Harry?'

'Downtown.'

'What about the meeting with the Bureau?'

Bosch didn't check his watch. 'We missed it. Call me if SID comes up with anything.'

He left Ferras there and started walking down the street towards the recreation centre, where the car was parked.

'Bosch, where are you going?' Hadley called. 'You're not done here!'

Bosch waved without looking back. He kept walking. When he was halfway back to the rec centre, the first TV truck passed him on its way to Samir's house.

EIGHT

Bosch was hoping to get to the federal building downtown before news of the raid on Ramin Samir's house did. He had tried to call Rachel Walling but got no answer. He knew that she might be at the Tactical Intelligence location but he didn't know where that was. He was banking on the idea that the growing size and importance of the investigation would dictate that it be directed from the main federal building and not a secret satellite office.

He entered the building through the law-enforcement door and told the US marshal who checked his ID that he was going up to the FBI. He took the elevator up to the fourteenth floor and was greeted by Brenner as soon as the doors came open. The word that Bosch was in the building had obviously been sent up from below.

'I thought you got the message?' Brenner said.

'What message?'

'That the status conference was cancelled.'

'I think I should've got the message as soon as you people showed up. There never was going to be a conference, was there?'

Brenner ignored the question. 'Bosch, what do you want?'

'I want to see Agent Walling.'

'I'm her partner. Anything you want to tell her, you can tell me.'

'Only her. I want to talk to her.'

Brenner studied him. 'Come with me,' he finally said.

He used a clip-on ID card to open a door and Bosch followed him through. They went down a long hallway and Brenner threw questions over his shoulder as he walked.

'Where's your partner?' he asked.

'He's back at the crime scene,' Bosch said.

It wasn't a lie. He just neglected to say which crime scene Ferras was at.

'Besides,' he added, 'I thought it would be safer for him there. I don't want you people leaning on him to get to me.'

Brenner stopped suddenly, pivoted sharply and was in Bosch's face. 'Do you know what you are doing, Bosch? You're compromising an investigation that could have far-reaching implications. Where is the witness?'

Bosch shrugged as if to say his response was obvious. 'Where's Alicia Kent?'

Brenner shook his head but didn't answer. 'Wait in here,' he said. 'I'll go get Agent Walling.'

Brenner opened a door that had the number 1411 on it and stepped back for Bosch to enter. As he stepped through, Bosch saw that it was a small, windowless interview room similar to the one he had spent time in that morning with Jesse Mitford. Bosch was suddenly shoved into the room and turned just in time to see Brenner out in the hallway, pulling the door closed.

'Hey!'

Bosch grabbed for the doorknob, but it was too late. The door was locked from the outside. He pounded twice on it but knew that Brenner was not about to open it. He turned away and looked at the small space he was confined in. The room contained only three items of furniture. A small square table and two chairs. Assuming there was a camera somewhere, he raised his hand and shot his middle finger into the air. He gave his hand a twirl to emphasise the message.

Bosch pulled one of the chairs out and sat down, ready to wait them out. He took out his cellphone and opened it. He knew that if they were watching him they wouldn't want him calling out and reporting his situation—it could be embarrassing for the Bureau. But when he looked at the screen, there was no signal. It was a safe room. Radio signals could not get out or in. Leave it to the feds, Bosch thought. They think of everything.

A long twenty minutes went by and then the door finally opened. Rachel Walling stepped in. She closed the door, took the chair opposite Bosch and quietly sat down.

'Sorry, Harry, I was over at Tactical.'

'What, Rachel, you people hold cops against their will now?'

She looked surprised. 'What are you talking about?'

'Your partner locked me in here.'

'It wasn't locked when I came in. Try it now.'

Bosch waved it away. 'Forget it. I don't have time to play games. What's going on with the investigation?'

She pursed her lips. 'What's going on is that you and your department have been running around like thieves in a jewellery store, smashing every goddamn case in sight. You can't tell the glass from the diamonds.'

Bosch nodded. 'So you know about Ramin Samir.'

'Who doesn't? It's already on I-Missed-It News. What happened up there?'

'A class-A fuckup is what happened. We were set up. OHS was set up.'

'Sounds like somebody was.'

Bosch leaned across the table. 'But it means something, Rachel. The people who put the OHS onto Samir knew who he was and that he'd make an easy target. They left the Kents' car right in front of his house because they knew we'd end up spinning our wheels.'

'It also could have worked as a payback to Samir.'

'What do you mean?'

'All those years he was on CNN fanning the flames. He could've been seen as hurting their cause because he was giving the enemy a face and heightening American anger and resolve.'

Bosch didn't get it. 'I thought agitation was one of their tools? I thought they loved this guy?'

'Maybe. It's hard to say.'

Bosch wasn't sure what she was trying to say. But when Walling leaned across the table he suddenly could see how angry she was.

'Now let's talk about you and how you have been single-handedly fucking things up since before the car was even found.'

'What are you talking about? I'm trying to solve a homicide. That's my—'

'Yes, trying to solve a homicide at the possible cost of endangering the entire city with this petty self-righteous insistence on—'

'Come on, Rachel. Don't you think I have an idea about what could be at stake here?'

She shook her head. 'Not if you are holding back a key witness from us. Don't you see what you are doing? You have no idea where this investigation is headed, because you've been busy hiding witnesses and sucker-punching agents.'

Bosch leaned back, clearly surprised. 'Is that what Maxwell said? That I sucker-punched him?'

'It doesn't matter what he said. We are trying to control a potentially devastating situation here, and I don't understand why you are making the moves you are making.'

Bosch nodded. 'That makes sense,' he said. 'You shut somebody out of his own investigation and it stands to reason you won't know what he's up to.'

She held her hands up as if to stop an oncoming train. 'OK, let's just stop everything right here. Talk to me, Harry. What's your problem?'

Bosch looked at her and then up at the ceiling. He studied the upper corners of the room and dropped his eyes back to hers. 'You want to talk? Let's take a walk outside, then we can talk.'

She didn't hesitate. 'OK, fine,' she said. 'Let's walk and talk. And then you'll give me Mitford.'

Walling got up and moved to the door. Bosch saw her glance quickly up at an air-conditioning grille high on the back wall and it confirmed for him that they were on camera. She opened the unlocked door. Brenner and another agent were waiting in the hallway.

'We're going to take a little walk,' Walling said. 'Alone.'

'Have a great time,' Brenner said. 'We'll be in here trying to track the caesium, maybe save a few lives.'

Walling led Bosch down the hall. Bosch saw Just as they were at the door to the elevator hall, then heard a voice from behind him.

'Hey, buddy!'

He turned just in time to take Agent Maxwell's shoulder in the chest. He was driven into the wall and held up against it.

'You're a little outnumbered this time, aren't you, Bosch?'

'Stop!' Walling shouted. 'Cliff, stop it!'

Bosch brought his arm up round Maxwell's head and was going to pull him down into a headlock. But Walling waded in and pulled Maxwell away, then pushed him back up the hallway.

'Cliff, get back! Get away!'

Maxwell started moving backwards up the hall. He pointed a finger over Walling's shoulder at Bosch. 'Get out of my building! Get out and stay out!'

Walling shoved him into the first open office and closed the door on him. By then, several other agents had come into the hallway to see what the commotion was about.

'It's all over,' Walling announced. 'Everybody just go back to work.'

She came back to Bosch and pushed him through the door to the elevator. 'You OK?'

'Only hurts when I breathe.'

'Son of a bitch! That guy is getting out of control.'

They took the elevator down to garage level and walked from there up an incline and out onto Los Angeles Street. She turned right and he caught up. They were heading away from the noise of the freeway.

Walling checked her watch, then pointed towards a modern office building. 'There's decent coffee in there,' she said.

It was the new Social Security Administration building.

'Another federal building.' Bosch sighed. 'Agent Maxwell might think that's his, too.'

'Can you drop that, please?'

He shrugged. 'I'm just surprised Maxwell even admitted we came back to the house.'

'Why wouldn't he?'

'Because I figured he was posted on the house because he was already in the doghouse for being a screwup. Why admit that we got the drop on him and have to stay in there longer?'

Walling shook her head. 'You don't understand,' she said. 'First of all, Maxwell has been wound a little tight lately, but no one in Tactical Intelligence is in the doghouse. The work is too important to have any screwups on the team. Secondly, he didn't care what anyone would think. What he did think was that it was important for everyone to know about the way *you're* screwing things up.'

He tried another direction. 'Let me ask you something. Do they know about you and me over there? Our history, I mean.'

'It would be hard for them not to know after Echo Park. But, Harry, never mind all of that. That's not important today. What is wrong with you? We've got enough caesium out there to shut down an airport and you don't seem all that concerned. You're looking at this like it's a murder. Yes, a man is dead, but this is a heist, Harry. Get it? They wanted the caesium and now they've got it. And it would help us if maybe we could talk to the only known witness. So where is he?'

'He's safe. Where's Alicia Kent? And where's her husband's partner?'

'They're safe. The partner's being questioned here and we're keeping the wife at Tactical until we're sure we have everything there is to get from her.'

'She's not going to be very helpful. She couldn't—'

'That's where you're wrong. She's already been quite helpful.'

Bosch couldn't hold back the look of surprise in his eyes. 'How? She said she didn't even see their faces.'

'She didn't. But she heard a name. When they were speaking to each other, she heard a name.'

'What name? She didn't say this before.'

Walling nodded. 'That's why you should turn over your witness. We have people who have one expertise: getting information from witnesses. We can get things from her that you are unable to get. We got them from her; we can get them from him.'

Bosch felt his face turning red. 'What was the name this master interrogator got from her?'

She shook her head. 'We're not trading, Harry. This involves national security. You're on the outside. And, by the way, that's not going to change no matter who you get your police chief to call.'

Bosch knew then that his meeting at the Donut Hole had been for nothing. Even the chief was on the outside looking in. Whatever name Alicia Kent gave up, it must have lit up the federal scoreboard like Times Square.

'All I've got is my witness,' he said. 'I'll trade you straight up for the name.'

'Why do you want the name? You won't get anywhere near this guy.'

'Because I want to know.'

She folded her arms across her chest and thought about things for a moment. Finally she looked at him. 'You first,' she said.

Bosch hesitated while he studied her eyes. Six months earlier he'd have trusted her with his life. Now things had changed. Bosch wasn't so sure.

'I stashed him at my place,' he said. 'I think you remember where that is.'

She pulled a phone from her blazer pocket and opened it.

'Wait a second there, Agent Walling,' he said. 'What was the name Alicia Kent gave you?'

'Sorry, Harry.'

'We had a deal.'

'National security, sorry.' She started punching in a number on her cell.

Bosch nodded. He had called it right.

'I lied,' he said. 'He's not at my place.'

She slapped the phone closed. 'What is with you?' she asked angrily, her voice getting shrill. 'We're running more than fourteen hours behind the caesium. Do you realise it may already be in a device? It may already be—'

'Give me the name and I'll give you the witness.'

'All *right*!'

He knew she was angry with herself for being caught in the lie. It was the second time in less than twelve hours.

'She said she heard the name Moby, OK? She didn't think anything of it at the time, because she didn't realise that what she had heard was a name.'

'OK, who is Moby?'

'There is a Syrian terrorist named Momar Azim Nassar. He is believed to be in this country. He is known by friends and associates as Moby. We don't know why, but he does happen to resemble the performer named Moby.'

'Who?'

'Never mind. Not your generation.'

'But you are sure she heard this name?'

'Yes. She gave us the name. And I have now given it to you. Now, where is the witness?'

'Just hold on. You already lied to me once.'

Bosch pulled out his phone and was about to call his partner when he remembered that Ferras would still be at the Silver Lake crime scene and would be unable to provide what he needed. He opened the directory on the phone, found the number for Kiz Rider and pushed the CALL button.

Rider answered immediately. Bosch's number had shown up on caller ID. 'Hello, Harry. You've been busy today.'

'The chief tell you that?'

'I've got a few sources. What's up?'

Bosch spoke while staring at Walling and watching the anger darken her eyes. 'I need a favour from my old partner. You still carry that laptop with you to work?'

'Of course. What favour?'

'I have a name. I want you to check to see if it's been in any stories in the *New York Times* archives.'

'Hold on. I have to go online.'

Several seconds went by. Bosch's phone started to beep because he was getting another call, but he stayed with Rider and soon she was ready.

'What's the name?'

Bosch put his hand over the phone and asked Walling for the full name of the Syrian terrorist again. He then repeated it to Rider and waited.

'Yeah, multiple hits,' she said. 'Going back eight years.'

'Give me a run-down.'

Bosch waited again.

'Uh . . . just a bunch of stuff from the Middle East. He's suspected of involvement in a number of abductions and bombings and so on. He's connected to al-Qaeda, according to federal sources.'

'What does the most recent story say?'

'Uh, let's see. It's about a bus bombing in Beirut. Sixteen people killed. This is January 3rd, 2004. Nothing after that.'

'Does it give any nicknames or aliases?'

'Um . . . no. I don't see anything.'

'OK, thanks. I'll call you later.'

'Wait a minute. Harry?'

'What? I have to go.'

'Listen, I just want to tell you, be careful out there, OK? This is a whole different league you're playing in.'

'OK, I got it,' Bosch said. 'I gotta go.'

He ended the call and looked at Walling. 'There's nothing in the *New York Times* about this guy being in this country.'

'Because it's not known. That's why Alicia Kent's information was so genuine.'

'What do you mean? You take her word for it that the guy's in this country just because she heard a word that might not even be a name?'

She folded her arms. She was losing her patience. 'No, Harry, we *know* he's in this country. We have video of him checking out the Port of Los Angeles last August. We just didn't get there in time to grab him. We believe he was with another al-Qaeda operative named Muhammad El-Fayed. They've somehow slipped into this country—hell, the border's a sieve—and who knows what they've got planned.'

'And you think they have the caesium?'

'We don't know that. But the intelligence on El-Fayed is that he smokes unfiltered Turkish cigarettes and—'

'The ashes on the toilet.'

She nodded. 'That's right. They're still being analysed, but the betting in the office is that it was a Turkish cigarette.'

Bosch nodded and suddenly felt foolish about the moves he had been making, the information he had held back.

'We put the witness in the Mark Twain Hotel on Wilcox,' he said. 'Room 303, under the name Stephen King.'

'Cute.'

'And Rachel?'

'What?'

'He told us that he heard the shooter call out to Allah before he pulled the trigger.'

She looked at him with the eyes of judgment as she opened her phone again. She pushed a single button. When her call was picked up, she delivered the information without identifying herself.

'He's at the Mark Twain on Wilcox. Room 303. Go pick him up.'

She closed her phone and looked at Bosch. Worse than judgment, he saw disappointment and dismissal in her eyes now.

'I have to go,' she said. 'I'd stay away from airports, subways and the malls until we find that caesium.'

She turned and left him there. Bosch was watching her walk away when his phone started to buzz again. He answered without taking his eyes off her. It was Joe Felton, the deputy coroner.

'Harry, I've been trying to reach you.'

'What's up, Joe?'

'We just swung by Queen of Angels to make a pick-up—some gang-banger they pulled the plug on after a shooting yesterday in Hollywood.'

'Yeah?'

Bosch knew that the medical examiner wouldn't have called to waste his time. There was a reason.

'So we're here now and I go into the break room to grab some caffeine, and I overhear a couple of paramedics talking about a pick-up they just made. They said the ER evaluation was ARS and it made me wonder if it could be connected with the guy up on the overlook. You know, since he was wearing the radiation alert rings.'

Bosch calmed his voice. 'Joe, what is ARS?'

'Acute radiation syndrome. The medics said they didn't know what the guy had. He was burned and he was puking all over the place. They transported him and the ER doc said it was a pretty bad exposure, Harry. Now the medics are waiting to see if they're exposed.'

Bosch started walking towards Rachel Walling.

'Where'd they find this guy?'

'I didn't ask, but I assume it was somewhere in Hollywood if they brought him in here.'

Bosch started picking up speed.

'Joe, I want you to hang up and get somebody from hospital security to watch this guy. I'm on my way.'

Bosch clapped the phone closed and began running towards Rachel as fast as he could.

NINE

The traffic on the Hollywood Freeway was all flowing into downtown at a slow crawl. Under the laws of traffic physics—that for every action, there is an equal and opposite reaction—Harry Bosch had clear sailing on the northbound lanes out. Of course, this was aided by the siren and flashing lights on his car, making what little traffic there was in front of him move quickly out of the way. *Applied force* was another law Bosch knew well. He had the old Crown Vic up to ninety and his hands were white-knuckled on the wheel.

'Where are we going?' Rachel Walling yelled over the sound of the siren.

'I told you. I'm taking you to the caesium.'

'What does that mean?'

'It means paramedics just brought a man with acute radiation syndrome into the emergency room at Queen of Angels. We'll be there in four minutes.'

'Damn it! Why didn't you tell me?'

The answer was that he wanted a head start, but he didn't tell her this. He remained silent while she opened her cellphone and punched in a number. She then reached up to the car's roof and flicked off the siren toggle.

'What are you doing?' Bosch exclaimed. 'I need that to—'

'I need to be able to talk!'

Bosch took his foot off the accelerator and dropped it down to seventy to be safe. A moment later her call was connected and Bosch listened to her bark commands. He hoped it was at Brenner and not Maxwell.

'Divert the team from the Mark Twain to Queen of Angels. Scramble a contamination team and get them there, too. Send back-up units and a DOE assessment team. We have an exposure case that may lead us to the missing materials. Do it and call me back. I'll be on site in three minutes.'

She closed the phone and Bosch hit the siren toggle.

'I said four minutes!' he yelled.

'Impress me!' she yelled back.

He pinned the accelerator again, even though he didn't need to. He was confident they would be first to the hospital. They were already past Silver Lake on the freeway and closing in on Hollywood. But the truth was that any time he could legitimately hit ninety on the Hollywood Freeway he took advantage. There were not many in the city who could say they had done that during daylight hours.

'Who is the victim?' Walling shouted.

'No idea.'

They were silent for a long period. Bosch concentrated on the driving. And his thoughts. There were so many things that bothered him about the case. Soon he had to share them.

'How do you think they targeted him?' he said.

'What?' Walling replied, coming out of her own thoughts.

'Moby and el-Fayed. How'd they zero in on Stanley Kent?'

'I don't know. Maybe if this is one of them at the hospital, we'll get to ask.'

Bosch let some time go by. He was tired of yelling. But then he called over another question. 'Doesn't it bother you that everything came out of that house?'

'What are you talking about?'

'The gun, the camera, the computer they used. Everything. There's Coke in litre bottles in the pantry, and they tied Alicia Kent up with the same snap ties she uses to hold her roses up in the back yard. Doesn't that bother you? They had nothing but a knife and ski masks when they went through that door. Doesn't that bother you at all about this case?'

'You have to remember, these people are resourceful. They teach them that in the camps. El-Fayed was trained in an al-Qaeda camp in Afghanistan. He in turn taught Nassar. They make do with what's available. You could say that they took down the World Trade Center with a couple of airliners or a couple of box cutters. It's all in how you look at it. More important than what tools they have is their relentlessness—something I'm sure you can appreciate.'

Bosch was about to respond, but they came up on the exit and he had to concentrate on weaving round the traffic on surface streets. In two minutes he'd killed the siren and pulled into the ambulance run at Queen of Angels.

Felton met them in the crowded emergency room and led the way to the treatment area, where there were six bays. A private security cop stood outside one of the curtained spaces and Bosch stepped forward, showing his badge. He split the curtain and moved into the treatment bay.

Alone in the curtained space was the patient, a small, dark-haired man with brown skin, lying beneath a spider web of tubes and wires extending from overhead medical machinery to his limbs, chest, mouth and nose. The hospital bed was encased in a clear plastic tent. The man's eyes were half-lidded and unmoving. Most of his body was exposed. Some sort of modesty towel had been taped over his genitals, but his legs and torso were visible. The right side of his stomach and right hip were covered with blooms of thermal burns. His right hand exhibited the same burns—painful-looking red rings surrounding purplish wet eruptions in the skin. A clear gel had been spread over the burns.

'Where is everybody?' Bosch asked.

'Harry, don't get close,' Walling warned. 'He's not conscious, so let's just back out and talk to the doctor before we do anything.'

Bosch pointed to the patient's burns. 'Could this be from the caesium?' he asked. 'It can happen that fast?'

'From direct exposure in a concentrated amount, yeah. It depends on how long the exposure was. It looks like this guy was carrying the stuff in his pocket.'

'Does he look like Moby or el-Fayed?'

'No, he doesn't look like either one of them. Come on.'

She stepped back through the curtain and Bosch followed. She ordered the security man to get the ER doctor who was treating the man. She flipped open her phone and pushed a single button. Her call was answered quickly.

'This is legit,' she said. 'We have a direct exposure. We need to set up a command post and a containment protocol here.' She listened and then answered a question. 'No, neither one. I don't have an ID yet. I'll call it in as soon as I do.'

She closed the phone and looked at Bosch. 'The radiation team will be here inside of ten minutes,' she said. 'I'll be directing the command post.'

A woman in hospital blues walked up to them carrying a clipboard. 'I'm Dr Garner. You need to stay away from that patient until we know more about what happened to him.'

Walling and Bosch showed her their credentials.

'What can you tell us?' Walling asked.

'Not much at this time. He's in full prodromal syndrome—the first symptoms of exposure. The trouble is, we don't know what he was exposed to or for how long. That gives us no grey count and without that we don't have a specific treatment protocol. We're winging it.'

'What are the symptoms?' Walling asked.

'Well, you see the burns. Those are the least of our problems. The most serious damage is internal. His immune system is shutting down and he's aspirated most of the lining of his stomach. His GI tract is shot. We stabilised him, but I'm not holding out a great deal of hope. The stress on the body pushed him into cardiac arrest. We just had the blue team in here fifteen minutes ago.'

'How long is it between exposure and the start of this produro-whatever syndrome?' Bosch asked.

'Prodromal. It can happen within an hour of first exposure.'

Bosch looked at the man beneath the plastic canopy enclosing the bed. He remembered the phrase Captain Hadley had used when Samir was dying on the floor of his prayer room. *He's circling the drain.* He knew the man on the hospital bed was circling it as well.

'What can you tell us about who he is and where he was found?' Bosch asked the doctor.

'You'll have to talk to the paramedics about that,' Garner answered. 'I didn't have time to get into it. All I heard was that he was found in the street. He had collapsed. And as far as who he is . . .' She raised the clipboard and read from the top sheet. 'He's listed as Digoberto Gonzalves, age forty-one. There's no address here. That's all I know right now.'

Walling stepped away, pulling her phone out again. Bosch knew she was going to call in the name, have it run through the terrorism data bases.

'Where are his clothes and his wallet?' he asked the doctor.

'His clothing and all his possessions were removed from the ER because of exposure concerns.'

'Did anybody look through them?'

'No, sir. Nobody was going to risk it.'

'Where was it all taken?'

'You'll have to get that information from the nursing staff.'

She pointed to a nursing station in the centre of the treatment area. Bosch headed that way. The nurse at the desk told Bosch that everything from the patient was placed in a medical-waste container that was then taken to the hospital's incinerator.

'Where's the incinerator?'

Rather than give him directions, the nurse called over the security guard and told him to take Bosch to the incinerator room. Before Bosch could go, Walling called to him.

'Take this.' She held out the radiation-alert monitor she had taken off her belt. 'And remember, we have a radiation team coming. Don't risk yourself. If that goes off, you back away. I mean it. *You back away*.'

'Got it.'

Bosch put the alert monitor in his pocket. He and the guard quickly headed down a hallway and then took a stairway to the basement. They then took another hallway that seemed to run at least a block in length to the far side of the building.

When they got to the incinerator room, the space was empty. There appeared to be no active burning of medical waste occurring. There was a three-foot canister on the floor. It was sealed with tape that said CAUTION: HAZARDOUS WASTE.

Bosch took out his key chain, which had a small penknife on it. He squatted down next to the canister and cut the security tape. In his peripheral vision, he noticed the security guard step back.

'Maybe you should wait outside,' Bosch said. 'There's no need for both of us to—'

He heard the door close behind him before he finished the sentence.

He looked down at the canister, took a breath and removed the top. Digoberto Gonzalves's clothes had been haphazardly dropped inside.

Bosch took the monitor Walling had given him and waved it over the open canister like a magic wand. The monitor remained silent. He let his breath out. Then he turned the canister upside-down and dumped its contents onto the concrete floor. He rolled the canister aside and once again moved the monitor in a circular pattern over the clothes. There was no alarm.

Gonzalves's clothes had been cut off his body with scissors. There were a pair of dirty blue jeans, a work shirt, T-shirt, underwear and socks. There was also a pair of work boots with the laces cut. Lying loose on the floor in the middle of the clothing was a small, black leather wallet.

Bosch started with the clothing. In the pocket of the work shirt were a pen and a tyre pressure gauge. He found work gloves sticking out of one of the rear pockets of the jeans, then removed a set of keys and a cellphone from the left front pocket. He thought about the burns he had seen on Gonzalves's right hip and hand. But when he opened the right front pocket of the jeans, there was no caesium. The pocket was empty.

Bosch put the cellphone and keys down next to the wallet and studied what he had. On one of the keys was a Toyota insignia. Now he knew that a vehicle was part of the equation. He opened the phone and tried to find the call directory but couldn't figure it out. He put it aside and opened the wallet.

There wasn't much. The wallet contained a Mexican driver's licence with the name and photo of Digoberto Gonzalves. He was from Oaxaca. In one of the slots Bosch found photos of a woman and three young children. There was no green card or citizenship document. There were no credit cards, and in the billfold section there were only six dollar bills, along with several tickets from pawnshops in the Valley.

Bosch put the wallet down next to the phone, stood up and got out his own phone. He scrolled the directory until he found Walling's cell number. She answered immediately.

'I checked his clothes. No caesium.'

There was no response.

'Rachel, did you—?'

'Yes, I heard. I just wish you *had* found it, Harry. I wish this could be over.'

'Me too. Did anything come through on the name?'

'What name?'

'Gonzalves. You called it in, right?'

'Oh, right, yeah. No, nothing. And I mean nothing, not even a driver's licence. I think it must be an alias.'

'I've got a Mexican driver's licence here. I think the guy's an illegal.'

She gave that some thought before responding. 'Well, it's believed that Nassar and El-Fayed came in across the Mexican border. Maybe that's the connection. Maybe this guy was working with them.'

'I don't know, Rachel. I've got work clothes here. Work boots. I think this guy—'

'Harry, I've gotta go. My team is here.'

'All right. I'm heading back up.'

Bosch pocketed his phone, then gathered the clothing and boots and put them all back in the canister. He put the wallet, keys and cellphone on top and took the canister with him. On the long walk back to the stairs, he pulled out his phone again and called the city's communications centre. He asked the dispatcher to dig out the details on the paramedic call that had brought Gonzalves to Queen of Angels and was put on hold. He got all the way up the steps and back to the ER before the dispatcher came back on the line.

'The call you asked about came in at ten-oh-five from a phone registered to Easy Print at 930 Cahuenga Boulevard. Man down in the parking lot.

Fire department paramedics responded from station fifty-four. Response time six minutes, nineteen seconds. Anything else?'

'What's the nearest cross at that location?'

After a moment the dispatcher told him the cross street was Lankershim Boulevard. Bosch thanked her and disconnected.

The address where Gonzalves collapsed was not far from the Mulholland overlook. Bosch realised that almost every location associated with the case so far—from the murder site to the victim's house to Ramin Samir's house and now to the spot where Gonzalves collapsed—could fit on one page of a Thomas Brothers map book. Murder cases in LA usually dragged him all over the map book. But this one wasn't roaming. It was staying close.

Bosch looked around the ER. He noticed that all the people who had been crowding the waiting room before were now gone. There had been an evacuation and agents in protective gear were moving about the area with radiation monitors. He spotted Rachel Walling by the nursing station and walked over to her.

He held out the canister. 'Here's the guy's stuff.'

She called over to one of the men in protection gear. She told him to take charge of the canister. She then looked back at Bosch.

'There's a cellphone in there,' he told her. 'They might be able to get something out of that.'

'I'll tell them.'

'How's the victim doing?' Bosch asked.

'Victim?'

'Whether he's involved in this or not, he is still a victim.'

'If you say so. He's still out of it. I don't know if we'll ever get the chance to talk to him.'

'Then I'm leaving.'

'What? Where? I'm going with you,' Walling said.

'I thought you had to run the CP.'

'I passed it off. If there's no caesium here, I'm not staying. I'll stick with you. Let me just tell some people I'm leaving to follow a lead.'

Bosch hesitated. But deep down he knew he wanted her with him. 'I'll be out front in the car.'

'Where are we going?'

'I don't know if Digoberto Gonzalves is a terrorist or just a victim, but I do know one thing. He drives a Toyota. And I think I know where we'll find it.'

HARRY BOSCH knew that the physics of traffic would not work for him in the Cahuenga Pass. The Hollywood Freeway always moved slowly in both directions through the bottleneck created by the cut in the mountain chain. He decided to stay on surface streets and take Highland Avenue past the Hollywood Bowl and up into the pass. He filled Rachel Walling in along the way.

'The call for paramedics came from a print shop on Cahuenga near Lankershim. Gonzalves must have been in the area when he collapsed. The initial call said a man was down in the parking lot. I'm hoping that the Toyota he was driving is right there. I'm betting that if we find it, we find the caesium. The mystery is why he had it.'

'And why he was foolish enough to put it in his pocket unprotected,' Walling added.

'You're basing that on him knowing what he had. Maybe he didn't. Maybe this isn't what we think it is.'

'There's got to be a connection, Bosch, between Gonzalves and Nassar and el-Fayed. He probably brought them across the border.'

Bosch almost smiled. He knew she had used his last name as a term of endearment. He remembered how she used to do that.

'And don't forget about Ramin Samir,' he said.

Walling shook her head. 'I'm still thinking he was a red herring,' she said. 'A misdirection.'

'A good one,' Bosch responded. 'It took the mighty Captain Done Badly out of the picture.'

She laughed. 'Is that what they call him?'

Bosch nodded. 'Not to his face, of course.'

He took the ramp up to Cahuenga from Highland. It ran parallel to the freeway and as soon as he checked he saw that he had been right. The traffic over on the freeway was frozen in both directions.

'You know, I still had your number in my cell's directory,' he said. 'I guess I never wanted to delete it.'

'I was wondering about that when you left me that mean message today about the cigarette ash.'

'I don't suppose you kept mine, Rachel.'

She paused a long moment before answering. 'I think you're still on my phone, too, Harry.'

This time he had to smile, even though he was back to being Harry with her. There's hope after all, he thought.

They were approaching Lankershim Boulevard. To the right, it dropped down into a tunnel that went beneath the freeway. To the left, it ended at a strip shopping centre that included the Easy Print franchise from which the call to paramedics had originated. Bosch's eyes searched the vehicles in the parking lot, looking for a Toyota.

He glided into the left-turn lane and waited to pull into the lot. He swivelled in his seat and checked the parking along both sides of Cahuenga. A quick glance showed no Toyotas, but he knew that the make had many different car models and pick-up trucks in the brand.

'Do you have a plate or any description?' Walling asked. 'How about a colour?'

'No, no and no.'

Bosch remembered then that she had the habit of asking multiple questions at once.

He made the turn on yellow and pulled into the lot. There were no parking spaces available, but he wasn't interested in parking. He cruised slowly, checking each car. There were no Toyotas.

'It's got to be in this area somewhere,' he said.

'Maybe we should check the street,' Walling suggested.

He nodded and nosed his car into the alley at the end of the parking lot. He was going to turn left to turn round and go back to the street. But when he checked to see if he was clear on the right, he saw an old white pick-up truck with a camper shell parked half a block down the alley next to a green trash Dumpster. The truck was facing them, and he couldn't tell what the make of it was.

'Is that a Toyota?' he asked.

Walling turned and looked. 'Bosch, you're a genius.'

He turned and drove towards the truck, and as he got closer he could see that it was indeed a Toyota. So could Walling. She pulled out her phone, but Bosch reached across and put his hand on it.

'Let's just check it out first. I could be wrong about this.'

'No, Bosch, you're on a roll.' But she put the phone away.

Bosch pulled slowly past the pick-up, giving it a once-over. He then turned round at the end of the block and came back. He stopped his car ten feet behind it. There was no plate on the back. A cardboard LOST TAG sign had been put in its place.

Bosch wished he had brought the keys he had found in Digoberto

Gonzalves's pocket. They got out and approached the truck, coming up on either side of it. Bosch noticed that the rear window hatch of the camper shell had been left open a couple of inches. He reached forward and pulled it up all the way. An air-pressure hinge held it open. Bosch leaned in close to look into the interior. It was dark because the truck was parked in shadow and the windows were darkly tinted.

'Harry, you have that monitor?'

He pulled her radiation monitor out of his pocket and held it up as he leaned into the darkness of the truck's cargo hold. No alarm sounded. He leaned back out and put the monitor on his belt. He then reached in and lowered the truck's rear gate.

The back of the truck was piled with junk. There were empty bottles and cans strewn everywhere, a leather desk chair with a broken leg, scrap pieces of aluminium, an old water cooler and other debris. And there, by the raised wheel well on the right side, was a lead-grey container that looked like a small mop bucket on wheels.

'There,' he said. 'Is that the pig?'

'I think it is,' Walling said excitedly. 'I think it is!'

There was no warning sticker on it or radiation-alert symbol. They had been peeled off. Bosch leaned in and grabbed one of the handles. He pulled it clear of the debris around it and rolled it to the tailgate. The top was latched in four places.

'Do we open it and make sure the stuff is in there?' he asked.

'No, we don't,' Walling said. 'We back off and call in the team. They have protection.'

She pulled her phone out again. While she called for the radiation team and back-up units, Bosch moved to the front of the truck. He looked through the window and saw a half-eaten breakfast burrito sitting on a flattened brown bag on the centre console. And he saw more junk on the passenger side. His eyes held on a camera that was sitting on an old briefcase with a broken handle on the passenger seat. The camera didn't appear broken or dirty. It looked brand new.

Bosch checked the door and found it unlocked. He realised that Gonzalves had forgotten about his truck and his possessions when the caesium started burning through his body. He had got out and stumbled towards the parking lot, seeking help, leaving everything else behind and unlocked.

Bosch opened the driver's door and reached in with the radiation monitor.

Nothing happened. No alert. He stood back up and replaced it on his belt. From his pocket he got out a pair of latex gloves, and put them on while listening to Walling talking to someone about finding the pig.

'No, we didn't open it,' she said. 'Just get them here as fast as you can and maybe this will all be over.'

Bosch leaned into the truck and picked up the camera. It was a Nikon digital, and he remembered that the lens cover found beneath the master bed at the Kent house had said Nikon on it. He believed he was holding the camera that had taken the photograph of Alicia Kent. He turned it on, and for once he knew what he was doing as he examined a piece of electronic equipment. He had a digital camera of his own. His wasn't a Nikon, but he was able to determine quickly that the camera he had just found had no photos in its memory because the chip had been removed.

Bosch put the camera down and began looking through the things piled on the passenger seat. In addition to the broken briefcase, there was a child's lunch box, a manual for operating an Apple computer and a poker from a fireplace tool set. Nothing connected and nothing interested him. He noticed a golf putter and a rolled-up poster on the floor in front of the seat.

He moved the brown bag and the burrito out of the way and shifted his weight to one elbow on the armrest between the seats so he could reach over and open the glove compartment. And there, sitting in the otherwise empty space, was a handgun. Bosch lifted it out and turned it in his hand. It was a Smith & Wesson .22-calibre revolver.

'I think we've got the murder weapon here,' he called out.

There was no response from Walling. She was still at the back of the truck talking on her phone, issuing orders in an animated voice.

Bosch returned the gun to the glove box and closed it, deciding to leave the weapon in place for the forensics team. He noticed the rolled-up poster again and decided for no reason other than curiosity to take a look at it. Using his elbow on the centre armrest for support, he unrolled it across all the junk on the passenger seat. It was a chart depicting twelve yoga positions.

Bosch immediately thought about the discoloured space he had seen on the wall in the workout room at the Kent house. He wasn't sure, but he thought the dimensions of the poster would be a close match to that space on the wall. He quickly rerolled the poster and started to back out of the cab so he could show Walling.

But as he was pulling out, he noticed that the armrest between the seats was also a storage compartment. He stopped and opened it.

He froze. There was a cup holder, and in it were several steel capsules resembling bullet cartridges closed flat on both ends. The steel was so polished it might have been mistaken for silver.

Bosch moved the radiation monitor over the capsules in a circular pattern. There was no alarm. He turned the device over and looked at it. He saw a small switch on its side. With his thumb he pushed it up. A blaring alarm suddenly went off, the frequency of tones so fast that they sounded like one long eardrum-piercing siren.

Bosch jumped back out of the truck and slammed the door shut. The poster fell to the ground.

'Harry!' Walling yelled.

She rushed towards him, closing the phone on her hip. Bosch pushed the switch again and turned the monitor off.

'What is it?' she yelled.

Bosch pointed towards the truck's door. 'The gun's in the glove box and the caesium's in the centre compartment.'

'What?'

'The caesium is in the compartment under the armrest. He took the capsules out of the pig. That's why they weren't in his pocket. They were in the centre armrest.'

He touched his right hip, the place where Gonzalves was burned by radiation. The same spot would have been next to the armrest compartment when he was sitting in the truck.

Walling didn't say anything for a long moment. She just stared at his face. 'Are you OK?' she finally asked.

Bosch almost laughed. 'I don't know. Ask me in about ten years.'

She hesitated, as if she knew something but couldn't share it.

'What?' Bosch asked.

'Nothing. You should be checked out, though.'

'What are they going to be able to do? Look, I wasn't in the truck that long. It's not like Gonzalves, who was sitting in there with it. He was practically eating off of it.'

She didn't answer.

Bosch handed her the monitor. 'It was never on. I thought it was on when you gave it to me.'

She took it and looked at it in her hand. 'I thought it was, too.'

Bosch thought about how he had carried the monitor in his pocket rather than clipped to his belt. He had probably switched it off unknowingly when he had twice put it in and removed it. He looked back at the truck and wondered if he had possibly just hurt or killed himself.

'I need a drink of water,' he said. 'I've got a bottle in the trunk.'

Bosch walked back to the rear of his car. Using the open trunk lid to shield Walling's view of him, he leaned his hands down on the bumper for support and tried to decipher the messages his body was sending to his brain. He felt something happening but didn't know if it was something physiological or if the shakes he felt were simply an emotional response to what had just happened. He remembered what the ER doctor had said about Gonzalves and how the most serious damage was internal. Was his own immune system shutting down? Was he circling the drain?

'Harry?'

Bosch looked round the trunk lid. Walling was walking towards him.

'The teams are headed this way. They'll be here in five minutes. How do you feel?'

'I think I'm OK.'

'Good. I talked to the head of the team. He thinks the exposure was too short to be anything serious. But you should still go to the ER and get checked out.'

'We'll see.'

He reached into the trunk and got a litre bottle of water out of his kit. It was an emergency bottle he kept for long surveillances. He opened it and took two strong pulls. The water wasn't cold but it felt good going down. His throat was dry.

Bosch recapped the bottle and put it back in the kit. He stepped round the car. As he walked towards Walling, he looked past her to the south. He realised that the alley they were in extended several blocks past the back of the Easy Print and ran behind all the storefronts and offices on Cahuenga. All the way down to Barham.

In the alley every twenty yards or so was a green Dumpster positioned perpendicular to the rear of the structures. Bosch realised they had been pushed out of spaces between the buildings and fenced corrals. Just like in Silver Lake, it was pick-up day and the Dumpsters were waiting for the city trucks to come.

Suddenly it all came to him. Like fusion. Two elements coming together and creating something new. The thing that bothered him about the crime-scene photos, the yoga poster, everything. The gamma rays had shot right through him but they had left him enlightened. He knew. He understood.

'He's a scavenger.'

'Who is?'

'Digoberto Gonzalves,' Bosch said, his eyes looking down the alley. 'It's collection day. The Dumpsters are all pushed out for the city trucks. Gonzalves is a scavenger, a Dumpster diver, and he knew this would be a good time to come here.' He looked at Walling before completing the thought. 'And so did somebody else.'

'You mean he found the caesium in a Dumpster?'

Bosch nodded and pointed down the alley. 'All the way at the end, that's Barham. Barham takes you up to Lake Hollywood. Lake Hollywood takes you to the overlook. This case never leaves the map page.'

Walling came over and stood in front of him, blocking his view. Bosch could now hear sirens in the distance.

'What are you saying? That Nassar and El-Fayed took the caesium and stashed it in a Dumpster at the bottom of the hill? Then this scavenger comes along and finds it?'

'I'm saying you've got the caesium back, so now we're looking at this as a homicide again. You come down from the overlook and you can be in this alley in five minutes.'

'So what? They stole the caesium and killed Kent just so they could come down here and stash it? Is that what you're saying? Or are you saying they just threw it all away? Why would they do that? I mean, does that make any sense at all? I mean, I don't see how that would scare people in the way we know they want to scare us.'

Bosch noted that she had asked six questions at once this time, possibly a new record.

'Nassar and El-Fayed were never near the caesium,' he said. 'That's what I'm saying.'

He walked over to the truck and picked the rolled poster up off the ground. He handed it to Walling. The sirens were getting louder.

She unrolled the poster and looked at it. 'What is this? What does it mean?'

Bosch took it back from her and started rolling it up. 'Gonzalves found that in the same Dumpster where he found the gun and the camera and the lead pig.'

'So? What does it *mean*, Harry?'

Two fed cars pulled into the alley a block away and started making their way towards them, weaving round the Dumpsters. As they got close, Bosch could see that the driver of the lead car was Jack Brenner.

'Do you hear me, Harry? What does it—?'

Bosch's knees suddenly seemed to give out and he fell into her, throwing his arms round her to stop himself from hitting the ground.

'Bosch!' She grabbed him and held on.

'Uh . . . I'm not feeling so good,' he mumbled. 'I think I better . . . Can you take me to my car?'

She helped him straighten up and then started walking him towards his car. He put his arm over her shoulders. Car doors were slamming behind them as the agents got out.

'Where are the keys?' Walling asked.

He held the key ring out to her just as Brenner ran up to them.

'What is it? What's wrong?'

'He was exposed. The caesium is in the centre console in the truck cab. Be careful. I'm going to take him to the hospital.'

Brenner stepped back, as if whatever Bosch had were contagious. 'OK,' he said. 'Call me when you can.'

Bosch and Walling kept moving towards the car.

'Come on, Bosch,' Walling said. 'Stay with me. Hang in there and we'll get you taken care of.'

She had called him by his last name again.

TEN

The car jerked forward as Walling pulled out of the alley and into southbound traffic on Cahuenga.

'I'm taking you back to Queen of Angels so Dr Garner can take a look at you,' she said. 'Just hang in there for me, Bosch.'

He knew that the last-name endearments were about to come to an end. He pointed towards the left-turn lane that led onto Barham Boulevard.

'Never mind the hospital,' he said. 'Take me to the Kent house.'

'What?'

'I'll get checked out later. The Kent house. Here's the turn. Go!'

She slipped into the left-turn lane. 'What's going on?'

'I'm fine. I'm OK.'

'What are you telling me, that that little fainting spell was—'

'I had to get you away from the crime scene and away from Brenner so I could check this out and talk to you. Alone.'

'Check what out? Talk about what? Do you realise what you just did? I thought I was saving your life. Now Brenner or one of those other guys will take the credit for the recovery of the caesium. Thanks a lot. That was my crime scene.'

He opened his jacket and pulled out the rolled-up and folded yoga poster. 'Don't worry about it,' he said. 'You can get the credit for the arrests. You just might not want it.'

He opened the poster, letting the top half flop over his knees. He was only interested in the bottom half.

'Dhanurasana,' he said.

Walling glanced over at him and then down at the poster. 'Would you start telling me what's going on?'

'Alicia Kent practices yoga. I saw the mats hanging on the wall of the workout room at the house.'

'I saw them, too. So what?'

'Did you see the sun discoloration on the wall where a poster had been taken down?'

'Yes, I saw it.'

Bosch held up the poster. 'I'm betting that this will be a perfect fit. This is a poster Gonzalves found with the caesium.'

'And what will that mean—if it's a perfect fit?'

'It will mean that it was almost a perfect crime. Alicia Kent conspired to kill her husband, and if it hadn't been for Digoberto Gonzalves just happening to find the tossed-out evidence, she would have got away with it.'

Walling shook her head dismissively. 'Come on, Harry. Are you saying she conspired with international terrorists to kill her husband in exchange for the caesium? I can't believe I am even doing this. I need to get back to the crime scene.'

She checked her mirrors, getting ready to make a U-turn. They were going up Lake Hollywood Drive now and would be at the house in two minutes.

'No, keep going. We're almost there. Alicia Kent conspired with someone, but it wasn't a terrorist. The caesium being dumped in the trash proves that. You said it yourself—there is no way that Moby and El-Fayed would steal this stuff just to dump it. So what does that tell you? This *wasn't* a heist. It actually *was* a murder. The caesium was just a red herring. Just like Ramin Samir. And Moby and El-Fayed? They were part of the misdirection as well. This poster will help prove it.'

'How?'

'Dhanurasana, the rocking bow.'

He held the poster up so she could glance at the yoga pose depicted in the bottom corner. It showed a woman with her arms behind her back, holding her ankles and creating a bow with the front of her body. She looked like she was hog-tied.

Walling glanced back at the curving road, then took another long look at the poster and the pose.

'We go into the house and see if this fits that space on the wall,' Bosch said. 'If it fits, that means she and the killer took it off the wall because they didn't want to risk that we might see it and connect it with what happened to her.'

'It's a stretch, Harry. A huge one.'

'Not when you put it in context.'

'Which you, of course, can do.'

'As soon as we get to the house.'

'Hope you still have a key.'

'You bet I do.'

Walling turned onto Arrowhead Drive and punched the accelerator. But after a block, she slowed down and shook her head again.

'This is ridiculous. She gave us the name Moby. There is no way she could have known he was in this country. And then up on the overlook, your own witness said that the shooter called out to Allah as he pulled the trigger. How can—?'

'Let's just try the poster on the wall. If it fits, I'll lay the whole thing out for you. I promise. If it doesn't fit, then I'll quit bothering you with it.'

She relented and drove the remaining block to the Kent house without another word. There was no longer a Bureau car sitting out front. Bosch guessed that it was all hands on deck at the caesium recovery scene.

'Thank God I don't have to deal with Maxwell again,' he said.

Walling didn't even smile.

Bosch got out with the poster and his file containing the crime-scene photos. He used Stanley Kent's keys to open the front door and they proceeded to the workout room. They took positions on either side of the rectangular sun-discoloration mark and Bosch unrolled the poster. They each took a side and held the top corners of the poster to the top corners of the mark. Bosch put his other hand on the centre of the poster and flattened it against the wall. The poster was a perfect fit. What was more, the tape marks on the wall matched up with tape marks on the poster. To Bosch, there was no doubt. The poster found by Digoberto Gonzalves in a Dumpster off Cahuenga had definitely come from Alicia Kent's home yoga studio.

Walling let go of her side of the poster and headed out of the room. 'I'll be in the living room. I can't wait to hear you put this together.'

Bosch rolled the poster up and followed. Walling took a seat in the same chair Bosch had put Maxwell in a few hours earlier. He remained standing in front of her.

'The fear was that the poster could be a tip-off,' he said. 'Some smart agent or detective would see the rocking-bow pose and start thinking: This woman does yoga; maybe she could handle being hog-tied like that; maybe it was her idea; maybe she did it to help sell the misdirection. So they couldn't take the chance. The poster had to go. It went into the Dumpster with the caesium, the gun and everything else they used. Except for the ski masks and the phoney map they planted with the car at Ramin Samir's house.'

'She's a master criminal,' Walling said sarcastically.

Bosch was undeterred. He knew he'd convince her.

'If you get your people out there to check that line of Dumpsters, you'll find the rest—the Coke-bottle silencer, the gloves, the first set of snap ties, every—'

'The first set of snap ties?'

'That's right. I'll get to that.'

Walling remained unimpressed. 'You'd better get to a lot of it. Because there are big gaps in this thing, man. What about the name Moby? What about the citing of Allah by the shooter? What—?'

Bosch held up a hand. 'Just hold on. I need some water. My throat is raw from all this talking.'

He went into the kitchen, remembering that he had seen bottles of water in the refrigerator while searching earlier in the day.

'You want anything?' he called out.

'No,' she called back. 'It's not our house, remember?'

He opened the refrigerator, took out a bottle of water and drank half of it while standing in front of the open door. The cool air felt good, too. He closed the door but then immediately reopened it. He had seen something. On the top shelf was a plastic bottle of grape juice. He took it out and looked at it, remembering that when he went through the trash bag in the garage he had found paper towels with grape juice on them.

Another piece of the puzzle fell into place.

He put the bottle back in the refrigerator, then returned to the living room, where Walling was waiting for the story. Once again he remained standing.

'OK,' Bosch said. 'When was it that you captured the terrorist known as Moby on video at the port?'

'What does—?'

'Please, just answer the question.'

'August 12th last year.'

'OK, August 12th. Then what? Some sort of alert went out through the Bureau and all of Homeland Security?'

She nodded. 'Not for a while, though. It took almost two months of video analysis to confirm it was Nassar and El-Fayed. I wrote the bulletin. It went out on October 9th as a confirmed domestic sighting.'

'Out of curiosity, why didn't you go public with it?'

'Because we have . . . Actually, I can't tell you.'

'You just did. You must have someone or someplace where you think these two might show up under surveillance. If you go public, they might just go underground and never show up again.'

'Can we go back to your story, please?'

'Fine. So the bulletin went out on October 9th. That was the day the plan to kill Stanley Kent began.'

Walling folded her arms across her chest and just stared at him. Bosch thought that maybe she was beginning to see where he was going with the story and she didn't like it.

'It works best if you start from the end and go backwards,' Bosch said. 'Alicia Kent gave you the name Moby. How could she have got that name?'

'She overheard one of them calling the other one that.'

Bosch shook his head. 'No. She told you she overheard it. But if she was lying, how would she know the name to lie about it? Just coincidence that she gives the nickname of a guy who less than six months ago was confirmed as being in the country—in LA County, no less? I don't think so, Rachel, and neither do you. The odds of that probably can't be calculated.'

'OK, so you're saying that somebody in the Bureau or another agency that received the FBI bulletin gave her the name.'

Bosch nodded. 'Right. He gave her the name so she could come out with it while being questioned by the FBI's master interrogator. That name, along with the plan to dump the car in front of Ramin Samir's house, would act in concert to send this whole thing down the wrong road with the FBI and everybody else chasing after terrorists who had nothing to do with it.'

'He?'

'I'm getting to that now. You are right. Anybody who got a look at that bulletin would have been able to give her that name. My guess is that would be a lot of people in LA alone. So how would we narrow it down to one?'

'You tell me.'

Bosch opened the bottle and drank the rest of the water. He held the empty bottle in his hand as he went on. 'You narrow it down by continuing to go backwards. Where would Alicia Kent's life have intersected with one of those people in the agencies who knew about Moby?'

Walling frowned and shook her head. 'That could have been anywhere. In line at the supermarket or when she was buying fertiliser for her roses. Anywhere.'

Bosch now had her right where he wanted her to be.

'Then narrow the parameters,' he said. 'Where would she have intersected with someone who knew about Moby but also knew that her husband had access to the sort of radioactive materials Moby might be interested in?'

Now she shook her head in a dismissive way. 'Nowhere. It would take a monumental coincidence to—'

She stopped when it came to her. Enlightenment. And shock as she fully understood where Bosch was going.

'My partner and I visited the Kents to warn them early last year. I guess what you're saying is that that makes me a suspect.'

Bosch shook his head. 'I said *he*, remember? You didn't come here alone.'

Her eyes fired when she registered the implication. 'That's ridiculous. There's no way. I can't believe . . .'

She didn't finish as her mind snagged on something, some memory that undermined her trust and loyalty to her partner.

Bosch picked up on the tell and moved in closer. 'What?' he asked.

'Look,' she insisted, 'take my advice and tell no one this theory of yours. You're lucky you told me first. Because this makes you sound like some kind of crackpot with a vendetta. You have no evidence, no motive, no incriminating statements, nothing. You just have this thing you've spun out of . . . out of a yoga poster.'

'There is no other explanation that fits with the facts. And I'm talking about the facts of the case. Not the fact that the Bureau and Homeland Security and the rest of the federal government would love this to be a terrorism event so they can justify their existence and deflect criticism from other failings. Contrary to what you want to think, there *is* evidence and there *are* incriminating statements. If we put Alicia Kent on a lie detector, you'll find out that everything she told me, you, and the master interrogator downtown is a lie. The real master was Alicia Kent. As in master manipulator.'

Walling leaned forward and looked down at the floor. 'Thank you, Harry. That master interrogator you love deriding happens to have been me.'

Bosch's mouth dropped open for a moment before he spoke. 'Oh . . . well . . . then, sorry . . . but it doesn't matter. The point is, she is a master liar. She lied about everything, and now that we know the story it will be easy to smoke her out.'

Walling got up from her seat and walked over to the front picture window. The vertical blinds were closed, but she split them with a finger and stared out into the street. Bosch could see her working the story over, grinding it down.

'What about the witness?' she asked without turning round. 'He heard the shooter yell "Allah". Are you saying he's part of this? Or are you saying they just happened to know he was there and yelled "Allah" as part of this master manipulation?'

Bosch gently tried to clear his throat. It was burning and making it difficult for him to talk. 'No. On that I think it's just a lesson in hearing what you want to hear. I plead guilty to not being much of a master interrogator myself. The kid told me he heard the shooter yell it as he pulled the trigger. He said he wasn't sure but that it sounded like "Allah", and that, of course, worked with what I was thinking at the time. I heard what I wanted to hear.'

Walling came away from the window, sat back down and folded her arms. Bosch finally sat down on a chair directly across from her.

'But how would the witness know it was the shooter and not the victim who yelled?' he continued. 'He was more than fifty yards away. It was dark.

How would he know that it wasn't Stanley Kent yelling out his last word before execution? The name of the woman he loved, because he was about to die not even knowing that she'd betrayed him.'

'Alicia.'

'Exactly. "Alicia" interrupted by a gunshot could become "Allah".'

Walling relaxed her arms and leaned forward. As body language went, it was a good sign. It told Bosch he was pushing through.

'You said the *first* set of snap ties before,' she said. 'What were you talking about?'

Bosch nodded and handed across the file containing the crime-scene photos. 'Look at the photos. What do you see?'

She opened the file and started looking at the photos. They depicted the master bedroom in the Kent house from all angles.

'It's the master bedroom,' she said. 'What am I missing?'

'Exactly.'

'What?'

'It's what you don't see. There are no clothes in the shot. She told us they told her to sit on the bed and take off her clothes. What are we supposed to believe? That they let her put the clothes away before they hog-tied her? Look at the last shot. It's the email photo Stanley Kent got.'

Walling looked through the file until she found the print-out of the email photo. She stared intently at it. He saw recognition break in her eyes.

'Now what do you see?'

'The robe,' she said excitedly. 'When we let her get dressed, she went to the *closet* to get her robe. There was no robe on that lounge chair!'

Bosch nodded. 'What does that tell us?' he asked. 'That these considerate terrorists hung the robe up in the closet for her after taking the photo?'

'Or that maybe Mrs Kent was tied up twice and the robe was moved in between?'

'And look again at the picture. The clock on the bed table is unplugged.'

'Why?'

'I don't know, but maybe they didn't want to worry about having any sort of time stamp on the photo. Maybe the first photo wasn't even taken yesterday. Maybe it came from a dry run two days ago or even two weeks.'

Rachel nodded, and Bosch knew she was committed. She was a believer.

'She was tied up once for the photo and then once again for the rescue,' she said.

'Exactly. And that left her free to help carry out the plan on the overlook. She didn't kill her husband, but she was up there in the other car. And once Stanley was dead and the caesium was dumped and the car ditched at Samir's, she and her partner came back home and she was tied up all over again.'

'She wasn't passed out when we got there. That was an act and part of the plan. And her wetting the bed was a nice little touch to help sell it to us.'

'The smell of urine also covered up the smell of grape juice.'

'What do you mean?'

'The purple bruises on her wrists and ankles. Now we know she wasn't tied up for hours. But she still had those bruises. There's an opened bottle of grape juice in the fridge and paper towels soaked with it in the trash can. She used grape juice to create the bruises.'

'Oh my God, I can't believe this.'

'What?'

'When I was in the room with her at TIU. That small space. I thought I smelt grape in the room. I thought somebody had been in there before us and had been drinking grape juice. I smelt it!'

'There you go.'

There was no doubt now. Bosch had her. But then a shadow of concern and doubt moved across Walling's face like a summer cloud.

'What about motive?' she asked. 'This is a federal agent we're talking about. To move on this, we need everything, even motive. There can be nothing left open to chance.'

Bosch had been ready for the question. 'You saw the motive. Alicia Kent is a beautiful woman. Jack Brenner wanted her, and Stanley Kent was in the way of that.'

Walling's eyes widened in shock.

Bosch pressed on. 'That's the motive, Rachel. You—'

'But he—'

'Let me just finish. It goes like this. You and your partner show up here that day last year to give the Kents the warning about his occupation. Some kind of vibe is exchanged between Alicia and Jack. He gets interested; she gets interested. They meet on the sly for coffee or for drinks or whatever. One thing leads to another. An affair begins and it lasts, and then it lasts to the point where it's time to start thinking about doing something. Leaving the husband. Or getting rid of him because there's insurance and half a company at stake. That's enough motive right there, Rachel, and that's what this case is about. It's not about caesium or terrorism. It's the basic equation: sex plus money equals murder. That's all.'

She frowned and shook her head. 'You don't know what you're talking about. Jack Brenner is married and has three children. He's stable, boring and not interested. He wasn't—'

'Every man is interested. It doesn't matter if they're married or how many kids they have.'

She spoke quietly. 'Would you listen and let me finish now? You're wrong about Brenner. He never met Alicia Kent before today. He wasn't my partner when I came here last year and I never told you he was.'

Bosch was jolted by the news. He had assumed that her current partner had been her partner last year. He'd had Brenner's image locked and loaded in his mind as he unfolded the story.

'At the start of the year, all partners in TIU were shuffled,' Walling explained. 'It's the routine. It promotes a better team concept. I've been with Jack since January.'

'Who was your partner last year, Rachel?'

She held his eyes for a long moment. 'It was Cliff Maxwell.'

ELEVEN

Harry Bosch almost laughed, but he was too shocked to do anything but shake his head. 'I can't believe this,' he finally said. 'About five hours ago I had the killer handcuffed on the floor right here!'

Rachel Walling looked mortified by the realisation that the murder of Stanley Kent was an inside job and the theft of the caesium was nothing more than a well-played misdirection.

'You see the rest now?' Bosch asked. 'You see how he would work it? Her husband's dead and he starts coming round out of sympathy and because he's on the case. They start dating, fall in love, and nobody ever raises an eyebrow about it. They're still out there looking for Moby and El-Fayed.'

'And what if we ever catch those guys?' Walling said, taking up the story. 'They could deny being a part of this thing until Osama bin Laden dies in a cave of old age, but who would believe them or care? There's nothing more ingenious than framing terrorists with a crime they didn't commit. They can never defend themselves.'

Bosch nodded. 'A perfect crime,' he said. 'The only reason it blew up was because Digoberto Gonzalves checked that Dumpster. Without him, we'd still be chasing Moby and El-Fayed, probably thinking that they had used Samir's place as a safe house.'

'So what do we do now, Bosch?'

'I say we set up a classic rat trap. Put them both in rooms, ring the bell and say the first one who talks gets the deal. I'd bet on Alicia. She'll break and give him up, probably blame him for everything, say she was acting under his influence and control.'

'Something tells me you're right. And the truth is, I don't think Maxwell was smart enough to pull this off. I worked with—'

Her cellphone started buzzing. She took it out of her pocket and looked at the screen. 'It's Jack.'

'Find out where Maxwell is.'

She answered the call and first replied to a few questions about Bosch's status, telling Brenner that he was OK but was losing his voice because his throat hurt. Bosch got up for another bottle of water but listened from the kitchen. Walling casually steered the call towards Maxwell.

'Hey, where's Cliff, by the way? I wanted to talk to him about that thing with Bosch in the hallway. I didn't like what he—'

She stopped and listened to the answer, and Bosch saw her eyes immediately become alert. Something was wrong.

'When was that?' she asked.

She listened again and stood up. 'Jack, I've got to go. Bosch is about to be discharged. I'll check in as soon as I'm clear here.'

She closed the phone and looked at Bosch. 'I can't stand lying to him. He won't forget it.'

'What did he say?'

'He said there were too many agents at the recovery scene. Just about everybody came out from downtown and they were standing around waiting on the radiation team. So Maxwell volunteered to go pick up the witness at the Mark Twain. Nobody had got around to it because I'd pulled off the original pick-up team.'

'He went alone?'

'That's what Jack said.'

'How long ago?'

'A half-hour.'

'He's going to kill him.'

Bosch started moving quickly towards the door.

BOSCH DROVE THIS TIME. On the way towards Hollywood, he told Walling that Jesse Mitford had no phone in his room. The Mark Twain wasn't much when it came to full service. Instead, Bosch called the watch commander at Hollywood Division and asked him to send a patrol car to the hotel to check on the witness. He then called the front desk at the Mark Twain.

'Alvin, this is Detective Bosch. From this morning? Has anyone come in asking for Stephen King?'

'Mmm, nope.'

'In the last twenty minutes, have you buzzed in anybody who looked like a cop or who wasn't a tenant there?'

'No, Detective. What's going on?'

'Listen, I need you to go up to that room and tell Stephen King to get out of there and then to call me on my cell.'

'I got nobody to watch the desk, Detective.'

'It's an emergency, Alvin. I need to get him out of there. It will take you less than five minutes. Here, write this down.' Bosch gave him his cellphone number. 'And if anybody but me comes in there looking for him, say he checked out and left. Go, Alvin, and thanks.'

He closed the phone and looked over at Walling. His face showed his lack of confidence in the deskman. 'I think the guy's a tweaker.'

Bosch increased his speed and tried to concentrate on driving. They had just turned south on Cahuenga off Barham. He was thinking that, depending on traffic in Hollywood, they could get to the Mark Twain in another five minutes. This conclusion made him shake his head. With a half-hour lead, Maxwell should already be at the Mark Twain.

'Maxwell may have already slipped in through the back,' he told Walling. 'I'm going to come in from the alley.'

'You know,' Walling said, 'maybe he's not going to hurt Mitford. He'll pick him up and talk to him, judge for himself if he saw enough at the overlook that he'd be a threat.'

Bosch shook his head. 'No way. Maxwell's got to know that once the caesium was found, his plan was going down the toilet. He's got to take action against all threats. First the witness, then Alicia Kent.'

'Alicia Kent? You think he'd make a move against her? This whole thing is because of her.'

'Doesn't matter now. Survival instincts take over now and she's a threat. It goes with the territory. You cross the big line to be with her. You cross it again to save your—'

Bosch stopped talking as a sudden realisation thudded in his chest. He cursed out loud and pinned the accelerator as they came out of the Cahuenga Pass. He cut across three lanes of Highland Avenue in front of the Hollywood Bowl and madc a screeching U-turn in front of oncoming traffic. He punched it and the car fishtailed wildly as he headed towards the southbound entrance to the Hollywood Freeway.

Walling grabbed the dashboard and a door handle to hold on. 'Harry, what are you doing? This is the wrong way!'

He flicked on the siren and the blue lights. 'Mitford is a misdirection,' he yelled. 'This is the right way. Who is the greater threat to Maxwell?'

'Alicia?'

'You bet, and now's the best shot he has of getting her out of Tactical. Everybody's up in that alley with the caesium.'

The freeway was moving pretty well and the siren helped open it up further. Bosch figured that Maxwell could have already rcached downtown, depending on what kind of traffic he encountered.

Walling opened her phone and started punching in numbers. She tried number after number, but no one was answering.

'I can't get anybody,' she yelled.

'Where's TIU?'

Walling didn't hesitate. 'On Broadway. You know where the Million Dollar Theater is? Same building. Entrance on Third.'

Bosch flicked off the siren and opened his phone. He called his partner, and Ferras answered right away.

'Ignacio, where are you?'

'Just got back to the office. Forensics worked the car for—'

'Listen to me. Drop what you're doing and meet me at the Third Street entrance to the Million Dollar Theater building. You know where that is?'

'Yeah, I know where it is. What's going on?'

'I'll explain when I get there.'

He closed the phone and hit the siren again.

THE NEXT TEN MINUTES took ten hours. Bosch moved in and out of traffic and finally reached the Broadway exit downtown. He killed the siren as he made the turn and headed down the hill towards their destination. They were three blocks away.

The Million Dollar Theater was built in a time when the movie business showed itself off in magnificent theatre palaces that lined Broadway downtown. But it had been decades since a first-run film had been projected on a screen there. Now the theatre waited unused for renovation and redemption while above it a once-grand office building was twelve storeys of midgrade office space and residential lofts.

'Good place for a secret unit to have a secret office,' Bosch said as the building came into sight. 'Nobody would've guessed.'

Walling didn't respond. She was trying to make another call. She then slapped the phone closed in frustration. 'I can't even get our secretary. She takes lunch after one so there'll be somebody in the office when the agents go to lunch earlier.'

'Where exactly is the squad and where would Alicia Kent be in there?'

'We have the whole seventh floor. There's a lounge room with a couch and a TV. They put her in there so she could watch TV.'

'How many in the squad?'

'Eight agents, the secretary and an office manager. The office manager just went out on maternity leave and the secretary must be at lunch. I hope. But they wouldn't have left Alicia Kent alone. It's against policy. Somebody had to have stayed there with her.'

Bosch turned right on Third and immediately pulled to the kerb. Ignacio Ferras was already there, leaning casually against his Volvo station wagon. In front of it was another parked car. A federal cruiser. Bosch and Walling got out. Bosch approached Ferras, and Walling went to look inside the fed car.

'Have you seen Agent Maxwell?' Bosch asked.

'Who?'

'Maxwell. The guy we put on the floor at the Kent house this morning.'

'No, I haven't seen anybody. What—?'

'It's his car,' Walling said as she joined them.

'Ignacio, this is Agent Walling.'

'Call me Iggy.'

'Rachel.'

They shook hands.

'OK, then he's gotta be up there,' Bosch said. 'How many stairwells?'

'Three,' Walling said. 'But he'll use the one that comes out by his car.'

She pointed to a pair of double steel doors near the corner of the building. Bosch headed over that way to see if they were locked. Ferras and Walling followed.

'What is going on?' Ferras asked.

'Maxwell is our shooter,' Bosch said. 'He is up—'

'What?'

Bosch checked the exit doors. There was no outside handle or knob. He turned to Ferras. 'Look, there's not a lot of time. Trust me. Maxwell is our guy and he's in this building to take out Alicia Kent. We're—'

'What is she doing here?'

'The FBI has a location here. She's here. No more questions, OK? Just listen. Agent Walling and I are going up in the elevator. I want you out here by this door. If Maxwell comes out, you take him down. You understand? You take him down.'

'Got it.'

'Good. Call for back-up. We're going up.' Bosch reached over and tapped Ferras on the cheek. 'And stay frosty.'

They left Ferras there and headed through the building's main entrance. There was no lobby to speak of, just an elevator. It opened at the push of the button and Walling used a key card to engage the seven button. They started going up.

'Something tells me you're never going to call him Iggy,' Walling said.

Bosch ignored the comment. 'Does this thing have a bell or a tone that sounds when it reaches the floor?'

'I can't remem— I think it does . . . Yes, definitely.'

'Great. We'll be sitting ducks.'

Bosch pulled his Kimber out of its holster and chambered a round. Walling did the same with her weapon. Bosch pushed Walling to one side of the elevator while he took the other. He raised his gun. The elevator reached seven and there was a soft bell tone from outside. The door began to slide open, exposing Bosch first.

No one was there.

Walling pointed to the left, signalling that the offices were to the left after they exited the elevator. Bosch lowered himself into a combat crouch and stepped out, his gun up and ready.

Again, no one was there.

He started moving to his left. Walling came out and moved with him on his right flank. They came to a loft-style office with two rows of cubicles—the squad room—and three private rooms that had been built freestanding in the open floor plan. There were large racks of electronic equipment between the cubicles and every desk had two computer screens on it.

Bosch stepped further in, and through the window in one of the private offices he saw a man sitting in a chair, his head back and eyes open. He looked like he was wearing a red bib. But Bosch knew it was blood. The man had been shot in the chest.

He pointed and Walling saw the dead man. She reacted with a quick intake of breath and a low-volume sigh.

The door to the office was ajar. They moved towards it and Bosch pushed it open while Walling covered them from behind. He stepped in and saw Alicia Kent sitting on the floor, her back to the wall.

Bosch crouched beside her. Her eyes were open but dead. A gun was on the floor between her feet, and the wall behind her was spattered with blood and brain matter.

He turned and surveyed the room. He understood the play. It was set up to look as though Alicia Kent had grabbed the agent's gun from his holster, shot him, then sat down on the floor and taken her own life. No note or explanation, but it was the best Maxwell could come up with in the short amount of time that he had.

Bosch turned to Walling. She had let her guard down and was just standing there looking at the dead agent.

'Rachel,' he said. 'He's gotta still be here.'

He stood and moved towards the door so he could search the squad room. As he glanced through the window he saw movement behind the electronics racks. He stopped, raised his weapon and tracked someone moving behind one of the racks towards a door with an exit sign on it.

In a moment, he saw Maxwell break free of the cover and dash towards the door.

'Maxwell!' Bosch yelled. 'Stop!'

Maxwell spun and raised a weapon. At the same moment that his back hit the exit door he started firing. The window shattered and glass sprayed across Bosch. He returned fire and put six shots into the opening of the exit door, but Maxwell was gone.

'Rachel?' Bosch called without taking his eyes off the door. 'OK?'

'I'm fine.'

Her voice came from below him. He knew she had hit the floor when the shooting had started.

'Which exit is that door?'

Walling stood up. Bosch moved towards the door, glancing at her, and saw glass all over her clothes. She had been cut on the cheek.

'Those stairs go down to his car,' she said.

Bosch ran from the room towards the exit door. He opened his phone as he went and pushed the speed dial for his partner. The call was answered on half a ring. Bosch was already in the stairwell.

'He's coming down!'

He dropped the phone and started down the stairs. He could hear Maxwell running on the steel steps below and instinctively knew that he was too far ahead. Bosch covered three more landings, taking three steps at a time. He could now hear Walling coming down behind him.

Then he heard the booming sound from below as Maxwell hit the exit door at the bottom. There were immediate shouts and then there were shots. They came so close together it was impossible to determine which had come first or how many shots had been fired.

Ten seconds later, Bosch hit the exit door. He came out onto the side-walk and saw Ferras leaning against the back bumper of Maxwell's fed car. He was holding his weapon with one hand and his elbow with the other. A red rose of blood was blooming on his shoulder. Traffic had stopped in both directions on Third and pedestrians were running down the sidewalks to safety.

'I hit him twice,' Ferras yelled. 'He went that way.'

He nodded in the direction of the Third Street tunnel under Bunker Hill. Bosch stepped closer to his partner and saw the wound in the ball of his shoulder. It didn't look too bad.

'Did you call for back-up?' Bosch asked.

'On the way.' Ferras grimaced as he adjusted his hold on his injured arm.

'You did good, Iggy. Hang in there while I go get this guy.'

Ferras nodded. Bosch turned and saw Walling come through the door, a smear of blood on her face.

'This way,' he said. 'He's hit.'

They started down Third in a spread formation. After a few steps, Bosch picked up the trail. Maxwell was obviously hurt badly and was losing a lot of blood. It would make him easy to track.

But when they got to the corner of Third and Hill, they lost the trail. There was no blood on the pavement. Bosch looked into the long Third Street tunnel and saw no one moving in the traffic on foot. He looked up and down Hill Street and saw nothing, until his attention was drawn to a commotion of people running out of the Grand Central Market.

'This way,' he said.

They moved quickly towards the huge market. Bosch picked up the blood trail again just outside and started in. The market was a two-storey-high conglomeration of food booths and retail and produce concessions. There was a strong smell of grease and coffee in the air that had to infect every floor of the building above the market. The place was crowded and noisy, and that made it difficult for Bosch to follow the blood and track Maxwell.

Then suddenly there were shouts from directly ahead and two quick shots were fired into the air. It caused an immediate human stampede. Dozens of screaming shoppers and workers flooded into the aisle where Bosch and Walling stood, and started running towards them. Bosch realised they were going to be trampled. In one motion, he moved to his right, grabbed Walling round the waist and pulled her behind one of the wide concrete support pillars.

The crowd moved by, then Bosch looked round the pillar. The market was now empty. There was no sign of Maxwell, but then Bosch picked up movement in one of the cold cases that fronted a butcher shop at the end of the aisle. He looked again closely and realised that the movement came from behind the case. Looking through the front and back glass panels and over the display of cuts of beef and pork, Bosch could see Maxwell's face. He was on the ground, leaning his back against a refrigerator in the rear of the butcher shop.

'He's up ahead in the butcher shop,' he whispered to Walling. 'You go to the right and down that aisle. You'll be able to come up on his right.'

'What about you?'

'I'll go straight on and get his attention.'

'Or we could wait for back-up.'

'I'm not waiting.'

'I didn't think so.'

'Ready?'

'No. Switch. I go head-on and get his attention and you come round the side.'

Bosch knew it was the better plan, because Walling knew Maxwell and he knew her. But it also meant she would face the most danger.

'You sure?' Bosch asked.

'Yes. It's right.'

Bosch looked round the pillar one more time and saw that Maxwell had not moved. His face looked red and sweaty.

Bosch looked back at Walling. 'He's still there.'

'Good. Let's do it.'

They separated and started moving. Bosch sprinted down an aisle of concessions one over from the aisle that ended at the butcher shop. When he came to the end, he was at a Mexican coffee shop with high walls. He was able to protect himself and look round the corner at the butcher shop. This gave him a side view behind the counter. He saw Maxwell twenty feet away. He was slouched against the refrigerator door, still holding his weapon in two hands. His shirt was completely soaked in blood.

Bosch leaned back into cover, gathered himself and got ready to step out and approach Maxwell. But then he heard Walling's voice.

'Cliff? It's me, Rachel. Let me get you some help.'

Bosch looked round the corner. Walling was standing out in the open, five feet in front of the deli counter, her gun down at her side.

'There is no help,' Maxwell said. 'It's too late for me.'

Bosch recognised that if Maxwell wanted to take a shot at her the bullet would have to go through both the front and back glass panels of the deli case. With the front plate set at an angle, it would take a miracle bullet to get to her. But miracles did happen. Bosch raised his weapon, braced it against the wall and was ready to shoot if he needed to.

'Come on, Cliff,' Walling said. 'Give it up. Don't end it like this.'

'No other way.'

Maxwell's body was suddenly racked by a deep, wet coughing. Blood came to his lips.

'Jesus, that guy really got me,' he said before coughing again.

'Cliff?' Walling pleaded. 'Let me come in there. I want to help.'

'No, you come in and I'm going to—'

His words were lost when he opened fire on the deli case, sweeping his gun and shooting out the glass doors all the way down. Walling ducked and

Bosch stepped out and straightened his arms in a two-handed grip. He held himself from shooting but keyed on the barrel of Maxwell's weapon. If the muzzle zeroed in on Walling, he was going to shoot Maxwell in the head.

Maxwell lowered his weapon and started to laugh, blood rolling down from both corners of his mouth and creating a freak clown look.

'I think . . . I think I just killed a porterhouse.'

He laughed again, but it made him start to cough once more and that looked painful. When it subsided, he spoke.

'I just want to say . . . that it was her. She wanted him dead. I just . . . I just wanted her. That's all. But she wouldn't have it any other way . . . and I did what she wanted. For that . . . I am damned.'

Bosch took a step closer. He didn't think that Maxwell had noticed him yet. He took one more step and then Maxwell spoke again.

'I'm sorry,' he said. 'Rachel? Tell them I'm sorry.'

'Cliff,' Walling said. 'You can tell them that yourself.'

As Bosch watched, Maxwell brought his gun up and put the muzzle under his chin. Without hesitation, he pulled the trigger. The impact snapped his head back and sent a spatter of blood up the refrigerator door. The gun dropped onto the concrete floor between his outstretched legs. In his suicide, Maxwell had adopted the same position as his lover, the woman he had just killed.

Walling came round the case and stood next to Bosch. Together they looked down at the dead agent. She said nothing. Bosch checked his watch. It was almost one. He had ridden the case from beginning to end in little more than twelve hours. The tally was five dead, one wounded and one dying of radiation exposure.

And then there was himself. Bosch wondered if he was going to be part of the tally by the time all was said and done. His throat was now blazing and there was a feeling of heaviness in his chest.

He looked at Rachel and saw blood running down her cheek again. She would need stitches to close the wound.

'You know what?' he said. 'I'll take you to the hospital if you take me.'

She looked at him and smiled sort of sadly. 'Throw in Iggy and you've got yourself a deal.'

Bosch left her there with Maxwell and walked back to the Million Dollar Theater building to check on his partner. While he was on his way, back-up units were pulling in everywhere and crowds were forming. Bosch decided he would leave it to the patrol officers to take charge of the crime scenes.

Ferras was sitting in the open door of his car, waiting for the paramedics. He was holding his arm at an awkward angle and was clearly in pain. The blood had spread on his shirt.

'You want water?' Bosch asked. 'I've got a bottle in my trunk.'

'No, I'll just wait. I wish they'd get here.'

The signature siren of a fire-rescue paramedic truck could be heard in the distance, getting closer.

'What happened, Harry?'

Bosch leaned against the side of the car and told him that Maxwell had just killed himself as they had closed in on him.

'Hell of a way to go, I guess,' Ferras said. 'Cornered like that.'

Bosch nodded but kept silent. As they waited, his thoughts carried him down the streets and up the hills to the overlook, where the last thing Stanley Kent ever saw was the city spread before him in beautiful shimmering lights. Maybe to Stanley it looked like heaven was waiting for him at the end.

But Bosch thought that it didn't really matter if you died cornered in a butcher shop or on an overlook glimpsing the lights of heaven. You were gone and the finale wasn't the part that mattered. We are all circling the drain, he thought. Some are closer to the black hole than others. Some will see it coming, and some will have no clue when the undertow of the whirlpool grabs them and pulls them down into darkness for ever.

The important thing is to fight it, Bosch told himself. Always keep kicking. Always keep fighting the undertow.

The rescue unit turned the corner at Broadway, working its way round several stopped cars before braking at the mouth of the alley and killing the siren. Bosch helped his partner up and out of the car and they walked to the paramedics.

MICHAEL CONNELLY

Home: Tampa, Florida
Most famous fan: Bill Clinton
Website: www.michaelconnelly.com

'I'm always looking at ways of shaking up the writing experience because I think it helps,' says Michael Connelly. *The Overlook* is the thirteenth in his successful Harry Bosch series but, while the books have brought him many fans and much critical acclaim, the author is aware that his main character's longevity presents its own challenges. 'My duty is to keep Harry Bosch interesting to readers and to me as the writer. When I start a book, knowing it's going to take me maybe ten or twelve months to write, then I have to take my time in the initial stages to make sure I have a story and a character that are going to keep me interested for that amount of time.'

When the editor of *The New York Times Magazine* recently asked Connelly if he would produce a serialised story specially for them, he knew it would be a great opportunity to try something new. He found the work more demanding than he'd expected. 'I had to write each instalment to fit a three-thousand-word hole,' he explains. 'For fifteen-plus years I have been writing chapters of my books without giving word or page count any thought at all, so it was hard to make each step of the story fit that space.' Once he realised the limitations on his style, he knew he'd eventually want to rework the story in order to publish it in book form. Surprisingly, perhaps, the chance to rewrite was a pleasure. 'I got to look at the story again with a totally fresh mind and take it apart and rebuild it and write it the way I prefer, with the pacing I wanted—also to throw in some new current events to make it more topical.'

Connelly was first inspired to become a crime writer when he studied journalism at the University of Florida. It was there that he came across the work of Raymond Chandler, author of such classics as *Farewell, My Lovely* and *The Big Sleep*. 'What was different about Chandler, and what really touched me, was that his writing is so evocative. Los Angeles is a character in its own right in his books. It turned my head.'

After completing the course, Connelly took jobs on the crime beat for two Florida newspapers and then on the *Los Angeles Times*. This enabled him to understand the world he wanted to write about, that of the police and criminals and the justice system.

'I didn't know anything about the world of cops other than what I'd seen in movies and read in novels. I wanted to get a realistic view of it,' he says.

Connelly's first-hand experience of their daily lives left him with a deep admiration for the work they do. 'I know that it has to be a tremendous challenge to do that job and remain whole, not to let the darkness get into you. I mean, how do you come home after seeing all the darkness of humanity, open the door and say to your wife, "Honey, I'm home."?'

The author has recently moved from Los Angeles to Florida, putting some distance between him and the city he has become so closely identified with. 'Now I'm writing about contemporary Los Angeles from memory,' he says. 'My process was to hang out, observe, research what I was writing about, and almost immediately go back to my office and write those sections. So it was a very close transfer between observation and writing.'

Michael Connelly is currently writing a new legal thriller featuring Mickey Haller, the defence lawyer he introduced in *The Lincoln Lawyer* (a former Select Editions choice). He is also writing a screenplay for a film version of a 1980s show called *The Equalizer*, about a shadowy former agent who helps others in order to make up for sins from his past. But loyal fans need not worry: plans are in the works for another Bosch mystery.

THE JAZZ-LOVING DETECTIVE

While Michael Connelly says that he and Harry Bosch are very different, they do share one important characteristic: they are both jazz fans. 'I listen exclusively to jazz when writing, because it is not as intrusive as music with lyrics and its improvisational nature is inspiring to me,' says the author. 'Invariably the music I am listening to ends up on Harry Bosch's CD player. I think the music he listens to says a lot about him.' Connelly recently put together a promotional CD called *Dark Sacred Night*, which features Bosch's favourite music, including works by artists such as John Coltrane (right), Sonny Rollins, Art Pepper and Louis Armstrong.

THE LAST TESTAMENT

SAM BOURNE

In the Middle East, a peace agreement between Israel and the Palestinians is imminent yet hanging by a slender diplomatic thread. The US government are sending in their top mediator, Maggie Costello, to see the process through.

In a dark back street in Jerusalem, a small clay tablet bearing an ancient script changes hands for a paltry sum that belies its significance. For it is one of the greatest archaeological discoveries ever made, and it could change the future of the Holy Land for ever.

PROLOGUE

Baghdad, April 2003

The crowd were pushing harder now, as if they scented blood. They charged through the archway and their combined weight pressed against the tall oak doors until they went crashing to the ground. As they rushed through, Salam moved with them. It was not a decision. He was simply a part of a moving, roaring beast made up of men, women and children, some even younger than him.

They burst into the first vast hall, the glass of the display cases glinting in the moonlight that spilt through the high windows. There was a brief pause, as if the beast were drawing breath. Salam and his fellow Baghdadis contemplated the scene before them: the National Museum of Antiquities, once Saddam's treasure house, bursting with the jewels of Mesopotamia, now laid wide open. There was not a guard in sight. The last of the museum staff had abandoned their posts hours earlier, and the few remaining security men had fled at the sight of this horde.

The silence was ruptured by a sledgehammer crashing through glass. On that cue, the room filled with thunderous noise, as one after another they wielded pistols, axes, knives, clubs—anything to spring these precious, ancient objects from their cases. Salam even noticed two well-dressed men setting to work methodically with professional glass-cutting equipment.

The ground trembled as wave after wave of people stampeded into the museum, ignoring this first exhibition hall, looking for fresh pickings elsewhere. They collided with those already struggling to get out, hauling their booty on handcarts, wheelbarrows and bicycles. Salam recognised a friend of his father striding out, his face flushed and his pockets bulging.

In all his fifteen years, Salam had never seen behaviour like this. Until a few days ago, everyone had moved slowly, head down, eyes averted. In Saddam's Iraq you knew better than to draw attention to yourself. Now the same people were stealing anything they could lay their hands on and destroying the rest. It was like a scene from the sacking of an ancient city, the participants slaking an appetite that had been pent up for decades.

Suddenly Salam was pushed forward again. A new group of looters had arrived and they were making for the stairwell; a rumour had spread that the museum staff had stashed all the best stuff in the storerooms. He saw a knot of men standing around a door that they had clearly just lifted off its hinges. Behind it stood a freshly constructed wall of cinder blocks, the mortar barely set. Two men began hacking away at the blocks with hammers; others joined them using metal bars, even their shoulders.

They turned to Salam. 'Come on!' They passed him a metal table leg.

Soon the wall gave way. The leader of the group stepped through the hole and at once began to laugh. Others joined him. Salam could soon see the source of their joy: the room was packed with treasure—stone carvings of princesses and kings, etchings of rams and oxen, statues of buxom goddesses, ceramic urns and bowls, copper shoes and fragments of tapestry.

Salam's eye caught a few of the labels that were stuck to these treasures. One identified a 'lyre from the Sumerian city of Ur, bearing the gold-encased head of a bull, dated 2400 BC'; that was soon carted off. Another was a 'white limestone votive bowl from Warka, dated 3000 BC'; Salam watched as it disappeared inside a football kit bag. He remembered a teacher once telling his class: 'Inside that museum lies not just the history of Iraq, but the history of all mankind.' Now it resembled nothing grander than a vegetable market, the customers scrapping over the produce.

Salam could hear raised voices: two men were arguing. One slapped the other and the pair began to fight, bringing a metal bookcase stacked with pots crashing to the ground. Someone produced a knife. Instinctively, Salam wheeled round, dived out through the hole in the wall and ran.

He rushed down the stairs, flight after flight, until he had left the crowds behind. No one was bothering to come this far down now with such easy pickings higher up. He would be safely away from them here.

Salam pushed open a door. In the gloom he could see overturned boxes of papers, their contents carpeting the floor. This was merely an office. He noticed a few dangling wires: someone had stolen the phones and fax machine. He tugged at the desk drawers, hoping they had missed something. But all he found were a few old sheets of paper.

Heading for the door, he caught his foot on a ridge. Salam looked down to find a loose stone square. Hardly thinking, he wedged his fingers into the crack between the squares and prised out the loose one. He felt for the ground below—but his hand just sank into a deep hole.

Now he felt something solid, cool to the touch: a tin box. At last, money!

He had to lie on the ground to reach it, his cheek against the stone, but at last he got the box out. It was locked, but as he stood up he noticed that its contents seemed too silent for coins and too heavy for notes.

Salam peered through the darkness until he found a letter opener lying on the desk. He slid it under the thin tin of the lid and levered up the metal all the way along one side. The box opened like a can of beans. His heart was pounding as he tipped out the object inside.

The second he saw it, he was disappointed. It was a clay tablet, engraved with a few random squiggles, like so many of the others he had seen tonight, many of them smashed on the ground. Salam was about to discard it, but he hesitated. If some museum guy had gone to such lengths to hide this lump of clay, maybe it was worth something.

Salam sprinted back up the stairs until he could see moonlight. He had come out at the back of the museum, where he could see a fresh horde of looters breaking in. He waited for a gap in the line, then stepped out into the night—carrying a treasure whose true value he would never know.

CHAPTER ONE

Tel Aviv, Saturday night, several years later

The usual crowd was there. The hard-core leftists, the men with their hair grown long after a year travelling in India, the girls with diamond studs in their noses, the people who always turned up for these Saturday night get-togethers. Holding candles or portraits of Yitzhak Rabin, the slain hero who gave his name to this piece of hallowed ground so many years earlier, they would form the inner circle at Rabin Square and hand out leaflets or strum guitars, letting the tunes drift into the warm night air.

Beyond the core there were newer, less familiar, faces. To veterans of these peace rallies, the most surprising sight was the ranks of Mizrahim, working-class North African Jews, who had trekked here from some of Israel's poorest towns, and were among Israel's most hawkish voters. Tough and permanently wary of Israel's Palestinian neighbours, most had long scorned the leftists who showed up at rallies like this. Yet here they were.

The television cameras—from Israeli TV, the BBC, CNN and all the major international networks—swept over the crowd, picking out more unexpected faces. An NBC cameraman framed a shot that made his director coo with excitement: a man wearing a kippah, the skullcap worn by religious Jews, next to a black Ethiopian-born woman, their faces bathed by the light of a candle cupped in her hands.

A few rows behind them was an older man: unsmiling, his face taut with determination. He checked under his jacket: it was still there.

Standing on the platform temporarily constructed for the purpose was a line of reporters, describing the scene for audiences across the globe. One American correspondent was louder than all the others.

'You join us in Tel Aviv for what's billed as an historic night for both Israelis and Palestinians. In just a few days' time the leaders of these two peoples are due to meet in Washington—on the lawn of the White House—to sign an agreement that will end more than a century of conflict. The two sides are negotiating even now, trying to hammer out the fine print of a peace deal in closed-door talks in Jerusalem. The location couldn't be more symbolic: Government House, the former headquarters of the British when they ruled here, which sits on the border separating mainly Arab East Jerusalem from the predominantly Jewish West of the city.

'But tonight the action moves here, to Tel Aviv. The Israeli premier has called for this rally to say "*Ken l'Shalom*", or "Yes to Peace"—a political move designed to show the world that he has the support to conclude a deal with Israel's historic enemy. Some angry opponents say he has no right to make the compromises rumoured to be on the table—no right to give back land on the West Bank or tear down Jewish settlements there and, above all, no right to divide Jerusalem. That's the biggest stumbling block. Israel has, until now, insisted that Jerusalem must remain its capital, a single city, for all eternity. But hold on, I think the Israeli leader has just arrived . . .'

A current of energy rippled through the crowd as thousands turned to face the stage. And when the Prime Minister appeared, this vast mass of humanity erupted. Perhaps 300,000 of them, clapping, stamping and whooping their approval. It was not love for him they were expressing, but love for what he was about to do—what, by common consent, only he could do. No one else had the credibility to make the sacrifices required. In just a matter of days he would, they hoped, end the conflict that had marked the lives of every single one of them.

He was over seventy, a hero of four Israeli wars. And though he had been in politics for nearly twenty years, he thought like a soldier even now, perennially sceptical of the peaceniks and their schemes. But things were different now, he told himself. There was a chance.

'We're tired,' he began, hushing the crowd. 'We're tired of fighting every day, tired of sending our children, boys and girls, to carry guns and drive tanks when they are barely out of school. We're tired of ruling over another people who never wanted to be ruled by us.'

As he spoke, the unsmiling, silver-haired man was pushing through the crowd, breathing heavily. '*Slicha*,' he said again and again. Excuse me. The wade through the throng was exhausting him; his shirt collar was darkening with sweat. He looked as if he was trying to catch a train.

A plain-clothes guard in the third row of the crowd noticed him, and whispered into the microphone in his sleeve. That alerted the security detail cordoning the stage, who began scoping the faces before them. It took them no time to spot him. He was making no attempt to be subtle.

The plain-clothes officer called out, '*Adoni, adoni*.' Sir, sir. Then he recognised him. 'Mr Guttman,' he called. 'Mr Guttman, please.'

People in the crowd turned round. They recognised him too. Professor Shimon Guttman, never off the TV and radio talk shows, scholar and visionary, or right-wing rabble-rouser, depending on your point of view. He was marching on, squeezing past a mother with a child on her shoulders.

'Sir, stop right there!' the guard called out.

Guttman ignored him. The agent began making his own journey through the crowd. He decided against pulling out his weapon; it would start a panic. He called out again, but his voice was drowned out by applause.

'We do not love the Palestinians and they do not love us,' the Prime Minister was saying. 'We never will and they never will . . .'

Guttman was now within shouting distance of the stage. He looked up towards the Prime Minister. 'Kobi!' he yelled, calling him by a long-forgotten nickname. 'Kobi!' His eyes were bulging, his face flushed.

Security agents were now closing in, two on each side, as well as the first man advancing from behind. They were ready to smother him to the ground as they had been taught, when a sixth agent, standing to the right of the stage, spotted a sudden movement. Perhaps it was just a wave, it was impossible to tell for sure, but Guttman seemed to be reaching into his jacket.

The first shot was straight to the head, to ensure instant paralysis. No muscular reflex that might set off a suicide bomb; no final seconds of life in which the suspect might pull a trigger. The bodyguards watched as the silver-haired skull of Shimon Guttman blew open like a watermelon.

Within seconds, the PM had been bundled off the stage. The crowd, cheering and clapping thirty seconds earlier, was now quaking with panic. Police used their arms to form a cordon round the dead man, who had fallen face down, but the pressure of the crowd made it almost impossible. People were screaming, stampeding, desperate to get away.

Pushing in the opposite direction were two senior military officers determined to get to the would-be assassin. One of them flashed a badge at a police officer and somehow ducked inside the small, human clearing.

The officer rolled the lifeless body over. What he saw made him blanch.

It was not the shattered bone or hollowed eye sockets; he had seen those before. It was the man's right hand. The fingers were not wrapped round a gun—but gripping a piece of paper, now sodden with blood. This man had not been reaching for a revolver, but for a note. Shimon Guttman hadn't wanted to kill the Prime Minister. He had wanted to tell him something.

Washington, Sunday, 9 a.m.

'BIG DAY TODAY, honey. Come on, sweetheart, time to wake up.'

'Nrrghh.'

'OK. One, two, three. And the covers are off—'

'Hey!'

Maggie Costello sat bolt upright and pulled the duvet back over her. She regarded the Sunday-morning lie-in as a constitutionally protected right.

Not Edward. He'd probably been up for two hours already. He wasn't like that when they met; back in Africa, in the Congo, he could pull the all-nighters just like her. But once they had come here, he had adapted pretty fast. Now he was Washington Man, out of the house in his shorts and vest just after 6 a.m., for a run through Rock Creek Park.

'Come on!' he said, shouting from the bathroom. 'I've cleared the whole day for furnishing this apartment. Crate and Barrel, then Bed, Bath and Beyond, and finally Macy's. I have a complete plan.'

'Not the whole day,' Maggie muttered inaudibly. She had a morning appointment, an overspill slot for clients who couldn't make weekdays.

'Actually not the whole day,' Edward shouted above the sound of the shower. 'You've got that morning appointment first. Remember?'

Maggie played deaf and reached for the TV remote. If she was going to be up at this hideous hour, she might as well get something out of it. The Sunday talk shows. She clicked onto ABC for the news summary.

'*Nerves on edge in Jerusalem after violence at a peace rally last night, where Israel's Prime Minister seemed to be the target of a failed assassination attempt. Concern high over the event's impact on the Middle East peace process, which had been hoped to yield a breakthrough as early as—*'

'Honey, seriously. They'll be here in twenty.'

She reached for the remote and turned up the volume. The show was hopping back and forth between correspondents in Jerusalem and the White House, explaining that the US administration was taking steps to ensure that all the parties kept calm and carried on talking. What a nightmare, thought Maggie. The last-minute external event, threatening to undo all the trust you've built, all the patient progress you've made. She imagined the mediators who had brought the Israelis and Palestinians to this point, imagined their frustration and angst. *Poor bastards*.

'*The time coming up to nine fifteen on the east coast—*'

'Hey, I was watching that!'

'You haven't got time.' As if to underline his point, Edward towelled himself in front of the blank TV screen. 'Besides, you don't need to follow all that stuff any more. It's not your problem now, is it?'

She looked at him, so different from the man in chinos and grubby polo shirt she had met three years ago. He was still attractive, his features straight and strong. But he had, as she would have said back in her Dublin schooldays, 'scrubbed up' since they'd moved to Washington. Now an official at the Commerce Department, he was always clean-shaven, his Brooks Brothers shirts neatly pressed and his shoes polished. Yet somewhere under that button-down exterior was the stubbled, unkempt do-gooder she had fallen for.

She stumbled into the shower, and was still drying off when the intercom sounded: the clients, down at the entrance to the apartment building. She buzzed them in. Allowing for the lift journey, she would have about a minute to get dressed. She scraped her hair back into a rapid ponytail and reached for a loose grey top, which fell low over her jeans. She flung open a cupboard and grabbed the first pair of low-heeled shoes she could see.

Just time for a glance in the mirror by the front door. Nothing too out of place; nothing anyone would notice. This had been her habit since she had come to Washington. 'Dressing to disappear,' Liz, her younger sister, had called it, when she was over on a visit. 'Look at you. All greys and blacks and sweaters a family could camp in. You've this drop-dead gorgeous figure and no one would know it. It's like your body's working undercover.' Liz, blogger and would-be novelist, laughed enthusiastically at her own joke.

Maggie told her to get away, though she knew Liz had a point. 'It's better for the work,' she explained. 'In a couples situation, the mediator needs to be a pane of glass that the man and woman themselves can look through, so that they see each other rather than you.'

She didn't dare let on that this new look was also the preference of her boyfriend. With gentle hints at first, then more overtly, Edward had encouraged Maggie to tie her hair back, and put away the fitted tops, tight trousers and knee-length skirts of her previous urban wardrobe. He always had a specific argument for each item: 'That colour just suits you better'; 'I think this will be more appropriate'—and he seemed sincere. Still, all his interventions tended to point her in the same direction: more modest, less sexy.

She wouldn't tell Liz that. Her sister had taken an instant, irrational dislike to Edward and she didn't need any more ammunition. Besides, if Maggie dressed differently now, that was her own decision, made in part for a reason she had never shared with Liz and never would.

She opened the door to Kathy and Brett George, ushering them towards the spare room reserved for this purpose. They were in the couples' programme devised by the state authorities in Virginia, a new 'cooling off' scheme, in which husbands and wives were obliged to undergo mediation before they were granted a divorce. Normally, six sessions did it, the couple working out the terms of their break-up without any need to call a lawyer, thereby saving on heartache and money. That was the idea, anyway.

She gestured to them to sit down, reminded them where they had got to the previous week and what issues remained outstanding. And then, as if she had fired a starting gun, the pair began laying into each other.

'Sweetheart, I'm happy to give you the house. And the car for that matter. I just have certain conditions—'

'Which is that I stay home and look after your kids.'

'Our kids, Kathy. Ours.'

The Georges were in their early forties, just a few years older than Maggie, but they might as well have come from another generation, if not another planet. For four weeks the two of them had slugged it out without taking a blind bit of notice of a word she said. She had tried it soft, saying little, offering gentle nods here and there. She had tried it hands-on, intervening in every twist and turn of the conversation, directing and channelling it. That didn't work either. They were in as much of a mess as when they first started.

'Look, Maggie, I hope this is already firmly on the record. I am more than happy to pay whatever maintenance budget we all decide is reasonable. I'm no miser: I will write that cheque. I just have one condition—'

'He wants to control me!'

'My condition, Maggie, is simple. If Kathy wants me to *pay* her to bring up our children, then I expect her to do no other job at the same time.'

'He won't pay child support unless I give up my career! You hear, Maggie?'

Maggie detected something in Kathy's voice she hadn't noticed before. 'And why would he want you to give up your career, Kathy?'

'Oh, this is ridiculous.'

'Brett, the question was directed at Kathy.'

'I don't know. He says it's better for the kids.'

'But you think it's about something else.'

'I wonder sometimes if, if . . . I wonder if Brett kind of likes me being dependent. Like, maybe he likes it when I'm weak or something.'

'Edward, what do you say to all this?'

'Excuse me?'

'I'm sorry. Brett. Forgive me. Brett. What do you make of this suggestion that you are somehow trying to keep Kathy weak?'

Brett spoke for a while, refuting the charge, and Maggie nodded throughout, making notes while maintaining eye contact. But she was distracted by her ridiculous slip of the tongue, and by the intercom, which had sounded while Brett was speaking, followed by the sound of several male voices. Regretting that she had opened up this theme—more therapist territory than mediator's—Maggie decided on a change of tack.

'Brett, what are your red lines?'

'I'm sorry?'

'Your three red lines. Those things on which you absolutely, positively will not compromise. Here.' She tossed over a pad of paper, followed by a pencil. 'And you too, Kathy. Three red lines. Go on. Write them down.'

Within a few seconds, the two were scratching away with their pencils. At last, she thought. A moment of peace.

She looked at this couple in front of her, two people who had once been so in love they had decided to share everything, even to create three new lives. When she had met up with Edward again after, after . . . what had happened in Africa, she had dreamt of a similar future for herself. Settle down and have a family life. Fifteen years later than the girls she had gone to school with, admittedly, but she would have a family and a life.

'You finished, Brett? What about you, Kathy?'

'There's a lot to get down here.'

'Remember, not everything's a red line. You've got to be selective. Come on, Kathy. Give us your three red lines.'

'Right,' Kathy said. 'Child support. My kids must have financial security.'

'OK.'

'And the house. I have to have that, so that the kids can have continuity.'

'And one more.'

'Full custody of the children, obviously. There's no shifting on that.'

'For Chrissake, Kathy—'

'Not yet, Brett. First you gotta give me your red lines.'

'OK. I want the children with me at Thanksgiving, so that they have dinner with my parents. I want that.'

'All right.'

'And spontaneous access. So that I can call up and say, I dunno, "Hey, Joey, the Redskins are playing, wanna come?" I need to be able to do that without giving, like, three weeks' notice. Access whenever I want.'

'No way—'

'Kathy, not now. What's number three?'

'Same as before. No child support unless Kathy is a full-time mom.'

'That is not fair! You're blackmailing me into giving up my career.'

And they were off again, back to shouting at each other and ignoring Maggie. Just like old times, she thought to herself. An image from her former life flashed into her mind, which she quickly pushed out.

But it gave her an idea. She snapped shut the file on her lap.

'OK, Brett and Kathy, I've made a decision. These sessions have become useless. A waste of time, yours and mine. We're going to end it here.'

The two people on the couch opposite suddenly turned and stared at her. She ignored them, busying herself with her papers instead.

'You don't need to worry about the paperwork. I'll get all that to the Virginia authorities tomorrow. Your lawyers can take it from here.' She stood up, as if to usher them out.

Brett seemed fixed to the spot; Kathy's mouth hung wide open. At last, Brett forced himself to speak. 'You can't just *abandon* us!'

Now Kathy joined in. 'We need you, Maggie. There is no way we can get through this without you.'

'Don't worry about that. The lawyers will get it sorted.' Maggie kept moving around the room, avoiding eye contact. Outside she heard the sound of people moving in and out of the apartment. What was going on?

'They'll kill us,' said Brett. 'They'll take all our money and make this whole thing even more of a nightmare than it already is!'

This was working.

'Look,' he said. 'We'll sort this out, we promise. Don't we, Kathy?'

'We do.'

'I think it's too late. We set aside a period of time to resolve everything—'

'Oh, please don't say that, Maggie.' It was Kathy, now imploring. 'There's not such a lot of work to do here. We're not so far apart.'

Maggie turned round. 'I'll give you ten minutes.'

In fact it took fifteen. But when they left Maggie's office and walked into the sunshine of a Washington September morning, Kathy and Brett George had resolved to share the costs of child support proportionate to their income, Kathy's financial contribution shrinking to zero if she gave up paid work to look after the kids. The children would live with their mother, except for alternate weekends and whenever either the kids or their father fancied seeing each other. The rule would be no hard and fast rules. Before they left they hugged Maggie and, to their surprise as much as hers, each other.

Maggie fell into a chair, allowing herself a small smile of satisfaction. She looked at her watch. Edward would be waiting for her outside, ready to hit the full range of Washington's domestic retail outlets.

She opened the door to a surprise. Flicking through one of Maggie's back numbers of *Vogue*, in the tiny area that served as Maggie's waiting room, was a man who oozed Washington. Like Edward, he had the full DC garb: button-down shirt, blue blazer, loafers, even now, on a Sunday.

'Hello? Do you have an appointment?'

'I don't. It's kind of an emergency. It won't take long.'

An emergency? What the hell was this? She headed down the corridor, opening the door onto the kitchen. There she saw Edward, signing on one of those electronic devices held out by a man wearing delivery overalls.

'Edward, what's going on?'

He seemed to pale. 'Ah, honey. I can explain. They just had to go. They were taking up too much space. So I've done it. They've gone.'

'What on earth are you talking about?'

'Those boxes you've had sitting in the study for nearly a year. You said you'd unpack them, but you never did. So this kind gentleman has loaded them onto his truck and now they're going to the trash.'

Maggie looked at the man in overalls, who stared at his feet. Now she understood what had happened. But she could not believe it. She stormed past Edward, flung open the door to the study and, sure enough, the space in the corner was now empty. She flew back to the kitchen.

'You bastard! Those boxes had my, my . . . letters and photographs and, and . . . whole life and you just THREW THEM OUT?'

Maggie rushed to the front door. But the trash guy, doubtless sensing trouble, had made his getaway. Swearing, she pressed the lift button again and again. 'Come on, come on,' she muttered, tensing her jaw. When the lift came, she willed it down faster. As soon as it arrived on the ground floor and the door opened a crack, she squeezed through it, running through the main doors of the building and out onto the street. She looked left and right and left again before she saw it, a green truck pulling out. She waved wildly at it, but it was too late. The truck picked up speed and vanished. All she had was half a phone number and a name: National Removals.

She rushed back upstairs, grabbed the telephone and called directory information. They found the number and offered to put her through. Three rings, then a recorded message: *We're sorry, but all our offices are closed on Sunday. Our regular opening hours are Monday to Friday . . .*

She went back into the kitchen to find Edward standing there, defiant. She began quietly. 'You just threw them out.'

'You're damn right I threw them out. They made this place look like a student shithole. All that sentimental crap. You need to move on.'

'But, but . . .' Maggie wasn't looking at him. She was looking at the ground, trying to digest what had just happened. Not just the letters from her parents, the photographs from Ireland, but the notes she had taken during crucial negotiations, private, scribbled memos from rebel leaders and UN officials. Those boxes contained her life's work.

'I did it for you, Maggie. That world is not your world any more. You need to adjust to your life now, as it is. Our life.'

So that's why he had been so keen to get her locked away in the consulting room this morning. He just wanted the garbage men in and out before she had a chance to stop them. At last she met his gaze. Quietly, as if unable to believe her own words, she said, 'You want to destroy who I am.'

He looked back at her blankly, before finally nodding towards the other end of the apartment. 'Someone's waiting for you,' he said coldly.

She almost staggered out of the room, unable to absorb what had happened. How could he have done such a thing? Did he really hate the old Maggie Costello so much that he wanted to erase every last trace of her?

She stood in the landing that served as the waiting area, her head spinning. The man in blue was still there, now turning the pages of *Atlantic Monthly*.

'Bad time? I'm sorry.'

'No, no,' Maggie said, barely out loud. On autopilot, she added, 'Is your wife coming?'

He made a curious smirk. 'She should be along soon.'

Maggie gestured him into the consulting room. 'You said it was some kind of emergency.' She was struggling to remember if he was one of the clients she said could contact her out of hours.

'Yes. My problem is that I'm finding it hard to adjust.'

'To what?'

'To life here. Normality.'

'Where were you before?'

'I was all over. Travelling from one screwed-up place to another. Always trying to make the world a better place and all that bullshit.'

'Are you a doctor?'

'You could say that. I try to save lives.'

Maggie could feel her muscles tensing. 'And now you're finding it hard to adjust to being back home.'

'Home! That's a joke. I don't know what home is any more. I'm not from DC; I haven't lived in my home town for nearly twenty years. Always on the road, on planes, in hotel rooms, sleeping in dumps.'

'But that's not why you're finding it hard to adjust.'

'No. It's the adrenaline I miss. The drama. Sounds terrible, doesn't it?'

'Go on.' Maggie was remembering what was in those boxes. A handwritten letter of thanks from the British Prime Minister, following the Kosovo talks. A treasured photo of the man she had loved in her twenties.

'Before, everything I did seemed to matter so much. The stakes were high. Now nothing even comes close. It's all so banal.'

Maggie stared hard at the man. His eyes were flat and cold. She began to feel uneasy. 'Can you say more about the work you were doing?'

'I started with an aid organisation in Africa, during a particularly vicious civil war. Somehow I ended up being one of the few people who could talk to both sides. The UN started using me as a go-between, and I became a sort of unofficial diplomat, a mediator. The US government hired me for a peace process that had stalled. And one thing led to another. Eventually they were sending me around the world, to peace talks that had hit the buffers.'

Maggie's mind was racing. Could she make a run for it? But something told her not even to glance at the door: she did not want to provoke this man. 'Then what happened?' Her voice betrayed nothing: years of practice.

'Then I made a mistake.'

'Where?'

'In Africa.'

Maggie's voice stayed low, even as she said, 'Who the hell are you? What are you playing at? Tell me now or I'll call the police.'

'You know who I am, Maggie. You know very well. I'm you.'

It wasn't a surprise. She had known that much the moment he had mentioned Africa and the UN. He had been telling her own life story back to her, including her—what had he called it?—mistake, pretending it was his own. It was a nasty little trick.

'I'm not here to taunt you,' he said.

'But you're not here for bloody divorce mediation either, are you?'

'There's no wife for me to divorce. I'm married to the job.'

'And what job is that exactly?'

'I work for the same people you used to work for. The United States government. My name is Judd Bonham.' He extended a hand.

Maggie ignored it. Slowly, she stepped back towards her chair. Initially, she'd had him down as some psycho stalker. But he was here on official business, no doubt about it. What on earth could it be? She hadn't done anything for the Agency or State Department since . . . then. That had been well over a year ago and she had cut all her ties instantly. If she'd had it her way, she wouldn't even be living in America. But somehow she'd ended up in Washington, inside the belly of the beast. To be with Edward.

'Gotta hand it to you, though. You haven't lost your touch. The old jet-on-the-runway trick, engines revving, ready to fly off. Love it.'

She looked up at him. 'What?'

'Threatening to walk out on Kathy and Brett. Didn't Clinton do it at Camp David? Get the chopper all fired up, blades spinning. The mediator says he—or she—will walk and the parties get scared. Realise that they need you, that any deal they'd make outside the room would be worse. And it brings them together, both sides desperate to keep the talks going. Genius.'

'You were listening.'

'It's the training, what can I say?'

'You arsehole.'

'I like how you say that. *Ahhhrse*-hole. Sounds sexy in your accent.'

'Get out.'

'Though I see you don't really do sexy these days. No more of the hair-tumbling-down-in-front-of-the-eyes routine. Is that Edward's influence?'

'Go. Before I call the police.' She reached for the phone.

'You won't do that. And we both know why.'

That stopped her; she put the phone down. He knew about her 'mistake'. And he would tell. The *Washington Post*, some blog, it didn't matter. The true reason for her exile, currently known only to a few diplomatic insiders, would become public. What was left of her reputation would be ruined.

'What do you want?' Almost a whisper.

'We want you to come out of retirement.'

'No.'

'The people I work for tend not to take no for an answer.'

'And who are they exactly? "The United States government" is a bit vague.'

'Let's say this has come from as close to the top as you can get in this town. You have a reputation, you know, Miss Costello.'

'Well, you can tell them I'm flattered. But the answer is no.'

'You're not even curious?'

'No I am not. I don't do that work any more. And I don't take emergency cases. Which means you have about one minute to leave.'

'I won't insult your intelligence, Maggie. You read the papers. You know what's happening in Jerusalem. We're this close to a deal.' He held his thumb and forefinger half an inch apart. 'But what happened yesterday in Tel Aviv could screw the whole thing.'

'The answer's no.'

'The powers that be have decided that this is too important an opportunity to be lost. They need you to go in there and work your magic. You've still got it. I could hear that just now. And this is something that really matters. Middle East peace, for Christ's sake. How could you pass that up?'

She thought of the pictures she had seen on TV that morning, and the feeling she'd had, but not admitted, even to herself. Envy. She had envied the people sitting at the head of the negotiating table in Jerusalem, charged with that weightiest of tasks, brokering peace. It was skilled, demanding work. But it was the most exhilarating activity she had ever known.

Bonham read her face. 'You must miss it. I mean, counselling couples is valuable, no question. But you're never going to feel the thrill you did at Dayton or Geneva. Are you?'

Maggie wanted to shake her head in agreement. But she resisted, turning instead to stare out of the window.

'Not that this is some kind of sport to you, I know that. It never was. Sure, you like the professional challenge. But that came second. To the *goal*. The pursuit of peace. You're one of the few people on the planet who knows how much these efforts matter. And few matter more than this one, Maggie. Thousands of Israelis and Palestinians have died in this conflict. It's gone on and on and on. And it will keep going. You'll turn on your TV set in ten years' time and there'll still be Palestinian kids shelled in playgrounds and Israeli teenagers blown to pieces on buses.'

'Look, I know only too well how much death and killing goes on in every corner of this planet. But I happen to have realised there is nothing I can do about it. So it's better I stay out of it.'

'The White House doesn't agree.'

'Well, the White House can just shove it, can't it?'

Bonham sat back, as if assessing his prey. After a pause he said, 'This is because of . . . what happened, isn't it?'

Maggie stared out of the window, willing her eyes to stay dry.

'Look, Maggie. We know what went on there. You fouled up badly. But it was one black mark on an otherwise exceptional record. The White House view is that you've done your penance. It's time you came back.'

'You're saying I'm forgiven.'

'I'm saying it's time to move on. But, yes, if you like, you're forgiven. After all, you're not going to bring back the lives that were lost because of what happened. Your mistake. But you can prevent more lives being lost. And that's got to count for something. Hasn't it?'

She said nothing.

'It's your choice, Maggie. If you believe that nothing else matters but your life here, your relationship here . . .'

She knew he'd heard the row in the kitchen.

'. . . you'll ignore me and send me away from here. But if you miss the work you were born to do, if you care about ending a conflict that's spread so much bitterness around the world, if you want to make things right, you'll say yes.'

'Tell me something,' she said after a long pause. 'Why the house visit? Why this cloak and dagger, pretending to be a client?'

'We tried phoning you. We've been leaving messages here since yesterday afternoon. We left a couple early this morning. But you didn't return our calls. I didn't think you'd let me into the building.'

'You called? But . . .' she stammered. She was sure she had checked, sure that there was nothing on the machine.

'Maybe someone deleted the messages before you got to them.'

She felt the air seep out of her lungs. *Edward.*

Judd threw a thick envelope on the table. 'Tickets and briefing material. The plane for Tel Aviv leaves this afternoon. The choice is yours, Maggie.'

CHAPTER TWO

Jerusalem, Saturday, 11.10 p.m.

After-dark meetings were part of the tradition of this office. Ben-Gurion had done it in the fifties, debating till the early hours; Golda, too, always worked late at night, most famously when the Egyptians launched their surprise attack on Yom Kippur in 1973. Somehow this small room lent itself to such encounters, with its single high-backed chair, reserved for the Prime Minister, and two couches forming an L-shape on which advisers or aides could sit around and talk for hours. Rabin used to sit here alone deep into the night, writing letters to the parents of soldiers—which, being Israel, meant every mother and father in the land.

Rabin was long gone now, taking the ashtrays that accompanied his chain-smoking habit with him. The current incumbent preferred, when stressed, to nibble on sunflower seeds, a habit that made him the peer of bus drivers and stallholders across the country. He gestured now to the man from Shin Bet, Israeli's internal security service, to begin speaking.

'Prime Minister, the dead man was Shimon Guttman. We all know who we're talking about: the writer and political activist, aged seventy-one. Our investigators found no sign that he carried any weapon. He was clasping a handwritten note, addressed to you. Intelligence say it will take some days to piece it together, the words were obscured by the blood—'

Grimacing, the Prime Minister waved him quiet. The head of Shin Bet put away the paper he had been consulting. The Deputy Prime Minister stared at his shoes; the Foreign and Defence Ministers stared at the PM, trying to gauge his reaction. None wanted to be the first to speak.

Amir Tal, special adviser to the PM and the youngest man in the room, filled the quiet. 'Of course, this has immediate political implications. We will be criticised for making a bad mistake, killing an innocent man. That kind of flak could come our way any time. But if we are about to sign a peace deal, this will make things much harder. The right are claiming their first martyr. They insist it is not a coincidence: Guttman was one of our loudest critics. Arutz Sheva was on the air an hour ago saying, "So now we know the government's plan; they want to silence dissent with gunfire."'

'Could they be right?' It was the Foreign Minister, addressing Tal, avoiding the boss's eye.

'Excuse me?'

'I don't mean that we deliberately killed him. But that it was not a coincidence. Could it be deliberate in the other direction? I mean, Guttman knew how things worked. You can't just rush towards the Prime Minister shouting, then reach into your jacket. He was a smart guy. He'd have known that.'

'Are you saying—?'

'Yeah. I'm wondering if Guttman *wanted* to get shot. If he was deliberately luring us in, daring us to kill a famous opponent of the government. After all, this is a guy who his whole life has gone in for the grand spectacular gesture, the great protest. And now, finally, it's the big one: we're about to make peace with the Arabs, to give away holy Judea and sacred Samaria.

To prevent such a calamity, Guttman would have to come up with the biggest possible gesture. One that might actually mobilise the right.'

'He would sacrifice his own life?'

'He would.'

The Prime Minister had uttered his first words since the meeting began. After a long pause, as if completing a thought that had been unspooling in his own head, he added, 'I know this man. Inside out.'

The Chief of Staff, dressed in pressed olive-green trousers and beige shirt, with a beret under his epaulette, broke the silence that followed with the question that everyone who had heard the eyewitness accounts on TV had wanted to ask from the beginning. 'How come he called you Kobi?'

'Ah,' said the Prime Minister.

'I thought he hated you. Yet here he talks to you like you're old chums.'

The PM sat back and looked into the middle distance. 'Kobi was the man I was a long, long time ago. It was what my friends called me. In the army. We were a good unit, one of the best. In '67 we took a hill, just us: thirty-odd men. And you know who was the bravest, much braver than me, despite what Amir here tells the newspapers? A young scholar from the Hebrew University by the name of Shimon Guttman.'

Jerusalem, Monday, 9.28 a.m.

For the first time since she got here, the people checking her bags were Arabs. Everyone she had met since coming off the overnight flight at dawn this morning had been an Israeli Jew. Now, at the entrance to the US Consulate on Agron Street, she was waiting to be processed by Palestinian Arabs—albeit wearing shirts bearing the crest of the United States.

Maggie was ushered into a small security lobby, staffed by a US Marine behind thick glass, watching a bank of TV monitors. Natural that the serious security would be entrusted only to an American. The use of Palestinian staff was also a statement, underlining that the consulate in Jerusalem was the US mission to the Palestinians, a wholly different operation from the embassy in Tel Aviv, which represented America to the Israelis.

As she gazed at the scene before her, she rewound her encounter with Judd Bonham for the dozenth time. He had played her like a master, making every move she would have made. He had appealed to her conscience and flattered her ego, just as she had done to countless delegates, ambassadors and presidential aides. He had both dangled a stick, revealing what he knew, and offered a carrot, designed to reach her weakest spot: her desire to wipe the slate clean. Bonham must have known it would be a breeze.

A door buzzed, opening up for a tall, fair-haired man. 'Welcome to the madhouse! Jim Davis, consul, good to see you.' He stuck out a hand.

They walked into a garden, a wide, square lawn laid out before a grand, colonial house. The noise of Agron Street was shut out now. The only sound was the hummed melody of an aged gardener, pruning a rosebush.

'As you can see, we work in the most beautiful pair of buildings the State Department owns anywhere in the world,' Davis said. 'And this is our newest acquisition, the Lazarist Monastery.' He pointed to his left, to a modest, fortress-like structure built in the pale, craggy stone that dominated this city.

Maggie looked up, shielding her eyes with the palm of her hand. The light was so bright here, bouncing off all that pale stone.

'The brothers have vacated most of the building,' Davis was explaining. 'A few of them are hanging on, in a little corner that will stay theirs. Otherwise it now belongs to the United States of America.'

He was babbling, a male reaction Maggie was used to. She had seen it in Davis's eyes the moment he had greeted her, the initial instant of surprise, followed by a concentrated effort to act normally. She had thought this would stop as she moved into her late thirties, that she would become less of a magnet for male attention. But even with the dressing-down, it hadn't faded much. She was still tall, at five foot nine, and her figure had held its shape pretty well. Her hair was still thick and warm brown, and when she let it down it was long enough to trail over her shoulders.

'So here's the deal.' Davis had led them to a cluster of iron chairs, shaded by some cypress trees. 'As you know, the White House is convinced that this is the week. Aiming for a permanent agreement signed in the Rose Garden within a matter of days. Just in time for election day.'

'Or re-election day, as I think the President likes to call it,' Maggie said. 'Is he going to get what he wants?'

'Well, we've had two delegations over at Government House sitting face to face for nearly two weeks now. That's a breakthrough right there.'

'What, that they've done two weeks?'

'No, I meant talks on the ground. It's never happened before. Camp David, Wye River, Madrid, Oslo, you name it. But never here. And the White House, in its infinite wisdom, decided that it would be good for the parties to do the business in their own back yard.'

'And are they? Doing the business?'

'Course not. These guys are leaking to their media more than they're talking to each other. You can't do a news blackout when you're in the middle of the freakin' conflict zone. So now we've got a billion Muslims on the edge of their seats, waiting to see what happens. Imams and mullahs from here to Mohammadsville, Alabama, preaching that this is the front line in the war between Islam and the evil West. If they all decide the Palestinians are being pushed into some kind of sell-out deal, then the whole region could go *boof.*' He made a little mushroom cloud of his hands. 'And that's World War Three right there.'

Maggie nodded, allowing Davis to know that his little dramatic exposition had struck home.

'Up till now things have gone OK. But it's crunch time now, R and J, and the parties are getting antsy.'

'They haven't talked about refugees and Jerusalem until now?' She wanted Davis to know that she knew the code. Like every field, diplomacy had its jargon; within that, Middle East diplomacy had its own dialect.

'There's been a ton of groundwork on right of return,' said Davis. 'Though don't let anyone catch you saying those words. It's not a "right", it's a claim. And it's not necessarily "return", because some of the Palestinians came from somewhere else first, blah, blah. You know all this.'

Maggie nodded, but she had stopped listening. She was remembering the row she'd had with Edward. He hadn't attempted to deny that he had deleted those messages from Judd; he simply said he had done it for her own good. She had been furious, accusing him of trying to cage her, to deny who she really was. After that, she had packed her bags and left for the airport. She felt a tremendous sadness, that her attempt at a normal life had collapsed so spectacularly. But she had boarded the plane, looked down at Washington as it receded, imagining Edward receding with it, then distracted herself by plunging into the 300-page briefing pack Bonham had prepared for her.

'So as you can imagine,' Davis was saying, 'this assassination thing has everyone extra jumpy. Which is why they sent in the cavalry.' He gestured towards her. 'Closing the deal.'

'Right. Though not in the room just yet.'

'How's that?'

'Washington has decided that the mood has "deteriorated" in the few hours I was in the air. Apparently, the moment is not "ripe" for me to come in just yet. So for now my immediate role is to keep everyone calm. Out and about, keeping the constituencies on side.'

'Ah, the "constituencies".' Davis made little quote marks with his fingers. 'Well, the Israeli right are the first guys who are gonna need stroking. They're saying the dead guy's a martyr.' A look of sudden comprehension crossed his face. 'So that's why you're going to the *shiva* house.'

'What?'

'The house of mourning. I just got told you're to go, as an unofficial representative. The Israelis asked for it, apparently. Shows respect for the guy, proof that he wasn't being taken out because he opposed the "US-backed" peace process; proof that no one regarded him as an enemy.'

'But not too official, or it looks like we're endorsing his views.'

'Right. The funeral was this morning, as soon as they got the body back. They do autopsies quick here; religious thing, like everything else in this place. But the *shiva* goes on all week. The details will be on your BlackBerry.'

'Ah. No BlackBerry, I'm afraid.'

'Oh, Comms will fix you up with one, no problem. I'll get—'

'I mean, I don't use a BlackBerry. Means you're listening to Washington or whoever when you should be listening to the people in the room.'

'OK.' Davis looked as if Maggie had admitted a heroin addiction.

'I wouldn't carry a cellphone either if I could get away with it.'

Davis ignored that. 'Your hotel's just a block away. You can freshen up, have lunch and the driver will take you there. Widow's name is Rachel.'

Jerusalem, Monday, 2.27 p.m.

THE STREET WAS JAMMED, cars parked on both sides. It was a well-to-do neighbourhood, Maggie could tell that much: the trees were leafy, the cars BMWs and Mercs. Her driver was struggling to get through, despite the discreet Stars-and-Stripes pennant flying from the bonnet.

The path to the building was packed, all the way to the front door. As she squeezed through, she noticed that look again from several of the men in the line, their eyes following her as she went past.

'You are from the embassy, no? Please, inside.' It was a man at the door, staff or relative Maggie couldn't tell. But clearly he knew she was coming.

Maggie was pressed into what would ordinarily be a large room. Now it was jammed with people, like rush hour on a subway train, and at the front a bearded man she took to be a rabbi.

'*Yitgadal, v'Yitkadash . . .*'

The room hushed for this murmured prayer for the dead man. Then the rabbi spoke a few sentences of Hebrew, turning occasionally to a row of three people sitting on strangely low chairs. Maggie guessed that they were Guttman's immediate family: widow, son and daughter. Of the three, only the son was not weeping. He stared straight ahead, his dark eyes dry.

Maggie was not quite sure what to do. She should wait her turn to meet the family, but the room was heaving and it would take an hour to get to the front. Yet if she left now, it could be interpreted as a snub.

She smiled politely as she inched her way through. Her black trouser suit persuaded most of the mourners that she was some kind of VIP and they made way for her. Still, she could only move slowly across the room.

Large bookcases lined each wall, floor to ceiling. They contained the odd ceramic pot or plate, including one with a strikingly ornate blue and green pattern, but mainly it was books. Most were in Hebrew, but there was a cluster of books on American politics, including several of the neoconservative tomes that had once dominated the *New York Times* best-seller lists. *Terrorism: How the West Can Win. Inside the New Jihad. The Gathering Storm*. She felt she had a good handle on this Mr Guttman. After all, Washington was not short of men who shared his politics.

At last, it was Maggie's turn to shake hands with the family. She nodded respectfully to each one. First the daughter, who gave her only a fleeting moment of eye contact. She looked to be in her mid-forties, attractive, with short, dark hair interrupted by a few strands of grey and a face that radiated solid practicality. Maggie guessed she was the person in charge here.

Then the son. He looked at her coldly. He was tall, and more casually dressed than she would have expected in a house of mourning, in dark jeans and a white shirt, both of which looked expensive. His hair, a full, dark head of it, was well cut, too. Late thirties, Maggie noted; no sign of a wife.

And finally the widow. Maggie bent down, so that the grieving woman could hear her, and offered her hand.

'Mrs Guttman, I am with the United States team in Jerusalem, negotiating for peace. I'm so sorry for your loss,' she said. 'We wish you to know that you and your family are in the prayers of the American people.'

The widow looked up suddenly. Her hair was dyed black, her eyes nearly the same colour. She gripped Maggie by the wrist, so that Maggie was forced to look into those dark eyes, which, still wet, focused intently.

'You are from the President of the United States? My husband had an important message. For the Prime Minister.'

'That's what I understand, and it's such a tragedy—'

'No, no, you don't understand. This message, he had been trying to get it to Kobi for days. He called the office; he went to the Knesset. But they would not let him anywhere near. It drove him mad!'

'Please don't upset yourself—'

Her grip on Maggie's wrist tightened. 'What is your name?'

'Maggie Costello.'

'His message was urgent, Miss Costello. A matter of life and death. Not just his life or Kobi's life, but the lives of everyone in this country, in this whole region. He had seen something, Miss Costello.'

Maggie crouched lower. 'What had he seen?'

'A document, a letter maybe—I don't know, but something of great importance. For the last three days of his life, he did not sleep. He just said the same thing over and over. "Kobi must know of this, Kobi must know of this."'

'Kobi? The Prime Minister?'

'Yes, yes. Please understand, what he had to tell Kobi still needs to be told. My husband was not a fool. He knew the risk he took. But he said nothing was more important. He had to tell him what he had seen.'

'And what had he seen?'

'*Ima, dai kvar!*' Mother, enough already. It was the son, his voice firm, the voice of a man used to giving instructions.

'He didn't tell me. I only know it was some document, something written. And he kept saying, "This will change everything."'

'What will change everything?'

The son was now getting up.

'I don't know. He wouldn't tell me. For my safety, he said.'

'Your *safety*?'

'I know my husband. He was a serious man. He would not suddenly go crazy and run and shout at the Prime Minister. If he had something to say, it must have been just as Shimon said—a matter of life and death.'

Beitin, the West Bank, Tuesday, 9.32 a.m.

HE WOULDN'T NEED to be here long. Just ten minutes in the office, collect the papers and leave. Except 'office' was not quite the right word. 'Workroom' was more like it, even 'storehouse'. Inside, it smelt like a potting shed.

The fluorescent strip lights flickered on to reveal shelves filled with stiff cardboard boxes. Inside those were fragments of ancient pottery, material that Ahmed Nour had excavated from this very village.

He worked this way on every dig. Set up a base as close to the site as possible, allowing each day's findings to be brought back, catalogued and stored right away. Even a few burnt pottery shards left lying around would soon vanish. Looters, the curse of archaeologists the world over.

Ahmed found the papers he needed for his meeting with the head of the Palestinian Authority's Department of Antiquities and Cultural Heritage on his desk. His young protégée, Huda, had left them in a neat pile: the permit renewal form, seeking permission to carry on digging in Beitin, and the application for a grant, begging for the cash to do it. Huda took care of all contact with the outside world now, so that he could bury himself in his work.

That's what he had done this weekend. And he would have carried on doing it if it hadn't been for this damned meeting. The head of antiquities was an ignoramus, little more than a political hack. He wore a beard, which meant that the politics in question were of the new variety: religious.

'My preference, Dr Nour,' he had explained to Ahmed in their first meeting, 'is for the glorification of our Islamic heritage.' No surprise there. The new government was half Hamas. Translation: I'll pay for anything after the seventh century; if you want to dig up anything older, you're on your own.

The irony of it was not lost on Ahmed. Once he had been a hero to the Palestinian political class, a founder member of a group of scholars who, decades ago, had insisted on looking at the ground beneath their feet in a radically new way. Until then, those taking a shovel to this landscape were looking for one thing only: the Holy Land. They weren't interested in Palestine or the people who had lived here for thousands of years. They were yearning to see the route Abraham trod, to gaze at the Tomb of Christ. They longed to find the vestiges of the ancient Israelites or of the early Christians. Palestinians, ancient and modern, were an irrelevance.

The new generation, Ahmed among them, was trained in biblical archaeology but they soon developed their own ideas. In the 1960s, several of them assisted a team of Lutheran Bible scholars from Illinois as they excavated Tell Ta'anach, a mound not far from Jenin in the West Bank, which was mentioned in the Bible as one of the Canaanite cities conquered by Joshua.

But Ahmed and his colleagues began to see something else. Their focus was not biblical Ta'anach but the Palestinian village at the foot of the mound: Ti'innik. These new archaeologists wanted to learn all they could about day-to-day life in this ordinary community, which had sat on the same spot for most of the last five millennia.

That put Ahmed Nour and his colleagues firmly into the bosom of the burgeoning Palestinian national movement. In whispers he was told that the Palestine Liberation Organisation, then still secret and run from abroad, approved of his work. He was nurturing 'national pride' and handily proving that the communities of these lands had the deepest possible roots.

His work here at Beitin had boosted his reputation yet further. Previous scholars had thrilled at this place as the Bethel of the Bible, the place where Jacob dreamt of angels going up and down a ladder. But Ahmed was determined to examine not just the ruins around Beitin but the village itself. For humble, tiny Beitin had been ruled by Hellenists, by Romans, by Byzantines, by Ottomans. You could still see the remains of a Hellenistic tower, a Byzantine monastery and a Crusader castle. To Ahmed's mind, that was the glory of Palestine. Even in a forgotten speck like Beitin, you could see the history of the world, one layer on top of another.

As he reached for the pile of papers, he heard a noise. Metallic.

'Hello? Huda?'

No reply. Probably nothing. He must have left the metal door to the workroom ajar and the wind had clicked it shut.

But then there was another sound. This time a footstep, unmistakable. Ahmed turned round to see two men coming towards him. Both were wearing black hoods that covered their faces entirely. The taller man was holding up a finger, which he theatrically placed over his lips. *Hush*.

'What? What is this?' said Ahmed, his knees buckling.

'Just come with us,' said the tall man, something strange in his accent. 'Now!' And for the first time Ahmed saw the gun, aimed straight at him.

The US Consulate, Jerusalem, Tuesday, 2.14 p.m.

'OUR INFORMATION is that the body, riddled with bullets, was dumped by two hooded men in Ramallah's main square about ten forty-five a.m. local time. The corpse was propped up and displayed to the crowd for about fifteen minutes, then taken away by the same two hooded men who'd brought it there.'

'Collaborator killing?'

'Exactly.' The CIA station chief turned towards Maggie, offering extra tuition to the newcomer to the class. 'This is standard punishment meted out by Palestinians to any Palestinian deemed guilty of collaborating with Israeli intelligence in any way.'

'What's the Israeli reaction? No chance they'd break off talks over this?' The questions came from a speakerphone at the centre of the table: the voice of the Secretary of State in Washington. He had left it to his deputy, Robert Sanchez, to manage this last stage of talks on the ground, keeping his distance in case of failure.

'We don't think so, sir. The talks are painfully difficult right now, but no one's walking away.'

'Still hung up on refugees?'

'And Jerusalem. Yes.'

'Remember, we can't let this go on for ever. If we're not careful, it's one delay, then another and before you know it—'

'It's November.' This from Bruce Miller, officially titled Political Counsellor to the President, unofficially his most trusted *consigliere*. His presence in Jerusalem confirmed what they all knew. That this push for peace was inseparable from American domestic politics.

'Hello, Bruce.' Maggie detected a sudden meekness in the Secretary of State's voice.

'I was just about to agree with you, Mr Secretary,' Miller began, his voice twanging between a down-home Southern accent and the Nicorette gum he chewed from morning till night. 'I mean, they've only had sixty years to think of an answer to all this. We can't maintain this pitch for ever.' His wiry frame was hunched forward over the telephone and his neck seemed to jut out at key moments, the two horns of hair bestriding his bald pate floating upwards as it did so. He reminded Maggie of a cockerel.

'We keep saying'—he gestured at a TV set in the corner, silently showing Fox News—'this is about to get resolved this week. Screw it up now and you go back to square one. Look what happened after Camp David. Israelis were shooting Arabs in the streets and Arabs were blowing up every café in Jerusalem. Because the folk who sat in these chairs screwed up.'

Silence, including from the speakerphone. They knew what this was: a rollicking from the top, doubtless with more to come.

'We do have more on this collaborator killing,' said the CIA man, in a tentative attempt to alter the mood.

'Yes?' The Secretary of State.

'Just a couple of oddities. First, the dead man was in his late sixties. That's much older than the usual profile for victims of these summary executions. Second, we've had a word with our Israeli counterparts today and they tell us this man was precisely what he seemed to be, an elderly archaeologist. He had done no work for them that they knew of.'

'So the Palestinians got the wrong guy?'

'That's possible, Mr Secretary. And death by mistaken identity would not be unheard of. But there are other possibilities. It could be the work of a rebel faction. Security's so tight in Israel just now that they can't pull off a terrorist outrage here. So killing one of their own, especially an innocent, well-respected Palestinian like Nour, is the next best thing. It sows dissension among the Palestinians and could provoke the Israelis into breaking off negotiations.'

'Sounds a long shot to me,' said Miller, still craning forward in concentration. 'Break off the whole peace process just because one Arab's blown away? Israeli public opinion would never swallow it. What else?'

'The other curiosity relates to eyewitness reports from Manara Square in Ramallah. The hooded men hardly spoke, but we're told that when they did they had unusual accents.'

'What kind of accents? Could they be Israeli?'

'It's a possibility.'

Miller fell back into his chair, took off his glasses and addressed the ceiling. 'Christ! What are we saying? That this might be an undercover Israeli Army operation?'

'Well, we know Israel has always run undercover units. This could be their latest operation.'

'Why the hell would they do that now?'

'Again, it might be an effort to destabilise the peace talks. It's widely known that elements within the Israeli military are fiercely hostile to the compromises the Prime Minister wants to make—'

'And if this got out, the Palestinians would be so pissed they'd walk away.' Miller rubbed his eyes. 'The killing of one of their national heroes.'

'Yes. And even if the Authority were prepared to let it go, the Palestinian street wouldn't let them.'

'Hence the accidentally-on-purpose slip of the accent.' The words were barely audible through the chewing.

'It's one of the lines of enquiry we're pursuing.'

'It's like a hall of mirrors here!' Miller replaced his glasses. 'We have the Israelis and the Palestinians at each other's throats. And now we've got rogue elements on both sides.'

'The possibility at least. Which is why we're taking a close look at the Guttman killing.'

'What's that got to do with it?'

'We're asking some questions about the security detail that protects the Prime Minister, wondering if it's possible it was infiltrated, and that the man who shot Guttman did so deliberately.'

Maggie leaned forward, about to mention her strange encounter with the Guttman widow, the previous night. *His message was urgent, Miss Costello. A matter of life and death.* Maybe it would sound flaky to bring that up here. On the other hand—

It was too late. Miller was getting up out of his chair. 'OK, people, that's enough for now. Mr Secretary, we're going to keep pushing the talks at this end as if none of this other stuff was happening. Is that OK with you?'

'Of course.'

'Anything else?' Miller looked towards Maggie, who shook her head, and then to the consul, who did the same. 'OK.'

The room broke up, every official eager to show the man from the White House that they were hurrying to return to their duties.

MAGGIE HEADED to the room Davis had set up for her, a work space for all State Department visitors. Just a desk, phone and computer. That's all she would need. She closed the door.

First, she checked her email. One from Liz, in response to a message Maggie had left on her phone, telling her of the sudden trip to Jerusalem.

> So, my serious sister, you've finally made it into my crazy online world. You know you're now a character in Second Life? You're in some Middle East peace talks simulation thing. It even looks like you: though they've given you a better arse than you deserve. Here's a link: take a look . . .

Maggie clicked on the link, intrigued. Liz had mentioned Second Life to her a couple of times, insisting it was not just another dumb online game but a virtual addition to the real world. Liz loved it, evangelising about the way you could travel and meet people—not orcs or dragon-slayers but real people—without ever leaving your computer. It sounded horrendous to Maggie, but her curiosity was piqued. What did Liz mean, that Maggie was now a 'character' in it? A 'peace talks simulation thing' she understood: there were several of those online, where graduate students would role-play their way through the latest round of Middle East negotiations. Impressive that they already knew she was in Jerusalem. She guessed there had been a paragraph in one of the Israeli papers.

The computer egg timer was still showing, before eventually freezing in defeat. A message popped up saying something about a security block on the consulate network. Never mind, thought Maggie. Some other time.

She went back through the inbox. Still nothing from Edward. She wondered if they would ever speak again, other than to arrange the removal of what was left of her stuff. Which, thanks to him, was not much.

She clicked her email shut, then, out of habit, brought up the *New York Times* and *Washington Post* web sites. The *Times* had a story about the Israel shooting on Saturday night, including a profile of the dead man. Happy for the distraction, she read through it.

> Shimon Guttman first came to prominence after the Six-Day War in 1967, in which he was said to have performed with military distinction. Seizing the chance to make the most of Israel's new control of the historic West Bank territories of Judea and Samaria, Guttman was among the activists who famously found an ingenious way to re-establish a Jewish presence in the heavily Arab city of Hebron. Disguised as tourists, they rented rooms in a Palestinian hotel, ostensibly to host a Passover dinner. Once installed, they refused to leave. In the stand-off with the Israeli authorities that followed, Guttman was especially vocal, insisting that the Jewish connection to Hebron was stronger than with anywhere else in the land of Israel. 'This is the spot where the Oak of Abraham stands, the ancient tree where *Avraham Avinu*, Abraham our father, pitched his tent,' he told reporters in 1968. 'Here is the Tomb of the Patriarchs, where Abraham, Isaac and Jacob are buried. Without Hebron, we are nothing.' Guttman and his fellow activists eventually struck a deal with the Israeli authorities, vacating the hotel and moving instead to a hill northeast of Hebron, where they established the Jewish settlement of Kiryat Arba. That hilltop outpost has since flourished into the modern city that exists today, though speculation mounts as to the town's fate in the new peace accord, which could be signed as soon as this week.

That would explain it, thought Maggie. Guttman was worried that the settlement he had founded was about to be surrendered to the Palestinians, along with scores of other Jewish towns and villages. He had been trying to persuade the Prime Minister to change his mind. And he clearly enjoyed the dramatic gesture. He had climbed a roof in Gaza a few years back and had, she now saw, seized a hotel in Hebron a generation before that.

She Googled him, looking into the handful of English-language web sites carrying Israeli news. They all told similar stories. Guttman had been first a war hero, then a right-wing extremist with a knack for the big stunt. It all seemed pretty straightforward. He was a hawk, determined to make his last stand by appealing to the Prime Minister direct. He got too close and was gunned down. Simple.

And yet there was something about what Rachel Guttman had said, and the way she had said it, that nagged at her. She had insisted that her husband had *seen* something—*a document, a letter*—that would change everything. Maggie rubbed her wrist, where the widow had gripped her so tightly.

There was a knock on the door. Without waiting for an answer, Davis walked in. 'OK, the United States has decided to deploy its secret weapon.'

'Oh yes, what's that?'

'You.'

Davis explained that, as feared, the Palestinian delegation to Government House were now threatening to pull out over the death of the archaeologist. They suspected the hand of Israel. 'We need you to talk them off the ledge.'

Maggie collected her papers and moved to turn off the computer. She was about to shut down the web site of the Israeli newspaper, *Haaretz*, which she had searched for information on Guttman, but changed her mind. Quickly she checked the front page, in case there was fresh word on the Nour case.

There was a news story, which she skim-read. It was written up as a straight collaborator killing: no mention of any possible Israeli involvement. But accompanying it was a picture of the dead Palestinian, what seemed to be a snap from a family album. The archaeologist was smiling at the camera, holding up a glass. A disembodied arm was draped over his shoulder, as if he were posing with an unseen friend.

Maggie got up to follow Davis, but something drew her back to the picture on the screen. She had seen something familiar, without being able to identify what it was. For a fleeting moment, she thought she had grasped it—only for it to slip back below the surface, out of reach.

CHAPTER THREE

Ramallah, the West Bank, Tuesday, 4.46 p.m.

Her first surprise was at the brevity of the journey. She had climbed into the back of one of the consulate's black Land Cruisers only fifteen minutes earlier and yet now her driver, Marine Sergeant Kevin Lee, was telling her that she was crossing the Green Line, an invisible border, out of 'Israel proper' and into the lands the country took in the Six-Day War.

'This is Pisgat Ze'ev,' said the Marine. 'Even the people who live here don't realise this is across the Green Line.' He turned to look at Maggie. 'Or they don't want to realise.'

Maggie stared out of the window. No wonder everything about these negotiations was a nightmare. The plan was for Jerusalem to be divided between the two sides—'shared' was the favoured US euphemism—becoming a capital for both countries. But she could now see that splitting it would be all but impossible: East and West Jerusalem were like trees that had grown so close they had become entwined.

'Now you get more of a sense of it,' Lee was saying, as the road began to bend. 'Pisgat Ze'ev on one side,' he said, pointing to his right. 'And Beit Hanina on the other.' Gesturing to the left.

She could see the difference. The Arab side of the road was a semi-wasteland: unfinished houses made of grey breeze blocks, sprouting steel rods like severed tendons; potholed, overgrown pathways, bordered by rusting oil barrels. Out of the car's other window, Pisgat Ze'ev was all straight lines and trim verges. It could have been an American suburb.

'Yep, it's pretty simple,' said Lee. 'The infrastructure here is great. And over there it's shit.'

They drove on in silence, Maggie's eyes boring into the landscape around her. Up ahead she saw two thin lines of people standing on either side of the highway. The lines stretched off to the side in each direction and into the distance. Some people were holding banners, the rest were holding hands. It was a human chain, broken only by the highway.

Maggie noticed that they were all wearing orange, the colour of the protest movement that had sprung up to oppose the peace process. WITH

BLOOD AND FIRE, YARIV WILL GO, said one placard. ARREST THE TRAITORS, said another. The first had mocked up a portrait of the Prime Minister wearing a black and white *keffiyeh*, the traditional Palestinian headdress.

'They call themselves "Arms Around Jerusalem",' the Marine explained. 'They say they're going to stay there until Yariv and all the other negotiators are gone and their city is safe again.'

Maggie nodded, and as they got closer she could hear a song drifting up from the hillside through the open window. It was out of time, as different people in different places struggled to keep up with each other, but even so it was a haunting, beautiful melody.

Against opposition this committed, people who were prepared to ring an entire city, day and night for weeks, or even months, Yariv surely had no chance, Maggie thought. Even if he were able to make the final push with the Palestinians, he had his own people to overcome.

Soon they were on a smooth road with hardly any traffic on it except the odd UN 4x4 or a khaki vehicle of the Israel Defence Force, the IDF. Any other vehicles, Lee explained, belonged to settlers.

'Where are the Palestinians?'

'They have to get around by some other way. That's why they call this a bypass road: it's to bypass them.'

Lee slowed down at a checkpoint. A sign in English indicated who was allowed to approach: international organisations, medical staff, ambulances, press. Below that: STOP HERE! WAIT TO BE CALLED BY THE SOLDIER! The driver reached across for Maggie's passport and passed it to the guard.

They were waved through, past an empty hulk of a building that Lee identified as the City Inn Hotel. It was pocked all over with bullet holes.

'During the second *intifada* they fought here for weeks.' He turned to smile at Maggie. 'I hear the room rate's real low now.'

Just a few minutes after driving through Israeli suburbia, they were in a different country. The buildings were still made of the pale stone she had seen in Jerusalem, but here they were dustier, more forlorn. Walking in the road, sidestepping the potholes, were children on their way from school, labouring under oversized rucksacks. She looked away.

On every wall and pasted on the windows of abandoned stores were posters showing the faces of boys and men, the images framed by the green, white, red and black of the Palestinian national flag.

'Martyrs,' said Lee.

'Suicide bombers?'

'Yeah, but not only. Also kids who were shooting at settlers or maybe trying to launch a rocket.'

They threaded through crammed roads, passing a coffee shop filled with women in black headscarves. Lee dodged a couple of wagons, pulled by young boys, loaded with fruit. Everyone used the road: people, cars, animals. It was slow and noisy, horns blaring and beeping without interruption.

'Here we are.'

They had parked by a substantial-looking stone building. A sign thanked the government of Japan and the European Union. A ministry.

Inside, they were ushered into a spacious office with a long L-shaped couch. A thickset man came in carrying a plastic tray bearing two glasses of steaming mint tea, for Maggie and her Marine escort, then left the room.

A short while later, he returned. 'Mr al-Shafi is ready. Please come.'

Maggie collected her small, black leather case and followed the guide into a smaller room. On one couch and in several chairs, assorted aides and officials. On the wall, a portrait of Yasser Arafat and a calendar showing a map of Palestine, including not just the West Bank and Gaza, but Israel itself. An ideological statement that said hardline.

Khalil al-Shafi rose from his seat to shake Maggie's hand. 'Miss Costello, I hear you came out of retirement to stop us children squabbling.'

The joke, and the inside knowledge it betrayed, did not surprise her. The briefing note from Davis had told her to expect a smart operator. After more than a decade in an Israeli jail, convicted not only on the usual terrorism charges but also on several counts of murder, he had become a symbol of 'the struggle'. He had learned Hebrew and English in jail, then taken a doctorate in political science. When the Israelis had released him three months earlier, it had been the most serious sign yet that progress was possible.

Now, though he held no official title, al-Shafi was recognised as the de facto leader of at least one half of the Palestinian nation, those who did not back Hamas but identified with the secular nationalists of Arafat's Fatah movement. The photos, of a stubbled face with broad, crude features, had led Maggie to expect a streetfighter rather than a sophisticate. Yet the man before her had a refinement that surprised her.

'I was told it was worth it. That you and the Israelis were close to a deal.'

'"Were" is the right word.'

'Not now?'

'Not if the Israelis keep killing us in order to play games with us.'

'Killing you?'

'Ahmed Nour could not have been killed by a Palestinian.'

'You sound very certain. From what I hear, Palestinians seem to have killed quite a lot of other Palestinians over the years.'

His eyes flashed a cold stare. Maggie smiled back. She was used to this. In fact, she did it deliberately: show some steel early; that way they'll resist the temptation to dismiss you as some lightweight woman.

'No Palestinian would kill a national hero like Ahmed Nour. His work was a source of pride to all of us. He was the last person on this earth who would collaborate with the Israelis, believe me.'

'Oh, come on. We know he couldn't stand Hamas.'

'He understood that we have a government of national unity in Palestine now. When Fatah went into coalition with Hamas, Ahmed accepted it.'

'What else could he say publicly? Last time I checked, collaborators weren't wearing T-shirts with "collaborator" written on the chest.'

Al-Shafi leaned forward and looked unblinking at Maggie. 'Listen to me, Miss Costello. I know my people. Collaborators are young or they are poor or they are desperate. Or they have some shameful secret. Or the Israelis have something they need. None of these fits Ahmed Nour. Besides—'

'He knew nothing.' Suddenly Maggie realised the obvious. 'He was an elderly scholar. He didn't have any information to give.'

'Yes, that's right.' Al-Shafi looked puzzled; the American had folded too early. 'Which is why it must have been the Israelis who killed him.'

'Which would explain the strange accent of the killers.'

'Exactly. So you agree with me?'

'What would be their motive?'

'The same as always, for the last one hundred years! The Zionists say they want peace, but they don't. Peace scares them. Whenever they are close, they find a reason to step back. And this time they want *us* to step back, so they kill us and drive our people so mad that Palestinians will not allow their leaders to shake the hand of the Zionist enemy!'

Something in al-Shafi's tone struck Maggie as odd. What was it? A false note, his voice somehow a decibel too loud. *Of course.* He was not speaking to her, she realised. He was *performing* for the other men in the room.

'Dr al-Shafi, do you think we could talk in private?'

Al-Shafi looked to the handful of officials and, with a quick gesture, waved them out. After a rustle of papers, they were alone.

'Thank you,' Maggie said. 'Is there something you want to tell me?'

'I have told you what I think.' The voice was quieter now.

'You've told me you believe that the men who killed Ahmed Nour yesterday were undercover agents of Israel. But you don't really believe that, do you? Is there something you didn't want to say in front of your colleagues?'

'Is this how you make peace, Miss Costello? By reading the minds of the men who are fighting?' He gave her a rueful smile.

'Don't try flattering me, Dr al-Shafi,' Maggie said, returning the smile. 'You suspect Hamas, don't you?' Taking his silence as affirmation, she pressed on. 'But why? Because he was a critic of theirs?'

'Do you remember what the Taliban did in Afghanistan, just before 9/11? Something that grabbed the world's attention.'

'They blew up those giant Buddhas, carved in the mountainside.'

'Correct. And why did they do this? Because the statues proved there was something before Islam, a civilisation even older than the Prophet. This is something the fanatics cannot stand.'

'You think Hamas would kill Nour just for that, because he found a few pots and pans that predated Islam?'

Al-Shafi sighed. 'Miss Costello, it's not just Hamas. They are under pressure from Islamists all around the world, who are calling them traitors for talking to Israel at all. Hamas may have felt they had to show their balls—excuse me—by killing a scholar who uncovered the wrong kind of truth.'

'But why would they disguise that as a collaborator killing? Surely they would make it look like a state execution, if they wanted to boost their standing with al-Qaeda.' Maggie paused. 'Unless they also wanted to make it look like Israel, so that the Palestinians would be too angry to go ahead with the peace deal. Is that possible?'

'I have wondered about it. Whether Hamas is getting, how do you say, cold feet?'

Maggie smiled. She was always wary of first impressions, including her own. But something about the knot of angst on this man's forehead, the way his mind seemed to be wrestling with itself, made her trust him.

'There's something else, isn't there?' she asked.

He looked up, his eyes holding hers. She did not break the contact.

At last, he got up and began to pace. 'Ahmed Nour's son came to see me an hour ago. He was very agitated.'

'Understandably.'

'He said he went through his father's things this afternoon, looking for an explanation. He found some correspondence, a few emails. Including one--a strange one—from someone whose name he does not recognise.'

'Has he spoken with colleagues? Maybe it's someone he worked with.'

'Of course. But his assistant does not recognise this man's name either. And she handled all such matters for him.'

'And the son thought this person may be linked to his father's death?'

Al-Shafi nodded.

'That he might even be behind it?'

He gave the slightest movement of his head.

'What kind of person are we talking about?'

Al-Shafi looked towards the door, as if uncertain who might be listening. 'The email was sent by an Arab.'

Jerusalem, Tuesday, 8.19 p.m.

MAGGIE LAY BACK on her bed at the David's Citadel Hotel, a cavernous, modern building a block away from the consulate. She and Lee had driven back from Ramallah in the twilight, the road even emptier than before, and in silence. Maggie had been thinking, doing her best not to believe that this mission, far from being destined to save her reputation, was doomed to fail.

What Judd Bonham had billed as a simple matter of closing the deal was deteriorating instead into another Middle East disaster. Maggie had learned to recognise the telltale signs, and high-profile killings on both sides, whatever the circumstances, were a reliable warning of serious trouble ahead.

She stood up and walked over to the minibar. With a glass honeyed by a whisky, she sat down at the desk and considered calling Edward. She wondered what they would say, whether he would apologise for throwing out her possessions, or expect her to apologise for having gone to Jerusalem. Was he right, that she always ran away, that she couldn't stick long enough at anything to make it work? Maybe he was. Draining her glass, she dialled his mobile. As she heard the first ring, she looked at her watch. One thirty p.m. in Washington. He picked up.

'Maggie.' Not a question, not a greeting. A statement.

'Hi, Edward.'

'How's Jerusalem?' A pause. Then, 'You save the world yet?'

'I wanted to talk.'

'Now's not a great time, Maggie.' She could hear the clink of silverware and low string music in the background. Lunch at La Colline, she reckoned.

'Just give me two minutes.'

Now she heard the muffled sound of Edward excusing himself from the table, finding a quiet corner. Truth be told, he wouldn't have been so unhappy to do it: interrupting a meal to take an urgent phone call was standard Washington practice, a way of signalling your importance.

'Yeah,' he said finally. *Fire away*.

'I just wanted to talk about what's going to happen with us.'

'Well, I was planning on you coming to your senses and coming back home. Then we could take it from there.'

'Coming to my senses?'

'Oh, you can't be serious about all this, Maggie. Playing the peacemaker.'

Maggie closed her eyes. She wouldn't rise to it. 'I need to know you understand why I was so angry. About the boxes. Because if you don't understand, if you can't understand—'

'Then what, Maggie? What?' His voice was rising.

'Then I don't know how—'

'What? How we can carry on? Oh, I think we're past that, don't you? I think you took that decision the moment you got on that plane. I offered you a life here, Maggie. And you didn't want it.'

'Edward, can we just talk—?'

'There's nothing more to say, Maggie. I've got to go.'

There was a click and eventually a synthetic voice: *The other person has hung up; please try later. The other person has hung up; please try later.*

Maggie expected to cry, but she felt something worse. A heaviness spreading inside her, as if her chest were turning to concrete. She leaned forward, elbows on her knees. It was over. Her attempt at a normal life had failed. And here she was again, in a foreign hotel room, quite alone.

It was all because of what happened last year, she understood that. She had thought her relationship with Edward might slay the ghost, but it had been consumed by it. She raised her head and gazed out of the window at the darkness of Jerusalem, and she stayed like that, staring and frozen, for the best part of an hour.

Then eventually another feeling surfaced, the sense that she had been handed a chance to break free of those dreadful events of a year ago, to balance the ledger somehow. She would have to make this assignment work.

OK, she thought, as she splashed her face with water, forcing herself to make a fresh start. What is the problem? Internal opposition on both sides, prompted by two killings: Guttman and Nour. First priority is to get to the bottom of both cases and somehow reassure both publics that there's nothing to worry about and that the talks should go ahead.

She checked the *Haaretz* web site again and saw the same picture she had seen five hours ago: Ahmed Nour, smiling that enigmatic smile. If they could only resolve his killing, then maybe things could get back on track.

Maggie had done her best with the Palestinian leader this afternoon, urging him to stick with the process. She had assured al-Shafi that if Hamas were going wobbly, there were things the US could do to bring them back on side. She stressed Washington's conviction that a Palestinian state could be theirs within a matter of days. She said he bore a historic responsibility and, not meaning to, had glanced up at the portrait of Arafat as she said it. There was no way of knowing if it had worked.

Now she scrolled down the page and saw that *Haaretz* had posted an extended 'appreciation' of the life of Shimon Guttman. The same details were there as before, but now there were more anecdotes and longer quotations. She was two-thirds down when her eye caught something.

> In the 1967 campaign and afterwards, Guttman combined his military prowess with a scholar's passion for this land's ancient history. He became what polite society refers to as a muscular archaeologist—and what the Palestinians call a looter in a tank. Every hill taken and every hamlet conquered were seen not only as squares on the war planners' chessboard but as sites for excavation. It is said that he amassed a collection of serious importance, a range of pieces dating back several thousand years. All of them had one quality in common: they confirmed the continuous Jewish presence in this land . . .

Maybe this was just a coincidence: Guttman and Nour, both archaeologists, both nationalists, both digging up the Holy Land to prove it belonged to them, to their tribe, both killed within twenty-four hours of one another.

Maggie returned to the Google window and typed in a new combination: Shimon Guttman archaeologist.

The page filled up. A decade-old profile from the *Jerusalem Post*; a Canadian Broadcasting transcript of Guttman interviewed in a West Bank settlement, describing the Palestinians as 'interlopers' and a 'bogus nation'.

Both made frustratingly fleeting reference to what the *Post* called his 'patriotic passion for excavating the Jewish past'.

Next came an article in *Minerva*, the International Review of Ancient Art and Archaeology, announcing the discovery of an unusual prayer bowl traced to the biblical city of Nineveh, written by Guttman and another author. She scoured the text for . . . she didn't know what. It made no sense to her, all the talk of 'embellishments' and 'inlays' and cuneiform script. Perhaps this was a dead end. Maggie glanced over at the minibar, pondering a refill. Then she looked back at the name next to Guttman's: Ehud Ramon. Maybe this man would know something. She Googled him, bringing up only three relevant results, one of them another reference in *Minerva*, all three appearing alongside Shimon Guttman. Of Ehud Ramon on his own, as an independent person in his own right, there was nothing. Who was this man, tied to Guttman yet who left no trace?

And then she saw it. She fumbled for a pen and paper, scribbling letters as fast as she could, just to be sure. Surely this name, apparently belonging to an Israeli scholar, couldn't be . . . And yet, here it was, materialising before her very eyes. An anagram, just like the ones Maggie had unscrambled as a teenager during dreary Sunday afternoons at the convent of her schooldays. Ehud Ramon was a scholar, an archaeologist. But he was the unlikeliest partner for Shimon Guttman, right-wing Zionist zealot and sworn enemy of the Palestinians. For Ehud Ramon was Ahmed Nour.

Baghdad, April 2003

SALAM PULLED his booty out from under the bed. But it looked drab and worthless. He wondered again what had sent him poking around in a dark basement when the dazzling glories of Babylon were there for the taking.

'What's that?' It was his nine-year-old sister, Leila.

Salam doubled over the clay tablet. 'What's what?'

'That thing. On your lap.'

'Oh, this. It's nothing. Just something I got at school today.'

'You said there was no school.'

'There wasn't. But I got this outside—'

Leila was already out of the room, skipping down the corridor to the kitchen: 'Daddy! Daddy! Salam has something he shouldn't have, Salam has something he shouldn't have!'

Salam stared at the ceiling. Now he would take a beating, for a worthless chunk of clay. He held the tablet, stood on a chair and began fiddling with the window. He would chuck the thing away and be done with it.

'Salam!'

He turned round to find his father in the doorway. Salam moved back to the window, working harder now, his fingers trembling. But it was jammed.

Suddenly he felt a hand gripping his wrist, pulling his arm back. The chair beneath him wobbled; he toppled over, landing hard on his backside.

The clay tablet was no longer in his hands. He looked up to see his father calmly pick it up from the bed where it had fallen.

'Dad, it's—'

'Quiet!'

How he wished he had never set foot in that museum. He began to explain: how he had got swept up in the fervour of last night, how he had been carried in there with the mob, how he had stumbled on this tablet, how everyone had taken something, so why shouldn't he?

His father was not listening. He was turning the object over in his hands. He paid close attention to the clay 'envelope' that held the tablet within.

'What is it, Father?'

The man looked up and fixed his son with a glare. Then he walked slowly out of Salam's bedroom, his eyes on the object in his hands. A moment later the boy could hear the muffled voice of his father on the telephone.

Salam perched on the end of his bed, thanking Allah that he had been spared a beating, for now. He stayed like that until, a few minutes later, he heard his father open the apartment door and step out into the night.

Jerusalem, Tuesday, 8.45 p.m.

AMIR TAL GLANCED down at the paper on the table before him.

'Gentlemen, scientists at the Criminal Identification Department have worked twenty-four/seven to see through the blood and tissue fragments and reveal the message that Shimon Guttman wished to convey to the Prime Minister. They warn that the version they have is provisional, contingent on final tests—'

The Defence Minister, Yossi Ben-Ari, cleared his throat and began to fidget with the yarmulke on his head. It was of the crocheted variety, a sign that Ben-Ari was a religious Zionist. He was the leader of a party whose core belief was that Israel should have the largest, most expansive borders possible. Guttman had denounced him as a traitor to their cause just for sitting in Yariv's cabinet, yet Ben-Ari believed he was doing vital patriotic work, preventing Yariv 'selling the Jewish people's birthright for a mess of pottage', as he liked to put it. And, if the Prime Minister went too far, Ben-Ari would simply quit the Cabinet, thereby unravelling Yariv's fragile coalition. That gave him enormous veto power, but if he ever used it Yossi Ben-Ari would be for ever cast as the man who prevented peace.

Tal saw the fidgeting and understood what it meant. He cut to the chase. 'It turns out this was more than a note. It was a letter. Guttman had written on both sides of the paper, in a tiny crabby script, which is why it took the technicians so long to decipher.' He read the letter aloud:

My dear Kobi,

I have been your enemy for longer than I was your comrade in arms, and you have good grounds to distrust me. Perhaps that is why every attempt I have made to contact you has been blocked. Forgive me for resorting to this desperate move tonight. I could not risk giving this letter to one of your staff, so that they could throw it in the trash.

I write because I have seen something that cannot be ignored. If you were to see what I have seen, you would understand. You would be changed profoundly—and so would everything you plan to do.

I have toyed with making this knowledge public, but I believe you have a right to hear it first. Accordingly, I have tried to keep this knowledge a secret—one so powerful it will change the course of history. It will reshape this part of the world and so the world itself.

Kobi, hear what I have to say: I will tell you everything. But I will tell only you. When you have heard it, you will tremble as I have done—as if God himself had spoken to you.

My number is below. Please call me tonight, Kobi—for the sake of our covenant.

Shimon

Tal put the paper down quietly, aware that a new atmosphere had entered the room, one he did not want to disturb by moving too briskly.

'He'd obviously cracked.' This from the Deputy PM, Avram Mossek.

Ben-Ari ignored that remark and nodded in the direction of the text. 'May I see it?' he asked Tal.

His eyes scanned it. 'It doesn't sound like Guttman at all. He was not an especially religious man. A nationalist, of course, but not religious. Yet here he implies that God himself has spoken to him. Maybe Guttman had indeed lost his mind.'

They all looked to the Prime Minister, waiting for his verdict. A one-word dismissal, even a gesture, and the matter would be forgotten. Yaakov Yariv sucked on a sunflower seed, and stared at the copy of the text Tal had handed him. Eventually he leaned forward.

'These are not the words of a madman. They are urgent and passionate, yes. But they are not incoherent. Nor is this a martyr's letter. If it were, he would have spoken clearly about the treachery of giving up territory and so on. He would have wanted a text to rally his troops. This is too'—he paused, sucking a tooth as he tried to find the right word—'enigmatic for that. No, I believe this is what it says it is: a letter from a man desperate to tell me something. The task now is to ensure that no one breathes a word of its contents. Amir will say that the lab tests were inconclusive, that no words can be made out clearly. If so much as a syllable of it leaks out, I will sack both of you and replace you with your bitterest rivals.'

Mossek and Ben-Ari drew back, astounded.

'Meanwhile, Amir, it is clear that Shimon Guttman harboured a secret for which he was prepared to risk his life. Your job is to find out what it was.'

Jerusalem, Tuesday, 10.01 p.m.

SHE WAS MEANT to travel nowhere except with her official driver, but there was no time for that. Besides, something told her this was a visit best paid discreetly, and it was hard to be discreet in an armour-plated Land Cruiser. So now she rattled towards Bet Hakerem in a plain white taxi.

She had moved fast. Once she had unpicked the anagram, everything else seemed to fit into place. She had stared at the photograph of Nour, trying to find whatever had nagged away at her when she first saw it. He was clearly standing indoors, in front of what seemed to be a bookcase. Visible was a complex floral pattern in blue and green. When Maggie zoomed on the image, she could see that this was not wallpaper, as she had first guessed, but a design on a plate, resting on the shelf just behind Nour's shoulder.

Of course. She had seen that pattern before; indeed, she had been struck by its beauty. Just twenty-four hours earlier, when she had made a condolence call at the home of Rachel Guttman, the ceramic plate had stood out. And here was Nour, standing in front of one just like it.

She looked again at the disembodied arm looped over Nour's shoulder.

Was it possible that it belonged to the fierce Israeli hawk,Shimon Guttman? Could the two of them have discovered this pottery together?

She had reached for her cellphone, about to call Davis with her discovery. But she paused. What exactly did she have here? A coincidence that was odd, granted, but hardly clear evidence of anything. It was all too speculative to be worth briefing colleagues about, at least in this form. She would find out what she could, then present her findings to her bosses. All she needed was to ask the Guttman widow a couple of questions.

That decision had been taken no more than half an hour ago. Now, the taxi pulled up on the corner of the Guttmans' street.

'I'll walk from here,' she told the driver.

Maggie passed a handful of activists with candles outside the house. She checked her watch. It was late to visit unannounced, but something told her Rachel Guttman wouldn't be asleep. She pressed the doorbell. No reply.

But the lights were on and she could hear a record playing. A melancholy, haunting melody. She tried the metal knocker on the door, and the door came open a little. It had been left ajar, just like the mourning houses Maggie remembered from Dublin, open to all-comers, day and night.

The hallway was empty, but there was a smell of cooking.

'Hello? Mrs Guttman?'

No reply. Perhaps the old lady had dozed off in her chair. Maggie stepped inside hesitantly, not wanting to barge into this stranger's house. She made for the main room, which last night had been jammed with people. There, on the shelving, between the tall, leather-bound volumes, was the ceramic plate, the pattern identical to the one in the newspaper picture of Ahmed Nour.

She tried again. 'Hello?' But there was still no response.

Confused, Maggie left the room and walked down a corridor, following the warmth and the smell to a door to what she guessed was the kitchen. She pushed at it but it was tightly shut.

'Mrs Guttman? It's Maggie Costello. We met yesterday.'

As she spoke, she turned the handle and opened the door. It took a few seconds for her eyes to adjust to the dark, to make out the shape of a table and chairs at one end, all empty. She looked towards the sink and the kitchen counter. No one there.

Only then did her gaze fall to the floor.

There, cold and lifeless, its hand gnarled around a small, empty bottle of pills, was the corpse of Rachel Guttman.

CHAPTER FOUR

Baghdad, April 2003

He only had a rumour to go on. His brother-in-law had mentioned it at the garage yesterday. He dared not ask him about it now. If he did, he would only demand why he was asking and before long it would get back to his wife and he would never hear the end of it.

No, he would find this out himself. He knew where the café was, near the fruit market in Mutannabi Street. Apparently everyone had been coming here.

Abdel-Aziz al-Askari took a seat near the back, so that he could see who came in and out. He signalled for mint tea and looked around. A few old-timers playing *sheshbesh*; several puffing on the *nargileh* pipe; a group clustered around a TV set watching footage of the statue of Saddam falling, apparently played on a loop. The talk was louder than usual, but there was none of the euphoria he had always imagined this day would bring.

People were holding back, just in case. What if the secret police burst in, announcing that the Americans had been defeated and anyone who had so much as smiled at Saddam's alleged defeat would be hanged? What if the pictures on Al-Arabiya were an elaborate hoax, designed by Uday and Qusay to flush out those who were disloyal to the regime? What, above all, if Saddam had not gone?

Abdel-Aziz sipped his tea and patted Salam's school satchel to be sure his son's discovery was still inside. He had been there a few minutes when a younger man, perhaps in his mid-thirties, came in, all smiles and confidence. He wore a black leather jacket and some kind of bracelet round his wrist.

'Good afternoon, my brothers!' he said, beaming. 'And how is business?'

There were nods in his direction, even a couple of hands proffered for shaking. 'Mahmoud, welcome,' said one man, by way of greeting.

Mahmoud. Abdel-Aziz cleared his throat. This must be him. I should seize the moment, talk to him right away.

But the newcomer had already spotted Abdel-Aziz, catching the look in his eye. 'Welcome, my friend. You are looking for someone?'

'I am looking for Mahmoud.'

'Well, maybe I can help you.' He turned towards the door of the café, pretending to shout. 'Mahmoud! Mahmoud!' Then, turning back: 'Oh, look! I'm right here.' His face disintegrating into an exaggerated laugh.

'I hear that you . . . that people who have—'

'What have they been saying about Mahmoud? Eh?'

'Sorry. Maybe I made a mistake—' Abdel-Aziz got up to leave, but he found Mahmoud's hand on his arm, pushing him down into a seat.

'I can see you're carrying something rather heavy in that bag of yours. Is that something you want to show Mahmoud?'

'My son got it yesterday. From the—'

'From the same place as everyone else. Don't worry. I won't tell. That would be bad for you, bad for me, bad for business.' He dissolved again into the fake laugh. Then the smile died. 'Bad for your son, too.'

Abdel-Aziz wanted to get away; he did not trust this man one bit. He glanced back at the others in the café. Most were still watching the TV.

'So shall we do some business, yes?'

'Is it safe? To show you here?'

Mahmoud shifted Abdel-Aziz's chair round so that they had their backs to the rest of the drinkers, and shielded their small, square table from view.

'Show me.'

Abdel-Aziz unbuckled the satchel, laid it flat on the table and slowly eased the object out. Mahmoud's expression did not change. Instead, he reached over and unsheathed the tablet from its envelope.

'OK,' he said. 'You can put it back now.'

'You're not interested?'

'Normally, Mahmoud wouldn't be interested in such a lump. Clay bricks with a few squiggles on it like this are ten a penny.'

'But—'

'But,' Mahmoud held up a finger, to silence him. 'But it does come in an envelope. And it's only had the odd knock. I'll give you twenty dollars.'

'Twenty?'

'You wanted more?'

'But this is from the National Museum—'

'Uh, uh, uh.' The finger was up again. 'Remember, Mahmoud doesn't want to know too much. You say this has been in your family for many generations and given the, er, recent events, you believe now is the time to sell.'

'But this must be very rare.'

'I'm afraid not. There are a thousand items like this floating around

Baghdad right now. If you want to do business with someone else—' He rose to his feet.

Now it was Abdel-Aziz's turn to extend a restraining hand. 'Please. Maybe twenty-five dollars?'

'I am sorry. Twenty is already too much.' He paused. 'But because you seem a good man, I will do you a favour. I will pay you twenty-two dollars. Mahmoud must be crazy: now he will make no money.'

They shook hands. Mahmoud stood up and asked the café owner for a plastic bag. He slipped the tablet into the bag, then peeled off twenty-two US dollars from a thick, grubby wad and handed them to Abdel-Aziz, who left the café immediately, his son's school bag now light and entirely empty.

Jerusalem, Tuesday, 10.13 p.m.

MAGGIE HAD SEEN plenty of dead bodies before. In the Congo, you would find them in forests, behind bushes, at roadsides, as regular as wild flowers. But never before had she been this close to one so . . . fresh. The fading warmth of the woman's flesh as Maggie touched her back appalled her.

Suddenly she heard the creak of a footstep on the floorboards outside. Maggie froze. The kitchen door swung open. She looked round to see a man's shape filling the doorframe, and the clear outline of a gun.

Slowly she raised her hands in the air, staring at the barrel of the revolver that was now aimed at her.

The gunman's arm made a sudden movement: Maggie braced herself for a bullet. But instead of firing, he reached for the light switch. In a flash, she saw him—and he saw the lifeless woman on the floor.

'*Ima?*'

He fell to his knees and began tugging at the arm, touching the body. Then he let his head sink onto the corpse's back, his shoulders shaking. It was as if every part of his being was crying.

'I found her here no more than three minutes ago, I swear.' Maggie hoped that this man recognised her as quickly as she had recognised him.

He said nothing, just remained hunched over the body of his dead mother. She tiptoed round him, towards the door. His face stayed hidden, his head still trembling in a dry sob over the body of his mother. But his hand was moving, reaching without sight for the revolver he had dropped.

Maggie stood rigid, as his arm lifted in a smooth arc until the gun was aimed straight at her face.

'I came here to tell your mother something. About your father,' she said. 'The front door was open. And then I found her, in there.'

The gun stayed locked onto her as the man holding it stood up. He seemed strangely at odds with the weapon, even though he handled it expertly. He certainly had the build for it: he was tall and muscular. But his eyes were not those of a gunman. They were too curious, as if they were meant to scan the pages of a book rather than lock onto a target.

'Please,' Maggie began, gambling that she had assessed him correctly. 'I came here to help. If I had come here to do harm, do you think I would be just standing here? Wouldn't I have killed you the moment I saw you?'

The gun wavered, the hand now shaking ever so slightly.

'I swear to you, someone else did this. Not me.'

Slowly the arm lowered, and he turned back to the corpse of Rachel Guttman. Maggie sat down and waited. She wanted to make him a cup of sweet tea, or at least fetch a glass of water. But she knew she could suggest no such thing. She had closed her eyes for perhaps five minutes when she heard an almost animal howl of pain. She opened them to see him standing over his mother's body. His face, once so pale, was now flushed red.

'What is it?'

He held out his hand. In it was a single sheet of paper. She stepped forward to take it.

Ani kol kach mitsta'eret sh'ani osah l'chem et zeh.

Hebrew, typewritten. 'I'm afraid I can't—'

'It says, "I am so sorry to do this to all of you."'

'Right.'

'Not right. WRONG!'

Maggie jumped back, shocked by the volume of his voice.

'This is meant to make us think my mother killed herself. She would never, ever do such a thing. Never. Remember how she took hold of you yesterday? She was desperate to do something, to take action. She wanted your help, to finish off whatever it was my father started.'

'A matter of life and death, she said.' As she recalled Rachel Guttman's words, and the way she had gripped her wrist, Maggie felt a twinge of guilt: this woman had tried to enlist her as an ally and she had done nothing.

'Yes. Does someone plead for something to be done and then do'—he gestured down at the body on the ground, unable to look at it—'this?'

'Maybe she had lost hope. Got frustrated that nobody was listening.'

'So she types a note on a computer. My mother, who does not even know how to switch on the TV. And saying sorry to "all" of us, not calling me and my sister by name. Believe me, I know my mother. She did not do this.'

'So who did?'

'Someone very, very wicked—' He stopped himself before he choked. He was standing close now, almost looming over Maggie. He looked scruffier than when she had seen him here yesterday, as if he had spent the intervening twenty-four hours hunched over, bent double with grief, his head cradled in his hands. And that was before this terrible thing had happened.

'Why would anyone want to kill your mother?'

'Remember, she said that my father knew something very important, something that would change everything. Someone must have thought she knew this thing too, and wanted to kill her before she told anyone.'

'But she insisted she didn't know what it was. She said your father wouldn't tell her. For her own safety.'

'I know that. But whoever did this was not so sure.'

'I see.' She looked down at the floor. 'Look, do you think perhaps we ought to call the police, get an ambulance maybe?'

'First, you tell me why you came here.'

'It . . . it seems ridiculous now. Really, you have so much to deal—'

'I don't believe someone working for the American government drives to a private home late at night unless there is a good reason. So you just tell me what business you had with my mother, OK?'

'Perhaps I ought to go, leave you some time to be alone.'

He reached for her arm, yanking her back. 'Tell me what you know. I . . .'

Maggie could see this was not an act of aggression, but one of desperation. For the first time, she saw the eyes of this grieving son glisten.

'If you trust me enough to tell me your name, I'll tell you what I know.'

'My name is Uri.'

'OK, Uri. My name is Maggie. Maggie Costello. Let's sit down and talk.'

Calmly, she led him out of the kitchen and sat him down. She told him what she had discovered. That Ahmed Nour, the Palestinian archaeologist slain earlier that day, had secretly worked with his father.

At first he refused to accept it. No way, he said, with the bitter pretence of a smile. An anagram? It was absurd. But once Maggie had mentioned the unusual but recurring ceramic pattern, Uri fell quiet.

'Look, if I'm right, it means that there may indeed be something going on here. Whatever secret your father was carrying, it seems to bring great harm to those who know it, or who are suspected of knowing it.'

'Then I know who will be the next to die.'

'Who?'

'Me.'

Baghdad–Amman highway, April 2003

MAHMOUD WAS REGRETTING this decision. He should be above this now, he said to himself, as the bus hit the thousandth bump in the road and he was thrown into the air yet again. He could have hired a runner, yet here he was, working as a humble courier himself. Ten hours down, five more to go on the clapped-out old charabanc they laughingly referred to as the Desert Rocket.

For the last couple of weeks he had been working on a different business model, with mobile phones the preferred means of communication. He would sit in the café on Mutannabi Street, waiting for pieces to come his way—and, let Allah be praised, they kept coming—and then pass them on via one of the countless boys who had emerged, like rats from a sewer, the instant Saddam was toppled. These teenage entrepreneurs would run the items across town, then pass them on to another runner, who would take the Desert Rocket to Amman. There the runner would meet al-Naasri or one of his rivals among the big Jordanian dealers. Al-Naasri would work out a price and the courier would take the cash back to Iraq. Thanks to the phone network, the runners knew better than to slice off a cut. If they did, there were no shortages of ditches along the Tigris for them to fall into.

Mahmoud had been doing that profitably for a while. Business had been constant since the statue came down, but there had been some—how should he put it?—*movement* of antiquities out of Iraq since the first war, back in 1991. The route, then as now, was Jordan and the conduit, then as now, was the al-Naasri family. Mahmoud had sent nearly a dozen runners to Amman in the last fortnight, carrying trinkets and pots from the eras of the Assyrians and the Babylonians, the Sumerians, the Persians and the Greeks. But something told him he was due a visit in person. With business expanding as it was, he wanted to be sure that al-Naasri was playing it straight.

So he had filled a holdall with his latest hoard of three or four items, including that clay tablet he had got from the nervous man in the café. As for the pièce de résistance, a pair of gold-leaf earrings that his valuer had estimated to be 4,500 years old, he wasn't about to entrust those to some spotty fourteen-year-old from Saddam City. All the more reason why he was spending fifteen hours on the sputtering bone-trembler that was the Desert Rocket. He knew the earrings were somewhere completely safe.

It was midnight by the time he got off the bus and breathed in the Amman air, inhaling the excitement of a place that wasn't Baghdad.

One of al-Naasri's boys was waiting for him, bored and listless by the railings. He said nothing as he set off for the short walk down King Hussein Street. Before long they were rushing along the cobbled alleys of the *souk*.

Most of the stalls were closed at this time of night. The boy was turning through the market, twisting left and right, so fast now that Mahmoud knew he would never be able to find his way out alone. He reached inside his jacket, under his arm, to check that his dagger was still there, in its holster.

Eventually Mahmoud caught a smell: fresh pitta bread. There must be a night bakery near here. Sure enough, the row after row of empty, unmanned stalls were broken by a cluster of lights just round the next corner. Tinny music was playing on a radio; men were sitting outside, drinking coffee and mint tea. Mahmoud sighed his relief. This felt like home.

He followed the runner inside, to a table where a man was sitting alone. The runner nodded curtly and left, still without saying a word.

Mahmoud did not recognise the man at the table. He was too young, younger than Mahmoud himself. 'I'm sorry, perhaps there has been some mistake. I am looking for Mr al-Naasri.'

'Mahmoud?'

'Yes.'

'I am Nawaf al-Naasri. I am my father's son. Come.'

He led Mahmoud outside, down another alleyway and into what looked like a souvenir shop: big glass windows and fifty-seven varieties of junk.

'Come, come. Some tea?'

Mahmoud nodded as he surveyed the merchandise. Clock faces on polished slices of timber; jars of coloured sand and bottles of water 'Guaranteed from the River Jordan'. It was crap, aimed at the Christian pilgrim market.

'Mahmoud! A pleasure.'

He wheeled round to see a beaming al-Naasri senior. Mahmoud, who had an eye for clothes, could see that the Jordanian was wearing a well-tailored suit. It had only been a matter of weeks since the treasure had started flowing from Baghdad, but already Jaafar al-Naasri had assumed the gloss that came with wealth. Maybe serious money worked its magic fast.

'So, my friend, to what do I owe this pleasure?'

Mahmoud flashed his own smile back. 'Shall we get straight to business?' he said, reaching into the holdall.

He brought out the first of the two seals that a young cousin had brought him within hours of what Mahmoud liked to think of as the museum's grand opening. Al-Naasri took it from him, checking its weight in his hands.

'It's real, I assure you. Mahmoud wouldn't spend fifteen hours getting his arse pounded on that bus for a fake—'

Al-Naasri halted him with an upward glance of the eyes. The expression demanded quiet. He was concentrating. 'OK,' he said finally. 'What else?'

Mahmoud produced the second seal, larger and more ornate. He had the sequence of items all worked out, building to an irresistible climax.

Al-Naasri submitted the seal to the same scrutiny, then said, 'You have done well here, my friend. I am impressed. Do I have the feeling the best is yet to come?' He flashed the teeth once more.

'You do indeed, my friend.' Mahmoud reached into the bag and brought out the clay tablet that had come to him in the café a few days earlier.

Al-Naasri extended his hands to take it from him. He held the envelope in one, and pulled out the tablet with the other. Suddenly he called over his shoulder to his son: 'My glass, please!'

Nawaf brought out a jeweller's eyeglass, which al-Naasri expertly lodged in his left eye. The older man studied the object closely.

'So what do you think?' Mahmoud couldn't help himself.

Al-Naasri leaned back, the glass still wedged in place, so that his left eye was magnified grotesquely. 'I think you have earned the right to see the al-Naasri collection.' He let the glass fall out, catching it in his hand.

Without prompting, Nawaf began to unlock a door behind the shop counter, which opened, Mahmoud presumed, onto a storeroom. All the big dealers worked like this: trinkets sold out front, the real deal hidden behind. Hurriedly, he stashed his hoard back in the bag and got up.

They walked in single file through the storeroom to a second door. It was sturdier and more heavily secured; al-Naasri had to use three keys to unlock it. To Mahmoud's surprise, it opened onto a decent-sized back yard.

'Nawaf, do you have the spade?'

Mahmoud swung round to see the young man holding a metal spade. Instinctively Mahmoud reached for his dagger and whipped it out.

'My dear brother, don't be so ridiculous!' said al-Naasri, laughing. 'Nawaf is not going to hit you. The spade is so he can show you our collection.'

Mahmoud's head was spinning. Sleep-deprived and confused, his eyes adjusted to see that the barren scrap of land was in fact covered with sandy brown earth, like a vegetable patch. And now, apparently unfazed by Mahmoud pulling a blade on him, Nawaf started digging.

'What's going on?'

'Wait and see.'

Al-Naasri and Mahmoud stood watching Nawaf as he dug into the earth in a smooth, easy rhythm. Slowly, out of the ground, a shape began to emerge. Then Nawaf threw aside his spade and crouched, scratching at the soil with his bare hands. In the moonlight, Mahmoud could make out a figure, an animal of some kind. Nawaf beckoned them over.

As he got nearer, Mahmoud saw it clearly. Pulled from the ground was a statue, a ram on its hind legs, its front hooves gripping a slim tree trunk, its horns caught in the tree's ornate flowers. As Nawaf dusted off the soil, and in the light of the night sky, Mahmoud could see the glint of gold. He gasped.

Al-Naasri senior smiled. 'You recognise it, yes?'

Mahmoud nodded, unable to speak.

'It is the Ram in the Thicket, found in the Great Pit of Death at Ur,' al-Naasri went on, enjoying the moment. 'You probably saw it on a school trip to the National Museum when you were a child.'

'You are showing me this so that I will know that what I have brought is worthless. Is that right? You want to humiliate me by this comparison.'

'Not at all, my friend. I am showing you this so that you might know what glories you are to live among.'

Mahmoud smiled with relief. 'Really? You think the pieces I have brought are worthy of being kept here, in the collection?'

'Not just the pieces, Mahmoud. I also plan to keep *you* here.' And, with barely a flick of his hand, he beckoned his son to move, precisely as they had planned. Before Mahmoud could move, the spade was thudding against his skull, knocking him to the ground. He oozed a final breath, but Nawaf pounded him with the head of the tool twice more, just to be sure.

'Strip him and bury him,' Jaafar al-Naasri ordered his son. 'Right away.'

He picked up the holdall, and as he was checking that the seals and clay tablet were still in place, he heard Nawaf laughing loudly. He looked up to see him standing over the fresh corpse, rocking back and forth in mirth.

Al-Naasri walked over to stand beside his son. He could not see the joke at first, until Nawaf pointed at the dead man's chest. There, glinting in the light of the stars, one attached to each of Mahmoud's nipples, were two fine, golden earrings. Mahmoud believed he had hit upon the perfect hiding place: their revelation was to be his grand finale. And so it turned out.

Jerusalem, Wednesday, 9.45 a.m.

SHE MET URI at the Restobar Café. Not that he called it that. 'Meet me at the café that used to be moment,' he had said, in a voicemail message on her mobile phone. She didn't understand it. Was it some kind of riddle?

She asked the hotel concierge, who seemed wholly familiar with the question and instantly gave her directions.

'But what does it mean?'

'That used to be the Moment Café. It was bombed a few years ago. A suicide bombing.' He pronounced both bs. 'So they changed the name.'

'But no one remembers the new name, so they all call it "the café that used to be Moment"?'

'Right.' He smiled.

Uri was already there, at a corner table, hunched over a cup of black coffee. Unshaven, he looked as if he hadn't slept for days.

Maggie took the seat opposite and waited for Uri to make eye contact. Eventually she gave up waiting. 'So when's the funeral?' she asked.

'I don't know. It should have been today. But the police are holding on to my mother's body, even though they say there is nothing to investigate.'

'What do you mean?'

'I mean—' He looked up, meeting her gaze for the first time.

His eyes, so black, were now ringed with red. Even like this, Maggie felt ashamed to notice, he was extraordinarily handsome. She had to force herself to look away.

'I mean they are insisting that it is suicide. I told them, over and over, that it is beyond doubt that my mother did not kill herself. Not my mother. My father maybe. This is the kind of macho stunt he might pull. The big heroic gesture, to get everyone's attention.'

She looked back at him. 'Uri—'

'It's his fault, you know.'

'You don't mean that.'

'No, I do. Always we had to suffer for his crazy beliefs. When we were kids, he was always arrested or he was on the TV or he was screaming at somebody. Do you know what that's like for a kid?'

'But he had principles. That's something to admire, isn't it?'

His eyes sparked with anger. 'Not if they are the wrong principles, no. All this worship of land: every inch must be ours, ours, ours. It's a sickness. And look where it led. He is dead and he has taken my mother with him.'

'Did your father know you felt this way?'

'We argued all the time. He always said that's why I stayed away, in New York. Not because it might actually have been good for my career, because there I had the chance to make movies properly—'

'You make movies?'

'Yeah, documentaries mainly.'

'Go on.'

'My father said I ran away because I couldn't face losing the argument.'

'The argument over—'

'Over everything. Voting for left-wing parties, working in the arts. "You live like some decadent dropout from Tel Aviv!" That's what he would say to me. Tel Aviv. The number one insult.'

Maggie stayed silent, looking away, then back at the man opposite her. 'Look, Uri. I know you're in pain. And I know there is so much to talk about. But we have to find out what's going on here.'

'Why do you care?'

'Because the government I work for doesn't want the whole Middle East peace process going down the pan over these killings, that's why.'

'You know my father would be happy if what you call the "peace process" fell to pieces. He called it the "war process".'

'Yes. But he wouldn't be happy to see his wife dead and maybe his son, too, would he, no matter how much you disagreed?'

'Look, the danger to me doesn't matter. I don't care about it. What I care about is finding the people who did this.'

She exhaled. 'Good. Well you can start by telling me what you know.'

FOR THE SECOND TIME in two days she was back on the West Bank, though now her guide was a man who called it Judea and Samaria, even if the phrase seemed to come wrapped in fairly large quotation marks.

Uri Guttman pointed out of the window. 'Down that road is Hebron, where Abraham, Isaac and Jacob, the three patriarchs, are all buried. And the matriarchs too: Sarah, who was married to Abraham, Rebecca, wife of Isaac, and Leah, second wife of Jacob.'

'I know my Bible, Uri.'

'You are a Christian, no? A Catholic?'

'I was born and raised that way, that's right.'

The guided tour was interrupted only once, when Uri turned on the radio news. The latest word was desperately bleak. Hizbullah had launched a rocket bombardment from Lebanon, breaking their own long-held cease-fire. Israeli civilians in the north were cowering in bomb shelters and Yaakov Yariv was under pressure to hit back. Maggie had discussed this with Davis on the phone that morning: Hizbullah did nothing without the backing of Iran. Which meant that Tehran expected a regional war. And soon.

They had driven around and then above Ramallah towards Psagot, a Jewish settlement perched on a hill looming over the Palestinian city. The road was winding and steep, but eventually they came to a boom gate. Uri slowed down, giving enough time for the guard on duty to emerge from his sentry box, decide that this car was Israeli and hence legitimate, and wave him on.

Once out of the car, Maggie tried to get her bearings. At first glance these Jewish settlements really did look like American suburbs transplanted into the middle of dusty Arabia, but an ugly concrete wall bordered one side of Psagot, shutting out any sight of the city below, and on closer inspection Maggie could see that the housing units were basic.

The central administrative building, into which Uri was leading her now, was drab and surprisingly empty. He explained that everyone was either at demonstrations in Jerusalem or in the human chain.

Eventually, a woman appeared at the front desk. She gave Uri a look of deep sympathy. Word about his mother's death had clearly spread, after an announcement on the radio that morning, and, whatever his personal views, Uri Guttman was the grieving son of settler aristocracy. She gestured for him to come into the office of the man who Uri had explained was the head not just of Psagot but of the settlements council of the entire West Bank.

The second Uri was through the door, Akiva Shapira was on his feet, striding over to welcome the younger man. Big and bearded, he placed his hand on Uri's head and uttered what Maggie took to be a prayer of condolence. '*HaMakom y'nachem oscha b'soch sh'ar aveilei Tzion v'Yerushalayim.*'

'Akiva, this is my friend Maggie Costello. She is from Ireland, but she is here with the American team for the peace talks. She is helping me.'

Maggie offered a hand, but Shapira was already heading back to his desk. Whether he was avoiding a handshake on political grounds, because she was a servant of an administration despised for imposing surrender on Israel, or on religious grounds, because she was a woman, she couldn't tell.

'You're both welcome,' he said, breathing heavily as he squeezed himself back into his seat. The first surprise: a New York accent. 'By rights I should be the one doing the visiting. You have suffered the most profound loss, Uri, and you know you have the wishes of all our people.'

'I need to talk to you about my father.'

'Of course.'

'As you know he was very agitated in the last days of his life, frantic.'

'He was desperate to see Yariv. To tell him what madness he was committing, but this so-called Prime Minister of ours wouldn't see him.'

'Is that what he wanted to say? That the peace talks were "madness"?'

'What else? He thought this was sane, giving up the very heart of our land? Are you serious? He knew it was the act of a people who have lost their collective minds. Give the enemy what he wants, without a fight, and call it peace. It is surrender, no more and no less. Am I wrong, Miss Costello?'

Maggie wished she hadn't come. Uri on his own would have been spared this performance. But he wasn't fazed.

Uri leaned forward, like an interviewer. 'Akiva. What I want to know is what specifically my father had on his mind in the last days of his life.'

'And just for this you came all this way? This you couldn't work out by yourself? Isn't it obvious what Shimon Guttman had on his mind? The self-destruction of the Jewish people. That is what he wanted to prevent.'

Uri raised a palm in request, like a pupil asking a teacher for permission to speak. Maggie could see he was struggling to hide his frustration.

'He told my mother he had seen something specific,' Uri began politely. 'Something that would change everything. Do you know what that was?'

Shapira turned towards Uri and softened his voice. 'Your father could be quite a private man, Uri. If he didn't want to share with you what he had seen, maybe there was a reason for that.'

'What kind of reason? You think he was protecting me?'

'He was a devoted father, Uri.'

'But what about my mother? He tried to protect her too. And look what happened to her.'

'Are you sure he didn't pass on whatever information he had to her, Uri?'

Uri reluctantly shook his head, as if he had been caught out.

Maggie realised that Mrs Guttman might have found something out last night. Maybe she had tried to make a call, and that had alerted her killers.

'You see, my dear Uri, the Almighty has a plan for the Jewish people. He gives us a glimpse of it, here and there, in the texts. Only a glimpse. But he performs miracles. The history of the Jewish people is a story of miracles. We suffer the greatest tragedy in human history: the Holocaust. The Nazis fall in 1945 and only three years later we have a state of our own. After two thousand years of exile, we return to our ancient land, the land God promised to Abraham. I'd call that a bona fide, copper-bottomed miracle.

'Now your government in Washington, Miss Costello, plans on robbing the Jewish people of its birthright, telling us to give up our promised land. And collaborating with you is a man we once trusted, a traitor ready to betray us. Then look! A hero of the Jewish people, Shimon Guttman, intervenes to stay the hand of the traitor and lo, the hero is slain. Now the people of Israel begin to understand. They see the threat that faces them: a government willing to shoot its own citizens. Even to kill the wife of the hero!

'This is the way the Almighty works. He gives us signs, clues if you will. Because he wants us to see what's going on. It's a message to us, Uri. Your parents and the tragedy that has befallen them is a message. It's telling us to say no to this huge American trick. To say no to mass Jewish suicide.'

All of this came at such a speed, and at such loud, full-throated volume, there was no choice but to wait for it to stop. When it appeared he had talked himself out, Maggie leapt in.

'Mr Shapira,' she began. 'It is clear that you suspect the hand of the Israeli authorities in the deaths of Uri's parents, and that you think it was done to silence them. Yet what you have described are the views Shimon Guttman held for many years. Why would the Israeli authorities act this way to suppress an opinion that was already well known?'

'Opinion? Who said anything about opinion? Not me. I've been using the word information. *Information*, Miss Costello. Different thing.'

'What kind of information?'

'Now you're asking too much of me, Miss Costello.'

'Does that mean you won't tell us or you don't know?' Uri asked.

Akiva ignored him. 'Take some advice from someone who's been around this neighbourhood a little longer than forty-eight hours, Miss Costello. What I know, you don't want to know. And, Uri, you don't want to know either.

Believe me, big things are at stake here. The fate of God's chosen people in God's Promised Land. A covenant between us and the Almighty. That's too big for a few jumped-up sleazeball politicians to try to tear up, no matter how important they think they are, whether here or in Washington. You can tell that to your employers, Miss Costello. No one comes between us and the Almighty. No one.'

'Or else?'

'Or else? You're asking "or else"? This is not a question to ask. But look around you. Uri, take my advice. Leave this alone. You have parents to mourn for. You have a funeral to arrange.'

There was a knock on the door. The secretary poked her head round and mouthed something to Shapira. 'Sure. I'll call him back.'

He turned back to Uri. 'Do yourself a favour, Uri. Mourn your mother. *Sit sheva*. And leave this thing alone. No good can come of poking around. Your father's task has been fulfilled. Not the way he intended, maybe. But fulfilled. The people of Israel have been roused.'

Uri had been doing his best, Maggie could see, to disguise his eye-rolling contempt for what he was hearing. Now he leaned forward to speak. 'Do you know anything about Ahmed Nour?'

Maggie leapt in. 'Mr Shapira, you've been very generous with your time. Can I thank you—?'

'What, you're blaming me for the death of that Arab? Is that what they're saying on the leftist radio already? I'm surprised at you, Uri.'

Maggie was on her feet now. 'It's been a very troubling time, as you can imagine. People are saying all kinds of things.' She knew she was babbling, but her eyes were doing the work, desperately trying to say to Akiva Shapira: *He's just lost both his parents. He's gone a little nuts. Ignore him*.

Shapira was now standing up, moving to embrace Uri.

'You can be very proud of your parents, Uri. But now let them rest in peace. Leave this alone.'

Amman, Jordan, ten months earlier

JAAFAR AL-NAASRI was not a man to rush. 'Those that hurry are those that get caught,' he used to say. He had tried explaining that to his sons, but they were too dumb to listen. It pained al-Naasri. Yes, he was a wealthy man now. Thanks to the United States military, the doors to the great treasure house of mankind had been flung wide open. The American soldiers who had placed the Ministry of Oil under round-the-clock armed guard did nothing to protect the National Museum of Antiquities. A single tank came, days too late. Otherwise, it was as exposed and available as a Baghdad whore. And Jaafar and his boys had feasted on her again and again, filling the collection in his back yard with enough delights to start a museum of his own. But al-Naasri could not say he was happy. He did not have sons he could rely on. He could rely only on himself.

Which is why he was stuck here, now, in his workshop, doing a job that was far too sensitive to entrust to anyone else.

The downside of Saddam's fall was that it had led to a tightening of the rules. Governments around the world had turned a blind eye to the trade in stolen Iraqi treasures before 2003, but after seeing the pictures of the Baghdad looting they felt they could no longer be accomplices to this great cultural crime. So the word went out to customs officials and auction houses and museum curators from Paris to Los Angeles: nothing from Iraq.

Which meant Jaafar had to be creative in concealing the products he was sending out. The item on the bench in front of him was a source of particular pride. It was a flat plastic box, divided into two dozen compartments, full of brightly coloured beads, under a clear lid—a jewellery-making set, aimed at young teenage girls. His wife's sister had bought it on a trip to New York. Jaafar had come across it a couple of months ago, quite by accident, and had realised its potential immediately.

Now he reached for a pink bead, threading it onto the string, which already carried a fake ruby, a purple sequin and a brassy miniature poodle. He smiled. It looked like the sort of tacky charm bracelet an adolescent girl might wear, break and never remember again.

Unless she looked too closely at one of the items on the string. It was a simple gold leaf, delicate and finely engraved. Had it been in a museum, resting on a cushion, then you might have guessed that this was an earring buried 4,500 years ago with a princess of Sumeria. On Jaafar's worktable, cheek-by-jowl with trash, it looked like nothing.

Next came the seals, small stone cylinders for rolling onto clay tablets, each embossed with a unique cuneiform signature. He reached down to the big brown carton that had arrived a week ago from Neuchatel, Switzerland. Inside was a bulk load of music boxes in the form of painted wooden chalets. Lift the roof and a slow, tinny melody would begin, picked out by the shiny metal mechanism within.

It had taken him months to source a music box with these exact specifications. Now he prised out the mechanism with his screwdriver, and saw that the central rotating drum, punctuated with tiny spears that caught a hammer to produce the melody, was hollow, as he had been assured. He looked again at the hoard of seals he had amassed, lined up before him like soldiers awaiting inspection. He felt confident that this would work.

He glanced over at the tea chest by a big roll of bubble wrap. Inside it were the several hundred clay tablets he had accumulated since April 2003. He had a plan for those, too. Not fiddly, but time-consuming.

All being well, he would have this lot boxed up, labelled as handicrafts and on its way to London by the spring. There was no need to rush. In the business of antiquities, time was never your enemy, only your friend. The longer you waited, the richer you became. And the world had waited 4,500 years for these beauties.

Jerusalem, Wednesday, 1.23 p.m.

THE DRIVE BACK from Psagot was tense. Maggie administered a bollocking to Uri before the engine had even started. 'Mentioning Ahmed Nour, what on earth was that for?'

'I thought he might have something to tell us.'

'Yeah, like, "Piss off before I kill both of you, too."'

'You think Akiva Shapira killed my parents? Are you out of your mind?'

Though she knew Uri was still in the initial shock of a double bereavement, Maggie was fed up with treading on eggshells. 'Tell me. Why is that so crazy?'

'You saw the guy. He's a fanatic, like my dad. These guys loved each other.'

'OK, so not him. Then, who?'

'Who what?'

'Who killed your parents? Go on. Who do you suspect?'

Uri took his eye off the road and looked at Maggie, as if in disbelief. 'You know, I'm not used to working like this.'

'Like what?'

'With another person. When I make a movie, I do everything myself. Interviewing, shooting, cutting. I'm not used to having some Irish girl next to me, chipping in.'

'I'm not "some Irish girl", thank you very much. That kind of sexist crap may play in Israel, but not with me. OK?'

Uri shot a glance back at Maggie. 'OK, OK.'

'As it happens, I'm not used to it either. When I'm "in the room", working, I'm on my own. Just me and the two sides. It works better that way.'

'How come you're so good at it?'

She guessed he was trying to make amends for 'some Irish girl'.

'At mediation, you mean?'

'Yes.'

She was about to tell the truth, to explain that it had been a while since she had engaged in an international negotiation, but decided not to.

'I got it from home, I suppose.'

'Don't tell me. Your mum and dad used to fight all the time and you became the peacemaker?'

'No, don't be soft.' Though she had to admit that the broken home appeared in the personal histories of dozens of mediators. 'The opposite. My parents were rock solid. Best marriage on the street. Not that that was saying much. Everyone else was rowing and fighting, husbands getting in drunk, mothers having it off with the milkman, all sorts. They used to come to my mother for advice. Couples would appear in our front room, asking my mother to arbitrate between them. "Let's see what Mrs Costello has to say." I watched what she did and I suppose I picked it up.'

Maggie couldn't remember the last time anyone had asked, 'How come you're a mediator?' She had enjoyed the chance to answer. And it struck her then that Edward had never once asked that question.

While they sped towards Jerusalem, she tried to focus on the meeting they had just had. Shapira seemed pretty clear: Guttman had told him what he had found—*You don't want to know what I know*—and, Shapira believed, the Israeli government had killed him for it. But Shapira was a big, puffed-up blowhard. It was possible he knew nothing, and simply wanted to make the Guttmans look like martyrs to the cause.

She was too lost in thought, and Uri the same, to look closely in the rear-view mirror and notice what was behind them: a white Subaru that kept three cars back. And never let them out of its sight.

THEY WERE BACK in the home of Shimon and Rachel Guttman. The doormat was piled high with notes and cards: well-wishers from abroad, no doubt. Everyone else would be at Uri's sister's house now, where the *shiva* for his father would continue and where the *shiva* for his mother would begin, once she had been buried. Maggie worried that Uri was absenting himself from a process he needed.

'In here.' He switched on a light.

The room they went into was, thankfully, at the opposite end of the house from the kitchen where she had discovered Rachel Guttman's body the previous night. It was small, cramped and lined with books, with piles of paper on every available surface. On a simple desk sat a computer, a telephone and a fax machine, with a jumble of gadgetry, including a video camera, pushed to one side. Maggie checked the camera: no tape inside.

'Where on earth do we start?'

Uri looked at her. 'Well, why don't you quickly learn Hebrew? Then it will only take us a few months.'

Maggie smiled. It was the closest thing to laughter they had yet shared.

'Maybe if you look at the computer. A lot of that was in English. I'll start on these piles.'

Maggie settled herself into the seat and pressed the power button. 'Hey, Uri. Can you give me the cellphone?'

He pulled out the transparent plastic bag he had collected from the hospital on their way back from Psagot. Inside it were the things his father had had with him when he was killed. He passed her the phone. She switched it on, then selected the message inbox. *Empty*. Then the SENT box. *Empty*.

'And you're sure your father used to send text messages?'

'I told you already. We used to text each other all the time.'

'So this phone has definitely been wiped?'

'I think so.'

'Then his email is likely to have gone too. But let's look.' She went straight for the email account. A box appeared, demanding a password.

'Uri?'

He was wading through a bundle of papers. 'Try Vladimir.'

'Vladimir?'

'As in Jabotinsky. The founder of Revisionist Zionism. My dad's hero.'

She keyed in the letters. Without fanfare, the screen filled up with email.

Uri smiled. 'He used to write love letters to my mother under that name.'

Maggie scrolled down, looking at the unopened messages. They had kept coming, even now, since his death. Bulletins from the *Jerusalem Post*; a soldiers' relief fund; circulars from Arutz Sheva, the settlers' radio station. Among those that had arrived before his death were some personal ones: a request to speak at a demo next Wednesday—that was today; an enquiry from German TV; a request for him to participate on a BBC radio panel. She hoped for a message that might explain the fevered words of Rachel Guttman in this very house just two days earlier. She checked the SENT box, but nothing in there stood out, and there was certainly no communication with Ahmed Nour or Ehud Ramon.

Maybe her assumption was right. Whoever had killed Rachel Guttman had stopped in here and deleted any emails of significance. She looked in the recycle bin, just on the offchance. Nothing in there since Saturday, the day of Guttman's death. Which meant that either someone had hacked into this computer and was skilled enough to cover their traces—or the dead man simply avoided using email for any communication that mattered.

'Are you certain your father used email? I mean properly.'

'Are you kidding? All the time. Like I said, for a man his age, he is very modern. He even plays computer games, my father. Besides, he is a campaigner. They live on the Internet, these people.'

That gave her an idea. Clicking the email away, she looked instead for the browser. She opened it up and went straight to the favourites. A couple of Hebrew newspapers; the BBC; the *New York Times*; eBay; the British Museum; Fox News. *Damn*. Her hunch had been wrong. She shut down the browser and looked hard at the icons on the desktop. A few Word documents, which she opened. Nothing. Whatever it was Guttman had wanted to say to Yariv, he had not left it lying around here.

Then, at the bottom of the screen, an icon she had on her own machine but had never used. She clicked on it and saw it was another Internet browser, just not a very famous one. She looked for the favourites, here called 'bookmarks', and there was only one: gmail.com.

It was what she had been hoping for. A separate email account, separate from his main one, effectively hidden away. Here, she had no doubt, was where Guttman's serious correspondence would be kept.

A box appeared, asking for a name and a password. She typed in Shimon Guttman, with Vladimir as the password, and waited. No luck. She tried Shimon on its own. Nothing. She tried Jabotinsky as the password, and what seemed like three dozen other permutations. No luck. Then it hit her. Without pausing, she pulled out her cellphone and punched at the numbers.

'The office of Khalil al-Shafi, please.'

Uri reared back when he heard the Fatah man's name. 'What the hell—?'

'Mr al-Shafi. This is Maggie Costello from the State Department. Do you remember you told me that Ahmed Nour had received some mysterious emails prior to his death, requesting a meeting? . . . That's right. From an Arab name his family did not recognise. I need you to tell me that name. It will go no further than me, I assure you.'

She checked the spelling back twice, knowing there was no room for error. She thanked the Palestinian negotiator and hung up.

'Do you speak any Arabic, Uri?'

'A little.'

'OK. What does *nas tayib* mean?'

'That's very simple. It means a good man.'

'Or, if we were to translate it into German, a *Gutt man, nein*?'

CHAPTER FIVE

London, six months earlier

Henry Blyth-Pullen tapped the steering wheel along to the *Archers* theme tune. He was, he decided, a man of simple tastes. He might have spent his working life surrounded by sumptuous antiques and precious artefacts, but his needs were modest. Just this—an afternoon drive through the spring sunshine—was enough to cheer his spirits.

He always enjoyed driving. Even this forty-five-minute run from the showroom in Bond Street to the cargo terminal at Heathrow Airport was a pleasure. He pulled into the car park, finding a space easily, and stayed to listen to the end of the episode. Then he got out, shot an admiring glance at his vintage Jaguar, and headed for the reception area.

'Hello again, sir,' said the guard the instant Henry walked into the Ascentis building. 'We can't keep you away, can we?'

'Oh, come on, Tony. Third time this month, that's all.'

'Business must be good.'

'In truth,' he said, mimicking a courtly bow, 'I cannot complain.'

At the window, he filled in the air waybill. On the line marked 'goods' he wrote 'handicrafts'. For 'country of origin', he wrote 'Jordan', which was not only true but suitably unremarkable. Imports from Jordan were entirely legal. He wrote down the string of digits Jaafar al-Naasri had given him over the phone, signed his name as an approved handling agent and slipped the form back under the glass.

'All right, Mr Blyth-Pullen, I'll be back in a tick,' said Tony.

Henry took his usual seat in the waiting area and began leafing through a copy of yesterday's *Evening Standard*. If he looked relaxed, it was because he felt relaxed. Sure, Customs would look at the forms, but he couldn't think of the last time they had asked to open anything up, let alone a crate that had been vouched for by a recognised, and highly respectable, agent like him. The truth was, they were not really bothered with the art trade. Trafficking, whether in drugs or people, that was their game.

Sure enough, Tony soon emerged with a set of papers and his usual smile: Customs must have nodded the forms through. Henry Blyth-Pullen paid the release fee, and he was shortly putting a single brown box into the boot of the Jag. One more signature, to confirm receipt, and the shipment was officially signed, sealed, delivered—and 100 per cent legitimate.

When he came to lever open the top of the crate in the back room of his Bond Street showroom, he felt the same pulse of pleasure he experienced whenever a truly special consignment arrived. Al-Naasri had told him to expect tourist souvenirs. Henry had been intrigued, assuming this was code for items brought to Jordan from somewhere else. But as he peeled off the first layers of polystyrene foam and bubble wrap, he felt uneasy. He saw a set of six music boxes, each in the form of a Swiss chalet in lurid colours. He lifted the lid of the first one, and it played a tune. '*Edelweiss*.'

Below them were horrible, shoddy glass frames an inch thick containing patterns of coloured powder, complete with a transparently fake sticker announcing each one as 'Genuin Sand from Jordan River'. Finally, encased in bubble wrap, were a dozen nasty charm bracelets. Of all the shipments he had received in his eighteen years in the business, this was easily the most disappointing.

Falling into a chair, he reached for the phone. He would get this sorted. Jaafar al-Naasri had never let him down before. He dialled and waited for the long drone of an international ring.

'Jaafar! Thanks for this latest arrival. It's—how shall I say—*surprising*.'

'Do you like the song?'

'On the music boxes? Yes, er, yes. Most . . . tuneful.'

'Ah, that is because of the workmanship, Henry. Look inside the cylinder drum; you can see a technique there that is very old. Ancient even.'

'I understand.' Listening to Jaafar, with the phone cradled to his ear, Henry moved back to the crate and picked out a music box. He wrenched the wooden roof off its hinges to get a closer look at the mechanism. Too impatient to find his tool box, he grabbed a kitchen knife and levered out the box's innards. There, inside, was a perfect example of a cylinder seal.

'Oh, I now see what you mean about these music boxes, Jaafar. The mechanisms are exquisite! They could only have come from the very birthplace of the, er . . . music box. The place where it all began!'

'And what about the sand displays?'

'Well, their immediate appeal is a little less obvious.'

'You know, of course, that every grain of sand was once a much larger stone. Look hard and you can see the rocks and stones of the past.'

Henry picked up the first display and smashed it against the desk, sending sand all over the carpet. He peered out through the doorway, hoping no one had heard the sound of breaking glass.

There, filling the palm of his hand, was a clay tablet. Etched on it was line after line of cuneiform writing. It was covered in sticky sand now, like party glitter, but it brushed off easily.

'Oh, and my dear Jaafar, these sands from the River Jordan are perfect. And I see you have sent me at least—'

'Twenty, Henry. Exactly twenty. And the bracelets are especially charming, don't you think? Do they not perhaps remind you of the leaves on the trees in springtime?'

Five minutes later, as Henry put the phone down, he marvelled at the ingenuity of it. Jaafar had surpassed himself. He had seen the opportunity of 2003, bided his time and then come up with a flawless disguise.

Now his task was to give Jaafar's hoard a patina of legitimacy. Governments had got heavy on the trade in stolen Iraqi antiquities since Saddam's downfall and no one would buy any of these treasures if they lacked 'provenance'. It was too risky: they could be seized and repatriated to Iraq, with meagre compensation.

The next day, Henry Blyth-Pullen called up an old academic acquaintance, Paul Cree. Henry suggested they operate in the usual way. Cree would take a look at the items, then submit an article for one of the journals, perhaps *Minerva* or the *Burlington Magazine*, which specialised in publicising new finds. Once they had been written about in a respectable outlet, they would be on a fast track to legitimacy; future buyers could check the *Burlington Magazine* and see that Henry was not flogging any old rubbish but rather works that had featured in a prestigious journal. Cree would be compensated handsomely for his time and expertise.

But Cree would not do business. 'I'm sorry, Henry, dear boy, but the mags have all clammed up. Tighter than a nun's whatchamacallit these days. They won't feature just anything. Not any more.'

'But, Paul, this is not just anything.'

'I know old boy, I know. But the *journeaux* worry when things might have . . . fallen off the back of a Baghdad lorry.'

'What am I supposed to do?'

'I'm sorry, Henry. But you'll just have to find another way.'

Henry was beginning to feel anxious. He knew these had to be items of serious value, or Jaafar would not have taken such care to disguise them.

He called Lucinda at Sotheby's, a move that smacked of desperation.

'Hello, darling,' she drawled, audibly exhaling cigarette smoke. 'What do you want this time?'

'Lucinda! What makes you think I want anything?'

'Because you never, ever ring me unless you want something.'

'That's not true,' Henry said, even though it was. Apart from one highly regrettable snog when tumbling out of the Christie's Christmas party, their relationship had only ever been about what Henry could get out of her. 'On the contrary, I have something of an opportunity.'

He went to see her that same afternoon, Lucinda being easily enticed by the promise of a gin and tonic afterwards.

'So what are these delights you have to show me, Henry?'

He produced a small jewellery box and popped it open, revealing a pair of fine gold earrings, each one consisting of a single leaf. Extracting them from the charm bracelets had taken a delicate touch, but it had not been too difficult. Luckily he had found a clear colour picture of them in a reference book. 'Photo reproduced by kind permission of the National Museum of Antiquities, Baghdad,' the caption had said.

'Good God, Henry. Those are . . . those are . . .'

'Four thousand five hundred years old.'

'Magnificent was what I was going to say. Four thousand five hundred years old? Incredible.'

'You know what I want you to do, don't you?'

'I can guess. You want me to sell them so that you can buy them off me. And that way they're kosher. "Purchased under auction at Sotheby's."'

'Lucinda, that's what I love about you. So quick.'

'Except you don't love me, Henry. Anyway, it's impossible.'

'Why?'

'Well, if we were actually allowed to sell pieces from . . . *you-know-where*, and there weren't half a dozen conventions banning it, these would go for an absolute bloody fortune. Far out of your reach. We'd have to lie about what they were. And that would defeat the object rather, wouldn't it?'

Henry stared into the puddle of gin at the bottom of his glass. 'Well, what the hell am I going to do? I have to sell these things somehow.'

'I'd sit tight, darling. Eventually this stuff will be in major demand. It's too good to go to waste. But now is not the time.'

When Henry spoke to Jaafar al-Naasri that evening, it was only after he had fortified himself with two more stiff drinks. He managed to spit out his basic message: Jaafar would have to be patient and he would have to trust him. Henry would hold back on the prestige, high-value items, which he could continue to keep in the showroom safe until the market was more propitious. 'You'll get the same story all over the world, Jaafar,' Henry told him when the Jordanian threatened to take his custom to a New York dealer. 'The Americans are even more uptight on all this than we are.'

Besides, it was not all gloom and doom. For the less glamorous items, Henry had a plan, a way to realise some value sooner rather than later. No, it would not be wise to go into details over the phone. But Henry knew exactly where those clay tablets would be going. He would take them there himself.

Jerusalem, Wednesday, 3.14 p.m.

'THEY'RE LIKE VULTURES.' Uri was standing at the window, pulling back the curtain just enough to see the street outside. 'Look at them, Channel 2 outside in their satellite TV truck. It's not enough the media all had to come here to show the world the death of my parents. They have to stay.'

'Hmm.' Her eyes fixed on Shimon Guttman's computer, Maggie was trying out her hunch on the gmail account. She logged in as Saeb Nastayib, the name of the man who had sent those mysterious last emails to Ahmed Nour—and, as it happens, a rough translation of Shimon Guttman. For the password, she tried Vladimir again. And got the message *Login failed*.

Damn. Maggie pushed the swivel chair away from the desk.

'We need to crack this password thing, Uri. The prompt seems to demand ten characters: Vladimir is only eight.'

'He always did Vladimir, on everything.'

'So we need two more characters. Is there any two-digit number that might be significant?'

Uri came over to the desk, standing by her side. He bent down, to get a closer look at the screen. She could see the stubble on his cheek.

'Try sixty-seven.' The year of the Six-Day War.

She typed in Vladimir67 and suddenly the screen altered, and a new page began loading: the email inbox of Saeb Nastayib.

At the top of the page, still in bold and therefore unread, was a name that gave Maggie a start: Ahmed Nour. The email was sent at 11.25 p.m. on Tuesday, a good twelve hours after he was reported dead. She clicked it open.

Who are you? And why were you contacting my father?

'It seems Mr Nour Junior knew as little about his father as you did about yours. Uri, do you mind if we look at the messages your father sent?'

He shook his head and she brought up the sent messages, all of which were to Ahmed Nour. The last one was sent at 6.08 p.m. on Saturday, just a few hours before the peace rally at which Guttman was shot dead.

Ahmed, we have the most urgent matter to discuss. I have tried your telephone but without success. Are you able to meet me in Geneva?
Saeb

Maggie scrolled down to the earlier messages and found several sent that day and the previous evening, all mentioning an upcoming trip to Geneva. As far as Maggie could see, Ahmed Nour had not replied to any of them. Had they fallen out? Was Ahmed blanking his Israeli colleague?

Uri had left the piles of papers and pulled up a second chair. He looked at the screen, clearly as baffled as she was. Predicting her question, he turned to her, shaking his head. 'I didn't even know my father had been to Geneva.'

'It seems there was quite a bit about him you didn't know. Did he keep any kind of diary? You know, like a desk planner.'

Uri began rummaging, while Maggie went back to the computer. She called up the browser's history, and as she scrolled through the cache of web pages Guttman had consulted in the last days of his life, she suddenly realised that she had made a stupid oversight.

'Uri, pass me the cellphone again.'

She had looked at the text messages, all of which had doubtless been wiped, but had not checked the call register, the record of outgoing calls. She grabbed the phone and stabbed at the keys until she pulled up the dialled numbers. There, at the top, was a call made on Saturday afternoon. It showed up on the display not as a number, but a name.

'Uri, who's Baruch Kishon?'

'At last, something that is not a mystery. He is a very famous journalist in Israel. The settlers love him; he has been denouncing Yariv every week for a year. He and my father were great friends.'

'Well, I think we ought to pay Mr Kishon a visit. Right now.'

Jerusalem, Wednesday, 3.10 p.m.

AMIR TAL was working hard to conceal his amazement, even his excitement. He had dealt with intelligence often; since taking this job in the Prime Minister's bureau, it was hard to avoid it. But he had never seen how it was done, how the raw information was gathered.

'Can I listen?' he asked, gesturing at the woman who sat at the centre of the multiple computer screens, with what looked like a DJ's mixing desk before her. She took off her headphones and gave them to Tal.

'The man's voice you hear is Uri Guttman, son of the deceased,' she said. 'The woman's voice is the American, Maggie Costello.'

'Irish,' Tal murmured, mainly to himself.

The voices were remarkably clear. Costello was asking Guttman for his father's cellphone. He could even hear papers rustling.

'And you can do all this from that TV satellite truck parked outside?'

'With directional microphones aimed at the windows—through the glass—you can do a lot. Better if you have something on the inside, too.' The woman gave Tal a crooked smile.

'You have something in there? How?'

'Well, there have been a lot of flowers arriving in that house, and food parcels, too. Let's just say one of the bouquets does more than look nice.'

Amir took off the headphones, and put his hand on the shoulder of the woman. *Keep up the good work.*

There was no point listening any further. Another operative was monitoring closely. Anything of substance, he would report it immediately.

'Amir, you might want to see this.' It was the man who had remained glued to a computer screen since they had got here, at least as far as Tal could tell. He had wondered what this man was up to, but hadn't dared ask.

Now what he saw disappointed him. It was a standard webmail page, an inbox no different from the one he used for his correspondence at home.

And then he saw it. The cursor moving around the screen without any apparent human intervention; the operator's hands remained still.

'What is this?'

'You're looking at Shimon Guttman's computer, the one his son and that woman are working on right now. We've got this neat little program that installs itself on someone else's machine and gains the kind of system-level privileges we need.' He could see that the penny hadn't dropped. 'It gives us total access to their computer. Anything they type, I see it. Right now, for example, they're trying to hack into his gmail account.'

The woman with the headphones called out: 'OK, we have a phone call. Costello's just dialled Khalil al-Shafi in Ramallah.'

Tal headed over, waiting to be passed a set of headphones. But the woman was concentrating too hard, listening to each word, to help the boss. By the time she had connected him, the phone call was over. Instead he heard Maggie Costello speaking to Uri Guttman.

'*OK. What does* nas tayib *mean?*'

A moment later and it was the computer operator who was getting excited. 'Hey, this is *interesting*,' he said.

'What are they doing?'

'Watch that window right there. They're logging on as that name we just heard. Saeb Nastayib. Now they're trying different passwords.'

'OK, let me know when you have something useful.'

Amir Tal didn't have long to wait. Within ten minutes the surveillance team parked in a Channel 2 truck outside the Guttman residence reported that Costello and Guttman Junior had left the house, apparently heading for the home of journalist Baruch Kishon. Meanwhile, computer analysis suggested a correspondence between the late Shimon Guttman and the late Ahmed Nour, the former using an Arab code name, combined with the password of Vladimir67. They were arranging to meet in Geneva.

'OK, gather round, people,' Tal began, enjoying taking command. 'I want whatever intel we can get on Nour: who was he, why did he die and what the hell was he talking about with Shimon Guttman? Talk to Mossad in Geneva. Find out whether they'd met before. Also Khalil al-Shafi. What's he been saying to Costello? Why did she call him? And what's his precise connection to Ahmed Nour? We need answers on this right away.

'I hope the most crucial thing goes without saying. We keep following Costello and Guttman. And we get to Baruch Kishon before they do. Go!'

Northern Israel, Wednesday, 8.15 p.m.

THEIR ORDERS were clear. Get in, search and destroy, get out. Above all, don't get caught. This was not to be a suicide mission.

There were four men in the rented Subaru. They had driven off the dirt track and concealed the car in a cotton field. The men changed into black clothing and had balaclavas to put over their faces. Each had a small torch in his pocket, a lighter, a knife and a Micro Uzi submachine gun. Two had cyclists' water pouches strapped to their backs, containing petrol.

They walked through the fields for twenty minutes until they could see the lights of the perimeter. Soon the crops gave way to the asphalt of the visitors' car park and service roads. They saw the sign in English and Hebrew, welcoming guests to KIBBUTZ HEPHZIBA, HOME OF THE LEGENDARY BET ALPHA SYNAGOGUE. One at a time, the four men ran in a low crouch towards the site entrance. The locked door was jimmied open and they slipped inside, into complete darkness.

They waited till they were deep within before switching on their torches, then shone them down onto the floor. It was an ancient mosaic, over 1,500 years old but perfectly intact, the colours of the countless tiny squares still vivid. The floor was divided into three distinct panels. Furthest away, what seemed to be a sketch of a synagogue. At the bottom, a primitive depiction of Abraham's sacrifice of his son Isaac. The larger, middle panel showed a circle, divided into twelve segments, one for each sign of the zodiac.

The four men knew what they had to do. Quickly, they got to work.

Ben-Gurion Airport, five weeks earlier

HENRY BLYTH-PULLEN hated flying at the best of times, even before the war on bloody terror, and the fear that some maniac with a pair of scissors was going to ram the plane into Big Ben. This time, though, Henry's anxiety had begun to build long before he got anywhere near the runway. Inside his luggage was a consignment of clay tablets, which he had decided to offload 3,000 miles away from London. They would not make his fortune, but they would at least make his monthly bank balance look a little bonnier. Besides, he needed to tell Jaafar al-Naasri he had at least sold something. The fact that he was taking the goods back to Jaafar's very own patch, or near as dammit, was a detail he would not share with anyone. It smacked so much of selling sand to the Sahara that he was embarrassed by it.

How to get them there, that was the issue. Jaafar had gone to great lengths to get them out; Henry couldn't just waltz them back in.

As it happens, it was lovable old Lucinda who hit on the answer. Not consciously, of course. No, she was burbling on about some ex-pat friends of hers who'd set up home in Barbados or somewhere, how the one thing they missed was the chocolate. 'Apparently the choccy there doesn't taste of anything,' Lucinda had said, flush with her third G&T. 'Now every time a friend comes over from Blighty, they're under strict orders to bring a *case-load* of proper choccy. Sophie says they've both put on at least a stone . . .'

That was it, Henry had realised before Lucinda even finished speaking. On his way home he had stopped at a garage and picked up one of almost every chocolate bar on the market. The next day he had sat in the back office at the showroom, trying to find a match for length, width, thickness and weight. Finally, he struck gold with a mid-size bar of Cadbury's Whole Nut.

He removed the paper sleeve carefully, then unfolded the inner foil as if handling the most precious gold leaf. He removed the chocolate bar, putting the clay tablet in its place. Then, to both the head and foot of the bar, he glued two rows of Whole Nut. Finally he refolded the foil and sheathed the whole hybrid chocolate-and-clay bar back in its paper wrapper. Soon he had twenty perfect specimens packed neatly in his small carry-on suitcase.

The security check at Heathrow was his first worry. Airport staff were more vigilant these days about previously ignored food items. But, Henry told himself, if he was stopped he would keep calm and stick to his story.

He placed the bag on the conveyer belt and walked through the metal detector, as nonchalantly as he could manage. As he reached for the bag, just off the belt, a hand stopped his.

'One moment, please, sir. Can you open the bag for me?'

'Yes, of course.' Henry smiled and unzipped the case.

'Computers must go in separately, sir. Please will you do it again?'

Henry could feel his hands go clammy. What were the chances that the twenty chocolate bars could evade discovery *twice*?

And yet, as the bag went through a second time, the man charged with examining the X-ray monitor turned away to share a joke with his colleague.

He stayed away from the screen for three or four seconds, just as the clay tablets, now bereft of the computer that had shielded them the first time around, lay exposed and in full view. Henry went on his way.

While his fellow passengers watched the in-flight film, Henry replayed that scene in his head, thanking God for his luck. But as the plane began its descent for Tel Aviv, relief gave way to more anxiety.

He had no luggage to collect, so he headed straight for immigration.

'And why you are in Israel?' the young woman asked him.

'I'm visiting my nephew, who's studying here.'

'And where is he studying?'

'At the Hebrew University. In Jerusalem.' Henry had a couple of Jewish friends whom he'd called up last week; he had asked casually after their sons, both of whom were on gap years, and promptly taken down and memorised all the details.

Only one more stop: Customs. As a white middle-aged man, the sorry truth was that he had always passed through Customs like a breeze. But for the first time ever, he was stopped. A bored, unshaven officer waved him over to one side and nodded wordlessly at Henry's suitcase. Henry pulled it up onto the metal counter between them and unzipped it.

The guard rifled through the Y-fronts, socks, toilet bag, before coming to the stash of chocolate. He looked up at Henry, raising a sceptical eyebrow.

'And what is this?'

'It's chocolate.'

'Why you bring so much?'

'It's for my nephew. He misses home.'

'Can I open it?'

'Sure. Why don't I help?'

Henry picked a bar at random, pushed up the chocolate an inch and tore off the foil to reveal a solid three squares of English milk chocolate. Without pausing, he broke off the squares and offered them to the Customs official. The man refused, then nodded his head towards the exit. Henry's examination was over. Which was lucky, because if the guard had looked closely he would have seen that the next row of the bar he had tested was strangely lacking in nuts and unappetisingly solid.

Clutching the handle of his suitcase more tightly than ever, Henry left the airport and joined the queue for a taxi. When it came to his turn, he said loudly, pumped up with relief, 'Jerusalem, please. To the Old City market.'

Tel Aviv, Israel, Wednesday, 8.45 p.m.

FOR A SMALL COUNTRY, Maggie decided, Israel wasn't half confusing. They had been driving less than an hour and yet she felt as if she had travelled through time. If Jerusalem was a town carved in the pale stone of biblical times, each narrow cobbled path coated in the stale must of ancient history, Tel Aviv was noisily, brashly, chokingly modern. On the horizon were gleaming skyscrapers, and by the roadside line after line of concrete apartment blocks, their roofs covered with solar panels and bulbous hot-water tanks. They pulled off the highway and into the city streets, home to a frenzy of billboards and shoppers, burger bars and pavement cafés.

'OK, this is his building,' Uri said. 'Let's park here.'

They were on Mapu Street, which, judging by the class of cars parked at the kerb, seemed to be one of Tel Aviv's more upscale neighbourhoods. They found the entrance and its intercom. Uri pressed number seventy-two.

There was no reply. Impatient, Maggie reached past Uri and pressed the button again, for much longer. Still nothing.

'Try the phone again.'

'It's been on voicemail all afternoon.'

'We could break in.'

'No, we can't. Imagine if I got caught—a government official. Is there any other way?'

Uri shook his head and punched his fist against the door of the building.

Maggie strained to think of a next move. Then, suddenly, Uri spun round.

'Uri? Uri, what is it?'

He was sprinting back towards the car. 'Just get in,' he shouted.

As they drove, Uri explained that in the army he had dated a girl whose brother had gone to India with Baruch Kishon's son. When he saw Maggie's face, a scrunch of incredulity, he smiled. 'Israel's a small country.'

A few calls later and he had a cellphone number for Eyal Kishon. Uri had to shout into the phone: Eyal was in a club. Uri tried explaining the situation, but it was no good. They would have to go there.

While they drove, Uri put on the radio news, giving a brief translation at the end of each story. Violence on the West Bank, some Palestinian children dead; Israeli tanks re-entering Gaza; more Hizbullah rockets in the north. Talks with the Palestinians now in the deepfreeze. Maggie shook her head: this whole thing was unravelling. Last item: 'They're getting reports of a fire at a kibbutz in the north. Might be arson.'

They parked on Yad Harutzim Street and walked straight into the Blondie club. The noise was immediate, a pounding rhythm that Maggie could feel in her guts. There was a steady bombardment of light, including one sharp, white beam that swept across the dance floor like a searchlight.

The place was hardly full, but already there seemed to be lithe, sweaty bodies in every corner. Maggie was struck by the range of faces. In front of her were two girls, blonde with porcelain skin, while just behind was a tall black man with an Afro and thin, sharp features. Dancing alongside were a man and woman, each with dark, corkscrew curls. All of them were gorgeous and skimpily dressed. In her elegant black trouser suit and Agnès B shirt, Maggie felt old and dull.

'He's over there.'

Uri gestured towards a man who was sitting back watching the dancing, his hand round the neck of a beer bottle, nodding to the music. He looked part stoned, part drunk—and fully out of it.

Uri sat beside him and, after a brief, seated embrace, spoke into his ear. While they spoke, Maggie scoped the club. By the entrance she could see a man, newly arrived, who looked as out of place as she was. He wore rimless glasses, which declared him 'adult' among these partying children.

She could see from Eyal's expression that Uri had reached the point in the story where he had lost both his parents. Eyal was shaking his head and pulling on Uri's shoulder, as if initiating another hug. But Uri was already bringing out the cellphone to show Eyal that the last call Shimon Guttman had made had been to Baruch Kishon.

Eyal shrugged apologetically; he didn't know anything. Uri kept up the questions, now turning back to Maggie with snatches of translation. When had he last spoken with his father? On Sunday morning. His father was off on 'assignment'. He didn't know where.

'Eyal, did your father mention a trip to Geneva?'

Careful, thought Maggie.

'As in, like, Switzerland? No. He usually tells me when he's going abroad. Likes me to check on his apartment. Pretty anal that way.'

'So you don't think he's abroad?'

'Nope.'

'But you haven't spoken to him since Sunday? And you're not worried?'

'I wasn't worried. Till you guys started freaking me out.'

They drove back fast, with Eyal, no longer blissed out, in the back. Uri kept up the questioning, extracting only one more detail: that when Eyal and his father spoke on Sunday morning, Baruch Kishon had seemed in a good mood. He said he had a 'hot' story to work on.

When they reached Kishon's apartment, Eyal seemed nervous about opening up the place. He walked in first, switching on lights, calling out his father's name.

'Eyal, look around,' Uri said. 'Look carefully. Tell us if you notice anything different, anything out of place. Anything at all.'

The place was preternaturally tidy. Maggie walked over to a desk in the corner of the living room. Just a phone, a fax, a blank message pad, a picture of Eyal and his sister, she guessed, as kids. She stepped away, then turned back. She pulled the pad towards her, picked it up and held it up to the light.

'Uri! Come here!'

There, engraved into the page, were the inkless markings of what she hoped was Hebrew handwriting. She imagined it: Baruch Kishon taking the call from Shimon Guttman, scribbling a note on his message pad, peeling it off, rushing out of the door—leaving the impression on the page below.

Uri saw it, too. He held the piece of paper up to the light, and squinted and grimaced until eventually he gave a small smile. 'It's a name,' he said. 'An Arabic name. The man we want is called Afif Aweida.'

Jerusalem, the previous Thursday

THIS WAS THE SOUND Shimon Guttman wanted to hear, the throb of carnival. The whistles, the pounding of dustbin lids, the clamour that could only be generated by a group of people strong in number and strong in conviction.

The crowd gathered here at Zion Square was enormous, some carrying placards, the rest waving their fists in the air or clapping in unison, all clad in orange: T-shirts, hats, shorts and face-paint. But what made Shimon tremble with pride was that this massed rally against Yariv and his treachery consisted entirely of the young.

When he had issued the call, he'd had no idea if it would be heeded. Conventional wisdom held that Israel's young had grown apathetic and wouldn't have the gumption to fight the way his generation did back in '67. Yet here was compelling evidence that such pessimism was misplaced. For this was shaping up to be a fight, good and proper. Facing the army of orange, separated by a thin line of police and the odd news photographer and TV cameraman, was another crowd, nearly as packed, almost as vociferous.

They had no single colour, but just as many placards, all saying simply, and in English: YES TO PEACE.

Shimon Guttman had been at the head of the orange column, one of only a half-dozen oldies granted such elevated status, but as the trouble started they were ushered out of the way. From his vantage point on the sidelines he could see that this would soon descend into a medieval pitched battle, two armies charging at each other. All that was missing were the horses.

I am not needed here, Guttman thought, smiling. He withdrew quietly, happy to let the young people get on without him. He checked his watch. The sensible course would be to slope off to a café and have a smoke before his meeting with Shapira and the Settlers' Council. But Guttman decided to grant himself a rare treat. He would go somewhere else entirely.

He walked briskly through the Jaffa Gate, and down the cobbled alleys of the *shouk*, as the Israelis referred to it, a soft 'sh' where the Arabs would sound an 's'. Not that Israelis ever came here. Since the first *intifada* in the late 1980s, few Jewish Israelis dared set foot inside the Old City, except of course for the Jewish Quarter and the Kotel, the Western Wall. After a spate of fatal stabbings, it had become a no-go area.

But Guttman was not frightened. He believed that Jews should have full access to all of their capital city, that they should not be intimidated into retreat from any part of it. True, he looked over his shoulder every five or six steps the instant he left behind the lit streets of the Jewish Quarter for the dust and noise of the Arab neighbourhoods. Still, he tried to walk like a man who was simply strolling in his home city. As if he owned the place. Which, as a matter of principle, he believed he did.

There were a few shops he stopped into whenever he was in the market. He checked in at the first, its entrance obscured by rails of leather bags. It had a pot that was intriguing but hard to date. The second and third shops were apologetic; they had sold the best stuff and were waiting for more. They didn't need to spell out that these new shipments would be coming from Iraq.

He was heading out when he caught a glimpse of the shop he had almost forgotten. Like the rest, it had no front window, just a pile of merchandise outside that extended inside. He entered, and began to survey the shelves.

'Hello, Professor. How nice to see you again.' It was the owner, Afif Aweida, emerging from behind the jeweller's counter at the far end, a glass case housing a collection of rings and bracelets. He offered his hand.

'What a remarkable memory you have, Afif. Good to see you.'

'To what do I owe this pleasure?'

'I was just passing through. Window shopping.'

Afif gestured for Guttman to follow him into a back office. The Israeli noted the large, bulky computer, the old calculator, the dusty shelves. Times had been hard for Aweida, as they had for everyone in East Jerusalem.

Afif saw Shimon check his watch. 'You are in a hurry?'

'I'm sorry, Afif. Busy day.'

'OK. Well, let me see.' He was on his feet, surveying his stock. 'Nothing too dramatic, but there is this.' He held out a cardboard box with a dozen mosaic fragments inside, arranged in the shape of a bird.

'Nice,' Shimon said, 'but not really my area.'

'Actually, there is something you can help *me* with. The usual terms, of course. A new shipment arrived this week.' He leaned down to pick up a tray from the floor. On it, arranged in four rows of five, were the twenty clay tablets Henry Blyth-Pullen had brought to him just a few days earlier.

Shimon Guttman checked his watch again: 1.45 p.m. He would get through these, then be off to Psagot for that three o'clock meeting. 'OK,' he said to Aweida. 'I'll translate all of them and keep one. Agreed?'

'Agreed.'

Aweida brought a notepad to his lap. Guttman brought the first tablet out of the tray, felt the pleasing weight of it in his palm. He moved it closer to his eyes, lifting his glasses to get a sharper view of the text.

The marks that gave cuneiform its name—the word translated as 'wedge-shaped'—never failed to thrill him. To the untrained eye, they looked like little golf tees, some vertical, in pairs or threes, some on their side, also in twos and threes, arranged in various patterns, filling line after line. But ever since Professor Mankowitz had taught him how to interpret them, he had felt the emotional charge of it. The idea of a written record that stretched back more than five millennia into the past was, to him, intensely moving. The notion that the Sumerians had been writing down their thoughts, their experiences, even trivial jottings, thirty centuries before Christ, and that they could be read on these small bars of clay, was exhilarating.

He dictated to Aweida. 'Three sheep, three fattened sheep, one goat . . .' he said after a glance. He could not read and understand these as quickly as he could English, but certainly as fast as he could read and translate, say, German. No one in Israel could match his knowledge, apart from Ahmed Nour (not that Ahmed would declare himself to be living in Israel).

The journals always said there were only 100 people in the world at any one time who could read cuneiform, but he suspected that was an overestimate.

He picked up the next tablet. Instantly, merely from the layout, he could see what this was. 'A household inventory, I'm afraid, Afif.'

The next one showed the same line repeated ten times. 'A schoolboy's exercise,' he told the Palestinian, who smiled and noted it.

He continued like that, setting the translated tablets onto Aweida's desk, until there were only six left in the tray. He picked up the next one, and read to himself the opening words as if they were the first line of a joke.

'*Ab-ra-ha-am mar te-ra-ah a-na-ku* . . .' He put the tablet down and smirked at Aweida, as if he might be in on the gag, then brought the tablet back to his eye again. The words had not vanished. Nor had he misread them. *Abraham mar Terach anaku*. I Abraham, son of Terach.

Shimon felt the blood draining from his face. His eye sped forward, as far as they could before the letters became cloudy and indistinct.

I Abraham, son of Terach, in front of the judges have attested thus. The land where I took my son, there to make a sacrifice of him to the Mighty Name, the Mountain of Moriah, this land has become a source of dissension between my two sons; let their names here be recorded as Isaac and Ishmael. So have I thus declared in front of the judges that the Mount shall be bequeathed as follows . . .

What reflex restrained Guttman at that moment, preventing him from saying out loud what he had just read to himself? Was it no more than the savvy of the *shouk*, the habit of a veteran haggler who knows that to show enthusiasm for any item doubles its price? Or was it a political calculation, made in a fleeting second, that what he held in his now-trembling hand could change human history no less dramatically than if he were grasping the detonator of a nuclear bomb?

'OK,' he said, hoping to hide the shakiness in his voice. 'What's next?'

'But, Professor, you haven't told me what that one said.'

'Sorry, my mind wandered. Another household inventory. Woman's.'

He proceeded to the next one, a tally of livestock in a farm in Tikrit. And somehow he ploughed through the rest, though he felt as if he were performing the entire task underwater. The hardest moment, he knew, was to come.

Guttman was no poker player. Would he be able to conceal his emotions?

He was not a politician, practised in the art of dissembling. Surely Aweida, a skilled market trader, would see through him instantly.

Then it came to him.

'So the usual terms?' he said, his throat parched. 'I can pick one?'

'As we agreed,' said Aweida.

'Good. I'll have that one.' He pointed at the ninth tablet he had examined.

'The letter from a mother to her son?'

'Yes.'

'Oh, but, Professor, you know that was the only one of any special interest. All the rest are so, how shall I say, day-to-day.'

'Which is why I want that one. Come on, your buyers won't care one way or the other.'

'Ordinarily that might be true. But I have a collector coming in from New York in the next few days. A young man, coming here with his own art expert. This story—a mother and a son—will appeal to him.'

'So tell him that that's the story of that one.' Guttman pointed at the tablet engraved with the schoolboy punishment.

'Professor. These buyers get such items independently verified. I cannot lie. It would destroy me.'

'I see that, Afif. But I am a scholar. This is what interests me historically. The rest are very ordinary.' He wasn't sure how long he could keep this up.

'Please, Professor. You know what these years have done to us. I earn a fraction of what we once could make. With this sale—'

'OK, Afif. I understand. I won't push you. It's fine.' He reached for the tablet that began *I Abraham, son of Terach*. 'I'll take this one.'

'The inventory?'

'Yes. Why not? It's not so dull.'

Guttman rose to his feet, slipping the tablet in his jacket pocket as casually as he could manage. He shook hands with Afif, only realising as they made contact that his own palm was clammy with sweat.

'Are you all right, Professor? Would you like a glass of water?'

Insisting that he was fine, that he just needed to get to his next appointment, Guttman said goodbye and headed briskly out. Gripping the tablet inside his pocket, he hurried back towards the Jaffa Gate. Only when he was beyond the walls of the Old City did he stop and pause for breath, gasping like a sprinter who had just run the race of his life. He felt as if he might faint.

For at that moment Shimon Guttman knew that he held in his hand the greatest archaeological discovery ever made: the last testament of the great patriarch, the man revered as the father of the three great faiths, Judaism, Christianity and Islam. In his hand was the will of Abraham.

CHAPTER SIX

Jerusalem, Thursday, 12.46 a.m.

Their first stop had been the central police station in Tel Aviv, dropping off a distraught Eyal Kishon so that he could file a missing person's report on his father. He was convinced that whatever curse had killed Shimon and Rachel Guttman had passed, like a contagion, to his family.

All the while, even as he drove, Uri was working his mobile, starting with directory enquiries, trying to get any information he could on Afif Aweida. The phone company said there were nine in the Jerusalem area alone. Uri had to use all his charm to get the operator to read them all out. There was a dentist, a lawyer, six residential listings and one Afif Aweida registered as an antiques dealer on Suq el-Bazaar Road, in the Old City.

Uri smiled and turned to Maggie. 'That's our man. Antiquities are about the only thing that could have made my father talk to an Arab.'

They knew it was pointless to head to the market and try to track down this Aweida immediately. All the shops would be closed, and without his home address it would be impossible to find him.

Uri drew up outside David's Citadel Hotel and pulled up the handbrake. 'OK, Miss Costello,' he said. 'This is the end of the line. All change here.'

Maggie thanked him, then unlatched her door. Before getting out, she turned back to him with a single word: 'Nightcap?'

HE WAS NOT A DRINKER, she could see that. He nursed his whisky and water as if it were a precious liquid that had to be observed, rather than consumed.

'So what about this film-making, then?' she said, removing her shoes under the corner table they had taken and enjoying the relief that coursed through her feet and upwards.

'What about it?'

'How come you're good at it?'

He smiled, recognising the return of his own enquiry. 'You don't know if I'm good at it.'

'Oh, I think I can tell. You hold yourself like a successful man.'

'Well, it's kind of you to say so. Did you see *The Truth about Boys*?'

'The one that followed those four teenagers? I saw that last year; it was brilliant. That was you?'

'It was. Thank you.'

'I couldn't believe what those lads said on camera. I thought there were hidden cameras or something, they were so honest. How on earth did you get them to do that?'

'No hidden cameras. There is a big secret though. Which you mustn't let on. It's commercially sensitive.'

'I'm good with secrets. You can trust me.'

'The secret is listening. You have to listen.'

'And where did you learn that?'

'From my father.'

'Really? I didn't imagine him as the listening type.'

'He wasn't. He was the talking type. So we had to listen. We got really good at it.' Uri smiled and took another sip of whisky. 'Anyway, you only answered half my question before. I get how you're a mediator, but not why.'

'You asked me "how come".'

'Right. And that's part how and part why. So tell me the why.'

He was leaning back in his chair now, relaxing for the first time since they'd met. Maggie was aware that this was some kind of respite for him, a break from mourning, a chance for lightness after the weight he had been carrying around for four days. Yet she couldn't just swat aside his question with a joke or a change of subject. She would be honest.

'The why sounds so corny no one ever talks about it.'

'I like corny.'

Maggie looked at him hard, as if she were handing him a fragile object. 'The very first time I'd been abroad was when I was an aid worker in Sudan during the civil war. One day we were driving back and we saw a village that had been razed to the ground. There were bodies on the roadside, limbs, the whole thing. But the worst of it were these children, alive, but wandering around aimlessly, stumbling really. Like zombies. They had seen the most awful things, their parents killed, their mothers raped. They were just dumbstruck. After that, I thought that if I could do anything, anything at all, to stop a war lasting even one day longer, then it would be worth it.'

Uri said nothing, just kept his eyes locked onto hers.

'Which is why I couldn't bear being away from it all this time.'

He furrowed his eyebrows.

'I haven't told you, have I? This is my first assignment for over a year. I've been brought back out of retirement.' Maggie drained her glass. 'Forced retirement.'

'What happened?'

'I was in Africa, again. Mediating in the Congo: the war no one ever talked about, even though millions died. Anyway, it had taken eighteen months, but we finally had all the parties on board for a deal. We were days away from a signing, very close. And I made—' She looked up at him, to see if he was still with her, and he was, his concentration absolute. 'I made a mistake. A terrible, terrible mistake.' Her voice was cracking now. 'And because of that, because of *me*, the talks broke down.

'I had to leave the Congo a few days later and when I did, when I took the road out to the airport, I saw them again. Those faces, those kids, that same stunned look in their eyes. And I realised that they were like that because of me, because I had fucked up so badly.' A tear trickled down her cheek. 'And those faces will haunt me for the rest of my life.'

Only then did Uri put down his glass and lean forward to touch Maggie's hand. He held it tightly, until he eventually stood up and brought Maggie up with him, so that her head was resting on his chest. Without saying a word, he stroked her hair, over and over, which only made the tears come faster.

THEY MOVED UPSTAIRS, to her room, in silence. Once the door was closed, they stood together for a while until, without any act of volition either of them could remember, their lips touched. They kissed slowly, shyly, their tongues making the lightest possible contact with each other.

Her hands were the first to move, placing themselves on his chest, feeling its muscled hardness. He moved gently, his right palm only grazing the side of her breast, a touch that made her shudder with pleasure.

When his left hand found the space between the top of her skirt and her shirt, his fingers tingling across her naked skin, she pulled away.

'What? What is it?'

Maggie stumbled backwards, until she was sitting on the bed. She leaned across and found the light switch, dazzling them both.

'I'm sorry, I'm sorry,' she said, shaking her head. 'I just can't do it.'

'Because of the man at home?'

It should have been because of Edward, she realised, but it wasn't. 'No. No, it's not that.'

The look in Uri's eyes changed, then he turned his face away from her.

'Uri, please. I want to tell you.'

He let his eyes meet hers, and lowered himself into the chair at the desk.

'You see, I didn't tell you everything about my mistake. Back in Africa. It wasn't a . . .' She struggled to find the right word. 'It wasn't a professional error. I didn't screw up the negotiations.' She gave a bitter smile, realising the linguistic trap she had just walked into. 'I screwed one of the negotiators. That was my mistake. A leader of one of the rebel groups.' She looked up at Uri, expecting the disapproval to be etched into his face. But he just listened. 'Of course, everyone found out. And when they did, they said I could no longer be impartial. The talks were suspended.'

Uri sighed. 'And that's why they sent you into exile? To punish you?'

'No, not really. That was me who did that. Punishing myself.' She gave a wan smile, her eyes blurred with tears. 'You know, people keep telling me I should move on. But I can't. Do you understand that, Uri? I can't. Not until I've made things right. And I won't do that if I make the same mistake again.'

'But, Maggie.' He smiled. 'I've got nothing to do with the peace talks.'

'No, but you're an Israeli. That counts as taking sides.'

'You're assuming people would find out.'

'Oh, they'd find out.' She was trying not to look at him, fearing that if she saw him as she'd seen him a few moments ago, her resolve would crumble.

She got up off the bed and opened the hotel-room door, wide enough so that both of them could see the corridor outside. Uri rose to his feet.

Her eyes still wet, Maggie said quietly, 'I'm sorry, Uri. I really am.'

Jerusalem, Thursday, 7.15 a.m.

MAGGIE SAT BOLT UPRIGHT, her heart thumping. She took a second or two to realise where she was. The phone had shocked her out of deep sleep.

'Yerrrr.'

'Maggie? This is the Deputy Secretary.'

Jesus. Maggie cleared her throat. 'Yes. Hello.'

'I need to see you in fifteen minutes. Meet me downstairs.'

Over coffee, Robert Sanchez set out just how bad things were. Both sides seemed to be trying to keep the lid on the violence, though there had been armed clashes in Jenin and Qalqilya and Israel had reoccupied whole swaths of the Gaza Strip. Worse still, the whole region seemed to be preparing for war. Not only was Hizbullah hurling rockets from Lebanon onto Israel's northern towns and villages, but now Syria was mobilising its troops around the Golan Heights. Egypt and Jordan had both recalled their ambassadors from Tel Aviv. The media were drawing comparisons with 1967 and 1973, wars that engulfed the entire Middle East.

'This time it will be worse,' said Sanchez. 'Half of these countries have got nukes now. They'll soon suck in the whole damn world.'

The prognosis could not have been gloomier. Yet Maggie found it comforting to be sitting with Robert Sanchez again. He was one of the very few people she knew in the current State Department, and the only familiar face in the US team in Jerusalem. She had worked with him twice before and had come to respect and trust him. He had led the second-string US team on the Balkans to which Maggie was attached when she was a novice, and she had watched his patient, deliberate method of working. He was a real diplomat, a career officer, not just some high-dollar donor to the party in power, rewarded with a juicy ambassadorship.

'It's only lucky we're not in Camp David or somewhere,' Sanchez was saying. 'If we were, the parties would have gone home by now. As it is, Government House is virtually empty, both sides having pulled back their negotiators for "consultations".'

'And this started with the killings?'

'Yep. First it was Guttman, then Nour. To say nothing of the Jenin raid on the kibbutz last night—'

'Sorry, Jenin raid?'

'Yep. Turns out it was some kind of Palestinian cell from Jenin. They crossed over and got through to Bet Alpha.'

'The Israelis know that for sure?'

'Yeah, the terrorists sprayed some slogan on the wall. *No sleep for Bet Alpha till there is sleep for Jenin*.'

'And the Israelis are saying that's grounds to break off talks?'

'Well, they haven't gone that far yet. But what's got them freaked is that since they built the wall the attacks from Jenin had stopped. Yariv's got the right wing saying he's been so busy sucking up to the Palestinians that he's left the country exposed, so now he's negotiating under fire.'

'And does Yariv know how they got through?'

'That's the thing, Maggie. Even our intel guys are stumped by it. The Israelis say they've checked the length of the wall—excuse me, the "security barrier", as we're supposed to call it—and they can't find a breach.'

'So what could it be?'

Sanchez lowered his voice. 'The Israelis are worried that maybe the Palestinians are stepping up the degree of sophistication. As a warning.'

'Have the Israelis responded?'

'Only a statement. Unless you count the killing last night.'

'What killing?'

'Didn't you get the CIA note?'

Doubtless sent at 6 a.m., thought Maggie. When the rest of the State team were already up, she was sleeping off a night in the bar with—

'There was a stabbing in East Jerusalem last night. Some trader.'

Maggie paled. 'A trader? What kind of trader?'

'I don't know. But listen, Maggie. We've got to raise our game here. Seems the bad guys on both sides are trying to derail this thing. OK. Shhh.'

Maggie turned round to see Bruce Miller strolling towards their table. *Damn*. She wanted to finish hearing what Sanchez knew.

The Deputy Secretary of State rose slightly for the President's man. 'Hello, Bruce. I was just bringing Maggie Costello here up to speed.'

Maggie offered a hand, which Miller took, keeping hold of it a moment too long. He did a tiny dip of his head—the Southern gentleman—as he said, 'Pleasure's all mine.'

She couldn't help but notice that this little performance allowed Miller to give her a good once-over, from her ankles to her chest.

'So,' he said finally. 'Whatcha got so far?'

Maggie told him that she believed there was a link between the Guttman and Nour killings and that she was using the relationships she had built up on both sides to discover what that connection might be. She said that she was certain it would explain the current threat to the peace process.

'What kind of connection, Miss Costello?'

'Archaeology.'

'Excuse me?'

'Both Guttman and Nour were archaeologists. I believe they had even worked together. Guttman had seen something that he told his wife would change everything. Two days later he's dead—and so's she.'

'Police said that was suicide. She couldn't handle the grief.'

'I know that's what the police say, Mr Miller. But her son is convinced otherwise. And I believe him.'

'You working pretty closely with him, Miss Costello?'

Maggie could feel her neck reddening. 'Uri Guttman has proved an invaluable resource.'

'Archaeology, you say?' Bruce Miller was tucking the napkin into his shirt collar. 'Does that make last night a coincidence or what?'

'Last night?'

'The attack on Bet Alpha.'

'You mean, the kibbutz?'

'Yeah, it's a kibbutz.' *Kiboootz*. 'Also the site of one of the great archaeological treasures of Israel. Please, take a look.' He passed over the English-language edition of *Haaretz*. 'Page three.'

The top half of the page was dominated by a photograph of a burning building. The caption identified it as the Bet Alpha Museum and Visitors' Centre, which 'last night appeared to have been the target of a Palestinian raid'. Inset was a smaller photo depicting a stunning mosaic, which was the floor of the oldest synagogue in Israel, dating back to the fifth or sixth century. 'Preserved intact for 1,500 years, experts now worry for its survival.'

'It's too much of a coincidence,' Maggie said. 'So far everyone hurt on both sides since this sudden deterioration has been connected with archaeology. With the past. I bet you it explains why these talks are in meltdown.'

'Face it, Miss Costello. Everything in this goddamn country—' Miller remembered himself and lowered his voice. 'Everything here is tied up to the past. That's the whole freakin' point. It don't explain nothing. We have a serious *political* problem here, which is gonna take some serious political solving. I need you to start living up to your damned five-star reputation and do some solving right now. Do I make myself clear, Miss Costello?'

Maggie was about to insist that she was not wasting her time when they were interrupted by Miller's BlackBerry announcing a new message.

'Israeli police have just confirmed the name of the man killed in the market last night.'

'I bet he was a trader of antiquities. Am I right, Mr Miller?'

He looked back at the handheld device and scrolled down the message.

'As a matter of fact you're wrong, Miss Costello. The dead man was, it seems, a seller of fruit and vegetables. Name of Afif Aweida.'

Jerusalem, the previous Thursday

SHIMON GUTTMAN'S HAND trembled as he put his key in the lock. The journey back home had been dizzy, his mind oscillating between excitement and alarm. Not once in all his years in Jerusalem had he ever feared mugging, but today he had eyed everyone who came near him with suspicion. He imagined the tragedy of it: some lout approaching him in the street, demanding that he empty his pockets. He couldn't let that happen. Not today. Not with this in his hand.

'I'm home,' he called as he walked inside. He prayed there would be no reply, that he would be alone.

'Shimon? Is that you?' His wife.

'Yes, I won't be long. I'll be in my study.'

Shimon headed straight for his desk, closing the door behind him. With his arm, he swept a pile of junk—video camera, digital sound recorder and piles of paper—to one side, to clear a space. Slowly he took out the clay tablet that Afif Aweida had given him an hour earlier.

I Abraham, son of Terach . . . As he read again those first few words, he felt his body convulse with anticipation. In the market he had been able to make out only the opening words. To decode the full text, he would have to study it closely, using some of his most arcane reference books.

He was desperate to find out what it said, but there was a feeling in his gut like a lead weight. What if he were wrong?

He breathed deeply and started again.

The text was in Old Babylonian language. That, thought Guttman, fitted: it was the dialect that would have been spoken eighteen centuries before Christ, when Abraham was commonly believed to have lived. He looked back at the text. The author gave his father's name as Terach and identified his sons as Isaac and Ishmael. It was conceivable that there had been other Abrahams who were sons of other Terachs, even possible that these other Abrahams had had two sons. But two sons with those exact names, Isaac and Ishmael? It was too much of a coincidence. *It had to be him.*

The door opened. Instinctively, Shimon hid the tablet with his hand.

'Hello, *chamoudi*. Aren't you meant to be with Shapira?'

The Settlers' Council meeting.

'Yes. I was. I mean, I am. I'll phone him.'

'What is it, Shimon? You're sweating.'

'It was hot out. I was running.'

'Why were you running?'

He raised his voice. 'Why all these questions? Leave me alone, woman! Can't you see I'm working?'

'What's that on your desk?'

'Rachel!'

His wife turned round, slamming the door behind her.

He tried to calm himself, looking back at the tablet, seeing the seal on the reverse side, in the space between the text and the date at the bottom, and repeated on the edges. It had not been made by a cylinder seal, the carved stone tube that could be rolled into the soft clay, leaving a unique marking. No, it was a much rarer pattern than that, roughly circular, formed by a criss-cross of lines. Shimon had seen it only twice before. It was formed by pressing into the clay the knot found at the fringes of a garment, of the kind worn by Mesopotamian men at Abraham's time. Such fringed garments had faded from history, with one exception: the Jewish prayer shawl.

Regardless of what it said, the importance of this object, no more than four inches high, less than three inches wide and barely half an inch thick, could not be overestimated. It would be the first significant archaeological evidence of the Bible ever discovered.

But what if it was a fake? Guttman thought back to the scandal that had spooked scholars and historians the world over. In 1983 the British historian Hugh Trevor-Roper had declared the Hitler diaries genuine and had paid for it with his reputation. His mistake was simple. He had *wanted* to believe they were real. Now, Shimon Guttman knew how Trevor-Roper must have felt: he wanted so desperately for this tablet to be what it seemed.

Guttman brought the tablet closer to his eyes: the angle of each line of cuneiform script, each syllabic character, was as it should be. And every phrase was idiomatically and historically fitting: *in front of the judges have attested thus* . . . There were only about half a dozen people in the world who could fake an item as well as this—and he, Guttman, was one of them.

But a fake made no sense. Trevor-Roper had overlooked a crucial fact. Someone had brought the Hitler diaries *to* him, wanting his validation. A vast fortune rested on his verdict. This was not like that. No one had come to Guttman, trying to pass off this tablet as the last will of Abraham. On the contrary, *he* had found it. If it hadn't been for his impulse visit to Aweida it would still be in that marketplace now, ready to be sold off to some know-nothing collector. A smile spread across Shimon Guttman's face. Logic was on his side. If this was a fake, the trickster would surely have brought it to Guttman demanding millions of dollars. It had to be real.

But how on earth had it got here? It had come to Jerusalem from Iraq, part of the huge outflow of antiquities since the fall of Saddam: that much was obvious. Maybe the authorities under Saddam had found it and hidden it from view; perhaps they had never realised its significance.

What fascinated Shimon Guttman was its earlier journey. The tablet was written in Hebron, where Abraham was buried. Did this mean that Abraham had lived his last days there? His two sons had been involved in his burial, but had there been a final deathbed scene, involving the father and his two heirs? Had there been a dispute the aged patriarch had to resolve? And how had the tablet got back to the land of Abraham's birth, Mesopotamia?

This, he realised, could be his life's work. Translating this tablet, decoding its history, displaying it in the great museums of the world. Scholars would tell and retell the story of how he had stumbled across the founding document of human civilisation in a Jerusalem street market.

Impatient to begin, Guttman reached for the three or four key volumes required in the deciphering of cuneiform and got to work.

I Abraham, son of Terach, in front of the judges have attested thus. The land where I took my son, there to make a sacrifice of him to the Mighty Name, the Mountain of Moriah, this land has become . . .

Guttman couldn't help it. He was overwhelmed all over again. Here was Abraham referring to one of the defining episodes in world culture, the *akeda*, when the great patriarch led his son up Mount Moriah, there to sacrifice him to the god in whom he had become the first believer. Abraham had raised his blade, only staying his hand when an angel descended to announce that God did not demand this act of child sacrifice after all. It was a moment that would bind Abraham and Isaac and their children to God for ever more, sealing them into the covenant between God and the Jews.

Mount Moriah, the Temple Mount, became Judaism's holiest site. Tradition held that this spot, where the angel had saved Isaac, was the centre of the world, the Foundation Stone on which the universe had been created. The Jews of ancient times had built their temple here and, when it was destroyed by the Babylonians, had built it again. All that was left now was the Western Wall, but this place remained the spiritual centre of the Jewish faith.

Yet Mount Moriah was holy to Muslims, too, to those who traced their ancestry to Ishmael. For them it was Haram al-Sharif, the Noble Sanctuary, the place where Mohammed had ascended to heaven on his winged horse.

> *. . . a source of dissension between my two sons; let their names here be recorded as Isaac and Ishmael. So have I thus declared in front of the judges that the Mount shall be bequeathed as follows . . .*

Here the characters were faded, as if the carving had gone less deep. Guttman opened a desk drawer and pulled out a magnifying glass. Some of the formations were novel: they required checking against other texts, looking for repetitions that might suggest a specific local usage.

More than two hours later and it was done.

Shimon Guttman gripped the desk in front of him. He needed to feel the solidity of the wood. For the enormity of these words was now apparent. Forget the fame and glory of an unprecedented historic discovery. What he had in front of him would change everything. People had fought for millennia over control of this holy site, all sides believing themselves to be the children of Abraham. And now he, Shimon Guttman, held the document that would settle this question for ever. All who regarded themselves as the descendants of Isaac and Ishmael, Jews and Muslims, would have to be bound by this, the word of the great father himself.

He quickly logged onto his computer and searched for a web site. Then he fumbled for his phone and dialled the number he had found.

'My name is Professor Shimon Guttman,' he said, his voice parched. 'I need to speak to the Prime Minister.'

Ramallah, the West Bank, Thursday, 8.30 a.m.

KHALIL AL-SHAFI knew that, in reality, this was only half a meeting. He had the head of the presidential guard, along with the heads of three other security forces here. But the leaders of the military wing of Hamas were not here, nor of the Gaza police. When he planned for this moment during those long stretches inside Ketziot jail, he had not factored in sufficiently the durability of Palestinian divisions. He had assumed that by the time serious talks came around there would be a single Palestinian leadership. They had cobbled together a coalition, but that was not the same thing.

He had always anticipated that the final straight of negotiations would be punctuated by outbreaks of violence on both sides. There would always be hardliners who would sabotage progress through atrocity. What he had not prepared for was this, attacks that no one claimed and no one could explain.

Al-Shafi turned to Faisal Amiry, head of the security operation that was the closest the Palestinians came to an intelligence agency.

'How is it possible that this attack was staged from Jenin? It's far, no?'

'It is far, sir. But if a team were able to get over the wall—'

'We would know about it. Wouldn't we?'

'There may be others who knew.' It was Toubi, a veteran of the old PLO struggles going back decades. He hated Hamas with a passion.

'The trouble is, it doesn't seem like Hamas,' Amiry replied. 'It's not their style. A raid, in then out.'

'With no martyrs,' said Toubi. 'I agree it's strange. If they wanted to blow up the talks they'd have blown up themselves. On a bus. In central Jerusalem.'

'Islamic Jihad?' asked al-Shafi.

'Our inside source says they're as surprised by this as we are,' said Amiry.

'What about the target?'

'That is the strangest thing. If you were aiming for loss of life, you'd have turned right out of the kibbutz fields, aiming for the residential buildings. But they were at the museum. Where they took only one life.'

Toubi was nodding. 'Or, once they got over the wall, they could have struck Magen Shaul. Why hike all the way to Bet Alpha?'

'I know why.' Al-Shafi had got out from behind his desk and was pacing. 'Bet Alpha is the site of an ancient synagogue. Fifteen hundred years old. The Zionists love it because it "proves" they've been here as long as we have. If it's gone, that's one bit less proof.'

'You're not serious.'

'Why not? This conflict is all about the *past*. All about who was here first, who has the prior claim. I think some Palestinian took it into his head to lend us a helping hand, to tilt the scales in our favour. "Look, there's now one less ancient Jewish site here. Maybe it never existed!"'

'I don't believe it.'

'Do you have a better explanation?'

There was silence, broken eventually by Amiry. 'And there's the trader. This man Aweida, stabbed to death in Jerusalem.'

'What can you tell me?'

'Not very much. Apparently there was some Hebrew message pinned to the body. A page of the Torah. A group nobody's ever heard of, the Defenders of United Jerusalem, is claiming responsibility.'

'Settlers?'

'Maybe.'

Al-Shafi rubbed his chin. 'In which case, Yariv is sweating right now.' He turned to Amiry. 'Find out whatever you can about the incident in Bet Alpha. Comb the Israeli papers: read the military correspondents. Anything the army finds out, they always leak. And see what people here know about Afif Aweida. Is there a reason why Israeli fanatics would kill a greengrocer?'

'Anything else?'

'Yes. I want to know what that American woman, Costello, is up to. She called me with more questions about Ahmed Nour. There are at least three mysterious murders here, my friends. Unless we understand what's going on, a lot more Palestinians will die—along with the best chance of independence any of us will ever see. I think you know what to do.'

East Jerusalem, Thursday, 9.40 a.m.

FOR THE SECOND TIME in a week, Maggie was entering a house of mourning. The house was full, as she had expected. It was noisy, with a piercing wail that rose and fell like a wave. She soon saw the source of it, a group of women huddled round an older woman, who was swathed in shapeless, embroidered black. Her face seemed to have been worn away by tears.

A path formed for Maggie as she made her way through the mourners. Eventually she reached the front of the room, where she found a woman of around her own age, dressed in simple, Western clothes. She was not crying, but seemed simply stunned into silence.

'Mrs Aweida?'

The woman said nothing, staring past Maggie, into the middle distance.

'Mrs Aweida, I am with the international team in Jerusalem trying to bring peace. I came to pay my respects to your husband and to offer my condolences on your terrible loss.'

The woman still stared blankly, seemingly oblivious to Maggie's words and the noise all around. Eventually Maggie placed her hand on the widow's, squeezed it and moved away. She would not intrude.

A man materialised to steer Maggie away. 'Thank you,' he said. 'Please, you to know we thank America. For you to come here. Thank you.'

Maggie nodded and smiled her weary half-smile.

'All he did was sell tomato and carrot and apple. He no kill anyone.'

'Oh, I know. It's a terrible crime that happened to your—'

'My cousin. I am Sari Aweida.'

'Tell me. Do you also work in the market?'

'Yes, yes. All of us, we work in market. I sell meat. And my brother he sell scarf, for the head. *Keffiyeh*. You know what is *keffiyeh*?'

'Yes, I do. Tell me, is there anyone in your family who sells old things? Antiquities? You know, old stones, pots, jewellery perhaps?'

'Ah, jewel, yes. My cousin, he sell jewel.'

'And antiques?'

'Yes, yes. Antique. He sell in the market.'

'May I see him?'

'Of course. He live near to here. I take you.'

'Thank you, Sari.' Maggie smiled. 'And what is his name?'

'His name also Afif. He is Afif Aweida.'

AS THEY THREADED through the back streets, narrow and made of the same pale stone as the rest of Jerusalem, Maggie realised that no one in the family had suspected that the Afif Aweida they were about to bury had been the victim of a case of mistaken identity.

She pulled out her mobile to dial Uri's number. A text message had arrived while she was in the Aweida house. From Edward.

We need to talk about what to do with your stuff. E.

Sari Aweida must have seen the expression on her face, the brow knotted. 'No to worry. We nearly there.'

She cleared the message without replying, and hit the green button for the last number dialled. She would speak as if last night had not happened.

'Uri? Listen. Afif Aweida is alive. I mean there's another Afif Aweida. A trader in antiquities. They must have got the wrong one.'

'Slow down, Maggie. You're not making any sense.'

'OK. I'm on my way to meet Afif Aweida. I'm sure he was the one your father mentioned on the phone to Baruch Kishon. He deals in antiquities. It's too much of a coincidence. I'll call you later.'

Like most people talking on a mobile while walking, Maggie had spoken with her head down. She now looked up to find no sign of Sari. He had obviously walked so fast, he hadn't noticed that she wasn't keeping up.

She walked on a few yards, peering to her left down an alleyway so narrow it was dark, even in this morning sunlight. In the distance she could see two kids, boys she guessed, kicking a can. If she went down here, perhaps she could ask their mother—

Suddenly she felt a violent jerking backwards, as if her neck was about to be snapped. A gloved hand was over her eyes and another was covering her mouth. She could feel herself being dragged backwards.

She tried to pull her arms free, but they were held fast. She was dragged into a dark alleyway and shoved hard against the wall, the bricks pounding against her spine. The hand covering her mouth moved down, clamping her throat. She heard herself emit a dry rasp.

Now the hand came away from her eyes but, for a second, she still saw only darkness. Then a voice, which she realised was coming from a face entirely covered in a black ski mask, barely an inch away.

'Stay away, understand?'

'I don't—'

The hand round her throat tightened, until she was gasping for air.

'Stay away.'

'Stay away from what?' she tried to croak.

The hand came off her throat, so that it could join with the other in taking hold of her shoulders. Then he rammed her hard against the wall again.

The pain shuddered all the way through her, reaching the top of her skull. She wanted to double over, but still he held her upright, as if she was a doll.

Suddenly a new voice—a second man, invisible in the shadows—whispered into her left ear. 'You know what we're talking about, Maggie Costello.'

The voice sounded strange, indeterminate. Was it Middle Eastern? Or European? And how many of these men were there?

Now she felt a hand squeezing a thigh. 'Do you hear me, Maggie?'

Her heart was thumping, her body still writhing in futile protest. She was trying to work out what kind of voice she was hearing—was it Arab, was it Israeli, or neither?—when she felt a sensation that made her quake.

The breath on her ear had turned moist, as she registered the unmistakable sensation of a tongue probing inside it. She let out the first sounds of a scream, but the gloved hand was back, sealing her mouth. And now the other hand, the one that had been gripping her thigh, relaxed—only to move upward, clamping itself between Maggie's legs.

Her eyes began to water. She was trying to kick, but the first man was pressed too close; she could hardly move her legs.

'You like that, Maggie?' The voice, its accent still so elusive, was hot and breathy in her ear. 'No? Don't like it?' She felt the tongue and face move six inches away from her. 'Then fuck off.' The first man let go of her shoulders, then pushed her to the ground. 'Or we'll be back for more.'

CHAPTER SEVEN

Jerusalem, Thursday, 11.05 a.m.

Tradition held that every Thursday morning at this hour Yaakov Yariv's informal kitchen cabinet of advisers met to digest and analyse events, spot mistakes, devise solutions and plot the next moves. Today the forum would consist of just Yariv and Amir Tal.

The talks at Government House were effectively on hold, only a skeleton presence maintained on each side. Neither Israel nor the Palestinians wanted to be accused by the Americans of pulling the plug, so they hadn't dared walk out. But no serious work was being done. The peace effort was collapsing.

Yariv spat a sunflower-seed husk into his hand. He felt confused, he now confided in Tal. 'Look, I expected a Hamas suicide bombing. They did it to Rabin and to Peres. Anyone gets close to a deal, they're on an Egged bus with dynamite strapped to their belly. I expected that. Even the *Machteret* I was expecting to hear from.' They had both assumed that a resurgence of the Jewish underground was on the cards. 'Maybe they'd firebomb an Arab playground or two. Even do the Mosque.'

He didn't need to say which mosque. They both knew the wilder elements of the *Machteret* dreamt of blowing up the Dome of the Rock, Islam's most cherished site in the Holy Land, thereby clearing the ground for the rebuilding of the Jewish Temple on the same spot.

'But these attacks make no sense. Why would the Palestinians attack some visitors' centre in the north, at night? If you want to screw up the talks, do it in the day! Kill lots of people!'

'Al-Shafi has denied all responsibility for it,' said Tal.

'Of course. But Hamas?'

'They have too. But—'

'But we don't know whether to believe them. And this stabbing in Jerusalem. I don't believe the claim of responsibility. Defenders of United

Jerusalem or whatever name they gave themselves. Why haven't we heard of them before? Could be just some street crime.'

'Not necessarily. You know we've been pursuing the Guttman investigation. We've had the son, Uri, under surveillance. He's working closely with Maggie Costello of the State Department—'

'The mediator? What the hell's she got to do with it?'

'It seems she was passed some kind of message by Rachel Guttman. And in the absence of any action at Government House, the Americans are letting her pursue it. As you know, Costello and Uri Guttman established a connection between the professor and the dead Palestinian, Nour. Well, we think there might be a further connection with last night's killing in Jerusalem.'

Yariv spat another sunflower-seed husk into his hand. 'Go on.'

'They visited Baruch Kishon's apartment in Tel Aviv last night. We didn't have much time to establish surveillance, but we did get a muffled voice recording. Apparently the pair found a piece of paper with a name on it.'

'What name?'

'Afif Aweida. It seems Guttman spoke to Kishon, mentioned Aweida's name. Suddenly Aweida ends up dead.'

There was silence, but for the sucking sound as a particularly fat seed lodged between Yariv's teeth. 'Well, who else was listening—?'

'That's why I'm glad we're here alone today, Prime Minister. Besides you and me, only military intelligence have access to our surveillance.'

'That's crazy. You think Yossi Ben-Ari, the Defence Minister of Israel, is running his own rogue operation? Killing this Arab in the market? Why?'

'I don't know. We'd have to know what this whole Guttman business was all about to understand that. But the bigger picture—'

'—is that he's trying to sabotage the peace talks. Bring me down; take over himself.' The Prime Minister leaned back in his chair, balling up the paper bag that had once been full of seeds, and sighed deeply.

'You know the army's attitude to what we're doing,' said Tal. 'They never liked the pull-out from Gaza; you think they're going to like this? Tearing down settlements in the West Bank? Handing over half of Jerusalem?'

Yariv smiled, the wistful smile of an old man who thought he had seen it all. 'I promoted Ben-Ari, you know. Made him a general.'

'What do you want me to do, Prime Minister?'

'Set up an intelligence team answerable solely to this office. Make sure they're loyal. Cut Defence out of the loop. And then, once you have the team in place, set them on Ben-Ari, maybe his chief of staff, too. Bug their phone calls and their meetings. I want to see their emails, their text messages, the colour of the paper they use to wipe their arses.'

'It's done.'

'And one other thing. Keep on Costello and Guttman Junior, too. Don't let them out of our sight. If they're about to find the explanation for all this madness, then good. They can lead us to it.'

Jerusalem, Thursday, 11.11 a.m.

SHE HAD NO IDEA how long she had remained on the ground. It might have been a minute, five or ten. She had stayed there, inert, since they dumped her and fled. She had not phoned for help. She had been too stunned for that.

Maggie had just begun to make the effort to pull herself together, to persuade herself that it could have been much worse, that they could have killed her, when a hand reached out.

It belonged to a man in a faded blue suit, with a long thin face and a head of closely cropped hair. He was staring down, his face a picture of concern and puzzlement. After a long while, the creases in his face briefly relaxed. 'You are the American lady. From the Aweida house.' Only to tense up all over again. 'What are you doing here?'

It forced Maggie to get up and dust herself down, to deploy the protective shell she had grown these last few years. She said nothing, gasping only at the pain that shot up her spine, fizzing like a firework, as she stood.

'Tell me. Why are you here on your own? Where is your protection?'

She felt her hands turn clammy. She wanted to call Davis at the consulate, or Uri, or Liz in London, anyone, but she feared this man's reaction. Would he snatch the phone off her? Would he grab at her? Who was he?

Maggie started heading up the alley. 'I really must go.'

'But where are you going to?'

Stumped, Maggie stopped walking. She didn't know where she was. 'My hotel is in West Jerusalem.'

'Why you not stay in East Jerusalem? It is beautiful here. You have the American Colony Hotel. All the Europeans stay there. Why never the Americans? You want only to see the Israelis.'

'It's not that at all,' Maggie muttered, and started walking again.

She could feel the man at her shoulder, and his closeness made her shudder, reminding her of the masked man and the hot breath.

'Please I ask again. Why were you here?'

'I wanted to see Afif Aweida's cousin. The other Afif Aweida.'

'Please. I take you.'

'No, no. There's no need. I just want to get back to my hotel.'

But he wasn't listening. He took her by the elbow and marched her back into the maze of streets and alleys of Jerusalem's Old City. Am I deranged? Maggie wondered as she followed a stranger through a strange city for the second time in—what was it, an hour? Two? This time, though, she was not distracted and careless. Her heart was racing. Was this a trap? Had Sari Aweida led her to her assailants? Was this man about to do the same?

She thought about making a run for it. But where? She would be lost instantly in these streets, which were getting fuller now, as they approached the *souk*. She saw a couple of women who looked like tourists. She could run up to them. But then what?

Now the man was guiding her through paths that twisted and turned, passing stalls teeming with goat-skin bongo drums, thick, woven carpets, tacky leather bags and purses, and wood-carved souvenirs.

Suddenly, they stopped at a jeweller's.

'Here. Please. This is Afif Aweida shop.'

Gingerly, she stepped inside, followed by her guide, who high-fived a young man sitting behind the counter. In Arabic she heard the man utter the word 'American' and gesture in her direction.

A moment later, from a back room, a middle-aged man in a V-neck sweater and dark-rimmed spectacles appeared behind a glass counter packed with silver and gold jewellery.

'A pleasure to welcome you here,' he said. 'Thank you, Nabil.'

Maggie turned round to see her guide heading out, a sheepish wave over his shoulder. She called out her thanks, but half-heartedly. A few seconds ago she had been suspicious of him, even feared him as a possible attacker. And yet he had turned out to be a stranger who simply wanted to help.

'Mr Aweida. I am so sorry about what happened to your cousin.'

'A terrible crime. Terrible.'

'Do you think you were the real target?'

'I'm sorry, I don't understand.'

'Do you think the men who killed your cousin got the wrong Afif Aweida?'

'How can there be the "wrong" Afif Aweida? My cousin was stabbed at random. It could have been anybody.'

'I'm not so sure. Do you know of any reason why your life might be in danger, Mr Aweida?'

To her surprise, the shop owner seemed genuinely puzzled by her question. Maggie realised she would have to start at the very beginning.

'Can we talk somewhere private, Mr Aweida? Perhaps in your back room?' Maggie nodded towards the door he had walked through when she arrived.

'No. No need, we can speak freely here.' He clapped his hands, urging the young man at the front to leave.

Maggie got up, walking towards the back door. She wanted to test him out. Sure enough, Afif Aweida leapt to his feet, blocking her path.

'Mr Aweida. I work for the American government, in the peace talks. I am not interested in your business dealings, or in whatever you keep behind that door. But you do need to help me. Your cousin was not killed at random. And many more people will die unless we can find out what's going on.'

Aweida paled. 'Go on.'

'Did you know Shimon Guttman?'

Again, Aweida seemed nervous, agitated. 'I know the name, yes. He was a famous man in Israel. He was killed on Saturday.'

Maggie leaned forward. 'Afif,' she began, 'I don't care what you buy and sell here. I just want to make sure this peace process is not stopped. If it is, many more Palestinians and many more Israelis will die. So I need to ask you again, in confidence. Did you know Shimon Guttman?'

He looked over Maggie's shoulder to check no one was near. 'Yes.'

'Do you have any idea why he might have mentioned your name to someone last week?'

At this, Aweida's brow furrowed. 'No, I have no idea.'

'When did you last see him?'

'Last week.'

'Will you tell me what happened?'

Reluctantly Afif Aweida sat down and explained about the brief, unannounced visit Guttman had made to the shop, his first for ages. At Maggie's prompting, he explained their 'arrangement', whereby Guttman translated a set of ancient clay tablets, keeping one for himself.

'And you say that none seemed especially significant?'

'No. They were all standard: household inventories, schoolwork.'

'Nothing else at all?'

'There was one item. A letter from a mother to her son.'

'And did Professor Guttman take it?'

'No. But he wanted it. He tried to persuade me to give it to him, but eventually he gave up. He let me keep it and took something else.'

Maggie leaned back. 'Did he fight you hard for that tablet from the mother straight away? Or after he had read all of them?'

'Miss Costello, this was a week ago.'

'Try to remember.'

'He read all of them. Then he decided that that one was the best.'

No, he didn't. She had done the same thing herself in negotiations: fighting for the apple so that she could get what she really wanted: the orange.

'And this tablet he took, do you have any idea what it said on it?'

'He said it was an inventory, a woman's. But I cannot read this ancient language. I only know what the professor told me.'

'One last thing,' she said. 'How did he seem when he left here? What mood was he in?'

'Ah, this I remember. He seemed rather unwell. As if he needed a glass of water. I offered, but he didn't take it. He had to rush off.'

I bet he did. 'And that was the last you heard of him?'

'Yes. Until what we heard on the news.'

'Thank you, Mr Aweida. I really appreciate it.'

Once outside, feeling safer now among the tourist throng, Maggie reached for her cellphone and dialled Uri's number.

'Uri, I think I know what's going on.'

'Good. You can tell me on the way.'

'On the way to where?'

'My father's lawyer just called me. He says he has a message for me.'

'Who from?'

'From my father.'

Jerusalem, Thursday, 1.49 p.m.

MAGGIE DID HER BEST to conceal what had happened. She strode confidently past the security guards on the hotel door to find Uri, pacing, head down, in the lobby. Fortunately, he didn't ask how she was, only what she had found out. She told him about the real Afif Aweida, the trader in looted antiquities who had lived while his fruit-selling cousin had been murdered.

'Dumb mistakes like that happen,' Uri said. 'Anyone could have made it.'

They were walking along Shlomzion Ha'Malka Street towards his car.

She had wanted to go to her room to freshen up, but Uri had been adamant: there was no time. As she got into the passenger seat, she explained what she believed had happened: that Shimon Guttman had visited Aweida's shop, translated several clay tablets and come across one of profound political significance. Some text that would have a huge impact on the peace process. He had called Baruch Kishon to discuss how they could best publicise his find. Then he had set about getting this information to the Prime Minister.

'For my dad to get so excited, it must have been something that showed the Jews have been here for ever. Some fragment in Hebrew going back a million years. We'll know what it was soon, I reckon. His lawyer was out of the country until today. He got back this morning and saw this letter waiting for him. Apparently my dad dropped it off last Saturday. By hand.'

Uri and Maggie looked at each other.

'I know,' said Uri. 'I thought the same thing. Like he knew something was going to happen to him.'

They drove in silence, trying to make sense of it all. Maggie considered telling Uri what had happened in the market that morning; maybe together they could work out who her attackers were. She was about to say something when Uri reached for the car radio, turning on the headlines. Once again he translated each story as it came.

'They're saying that there are fears across the world for the Middle East peace process after both sides admitted they had effectively broken off negotiations. Apparently the President of Iran has said that if Israel refuses this last chance to be accepted in the region, then the region will have to remove Israel once and for all. Cast this cancer out, he said. Washington has said any first use of nuclear weapons against Israel will be punished, er, how do you say that? "In kind"?'

Jesus. Failure in Jerusalem could trigger a geopolitical catastrophe. Then she heard in the stream of Hebrew two familiar and unexpected words.

'Uri?' she said. 'What's happened?'

He held up his hand to silence her, paling visibly. Finally he spoke. 'They said tributes are coming in for veteran journalist Baruch Kishon, killed in a car accident in Switzerland. Just outside Geneva.'

'Uri. Pull the car over. Now.'

Maggie's mind was racing. Somebody was one step ahead of every move they were making. She and Uri had deciphered the name of Afif Aweida at Kishon's apartment; within hours a man called Afif Aweida was lying in a pool of blood. They had been the only people to discover that Kishon had received Guttman's last phone call. Now he too had been hunted down. It could only mean one thing: they were being followed and their every conversation bugged. There could be no other explanation.

Uri was hooting at the cars in front, desperately trying to pull over.

Unless . . . Where did Uri say he had done his army service? In intelligence. He was the only person who knew all she knew. She had trusted him immediately and completely. Maybe she had made a mistake.

She felt queasy as she looked at him. She thought of the masked man who had grabbed her that morning, his hand squeezing her *there*. His accent was so strange; maybe, she wondered, it was the sound of someone disguising his voice. Could he have been . . . ? She waited for the traffic to bring the car to a halt and, when it did, she swiftly reached for the handle.

But Uri got there first, using the button on his side to lock all the doors.

'Uri, I want to get out.'

He turned to her and in a calm voice said, 'You're not going anywhere.'

'Let me out. NOW!' Maggie only very rarely raised her voice and she knew the sound of it was shocking.

Uri finally pulled over.

'You can't walk out on me now. Just because this is getting frightening.'

'It's you I'm frightened of, Uri.'

'Me? Are you crazy?'

'Whenever we've found a name, that person has ended up dead. First Aweida, now Kishon. And I know *I* didn't kill them.'

'So you think it was me?'

'Well, you're the only one who knew what I knew.'

Uri was shaking his head in disbelief. 'This is insane, Maggie. How could I have run a guy off a road in Switzerland, when I was here?'

'You could have told someone.'

'I didn't even know he was there!' He tried to collect himself. 'Look, I just want to find out what happened to my parents. Someone killed my mother, Maggie. I'm sure of it. And I want to know who it was. That's all.'

She felt the anxiety recede, as if the blood in her veins was subsiding. 'But you could be passing on what you know to Israeli intelligence.'

'Why would I do that? It was Israeli security who shot my father, remember? They may even be the people behind all this.'

It was true. It didn't make sense. She had allowed herself to panic.

'OK. I believe you. Now unlock the doors.'

He clicked them open and waited for her to get out. When he saw that she wasn't moving, he spoke. 'I only locked them because I need you, Maggie. I can't do this alone. I don't want you to go.'

She saw in his eyes what she had seen there last night. The same warmth, the same spark. She wanted to dive into that look, to stay inside it. Instead she turned away, nodding, as if to signal that it was time for him to drive on.

He had driven about a hundred yards when, in a sudden movement, he reached for the volume knob on the radio and cranked it up loud. Then he retuned until he had found some pounding rap music.

'What the hell are you doing?' she shouted, her head hurting.

Uri looked back at her, his eyes wide. *Bugs*, he mouthed silently. *The car could be bugged*.

Of course. Suddenly she felt very stupid. He was right: they needed to assume they were being bugged.

When they reached a traffic light, Uri leaned across to her, so that he could whisper into her ear. 'The computers, too.' She could feel the words as much as she could hear them, Uri's breath caressing her ear. 'They will have seen whatever we saw. From now on, talk just like normal.'

He turned the music back down. 'You don't like it? Rap's very big in Israel right now.'

Maggie was too thrown to play-act. If their session on Guttman's computer had been monitored, then whoever was doing the monitoring would know all they knew—including the truth about Ahmed Nour. And now something had got them rattled—rattled enough to want to scare her off.

Uri pulled over. Once they were out of the car, she began speaking immediately, only for Uri to put his finger across his lips. *Hush*.

'Yeah, there's a really thriving music scene here now,' he said, still in fake chat mode. 'Mainly Tel Aviv of course.' He beckoned for her to follow.

Maggie couldn't think of a thing to say. She gave him a baffled look.

He leaned in to her ear. 'Our clothes too,' he whispered.

Reflexively, she patted her pockets, feeling for a tiny microphone. He smiled, as if to say, There's no point, you'll never find it.

They were walking towards what looked like an apartment building, not the law office she was expecting.

Uri pressed the buzzer by the main entrance. 'Hi, Orli?'

Maggie heard a woman's voice crackle through the intercom. '*Mi zeh?*'

'Uri. *Ani lo levad.*' I'm not alone.

The door buzzed open and after two flights they came to an apartment door that was already open. Framed in the doorway, looking bewildered, was a woman at least five years younger than Maggie—and unnervingly beautiful. With long dark hair that fell in easy curls, wide brown eyes and a slim figure that even loose, faded jeans could not conceal.

Instantly, the pair embraced, a long, closed-eyes hug that made Maggie want to disappear. Were they family? Was this woman consoling Uri on his double loss? A moment later, they were inside, Maggie still unintroduced.

Uri made straight for the stereo, putting on a CD and turning up the volume. Over Radiohead, he began explaining to Orli what had happened and what he suspected. Then, to Maggie's surprise, he pointed towards what she assumed was the bedroom, urging them to follow him. Still whispering over the music, Uri introduced the two women to each other, and each offered an embarrassed half-smile. Then he turned to Maggie and explained that, first, Orli was an ex-girlfriend and, second, Maggie needed to get undressed.

Then in a louder, more deliberately normal voice, he continued: 'Orli trained as a designer in London. I thought maybe you'd like to take a look at some of her latest clothes.' He made a listening gesture, cupping his ear with his hand, then started pointing. The bug could be anywhere: shirt, shoes, trousers, anywhere.

Next, Uri opened up a cupboard and began to pull out men's clothes. Were those his, still stored here? Or did they belong to Orli's new boyfriend?

She couldn't stare for long, because Orli was now standing Maggie before her own closet, assessing her up and down with the brutality women reserve only for each other. As it happened, though Maggie might not have Orli's skinny arms, most of the clothes on the rail would fit her.

Orli picked out a long, shapeless skirt. 'What about those?' Maggie countered, indicating a pair of neat, grey trousers. She saw a T-shirt and cardigan that would complete the outfit just fine. Reluctantly, Orli handed them over. Pushing her luck, Maggie also nominated a pair of chic leather boots.

Orli left the clothes in a pile on the corner of the bed, turned on her heel and strode off. Within a few minutes, they were saying their goodbyes, Orli drawing out her embrace with Uri a second or two longer than was strictly necessary. He and Maggie headed down the stairs not only wearing new clothes but also, at his insistence, having ditched everything else that might contain a device: shoes, bag, pens, the lot.

'You'd be amazed where they can put a microphone or even a camera these days,' he said, as they walked towards the car.

She looked at him.

'We've done it all, for TV documentaries,' he added.

'Sure, Uri.' She suspected this knowledge was acquired wearing the uniform of the IDF rather than in the edit suites of Tel Aviv TV-land.

Once in the car, he put the music back on and they drove in silence. It was Maggie who broke it.

'So what's the deal with Orli, then?' She hoped it sounded matter-of-fact.

'I told you. An ex-girlfriend.'

'How ex?'

'Ex. We stopped seeing each other more than a year ago.'

'I thought you were in New York a year ago?'

'I was. She was with me. What is this, an interrogation?' Uri took his eye off the road to smile at her.

She knew how she sounded. She decided to shut up, to look out of the window and say nothing more. That lasted at least fifteen seconds.

'So what happened between you?'

'She said she was sick of hanging around in New York waiting for me to commit. So she came back here.'

'And is it over? Between you?'

'Maggie, what is this? Until this week I hadn't spoken to her for nearly a year. She called me about my parents, said if there was anything I needed, I should call. We needed something; I called.'

Maggie was about to apologise, but the chance was taken from her. Her phone rang, displaying the number of the US Consulate. She gestured at Uri to pull over, so that she could get out and speak, away from the car and the assorted microphones it might be concealing. The phone could be tapped, of course. But she couldn't ignore a call from the consulate.

'Hi, Maggie, it's Jim Davis. I'm here with Deputy Secretary Sanchez and Bruce Miller.' There was a click, as she was put on speakerphone.

'Maggie, it's Robert Sanchez here. Things have got a little worse in the course of the day—'

'A *little* worse?' It was Miller, his Southern twang cutting through Sanchez's soft baritone. 'This whole country's burning up faster than a Klansman's cross.'

'I understand.'

'I hope you do, Miss Costello. ''Cause I gotta tell ya, the President and a whole lotta other folks have put way too much into this peace process to see it turn into a pile of buffalo shit now.'

This, Maggie knew, was the kind of talk that made Bruce Miller such a force of nature in Washington, overwhelming anyone unlucky enough to stand in his way. His trademark blend of farm-boy argot and cut-to-the-chase political insight made him a staple on all the talk shows.

'We got three big motives in play here. First up, my job is to get the President re-elected in November. Peace treaty in Jerusalem makes that a sure thing. Second, Mid-East peace wins the President a place in history. I like that, too. I like that a lot.'

Maggie was smiling despite herself. Undiplomatic candour like Miller's made a refreshing change.

'But here's the point, Miss Costello. We got ourselves a chance to do the right thing *and* win a ton of votes doing it. Stopping the Jews and Arabs fighting, that's the right thing to do. We owe it to them not to fuck it up.' He paused, to make sure his homily had sunk in. 'So what you got?'

Maggie flannelled, claiming progress on both sides, then fell back on her insistence that their best shot at halting the violence would be finding the specific cause she believed lay behind several, if not all, of the incidents. She was getting closer to uncovering that cause, but it would take time.

'Time's what we don't have, Maggie.'

'I know, Mr Miller,' Maggie said, feeling a surge of guilt that she had been entrusted with this vital task and she was fumbling it. She hung up, promising another progress report later that night, and got back in the car.

For a long time she sat in silence, contemplating a second, lethal failure. Uri drove on, asking no questions.

By the time they stopped outside the lawyer's offices, the light was mellowing into afternoon. They walked up a single flight of stairs to a door marked DAVID ROSEN, ADVOCATE. Uri knocked gently, then pushed at the door. There was no one at the reception desk.

'Probably knocked off early,' he said out loud, unperturbed, and confident that he had now shaken off whatever bug had been pinned on him. Or her.

They looked in the first room: no one there. The next room was the same.

'What time was he expecting us here?' Maggie asked.

'I said I would come straight over.'

'Uri! That was ages ago. We wasted all that time at Orli's.'

Uri poked his head round the last door which, as he hoped, revealed the grandest office. The colour drained from his face.

This office was not empty. David Rosen was still at his desk. But he was slumped across it, his body as still as a corpse.

Tekoa, the West Bank, Thursday, 3.13 p.m.

THERE WERE ONLY FOUR of them gathered here, in a meeting whose existence, they agreed, would be denied by each of them. Akiva Shapira and the man at his right were the only two who held formal positions within the settler movement. The man in the chair had gained fame, and notoriety, another way, as the quartermaster of the *Machteret*, which had made several terrorist attacks on Arab politicians and others more than two decades earlier. He had served time in jail and had, officially, retreated from public life. Most Israeli journalists believed that he now lived abroad. Even so, here he was, deep inside the West Bank.

And yet, should an Israeli camera crew have stumbled upon this gathering, it would have been the figure seated directly opposite Shapira whose presence would have shocked most. This man was the personal aide to none other than Yossi Ben-Ari, the Defence Minister of the State of Israel.

'We're here, as you know, to talk about Operation Bar Kochba,' the quartermaster began. 'Our preferred option remains mass disobedience within the ranks of the IDF. Yariv can have no peace deal if the army refuses to implement its terms. If he gives the order to dismantle a settlement like this one, like Tekoa, then our people will refuse to obey.'

'But there was Gaza,' said Ben-Ari's man.

'Precisely. There was Gaza. We expected mass refusal then and it didn't happen. But now we have highly trained young men who will throw off their IDF uniforms and take up arms to protect their homeland.'

Shapira looked over at the aide to the Defence Minister. That he was here at all was symbolic enough. But that he was listening, without protest, to a plan by Israelis to take up arms against the army of Israel was extraordinary. That they had this man, and so, by implication, Ben-Ari himself, on side was proof of their strength and confirmation of Yariv's great weakness.

'I repeat, we deploy these forces only once an agreement is signed and once the government starts enforcing its terms. In the meantime, we are taking steps to prevent any such deal. You will have seen our claim of responsibility for the latest action in the Old City market.'

The others nodded.

'These pre-emptive steps then, aimed at destabilising the government before it can commit national surrender, will be the focus of our energies. We have in the last few days established a small unit dedicated to precisely these activities. For now, gentlemen, our fate is in the hands of these men. Tonight at the evening service, I suggest we each offer a silent prayer for the good fortune and success of the Defenders of United Jerusalem.'

Jerusalem, Thursday, 3.38 p.m.

URI APPROACHED the desk gingerly, Maggie following behind, her spirits plunging. There was no denying it: anyone who had been close to Uri's father ended up dead. Shimon's wife, poisoned with pills; Aweida, stabbed in a street market; Kishon, driven off a mountain in Switzerland. And now this man, David Rosen, a lawyer who had been entrusted with Guttman's last words, slumped over his desk before he had time to impart them.

When he was within touching distance of the body, Uri reached out to search for a pulse. A second after he had pressed his fingers into the neck, he leapt back, as if recoiling from an electric charge. At the same instant the body stirred and David Rosen sat bolt upright.

'Uri, what the hell are you doing here?' Silver-haired with large, unfashionable glasses, Rosen was thin, with spidery arms and legs. As he collected himself, Maggie could see faint red lines etched down one side of his face, the creases of a man who had fallen asleep on his desk.

'You asked me to come here, Mr Rosen! You called me. Said there had been a letter from my father.'

'Yes, yes, that's right. I only arrived from London this morning. Overnight flight. I'm exhausted. I must have fallen asleep.' Suddenly Rosen pulled himself up to his full height. 'Uri, I'm so sorry. I don't know what I was thinking. Please, come here.'

Uri approached and lowered himself, like an adolescent boy receiving a kiss from a tiny grandmother.

Rosen hugged him, muttering what seemed like a prayer. Then, in English: 'I wish you and your sister long life. A long life, Uri.'

Maggie gave Uri a stare.

'Oh, yes. Mr Rosen, this is Maggie Costello. From the American Embassy. She's helping me.'

'What do you mean? Why exactly is Miss Costello helping you?'

Uri did his best to explain, without giving away specifics. His mother had trusted this woman, he said, and, now, so did he. She was helping solve a problem that seemed to be expanding exponentially. Uri's eyes said something even simpler: I trust her, so should you.

'OK,' said Rosen finally. 'Here it is. He delivered it by hand last week.' And, with no more ceremony than that, he handed over a white envelope.

Uri opened it slowly and looked inside, a puzzled expression spreading across his face. He pulled out a clear plastic sleeve containing a single disc.

'A DVD,' said Uri. 'Can we use your machine?'

Rosen began fiddling with his computer until Uri moved round to his side of the desk, placed his hands on the old man's shoulders and gently shifted him out of the way. No time for courtesies, not now.

He inserted the disc and waited for the program to boot up. A screen within the screen appeared, black at first, then, after a second or two, filling up with a line of white characters. Hebrew.

'Message to Uri,' said Uri, translating.

Then, fading up from the black, a moving image appeared: Shimon Guttman, sitting at the desk where Maggie herself had sat just last night, his face haggard. He must have filmed this himself, alone, Maggie guessed, remembering the video camera and other paraphernalia in his study.

'Uri *yakiri.*'

'My dear Uri,' Uri begain translating in a low murmur, 'I hope you never need to see this, that I will come back to Rosen's office in the next week or so and remove this envelope, which I asked him to deliver to you only in the event of my disappearance or, God forbid, my death. With any luck, I'll be able to solve this problem by myself. But if I do not, then I could not let this knowledge die with me. You see, Uri, I have seen something so precious, so important, that I genuinely believe it will change anyone who sees it. I know that you and I disagree on almost everything, and I know you think your father exaggerates, but you will see that this is different.

'In the last couple of days I have come across what is the greatest archaeological discovery of my career. Of anyone's career, for that matter. To get to the point, I have seen the last will and testament of *Avraham Avinu*. You heard right. The final will of Abraham, the great patriarch. And here it is.'

Maggie's eyes opened wide. Uri stopped talking and they both stared at the screen, David Rosen as dumbfounded as both of them. Shimon Guttman, now with sweat beading on his forehead, had produced a small object from below, out of vision, which he held up to the camera. It was brown and about same size as an audio cassette.

'No one tried to sell me this,' Uri said, translating once more. 'I found it, by chance, in a shop in the Jerusalem market. My guess is that it was stolen from Iraq, from the National Museum. Whether the museum knew what they had, we will never know. But this text is real. In it, Abraham is an old man who has reached Hebron. It seems his two sons, Isaac and Ishmael, are close by. There seems to have been a dispute over Abraham's will. We know from the Torah that Abraham bequeathed the Land of Israel to Isaac and his descendants, the Jewish people. But Jerusalem, it seems, was a more complicated matter. In this text'—on screen, Guttman held up the tablet once more—'it's clear that Isaac and Ishmael had been arguing and that Abraham had to settle the dispute before he died. He must have called for a scribe to come to Hebron and take down this testament. So that there would be no confusion.

'In the text, the old man speaks only of Mount Moriah, the place where he was ready to kill his son Isaac. There was not yet the Jerusalem we know today. It is the ownership of this spot that Abraham decides in this text.

'My dear Uri, you know the significance of this. The government of Israel now includes three different religious parties. If this text shows clearly and unambiguously that Abraham gave the Temple Mount to the Jews, they will not be able to stomach a peace accord that compromises on that sovereignty. And what about the Palestinians? Their government includes Hamas, devout Muslims who revere Abraham. If this text says the Haram al-Sharif belongs to the heirs of Ishmael alone, how can they defy that will? More to the point, what of the first possibility, that this document gives that sacred land entirely to the Jews? How would the Muslim fundamentalists cope with that?

'That's why I am sure that if either side were to know even about the existence of this tablet, they would take extreme measures to prevent it seeing daylight. That's why I need to handle this carefully. I need to get this information to those who will treat it properly. Later today I will try to speak to the Prime Minister. But if something happens to me, this grave responsibility will become yours, Uri.'

Maggie placed a hand on his shoulder.

'You'll notice that I do not say here what the text reveals. I cannot risk that, in case this recording falls into the wrong hands. But if I am not here, it will be your job to find it. I have put it somewhere safe, somewhere only you and my brother could know about.

'I know you and I have had our differences. But I need you to put them aside and remember the good times, like that trip we took together for your Bar Mitzvah. What did we do on that trip, Uri? I hope you remember that.

'I can tell you only that this search begins in Geneva, but not the city everyone knows. A better, newer place, where you can be anyone you want to be. Go there and remember the times together I just spoke about.

'*Lech lecha*, my son. Go from here. And if I am gone from this life, then you shall see me in the other life; that is life too. Good luck, Uri.'

The screen went black. David Rosen sat in his chair, stunned by what he had just seen. Maggie was speechless. Uri, however, was furious.

He started pounding at the computer keyboard, trying frantically to find something else on the DVD, some further element they had missed. 'It can't finish there! It can't!' He was skipping back through the speech they had just watched. He played the last line again. '. . . Good luck, Uri.' Once more, the screen faded to black. Uri put his head in his hands. 'This is so typical of that bastard,' he said quietly.

'What's typical?' asked Rosen.

'This. Another dramatic gesture. He has a secret that got his wife killed, that could get his son killed, and does he reveal it? No. He plays games.'

'But, Uri,' said Maggie, trying to calm things down, 'wasn't he trying to tell you where it is? He said we have to start in Geneva.'

'Oh, don't listen to any of that crap. Not one word of it makes sense.'

'What do you mean?'

He looked up, his eyes blazing. 'Well, for a start he said, "I've put it somewhere safe, somewhere only you and my brother could know." It's nonsense.'

'Nonsense? How?'

'It's simple.' He looked her in the eye. 'My father didn't have a brother.'

BOTH MAGGIE AND URI were too fazed by that, too shocked by what they had seen on the DVD and too rapt in conversation to listen closely as they left the offices of David Rosen, Advocate. If they had, they might have heard the veteran lawyer pick up the telephone, asking to speak urgently to a man both he and the late Shimon Guttman regarded as a comrade, an ideological kindred spirit. 'Yes, immediately,' he said into the receiver. 'I need to speak right away to Akiva Shapira.'

Rafah refugee camp, Gaza, two days earlier

THEY WERE RUNNING out of places to meet. The golden rule of an armed underground—never in the same place twice—required an infinite supply of safe houses, and Salim Nazzal feared that theirs was dwindling. The peace talks in Jerusalem had been bad for business; the Palestinian street was suddenly less sympathetic to those who would bomb Israeli buses and Israeli shopping malls. Give the talks a chance—that had become the favoured position of the man in the café. No one's saying we can't go back to armed struggle if—when—the talks fail. But, for a few weeks, let's see what the negotiators can bring us.

In that climate, there was a limited number of Gazans ready to open their doors to a breakaway from Hamas, which, everyone knew, was out to sabotage the talks. The risks were insanely high. If anyone found out who was under your roof, your home could be flattened by an Israeli shell. Or you could be shot dead by the Fatah men who, while officially in coalition with Hamas, had not forgotten the street battles they had fought with the organisation not that long ago. Or you could be murdered by your former brothers in Hamas itself, disciplined for daring to rebel against the party line.

So Salim bowed graciously to his host, a man, like himself, in his thirties with the neat, short beard of an Islamist. The house was like all the others here: a basic box made of breeze blocks, its floors covered with thin, threadbare rugs and equipped with a TV set, a cooker and a few mattresses on which an entire family would have to sleep. It wasn't the tent city that international visitors would often expect from the words 'refugee camp'. It was more like a shantytown, an urban slum.

Tonight's meeting was even more clandestine than usual. Salim had crucial, and highly confidential, information to impart. A technician at Jawwal, the Palestinian mobile phone company, had been closing down the account of the late Ahmed Nour when he had noticed an unplayed message in the dead man's voicemail box. Curious, he listened to it: a rambling, excitable message in English from a man who seemed to be an Israeli scholar. The technician had then made contact with Salim, saying he wanted to pass this knowledge to Palestinian patriots and faithful Muslims.

'We have heard news that will have a great bearing on our struggle,' Salim began. 'A Zionist activist and archaeologist claims to have bought, from an Arab in Jerusalem, a tablet expressing the last will and testament of Ibrahim.' He paused. 'Ibrahim Khalil'ullah.' *Abraham, Allah's friend*.

The men's expressions broke out into a series of sceptical smiles.

'My reaction too, my brothers. But the indications are—and I beg of you that not a word of this travels beyond this room—that the document could well be genuine. Doubtless, this man will claim that this text supports Zionist claims to Jerusalem. We all know what the Hamas leadership will say to this. Either that this is Zionist theft of Arab heritage, looted almost certainly from Iraq, or that it is a fake and a forgery that only the Zionist media cannot see through, and so on. We would say the same.'

The six men in the room nodded. Salim was younger than most of them but he was respected. In the second *intifada* he had played an active role in the Izz-ad-Din al-Qassam brigades, Hamas's military wing. He was a bomb-maker, one of the few who had avoided the crosshairs of the Israeli military's targeted assassination policy.

'But none of that will matter. The Israeli right will not give up an inch of the Haram al-Sharif if they can point to some text that says Ibrahim gave it to them. The peace talks will be over.'

'What if the document says the Haram belongs to us?'

'I think it's safe to assume that if a Zionist scholar had found such a text in the ground he would have put it straight back there.'

The questioner smiled, nodded and sat back.

'Many Palestinians will work hard to prevent this document coming to light in the belief that, if Ibrahim's will is known, it will weaken the Palestinian claim on Jerusalem. But there is another view. That if this tablet emerges, and it gives the Zionists all they want, they will definitely not agree to the arrangements they have been discussing at Government House. Why would they share Jerusalem when Ibrahim has said it belongs to them, all of it?'

'They will call off talks immediately,' chipped in one of Salim's most reliable lieutenants.

'They will. And this sham of a peace process will be over. No more non-sense about a truce with the enemy. We can return to the legitimate struggle, one the Prophet, peace be upon him, has determined we shall win.'

'So,' began another. 'You're saying it is in our interest for this document to become public?'

'If we want this betrayal of our people to end, I believe so, yes. But first we have to find and capture it. Whatever has to be done to get it, must be done. Do I have your agreement?'

The men looked at each other, and in chorus they replied, 'God is great.'

CHAPTER EIGHT

Jerusalem, Thursday, 6.23 p.m.

Uri drove Maggie back to the hotel in silence. He had turned up the rap music again, so that they could drown out whatever bug was listening, but Maggie couldn't stand it. She would prefer to say nothing than have her head pounded with noise. And she knew that if they were being bugged, they were almost certainly being followed.

Back at the hotel she led Uri straight to the bar, ordered a Scotch for each of them and all but forced him to down his before ordering another round.

'What about this brother then, Uri?' she said, glancing at the notes she'd made during the Guttman video message.

'There is no brother.'

'You sure? Could your grandfather have had an earlier marriage? A secret family he kept hidden?'

Uri looked at her. 'After everything else, nothing would surprise me.'

'So it's possible?'

He seemed tired. 'If you can keep one secret, maybe you can keep many.'

Without thinking, Maggie placed her hand on his. It felt warm. She let it linger, even after she felt self-conscious, just for a second or two. 'OK, let's put the brother thing to one side for now.'

At the other end of the bar Maggie noticed an orthodox Jewish man munching peanuts and reading the *Jerusalem Post*. She couldn't remember if he had been there when they arrived.

'Come,' she said suddenly. 'I need to sit on a proper chair.'

She eased herself off the stool, beckoning Uri to follow. Finding a spot directly behind the peanut-muncher, she placed her drink on the table and sat where she would have a clear line of sight. Now if the man wanted to watch them, he would have to turn round and reveal himself.

She called over a waiter and ordered some food. Then, on impulse really, with no planning, she began to tell Uri what had happened that morning in the market, keeping it brief and factual. She spared some of the details, but still she saw Uri's face turn from horror to anger.

'The bastards—' he began, rising to his feet.

'Uri! Sit down.' She tugged him back into his seat. 'Listen, I'm angry too. But the only way we're going to find these people is if we keep calm.'

The waiter brought over two plates of sandwiches. Maggie was glad of the diversion.

'Look,' she began, once she was sure Uri would not bolt again. 'You know what I can't work out? Why they follow us, but don't strike. Why they don't just take us out. They're killing everyone else.'

Uri chewed for a while, as if trying to swallow his rage. Eventually he spoke, making a clear effort to sound lighter than he felt. 'Speaking as an ex-intelligence officer of the Israel Defence Force, I'd say when you follow like this, but don't strike, it can mean one of two things. Either the target is too risky to take out. If these are Palestinians who are following us, the last thing they need is to kill an American official. Especially a beautiful, female one. Imagine how the American public would react.'

Maggie looked down, unsure how to reply. 'All right, I get the picture,' she said. 'The same would be true of the Israelis.'

'Even worse for them in a way,' said Uri.

'So what's the other possibility? You said there were two.'

'Oh, the other time you stalk but don't strike is when you want the subject alive. To lead you somewhere.'

Maggie took a swig of the drink, letting an ice cube slip between her lips, enjoying its chill on her tongue. So they wanted her to pursue this Guttman trail, whoever 'they' were. They would keep away for as long as she was useful. 'But the people who attacked me today told me to back off.'

'I know,' said Uri. 'So maybe they're in the first category. They're only not killing you because killing you would bring too much trouble.'

'Or maybe more than one group is following us. All for different reasons.'

'Maybe.'

Maggie pulled out the note she had scribbled in Rosen's office. 'Your father said something about the "good times". Some trip you took together for your Bar Mitzvah. He said he hoped you would remember that.'

'I do remember it. He took me with him on a working trip to Crete. He wanted to check out the excavations at Knossos. Imagine it: I was thirteen years old, and I was looking at dusty old relics.'

'Did anything specific happen?'

'It was a long time ago, Maggie. I just remember waiting around a lot. And I liked the plane ride. I remember that.'

'Think Uri, think. There must be some reason your dad mentioned this in the message. Did something important happen there?'

'Well, it felt important to me at the time. It was a big treat to be alone, just me and him. It hadn't happened before. And it didn't happen again.'

'Did you talk about something?'

'I remember him talking about the Minoans, saying they had once been this great civilisation. And look at them now, he said. They don't exist any more. That could happen to us, he said; to the Jews. It nearly *has* happened, lots of times. That's why we need Israel, he said.'

Anything specific, Maggie was thinking impatiently, straining to stick to her own rule: to let people talk until the crucial sentence tumbled out.

'He told me about his parents, how his mother had been killed by the Nazis, how his father had survived. That was an amazing story. He hid, my grandfather, with a family of non-Jews, on a farm in Hungary. They kept him in the pig sty. At the end of the war, he escaped by crawling through two miles of sewers.'

Maggie suddenly remembered the rows about the Swiss banks that had kept their hands on long-dormant accounts held by Jews who had been murdered by the Nazis. Could there be a connection? 'Uri. You know the message mentioned Geneva? Might your family have left—?'

'My family had no money. Poor before the Nazis and poor after.'

'OK, so not money. But what about a safe-deposit box in Geneva? Maybe your father hid the tablet in a Swiss bank.'

'I just don't see it. A vault in Geneva? That would cost serious money. Besides, when would he have had the time to put it there? He said on the DVD he'd only just found the tablet.'

Maggie nodded; Uri was right. Geneva must mean something else.

'And what about all this stuff at the end? "And if I am gone from this life, then you shall see me in the other life; that is life too." I was under the impression your father was not a religious man.'

'Maybe that's what happens when you hold the words of Abraham in your hand. And if you fear death. Maybe you start talking like a rabbi.'

'I'm sorry about all this, Uri.'

'It's not your fault. But it's horrible to realise you hardly knew your own father. All these secrets.'

'Look,' she said. 'They're closing up here. We'd better go.'

But instead of heading for the lifts, Maggie strode over to the front desk.

Uri watched as she launched into a long story about allergies and dust and how she simply couldn't sleep another hour in her room. The night manager put up some resistance but soon surrendered. He took her old key, replacing it with one for room 302, and despatched a porter to move her things.

As she turned round, she gave Uri a wink: 'No bugs in room 302.'

He insisted on walking her to her room. Once they got there, she asked where he was going to sleep. He looked as if he hadn't thought about it.

'Well, my apartment is being watched. And so is my parents' house.'

'Seems like the only reason they're not killing you is because you're with me,' said Maggie, smiling up at him.

'Well, I'd better stay with you, then.'

SHE KNEW she should have said no, should have insisted that he take the lift back down, that he sleep in the car if necessary. But she told herself that he would sleep on the sofa and that would be that. She even opened a cupboard, looking for extra blankets and pillows. But when she turned round, Uri was standing behind her, unmoving, as if refusing to play along with this charade.

'Uri, listen, I explained—'

'I know what you said,' he replied, placing a finger on her lips.

Before she could say another word, he was kissing her, gently at first, but soon it was urgent and the current of electricity came from her.

She kissed him hungrily, her hands moving through his hair, tugging at it, wanting to bring his face, his smell, closer. It was a sort of devouring, and they both felt the urgency of it. His hands were caressing the side of her face, then her neck, until now they were tearing at her top.

A moment later they had fallen onto the bed. Each caress, each taste, brought a new flash of intense sensation, until their bodies were joined. She was sure she could feel not only his desire but also his longing, his need, even his grief. And as she howled her release, she knew he could hear her own need, her yearning to be free after so long.

WHEN SHE WOKE up, sometime after 2 a.m., she was too wired to get back to sleep. Uri was slumbering beside her, and for nearly an hour she lay there on her side, just watching him breathe.

Eventually she grew restless. She got out of bed, grabbed a T-shirt and crept over to the desk. She flipped open the lid of her laptop and opened up her email. Top of the list was a message from Liz.

Mags. My Second Life account tells me you never used that link I sent you. So knew you wouldn't! But you should. Not only is it proof of your 2L stardom, but there's also some pretty cool stuff on there. Just go on as me . . . btw, we must talk about Dad's 70th. I reckon a big do, you know, fly him and Mum to Vegas, strippers, the works. What do you reckon? Just kidding xx L

The next one was from Edward. She braced herself.

M. Not that you would care but am off to Geneva this evening. Government business, can't get into it in an email. We have some practical matters to resolve when we both return. Please advise on your plans. E

Maggie let herself fall back into her chair. *Please advise*. Had this man really once been her lover? She looked over at Uri, the outline of his sleeping body visible under a single white sheet, and she smiled.

Maggie clicked back to Liz's message. Such a sweetie. She was about to hunt out Second Life when she had a sudden sinking feeling. Their phone calls were bugged, they were being followed and, it seemed, her work on Shimon Guttman's computer had been watched. Someone was probably reading this right now. She snapped the lid shut.

She knew she wouldn't sleep, she was buzzing too much. So she pulled on some clothes, creaked open the door and tiptoed down the corridor to the hotel's business centre. In the era of the BlackBerry and wi-fi, such centres were hardly used any more, and there was just one single, forlorn terminal in the room. But it worked, asking her for her room number and nothing else. That was OK: hotel staff could see what she was doing, it was just the electronic eavesdroppers she wanted to avoid.

She called up Liz's email again, scribbled down the user name—Lola Hepburn!—and password she had given her, and clicked on the link. The screen instantly went black, then displayed a message.

Welcome to Second Life, Lola.

She entered her details, then watched as a computer-generated landscape began to fill the screen, as if to herald the start of a video game. In the foreground, with her back to Maggie, was a stylised version of a lithe young woman wearing tight jeans and a Union Jack bra top. This, Maggie realised, was Lola Hepburn, Liz's embodiment in Second Life, her 'avatar'. Maggie looked at the set of buttons that appeared at the foot of the screen: MAP, FLY, CHAT and a few others whose meaning eluded her. There was an instruction to use the keyboard's arrows to move backwards and forwards, left and right. She tried it and watched, amazed, as the buxom siren on screen moved ahead, jerkily, with arms swinging, in a simulation of human walking.

She seemed to be in some kind of virtual garden, with brown autumnal trees swaying in the wind. It was as if Maggie were operating a camera, lurking several feet behind and above the avatar, one that followed its—her—every move. It was bizarre and strangely mesmerising.

Maggie looked down at the scribbled instructions taken from Liz's email. To get to the venue for the peace-simulation game, she had to hit the MAP button, find the MY LANDMARKS pulldown menu, select Harvard University, Middle East Studies and then hit TELEPORT. She smiled as the computer gave off a suitably sci-fi *whoosh* sound, suggesting a *Star Trek*-style leap across the universe. The screen darkened, lit up with a message that said, 'Second Life, Arriving . . .' and an instant later she saw the girl in the jeans and crop top standing somewhere else entirely. She was surrounded on all sides by buildings, some rendered in traditional brick, some in more modish steel and glass, arranged as if on a university campus.

As the avatar walked ahead, Maggie noticed a ramp in front of her, with the words WELCOME TO THE FACULTY FOR MIDDLE EAST STUDIES printed on it. She moved upwards, marvelling at the change in perspective as she did so. There was a reception desk in the lobby and, at shoulder level, a series of signposts. Maggie took the one marked Peace Simulation.

Suddenly she was inside a room laid out in classic negotiation style: a long wooden table with space for more than twenty people round it. Avatars were sitting in every place, name cards in front of each one. There was one for the American President, another for the UN Secretary General and several more for the leaders of assorted interested parties: the perennial 'moderate' Arab states, Egypt and Jordan, the European Union, Russia and others. Ringing the room were chairs laid out for officials, from the US Secretary of State down. She moved her cursor over the American team, until she came across a female avatar, with long brown hair, a trim figure and a vacant expression. A black information bubble appeared: Maggie Costello, US mediator.

'At least I'm in the room,' Maggie muttered to herself. She guessed these were dumb avatars, inert mannequins installed inside Second Life as props to add to the authenticity of the scene. You had to give it to the geek community: they certainly cared about detail.

Then Maggie noticed that two of the figures round the table were not still, but wobbling. They were facing each other, identified in on-screen bubbles as Yaakov Yariv and Khalil al-Shafi. They had the faces of the two men too, or a close computer simulation of them. Only the bodies and clothes didn't fit, unless Israel's aged Prime Minister still maintained an ostentatiously muscled chest, while the Fatah leader secretly dressed like an urban clubber. Now that her avatar was this near, she could eavesdrop on their conversation. She checked her watch. Early evening on the east coast: these were probably a couple of postgrads putting in some extra hours of role-play.

A speech bubble appeared by the Yaakov Yariv avatar. A line of yellow text: Hello? Can we help you? Are you taking part in the peace simulation?

There was only one thing for it. Maggie would have to pretend to be someone else. Valley girl, she decided. She hit the CHAT key and typed. As the words appeared on the screen, she noticed her avatar's arms rise and her hands start flapping, in a mime of typing.

hope i'm not crashing in here guys, but i'm doing my major in int rels and if i could listen in it could really help.

Yariv came back a second or two later, the hands of his avatar now waggling in front of him, as if hitting the keys of an unseen keyboard.

Where do you study?

Maggie hesitated, looking again at Liz's avatar.

burbank community college.

There was a pause.

OK.

Maggie waited, enjoying this strange game. She wondered what Liz got up to here. Did she have the boyfriend in Second Life that she lacked in the first?

The al-Shafi character began. Have you seen the latest Silwan map?

There was a delay of a second or two. Then a bubble popped up by the Yariv avatar. We saw it. It involves a bypass route for the water main.

Khalil al-Shafi: Yes.

Yaakov Yariv: Who would pay for that?

Khalil al-Shafi: We propose three years from the EU-UN fund, eventually to be self-sustaining.

Yaakov Yariv: With access to the Jordanian aquifer?

Khalil al-Shafi: We imagine so. But we would need your in-principle agreement before we would put that to the Jordanians.

Maggie nodded her head in professional admiration. You had to hand it to these kids: they were certainly taking their studies seriously, getting into the real detail of the negotiations. Water was one of those issues whose importance eluded most outsiders to the Middle East conflict—too busy thinking about oil.

Good for them, she thought. She went back to her keyboard, back to the busty Valley girl.

you guys are really smart! thanks a bunch but i think i'd better study some more before i'm ready for this stuff, wish me luck!

Having said her goodbyes, Maggie exited the room then hit the FLY button. Sure enough, the glamorous avatar rose from the ground and, with a little help from the forward arrow, took flight.

Immediately, she collided with a neighbouring building, smacking her virtual head on it, watching her virtual self flinch. But a few moments later she was soaring above the Harvard campus. The graphics were extraordinarily detailed, showing the white stucco cladding on the Dunster House clock tower, even the newsstands and bicycle racks of Harvard Yard.

She carried on flying, her arms outstretched, her body horizontal, like a heavy-chested Superman. She was zooming over seas, palm-fringed islands, city streets, occasionally descending to take a closer look.

Maggie went back to the MAP key, taking a few seconds to work out what she had to do. Homesickness decided her first destination. She typed in 'Dublin' and then hit TELEPORT.

A *whoosh* later and she was standing in a landscape that felt instantly familiar, even reproduced like this. The water on the Liffey was too static, but the Temple Bar area was there, complete with the clubs and pubs she remembered so well from her teenage years, when she and the other convent girls drank vodka like Russian sailors. But it looked desolate tonight, just her and a few wastrels mooching down Dame Street.

She sniffed at the thought of it. Pathetic really, a grown woman staring at a screen in the middle of the night to remind her of home. She shut the computer down, crept out of the glass-walled business centre and headed for the lifts. She thought of the Dublin she had just seen. Not like any Dublin she remembered. Cleaner, tidier and infinitely lonelier.

It was only as the lift doors slid shut that it hit her. *Of course*. That's what Shimon Guttman had meant. How could she not have seen it till now?

'Come on, come on,' she said, desperate to get back and wake Uri. She looked up at the numbers, counting the floors. *Seven, eight, nine*. Here.

Hesitantly, she peered out of the lift doors, just in case whoever had been following her had stationed himself outside her room. No one there.

She padded along the corridor and slid her keycard into the lock until it flashed green. She pushed the door open, and had begun crying out Uri's name when she felt a hard, quick blow to the back of the neck.

Jerusalem, an hour earlier

FIRST HE HEARD the double click, the signal that they were speaking on a secure line. As always, the boss got straight to the point.

'My worry is that things are spiralling out of control.'

'I understand.'

'We need that tablet. The cure is beginning to look worse than the disease.'

'I know how it looks.'

He could hear a deep sigh on the other end of the phone. That was the drawback of a job like this, working for a big decision-maker. Such men always expected action immediately.

'But now we've started, I don't see how we can stop. You've seen the latest. Hizbullah firing rockets at towns in the middle of the night, maximising risk of casualties. We can't let ourselves be dictated to by them.'

'What about Costello? Has she got anything?'

'I think she's making progress. And what she knows, we know.'

Another sigh. 'We need to have this tablet in our possession. We have to know what's on it before they do. So we can act first. Shape events.'

'You know it's always possible that no one will get it. I mean if Costello fails to lead us to the tablet, it would be as if the whole issue never arose.'

The voice on the end of the secure line did not need to hear more. He could put the pieces together. 'That's not bad.'

'Almost a win-win.'

'OK. Let's talk in the morning.'

He heard the familiar second click, then terminated the call and scrolled through his contacts to find the number of the surveillance team, the unit tracking Guttman and Costello. He was connected within a single ring.

'Do you have the subjects within view? . . . Good. We need to talk about a change in plan.'

Jerusalem, Friday, 3.11 a.m.

AT FIRST she wasn't sure if she had opened her eyes. The room was in complete darkness. She raised her neck, a reflex, to check the clock, but immediately felt a spasm of pain. Where was she? Flat, the palms of her hands detected the cotton softness of bedclothes. She was, then, still in her room.

Suddenly there was a voice, alarmingly close to her ear.

'I'm so, so sorry. I'm sorry, Maggie.'

Uri.

She tried to haul herself up, but the pain shot through her again.

'I woke up and saw the bed was empty. I thought maybe something had happened to you. I waited by the door and then—'

'And then you hit me.'

'I didn't know it was you. I'm so sorry. How can I make it better?'

Maggie decided to push through the pain barrier and sit up. Uri instantly propped her up on some pillows, passing her a glass of water. As her eyes adjusted to the dark, she could see that he was kneeling by the bed.

'Where the hell did you learn to hit like that?'

'You know the answer to that.'

'You Israelis don't mess around, do you?' she said, rubbing at the pain.

'Here.' At his side was a towel, the edge of which was soaked. He placed it at the back of Maggie's neck. The towel was cold, soothing.

'Uri!' she said suddenly, grabbing the towel from him so that she could face him. 'Turn on the light. And pass me my jacket, on the chair.'

He got up and brought back Maggie's coat. She patted through the pockets, till she found it: the notes she'd made in Rosen's office.

'OK. Listen. Your father said, "I can tell you only that this search begins in Geneva, but not the city everyone knows. A better, newer place, where you can be anyone you want to be. Go there." Remember?'

'Yes.'

'I think I know where that is.' Maggie scanned ahead, to her last scribbled line. 'Then he said, "And if I am gone from this life, then you shall see me in the other life; that is life too." Uri, what were his exact words. In Hebrew.'

'I don't understand a word you're saying.'

'You will. Just tell me what he said!'

'OK. "*Im eineini ba-chaim ha'ele, tireh oti ba-chaim ha-hem.*"'

Maggie looked down at the note. 'And that means, "If I am gone from this life, you shall see me in the other life", right?'

'Yes. Then he said something odd. "*B'chaim shteim.*" Meaning, "in life two".'

'As in "that is also life".'

'No, no. Not "too" but "two". *Shteim* is the number two.'

Maggie felt the adrenaline coursing through her. 'So he was actually saying: "You shall see me in the other life; that is, life number two"?'

'Right.'

'Or to put it another way,' she said triumphantly, 'Second Life.'

For the first time, Maggie felt this was a problem that could be solved. Shimon Guttman was sharp, and Uri had told her that his father was at ease with new technology. Didn't he even say the old man played computer games?

What he had done was utterly in character. Under pressure, aware that he was holding in his palms a geopolitical timebomb, he had decided to hide the Abraham tablet, or the secret of its location, where no one would think to look. Nowhere in the real world at all. But in the virtual realm, *A better, newer place, where you can be anyone you want to be*. Second Life.

And then her stomach gave way. *Oh, no*. To have come this far and to have screwed up now. How could they, how could *she*, have been so stupid?

'What is it?' asked Uri, still baffled.

Maggie said nothing, simply placing her finger over her lips. *What idiots*. They had forgotten that they were being listened to. It wasn't enough that they had changed rooms; their pursuers had had several hours to catch up. Which meant that they could now know her crucial discovery.

Maggie reached for the hotel message pad by the phone, scribbling fast: *Get dressed*. There was no time to waste. She had to get onto Second Life before they did. She was tempted to use her laptop and be done with it. But it was too risky: if they had already hacked into that, they would discover whatever she was about to find the instant she found it.

When Uri was dressed, she led the way downstairs, back to the business centre. She powered up the machine, reassured by its anonymity, and logged into Second Life, using the name and password Liz had given her.

Uri stood over her shoulder, his face lit up by the screen. When Liz's avatar materialised, his eyes widened. 'Wow. Hey, Lola!'

'She's not mine; she's my sister's.'

'Your sister looks like a fun girl.' For that, she slapped him on the arm.

Feeling like a veteran now, Maggie called up the TELEPORT prompt and keyed in the six letters she hoped would unlock this puzzle once and for all.

Her avatar had now landed in the scrubbed streets of virtual Geneva. She began walking down Rue des Etuves, turning into Rue Vallin. There was hardly anyone about, save for a couple of rabbit-headed avatars on a street corner. Maggie headed down Rue du Temple to avoid them.

'You're saying my dad came to this . . . place?' asked Uri.

'"Geneva, but not the city everyone knows." He must have mentioned something about it to Kishon. But Kishon went to the wrong Geneva. What your father had was hidden here somewhere. We'll have to work it out.'

She reached into her pocket, looking again at her notes. *I have put it somewhere safe, somewhere only you and my brother could know*. If only she understood what the hell that meant. She read on. *I need you to remember the good times, like that trip we took together for your Bar Mitzvah. What did we do on that trip, Uri? I hope you remember that . . .*

'What did you do on the trip, Uri? Think.'

'I told you. We went to Crete. I got bored.'

'All right. Let's see if Geneva has a Greek museum or something.'

'Minoan,' he said. 'Crete is Minoan.'

Maggie gave Uri a glare. 'Thank you, Professor.' She tried to see if there was a directory of buildings of this virtual Geneva. Nothing.

'The funny thing is,' Uri was saying, more to himself than to Maggie, 'the only really strong memory I have of that trip is the flight; it was the first time I had ever been on a plane. That's what really stuck in my mind. I told my father that, probably hurt his feelings. But it was true. We sat together, by the window seat, and I found it amazing, looking down at this beautiful blue water, while he pointed out the different islands below.'

Maggie suddenly turned to look at him. She could hear Guttman's voice: *What did we do on that trip, Uri? I hope you remember that*.

'He wants us to do that here,' she said, hitting the arrow keys with new vigour. 'He wants us to fly over Lake Geneva, looking for islands.'

The avatar was hovering above the virtual city, as Maggie directed it first west, then east, looking for a big patch of blue. Once she had found the shoreline, she slowed down so that her avatar could fly low and close.

'There's one!' said Uri, pointing to the bottom left of the screen.

Clumsily, Maggie turned herself round and hovered over a cartoon depiction of a desert island. It had a flag planted in the yellow sand announcing times for a weekly poetry discussion group. Maggie hit the up arrow.

There were several islands in the lake, but none had any connection to Shimon Guttman. Maggie was growing anxious.

'Come on,' said Uri. 'Keep flying. If it's here, we'll find it.'

Maggie kept it up, looping and dipping over the blue of Second Life's version of Lake Geneva, concentrating hard to stay at the right altitude.

'Hey, what's that?' said Uri, pointing at a small patch of land below. Maggie had to double back, steering Lola down.

'I don't believe it,' Uri said, shaking his head. 'Even here.'

'What is it, Uri? What?'

'See the shape of that island?' He was pointing at the yellow pixels on the screen. 'On the left? That's Israel. And that big bulge? That's Jordan. This is the map of Eretz Yisrael, the complete Land of Israel, according to right-wing fanatics like my father. They have this shape on their T-shirts. I grew up with this shape, Maggie. Believe me, my father must have done this.'

Maggie clicked to stop flying, landing splashily on the water lapping against the island's shore. She walked forward, but was pushed back. A red line, like a laser beam girdling the island, materialised each time the avatar got too near. She could see it was made up of words: NO ENTRY NO ENTRY NO ENTRY. A small message appeared: cannot enter parcel—not member of the group.

'Damn. It's locked somehow.' Her avatar was static. Maggie looked at the bottom of the screen, trying to find a box for keying in a password.

'Hey, Maggie. Who's this?'

She looked up and felt a chill run through her. Two avatars were hovering close by. They had the same, eerie bunny-heads she had seen before, but now both were clad in black.

Maggie looked up at Uri. 'They're following us, trying to get whatever information your father stored here before we do. What should I do?'

'Can you talk to them?'

Maggie hit CHAT and typed, trying to stay in character, hey guys, what's up?

She waited for a reply. Three seconds, four, five. She waited till the Second Life clock in the corner of the screen turned a minute. Nothing.

'They're waiting for us to make a move.'

Maggie imagined their operators running de-encryption programs, working out how to smash through Guttman's little barrier. If these people were clever enough to have followed Lola Hepburn to this spot within Second Life, they would hardly let one piffling cordon stand in their way.

'I'm going to get something,' Uri said, heading for the door. 'I'll be back in a second.'

Puzzled, Maggie watched him leave. As she turned back to the screen, there was a *whoosh* sound and everything went blank. Suddenly the screen was loading with a landscape Maggie did not recognise. She had been teleported somewhere else within Second Life, even though she had clicked no button. Could she have fumbled the keyboard without realising it?

Then she saw them. Four rabbit-heads now, surrounding her. She pressed the forward arrow and moved a few paces, then froze. She turned into a side alley. The rabbit-men were behind her, gaining ground. She froze again.

Maggie could feel her own, real-life, breath coming short and fast. Whoever was behind the rabbit-heads was paralysing her avatar. Now she wouldn't be able to return to the island in Lake Geneva. Whatever message Shimon Guttman had locked there would be out of reach.

Maggie heard the sound of the door opening and turned to see Uri clutching a neat pile of light brown clothes. Without explanation, he began unbuckling his trousers and removing his shirt, before stashing them out of view. That done, he started putting on the items he'd brought in: the uniform of a hotel bellboy.

'What on earth—?'

'Anyone who's ever worked night shifts in a hotel, as I have, knows they all have a laundry room somewhere. You just have to find it and break in.'

'But why?'

'We've got to get out of here. Now the people who have been bugging us have what they want. They know the answer is on that island and they'll get it. They don't need us any more, Maggie. We're in the way.'

Her heart hammering, she turned back to the screen, where Lola was now surrounded by six rabbit-headed men. She hit the FLY button, to escape. It didn't work. The avatars in black were closing in.

And now something else was happening. The face on Lola Hepburn, the fresh-faced Valley girl with the ponytail, was starting to change. The eyes began to droop, as if they were about to dissolve into tears. Now the nose began to descend too, the face of this electronic creature no longer perky but increasingly hideous. Soon Lola's entire body was a pool of sludge. Their only chance to find out what Shimon Guttman knew had gone.

'Maggie.' It was Uri, at the door, about to leave. 'In three minutes' time, go down the fire escape.' He pointed to the entrance. 'Walk down the stairs as far as you can go. You'll come out in the kitchens. Turn left, and head for the loading bay. Get out there and I'll be in a car.'

'How are you going to get—?'

'Just do it.'

And then he vanished, for all the world a member of the night team of the David's Citadel Hotel.

Psagot, the West Bank, Friday, 4.07 a.m.

HIS WIFE HEARD the ringing of the phone before he did. He had always been a heavy sleeper, but now that he was carrying perhaps twenty or thirty pounds in excess weight, his descent into slumber was positively leaden. His wife was shaking him vigorously when he finally awoke.

'Akiva, come on. Akiva!'

Akiva Shapira groaned before squinting at the clock on the nightstand. It was gone four in the morning. Who on earth could be calling so late?

He picked up the receiver. 'What the hell—?'

'Akiva, in the last hour I have spoken to the other members of our group, seeking permission for a specific action which has just become possible. If we all agree, we have to act at once.'

Shapira recognised the voice of the Defence Minister's aide, who had been present at the meeting the previous afternoon. 'I'm listening.'

'The subject we discussed. She is now in our sights. We can strike.'

'Risks?'

'Arrest and capture, minimal. Our snipers are highly skilled.'

'OK,' said Shapira. 'Do it.'

CHAPTER NINE

Jerusalem, Friday, 4.21 a.m.

She got out of the hotel more easily than she expected. Uri's instructions were accurate and the kitchen was empty. She unbolted the door at the back and stepped out onto a raised concrete platform, looking down into a square gulch built for reversing delivery trucks.

Two minutes later, she saw the beam of headlights coming into the area then swerving round and reversing towards the loading bay. A sleek silver Mercedes was nudging backwards in her direction. It's rear lights meant that she could now see a set of steps off to the side. She thought about heading down them, then hesitated. What if it wasn't Uri?

She stayed in the shadows until she heard the slow glide of an electric window, followed by a whispered 'psst'. Uri. She leapt down the stairs and bundled herself into the passenger seat.

'Nice wheels. How did you pull this off?'

'By strolling over to the concierge desk, finding the valet parking box and taking the first key I saw.'

'Hence the uniform.'

He nodded. 'So now you've got the limousine, where do you want to go, Miss Costello?'

'Anywhere with a computer. The rabbit-heads melted me. They're going to get through to the island before we do.'

'Even if they do, they might not understand what they see. To judge from my father's message, that requires knowledge that only I have.' He paused. 'Why did he have to make everything so complicated, though?'

'Actually, I kind of admire it. There are a lot of serious people who want the discovery he made and none of them have got their hands on it.'

'Not yet.'

'All right. But it's pretty impressive if you ask me.'

Uri drove on in silence.

'So where are you taking me, Mr Chauffeur?'

'One of the few places in Jerusalem that stays open all night. And certainly the only one with a computer we can use.'

He parked the car at the bottom of a pedestrianised area and guided her through to a maze of narrow, catacomb streets, where each arch or vaulted entrance led to a shop or office; modern life carved out of ancient stone.

'Here we are. Someone to Run With.'

'That's its name?'

'Yeah. It's become a Jerusalem institution. All the runaways and dropouts come here. Named it after a novel.'

'Someone to run with, eh? Like you and me.'

Uri smiled and ushered Maggie inside. She surveyed the room. There were no chairs, only enormous cushions arranged on stone benches and window seats. The air was heavy with the smoke of tobacco and assorted varieties of weed. In one corner a boy was hunched over a guitar, a curtain of lank, dark hair hiding his face. The kids barely glanced up at her or Uri—too stoned to notice probably.

Uri nodded at the sole, unused computer in the corner of the room. While he went to the counter and asked a girl with a stud in her nose for coffee, Maggie switched on the machine and called up Second Life.

At the name prompt she typed 'Lola Hepburn', only for an error message to appear: Invalid username and/or password, please try again. Liz's avatar had been eradicated from the system. She would have to enter as someone else. Who?

Then she heard it again, the voice of Shimon Guttman, as clear she had heard it twelve hours ago in Rosen's office.

You shall see me in the other life, not this one but the next one.

Of course. She was meant to enter Second Life as Shimon Guttman himself. That was surely how the coding worked: the island in Geneva would open up to no one but him.

As she typed his first and last names, and Vladimir67 as the password, she hoped that, just this once, the old man had made it easy.

Invalid username and/or password, please try again.

Uri arrived with an oversized cup of steaming coffee. Merely inhaling its aroma made Maggie realise how tired she was. She had been living on adrenaline for days now, and her body was feeling it.

Uri watched what she was doing. 'Why don't you try the name my father used to email that Arab guy?'

Maggie gave Uri a downturned smile, as if to say, not a bad idea. She typed in Saeb Nastayib and repeated the previous password, Vladimir67, and beamed when a lean male figure materialised on the screen.

She hit MAP, typed 'Geneva', hit TELEPORT and, after a few seconds, she was hovering over the blue water and green banks of the lake. Anxiously, she searched for Guttman's uniquely contoured island. Finally a green stain appeared on the blueness of the lake which, as the avatar drew near, revealed itself as the replica Greater Israel Uri's father had created.

This time there was no electronic cordon; there wasn't even a password.

'We're in,' she said with relief.

'Now what?' asked Uri, leaning forward, cradling his cup of coffee.

'Now we look.'

They didn't have far to go. The island had only one structure, a glass-and-steel box. Inside it was a chair, a desk and a virtual computer. Maggie pushed the Guttman avatar forward and sat him on the chair. The instant he did, a text bubble appeared:

> Go west, young man, and make your way to the model city, close to the Mishkan.
> You'll find what I left for you there, in the path of ancient warrens.

'So, Uri. What do we have here?' She looked round, expecting to see Uri peering at the words with her. But he was gone.

Khan Yunis, Gaza, Friday, 2.40 a.m.

HE WAS NOT ASLEEP, so he heard the footsteps himself. Instinctively, he removed the safety catch on his pistol and waited in the dark. He saw a curve of candleglow before he heard a voice.

'Psst. Salim, it's Marwan.'

'Come in, brother.'

Warily, the younger man tiptoed into the room where Salim Nazzal was bedded down for the night. He looked around, counted three teenage boys, all fast asleep on a single mattress. He had no idea whose house he was in, which family had opened its doors to their leader for tonight.

'Salim. They say they have something. A sighting, in Jerusalem.'

'Of this tablet?'

'Of the Zionist's son. And the American woman.'

Nazzal replaced the safety catch on his gun. He wanted time to think.

'The unit on the ground want to know whether they should strike.'

One of the boys stirred. Salim waited until he was sure he was asleep.

'Tell them,' he said eventually, 'that they are free to act—'

'OK—' He strode away at once.

'Marwan! Come back. They are free to act, but only if by acting they secure the tablet or discover, for certain, its location. No point killing Guttman and the American if we don't get the tablet. Do you understand?'

'I understand, Salim.'

'I mean it, Marwan.' And he cocked his weapon again, to leave no doubt.

Jerusalem, Friday, 5.23 a.m.

SHE SEARCHED among the blissed-out faces for Uri, but he had vanished. She stood up, walking towards the entrance. Then she saw him, his forehead lined with anxiety. He was in the doorway, staring hard into the street.

'Uri, what is it?'

'I don't know, but I heard something. Could be a car. We've got to get out.'

'Yeah, but first you have to tell me what this means!'

'Maggie, there's no time. If they're on to us they'll kill us.'

'Uri, I'm not leaving here until you work this out.'

Shaking his head he strode back to the machine, peered at the small bubble of text on the screen and repeated the riddle his father had hidden there. Then he said simply, 'All right, let's go.'

As Maggie closed down the machine, the nose-studded barista appeared and murmured in Hebrew to Uri, pointing to an exit at the back end of the café. He thanked her, grabbed Maggie's wrist and dashed to the fire door.

Outside, they climbed some stone steps into an alleyway. Uri tugged her along, first right, then left, then down a cobbled slope and eventually to a main street, where the silver Mercedes was parked and ready. They got in.

'Where are we going?'

'I don't know. Away from Jerusalem. We'll go back when it's clear.'

Maggie looked out of the window, watching the first glimmers of a blue, hazy light over the horizon. 'What about this message of your father's? "Go west, young man, and make your way to the model city, close to the Mishkan", whatever that is. "You'll find what I left for you there, in the path of ancient warrens." So what do you think?'

Uri took his eyes off the road to fix Maggie with a glare. 'Do you have any idea how much I hate my father right now? All these games he's putting me through? As if it wasn't enough that this madness has already killed my mother. And for what? For some biblical relic that will prove that he and all his right-wing nutcase friends were right all along! He couldn't make me join him when he was alive, but somehow he has me working for him, like some disciple, now that he's dead.'

'Is that where he's hidden it? In some right-wing nutcase place? On the West Bank?'

'No. It's in a much more obvious place.'

'You've worked it out already?'

'What's this whole thing about? It could only be in one place.'

'You mean it's on the Temple Mount.' Maggie smiled at the ingenuity of it. Of course he would bury the tablet there. Where else did it belong?

'That's the Mishkan: the Temple, the palace. It refers to that whole area. Except whatever he's left is not on the Temple Mount. Jews hardly ever go there: too holy. He's hidden it underneath.'

'Underneath?'

'A few years ago, they excavated the tunnels that run alongside the Western Wall. My father and a few other archaeologists. Not the famous part, where people stick notes to God in the crevices. But the stretch that was buried under the Muslim Quarter. Everyone went nuts.'

'You mean the Palestinians?'

'Of course. What did my father expect? The Arabs said the Jews were trying to undermine the foundations of the Dome of the Rock. It's where they think Mohammed ascended to heaven. And here are the Jews tunnelling underneath. Then, to make matters worse, they decide that the tourists need an exit at the other end, rather than having to walk all the way back through the tunnels. So they build one. And it pops out right in the Muslim Quarter.'

'A provocation.'

'Exactly.'

'So that's what he means by "ancient warrens": the tunnels. "Go west", the Western Wall. Clever. And of course Jerusalem is the model city; it's the holiest place on earth. But what—?'

Maggie could see Uri suddenly transfixed by his rearview mirror. She looked behind and saw a car, its lights set to full beam. They had left the city now, descending instead on a winding mountain road.

'They're getting closer, Uri.'

'I know.'

'What the hell are we going to do?'

'I don't know. Let me think.'

He was being dazzled by the reflection in the mirror, which seemed to fill the car with yellow light. Uri accelerated but the car caught up effortlessly.

'Can we turn off?'

'Not unless we want to go tumbling down the mountain.'

'Uri, we've got to do something.'

'I know, I know.'

After a few seconds, he spoke again. 'OK. At the next bend there is a lookout spot. I can pull in there. When I do, you have to open your door immediately and slip out of your side. Don't wait for the car to come to a complete stop. Keep very low, and then just run over the edge. It's a short drop, and there's flat ground for a while, like a ledge. OK?'

'Yes, but what about—?'

'Don't worry about me. Once you're out, I'll be right behind you. OK?'

'OK.' Maggie unbuckled her belt.

Uri began to squeeze the brake, looking in his rearview mirror. Then he swerved into the space and yelled: 'Now! And keep low!'

Maggie pulled on the door handle, pushed it and ducked out of the car, tripping on the moving road, running in a crouch to the edge of the paved surface. Instinct, in this half-light of dawn, told her this was a sheer drop and that to run off it was to guarantee death. Yet she had to trust Uri. She stepped off the edge.

The drop came—but it was a tiny one, like missing the bottom stair in the dark. She stumbled on until she was out of sight of the road. As the sound of her breath quieted, she looked around to see that she was quite alone. A second later she heard a gunshot from the road above, and knew, with a certainty that chilled her, that it was Uri who had been hit.

SHE HELD HERSELF very still, wary even of her own breath. Her muscles were quaking, her face trembling, but some instinct of self-preservation took over, forcing her feet to make no movement, determined that no one would hear so much as a crunch of a stone under her.

She stood like that for seconds that stretched into long minutes, her eyes closed so that she could concentrate on her ears. In the seconds after the gunshot, as she played back the memory of it now, she had heard a thud and the sound of footsteps on the gravel above. Then, a minute later, car doors slamming shut and an engine roaring away.

She had prayed that she would soon hear something else: his footsteps coming towards her, perhaps, or his voice calling out from the road above. Then she pictured his body, unmoving and bloody, on the gravelled road, and her own body convulsed at the thought of it. She knew she had to keep quiet, but it was no good: she was sobbing noisily now, for the man she had held in her arms, pulsing with life, just a few hours ago.

Eventually, she took a step forward, then another, and another, until she had a view, albeit restricted, of the road. She could see nothing. No cars, not even the Mercedes they had been driving. Above all, there was no Uri.

Maggie didn't know what to feel. She exhaled her relief that there was no corpse. Was it possible that Uri had somehow escaped, that the sound she had heard had been Uri, driving himself to safety?

But that, she knew, made no sense. He would have come back to get her. No, she knew what was more likely, her mind supplying the image: masked men picking up Uri's lifeless body, one taking the arms, the other the ankles, and swinging it into the boot of the Merc, then driving the car away.

She turned her back to the road, only now noticing the beauty of this view. The sky was a pale morning blue, the sun strong enough to light up the brittle, sandy landscape: the hills, stepped in terraces, punctuated by isolated olive trees. Something in this view hardened her resolve. She would find that goddamned tablet if it was the last thing she did. She would do it for Uri's sake, and for the sake of his father and mother too.

And then she heard it, faint at first. She was struck, as she had been the first time, by the beauty of the melody, a haunting series of notes. It was human voices singing, their sound carried on the breeze. She walked down to the edge of the ledge and saw that there was still no sheer drop, but rather a downward slope. Thanking Orli for the boots she was now wearing, instead of the shoes she had left at the ex-girlfriend's apartment, she pushed down the hillside towards the sound of the voices.

Soon she had flat ground in view. And she could see the source of the song. It was the Arms Around Jerusalem protest, still going strong. Maggie had never been so glad to see a political demonstration in her life, never more grateful for the protesters' stamina in maintaining it around the clock. Even now, not much after dawn, there was a group of activists, holding hands at the foot of this hill.

'Are you journalist?' It was a woman wearing a vast pair of glasses, her arms extended to a teenage girl, perhaps her daughter, on one side and a rabbinic-looking man on the other.

'Oh, no,' said Maggie, immediately and without forethought, exaggerating her Irish accent. 'I'm a visitor.'

'What, tourist?' *Turrrist*.

'Not quite, dear. I'm more of a pilgrim.' It was blatant, an impersonation of the nuns at school. But Maggie prayed it would work.

The rabbi stopped singing and joined in the conversation. 'You need to get to Bethlehem?' He positioned himself to give directions.

'No, actually, I'm on my way to Jerusalem. And it seems I've been tricked, I'm afraid.'

'Tricked?'

'By a taxi. Said he would take me there. He dropped me on the roadside there.' She pointed up the hill. 'He said I should enjoy the view. Then, would you credit it, he only offs and leaves. With my coat and everything.'

'He was Jewish, this driver?'

Maggie was stumped. What was the right answer? Would it be an insult to accuse a Jew of this act of perfidy? Or would it be seen as a greater treachery to have hired a Palestinian driver in the first place?

'You know, I never asked him. But I do feel as if I've been terribly naive. I thought, this being the Holy Land and all—'

'Listen, lady.' It was the rabbi, now broken out of his place in the circle. 'Where do you need to get to?'

'Oh, I don't want to trouble a man of God like yourself.'

'No trouble, really. We have a driver.' And before she had had a chance to say another word, he had produced a walkie-talkie. 'Avram? *Bo rega*.' He looked at Maggie and nodded, as if to say, don't worry, it's all under control.

Within a few moments a car had arrived, a rugged, muddied SUV. Maggie sized it up and concluded that these rebels were supremely well organised, funded possibly by Christian evangelicals in the States. Once again, she was reminded that, even if the parties came back to the table, the peacemakers would face the most enormous obstacles.

Maggie thanked the rabbi and got in the car. A dark, burly man in shorts sat in the driver's seat. He raised his eyebrows in a question.

'Could you take me to the Old City, please?'

Within a few minutes they were back on the main road, retracing the dawn journey she had made with Uri, winding steadily upwards back to the centre of Jerusalem.

Jerusalem, Friday, 7.50 a.m.

THE CAR TURNED through the Jaffa Gate, stopping almost immediately in a small square, a paved plaza fringed by a souvenir shop selling the usual kitsch, and a couple of backpacker hostels. She would have to walk from here. Maggie thanked the driver, waved him off and took a good look.

Straight ahead of her was what looked to be a central police station, complete with a tall communications mast sprouting multiple aerials. She began to walk towards it. She would report Uri missing. She would tell them about the shooting, they would send out patrol cars and find Uri and . . .

But then she stopped still. She would have to explain the stolen car and why they were being chased in the dead of night, why Uri was dressed in a stolen bellboy uniform. No one would believe a word of it. The police would immediately get on the phone to the consulate to check her out and she only had to imagine that call, as Davis, Miller and Sanchez were told that Maggie Costello had spent the night with Uri Guttman.

She stood there, frozen. If Uri was alive, he needed her help. But she had no one to turn to, no one who would understand or believe what they now knew. Her only hope was the tablet. If she found that, she would have her own bargaining chip. Then all she had to do was decide how best to use it.

She looked around, trying to get her bearings. Seeing a man with an oversized camera round his neck, she stopped him and asked for the

Western Wall. He pointed at an archway directly opposite the Jaffa Gate. This, she remembered, was the way to the *souk*.

The market seemed different today. It was still early; almost all the stalls were locked up behind green metal shutters, and, instead of the thick crowds of tourists and shoppers, there was just a boy pushing a handcart.

Finally she saw a handwritten sign in English: *To the Western Wall*, with an arrow indicating a right turn. She followed it down some steps until she saw another, more formal sign: YOU ARE ENTERING THE WESTERN WALL PLAZA. VISITORS WITH PACEMAKERS SHOULD INFORM THE SECURITY PERSONNEL . . .

There was an airport-style metal detector to go through, watched by a couple of Israeli police guards. A policewoman frisked her, all the while laughing and chatting with her colleagues, then waved her through.

And now it stretched before her, a sloping, paved plaza teeming with people and at one end of it the solid, enormous stones of the Western Wall. It seemed to belong to another world: its scale was not human. One stone was almost as tall as a man. And yet this dated from a temple built here some 2,500 years ago.

People were milling everywhere. Bearded men striding about as if they had trains to catch, others handing out skullcaps, while still a few more were buttonholing pedestrians for a chat. There seemed to be a dozen different gatherings and services taking place.

Perhaps four-fifths along the wall a partition emerged to bisect the crowd. On the left side of it, the crowd was much thicker. She walked closer, to work out what this division could mean.

Ah. Men on the left side, women on the right. There was another sign, addressed to the women. YOU ARE ENTERING AN AREA OF SANCTITY. WOMEN SHOULD BE IN APPROPRIATE MODEST DRESS. But it was the men she looked at. Many were draped in large black and white shawls, facing the wall. Some let the shawls cover their heads, others wore them over their shoulders. All seemed to be rocking back and forth on their heels, their eyes closed.

Maggie had to find out where to go. She saw a policeman, armed, and asked for the Western Wall tunnels. He pointed at a small archway built into the long wall that ran perpendicular to the wall itself.

Outside was a group of maybe thirty men and women, kitted out with water bottles and video cameras. *Perfect*.

She loitered at the back, then followed them through the archway, her eyes down, and fidgeting with her phone.

'All right, people. If we can all listen up. Thank you,' said the tour guide: American, late twenties, with a whiskery beard and bright, shining eyes. He clapped his hands three times and waited for silence. 'Great. Thanks. My name is Josh and I'm going to be your guide on this tour of the Western Wall tunnels. If you just follow me through here, we can begin.'

He led them into an underground cellar, its shape described by a vaulted arch. 'OK, do we have everybody?' His voice was bouncing off the walls. 'All right. We're in a room the British explorer Charles Warren called the Donkey Stable. That may be because that was what this room was once used for—or perhaps it just looks that way.'

There was polite laughter from all those who were not framing up a shot on their camera phones. Maggie started scoping the walls for any kind of opening in which Guttman might have stashed his precious discovery.

'We are now close to the area known as the Temple Mount. Our tradition holds that on this spot stood the Foundation Stone, from which the world was created. We also know it as Mount Moriah, where Abraham was asked by the Almighty to sacrifice his son Isaac, and where Jacob predicted that the House of God would be built. Sure enough, the First Temple was built by Solomon nearly three thousand years ago, and the Second by Ezra about five hundred years after that. When the Second Temple was destroyed by the Romans in the year 70, the only part left standing was the Western Wall . . .'

While he spoke, Maggie scanned every crack between the stones. *You'll find what I left for you there, in the path of ancient warrens*, Guttman had said. Could that refer to something in this room?

'. . . most people don't realise is that the giant wall we just saw outside, with everyone praying, is not the entire Western Wall. It continued on, northwards, for *four times* as long again. Trouble was, over the years, people built layer on layer of homes against it, and eventually *over* it. But we've been able to dig out a tunnel along the entire length of the wall. Now we can see all those layers of history . . .'

While the men in shorts and women with sweaters tied round their waists ooh-ed and aah-ed, Maggie examined the ground, wondering if there was a trap door, a staircase perhaps, that might lead to a vault.

'OK. We're going to follow that little light you can see there—and head down the Secret Passage.'

A teenage boy made a ghost sound as the group walked in single file down a long corridor beneath a low ceiling. There was no daylight now, just the orange glow of electric lights embedded at intervals along the ground.

The guide raised his voice to be heard above the footsteps. 'Legend has it that this was an underground walkway used by King David so that he could travel unseen from his palace, west of here, to the Temple Mount . . .'

Maggie looked above her and at the walls. Could Guttman have loosened one of these ancient stones and hidden the tablet behind it? The light was too weak for a proper search and, if she stuck with this group, there was too little time in each stop along the tour. She thought of Uri, cursing his father and his elaborate schemes, and understood his exasperation. Leading them here was all very well, but not if they had no chance to find the tablet.

She suddenly became self-conscious. She glanced up to see a man gazing at her, then looking away. Had she been muttering? It wouldn't have surprised her if, in her tiredness and desperation, she had started thinking out loud. She felt her cheeks grow hot.

They were now, the guide explained, walking through a series of cisterns whose arches supported the houses built above. 'See the holes in the ceiling,' he said, as everyone looked up. 'They would drop a bucket from those, then pull it up, full of water.'

Maggie was barely listening, studying instead two illuminated signs that listed the foreign donors who had made these excavations possible. She scanned the names, looking for a Guttman or an Ehud Ramon or anything that might give her some clue. This place was so big, a maze of tunnels; how on earth was she meant to find anything here?

The guide called them forward, to see what he introduced as Wilson's Arch, an opening through which they could glimpse again the stones of the Western Wall, no different from those outside.

Enough of this, Maggie decided. She needed to search properly. And that meant alone. She walked casually towards a flight of metal stairs that she had spotted when they came in, and went down them as quietly as she could.

At the bottom, she saw a group of men in yellow hard hats working: Arabs, Maggie couldn't help noticing, conscious of the irony that the Jewish settlements on the West Bank, like Israel's security barrier, so hated by the Arabs, were almost always built by Arab hands.

Facing her was the newly exposed section of the Western Wall. She skim-read the sign telling her that one stone was longer than a bus and weighed more than a 747 loaded with passengers and all their luggage.

When was she going to see something that made sense?

She took the next opening and found herself on a narrow path, faced on one side by an enormous arch that seemed to have been bricked up, filled in with a coarse, craggy rubble. Next to it was a sign: WARREN'S GATE.

Thank God for that. Both she and Uri had taken the 'path of ancient warrens' to mean this warren of ancient tunnels, but Guttman had been cleverer than that. He meant this place: not warrens at all, but Warren's.

She looked up, down and around, confident that the hiding place was about to reveal itself. Yet all she could see was this wall of stone and brick. She began tapping and pulling, hoping to find a loose brick. None yielded.

Her confidence waning, she fell to her knees. She would work methodically, starting with the bottom line of stones. She began grabbing and tugging, the skin of her fingers tearing on the coarse brick. Her hands moved frantically across the next line of stones, then the next. Nothing.

She stood up to look at the wall opposite. Perhaps the hiding place was here. She gazed high above, then below. Where in God's name was it?

And then she saw him.

The same man she had made eye contact with during the tour, except now he was standing, alone, at the other end of this narrow pathway. Maggie registered no embarrassment, only recognition.

She had seen his face before. But where? Her mind was so addled with exhaustion, it was like wading through deep water to find the memory. At the hotel? At the consulate? No, she suddenly realised. Oh, no.

It had been at the nightclub in Tel Aviv where she and Uri had tracked down Baruch Kishon's son. Maggie had noticed him at the entrance, shortly after they had arrived. She had almost given him a sympathy smile: another thirtysomething, out of place in a club heaving with gorgeous kids. He had followed her then, and he had followed her now.

His purpose was beyond doubt. Whatever she was about to discover, he would pass on to the men who had killed Uri's mother, Kishon, Aweida and maybe even Uri. The men who would doubtless do the same to her, right here, right now, in this catacomb of age-old secrets.

HER LEGS MADE the decision before she did. She ran, pushing through a narrowing of the passageway, in which perhaps a dozen women stood holding prayer books, their faces pictures of intensity as they touched a wall that was trickling with water. As Maggie rushed past them, she looked over her shoulder to see the stalker had now been joined by another man, a video camera round his neck. They were getting closer. She picked up speed.

Now the pathway became a low, narrow tunnel. She ran on, hunched over. When she glanced back she saw them still gaining on her, even as they ran in their own awkward crouch. As she dashed forward, the ground beneath her feet changed: a glass square looking down onto a cistern below. The men were only about ten yards behind her.

Suddenly the tunnel passageway ended, opening out into another cistern. She was desperate to find a way off the official path, but there only seemed to be one opening each time. She would just have to keep going until she could break back out into the daylight. But how much longer would that be?

The path narrowed again, turning ninety degrees away from the Western Wall. She seemed to have entered some kind of underground gorge, a canyon of steep walls, as high as a cathedral, on both sides. They were wet and made up of solid, striated layers like the inside of a cake.

'Stop!' shouted one of her pursuers.

As she glanced over her shoulder, she thought she saw the second man draw a weapon and aim it at her. She yelped and ducked, but he could get no clear line of sight: the rocks twisted and turned too sharply.

At last she came to a set of narrow, metal stairs. She clattered up them, breathing raggedly. Once at the top, she had to turn sideways just to get through, so tight was the gap. Behind her she heard a woman's scream: someone had just seen the gun.

Then the space opened out again, and once her eyes adjusted she could see a pool, full of thick, stagnant water. She stood for a second, her lungs screaming to extract oxygen from this musty, humid air. Where did this pool lead? Maybe it came out somewhere outside, away from here. She stood at the edge, contemplating a dive. She had always been a good swimmer. Perhaps she could hold her breath . . .

But then she heard the footsteps, and she instinctively turned away from the pool and scrambled through the only opening instead. The second she had, she was flooded with relief. For now she could see daylight. Up a path, through a turnstile, and she was out.

Gulping at the air, blinking at the sudden sunlight, she found herself in a narrow street, busy with people. Opposite her was a sign: SANCTUARIES OF THE FLAGELLATION AND THE CONDEMNATION. She was on the Via Dolorosa, Christ's route to the Crucifixion.

Maggie would have felt a moment's Catholic comfort in the familiarity of it, if she had had the time. But she had no such luxury. Waiting for her at the exit were two men, their faces covered, who stepped forward and, calmly and with minimal exertion, grabbed her.

GLOVED HANDS gripped her wrists so hard it was as if they were made of steel rather than flesh and blood. She gasped but made no sound: other hands had already placed a small roll of cloth into her mouth.

They moved her backwards, off the street and back into the tunnels, away from public view. 'What are you doing? Who are you?' she tried to say through the gag, but she knew her words were useless.

Two of the men in front of her stepped forward, and instinctively she tried to lash out. But her arms were now bound in what felt like tight plastic tape. She tried to scream, but this made her retch on the material jammed into her mouth. Now she was panting even harder, her lungs forced to sate their craving for air through her nose.

The two masked men came closer, so that she could see their eyes. Those of the taller man were dark, flat and glassy, like a pond frozen in winter. Maggie looked at his partner, hoping to find some spark of the human. But what she saw chilled her. For the green eyes of this man did indeed betray an emotion, and that emotion was pleasure.

It was he who approached now with another strip of material in his hands. As he tied the blindfold round the back of her head, his face inches away from hers, she came to a cold, certain realisation. He was the man who had assaulted her a few hundred yards away from here, in the market.

She felt a shove in the centre of her back and stumbled forward, someone catching her arm to prevent her falling. After a few minutes of staggering in this manner, she detected a change in the acoustics, a lifting of the cold dankness of the air. As her feet stumbled on the uneven surface, she heard street noise: people, cars, footsteps. Then the colour of the dark under her blindfold altered and she felt the warmth of sunlight on her skin.

Suddenly she felt the same metal hand that had gripped her wrists now grasp her neck from behind and push it downwards. He was pushing hard, but she resisted, holding her back firm, refusing to be folded. He pushed harder. Eventually a male voice behind her uttered a single word: 'car'.

So that was it. They were shoving her into the back seat of a car. She gave way, glad for her little show of resistance. It wasn't much, but it had forced these men to break the silence they had maintained since they cornered her outside the tunnels. They hadn't wanted to speak, but they had to, to win her cooperation. She may have been bound and gagged but, in mediation terms, she decided she had won the first round.

They drove for what she guessed was ten minutes. She sat jammed into the back seat of the car, her legs pressed against those of the men on either side of her. Her skin crawled.

Finally she felt the car slow down, then bump over a ridge, as if entering a driveway. She heard the driver's window wind down and then back up a moment later; perhaps he had had to show papers at a checkpoint. Was this an Israeli team, taking her to the West Bank?

The sound changed again. The car had gone down a ramp and now seemed to be indoors. Maybe they were in an underground garage. The car stopped and she heard the rear doors open. Then the metal hand was on her back again, shoving her out. She didn't resist this time: she wanted to be out of that suffocating, confined space.

If it was a garage, they weren't in it for long. The car seemed to have been parked right by a door. She was pushed through it, then up some stairs, guided by the man stuck to her right side. A few more paces forward and a door shut behind her.

'OK.'

She was so taken aback to hear a word spoken that she hardly paid any attention to the voice that had spoken it. It was male, but more than that she couldn't tell. What accent was it? She imagined it as Israeli and, playing the sound back in her head, it could have been. But then she tried the memory of it as Palestinian and it fitted that too. It could have been anybody, from anywhere, in any language.

A few seconds later she understood what the word meant. It was an instruction, a go-ahead. For now she felt a series of hands on her, some touching her legs, others moving around her back, up and down each leg and down her arms, like an airport security check. *Of course*, she realised. They were searching her for the tablet. She felt them go into her trouser pockets, pulling out her mobile phone and the small wallet she carried. They would see her ID. But these people knew who she was.

There was a pause, in which she imagined that some kind of silent consultation was taking place. Perhaps they had realised she had nothing.

But a few seconds later, the hands were back, rapid and determined. First they removed her shoes. Then she felt hands undoing the buckle of her belt, before tugging down the zip of her trousers and pulling them clean off her.

Meanwhile another pair of hands unbound her wrists so that her T-shirt could come off. She screamed into her gag, as every item of borrowed clothing was taken from her. She had never felt weaker.

Then the voice spoke again. 'OK.'

SHE COULD SEE the scene as if she was outside herself. She could picture it: her naked body presented to this group of masked men for their probing inspection. She fought the urge to weep. She couldn't give them that victory. To deny them tears, that was her only resistance now.

There was a sound of a door opening, of someone else entering the room.

'That's enough,' said a voice, just a few feet away. Amid the pounding of her heart and the effort to swallow back her tears, she couldn't make sense of the voice, couldn't even tell if it was the same man who had spoken before. Until he spoke again.

'Get her dressed.'

Now it came to her, unmistakable. She knew that voice all right. Because she knew that man.

'THEY DON'T USUALLY show people this part of the building, Maggie. It's a pity. Perhaps they should.'

As he spoke, she could feel multiple hands fussing over her, sliding the T-shirt back over her head, placing her legs back into her jeans. They came to her face last, untying the gag—which triggered an instant spasm of coughing—and finally removing her blindfold. With that, they pushed her downwards, into a hard, wooden chair.

In the time it took her to adjust to the light, the men in ski masks had cleared the room. It was bare and featureless, the walls a dirty white; there were no windows and nothing on the walls. In front of her was a table. And he was sitting on the other side of it, on a simple chair, just like hers.

'I can only apologise for what just happened, Maggie. The strip-search, the body cavity thing. Horrible. Wouldn't wish that on my worst enemy.'

She thought she would want to rush at him, to strangle him. But those feelings were subsumed by sheer disbelief, her dumbfounded incomprehension at the sight of this man here, in this place.

'What on earth are you doing?' was all she could manage to say.

'Not so fast, Maggie. First I need to know the location of that tablet.'

'But, you? Why would you . . . ?'

'The question is, if you haven't got it on you, then where the hell is it?'

'I don't know.'

'Oh, come on, Maggie. I know you've got it all worked out. You expect me to believe you don't know where it is?'

'And you expect me to talk to you, after what your thugs just did to me? I'll never say a word to you again.' And then, a surprise to her as much as to him, she spat in his face.

'I like that, Maggie, you know I do. A girl with spunk. And you look good naked, too. That's what I'd call a killer combination.'

Maggie could say nothing. If her body was still reeling from the humiliation it had endured in this room, her mind was going through the very first convulsions of shock. Here was a man she had trusted, whom she had believed wanted the same things she wanted.

'Does this mean you were behind it all? All those killings?'

'It's our policy never to discuss the details of intelligence operations. You know that, Maggie.'

And he smiled. The knowing, complicit smile of one cynical political insider to another. The smile that Bruce Miller, Political Counsellor to the President of the United States, had flashed a thousand times before.

CHAPTER TEN

Jerusalem, Friday, 9.34 a.m.

'Who the hell are you working for?' It was as if the blood was finally reaching her brain. 'You're a traitor. You've betrayed your country. You've betrayed your own president.'

'Maggie, can we skip the whole Irish outrage thing? You, Bono, that other asshole, what's his name, Bob Geldof? Every other do-gooding, bleeding heart coming on with that big, guilt-tripping accent. It's not going to work this time.' He was leaning back, pivoting the chair on its two hind legs. 'This is not some negotiation with a bunch of banana-munchers in Africa. You have something that I need. And you have no cards to play, Maggie. Not one. So tell me. Where is the tablet?'

Negotiation. The mere mention of the word was enough to make her snap back into herself. She had always been good at what the shrinks call 'compartmentalisation', and now, consciously, she forced herself to perform the trick again. To forget what had just happened, and do her job. To negotiate.

'I won't tell you a thing until you tell me what the hell is going on here.'

'Look, Maggie. I don't want to repeat myself. But you have no leverage here. I can force you to tell me what you know, if I have to.'

'Oh, really? The President's most trusted adviser personally directing the assault of a US citizen, a senior US diplomat—in an election year. That should play well in the polls.'

'No one's going to believe a word you say. A washed-up slut who can't keep her legs closed, banging first the Africans and then some Israeli. How do you think that'll look on the front page of the *Washington Post*?'

Maggie closed her eyes, involuntarily. She knew he was right. In a contest of credibility, which is what most political scandals came down to, she would lose to Bruce Miller every time.

'Yeah. And the soccer moms are going to just love a president whose main man instructs masked goons to strip and assault one of his female colleagues. You're already in deep shit. So why don't you talk to me and then maybe I'll talk to you?'

Miller eyed Maggie up, the suggestion of a smile on his lips. She could sense a poker player about to fold.

'Like I said, you got spunk, Costello. In a different life, I could imagine you and me getting on, if you know what I'm saying.'

Maggie kept her expression fixed, not wanting to make the slightest move that might divert him, break the spell.

'It's not that complicated, really.'

She wanted to exhale her relief: he was going to talk.

'We need a peace deal here, Maggie. And we were pretty close. Then last weekend we hear there's some tablet floating around that could be Abraham's last will and testament—'

'How did you hear?'

'Your boyfriend's dad. Guttman. He calls Baruch Kishon, the Israeli journalist, and tells him. Not the whole story, but enough of it. Mentions the trader Afif Aweida, mentions his pal Ahmed Nour. As luck would have it, we had someone listening in.'

'As luck would have it.'

'OK, it wasn't luck. We'd been bugging Kishon for years.'

'Kishon? Why the hell would you be bugging him?'

'You not been reading the files, Maggie? Kishon's the guy who broke the Tel Aviv connection story all those years ago.'

Maggie cursed Uri for not mentioning it. He must have known. It had been the biggest diplomatic rift between Israel and the US for decades: three CIA agents had been double-crossing the Agency, leaking secrets to the Israelis. To this day, the Israelis constantly demanded the spies' release; even the most pliantly pro-Israel presidents refuse.

'So once you heard what Guttman had told him, you decided to kill him.'

'Oh, don't start preaching to me, young lady. We knew what was at stake here. The Arabs and the Israelis are about to split Jerusalem down the middle, and now we've got God Almighty himself, or near as dammit, saying that no, it belongs to the Jews. The whole deal would be off.'

Maggie had to work hard to stay cool. *He had seen the text; he knew what it said*. She couldn't let him know that she hadn't and didn't. 'So you were frightened that the Israelis would walk away, because Abraham bequeathed the Temple Mount to them?'

'Or to the Muslims. It made no difference which one got it. Either way, the peace process would be over.'

That allowed her a moment of relief: Miller was not ahead after all. She would stay on the offensive. 'So it's been you all along. Killing Kishon, Ahmed Nour, Afif Aweida, Guttman, Guttman's *wife*—anyone who might know what's on the tablet and who might talk.' She didn't want to mention Uri; saying it might make it true.

'Don't get carried away, Costello. Guttman was killed by the Israeli secret service. The guy looked like he was about to pull a gun on Yariv.'

'And that kibbutz in the north. The arson attack. That was you too?'

'Guttman was one of the main archaeologists of that site. We thought he might have hidden it there.'

Now it was Maggie's turn to say nothing. She stared at her wrists, red welts etched deep into both of them. She started shaking her head.

'What's that for?' Miller asked, irritated. She said nothing. 'Why are you shaking your head?' he shouted.

She looked up, glad she had needled him. 'Because I cannot believe how deeply, profoundly stupid you are. You did all this because you were worried that the release of the testament would derail the peace process? All this killing, of people on both sides?' There was a mirthless laugh in her voice. 'You did all this to *prevent* the breakdown in the peace process? Did you not think, for one second, that tit-for-tat killings, in the most delicate stage of negotiations, might actually fuck the peace talks up all by themselves?'

'You have no right to lecture me—'

'I have every right. I have been running around this country, risking my life, desperate to get to the bottom of whatever was causing all this violence, to help save the peace process. And now I find the real source of the trouble and of the violence that's been destroying everything wasn't Hamas or Fatah or the settlers or any of them. It was you!'

Miller had collected himself. 'I always knew you were naive, Maggie, but this is too much. You don't think these guys would have got started the moment they knew about the testament? Of course they would. The peace talks would be deader than a turkey in November the second that tablet got out. That's the real world, my girl. You're facing a disease that's 'bout to spread, you kill the first beast that gets it. Otherwise, it'll kill the whole herd.'

'So that's what this was, eh? You derail the peace process a bit, before the lunatics derail it even more.'

'There are no good choices in this game, Maggie. You know that.'

'And I suppose it was working. Until I came along and started poking around, obsessing night and day to uncover what you had decided should stay hidden. What a bloody fool I am.'

'You want to ease up on yourself, Maggie.'

'Why should I do that?'

'Because you've done exactly what we wanted you to do—from the very beginning.'

'What is that supposed to mean?'

Miller smiled. 'Oh, come on, Maggie. Let's not dwell on this. We've got work to do. Believe it or not, we have a peace process to save.'

'Like you care.'

He gave Maggie a look of deep disgust. 'You just don't get it, do you? You love all the talks, the plans, the counterplans, the roadmaps, the UN resolutions, the White House handshakes—you love all that. But d'you ever stop for one second and wonder how it's all possible? You ever wonder what drags bloodthirsty bastards like Slobodan Milosevic to sit down for one of your peace treaties? It's because someone like me was threatening to drop a megaton of dynamite on their heads if they didn't. And not just threatening.

Sometimes we did it, too. So don't fool yourself, missy. There'd be no peace unless there were guys like me ready to make war.'

Maggie took a deep breath. 'And that's what you were doing here? A bit of war so that we could make peace, that's what—?'

'You're damn right, that's what we were doing. And it made sense, too. The two sides are still in the room—'

'Technically.'

'There's a back channel too, so they're talking, believe me.'

'Did everyone know apart from me?'

Miller was quieter now, examining his own fingers. 'The opposite. This was need-to-know. Me and a small team of ex-special forces.'

'And the rest of us were out of the loop? The Secretary of State? Sanchez?'

'All of them. Except you. You should feel proud.'

'Proud? What the hell are you talking about?'

'Of what you did. You nearly got us the tablet. Just like we hoped.'

'I don't understand.'

'Oh, come on. Why do you think we sent Bonham over there to get you?'

'To close the deal. The two sides were nearly there and you wanted me to close the deal. That's what Bonham said.' Maggie's voice was wobbling.

'Course that's what he said. But come on, Maggie. You think the State Department's not crawling with skilled diplomats who could do this job? Specialists on the Middle East conflict? Didn't you wonder why, out of all the people we had, we had to have you? We needed you because of your—how can I put this delicately?—because of your unique expertise.'

Maggie could feel herself paling. 'What are you saying?'

'We needed someone to get close to Guttman Junior. If anyone knew where the old sonofabitch had hidden this tablet, it would be him.'

'You brought me here to, to . . .' She couldn't say the words.

'Well, let's face it, Maggie, you had the right résumé. You got close to that lunatic in Africa and we thought, given the right context, you'd do the same here. And you did. Like I said, you should be proud.'

It was as if she was being crushed from the inside. So that's what this was about, that's what it had been about from the very beginning. Maggie heard again the voice of Judd Bonham, recruiting her for this enterprise. *This is your chance*, he had said. Cancelling out the sin through repentance. But it was the opposite of the truth. He did not want her to come to Jerusalem to undo her mistake in Africa, but to repeat it.

She was nothing more than a honeytrap, that lowest form of espionage life, sent in to win the affection of Uri Guttman. The fact that she had succeeded only increased her nausea. What did that make her? Nothing more than a whore for the American government.

Instinct launched Maggie from her chair. She slapped Bruce Miller hard across the face. Feeling the sting, Miller put his hand to his cheek, then, with a smirk that oozed lechery, slapped her back. As she reeled, he pressed a button under the table, bringing two masked men back into the room.

'OK, Maggie. This has gone on long enough. Not that I'm not enjoying myself. But you need to tell me where that tablet is.'

'I don't know,' she said, her words slurred by the blow to her face.

'That's not nearly good enough, Maggie. Now, I think you know I got some boys here who've enjoyed getting acquainted with you. They might like the chance to get to know you a little better.'

'So now you're going to have the White House implicated in a rape.'

'Not at all. We would issue a statement mourning the loss of a fine American, brutally assaulted and then murdered by terrorists. The United States wouldn't rest until your killers were brought to justice.'

Maggie felt herself trembling, with rage, fear and a terrible sadness.

'Do I have your attention now, Miss Costello?'

She dug deep into her own reserves—of restraint, of self-control and of that mysterious inner drug she seemed able to generate when the moment truly demanded it, the one that numbed the pain.

'I don't know any more than you already know,' she heard herself say calmly. 'You saw the message that sent us to the Western Wall tunnels.'

Miller gave a tiny movement of his head, and the two men came closer, each taking an arm. They pulled Maggie up from her chair and, careful to synchronise their movements, wrenched her arms until they were both flat and high against her back: a full nelson. She roared with pain. The men yanked harder, pulling her arms higher. The pain was so intense she could see it: a bubbling redness in front of her eyes. She was sure they were about to pull her arms right out of their sockets.

Then it stopped and she was dropped back in the chair, limp as a doll.

Miller spoke again, his voice unchanged. As if he had merely paused to take a sip of water before picking up their conversation where they had left off. 'And you didn't see anything when you were in there this morning?'

All she could muster was a croak. 'You know I didn't. You searched me.'

Miller leaned forward. 'Not only that, but I've had people searching the tunnels area since you led us there. And still nothing. Which means—'

'That the old man didn't play it straight. He said it was there, but it wasn't.'

'Or that Uri was tricking you. Sent you off chasing wild geese in those cellars, so that he could go and get his inheritance all by himself.'

'Maybe.'

Even through the haze of agony and rage, Maggie was considering it. After all, she now understood, any kind of betrayal was possible. Uri could have faked the shooting on the road that morning, then headed off to collect the tablet alone. Maybe he realised who Maggie was before she had: a honeytrap, to be avoided. She was the only one who had not seen it.

'Or maybe there's nothing to know.' She could barely hear her own voice.

'What does that mean?'

'Maybe we couldn't find where Shimon Guttman hid the tablet because he hadn't yet hidden it.'

'Explain.'

'The messages Guttman left—the DVD, the one in Second Life—they were all done on Saturday. So was the call with Kishon. But what if he hadn't finished doing what he needed to do? Maybe he *planned* to hide the tablet in the tunnels, after the peace rally, but events intervened: he got killed.'

Miller was listening closely. 'So where's the tablet now?'

'That's the whole point. I don't know. And if *I* don't know—when I've seen his last messages and had his son explain his childhood memories—that means nobody knows. And nobody will know.'

'The tablet will be lost.'

'Yes.'

Miller nodded slowly, as if he were weighing the pros and cons. He got out of his chair and began to pace. Finally he delivered his verdict.

Jerusalem, Friday, 10.14 a.m.

THE DRIVER TOOK HER the short distance to the hotel, but she didn't want to go in straight away. She had seen so little daylight, she just wanted to absorb some of it now. She turned away from the busy entrance and walked on. Every part of her ached, her arms and neck especially. She yearned for a long soak in a hot bath and a deep sleep. But she was not ready for that now; her mind wouldn't let her rest.

She found instead a park, almost empty and looking unloved. The lawns were unkempt at the edges, the metal struts that supported a gazebo canopy in the middle had been allowed to rust. Maggie noticed that even the paving stones, and the benches, were made of Jerusalem stone.

She sat on a bench and stared. When Miller told her she was free to go, that he had concluded she had nothing more to reveal, she had felt relief but no pleasure. It wasn't only the pain and the humiliation that still coursed through her, nor even what Miller had revealed was the true nature of her mission to Jerusalem. No, what Maggie felt was something she guessed only another mediator would understand: the gnawing anxiety that comes when the other side has given in too easily. Miller had folded too soon and she didn't know why.

She went over his words again and again, including the final statement he had delivered as he left the interrogation room. He warned her that if she tried to reveal what had happened, he would ensure that the *Washington Post* was briefed that poor Miss Costello had suffered a breakdown in Jerusalem, leaving her delusional and irrational, following a second affair while on duty. If she tried to fight it, they had the tapes and photographs showing her with Uri, late at night, drinking, kissing . . .

Then Miller had surprised her. His expression, the cocky, jabbing neck movements, gave way to something else, something she hadn't seen before. He leaned his head to one side and his eyes seemed to radiate sympathy. 'We have to do horrible things sometimes,' he said quietly. 'Really horrible things. But we do them for the right reason.'

What maddened her now, as she sat in this barren piece of parkland, was that she almost agreed with him. She was not some pacifist who thought all power was inherently evil. She understood how the world worked. Specifically, she understood—better than anyone—how critical it was to keep this tablet out of the combatants' hands. Miller was right to do whatever it took to find it before they did. The President wanted to get re-elected and that meant he needed an Israeli–Palestinian peace deal. Who cared if his motives were shoddy? At least these two nations would finally get the accord they needed.

What Maggie resented was that Miller hadn't trusted her to know what the big boys knew. She was merely a tool to be deployed.

It was getting cold, or at least she was. Probably the tiredness. She would go back to the hotel, speak to no one and, once she had slept, she would go to the airport. Where would she go? She had no idea.

Once back in the cavernous lobby of the Citadel, she walked with her head down, determined to make eye contact with no one.

'Miss Costello! Hello!' It was a clerk at reception, waving a piece of paper, calling loudly across the lobby. 'Miss Costello, please!'

If only to shut her up, Maggie marched across the polished floor.

'Ah, Miss Costello. He said it was most urgent. You just missed him. He was here a minute ago. I told him—'

'Please, you'll have to slow down. Who said what was urgent?'

'The man who came here. He wanted me to give you this.' She handed Maggie a piece of paper, torn from the hotel's message pad.

Meet me in an old moment. I know what we have to do.

Vladimir Junior.

Jerusalem, Friday, two hours earlier

THE THROBBING was softened now, reduced to a rhythmic ache. He wondered if they had given him something, perhaps a jab in the thigh as they bundled him back into the Merc. He wouldn't have noticed if they had.

He had come round half an hour ago. Or maybe it was an hour. It had taken him a while to realise that he was not staring into a darkened room, but was blindfolded. Then he remembered the bullet and wondered, in earnest, if he was experiencing the consciousness of the dead.

Sensations returned only slowly, as if in succession. After the eyes came his arms, which told him they were immobile. Might he be paralysed? He did not panic. Instead he felt his heart plumb to the slow, low pressure deployed *in extremis*. It was as if the body went into emergency deep-freeze, knowing it was now in a battle to survive.

Coolly, he remembered the incident on the Jerusalem highway: it must have lasted only thirty seconds. He had seen the car behind, unmistakably following them. He had slowed down, swerving into the lay-by at an angle he hoped would allow Maggie to drop out unseen. Once she was clear, he had attempted to spin the car round and repeat the manoeuvre, so that he too could bail out. But the turn had proved impossible and by then the pursuers had caught up. He had taken no more than a step outside the car when the bullet had struck his leg. He had fallen, like a puppet whose strings had been severed.

Now came a new signal, from his wrists. The messages were reaching his brain so slowly, but the wrists were saying, he finally realised, that they were bound. The blindness, the immobility, were signs not of a physical shutdown preceding death but of something less final. He had been shot and bundled in the car not as a corpse, but as a prisoner. His heart began to beat faster.

He began to struggle, to jiggle his wrists. He soon understood that they were not only bound to each other, but to the chair he was sitting on. He wanted to inspect his wound, but he could not touch it, and in the blackness he could barely be certain which leg it was that had been struck.

Who had taken him? He pictured masked men, dressed in black, but that could have been a trick of the memory. He tried to remember what he had heard when they shoved him in the car. The name Daoud surfaced. He had heard someone call it, as if in a question, twice. It must have been a symptom of his delirium though, because in Uri's mind he thought he heard the name being called out in a distinctly American accent.

The thoughts were flowing more freely now. Uri wondered what Maggie had done. He guessed she had somehow found her way straight back to the subterranean catacombs of the Western Wall. But where would she have even begun? They covered a significant distance, he knew.

In the dark like this, Uri at last had a chance that had not come since he took the phone call six days ago. In truth, he had avoided it. But now he had little alternative but to think about his father. He had surprised him more in death than he ever had in life. Until this week, Uri would have described his father as predictable, the way all ideologues are predictable. They were unbending and therefore, to Uri's mind, irretrievably dull.

Yet in the last few days, his father had proved him wrong. He had harboured many secrets, including one that had clearly given him the greatest thrill of his career—and they had cost him his life.

He heard a door unlock, followed by the sound of men. He knew what was coming and felt oddly armed against it. He would do what he had read all survivors of brutality had done: he would stay within his own head.

He heard a voice with an American accent, the one he thought he had imagined in the car. 'OK, let's go to work.'

Next he could feel a bandage on his right leg being steadily unwound. Perhaps he was in hospital and these men were not torturers, but doctors.

He was about to speak when he felt fingers exploring the outside of his wound; he inhaled sharply at the sting. And then, a moment later, he felt a pain that made him howl as he had never howled before.

'Funny, ain't it, what one little finger can do?'

The pain stopped for a second.

'That's all it is, one little finger. All I have to do is push it right there, into this hole in your leg, and—'

Uri screamed in agony. He had vowed not to let them see him suffer. But he could not hold back the pain.

'Get off me, you bastards, get off!'

At that, the pain leapt in intensity then disappeared, as if off the register. This blankness lasted only a few seconds, before he heard a faraway voice.

'. . . in fact, if I kept on pressing, I'd probably be able to touch your bone. Like that.'

'What do you want? I don't know anything!'

Blackness again, for just a few short seconds. When it ended, Uri realised what was happening: the agony was so excruciating, he was moving in and out of consciousness.

'Just tell us what you know.'

'You know what I know.'

Next he heard the wailing as if it were someone else. And suddenly a voice in some inner chamber of the self spoke to him. Now, it said. This is your chance. Detach yourself from the pain. *Stay inside your head*.

He tried to remember where his thoughts had been just before the men came in. He had been thinking of his father's ingenious code name, Ehud Ramon. Hold on to it, he thought; hold on. He repeated the name to himself, even as he felt his own body tremble from the agony. *Ehud Ramon. Ehud Ramon. Ehud, Ehud, Ehud* . . .

And then a memory surfaced that had lain buried for decades, a memory of the bedtime story he had loved as a child, the one he made his father read to him over and over, about a wonderfully naughty little boy. For a fleeting second, Uri pictured the book cover: *My brother, Ehud*. What had his father said in that video message? *I have put it somewhere safe, somewhere only you and my brother could know*.

Of course, Uri thought, willing himself to stay on this train of thought and not to fall into the pits of hell below. Of course. It hadn't been a real brother that his father had spoken of. Rather he was referring to the fictitious brother in a story he assumed his son would remember. And it was meant to lead him to another fictitious creation, the mythic Ehud Ramon.

The probing into his wound intensified now; they were using some kind of implement. And the questions kept on. Where is the tablet? Where is it?

But Uri stayed in his head. What a typical Guttman rhetorical flourish, he thought. The professor had just seen the ancient words of Abraham, speaking of his two sons, Isaac, the father of the Jews, and Ishmael, the father of the Muslims. Two brothers, Jew and Arab. 'My brother . . .' Shimon Guttman had said. If he could have, Uri would have smiled. His father, the flint-hearted nationalist, was using that weariest cliché of the Kumbaya-singing, hand-holding left—that Jews and Arabs are brothers.

He felt a surge of admiration for his old man: it was a brilliant piece of cryptography. Was there a codebreaker in the world who would realise that when a fanatic hawk referred to 'my brother', the man he meant was none other than the stubborn Palestinian nationalist Ahmed Nour?

Jerusalem, Friday, 11.50 a.m.

MAGGIE STARED at the message, her brow slowly smoothing into a smile. She only knew one Vladimir, and that was Vladimir Jabotinsky, mentor and pseudonym of Shimon Guttman. Vladimir Junior could only be one person.

When she opened the door of the café that used to be Moment, she saw him immediately. He was in the same seat she had found him in two days ago. Except now he was looking up, straight at her.

'You know,' she said, 'I normally insist on going somewhere new for a second date.'

He tried to smile, but only a wince came. She sat beside him, planting a long kiss on his lips, but when she moved to hug him he yelped.

Pointing at his leg, he explained that underneath his jeans was a thick bandage covering a bullet wound. He told her about the shooting and the interrogation, and he told her how his tormentors, in the middle of their work, had received a phone call, one that made them stop. They had dressed him in new clothes and driven him to the centre of town, dumping him ten minutes from here. They left him with a warning: 'You saw what happened to your parents. If you don't keep your mouth shut, the same will happen to you.' He had been blindfolded throughout.

'Uri, did the men who . . . did they ever tell you who they were?'

'They didn't have to.'

'You guessed?'

'I guessed even before they spoke in English. They were speaking to each other in Arabic. Calling their leader Daoud, the whole thing. Their accents weren't bad. But they were like mine.' He tried to smile. 'You know, an accent learned in a classroom. I wondered if they were Israelis at first. I spoke to them in Hebrew.' He shook his head. 'Not a word. So I worked it out. Later, when they were torturing me, they didn't even hide it. That's what frightened me the most. When they don't care if you know who they are, that can only mean that they're going to kill you.'

When she described what had happened to her, his face registered fury and resolve but, above all, sorrow. Finally he said: 'Are you OK?'

She tried to speak, to say that she was all right, but the words caught in her throat. Her eyes were stinging too. Uri held her hand, squeezing it as if in compensation for the words she wasn't saying. And he kept holding it.

When she told him about Miller, his face showed only mild surprise. 'You do realise,' she said, 'that this goes all the way to the top.'

'Of course it does. Special forces don't just deploy themselves.'

And then she felt it again, that same unease she sensed when Miller had let her go. She reached into her pocket, pulling out the piece of paper from the hotel, with Uri's message on it. On the other side, she scribbled a question. *When did they let you go? What time did the phone call come?*

Uri looked puzzled for a second, then wrote down a guess at the answer. If Uri was right, he had been released just minutes after her. The phone call must have come from Miller. We're letting her go; now let him go too.

Maggie pulled back the piece of paper. 'So, Uri, I need to eat. What do they have here?' As she spoke, she was writing furiously. *They set us free to follow us. They haven't given up. They want us to lead them to it.*

'Well,' said Uri, reading Maggie's note and nodding. 'The eggs are not bad. And the coffee. They serve it in big cups. Almost like bowls.'

They carried on like that, chatting about nothing. They spoke about what had happened, knowing it would sound strange if they didn't. But of what they would do next, they said not a word. At least not out loud.

THERE WERE FEWER CARS on the road now: Shabbat was coming, Uri explained. Jerusalem was getting more and more orthodox these days, and driving from Friday afternoon till sundown on Saturday was frowned upon.

Uri hailed a cab, speaking to the driver, who promptly cranked up the volume on the radio.

'OK, Vladimir Junior,' said Maggie. 'What's going on?' She made a dramatic face before quoting his message: '"I know what we have to do."'

Uri explained that he had worked it out as the pain intensified. They were torturing him for information he didn't have. But by the time they let him go, he had something. *My brother*, his father had said. Who else could he mean?

He had gone back to the Internet café, logged on as his father again and found the email that Ahmed Nour's son had sent. *Who are you? And why were you contacting my father?* Maggie and he had done nothing about the message, assuming that Nour Junior knew as little about his father as Uri did about his. This time Uri had replied, and there had been a quick response. Uri had been careful to say little, just that he had information on the death of Ahmed Nour and was keen to share it. The two bereaved sons, Israeli and Palestinian, agreed to meet at the American Colony Hotel, just fractionally on the eastern, and therefore Arab, side of the invisible seam that divided Jerusalem. They would be there in just a few minutes.

Maggie nodded. She had stayed there the last time she was here. The place was a legend: watering hole for visiting journalists, diplomats, unofficial would-be peacemakers, assorted do-gooders, and spies, for all she knew. After a day seeing Third World poverty and often bloody violence, coming back to the Colony was like returning to a safe haven.

That's how it seemed now, too, as they paid the taxi and walked in. The cool stone floor of the lobby, the old-world portraits and drawings on the walls, the bowing welcome of the staff. 'Colony' was right; the place could have been air-dropped straight out of the 1920s.

Uri didn't linger. Limping heavily, he headed towards the one place the Colony's guests rarely used. If there was anyone else but Nour's son there, they would know just how closely they were being pursued.

Sure enough, the swimming pool was empty. Even when the weather was good, no one really sunbathed in Jerusalem. Not that kind of city. There was only one person here, and when he saw Uri and Maggie approach, he stood up. The man was tall, with hair cut short, almost shaven. As her eyes adjusted to the bright sunlight, Maggie registered that he was probably in his early thirties, with sharp, clear green eyes. He wore jeans and a loose T-shirt.

Uri offered a hand, which the Palestinian took hesitantly.

'I realise,' Uri began, 'that I don't even know your name.'

'It's Mustapha. And you're—'

'I'm Uri and this is Maggie.' They were speaking over each other. Nervousness, Maggie decided, and unfamiliarity: Israelis and Palestinians hardly ever did anything as simple as talk.

Each gestured for the other to continue. Then Uri remembered himself, dipping into his shoulder bag to produce the portable radio he had picked up that morning. He turned it up loud, before mouthing, by way of explanation, the single word: bugs. Then he got down to business.

'Mustapha, thanks so much for coming here. I know it's not easy.'

'I'm lucky to have Jerusalem residency. Otherwise, from Ramallah, it would have been impossible.'

'Look, as you know, our fathers knew each other.' Uri went on to explain the discovery of the anagram and the coded emails. Then, taking a deep breath, he explained everything else: the tablet, the video message from his father, the tunnels. How Uri knew they were close, but not close enough.

'And you think my father knew where this tablet was hidden?'

'Maybe. After my father, yours was the very first killed. Someone thought he knew something.'

Mustapha Nour, who had been holding Uri's gaze, now looked over at Maggie, as if for validation. She gave a small nod.

'You know,' he said finally, looking down at his fingers, 'I always stayed out of politics. That was my father's business.'

'I know the feeling,' said Uri. 'But did he talk to you, in the last few days? About some kind of discovery?'

'No. We didn't talk much about his work.'

Uri leaned back, exhaling noisily. Maggie could tell that he was about to give up; this had been his last good idea.

I have put it somewhere safe, somewhere only you and my brother could know. A wheel turned slowly in Maggie's brain. She thought of how Shimon Guttman's messages had worked so far, urging Uri to remember things he already knew. Perhaps he had done the same with his 'brother', Ahmed Nour.

'Mustapha,' Maggie began, 'did it come as a complete surprise to you that your father knew an Israeli?'

'Yes,' he said, looking up at her, the green eyes piercing. 'And no.'

'No?'

'Well, it did when I first heard from you.' He nodded towards Uri. 'But the more I thought about it, the more it kind of made sense. I mean, he knew a lot about Israel, my father. He was an expert in the languages of this region, including, by the way, the script those ancient tablets are written in. And of course he knew Hebrew. He knew a lot about the way this country worked. So . . . well, it makes sense that he couldn't only have got that from books. Maybe he had someone to show him around.'

'OK. Did he ever mention—?'

'Like I know he went to the tunnels, under the Haram al-Sharif. Not many Palestinians have done that. And he disagreed with them passionately. "They're a Zionist attempt to undermine the Muslim Quarter," he said.'

'But he went anyway.'

'He was an archaeologist. He was curious.'

No wonder Guttman had wanted to speak to Nour about the tablet, Maggie thought. They might well have been the only two people in this divided land able to read what it said—and to understand its true meaning.

'Mustapha, I know it's hard. But can we tell you the exact message Shimon Guttman left behind? See what it means to you?'

Mustapha nodded.

Maggie repeated it word for word, from memory. ' "Go west, young man, and make your way to the model city, close to the Mishkan. You'll find what I left for you there, in the path of ancient warrens." '

Mustapha shut his eyes as he listened to her. Finally, he spoke. 'He has to mean the Haram al-Sharif, the place you went. Warrens are like tunnels, yes? And the model city. It's how we all speak of Jerusalem, Jews and Muslims.'

'Sure, but where?' Uri was showing his frustration.

'Could "Go west" tell you the way to go through the tunnels?'

'There is only one way through and I've done it.' It was Maggie, her own exasperation no longer contained.

'I am sorry.'

'No,' said Maggie, remembering herself. 'It's not your fault. We just thought there was something you might know.'

They began to walk back into the hotel. Maggie realised that she had barely offered her condolences to Mustapha. Out of politeness, she asked after his late father, how many children he had left, how many grandchildren.

'And he was still working?'

'Yes,' he said, explaining about the dig at Beitin. 'But that was not his life's dream. His real dream, he will never see.' His eyes were glittering.

'What was that, Mustapha?' Maggie asked.

'He wanted to build a Palestine Museum, a beautiful building full of art and sculpture, and all the archaeological remains he could collect. The history of Palestine in one place.'

Uri looked up, suddenly alert. 'Like the Israel Museum?'

'That's right. In fact, I remember him saying that one day we should have something like that. In our part of Jerusalem. Something that would show the world what used to be here, so they could see it for themselves.'

Uri's eyes widened. 'He said that?'

'Yes.' Mustapha was smiling. '"One day, Mustapha," he said, "we shall build what they have, to show the world the history of *our* Jerusalem."'

'My father must have shown it to him,' Uri said quietly.

'Uri?'

He gave her a brief glance. 'I'll explain on the way. Mustapha, can you come with us?'

Within a minute, the three of them were in a taxi, heading west across the city. The smile barely left Uri's face, even when he was shaking his head, saying 'of course' to himself, again and again. When Maggie asked where the hell they were going, he looked at Mustapha and grinned broadly.

'Thanks to our two fathers, I think our journey is about to end.'

SITTING IN THE FRONT SEAT, alongside the driver, and against a pounding techno beat from the radio, Uri took delight in explaining his father's clue.

'You see, I read it too quickly. I assumed that "Go west, young man" had to refer to the Western Wall. But it was too obvious. He meant go west across Jerusalem, to the west of the city. To the place that "my brother"—your father, Mustapha—would know. The clue was in the word *Mishkan*. It can refer to the Temple, but also this place, the Knesset.' Right on cue, they passed Israel's parliament.

'What about the rest? The path of ancient warrens?'

'Don't worry, Maggie. We'll see it when we get there. I'm sure of it.'

He then turned back towards the driver, asking to borrow his mobile phone. He had done the same thing the instant they had left the Colony, then, as now, speaking intently in Hebrew for a while, before smiling and hanging up. Maggie wondered who he had just phoned and was about to enquire when Uri's face seemed to darken. Maggie asked him what was wrong. He came back with a single word: 'Shabbat.'

They pulled into a car park, one that was worryingly empty. Uri did his best to bolt out of the car, hobbling over to the ticket office, whose windows were all closed. By the time Maggie and Mustapha had caught up, Uri was already gesticulating desperately to a security guard on the door. As he feared, the Israel Museum was closed for the sabbath.

After much pleading, the guard grudgingly passed Uri a cellphone, apparently already connected. Uri's voice instantly became lighter, full of warmth and humour. Maggie had no idea what he was saying, but she felt certain that Uri was speaking to a woman.

Sure enough, a few minutes later an attractive young woman appeared at the gate. She was carrying a walkie-talkie and had a name tag pinned to the front of her dark blue jacket. As she approached, Uri turned to Maggie and Mustapha and whispered: 'We're a TV crew from the BBC, OK?'

The woman had a quizzical look on her face, but it was not hostile, and Maggie could only admire as she watched Uri go to work. He gave this girl both barrels the fixed eye contact and the occasional shake of the head, to get the long curls of hair out of his eyes, even the hand landing, as if inadvertently, on her forearm. It was a charm offensive that offended Maggie much less than it charmed the girl, at least if the sudden unlocking of bolts and creaking opening of the gate were anything to go by.

As the guard ushered them in, the woman pointed at her watch as if to say 'just five minutes'. Maggie gave Uri a bewildered look.

'Media relations officer,' Uri said. 'Told her we'd met a few years ago and how sad I was that she'd already forgotten me.'

'And did you meet her a few years ago?'

'I have no idea.'

Uri had played the film-maker, somehow persuading the young woman that they were part of a documentary crew due to fly back to London tonight. Maggie was the reporter. They desperately needed to get one last shot, a long-distance zoom. The cameraman was over there, Uri had said, pointing at the faraway trees just below En Kerem. The camera would begin with Maggie in shot, then pull out to show the full, extraordinary panorama. The whole thing would take just five minutes and they would be gone.

'And she bought that crap?'

'I think she liked that I still remembered her.'

They were walking through what seemed like a university campus, or a private garden. All around was playful modern sculpture, including a giant steel dog whistle, painted red. They passed an enormous white structure, shaped like the lid of an urn, set in a square pool of shallow water. The surface, Maggie could see, consisted of a thousand tiny white bricks.

'Shrine of the Book,' Uri said briskly, marching ahead. 'Where they keep the Dead Sea Scrolls.'

He led them up onto a raised stone platform, where they stood looking across at a sweeping view of Jerusalem. On her right, Maggie could see the various government buildings Uri had pointed out en route. Opposite, and in the distance, was indeed a thick covering of trees; Maggie half expected to spot a cameraman, waiting for their signal.

But that was not what Uri was looking at. Instead, leaning over the observation bar, he was gesturing to what lay beneath.

And now Maggie saw it. Laid out on the ground below was a miniature city, its walls, its streets, its houses. Everything was perfect, down to the little red roofs, the tiny trees and the minuscule bricks in each wall. There were courtyards, turrets, even a coliseum. A marble structure loomed over all the rest, its entrance framed by four Corinthian columns, each crowned in gold, leading to a roof that seemed to blaze with precious metal.

A heartbeat later and she understood. This was a model of ancient Jerusalem and *that* was the Temple, its dominating vastness clear now in a way it had never been before. This was how the city would have looked two thousand years ago, when the Jews' Temple still stood.

Go west, young man, and make your way to the model city . . .

Maggie wanted to laugh at the simplicity of it. Guttman had been both ingenious and obvious, so long as you knew where to look. He had, Maggie realised now, been thorough too. If 'my brother' Ahmed Nour had been alive, he might well have known to come here straight away. But if he was gone, there was an alternative path to this place, via Second Life.

Uri had already taken the stairs down, so that he was now at the same level as the model. Most of the city barely reached the height of his knee.

'OK, Maggie,' he called up, his voice different. 'We'll need you over there, I think. For the shot. Musta— Mark, if you can join me down here, we can work out the angle.'

As Maggie climbed down the stairs, she realised that Uri was pointing at one of the outer retaining walls of the vast Temple courtyard—the Western Wall, the very spot where she had walked, underground, that morning, in the real world. Now they would do the same here, in the model version.

'Take this,' Uri said, handing her the mobile he had borrowed from, and not returned to, the cab driver. 'I've called it already and it's on speaker. Leave it on and it'll be an open line between us.' He then added firmly, 'If anything happens, just do exactly what I say. Understand?' When Maggie asked what he meant, he shook his head: 'No time. As soon as they see what we're doing, they'll throw us out.'

She stepped gingerly over the low rail and miniature moat surrounding the model, and tiptoed between the dwarf dwellings, feeling like Gulliver in ankle boots. She looked back to see Uri pointing at a particular spot on the wall. It was a staircase, side on, which ascended to a small opening. *Of course*. This was Warren's Gate, where she had been this morning. Directly behind it, just yards away, was the Foundation Stone itself, the place where Abraham had been ready to kill his son. *You'll find what I left for you there, in the path of ancient warrens.*

Maggie was now looming over this tiny staircase. She crouched down to see the top of the stairs, the flat surface that led onto the gate. She touched it, but felt only dust. Even this, she thought, the model-makers had got right: the same Old City dust she had had on her feet that morning.

She scratched away at the dust until she felt a gap, a line between the wall of the staircase and what was meant to be its top landing. She dug in her nails, and tugged. There was movement, she could feel it. Finally the small rectangle of ground gave way in her hand. At long last, she had found it.

Suddenly, she heard the sound of a woman's screams, followed by the thundering noise of male footsteps, charging as if in an animal stampede. She had barely stood up to her full height when she heard a single word bellowed out at terrifying volume.

'FREEZE!'

Stationed all around the model city, surrounding it from every angle, were half a dozen men, all dressed in black, their faces covered in masks. And each one of them had an automatic weapon aimed at her head.

CHAPTER ELEVEN

Jerusalem, Friday, 1.32 p.m.

Her eyes searched for Uri, but could see no sign of him. Nor of Mustapha. She remained frozen to the spot.

'Put your hands in the air. Now!'

Maggie did as she was told, phone in one hand and the clay tablet in the other. Her heart was thumping, powered by the excitement of finding what she felt sure was the tablet and, now, by sheer mortal terror.

Then a familiar voice. 'Thank you, Maggie. You surpassed yourself.'

He had been the last to arrive, coming down the stairs only now to join his men on the same level as the model city. 'I'm grateful. Your country is grateful.' She had to move her eyes to the left to see him: Bruce Miller.

'So why don't we do this cool and calm. You just stay there, and one of my boys will approach and relieve you of the tablet. Try anything stupid and we'll blow your brains out.'

Maggie could barely think above the throb of her own blood. What option did she have but to surrender? After all she and Uri had been through, she had to face reality. He and his gang of torturers had won.

It was then she heard another voice, nearer than Miller's yet not as clear. It took her a second to realise where it was coming from.

'Maggie, it's Uri.' The mobile phone, on speaker, crackling away inside her own hand. 'Listen very carefully. Tell Miller there is a live camera on him right now, streaming pictures of this onto the Internet.'

She looked around again; no sign of Uri. He must have seen the men coming and fled down the hillside. And what was this lunacy about cameras and the Internet? Blagging your way into a museum was one thing. Trying to bullshit a henchman to the American President was madness.

Then she remembered the moment on the highway, when she had trusted Uri—and she had been right.

'Now be a good little girl and give us the tablet. Otherwise my boys might want to finish what they started. Don't think they didn't enjoy inspecting that tidy little body of yours. But, gotta tell ya, they found it a little frustrating, being restricted to the use of their hands and all.'

Uri's voice again. 'Tell him to call the consulate. Get them to look at www.uriguttman.com and tell him what they see.'

Maggie hesitated; a plan was forming in her head. Then she spoke.

'Is that any way for Bruce Miller, Special Assistant to the President of the United States, to be talking?'

'I'm the Political Counsellor to the President, if you don't mind, young lady. Now give me that tablet.'

Maggie smiled. Nothing was more important to a Washington man than his title.

Uri's voice crackled again: 'Maggie, what are you doing? Tell him about the camera! Tell him to call the consulate!'

Not yet.

'You mean this?' She held up the tablet, keeping it as straight and steady as she could. 'What could be so important about this little object that you've got six men aiming their guns at me, an innocent woman—Maggie Costello, negotiator for the United States State Department?'

'We've been over this, Maggie.'

'It's just a little bit of clay. What could be so important about that?'

Uri was boiling over. '*Tell him!*'

'Are you bluffing, Costello? Is that some dummy tablet in your hand? 'Cause if it is, you ain't got no bargaining chip, no leverage.'

'Oh, I've got the real thing here, Bruce Miller, believe me. The last will and testament of Abraham. That's what you're looking for, isn't it?'

'*Maggie!*' Uri was getting desperate.

But she wasn't done yet. 'And that's why Rachel Guttman had to die. And Baruch Kishon. And Afif Aweida and God knows who else. You got your men to kill those people, just because of this, didn't you?'

'Maggie, come on. You know why we had to take those people out. If we didn't get that tablet into safe hands, many more would die.'

'So you're not ashamed of killing those people, even though they were innocent? You're not ashamed of assaulting me and torturing Uri Guttman? Tell me honestly, Bruce Miller. Look me in the eye and tell me.'

'Ashamed? I'm proud of it.'

'All right. I'll give the tablet to you,' she said, doing her best to keep her voice steady. She had heard what she needed to hear.

The guns remained locked on her.

'But there's something you ought to know, Mr Miller. You've just made what could be your greatest-ever TV appearance. There's a camera on you right now, relaying this whole conversation onto the Internet. Call the consulate. Get someone to log on to www.uriguttman.com. Ask them to describe to you what they see. Go on. If I'm lying you'll soon find out and then you can do what the hell you like to me.'

She saw Miller pull out his mobile phone and whisper into it.

A pause, then she heard the two words of confirmation, from Miller's own mouth. They were said quietly, but their meaning was unmistakable.

'Holy shit.'

God only knew how, but Uri had not been bluffing. He did indeed have Miller on camera; it had held steady on his face as he had identified himself and confessed everything.

'That's mighty clever, Miss Costello. I'll hand it to you. But no one was watching that no-name web site. It went into the ether and now it's vanished.'

'Not quite. We're recording this as it goes out. People will be able to play it again and again.' It was Uri's voice, though this time it was not coming through the phone. He was emerging from the hillside with a small, hand-held video camera at his eye. Walking beside him was Mustapha. Maggie could only smile at the sheer cheek of it.

'Right now, we've got the news editor over at Channel 2 looking at these pictures. And who was it you just phoned, Mustapha?'

'Al Jazeera. Ramallah bureau.'

'They're all watching this little scene. And before you get any ideas, Mr Miller, this is only a second camera. Getting what we call B-roll. The main camera is down there, safely hidden from view. You blast me now and my friend there will capture it in glorious Technicolor.'

Maggie could see Miller paling. 'Who's going to believe this cock and bull story of yours?' he stammered.

'No one would have believed it, Bruce,' Maggie conceded. 'Not until you confirmed every last detail just now. When this bit of video finds its way onto YouTube and CNN and ABC and all the rest, I don't think even you will be able to talk your way out of it.'

A mobile phone rang. Miller's. He turned his back to Uri's camera before answering, though his voice was still audible.

'Yes, Mr President. I can hear you clearly, sir . . . I understand: you can see me too. I agree, technology is an incredible thing, sir.' He said nothing for a good half-minute, then spoke again. 'I will draft the letter of resignation immediately, sir. And yes, I will make clear that this was a rogue operation, wholly my own initiative. Goodbye, Mr President.'

Without another word, Miller gestured at the armed men. Their weapons still raised, they slowly withdrew back up the steps, forming a protective cordon round Miller's retreat. A few seconds later and they were gone.

Uri lowered his camera and walked over to Maggie. As they hugged, he pointed towards the trees. 'That's who I was calling from the car. An old cameraman friend of mine who lives in En Kerem. I told him to get in position and aim his longest lens here. Oh, and to bring his smallest microwave transmitter with him. I'd say it was my best work.'

Maggie suddenly broke off the hug, seized by a thought.

'Is that thing still on?'

Uri nodded.

'Point the camera at me,' she said to Uri. 'Right now.'

He brought the viewfinder to his eye, and gave her a thumbs up.

'My name is Maggie Costello. I'm a peace negotiator working for the United States government in Jerusalem. This'—she held up the tablet—'this tablet is nearly four thousand years old. Over the course of the last week, an American covert-ops team have bugged, burgled and murdered their way across this country and beyond trying to get hold of it. You heard Mr Miller confess to that a moment ago. He wanted to keep the fact of this tablet's existence, and above all its contents, a secret. And here's why.'

At last she took a good look at the object she had been gripping tightly in her hand. When she finally saw it up close, she was almost disappointed. It was so small, the characters etched on it so tiny. The whole thing was no bigger, and much slimmer, than a cigarette packet, hewn from rough, earthen clay. And yet her own government had been prepared to kill for it—along with any number of fanatics among the Israelis and Palestinians. Whatever this small chunk of clay said, it could only spell victory for one side and disaster for the other.

As she turned it over, she looked for a small piece of tape on the bottom edge which she had noticed when she peeled the tablet from its hiding place by the miniature Warren's Gate. She had assumed it was part of the fixing that Shimon Guttman had devised to keep this treasure hidden in the shadows of the model city. But when she brought it up to her eye, she saw that it was not just tape, though it was sticky on one side. It was instead a tiny clear plastic envelope, a smaller version of the kind traffic wardens use to keep a parking ticket dry. Carefully, she peeled it away from the tablet. Then she removed from it a small white square of paper bearing three neat, if tiny, blocks of print. The first was in Hebrew, the second in Arabic and the third in English.

She began to read aloud, into the camera. 'This is a tablet dictated to a scribe by Abraham the patriarch, shortly before his death in Hebron. The translation of his words reads thus:

I Abraham, son of Terach, in front of the judges have attested thus. The land where I took my son, there to make a sacrifice of him to the Mighty Name, the Mountain of Moriah, this land has become a source of dissension between my two sons; let their names here be recorded as Isaac and Ishmael. So have I thus declared in front of the judges that the Mount shall be bequeathed as follows—'

She fell silent the instant the shot rang out. When she hit the ground, her hand stayed wound round the tablet, clinging on to it, as if to life itself.

THE CAMERA FELL from his hand with a thud. Uri dashed over, crouching over her body to see where she had been hit. Less than a second later he heard a bullet whizzing past his own ear. Now he too fell flat, lying on top of Maggie to shield her from the incoming fire.

He looked across and saw Mustapha, also prone on the ground. The Palestinian gestured for Uri to look upwards. There, directly above them, leaning over the parapet, were the barrels of several guns, firing into the trees opposite. Were Miller's men trying to kill the hidden cameraman, as if that would somehow save them and their boss?

A rustle came from the trees, then a Hebrew cry of '*Al tira!*' Don't shoot.

From above, Uri heard a response: '*Hadel esh!*' Hold your fire.

As Uri and Mustapha gradually raised themselves up, more than a dozen men pounded down the steps: Israeli police. Their semiautomatic weapons were aimed at two men standing on the hillside just below the model.

'Identify yourselves!' the police commander barked.

There was silence.

Were these Palestinians, their Hebrew learned in jail, come here to mount some suicide mission? If they hesitated even a second longer, Uri knew what would happen: they would be shot in the head, the only sure way to prevent them setting off a bomb.

'We are the Defenders of United Jerusalem,' said the elder of the pair. And as the police circled them, Uri could see they each wore a knitted kippah, or skullcap—the unambiguous badge of the settler movement.

'So, they were after us as well.'

Uri wheeled round to see Maggie sitting up, rubbing her eyes.

'Maggie! You're alive!'

'Sorry about that. I didn't know I was such a wuss. I'm meant to be a big strong diplomat. I'm not meant to faint the moment someone fires a gun.'

THE POLICE KEPT all three of them, Uri, Maggie and Mustapha, for several hours, asking them to give long, detailed statements. At their side throughout was a lawyer, Uri's brother-in-law, who insisted on his clients' right to keep their private property, including the clay tablet, private. After his intervention, the tablet stayed with them at all times. As for the tiny white square of paper, Maggie hid that deep in a pocket and never let it go.

When they emerged from the police station, hundreds of camera lenses were aimed at them, flashbulbs strobing. There was a collective roar, as dozens of reporters called out: 'Maggie! Maggie! What did he say? Maggie, what did Abraham say? What does the tablet say?'

Uri and Mustapha flanked her on either side, and they shoved their way to a waiting taxi. The driver had to do two full circuits before he had shaken off the chasing vans and motorcycles, eventually reaching Maggie's hotel.

In the sanctuary of her room, Maggie switched on the television. She had some clue what to expect from her mobile phone, returned to her by the police with a full inbox: voice messages from the BBC, CNN, Reuters, AP, the *New York Times*, all requesting an interview. There were also several messages from the White House.

Now when she clicked through the channels she kept catching sight of herself, holding the clay tablet up to Uri's camera. Fox News was playing the tape of Bruce Miller confessing his sins, culminating in the line, 'Ashamed? I'm proud of it.'

As Maggie perched on the end of the bed, Uri came over, clutching a laptop computer. He clicked through a series of web sites: *Al-Ahram*, the *Washington Post*, the *Guardian*, the *Times of India*. They were all covering the same story. Finally, he clicked on the *Haaretz* site and brought up a news account of the arrest of settlers' leader Akiva Shapira, the suspected leader of the Defenders of United Jerusalem. What's more, the police spokesman added, they had gathered evidence that Uri Guttman and Maggie Costello had also been within the sights of a radical Islamist cell linked to the wanted militant Salim Nazzal.

There were endless columns and debates devoted to discussing what Abraham might or might not have said, and cries on all sides that it must be a fake, and that the timing of the tablet's release was just too neat to be real.

'You know, Maggie, you're going to have to get the truth out, the full text of the testament. It can't wait.'

Maggie looked back at the TV. It now showed the British Prime Minister, standing in Downing Street, declaring that 'History is holding its breath'.

Maggie sighed. 'I know, Uri. I just need to work out who should be the one to say it.'

SHE LAY on the hotel bed, allowing herself to drift off into a few minutes of exhausted sleep. She dreamt she was roaming the streets of Jerusalem, not in her own body, but as her sister's bra-topped avatar in Second Life. She was floating above the golden Dome of the Rock, soaring high above the Western Wall . . .

She woke suddenly, her forehead clammy with sweat. A single sentence that Bruce Miller had uttered now flashed through her mind.

There's a back channel too, so they're talking, believe me.

Could it be? Was it possible? She grabbed the computer and headed straight for Second Life, logging on again as Shimon Guttman's alter ego, Saeb Nastayib. She teleported straight back to the seminar room at Harvard University. *Please be there.*

Sure enough, there were the avatars she had seen before: Yaakov Yariv and Khalil al-Shafi. She approached, hit the CHAT button and typed a simple message: I have the information the world is waiting for.

The reply did not come instantly, for reasons she would later understand. It turned out that both Yariv's office and al-Shafi's would dump 'sleeping' avatars in Second Life's Harvard seminar room, just to maintain a presence there. That way they could keep the channel open, ensuring that each side was available to the other twenty-four hours a day. Amir Tal, the personal aide to the Israeli Prime Minister, would check in hourly during the day and several times at night, while his Palestinian counterpart would do the same. It had been al-Shafi's idea: he had read about Internet simulations of the Middle East peace process while in jail and had logged on to one, taking the role of Khalil al-Shafi, soon after his release. All it needed, he realised, was a senior Israeli to join in and they would have their own back channel. No need for midnight flights to Oslo or clandestine weekends in Scandinavian cabins. This dialogue could take place in full daylight, with total deniability. And if anyone asked what was going on, 'Yaakov Yariv' and 'Khalil al-Shafi' could say they were simply American students, playing a game.

The first reply came from al-Shafi. She asked him to telephone her, to verify that it was really him and, sure enough, she heard that familiar voice down the telephone. She arranged to meet his aide in an hour's time.

Then she made the same arrangement with Amir Tal.

They gathered in the plush West Jerusalem home of an American businessman. Maggie was too tired for pleasantries and got straight to the point.

'As you know, I have the tablet. Today I was about to reveal the full text on camera because I feared that if I didn't, if something happened to me, the last testament of Abraham would be lost for ever. But now it is safe.'

She explained that she would not yet show them the tablet—that would have to wait until the leaders themselves met. She produced instead Guttman's translation, and read the English out loud. The two men paled.

She passed the paper so that the two of them could read the words again, in their own languages. 'Of course you'll have every chance to verify the authenticity of the tablet and this translation as soon as we move to the next stage,' Maggie said quietly, anxious to give them as much time as they needed to absorb what they had just read.

'And what is the next stage, Miss Costello?' the Palestinian asked.

Maggie explained that it was up to the two leaders to tell the world what Abraham had decided. It wasn't right for the announcement to come from her, an outsider. Instead they should call a joint press conference for the next day. Uri Guttman and Mustapha Nour would be at their side, representing their late fathers, as the two leaders made the announcement.

MAGGIE WATCHED the press conference on television. It would have been fun to be there, but in the background was where she belonged.

Al-Shafi went first and he spoke in English, introducing this as the tablet dictated by Abraham the patriarch and then reading the text: '*I Abraham, son of Terach, in front of the judges have attested thus. The land where I took my son, there to make a sacrifice of him to the Mighty Name, the Mountain of Moriah, this land has become a source of dissension between my two sons.*'

Then he paused and Yaakov Yariv took over, also in English: '*Let their names here be recorded as Isaac and Ishmael. So have I thus declared in front of the judges that the Mount shall be bequeathed as follows—*'

Then the two men paused, veteran showmen the pair of them, before reading on, in unison, their voices chiming perfectly:

'*That it shall be shared between my two sons and their descendants in a manner of their choosing. But that they be clear that it belongs to neither one of them, but to both, now and for ever. That they be entrusted as its guardians and custodians, to protect it on behalf of the Mighty Name, the one Lord who is sovereign over everything and all of us. Sworn with the seal of Abraham, son of Terach, witnessed by his sons, in Hebron, this day.*'

EPILOGUE

Jerusalem, two days later

She had all her papers on her lap, in a neat black portfolio case. Less was always more when it came to a negotiation, she believed: a blank note pad should really be enough. Only at the very last stage did you need sheaves of documents, usually maps. And they were not at that stage. Not yet, anyway.

She took a look at this room, at the large table stretching out before her, its faded elegance typical of this building. Government House. She looked at her watch, again. Another five minutes and they would get started.

The joint press conference had had a more powerful effect than anyone had anticipated. The television images of those two old warhorses joining together, incanting the words of their common ancestor, had proved irresistible. The pundits even began wondering if peace was in fact the Middle East's age-old destiny, a destiny of which it had been cruelly cheated.

A euphoric Amir Tal and his Palestinian counterpart had been on the phone just before midnight on Saturday, asking Maggie what she wanted in return for allowing their bosses to take credit for a discovery that would endow them both with enormous, enduring authority.

'Only that the two sides resume face-to-face talks immediately,' she had said. Just the two leaders in a room with a single mediator.

The two officials offered their provisional agreement. Maggie pressed home her advantage. 'And there's one last thing I want.'

'And what is that, Miss Costello?'

'Well, it relates to the identity of the mediator.'

THAT HAD BEEN two days ago. She had spent the forty-eight hours since that phone call preparing herself. She had read every note, every minute, of the talks so far, every official document prepared by both sides.

In between it all, she saw Uri. After the press conference on TV they had met up at Someone to Run With, the late-night café where they had hammered away at the computer before fleeing. 'We're still the oldest people here,' she said. And he smiled. Each asked the other about their plans and each shrugged. Uri said he had some things to sort out here in Jerusalem, his parents' house, his father's papers.

'Your father gave you one last surprise, didn't he?'

'You know, it's funny. The whole world is going crazy over this tablet. Everything it means. But for me the most amazing thing is that my dad did so much to keep it safe. Even though it says what it says.'

'He was a scholar.'

'Not just that. Remember what he told my mother, over and over? That this changes everything? Maybe it changed him.'

Hesitantly, Maggie had steered the conversation round to Bruce Miller and why she had been sent to Jerusalem, that she had been—she hesitated before the word—a honeytrap. She told him how ashamed it made her.

He listened hard, unsmiling. 'But you didn't know you were a trap, did you, Maggie? You can't be a trap if you don't know you're a trap. And it's my fault for walking into you. Besides, you're much rarer than honey.'

They hugged, a long, tight hug, and then shyly, like teenagers at summer camp, they exchanged email addresses. Neither had a physical address they could be sure of. When Maggie began to say goodbye, he placed a finger over her lips.

'Not goodbye,' he said. '*L'hitraot*. It means "Until we see each other again". And we will. Soon.'

And both knew that promise was not vain.

Now a distant grandfather clock struck ten, the clock no doubt a parting gift of the British who had built this Government House when they ruled Palestine. Maggie could hear a sudden surge of noise outside: the sound of several cars pulling up, and a press ruck, questions being shouted, bulbs flashing. A minute or two later, and the same thing all over again.

Then, the sound of footsteps down two corridors; the leader of the Israelis and the leader of the Palestinians walking from opposite directions, each man alone, towards this room. She took a deep breath.

She shook both their hands, then invited them to shake hands with each other and gestured for them to take their seats.

'Thank you, gentlemen,' Maggie Costello said, aiming a warm smile at both of them. The smile was genuine. It was the smile of a woman who, at long last, was back where she belonged.

She cleared her throat. 'Shall we begin?'

SAM BOURNE

Real name: Jonathan Freedland
Inspiration: George Orwell, John le Carré
Home: Stoke Newington, London

RD: Why do you think religious thrillers have become so popular recently?

SB: Probably because religion seems to matter so much more than it once did. Indeed, I reckon that the persistence of religion is the first great theme—and surprise—of the 21st century. I even like to joke that 'religion is the new politics', meaning that if it was politics and ideology which motivated people in the last century, then faith does that today. For thriller writing, that has an immediate effect. The old Cold War thrillers were about clashes of ideology—Communism against the West. Today's thrillers are about today's clashes and the forces that now motivate people—and that, often, includes faith.

RD: What gave you the idea for *The Last Testament*?

SB: The initial inspiration was seeing an event I consider to be one of the most dramatic of recent times: the looting of the National Museum of Antiquities in Baghdad, directly after the American and British invasion in 2003. Many, many precious objects were stolen in that chaos—*The Last Testament* imagines the fate of one of them.

RD: In 2002, you chaired a three-day dialogue between Israelis and Palestinians on behalf of the *Guardian*. Did this inform the way you wrote the book?

SB: I certainly drew on that experience when writing my lead character, Maggie Costello, who is a peace negotiator. She comes up against some of the obstacles, and deploys some of the tricks, that I saw at first hand during that process. I also used some of the experience of organising that 2002 dialogue—coaxing the players to take part—when crafting a number of the scenes involving politicians, Israeli and Palestinian: how they are with their aides, what their offices look like, that kind of thing.

RD: Did you worry about upsetting any of the factions involved in the Middle East?

SB: I have learned that when you write about the Middle East conflict, it is *always* possible for people to get upset. The issues are just so sensitive. Nevertheless, I hope the book is accurate in what it says about both sides—and so far there have been no complaints.

RD: Did the charismatic character of Maggie Costello arrive in your mind fully formed, or did she develop along with the plot?

SB: She certainly did develop—there were points in the story where I did not know until I got there how she would react. But I had a very good sense of her very early on, chiefly because she was very much inspired by a woman I know and admire. So I had that woman's voice, her manner, in mind when writing Maggie Costello.

RD: Why did you pick a woman to be the mediator in such a male-orientated world?

SB: I was always very struck by the example of Mona Juul, the Norwegian diplomat who, together with her husband, played a key role in negotiating the 1993 Oslo Accords between Israel and the Palestinians. Accounts of those secret talks reveal that the two sides were often wrongfooted by the presence of this young—she was then in her early thirties—attractive woman. These hardened men of war found themselves competing for her favour, compromising to win her approval or even just a smile during the lunch break. When I first read of that unusual human dynamic, I thought that a woman peace negotiator absolutely belonged in a novel.

RD: What research did you do into antiquities looted from the Baghdad museum?

SB: A lot. I interviewed a lawyer who specialises in stolen antiquities, as well as the policeman who founded Scotland Yard's Arts and Antiquities squad. But the key source was Dr Irving Finkel of the British Museum. He is the world authority on the ancient language of Babylonian cuneiform. I spent many hours with him and admire him greatly.

RD: Has the huge success of your first novel, *The Righteous Men*, selected by the Richard & Judy Book Club on Channel 4, made it more daunting to write?

SB: In a way, because this has now gone from being a journalist's hobby, a project on the side, to being slightly more serious. But I guess the trick is not to think about success or failure but just to get on with telling the story.

RD: How do you fit in novel writing alongside a family life and a demanding career in journalism?

SB: That, I confess, has not been easy. It just meant working horribly hard in 2006, lots of very long days and far too many weekends at the desk. I've now lightened my journalistic load a bit—I'm taking a break from my column for the London *Evening Standard*, for example—and really hope to get the next book written without encroaching too deeply into weekends. Writing at home does mean that I get to see my kids a lot, even when I'm hard at it. I'll often take a break for their bathtime and bedtime stories, and then go back to the writing afterwards if I have to.

RD: Why did you decide to use a pseudonym?

SB: It was my agent's idea. He thought 'Jonathan Freedland' didn't sound like a thriller writer's name—and that it was best to keep my day job and this new venture separate. So far, I reckon he was right.

The Untold Story of the Tragic 1979 Fastnet Race

LEFT FOR

Nick Ward

with Sinéad O'Brien

DEAD

As the start gun for the 1979 Fastnet Race was fired, Nick Ward was brimming over with excitement, honoured to be taking part in one of the most challenging yacht races in the world. On that sunny morning off the south coast of England, nothing prepared him for the drama that was to unfold within a few short hours . . . Twenty-seven years later, Ward decides to tell his gripping story.

Breaking the Silence

It is over twenty-six years since I sat alone at a bedside table with paper and pen supplied to me by Treliske Hospital in north Cornwall. Then I thought it important to record the facts, as I knew them, while they were still vivid in my mind. I was tired and overcome, but the words wrote themselves. The date was August 15, 1979—the day after the most shattering event of my life. This last quarter-century has given me plenty of time to reflect on the longest fourteen hours of my life, which I shared with my friend and crewmate Gerry Winks aboard the yacht *Grimalkin*.

Four days before, on August 11, 1979, I had set sail on my first ever Fastnet Race, part of a crew of six men: David Sheahan (owner and skipper of *Grimalkin*), his son Matthew, Gerald Winks, Mike Doyle and David Wheeler. All of us were excited and proud to be taking part in this 600-mile offshore classic. The race began in near-perfect conditions, but on day three *Grimalkin*, along with many of the other yachts, got caught up in the deadliest storm in the history of modern sailing.

In the months following the disaster I gave several interviews. I know now that I never portrayed my true feelings nor gave the full story. I was a twenty-four-year-old man in deep shock and in no position to evaluate my situation objectively. Much of what I read about the circumstances surrounding my story caused me such pain that I simply wanted to block it all out. In 1980 I took the decision not to be interviewed again.

That was until September 2004, when I was approached by Sinéad O'Brien, a documentary film-maker who was interested in pursuing the story. Over the next few months, Sinéad, this bright, young, vibrant, tenacious Irish woman, was to tease out memories from me, some long covered up. In front of this stranger I began to purge myself of twenty-five years of pent-up emotions.

After much indecision I decided to finally put down on paper the feelings of anger, helplessness, despair and pure bloody-minded frustration I had felt while trying to survive the near impossible.

Once she realised I had a story to tell, Sinéad brought her incisive style and her structuring skills to the writing of this book. She showed me how to add without veering off the line of being true to myself. Without Sinéad this story would have been left as a private journal, unpublished.

This book is as much for Gerald Winks as it is for me—for if it were not for him, I would not be here to tell this story. This is the, until now, untold story of what became of Gerry and me on that day, August 14, 1979.

I WAS BORN in the little south-coast village of Hamble, in Hampshire, the youngest of four children. Hamble is no ordinary village; some of the finest national and Olympic sailing champions were born here, sailed here or are connected with this place. If you are born in Hamble, it is inevitable that sailing will play some part in your growing up.

Certainly my father instilled in his three sons a love of all things nautical. My first sailing lessons were at the age of four on the River Hamble, in a pram dinghy Pa built for me during the winter of 1959/60. Perhaps because I was the youngest and he was that much older when I was growing up, Pa had the time to do things for me he had not had for the others. I spent far more time with him than my siblings had, and although I adored both my parents, Pa and I had a particular affinity. He was well built, six foot two, and for as long as I knew him had white hair and an untipped Senior Service cigarette in his hand. He captivated me with tales of the sea. He read me classic accounts of ships and their crews sailing the southern oceans and rounding Cape Horn. I wanted to be there with the characters in the books. I can remember the thrill I felt when we launched the dinghy down at Hamble quay the following spring—and also the crowd that it drew. Pa had named her *Fred* after my uncle, and I recall someone saying to him, 'You can't call her *Fred.*'

'We'll call her whatever we like,' said my father. 'Won't we, son?'

Standing alongside *Fred*, knee deep in water, I waited for Pa to lift me in. Then finally, with the crowd cheering, I was off on my first sail in *Fred* with Pa. I felt like a sailor heading off to the southern oceans to follow his dreams.

Over the summer of 1960 Pa taught me the basics of sailing. At such a young age I had no fear and my confidence grew quickly. I revelled in the water and everything about it, sometimes taking risks that Pa strictly warned me against. One of the first rules he instilled in me was that if the dinghy capsized, I was to stay with it.

'Stay with the boat, son. Hang on to it—she will save you.'

This beautiful navy-blue and snow-white dinghy was my first love. And I had fallen not only for *Fred*, but for the river too. These lessons with Pa began a lifelong passion.

WHILE I WAS STILL very young, I heard about the Fastnet Race from my next-door neighbour, Dick Langton, a seasoned off-shore sailor. The race starts off at Cowes, on the Isle of Wight, and continues westwards along the English coast until it passes Land's End. Its course then takes it up and across the approaches to the English Channel and into the Irish Sea, rounding the southernmost point of Ireland, the Fastnet Rock lighthouse—known as Ireland's 'teardrop'. The race then backtracks, going inshore to its finishing point in Plymouth off the famous breakwater. Dick, who had competed in three Fastnet Races, told me of the notorious stretch of water between the mainland and the rock, and all the variations in weather he had experienced. He described the stunning sunsets off the south coast of Ireland where the Irish Sea and Atlantic Ocean meet, and how he'd never seen anything like them. He told me of lightning, thunder and summer gales, but he also told me that the finish and the reception at Plymouth justified every minute of the 'hardship'. His stories gave me an idea of how important this race was. In my young mind it began to take on mythical form.

Pa had also increased my appetite for the Fastnet by taking me when I was seven to Cowes Bay to see the race's start. This was in the early 1960s, and Pa drove the launch *Snapdragon* for Eileen Ramsay, a famous marine photographer. Even at this age I was aware of the significance of this great race, the last in a series of five that make up the Admiral's Cup competition, the world championship of yacht racing. To this day the Fastnet Race is considered to be the jewel in the crown of offshore races.

It took under an hour to travel across the Solent to Cowes. We anchored in the bay and waited as hundreds of yachts filled the bay. The atmosphere made the hairs on the back of my neck stand up. I stood by Pa. 'One hand for yourself, one for the boat, Nicholas,' I remember him telling me. And I promised myself that one day I would be among the boats on the start line.

As I grew older sailing became my whole life—at least, that's how it felt to a teenage boy without a worry in the world other than would the weather be OK for that night's sailing. I loved every minute I spent afloat. All other activities—social, academic or otherwise—were secondary. I belonged to the Hamble River Sailing Club, which over the years has produced more champions and medal winners than almost any other club in the country.

Pa was soon taking me round the country to open meetings, trailing our dinghies and winning a few cups and medals on the way. I had a long apprenticeship in dinghies before I made my first Channel crossing in my early teens and started to race small keelboats offshore. I was dead set on a career in the merchant navy. I was also very clear about which offshore races I wanted to race in. I reckoned seventeen was the right age for my first Fastnet. On completion of that I would move on to the Sydney to Hobart Yacht Race and the Bermuda Race. But the Fastnet was to be first.

At the age of fifteen, in my final year at secondary school, I had an unexpected setback. I suffered a brain haemorrhage. The previous day I had been playing hookey with my good friend Mark Parkin. We had enjoyed a long walk to Totchfield Haven. It was a very hot March day and I had a nasty headache, which fortunately eased off by the time I went to bed.

The next day, March 24, 1971, was again hot. In the afternoon I played a hard-fought game of hockey and was exhausted after it. School friends told me afterwards that I collapsed on the hockey pitch, but this I don't recall. I simply remember having a violent headache, like a migraine but worse. When I got home I went straight upstairs to bed.

My headache got more severe as the evening wore on, so severe that I started to bang my head against the wall of my bedroom to try to stop the pain. I was sick several times. Turning over in bed, I tried supporting myself with my left arm and it collapsed beneath me, useless. The vision in my left eye became blurred, as if there was a screen being erected on my left side, blocking things out. My curtains were closed because I couldn't bear any light. Soon I had lost all sensation in the whole of my left side.

An ambulance was called and I was taken directly to hospital in Southampton. Ma was with me. I felt every bump the ambulance went over, and its flashing blue lights and the sound of its siren hurt my eyes and ears. I remember looking up at Ma as she squeezed my hand—there was fear in her eyes. I began to understand that my condition might be serious. I was transferred to the Wessex Neurological Centre.

The next day my condition deteriorated further and I was rushed into the operating theatre for an operation that lasted around three hours. I found out months later that I was given no more than a fifty-fifty chance of survival. There was never an explanation of exactly what had happened, only that some abnormal blood vessels were found, which I had probably been born with. Brain haemorrhages are sudden in onset and can occur at any time of life.

I spent months in hospital, and found out that the longer-term effects of my haemorrhage were a left-sided weakness and epilepsy. I felt as if life, barely begun, had passed me by. All my hopes were thwarted. I had to struggle to relearn basic skills, such as walking. If it hadn't been for my family, I could not have got through this. And as well as their support, I had a special form of therapy awaiting me—sailing.

One year later I plucked up the courage to sail again. I went on the river with Mark. I was reluctant; people had gathered on the quay to wish me well and I did not want to make a fool of myself. Christ, here I was standing knee-deep in water that felt particularly cold on my left side, as if someone had poured liquid nitrogen on it—cold, cold, cold. Then I thought: I can't back down now. I had something to prove to myself. Sod it, here goes. I struggled over the transom and sat in the dinghy. At once, it was as if I'd never been away. This was no problem, familiar territory—I could cope with this.

Mark jumped in and off we went, not far, but far enough. It was brilliant, absolutely brilliant, to be sailing again. I can do this, I thought; I was born to it. This first sail was so confidence-building that it fired me up like never before. I was now determined to prove to myself that I could achieve my ambitions, even if perhaps not as quickly.

I worked in a riverside chandlery, the biggest around, which at this time supplied most of the well-known ocean-racing yachts. Soon I was also boosting my income delivering boats, locally and abroad, gaining sea time and experience. Most weekends I was sailing and racing competitively offshore. I had given up my dream of joining the merchant navy, but I had made a life for myself on the sea. I had no complaints.

By 1977 I felt ready to do the Fastnet Race, but most skippers like to retain their crew for a full season and I wasn't able to make the commitment that year. In June 1979 I was asked by David Sheahan, one of my customers, to join him as crew for the forthcoming Channel Week series of races. I was thrilled and took up the offer without a second thought. I knew that by participating in this series the boat and her crew would automatically qualify for the Fastnet Race. This could be the year!

I didn't know David well at that time, only that he was an accountant in his mid-forties; I was better acquainted with his son, Matt, who I often saw racing his sailing dinghy on the Solent. I knew that his father owned and raced a thirty-foot yacht called *Grimalkin*—she was sister ship to *Silver Jubilee*, the world-cup-winning boat of 1976. *Grimalkin* was the type of boat I was used to sailing and, most importantly, David seemed a man to trust. When he asked me to join his crew, he already knew my physical capabilities, my strengths and my 'weaknesses'.

Less than a week after taking up his offer, I got a letter from David. I remember the excitement I felt when I read it: Channel Week would be a good introduction to his boat, he said, 'in contemplation for the longer Fastnet Race in August'. This was getting more and more real. I was getting to know Matt better too. At seventeen, he was confident and self-assured, articulate and sometimes outspoken. Stocky in build, around five foot eight or nine, he was strong and athletic. I didn't regard Matt as a really close mate, but we were friends who shared a goal and a passion.

The first race of the series began on Friday, July 6. It was the well-known 165-mile offshore race from Cowes to Saint-Malo. *Grimalkin* sailed with a six-man crew. David Sheahan was one of the best skippers I had crewed for. He was extremely good-humoured, and appreciated effort and attention to detail. In many ways David reminded me of Pa. They never met, but if they had, I know they would have got on famously. They were both polite and courteous men, though neither would 'put up with any nonsense', ashore or afloat. David was even of similar countenance to Pa, but shorter, around five foot nine, and of slighter build.

The great thing about this week's racing was that I had the chance to get to know the rest of the crew. Matt was almost simian in his agility in front of the mast, always eager to get the best from *Grimalkin*. But there were times when he became frustrated and gave in to 'stroppy' behaviour—which the rest of us found quite amusing. He adored his father. There was equality in the relationship, too—they were like best mates as much as father and son. Gerry Winks was second-in-command and navigator. He was a large man, around fourteen stone and well over six foot tall, but surprisingly softly spoken and affable. I took to him at once.

Mike Doyle was a likable young guy who smiled a lot. He was tall, dark-haired and had an incredibly deep voice, which I was sure he used to great effect in chatting up women. He also had a large repertoire of jokes and was good at raising a laugh.

I had rather less time for Dave Wheeler. He had a good nature but was somewhat young in outlook. I found out fairly early in the race that when put under pressure he developed a bit of an attitude problem. But he was also funny. He had a never-ending supply of filthy jokes, and he also broke wind constantly—more to his own delight than anyone else's.

If there wasn't much going on, it was hard not to get swept along with Dave's silly jokes. I remember on occasion laughing so hard I nearly fell overboard. At times Dave had to be reminded by the skipper that he wasn't just along for the ride. Looking back now, I can see that he was very young—about nineteen—and while his intentions were good he possibly *was* just along for the ride.

This first race passed without incident, and I enjoyed it. On the leg across the Channel to Saint-Malo we had the pleasure of seeing a fantastic all-colour summer sunset. It brought back what Dick Langton had told me years before about the Fastnet sunsets. If we qualified for the race, I hoped those sunsets would appear for us too.

Overall we had a fantastic week. *Grimalkin* performed well. We endured some close racing, some success and also our share of bad weather, which *Grimalkin* and her crew stood up to without difficulty. We sailed together well. All in all, I felt that David's crew was a good mixture of experience and youth. And apart from the usual friction caused by such proximity, there was absolutely no animosity on the boat.

Although we were forced to retire from the last race, David judged the week a success because we qualified for the Fastnet. He entered the boat, and confirmed that I would be in the crew. I knew, finally, that it was a certainty that I'd be on the 1979 Fastnet Race start line. I felt great; everyone did. We had a few beers that night, and sang *Grimalkin*'s praises until we could sing no more.

A couple of weeks before the Fastnet Race, David Sheahan sent a letter with detailed preparations to each member of the crew. He was very specific, allotting individual responsibilities, duties and domain aboard. He also included a watch schedule. I was really pleased to read that I would be off watch for the first twelve hours of the race. All I would have to do was hand the crew sandwiches. I was no cook—David had already 'awarded' me *Grimalkin*'s burnt spatula, the result of my labours in the galley during Channel Week, but I was fine with this; I'd much rather be trimming a sail than cooking.

David did not skimp on anything. As well as ensuring the boat was in a state of perfect preparation, he also ensured that his crew were the same, even insisting we all pay a pre-race visit to the dentist. He was a perfectionist —which is why I loved sailing with him.

During the week before the Fastnet, I checked the weather daily. The conditions seemed perfect, and I couldn't wait to set off. No part of the route is easy, so I knew it would be tough, and in sailing terms my greatest challenge, but I was ready for it.

Ma was concerned for me. Throughout the week before the race, she kept saying to me, 'Now, you won't forget your medication, will you?'

My epilepsy required me to take phenobarbitone, an anticonvulsant drug, twice daily. This was the one thing I never needed reminding of. But I suppose Ma could only picture the worst. What if I did forget, or mislaid it? What if there was bad weather and I had a convulsion? Ma and Pa were both well aware of the many risks involved in offshore sailing.

The night before the race I stayed at home with Ma and Pa. We ate an early supper and Pa got out his stamp album. He was adding a Japanese commemorative stamp, a version of Hokusai's famous woodcut entitled *Behind the Great Wave at Kanagawa*. It depicts a huge wave topped with white foam that almost blocks the view of Mount Fuji. I admired not only the stamp but also the yellow-gold Indian-ink words beneath it in Pa's beautiful handwriting. Just as I always did, I wished that my hand was as steady and accurate as Pa's.

The next morning, after an early breakfast with Ma, I packed the last of my kit, including my medication. I closed the bedroom door, stroked our black cat Tom, then went down the stairs. Pa waited in the drive in his white Escort estate.

As Pa drove off I turned in my seat and saw Ma framed by the high privet hedge either side of the gate. She smiled broadly and gave me a huge sweeping wave.

Pa drove me the half-mile or so to Hamble Point where *Grimalkin* was berthed. He was deep in thought and I knew that he was concerned for me, but, typically, he did not voice it. We reached the marina. Only five minutes away was *Grimalkin* and my starting point to the Fastnet Race.

I retrieved my kitbag from the boot. Pa got out too and we shook hands rather formally, then he put his arm briefly round my neck. 'Do as your Ma says—take care.'

He went to lean on the railings of the marina. I walked away, turning and waving once. Pa's white hair made him easy to spot.

It was early in the morning of Saturday, August 11, 1979, and the next four days were going to change our lives irreversibly.

Watches and Lighthouses

I strolled along the wooden decking in Hamble Point Marina. It was busy with crews preparing to sail: some on the Fastnet Race, others just going out to watch the start. The excitement I was feeling seemed to run through the entire marina. There were more boats than usual, of every colour and size, and every berth was taken. The atmosphere was electric, Fastnet electric—I felt it, could almost taste it. I also heard the sounds of rapping halyards: wire against aluminium, the background music in any marina. I passed a yacht with familiar faces on board, three guys sitting in their cockpit drinking coffee and smoking. They were customers of mine, and also off on the race.

'Hey, Nick,' one of them hollered. 'What do you think your chances are against us?'

I couldn't help smiling at this. 'We'll just have to see!'

Seeing these guys smoking reminded me I had a half-full packet of Marlboro Reds in my pocket; they had to be transferred into my kitbag as David forbade smoking on board. Despite this, Matt and I did light up occasionally, unknown to our skipper.

Thoughts of nicotine vanished as, ahead of me, I glimpsed *Grimalkin*—I could see her mast, her rigging and most of her light blue painted decks, and her white hull with her name beautifully painted in dark blue script. This thirty-foot boat was light, buoyant and wide. Ron Holland, her designer, had created a yacht for speed and comfort. I loved the shape of her transom. Ron must have been thinking of a woman when he drew those lines. She was a fantastic-looking boat. All of a sudden, my mouth was dry.

I saw that Matt was in the cockpit—I knew at once it was him because he was wearing his green tartan flat cap. It did nothing for him whatsoever but despite some serious ribbing he always seemed to have it on. David stepped down off the deck and greeted me with a friendly smile and a firm handshake. Four people stood alongside the boat—I immediately recognised Gay Sheahan, David's wife, and Matt's younger brother and sister, but not the fourth person. Gay introduced her as Gerry's wife, Margaret. She seemed excited, but nervous. Her hair was dark and her face was pale. Just past her I saw Mike and Dave busy on the foredeck. I was the last to arrive.

Matt grabbed my kitbag and Gerry helped me over the guardrail.

'Glad you could make it . . . Mr Ward.'

Redhead Gerry had a very dry sense of humour. We had clicked the first time we met. I smirked back at him.

'Wouldn't have missed it for the world, Mr Winks.'

'Come on, guys, we need to keep going.' This was David, calling us to order. We all responded to our skipper's command.

I started unlacing my brown Docksides shoes. Like Matt's tartan cap, they were pretty odd-looking. I had got them when I was sixteen and I hadn't raced without them since. What a superstitious breed sailors are. Pa had told me that green was an unlucky colour to carry on board and since then I had never had anything green among my belongings while on a boat. Many other things are deemed unlucky—to race on a Friday, to change a boat's name, to lose a bucket at sea, even whistling on board could bring bad luck. Worst of all was to have someone die on board, and then to sail with the dead body. I had no doubt that every sailor on this race—all 2,500-odd of them—carried some sort of lucky item and had rituals he or she carried out, unnoticed by their crewmates.

I pulled on my nonslip waterproof sea boots and climbed down the vertical six-runged companionway ladder into the cabin. Once down there I inhaled *Grimalkin*'s familiar smell, the blend of natural and man-made materials that gives any racing yacht its individual identity. *Grimalkin*'s cabin was not the largest space to share with five other blokes, but I'd had experience of smaller boats and this was light and functional in comparison.

To my right was the navigation table, with the VHF radio and echo sounder just above. As well as the VHF, David had two other radios on board: the Callbuoy and an AM/FM radio receiver; he was leaving nothing to chance. Two folded charts were laid on the table's hinged top. It looked like David had been plotting our course. Opposite the navigation table was the port quarter berth. The bunks were made out of strong blue material laced to aluminium poles. Each had a waterproof stowage bag for personal items. The shelves above the galley were filled with cans and jars of food, retained by wooden slats—every available space was used.

As I unpacked, I began to visualise our forthcoming trip by means of the lighthouses we would pass, just as I always did on races. It was a memory map, going westwards from our start off Cowes: Hurst Point, the Needles, Anvil Point, Portland Bill, Berry Head, Start Point, Eddystone Light, St Anthony's, Lizard, Tater Du, Longships, Wolf Rock, Seven Stones/Sisters, Peninnis (Scillies), Round Island (Scillies), Bishop Rock and finally Fastnet Rock Lighthouse before turning back.

I knew that we would not necessarily pass each one in this order because wind, tide and weather conditions would dictate changes, but it felt good that my map was firmly in place. I placed my medication safely on the shelf above the port bunk and climbed back up into the cockpit. The rest of the crew were hard at work preparing and rigging the boat, so I got stuck in too.

We had planned to leave at 10.30 a.m., leaving plenty of time for our 1.20 p.m. start time. On the foredeck Matt and I unpacked *Grimalkin*'s number-one genoa from its sail bag, while Mike and Dave attached sheets with tight bowlines.

'Hold on to your bollocks, guys,' said Dave.

Dave could always be relied upon for juvenile comments. As we carried on rigging *Grimalkin*, the banter got sillier and sillier, particularly between Gerry and Dave, whose high spirits led them to talk in Donald Duck voices. They lisped and rasped away like two madmen.

One of the last jobs we did was to tie the white, flexible PVC panels that bore *Grimalkin*'s sail number—K5637—in black fifteen-inch-high letters. These identification panels were a requirement of the race organisers and rescue services alike.

Once we were prepared on deck, David called us into the cabin. As on all our previous races, he was meticulous in explaining where everything was—from the safety equipment, such as fire extinguishers, the first-aid kit and flares, to food supplies and the quantities of water we could each use. The boat's water tanks held twenty-five gallons and we were to be frugal in using it: daily consumption no more than three gallons.

With the serious instructions out of the way, David simply wished us all good luck. He was as excited as the rest of us but in a very British way. David was not one for hype—he hated bullshit. He was just a decent, down-to-earth bloke.

Then it was time to say goodbye. Not knowing Gay that well, my goodbye to her was pretty formal, as were Mike's and Dave's. She was a bit like a younger version of my own mum, and I suspected that, like Ma, she was anxious, seeing off not only her husband but also her son. Gerry said goodbye to Margaret. Margaret was noticeably more emotional than Gay.

David, hugging his wife tightly, said, 'I'll see you in Plymouth.' It was a bank-holiday weekend on our return and David had planned a family cruise. Gay now pulled Matt into a group hug and I overheard her say to them, 'Now, you two . . . You must look after each other.'

David reassured his wife that everything would be OK, then turned to the crew, 'Everyone ready?'

Without another word we singled up, untying the bow and stern spring ropes. David was now standing at the helm with the tiller in one hand. He said the magic words, 'Cast off.' As we quietly slipped away, Matt's younger brother followed as far as he could, holding on to the barnacled pile at the end of the pontoon. I was reminded of the times I'd waved my own father and older brother off on races when I was too young to take part.

We soon made our way towards the mouth of the river—I was sitting forward, my back against the mast, determined to absorb every detail of my first Fastnet Race. Even the gentle rush of water against the knuckle of *Grimalkin*'s forefoot as she sped along sent a shiver down my spine. To me the most wonderful sound in the world is the sound of a racing yacht's bow moving through water. Hearing the boat's bow slice effortlessly into the gentle chop was magic. I knew that sailing was something I could never get enough of, ever.

Further downriver we passed the old Fairey Marine slipway. The River Hamble's most prominent feature, its Spit, a shingle bank marked by a tall black post called Spit Pile, was half uncovered. All around was familiar territory: my playground, the safe training ground in which I had been taught to swim, sail and scull—almost in preparation, it seemed, for this race.

We passed Hamble Point buoy, then, a quarter of a mile further on, Coronation buoy, where on July 21, 1962, Chris Bell, a dinghy sailor from my club, had drowned. Chris, twenty-one years old, a good friend of my eldest brother, had been a great sailor, full of potential. The following year a race was established in his memory that still runs to this day. As we motored by I thought about his headstone in Hamble's cemetery. It said, simply, 'Claimed by the Sea'. We surged on and I turned and looked at Hamble. Holding on to the end of the main boom, I said my own farewells.

The weather was sunny and fairly warm. As we rounded Calshot Spit, two miles out, the sails were hoisted but we continued to motor-sail while the wind picked up and filled the sails. There was silence as David killed the engine and *Grimalkin* accelerated, responding quickly to the trimming of her sheets. This was what we all went sailing for. Matt was revelling in it already. He was sitting on the top rail of the pushpit, looking forward, as *Grimalkin* made her way hastily over to Cowes as if she, too, was impatient for the start.

Within an hour or so we reached Cowes Roads, off the Isle of Wight. The sight was breathtaking. This view took me back seventeen years to my first-ever experience of a Fastnet start, as a spectator with my father. The mouth of the River Medina was filled with yachts and powerboats celebrating both the start of the Fastnet and the finish of Cowes Week. With all this commotion the normally calm water was chopped up. *Grimalkin* was holding her own, coping with the wash, responsive to the helm.

We saw the larger classes, Class 0, the maxi yachts, such as *Condor of Bermuda*, at seventy-eight feet. For this Fastnet she was skippered by Peter Blake, New Zealand's equivalent of one of my sailing heroes, Eric Tabarly. *Tenacious* sailed past us, forty-one-year-old media mogul Ted Turner at the wheel of his white, sixty-one-foot sloop, looking as cool as only a Fastnet-course record holder could. I saw *Morning Cloud*, the second largest of Britain's three-boat team, through the crush of boats around us. This forty-four-foot yacht looked truly magnificent as she glided through the choppy water. I caught a glimpse of Dick Langton on the foredeck, working hard as usual. I yelled across to him, 'Good luck, Dick.'

He saw me and waved. As *Morning Cloud* passed by, all six of us stopped and watched. I could hear the incessant clicking of cameras as photographers on smaller boats pursued her. Seeing her in all her glory I knew that she and her owner, the former prime minister Edward Heath, deserved all the respect and attention they got.

Everywhere I looked there was something going on. Mesmerised, I managed to remember how Pa had taught me to be careful close to manoeuvring boats, how to cope with their unpredictable wash, how best to deal with the strong tides off the Medina's mouth. Much of what he had taught me had become instinctive, like a third hand, a third hand that most Solent-born lads possessed.

Gerry yelled, 'Bear off a touch, David, there's a boat on starboard.'

It was *Green Dragon*, the fastest boat in our class and favourite to win, crossing us on starboard tack. We gave her a wide berth, while keeping a close eye on her movements. David had told us that her crew were local and there were few, if any, better boats to shadow.

We milled around the start line, waiting for our 1.20 p.m. start and sussing out our competition, sailing close by, tacking under their bows, seeing how they were reacting. This gave David a benchmark. It was exhilarating for everyone, the hustle and bustle of pre-start manoeuvres.

We were so close to our competition that sometimes the seawater generated by a tacking boat would spatter *Grimalkin*'s genoa or slop into the cockpit. Throughout this period we ensured that David was aware of *Green Dragon* and her position at all times—one of us relaying to him exactly when she was tacking, making a move to one end or other of the start line.

We then practised our start a couple of times, lining up transit points from the shore and the outer distance mark, sailing along the line and putting in a few practice tacks. These practice tacks, although second nature to us all, still had to be done because we knew that after the start there was a long beat to windward, against the wind. David's instructions from the helm were brief. As on any racing yacht, there was no need for talking. Energy was better used on rope, winch or concentration. Choreography between a good skipper and crew is fluent, requiring only the nod of a head, a look or sometimes the pointing of a finger. So close to the competition, raising an arm or pointing to a buoy or another boat was taboo. This could indicate a change of tactic or an altering of course. It was a game of chess, with nothing given away.

David was now able to prepare for our start. The breeze was light to fresh so we set full sail and then sat in wait. David, Matt and Gerry counted off the minutes and seconds on a stopwatch. Mike, Dave and I kept an eye out for boats getting too close.

The starting gun fired. *Grimalkin* was one of the first boats across the line, vying for position with *Green Dragon*. Using little rudder movement and letting the sails do most of the work, David had timed our Class V start to perfection. The first tack we put in was a slick one—we were in the groove. *Grimalkin* rolled nicely through the eye of the wind, carrying her way, losing no speed while tacking.

'Keep it up, this is great!' yelled David.

He was not afraid of mixing it and before long we were in some closely fought duels with French competition. Close-call tacking was fantastically exciting, especially if the crew worked as one—easing, clearing, tailing and winching the genoa, each of us had more than one job to do. As we steamed along we kept clear of the French boats by either bearing away round their sterns or tacking away in another direction. Every tack counted, but we were smooth and more often than not came out the better.

I could see *Green Dragon* slightly ahead, her varnished transom like a target as we made our way down the Solent. I also saw Hurst Point lighthouse, number one to tick off on my memory map. We were well up with the competition and had earned third place as we passed the Needles. This lighthouse, number two on my memory map, with its white, needle-shaped, chalk cliffs, is one of the most striking sites round the British coast.

We were concentrating, working hard on the many short tacks along this last stretch of the Solent before reaching the buoy marking its entrance. Excitement gave energy to aching muscles as we diced with the many other boats in Class V. Like *Green Dragon*, David had chosen the island shore, and now other boats in Class V, realising there was more wind and tide where we were, tacked across from the mainland shore to join us.

Within a few short hours we had left our familiar home waters to join those of Christchurch Bay and the English Channel. By 6 p.m. we had cleared the Fairway buoy on the western exit of the Solent. The wind had dropped slightly but we were slipping along at a good speed, still maintaining third position in our class. The crew concentrated hard on the boat speed and sail trim, but we hadn't had a break and we were all beginning to feel it. The muscles in my right arm were painful, making concentration harder to maintain. Dave was in the cockpit, drumming his fingers on the side deck and not doing much else, apart from breaking wind. I could feel my blood rising, and under the incessant drumming I snapped.

'Jesus, Dave, give it a break.'

Dave laughed this off. 'Ohhhhh, feeling a bit touchy there, Nick?'

David butted in and instructed the crew to—in turn—take a break and eat some sandwiches. I grabbed a drink to help revive my tired muscles. By the time I returned to deck, the drumming had stopped—Dave had dozed off in the cockpit. Good, at least he was quiet. I sat on the windward rail with Matt and Mike, legs under the lower lifeline. It was standard practice for crew not tending sheets to sit in this position to gain maximum weight to the weather side, balancing the boat as she heeled into the wind. Also, *Grimalkin*'s cockpit seats were narrow and hard. It was a racing boat's cockpit, one that encouraged the crew to either work or rest below. Apart from her bunks, the most comfortable place to sit aboard *Grimalkin* was on her weather rail. Our gaze was directed at our competition and at the soft, fast-receding coastline of the Isle of Wight. I kept a close eye on *Green Dragon*; so far we were doing fine, going nicely.

By 7.45 p.m. the winds had become lighter. We sailed into Christchurch Bay. The visibility we had enjoyed bearing down the Solent was now not so good. I couldn't pick out any of the lights or features and was unable to see the illuminations on Bournemouth Pier.

Grimalkin's watch system started at 8 p.m. on Saturday evening. The system ensured there were always two people on watch at any one time, and that, in rotation, one person—excluding the skipper—always got a twelve-hour period off watch. This meant that the crew would alternate four hours on deck and four hours below. The off-watch crew's duties included preparing meals and keeping the interior of the boat in good order, although the most important thing was getting adequate rest. The on-watch crew's duties and responsibilities included keeping the boat on course. Every hour, they were required to enter the boat's speed, the barometric pressure, the course steered, the depth of water and other details into the boat's log, as well as taking note of any obvious changes in weather or tidal situations.

I was off watch for the first twelve-hour period, from 8 p.m. on Saturday evening until 8 a.m. Sunday morning. I spent the first hour passing round sandwiches, washing up and making hot drinks. The wind began to drop as the evening got darker. We sailed across Christchurch Bay to Anvil Point Lighthouse, number three on my list. At 9 p.m. I went below to rest.

As I lay in my bunk I could hear other boats around us: the ratcheting of turning winches, the unmistakable sounds of other crews. It sounded as if our competition were doing some sail changes. I found it impossible to sleep, so I joined the others on deck; they were altering sheet positions, getting a fuller shape in the sails to accommodate the lightening winds and to keep our speed to maximum. By half past ten we had done all we could. Satisfied I could do no more, I went below, this time to sleep.

Ochre Sky

At around 7.30 on Sunday morning, I woke from a deep sleep. I wondered how we were doing, whether there was much wind. It didn't feel like it. I looked out of *Grimalkin*'s cabin window and saw Dorset's coastline for the first time. Although it was somewhat indistinct, there was no mistaking the green rolling downs of Hardy's Wessex.

Up on deck, I saw that not much had changed during the night. There was a slight mist yet to lift—it always took a while for the early morning sun to heat up and burn the last of it off. The sea was lazy and flat.

'It looks like we're doing OK,' called Matt from the helm. 'What do you think?'

Undecided, I found myself scanning the horizon for signs of any of the other Class V yachts. Matt and I agreed that it was a little odd that there were no other boats in our class around us. We never assumed anything during a race, but Matt and I felt justified in thinking, rather excitedly, that *Grimalkin* could well be up front of our fifty or so competitors in Class V.

Matt updated me on the latest weather forecast: force 4 to 5 southwesterly winds were predicted for the morning, increasing to force 7 or perhaps 8 later in the day. This was at odds with the winds we were sailing in, which were no more than force 2, but that was not unusual. I knew from delivering yachts up and down this coast that a southwesterly sea breeze sometimes did not fill in until hours after it had been predicted. Therefore, although frustrated by the lack of wind, none of us was greatly concerned.

My first four-hour watch period was fantastic. It started well, with a cup of coffee made by my watch-mate, Mike. He was around the same age as me and was easy to talk to. I knew that, like Dave, he was not as experienced as the rest of *Grimalkin*'s crew, but I found him fine to work alongside—physically strong, sure-footed and able to cope with most situations aboard. We went about our routine, alternating half-hour turns at the helm.

Intermittently, Matt poked his head up from the cabin, wanting to know what was going on. Sailing in his dad's boat meant so much to him, and he was enjoying his first Fastnet Race at least as much as any of us.

'Better than work, eh, Nick?' he'd say.

'You bet,' I'd reply.

Not much happened during this watch except the passing of two ships, one a container vessel, the other a coaster. They were a fair distance from us and posed no threat, but the sound of their foghorns brought David up on deck. He checked our course, which was spot on. There was no wind change so there was nothing we could do other than keep our eyes peeled for 'cat's paws', tiny ripples on the surface of the water indicating wind.

To pass the time we played 'I spy' until we ran out of things to spy. Then we just sat in silence. Despite the frustrating lack of wind, there was a certain peace to be enjoyed in these dead-calm waters. I spotted the dark shape of a cormorant in the distance. I wanted to get a closer look, but it was keeping well clear. The only birds close to us were gulls, either floating in the water or circling round us in flight. Near the end of my watch the sun was shining brightly through the mist and my eyes were sore from squinting.

When Matt and Dave came up to take over from us, we all stayed together in the cockpit for a while. The mood was good as we talked about the race and how we were doing. A discussion began about rounding the infamous Fastnet Rock in a day or so. I thought about what Matt and I had discussed earlier that morning—if we all kept our heads, then there was every chance of a victory in Class V.

With that uplifting thought, I gave the horizon a quick 360-degree scan before going down to my bunk. I rarely had trouble catnapping, day or night. David was not so lucky—I could hear the sounds of him retching into a bucket. I offered him assistance, which he politely rejected. Best thing to do was let him sort himself out. I drifted off to sleep.

At around 3 p.m. my sleep was disturbed by David talking to his wife, Gay, via the VHF radio. I heard him confirming to her that everyone was well and not to worry about a thing. I smiled at him; he looked much better now, a bit of colour back in his face.

'She's going to phone everyone and let them know we are all fine.' He winked at me. 'Give me a hand with this, Nick.'

I hopped off my bunk and helped David mop the bilges out with a sponge and bucket. One of our skipper's characteristics I admired the most was his easiness in doing any of the most menial jobs on board.

I rested for a while before going back on deck for my second watch, from 4 p.m. until 8 p.m. Again, not much happened. The visibility was not brilliant and the wind was still holding at about force 2, if that. Mike and I coaxed *Grimalkin* along, gently trimming her sheets in the shifting puffs of wind, which were difficult to anticipate. Later that afternoon, as we rounded Portland Bill, we saw that our hard work was paying off. With improved visibility we were able to pick out Class IV, Class III and even some stragglers from Class II, and there was still no sign of *Green Dragon*—good. There was every chance we were ahead of her.

I was off watch at 8 p.m., but due back on a double shift from midnight until 8 a.m., so as soon as I could I climbed down the companionway ladder into my bunk. I realised I'd almost forgotten to take my medication. I reached for my pills. Just as I was about to doze off, David called down from the cockpit for me to move to a bunk on the opposite side of the cabin. This was to balance the boat correctly—not an unusual request in light winds.

It was dark outside when I woke. I looked at my watch: 11.45 p.m. There were quiet, muffled sounds in the cockpit above me, so I knew the weather had not changed. I was surprised the wind had still failed to fill in. I got up. Moving past the navigation table I glanced at the charts and saw that I had missed the passing of lighthouses five and six—Berry Head and Start Point.

Up on deck, David, Gerry, Matt and Mike were having what seemed to be a serious conversation. The complete lack of wind, coupled with our slow speed, was beginning to give rise to concern about whether our fresh water and food would last. Some yachts sacrificed provisions, which took up weight and space, for an extra sail—which was what we had done. If these weather conditions continued there would be no chance of us finishing in the five days David had estimated. Watching the sails limply flopping around, I knew this was a realistic concern. If this weather continued the race might have to be cancelled. As far as I knew, despite a few close calls, this had not happened in the race's history.

I could sense that morale was dipping. For the Fastnet Race to be postponed or called off would be more than a mere inconvenience. This race was something we'd prepared for, all six of us, physically and mentally.

David went below. After scanning several different broadcasts, he found a forecast. This, along with the others we had heard over the previous few hours, now really began to puzzle us. The conditions we were experiencing conflicted entirely with what had been forecast. We did not have, as they suggested, force 5 to 7 southwesterly winds. Rather, we had wind strength zero and wind direction zero.

'What are they on about?' Gerry said, shaking his head.

I shrugged. Matt and Mike were equally stumped.

'Let's not get into a panic yet,' said David, coming back up. 'There's nothing that would surprise me about August weather.' It was a clear attempt to dispel the anxiety that was building up. 'OK, Gerry and Nick,' he continued, 'concentrate on getting as much out of her as you can. And, you guys, go and get some rest.'

The first part of my watch, from midnight until 4 a.m., was with Gerry—I was glad to spend some time with him. Soon into the watch we passed by the Eddystone and St Anthony's lighthouse, but we saw neither because of reduced visibility. We kept our eyes peeled in the black murk. Vigilance was needed in the busy English Channel. We were crossing shipping lanes and there was always the possibility of collision.

Gerry and I spoke at length about the flat, still, almost lakelike waters we were sailing in. We both agreed that we had never experienced anything quite like this. Noises were weirdly muffled, the moist fog acting like a silencer. On a couple of occasions, despite our best efforts, *Grimalkin* simply stopped, completely becalmed. And when there was any wind, it shifted direction. On the rare occasions we got near to a fellow competitor, we could tell neither what class of boat it was nor whether it was longer, as the navigation lights were blurred in the fog-bound darkness.

Gerry was telling me how he wanted to progress in offshore racing and how this, his first Fastnet, had been one of his abiding ambitions—much like the rest of us. Later, as the damp atmosphere worsened, I noticed that he kept rubbing his hands together. His joints were beginning to ache, he said. I knew that he suffered from arthritis and that it was fairly severe for a man so young.

Just after 3 a.m., David climbed out from the cabin and checked the log. He went back below and then returned a few minutes later, announcing a change of course to take advantage of the tide. I looked at the log entries—our last three hours had seen us travel seventeen miles, an average of just under five knots. Matt came up on deck at least twenty minutes before his watch was due to begin and relieved a tired and aching Gerry early. No sooner had Gerry gone below than Matt whispered, 'Any ciggies, there, Nick?'

That question had been a long time in coming. 'Not on me. Anyway, your dad's up and about. He'd shoot me.'

Matt winked at me. 'What he doesn't know won't hurt him. Come on, where are they?'

I relented. 'In the Tupperware box.'

Matt sloped back down below. Our common bond, besides sailing, was that we both enjoyed family life, were close to our parents and had siblings we cared for. This was perhaps why we had more of a connection than either of us had with Dave or Mike. A few moments later he returned above deck and watchfully lit up. We shared the cigarette, like two silly kids who'd just found a butt on the top deck of a bus. This was what I liked about Matt —without being irresponsible, he occasionally threw caution to the wind.

There was no sign of the fog clearing or the wind shifting, but David's plotting of our course through this grey soup was a sound one. He and Gerry together gauged and worked the tides correctly. *Grimalkin* made her way westwards towards Land's End. As dawn broke around 5.30 a.m., we could detect an airborne smell like freshly mown grass or compost—odd but recognisable to any experienced sailor. It was the smell of silage drifting from the fields off the West Country coastline. There was insufficient light to distinguish anything at all. Not even the horizon itself was discernible. There was only blurred vision.

'Hey, Nick,' Matt said suddenly, pointing ahead. 'There's something over there . . . A lobster pot maybe?'

Looking to windward I saw he was right. Hardly distinguishable in the mist, there were in fact quite a few. 'Well spotted,' I said, making a small adjustment to the course. It was not just other boats we had to beware of in these conditions. A mile or even two miles offshore, it was not uncommon to see long lines of lobster pots.

At the end of our watch, we had covered twenty-six miles, a pitiful distance. The mood on board was seriously dampened—we needed some wind.

Exhausted, I went below, downed a mouthful of breakfast and climbed into my bunk, still warm from its previous occupant. It seemed like I had been asleep only moments when I was wakened by my name being called loudly from the deck—it was Matt. I opened my eyes and knew immediately that things were changing, for the better.

'There's a breeze beginning to fill in out here.'

It was 11.15 a.m. I was still sleepy, but the excitement in Matt's voice fired me up. I wanted to see what was happening. I stepped up onto the deck and saw that Matt was right; the sea breeze had finally filled in. This felt different to the light, shifty winds of the previous days. It was fresher, more assured, as if it was here to stay.

At around 1 p.m., we passed the Wolf Rock lighthouse—number twelve on my list. Several others had been passed while I slept. The mist was slowly lifting and we were beginning to spot bigger boats. David listened to the 1.55 p.m. BBC shipping forecast for the Fastnet area. It told him that the winds would be southwesterly, force 4 to 5, locally force 6 to 7, veering in direction westerly with occasional rain and showers. After the wind had changed direction and increased slightly, David set a course for the Fastnet Rock and awaited the next forecast from the BBC, due at 5.50 p.m.

By 2.30 p.m., the winds had settled enough in strength and direction for Matt to rig the spinnaker. *Grimalkin* accelerated like a racehorse down the back straight, creating a great, arcing quarter wave that would have graced a yacht twice her length. She had settled beautifully in on her new course, her speed almost doubling. God, this felt good. The increasing wind seemed to lift everybody's spirits. Our worries regarding lack of water and food supplies disappeared.

By 3 p.m., we were flying along doing a constant eight knots, and over the next hour this rose to ten or twelve. Terrific, absolutely glorious—*Grimalkin* at her very best, performing wonderfully. It seemed that the theory about August weather had proved correct. *Grimalkin* picked up her skirts and flew.

By the time my watch finished at 4 p.m., adrenaline was pumping through my body and my head was the clearest it had been since the start of the sluggish weather. My right hand and biceps were aching from pumping the spinnaker's sheet, but I knew that a couple of hours' rest would settle that. Before I went below I looked round me, taking it all in, imagining what it must have been like for the crews on the very first Fastnet Race, back in 1925. In the distance, about half a mile away, were some bigger yachts—still no sign of our nemesis, *Green Dragon*, though; maybe she was up ahead.

I climbed into one of the blue canvas bunks—mine for the next four hours—and peered out of the cabin window. The sea beyond looked as if it had turned a deeper, darker shade of grey-green, as if under pressure. I was exhausted but excited, and my thoughts turned to the first sighting of the Fastnet and then the rounding of it. If the wind kept up, this would happen during my next watch period, beginning at midnight.

I WAS DISTURBED from a deep sleep by the increased volume of seawater passing by outside just inches from my head, and a series of loud winching noises that reverberated through the fibreglass cockpit floor above me. I was surprised to see that it was only 5.30 p.m.—I had been asleep less than an hour. As I sat up, I became aware that *Grimalkin* had taken on a different motion in the water. The cabin was empty; the whole crew were on deck. This could mean only one thing: they were making a sail change. Despite my lack of sleep I dressed quickly. I had to see what was going on.

From the third step of the companionway ladder I could see *Grimalkin*'s mainsail and genoa—they looked superb, brilliant white, contrasting beautifully with the sea and skyline. Moving up the ladder I felt stronger winds surrounding me, then I saw greyish clouds scudding across the sky. There was also a greatly increased chop in the water—some of the waves must have been up at around twenty feet. But most noticeable of all was *Grimalkin*'s speed, which must have increased by at least four or five knots in the short time that I had been asleep. I was fired up about the prospect of getting out of the last vestige of lee provided by the English mainland and beginning to sail deep into the Irish Sea.

Gerry was at the helm.

'Jesus . . . She's going like a train,' I called over to him.

Clearly exhilarated, Gerry smiled back. 'It's incredible. If this keeps up a course record could be set, mark my words.'

It was then that I noticed the combination of colours in the sky—reds, oranges and ochres, weird but exquisite, unlike anything I had seen before. I joined Matt, Mike and Dave on the windward rail looking intently to the west, all of us transfixed by the beauty of this skyline. With sunset not due until around 8.30 p.m., I was baffled by the colour scheme this deep orange sun created in the sky so early in the day. None of us had ever seen anything that could touch this. I regretted not having a camera.

Yachts that had been to windward of us had gone. The only boats I could see were two or three larger ones from Class IV, slightly ahead, holding the same course as *Grimalkin*.

The vista around us was clean, vibrant and open. It was obvious we were the only Class V boat in the vicinity. I couldn't help smiling to myself at the thought of us leading our class. As *Grimalkin* planed through the water, she looked neat and fresh, her gleaming white topsides and sky-blue deck paint reflecting light as if she'd just been scrubbed.

Mike commented, 'The horizon seems like it's changing all the time . . .'

I had to agree. The horizon was looking uneven, almost ruffling itself up by the minute. I was mesmerised. I wondered if I was experiencing some kind of optical illusion, so I turned away and looked back—but it wasn't an illusion. Rapidly, the horizon was becoming more and more distorted, the weird colours of the sky reflecting off the clouds.

Matt began to voice what we were probably all thinking. 'I wonder what it means . . . More wind or less? What do you guys think?'

Nobody ventured an opinion because nobody knew. Was this sky a sign of bad weather? Or was it just one of those stunning Fastnet sunsets that Dick Langton had told me so much about?

Despite the thrill the turnaround in the weather had given us, a level of anxiety was also growing. Another thing I had noticed, but didn't voice, was that all the gulls had disappeared—there was no longer a bird in sight.

David came up from the cabin and began discussing a course change with Gerry, then he too looked up.

'That's a pretty odd-looking sky.'

'What do you think, David?' Dave's anxiety was showing.

'There's a forecast due in ten minutes. If there's anything untoward up, we'll know about it soon enough.' He smiled. 'I'm sure it's just a beautiful sunset . . . Enjoy it, guys.' He went back down below.

I didn't want to leave this extraordinary sight, but I knew I ought to get some more sleep. I descended the companionway ladder. David was back at his navigation table with the radio tuned in. The 5.50 p.m. BBC shipping forecast was of winds from a mainly southerly direction, force 4, force 6, increasing to force 8, changing direction to northwesterly later. This forecast did indeed indicate nothing untoward. These wind strengths weren't something to be worried about; we'd all coped with force 8 on numerous occasions before. I closed my eyes.

A short time later I heard Gerry come down into the cabin to cook up a stew that his wife, Margaret, had made for us. He was completely soaked, having been at the helm for the last few wind-driven hours. He winked at me, taking off his dripping wet life jacket and harness.

'Don't get too cosy, Nick. It's getting pretty rough out there.'

The swaying motion on board had become so strong that Gerry was forced to use the webbing galley strap round his hips to maintain balance, but this didn't stop him from telling a few jokes about our newly elected prime minister, Margaret Thatcher, and the handbag she always seemed to carry, which looked like it could—and would—be used to concuss anyone who opposed her. Gerry knew how to lighten the mood; I even heard a chuckle coming from David's direction.

The result of Gerry's labours smelt delicious. I got up and helped him pass the thick plastic mugs of stew round the boat. It tasted as good as it smelt. I was off watch so I did the washing-up. Like Gerry, I had to brace myself against the galley lockers to do so. Tired and well fed, I climbed back up into my bunk and closed my eyes.

At around 7.30 p.m., I was woken by a good deal of increased movement above my head. The on-watch crew—Matt, Gerry and Dave—were clearly moving from the weather rail into the relative shelter of the cockpit. I was tired, but such was the motion of the boat I found it difficult to get back to sleep. I looked to the opposite bunk and saw that Mike was also awake. With conditions like this below, it was not surprising the crew above had moved to the cockpit. David was still at the navigation table.

'How are we doing?' I asked.

He looked up. 'We're just passing the Bishop Rock lighthouse.'

Bishop Rock lighthouse? We *were* doing well—this was the last lighthouse before we reached Fastnet Rock.

Again I closed my eyes, trying to entice some sleep. It didn't work, but at least I was resting. Over the next half an hour, I noticed that weather conditions were changing at an almost astonishing rate.

Mike, in his bunk, must have noticed too. 'There's some gale blowing out there.'

David nodded. 'It's certainly building.'

I could tell by David's tone that he was puzzled. The next official shipping forecast from the BBC, for all areas, was not due until after midnight, so David tuned in and out of stations until he finally found a forecast for our area. It was in French, but we were familiar with French broadcasts, having relied on them before. The calm, clear voice anticipated winds of between force 8 and force 10.

Mike immediately sat up in his bunk. 'Oh my God, did I hear that right?'

David concurred, turning up the set's volume to its highest point. The forecaster repeated this warning conclusively—force 10 winds in the Fastnet and Lundy area, the very area we were sailing into. With the volume turned right up, the crew above deck picked it up too.

All six of us knew, as did every sailor on this race, the deadly difference between a gale-force 8 and a storm-force 10 wind. Force 8 was a bad headache, no more—force 10 was a brain haemorrhage. The winds, and particularly the wave heights, would be multiplied by two, perhaps even more. These were not the conditions for any small yacht to sail into. Matt and Gerry clambered down into the cabin, leaving Dave at the helm. Everyone began talking at once.

'OK, everybody!' yelled David. 'We need information, and quickly, and for that I need silence.'

He got it. Three nerve-racking minutes passed before we overheard a French boat calling Start Point Radio. This was against the rules of the race, but in light of the news we had just heard, not surprising. The boat's skipper asked the coastguards to confirm that the BBC's 5.50 p.m. forecast was correct. We waited for the response, nobody uttering a word. Finally, the coastguards confirmed that the 5.50 p.m. BBC forecast had been the correct one. A wave of relief went through the cabin—thank God, our race was not over.

'Should we maybe think about a course change, as a precaution?' said Mike to David.

David answered carefully. He reassured us with his faith in the BBC forecast and in *Grimalkin*'s ability to cope with the anticipated conditions. He also pointed out, quite rightly, that any abandonment of the race by our fellow competitors would have been apparent by the reappearance of the larger classes of boats. We would have seen them returning in the early-evening light.

After the windless inactivity of the last couple of days, David did not have to try hard to sell these reassurances. A renewed sense of excitement motivated us all. As far as I could see, there was absolutely no disagreement among the crew—we all backed our skipper's decision unreservedly. With that, David instructed us to get ourselves and *Grimalkin* fully prepared for the night's leg. Our predicted course was out into the Irish Sea, towards the rock. Without need of further encouragement, the whole crew got togged up, layering up to protect ourselves against the cold, wet and windy conditions that had been forecast.

On deck, I noticed the sun had disappeared entirely, leaving not a trace of the wonderful colour display we had seen earlier. The sky was filling with dark, fast-moving clouds that were closing in on *Grimalkin*, as if a curtain was being pulled round us.

It looked and felt strange—as if it was not quite day and not quite night. It was something like an early-morning eclipse of the sun I had witnessed some years before. When the moon had eclipsed the sun, we had been left with an unnatural-looking light, as though it were artificial. I wanted to say something to the others but time was of the essence—*Grimalkin* had to be prepared, and quickly.

We knew we were in for a substantial blow, so things needed to be made secure. All loose, unused halyards were made fast. The strap that held the main boom down was winched in, tensioned as hard as we could get it. The spinnaker and jockey poles were checked, clipped and lashed. Working together, we got *Grimalkin* ready for the worsening conditions; ready as any boat in the race could have been. By about 8.30 p.m., we were done. David turned on the navigation lights—red and green at the bow, white at the masthead and stern. At the same time he checked the batteries of the separate, emergency navigation lights.

Mike and I knew our midnight watch was going to be long, wet and tiring, so we decided to try to get a couple of hours' sleep in. David was at the navigation table. I wanted to talk, to discuss the race, but I knew he was concentrating hard on the charts. I tried to stay still but I couldn't. There was no chance of sleep.

Just after 9 p.m., I got up again and got fully dressed, this time putting on an additional waterproof jacket over my orange oilskins. I heard *Grimalkin*, slightly free, a couple of points off the wind, at speed. Her bows plunging into seas, she was now forcing her way through the increased swell. Often her lee bow slapped onto a crest, making her yaw, the noise of it echoing up in her forepeak. As I moved across the cabin I was forced to grab on to the navigation table for support, knocking into David.

'Clip on out there, Nick. It's building far faster than expected.'

David's expression told me that he was concerned by the speed with which conditions were worsening. I looked up through the half-open companionway hatch and saw seawater cascading into the cockpit. The cockpit was self-draining, but my crewmates were completely drenched. As I climbed the companionway ladder I heard a spooky sound—almost like an animal screech. I realised it was the number-three headsail's starboard sheet straining. I blinked and tried to adjust to the dark after the relative brightness of the cabin. I clipped my safety harness to the stout U-bolt before climbing the final four steps out onto the cockpit. Sitting down safely with Dave, Gerry and Matt, I got a full view of the conditions. What a transformation. The pace of change was incredible. Some waves were now at about thirty-five feet, and appeared to have a different pattern—they were longer, steeper.

'Jesus, she's really cracking along,' I shouted over to Matt on the helm. 'How's the wind direction? Is it changing?'

'Yeah, all the time!' he yelled back. 'It keeps heading us.'

As if to illustrate the point, *Grimalkin* heeled to a heavy gust. Matt reacted by pushing the tiller away from him, heading up into the gust. This took the pressure off the sails. Like an aircraft's wing stalling as a result of too steep a climb, *Grimalkin* responded and settled to a more even angle of heel, dumping a sizable wave on the foredeck as she did so.

Matt shouted more information to me. 'The wind hasn't even peaked yet—we're making great time. This could be our year, Nick.'

It certainly looked like it might be, if these winds kept up. Matt then told me they had shortened sail because of the increasing wind strength. They had put two slab reefs in the mainsail. They had also changed headsails, down to the number-two, then the number-three jib; this made the boat safer in the current wind.

I looked over at the combined speedometer/anemometer dial. The needle was swinging wildly, registering between thirty and thirty-five knots of wind, the top end of a force 6, near on force 7. This was good, really good.

We were likely to experience up to a force 8 in the next hour or two. With these wind strengths it would be during my midnight to 4 a.m. watch that we would round the rock. I also knew that the plotted course we were sailing into, where the influence of the Gulf Stream was strong, had one of the highest tidal ranges in the world.

David poked his head above deck and clipped himself on. He shouted to Gerry, 'Have you ever seen winds build this quickly?'

Gerry shook his head. It had been only fifteen minutes or so since I had come up on deck and I, too, had seen the weather change. The waves were now up to at least forty feet.

David took the tiller from Matt's grip. Looking back and forth from the compass dial to the speedometer/anemometer dial, he computed the wind speed and direction. I saw him mouth the word '*merde*' and saw the glance he shot Gerry—a glance that said it all. He was not happy. This escalation of the weather was beyond comprehension.

'Course held OK?' David asked Matt.

Matt nodded. 'It's seriously blowing. Much more and I'll think about another reef in the main. Maybe even the storm jib?'

David agreed. 'Let's make it a safe and quick change.'

The smallest sail *Grimalkin* possessed, her storm jib, was prepared and hoisted, replacing the number three. This took about fifteen minutes. Immediately the smaller sail was sheeted in, *Grimalkin* seemed to utter a sigh of relief. The relief was short-lived, however.

I watched white-crested waves flood the foredeck, and listened to the thudding against the bows and on the deck. Behind us the waves stacked high, their heights building at an extraordinary rate. The anemometer now showed force 8.

'Do you think it's peaking?' said Mike to David.

'It should be.'

We were getting repeatedly drenched with freezing cold, salty water. Our tightly drawn hoods didn't help much. Spray blowing viciously in our faces made it difficult to see. The sky was darker than dark; the full moon masked and invisible. There was an occasional glimpse of fast-moving clouds. Most noticeable were the ever-increasing gusts of wind—they built up inexorably, gust upon gust, increasing the noise level around us.

Grimalkin continued to press her way through the worsening seas. I glanced down at the anemometer needle. Shit, it was forty-five, sometimes touching fifty knots. This was the top end of force 8 and 9, approaching force 10. It was happening in the space of minutes.

The compass was swinging wildly now. It showed a course of 330 degrees, but the course kept changing, determined by the gusting wind and seas.

'Take over the helm, Gerry,' yelled David. 'I have to check our position, check for a forecast, try to find out what the hell's going on here.'

David made his way towards the cabin. The wind was so ferocious he could barely keep upright. He stumbled, falling forward—luckily grabbing the lip of the coach-roof hatch, halting a bad fall. He paused on the companionway ladder, cupped his hands round his mouth and shouted: 'Inflate your jackets. Thumbs up, everyone.'

I released the yellow inflation tube from the collar of my life jacket, blew into it, then put my thumb in the air. The others did the same.

Illuminated in the companionway by the dim cabin light, David gave further instructions. 'Right, the mainsail has to come off.'

We were in a full-blown, volatile storm. David wanted a clear deck, and a clear cabin-top for ease of movement and communication. He also wanted the on-watch helmsman to have a clear view ahead, and that was currently obscured by the mainsail and its boom.

David went below and we set about removing the mainsail—not easy in conditions like these. Matt clipped into the windward jackstay and after looking back at us, no smile, crawled forward to the mast to gather in the now flogging sail. Spray bounced off its leach as waves swept the foredeck. I saw a sail batten fly out of its pocket, missing Mike's head by inches. Crouched over the coach-roof-mounted winch, Mike took the halyard's tension by putting two turns round the winch and wrapping the halyard round his open fist. I released the clutch handle. With the mainsail's halyard now freed, Matt pulled and yanked on its boltrope like a man possessed, inching the sail down the mast.

All of us continually faltered in the face of the elements. Even with our harnesses clipped on and our life jackets fully inflated, we were exposed and vulnerable. Finally, the mainsail was off, tightly flaked, wrapped to the boom. The boom was securely lashed to the deck and control lines were made fast. We retreated to the relative safety of the cockpit.

From that point on we saw only ourselves, the boat and the weather. As we sat there, waiting for news from our skipper, one thing was for sure: the atmosphere on this boat had changed. Dave caught my glance.

'Do you think this lot will blow itself out soon, Nick?'

I had no idea of the answer. It was clear to me that this sometimes irritating but nonetheless likable young man was frightened. I nodded, reassuringly. 'It should do.'

But my instincts told me otherwise. I mulled over the disparate forecasts we'd heard, in particular the BBC's at 5.50 p.m. I had listened to many BBC shipping forecasts and had always accepted what was said, good as gospel. Tonight was different. The forecasters had not seen the ochre sky. If they had, would they have revised the forecast? Pulling up the sleeve of my oilskin, I pressed the button of my LCD watch, illuminating its face: 10.15 p.m. Time was flying.

David struggled into the cockpit and told us that he had not been able to get any more information about the weather situation, nor had he been able to update his last plot. He looked shaken.

'OK . . . We're going to close up below and all stay in the cockpit.'

The washboards were put in place and the sliding companionway hatch closed tight so no water could find its way below. Everything was as secure as we could possibly make it. The six of us now huddled together in the open cockpit. We were headed for the unforgiving Irish Sea, nigh-on 10,000 square miles of it. Were any boat to founder, I thought, lifeboats would come from both coasts, from Waterford, maybe Cork, Baltimore on the Irish side, from Penzance, Newquay on the Cornish side, St Mary's in the Scillies. They could come, sure. But would they find?

That damn multicoloured sunset, that ochre sky had been beautiful but malign. David had based his judgment on the BBC shipping forecast as I was sure our fellow competitors had. The French forecast of force-10 gales, the one we had been told to ignore, must have been correct.

'Try heaving-to,' David shouted to Gerry.

This was the obvious next step in a heavy storm. It meant setting the boat on a predetermined course into the oncoming sea, unmanned apart from one crewmember on watch—almost the equivalent of autopilot. This would be achieved by determining the safest course, then lashing the tiller securely. The idea was that the yacht could ride out the storm safely. It would also allow the crew to get some much-needed rest and food, while they waited for the wind and weather to subside.

We tried this tactic, but *Grimalkin* was having none of it, simply refusing to stay where she was put. The seas were too steep. She slid down the faces of waves I'd never seen the like of before. The wind was gusting so hard that we kept risking a broach on a wave top, being turned side on to the wind and the sea, which would leave the hull vulnerable. And a serious broach could lead to a knockdown or capsize.

We were all nonplussed over *Grimalkin*'s refusal to heave-to. Heaving-to in big boats was easier; I had done it many times before to ride out storms. But as I looked at the conditions that surrounded us, I began to think that no boat could have ridden this out.

We were caught in the middle of a phenomenal weather pattern, something none of us had experienced before. And we were now far out in the western approaches. It would be fatal to simply turn round on a reciprocal course—the seas were too steep. Somehow, somewhere, somebody had got this forecast desperately wrong. We were left with no option but to tough the night out. We had already sailed into the eye of this unforeseen storm.

Grimalkin had reached the point of no return.

Off the Scale

It was 11.25 p.m. and there was no sign of the storm subsiding. In fact, the barometer was falling, which meant there was worse to come. *Grimalkin* was already fighting her way through mammoth walls of water; how could she cope with anything greater than this?

Gerry was still at the helm. He was sawing away as best he could, the tiller almost thrust from his grasp as he directed *Grimalkin* uphill through monstrous waves. Each time the boat mounted then crested a wave, he prepared for the smashing of her bows into the trough at the bottom. He hung on grimly; it looked as if his freezing hands were hurting badly.

A loud, gunfire-like noise sounded—it turned out to be nothing more than the storm jib and its sheet being whipped against the starboard shrouds. I noticed suddenly that we were sailing far too close into the wind. At once everyone started yelling.

'To the RIGHT, Gerry . . . Pull the helm up!'

With all the commotion, Gerry had had a momentary lapse in concentration. In an instant, *Grimalkin*'s bows became fully exposed to the fury of oncoming wind and waves, almost throwing the boat aback. Had we been taken aback, we would have pivoted on the peak, the highest part of the wave. As it was, we barely escaped capsizing.

David understood that Gerry's ability to concentrate had gone; his momentary lapse had put us all in danger. He instructed Gerry to go below to try to get warm. Gerry was exhausted. Mike and Dave slid the hatch forward and removed the two vertical washboards for Gerry to go below. I didn't fancy his chances down there as I watched him descend the companionway ladder. Even over the deafening racket above, loud noises could be heard coming from down below. Cans of food were flying around at head height. David shouted for me to take over the helm.

Once I was sitting where Gerry had sat, I knew why he could no longer continue. Perched up here at the helm, right back aft, God knows how far above the true surface of the sea—forty feet, maybe more—the sight was breathtaking. The seas appeared to be higher than twice the length of *Grimalkin* at times.

At first I felt excitement as I took control of the boat, but this swiftly turned to fear. I saw and felt the magnitude of these black, storm-ridden seas with their white-capped peaks. The winds blew from every direction, leaving me bodily dishevelled and mentally bewildered.

Keeping *Grimalkin* pointed into the wind was near impossible. She fought the waves as best she could, but it would take only the smallest lapse in concentration at the peak of one of the waves to send her aback—as Gerry had almost done. It felt as if the storm jib was overpowering her. *Grimalkin*'s smallest foresail was tiny in area but with these seas and in this wind strength, it was still far too big. If we weren't to be completely overwhelmed, it had to come off.

As if sensing my thoughts, David yelled, through cupped hands, to the crew: 'We have to get the storm jib down.'

After a disjointed discussion, David remained in the cockpit while Matt, Mike and Dave started preparing themselves. Eventually it was Matt who ventured up onto the violently bucking foredeck. I was glad—his surefootedness had already been proven up there an hour or so earlier. All I could see of him was his silhouetted profile, white spray crashing against his back. Ever so carefully he clipped himself on at the mast. Keeping a continuous watch for rogue waves, he began to gather in the soaking-wet sail.

All the while David looked on, willing his son to hold firm.

Matt was finally finished; Dave and Mike leaned forward and lowered the halyard. Then all three of them tied the storm jib securely so it could not blow free and tangle itself round *Grimalkin*'s shuddering mast. I saw relief, even a brief glimmer of pride, as David helped his son back down. Everyone, including Gerry—who was now back on deck, having eaten and changed—huddled back into the relative safety of the cockpit.

The respite was agonisingly short-lived. The effect of *Grimalkin* being bare-poled—having no sails up whatsoever—quickly became apparent. It was not good. There was absolutely no way that she was going to keep her bows into the wind. This was dreadful. If she had done as expected and remained pointing into the wind and seas, then we would have had time to tie the tiller and could then have followed one of the well-known methods of riding out heavy weather. This attempt had failed utterly. We were being totally overwhelmed.

The seas were now like huge blocks of flats but twice as wide—it was a surreal environment. From my heightened position at the helm, I looked over the crew's heads, down into the waves. While searching for a flat spot to aim for, it became obvious to me that *Grimalkin* was in danger of being pitchpoled. Her bow, plunging into the face of a wave, risked being overtaken by the stern, which would cause her to cartwheel through the water. We would then be thrown forwards and downwards by gravity, and brought up short by the tension of our harness lines. This is one of the worst consequences of downwind sailing. Now, here, upwind, sailing under bare poles in heavy weather, we were in the same danger.

It occurred to me that we might have a chance if we streamed every spare sheet, guy and warp out behind us. Then we could turn the boat round and run with the seas, the wind and waves behind us. This procedure, again, was a well-known tactic, used as an alternative when heaving to was not an option. The idea was that the trailed lines—two lines of nearly 500 feet, from the rear of *Grimalkin*—would induce some drag, slowing the boat down. Trailing lines also had the effect of breaking wave crests—the most dangerous part of a wave—prematurely. This lessened the probability of a huge wave crest dumping itself onto the stern or deck of the boat.

I told David my idea. After observing the situation from my position, he concurred—we had to try something. Doing this would mean a course change, but that didn't matter. There was no reluctance from my crewmates. I'm sure that everyone on board knew that our race was done. Our Fastnet was over.

I stayed on the tiller, while the rest of the crew opened all of *Grimalkin*'s cockpit lockers, locating every possible length of suitable rope or line, including mooring warps. Then everyone, with cold hands, fumbled with reef knots, sheepshanks and bowlines, making up two separate lengths of warp to tow. Once this was done, David prepared the crew so that when I swung *Grimalkin* round, with the sea, they could deploy the lines over the side without them twisting and further endangering the boat.

Before attempting this precarious turn through the wind, I had to get my timing in sync with the seas. If my timing was out, *Grimalkin* would capsize. I was deeply afraid. Sitting on the floor of the cockpit, knees bent with both feet planted against the cockpit's side, gave me extra leverage on the tiller. Judging what I deemed to be the safest time to turn, I signalled to David that I was ready to go.

Never before had I exerted as much pressure on a tiller, and at one point I was sure it would snap, but gradually *Grimalkin* responded and I felt her begin to swing. Midway through the turn she heeled at an extraordinary angle and her pitch changed—taken by surprise, I nearly had the tiller yanked from my arms. I saw Gerry, Matt, Mike and Dave, streaming the warps under David's watchful eye. As *Grimalkin*'s bows dipped into a trough, I centred the shuddering tiller to complete our 180-degree turn. Almost everything had gone to plan, the warps were successfully streamed and *Grimalkin* was roughly on the course we anticipated. Most noticeable was the lessening of the cacophony around our ears. The pressure was off somewhat—or so we thought.

Mere seconds after *Grimalkin* completed her turn, the wind noise returned with a vengeance and the deadly helter-skelter ride began. Travelling now at a far greater speed, we had even less control. As the first wave smacked beneath her I was nearly ousted from the cockpit. We were now travelling 'downhill'—being blown along with the wind, rather than against it—away from our supposed destination, the Fastnet lighthouse. It was a bit like putting your foot down on the accelerator of a sports car while travelling down a very steep hill. It became obvious that *Grimalkin* could no longer be helmed by just one person. I motioned this to David—promptly, he instructed my on-watch partner, Mike, to join me on the helm. We now jointly guided her at ludicrous speeds and dangerous angles down the faces of massive waves. Even though we were no more than an arm's length apart, we had difficulty communicating. The view ahead was of row after row of white-crested ridges.

We squinted ahead, lip-reading the shouts of the others as we tried to guide *Grimalkin* through walls of water. As well as the wind-borne spray, *Grimalkin* was creating her own enormous wake: sheets of water raced up her topsides, many feet above us. The lines we had streamed did not have the anticipated effect. While they helped to slow the boat, phosphorescent spray was flying off them, with the rollers beneath the crests continuing to overwhelm us. Even worse, the chance of *Grimalkin* pitchpoling was now even more likely. This tactic was not designed for such immense seas, but how could we have known?

The main priority for Mike and me now on the helm was to prevent *Grimalkin* from either pitchpoling at the bottom of a trough or broaching on the wave's peak. It took all of our physical strength to keep *Grimalkin* upright. We pushed and pulled the tiller with aching arms and blistered hands, guiding the boat into the next black abyss.

We had all endured broaches and even knockdowns before. It is common, while racing, for boats to broach in strong winds. Knockdowns—known as B1 and B2—are more violent than any broach. A B1 knockdown levels a boat at a ninety-degree angle in the blink of an eye—and there she stays until she manages to right herself. Like whiplash, it cannot be stopped. If you are lucky enough to remain with the boat during a B1, you end up either crumpled in a corner of the cockpit, usually with a crewmate on top of you, or on the side deck, clinging to a guardrail. If unlucky, you land in the sea. Once the boat rights herself, you have to drag yourself back on board by the rope of your safety harness.

A B2 knockdown is more extreme and follows through to a 180-degree capsize—at which point the boat stays there, inverted. Crew are trapped in or under the boat, either in the cabin or in the cockpit, or thrown clear of the hull and are thus in danger of being dragged along and then forced under the surface, if their harness ropes are still attached. An extra hazard is the mast snapping under the force of the water, risking further injury to crew trapped underwater. A yacht can be righted from capsize, either by the force of wind and waves or by the crew climbing onto the upturned hull and exerting force on her keel to right her. At its worst a B2 knockdown causes a yacht to sink, usually resulting in loss of life.

The spine-chilling thought of a knockdown stayed with me as Mike and I, hands tight on the tiller, roared our way through the darkness. As the waves got bigger, our fears became greater. David offered to take over from either of us at the helm, but Mike and I held on. We seemed to be glued to the tiller.

As I peered with my salt-sore eyes into the madness ahead, I thought I saw navigation lights in the near distance. I wondered if, such was my state of exhaustion, perhaps I was imagining this. But once again, then twice, to our left, I caught glimpses of red, white or green glows. Jesus, there were other people out here too, trying to cope with these conditions, and they were close to us, too close. I nudged Mike.

'Look . . . Nav lights . . . Can you see?'

Mike confirmed that yes, he could see them too. We alerted the rest of the crew, pointing frantically. Although unnerving, this also cleared my head and focused my concentration more intently on the noisy waste of ploughed-up sea ahead of us.

I glanced at my watch—it was just after 1.30 a.m. The wind speed was now between sixty and sixty-five knots, which roughly translated to seventy-five miles per hour, a Beaufort scale of force 12. The Beaufort scale does not go any higher than 12. Force 12 going downwind under bare poles in southern-ocean-sized seas—unreal.

This storm was bigger than any of us or any race. *Grimalkin* and her crew were being crushed by this heavyweight bruiser. Each time *Grimalkin* was pitched into a monster wave, we were violently flung about, thrown against a combination of wood, metal, fibreglass and each other.

Nobody could have prepared us for this. We were fighting for our lives.

BY 2.45 A.M. on Tuesday, August 14, the seas were indescribable. Over the last hour or so, *Grimalkin* and all six of us in her had been like a cork in rapids, just about keeping our heads above the boiling water. I did not know how much more I could take at the helm. Mike and I still grimly shared the tiller, negotiating wave after wave, each totally out of sync with the next. We were travelling at what seemed like three times the speed *Grimalkin*'s hull was designed for.

'Behind you . . . To port . . . LOOK!' Matt and Dave were shouting with, if it were possible, an even greater sense of fear and urgency in their voices.

Mike and I looked behind us. An unusually large wave was poised above us, its curling lip about ten feet above our heads. At this time we were surfing along at a terrifying angle down the face of a breaker—as we bottomed out in the trough, we had no choice but to go with it.

'HANG ON!'

The wave roared under us and lifted *Grimalkin*'s stern up. It wrenched the tiller from our hands and rendered the rudder useless. *Grimalkin* was out of control. I felt the straps of my harness tighten and a huge gaping pit seemed to open in my stomach. My attempts to cling to something, anything, failed. I was sucked from my seat and thrown through the air. Was this it? Was *Grimalkin* going to hold on, or this time be pitchpoled or knocked down? While in the air I caught sight of the foredeck and the mast toppling into the sea and staying there. I was both spectator and participant. Yes, this was it, a knockdown.

A terrifying, thundering, rolling racket penetrated my eardrums. I landed with a thud, squashed up against a stanchion with cold sea engulfing me. My harness line had brought me to a body-blow standstill, just short of the water. I sucked air in hard but coughed and choked on freezing seawater.

Checking I still possessed my legs, my arms, my hands and feet, I held on to the stanchion for my life.

We must have suffered our first B1 knockdown. I looked around and saw nobody. Where in God's name were the others? Then I saw someone to my left, slightly behind me. Was it Matt?

'Matt, Matt, are you OK?'

A deep voice roared back. It wasn't Matt, it was Mike. I now saw him only feet away—he looked as disorientated and as distressed as me. I heard another voice yelling.

'David here . . . Gerry's with me . . . Anybody else there?'

Mike and I responded, then kept a keen ear out for the others.

'Matt, Dave . . . Matthew!' David yelled again.

I could hear the panic rising in his voice. About thirty excruciating seconds passed before we heard, in the distance, the voices of our other two crewmates. Thank God—all six of us accounted for. Now we just had to hang on while *Grimalkin* righted herself. Although it felt far longer, in reality it was only two, maybe three minutes before she shook herself free of the mass of water around her. Gripping onto the guardrails and each other, Mike and I dragged ourselves into the relative safety of the cockpit. As I slumped there, catching my breath, totally shaken, I saw a jumble of bodies do much the same, Gerry being dragged along by David and Matt.

'Come on, Nick, come on! We have to get back to the helm . . . This is way out of control,' shouted Mike.

Grimalkin's tiller was unmanned, allowing her to be swept along at merciless speed. I grabbed a line and clawed my way towards the back of the cockpit. Mike was opposite me again. Somehow he had found his way back too. We grabbed at the tiller and managed to bear *Grimalkin* away again, away from the eye of the wind. *Grimalkin* was once again under a control of sorts from her two bruised, drenched, bewildered helmsmen.

I saw that Matt, David, Gerry and Dave were safe with us in the cockpit. Thank Christ—nobody had been washed overboard. We had all either been retained within the boat by her guardrails or been brought up short at the end of our lifelines. This last wave had unleashed so much energy—as if it were alive and we were the target of its inexplicable fury. From where I sat and from what I could see, it was apparent that this knockdown was merely going to be the first of many.

And so it proved. As *Grimalkin* hurtled through the darkness, this was an experience the whole crew went through time and time again. Each knockdown sent all six of us hurtling through the air then crash-landing on the boat or, worse, in the water—whichever way, we were either awash or completely immersed in bitterly cold sea.

Grimalkin behaved marvellously—each time righting herself within minutes of a ninety-degree B1 capsize. On several occasions, she teetered on the brink of a full 180-degree capsize—but she managed to hold her own. The conditions were still, unbelievably, worsening, and I think we all knew it was only a matter of time before the worst happened. All we could do was to concentrate hard on the roaring obstacle course behind and in front of us.

I had seen enough over the last couple of hours to understand that these seas were capable of anything. I had never heard of anything like this. Mike and I still gripped the tiller, and just as we caught one acutely angled, steep wave, we made a misjudgment of timing and shot into the back of the wave in front. *Grimalkin*'s foredeck—from her bow right back to the mast—was forced underwater. The back of the next wave threatened to push us completely under.

The force that threw all six of us out into the water was so violent that I heard almost nothing but screams—and above them all, my own. Miraculously *Grimalkin* righted herself and we clawed our way back up our six-foot-long safety-harness lines onto the deck, grabbing whatever we could. Numb with cold, we set about clearing the warps and ropes that had been trailing behind us and which were now a jumbled mess in the cockpit. David manned the tiller while the rest of us threw the lines back astern. Once this had been done, David shouted at the top of his voice for Dave to join him at the helm. I watched the two of them as they peered ahead through the rain, spray and spume, desperately trying to orientate themselves to the crazy rhythm of the boiling black liquid.

In the cockpit, I huddled up against Mike to try to gain some warmth. Matt and Gerry sat opposite, also huddled together. I looked at my watch—it was 5 a.m. and still dark. Not a sign of daylight, and not a sign of this force-12 storm relenting. All four of us concentrated on the seas around us, trying to indicate to David and Dave, at the helm, the direction of the next onslaught. I found myself becoming transfixed by the surreal beauty of these slow-moving mountains. I thought of Pa's Japanese stamp. Had he heard about the storm? Oh God, Ma would be worried, they both would. In my dreamlike state I saw Matt shouting, then screaming at me. I stared back, seeing him but not reacting to him.

'For God's sake, Nick, hold on!' Mike had grabbed me and shaken me hard.

Too late—one of these slow-moving mountains of water poured down onto *Grimalkin*, throwing us all upwards before smashing us back into the cockpit in a heap. I landed on top of Gerry—poor guy, his whole body seized up with pain. With these conditions it was impossible to prevent collision in the confines of the cockpit, but I knew I had to concentrate harder to try to prevent a serious injury.

Once more *Grimalkin* steadied herself and each of us braced ourselves for the next onslaught.

'Check the harness lines!' screamed David.

With numb hands, Matt, Mike and I scrambled through the rope tails on the floor of the cockpit.

'All fine, no snags, all attached!'

We were still interacting with one another, but communication was reduced to stilted words and minimal gestures. None of us ate; none of us wanted to. I thought of the odd ochre sky we had seen. How many hours ago was that? We were now a seriously weakened crew. I prayed for daylight, feeling sure it would give us back some conviction and a renewed ability to deal with this storm.

AT 5.30 A.M. the first traces of light appeared. But the dawn brought with it an unexpected shock—the fear on each other's faces that had been unseen in the dark. Anxiety gripped me. For the first time it struck me: we might not survive this.

Nothing could have prepared us for the horror of our surroundings. The noise was cacophonous; dawn had turned the volume up. The low light magnified the height of the waves. Menacing and unpredictable, these monstrous white-topped bodies of water swept everything aside. I said nothing; nobody did. I just sat there and thought: what on earth have I got myself into? It was clear to me that my prayers had not been answered. There was no new conviction among the crew. There were no smiles between us, just looks of uncertainty and disbelief.

I thought about the guys I'd waved to on the marina before we left Hamble—were they somewhere around us in this deafening sea? Where were *Green Dragon* and the French Class V boats we'd been duelling with soon after the start? Was this weather affecting all the 300-strong fleet in the same way, or was this storm localised?

Dawn also revealed how entirely out of control *Grimalkin* was, sheering off downwind, running and surfing at unbelievable speeds beyond the control of David and Dave at the helm. Where the hell was this storm taking us? We could end up anywhere in these conditions—shoal waters, the shoreline, crashing into rocks. We could be headed directly for the Scilly Isles, the Seven Stones or even southern Ireland—we had no idea. It felt as if we were on an involuntary suicide mission, being carried along by these forty- to fifty-foot waves. I found it increasingly difficult to do anything other than stay clipped on in the cockpit and watch for rogue waves. I wondered how much longer *Grimalkin* could survive.

I looked across at Gerry, sitting on the other side of the cockpit—my deepest worry was for him. He was showing marked signs of deterioration and his reactions were noticeably slower than I was used to from him. His fingers were white and wrinkled, his knuckle joints swollen. I feared now that his arthritis had got the better of him. Had he had time to take his medication since the maelstrom had begun? He was shivering uncontrollably and his face was paler than anyone else's; I was sure he was not far from becoming dangerously hypothermic. I now stared over at Matt—for the first time he really looked his age. His tough, confident veneer had gone, and he looked absolutely terrified. He was slumped in the cockpit, his eyes fixed on Mike, who was struggling to shift Gerry's dead weight into a more comfortable position. I wondered why Matt didn't help. Then I realised I was doing exactly the same—just staring. I wanted to stand up and help lift Gerry back to some sort of comfort, but I couldn't.

Everyone was done in. It was as though we were all too scared to say anything, as if acknowledging our greatest fear would make it more likely. 'There may be no way out of this.'

'Hold on, I'm bearing off . . . Hold on, hold on!'

My train of thought had been interrupted by Dave roaring at us from the helm. All of us in the cockpit braced ourselves. *Grimalkin* dipped her bows and her stern rose so violently that I shot across the cockpit at speed and was then lifted up high. This knockdown was without doubt the most violent yet. As I was hurled through the air I looked down and could see, as if in slow motion, the rest of the crew below me being thrown in the same manner. This was truly petrifying. *Grimalkin* ploughed into the trough of the wave and I was once again catapulted into the ferocious seas.

The water was so cold that the breath was forced out of me. My safety harness tightened round my chest as I was towed along. The rush of freezing seawater undid the fastenings of my oilskin top and found its way down through the opening at the neck. The inner, thermal layers of clothing, including my socks, soaked up water; I was being dragged down like a sack of cement. The intense cold of the sea made me want to inhale; this involuntary reflex choked me. If I swallowed much more of this black liquid, one thing would lead to another: more swallowing, more choking, then drowning. I began to panic. My leg, the left one, was hurting like hell. I knew straight away that I was badly injured as this was the first time I had felt any sensation in this leg since my brain haemorrhage eight years earlier. But I had no time to think about this now—simply grabbing enough oxygen to keep me conscious was all I could cope with. Somehow I had to get a grip. I twisted my head round and saw the outlines of David and Matt just above me, aboard the boat. Thank God. They were leaning over the guardrails, yelling at me. I yelled back.

'My leg . . . My leg!'

I have no idea whether they heard me. Their arms were stretched out to me. I reached my right arm up but the speed and the motion of the boat kept dragging me away from them. I made several attempts to lever myself those few crucial inches up my safety-harness tether but could not do it. I fixed my eyes on David.

'Come on, Nick, pull yourself up . . . You can do it!'

Both my hands were raw and bleeding—I had to let go, be dragged helplessly along. From my position in the water three or four feet below, all I could see were my crewmates, yelling ferociously down at me. Why the hell weren't they doing anything?

Anger welled up inside me. It gave me a much-needed adrenaline boost. I grabbed my safety-harness tether and yanked myself up, managing to get my injured left leg onto *Grimalkin*'s toe rail, but she was travelling at such speed I was forced back into the freezing water. On my second attempt, I swivelled round with my back to the seas, the flow of water supporting my damaged leg. I reached up and finally felt a firm grip on my right arm. I had no idea who it was but I clung on. Between them, they pulled me over the guardrails and onto the deck.

I coughed and vomited endless amounts of water. Crouched there, on my hands and knees, the anger I had felt towards my crewmates was instantly replaced by gratitude. As Matt and David helped me back into the cockpit, I began to comprehend that I had been saved from drowning. Huddled back in the safety of the cockpit I looked up at them both, father and son—they had just saved my life. Still coughing and spluttering, I gasped, 'Thanks.'

David put a firm arm on my shoulder—I knew he was trying to tell me that everything was fine. I looked down at my left leg, fully expecting to see my femur protruding through my oilskin trousers, but no, nothing. I couldn't understand—it had hurt so much. I carefully moved it back and forth: no sensation. Had I imagined the pain? I moved it again, this time a little further—I seized up in agony. I wanted to explain to everyone that I normally had no feeling in this leg and how amazing it was to feel even severe pain, but I was beyond exhaustion. With Mike's help I placed the injured leg into a more comfortable position.

I looked round at Gerry, by now impassive, apparently oblivious to what was going on; it was probably better this way. I looked at Mike, who was scared, and then at Dave, who was helming, doing his best, but he was frozen, almost beat. David was knackered too—I could sense that he had begun to wonder what the hell to do next. The immersion in the sea had left me more scared than I had ever felt before. This couldn't go on; we couldn't take much more of this.

All five of us looked to David, our skipper. Decisions had to be made.

'We're going to make a mayday call for rescue.'

A silent wave of relief went through us all. David's decision was a prudent one, given our circumstances. Up until now it had been considered too great a risk to go below into the cabin; that area of the boat was untenable in a storm of this magnitude. But in the rapidly deteriorating conditions, this became a risk that had to be taken.

David and Matt struggled against the storm towards the cabin. Matt slid the horizontal hatch forward. He then removed the two wooden washboards that prevented seawater from getting in.

Amid the mess and debris in the cabin, I saw David attempting to make contact through the VHF radio to *Morningtown*—the Royal Ocean Racing Club observation boat for the race. *Morningtown* then transferred David's call to Land's End Radio to verify our position. I knew that giving our exact position was going to be difficult—we had not had a decent plot since the previous evening. We all waited in anticipation—then finally David shouted up to us. 'They're coming . . . *Morningtown* is sending a helicopter.'

David now turned to Matt.

'Flares . . . Quick, get them.'

Matt grabbed the flare container from beneath the navigation table and passed it up the companionway ladder. Mike grabbed the container. I could see Matt's face—he was elated. For the first time in hours we experienced hope; contact with *Morningtown* had given us all a morale boost. Someone, some authority, now knew of our predicament.

Mike opened the container, took a parachute flare and crouched to port, cowering as far forward as the cockpit allowed. It was immediately clear he was having difficulty. In normal circumstances Mike would have been able to let off one of these flares within seconds. After an agonising wait, two flares went off—neither of them vertical. The ideal trajectory would have been angled into the wind so that the flares drifted back over us at about a 200-foot zenith. One went into the waves, the other flew off at an odd angle. We watched as their smoke wafted pathetically over the boat. Who would see the flares? How close was *Morningtown* or a helicopter to us? How close was anything, for that matter?

Tempers quickly got heated. We knew we had to get at least one flare vertical for any chance of making our position clear to oncoming rescue. Matt roared angrily up from the cabin.

'Come on, guys, get on with it!'

These yells did nothing but hinder Mike's efforts, his soaking hands fumbling and losing grip on the long slippery tube of another parachute flare. Just then a wave smashed on the foredeck, completely enveloping Mike in spray. Pandemonium broke loose as we all started blaming each other. In the midst of this, I heard David's voice.

'Nick, help him, for God's sake!'

I grabbed a flare and attempted to operate the firing mechanism of the parachute. My hands were trembling with the cold and the flare continually slipped from my grip—I could do no better than Mike.

Just at that moment there was an almighty bellow from Dave at the helm.

'Hold on . . . Hold on . . . We're bearing off!'

Grimalkin's stern began to lift. I looked up and saw a rogue wave towering above us. The situation had turned so chaotic that we had all dropped our guard. I yelled down into the cabin, 'Hold on . . . Hold on!' Again it was too late. The colossal wave pitched *Grimalkin*'s stern up at such a crazy angle that the boat rolled forward, leaving David and Matt helpless. They were flung round the cabin along with the other flying objects in the boat's churning interior.

I was thrown upwards but this time I landed back in the cockpit. My relief was short-lived when Gerry's full weight came crashing down on top of me. My face was crushed against the cockpit floor. Again everything speeded up into fast jerky movements. With Mike's help I struggled from underneath Gerry and we shifted him upright. We checked and saw that Dave had managed to hold on at the helm.

'Jesus Christ, David and Matt.'

The rain and spray prevented us from seeing into the cabin so we attempted to climb out of the cockpit, but the strength of the gale forced us back. We began yelling down into the cabin, 'David . . . Matt . . . David!'

We waited for a shout for help—something, anything. But there was nothing, not even a whimper. Mike tried again to crawl towards the cabin entrance, but was forced to retreat. The elements were in control. We found ourselves staring at each other, terrified. Then, through the howling wind, we heard Matt's voice.

'Help me! I need help down here!'

Mike and I both pushed forward against the oncoming gale, this time refusing to give in. Matt finally came into view, holding his father in his arms. He was distraught, his eyes wide with fear.

'He's injured . . . Dad is injured.'

We could see that David's head was gashed—blood pumped from a gaping wound. Matt by now had David popped up against the companion-way ladder, his free hand pressed against his father's head wound, desperately attempting to stop the flow of blood.

Mike grabbed hold of David and hollered at Matt, 'The first-aid kit!'

Matt grabbed the red plastic box from its fixed position on a shelf and tore off the lid. I crouched down, looking directly at the back of David's bare head. The gash was about two and a half inches long, easily visible through his thinning hair. In normal circumstances this wound would not have been life-threatening, but David's circumstances were by no means normal. Matt grabbed some plastic skin from the first-aid kit and protected the wound as best he could. He handed me the spray and I did as well as I could with it though the can kept slipping through my hands. Matt then pulled David's balaclava back on his head and his oilskin hood up over that, to afford him some protection. Somehow, with *Grimalkin* still pitching and rolling, Matt swivelled round, and with his father's full weight in his arms gained a toehold on the companionway ladder. With our help, he managed to get David out from the nightmare below and into the cockpit.

It was then that I caught a proper look below deck. The cabin was unrecognisable—it was submerged: perhaps only nine inches, but enough to allow the floorboards to float free. There were cans of food, saucepans, batteries, personal gear and other general detritus, all flying round inside the boat at great speed. Everything was wrecked—the engine, its housing and the chart table. It was a miracle the first-aid box had remained on its shelf.

Mike shook his head in shock. We slid the cabin hatch shut.

Grimalkin continued downwind, at a frantic rate. We were all freezing, wet, exhausted and terrified. Matt, white with fear and distress, had his arms protectively round his father, who appeared to be slipping in and out of consciousness.

'Try another flare!' shouted Dave from the helm.

Grimalkin's regulation flare pack contained four parachute flares, three of which had been wasted. Mike grabbed some hand flares. After some fumbling, they went off, one after the other. These hand flares were less effective, less visible, but easier to ignite. Mike then threw the two buoyant orange ring-pull smoke canisters over the side, one after the other. In desperation, he ripped open the yellow sachets of sea marker dye, dropping them over the side.

'This is the last one . . . Should I let it off?' yelled Mike.

Matt, Dave and I simultaneously roared yes.

The last flare went off. It glowed bright for a couple of minutes, sparks falling onto the deck as he held it aloft in his right hand. Then it was gone.

Mike became agitated. 'How long should we wait?'

Matt and I shrugged.

'We have to prepare the life raft.'

From the helm Dave yelled in agreement. I was horrified. The unwritten law for any sailor is 'never leave the boat', not unless she is sinking. *Grimalkin* was the biggest, safest life raft we had. Her cold, hard fibreglass, was much better than any soft, inflated rubber raft. For me this was not an option, not yet anyway. I looked at Matt, who said nothing—he was more preoccupied with his father. I felt I had to answer for the two of us.

'No way.'

Mike seemed to lose it at this point. 'One more knockdown and we're done for. We have to get off this boat!'

'No way . . . we're *not* leaving the boat, not unless she's going down.'

I was furious. We had to keep giving *Grimalkin* a chance. She'd performed miracles so far. Gut feeling told me that David and Gerry would never agree to leave the boat, were they in any state to contribute to the debate. From the helm Dave joined in, shouting over his agreement with Mike. I turned to Matt for support.

'Tell them, Matt . . . It would be crazy.'

Matt looked at his dad, who was clearly incoherent. Matt had always followed his father's decisions to the letter. Now, holding his badly injured father in his arms, he spoke softly.

'Dad, what shall we do? Should we prepare the life raft?'

David nodded in semiconscious agreement. Avoiding eye contact with me, Matt now nodded to Mike. I could not believe it. It had all gone beyond my control in a matter of seconds—less than that.

Up until this point, David had followed the right course of action and had acted with all caution. Now, semiconscious and delirious, he had clearly become overwhelmed. I thought of what Pa had told me once: that you do not become a survivor until you have been rescued. In these surreal conditions, I thought that with us pulling together it would be possible to survive. I tried to reason with Matt.

'It would be suicide to leave, Matt . . . Help is on the way.'

Matt, almost skipper by default, now appeared to be a bewildered young man. In adversity, it looked as if he would take a snap decision—not the considered one his father would take.

'Dad needs help . . . I have to get him off the boat!' Matt yelled.

Mike spoke up. 'OK, we have to prepare the life raft.'

Jesus Christ, how the hell had this happened? I was angry with Mike. I was sure that once the life raft was prepared, he would opt for abandoning ship. Serious hostility set in, both of us refusing to give in. Meanwhile, the seas continued their unrelenting attack. It was then that I heard an unfamiliar noise. I looked around. The clouds seemed to be lower, more sinister; there was no definition between sea and sky. What did have definition, however, were the noises.

'Listen, listen . . . Can you hear it?'

Everyone listened, looking upwards. We couldn't see a thing but we knew it was the noise of jet engines—an RAF Nimrod search aircraft was circling somewhere above us.

Matt was suddenly ecstatic. He looked to his dad. 'They saw the flares, Dad . . . They've spotted us.'

Human nature soon had all of us believing that we had been spotted and we were nigh on rescued already.

Mike jumped up, 'The life raft has to be ready!'

But everything was moving too quickly. If the engine noise was, say, a Nimrod aircraft, all they do is search and find. The rescue comes from shore-based helicopters. Signals have to be sent. I thought of last night, when I had glimpsed other navigation lights in the dark. There must be other boats out here in the same fix as us. How far down the list of casualties were we? How could we know they had seen us?

'Get real, will you?' I said to Mike. 'Look at the seas. They're huge, look. Once the raft's launched there's no going back. It's a parachute—only one chance, no back-up.'

With that, everyone started yelling at each other. It was impossible to make sense of anything. All I knew was that no one agreed with me. They had already decided on their next move. David, Gerry and me, all incapacitated in one way or another, were excluded from the decision. I knew, too, that with my injured leg, I would have no chance if left on board on my own. I had to go with them on the life raft if they decided to go.

So, with David's semiconscious agreement, *Grimalkin*'s cockpit floor was lifted to reveal the six-person life raft. The raft, sitting there, almost had a sign on it saying, 'Use me.' But Pa's words were embedded in my brain: 'Never leave the boat.' Even as I was hearing his words I was helping with the raft's preparation. How could I argue with them? With every passing moment, *Grimalkin* was close to capsizing again. With everyone's eyes full of terror, how the hell could I argue?

The life raft was now prepared but still securely fixed to a strong attachment point, bolted right through the cockpit floor.

We waited, for God only knew what. I began to wonder if what I had gleaned from Pa, Dick Langton and many other respected sailing friends, all professional, was right. I began to wonder if 'never leave the boat' was the way forward. If they were here now, with us, in this cockpit, would they put into practice what they had been preaching to me over the years?

Then, within the blink of an eye, unseen by any of us, a huge wall of water, far bigger than any other wave we had encountered so far, advanced on us. I felt *Grimalkin* lifting, being thrust upwards. This overwhelming rogue wave was iridescent at its top—what little light there was radiated through its curling lip. This is what I remember about it: its high curling lip on top of its crest, that seemed to be hanging in wait, even while the wave itself was moving at speed. It was as if the constituent parts had minds of their own—each piece with its own destructive agenda.

Something crashed violently against the back of my head, forcing it downwards into a grey, quickly fading pit. I was immediately overwhelmed, all train of thought gone, all senses blocked. Everything moved from light to dark, as if someone were turning a rheostat in my head, dimming the light. I tried to fight the closing of my eyes; I tried to see the indistinct bodies, I guess those of my crewmates, miming silent noise in front of me. The intoxicating sea seemed to want me.

I yelled, but nobody heard me. I was losing the battle for my consciousness. Everything was fading to freezing-cold black.

Muddled Mind

I could feel my head being slammed against something hard, over and over. My ears rang with the noise of hissing, like static. It was like being in a whirlpool. I slowly opened my eyes. Within seconds I experienced a terrifying surge of fear—I was underwater, in dark, murky, turbulent waters. My body was being dragged along by my safety harness. How long had I been in the water? I tried to move but couldn't—my legs were completely tangled up in rope, restricting any movement. Suddenly my inflated life jacket ejected me to the surface, long enough for me to gasp in some air. I was dragged underwater again. Once more I was ejected to the surface, and this time I managed to keep my head above water.

I could now see that *Grimalkin* was upright. The seas around her were still raging—huge, terrifying and relentless. I felt tiny, minuscule. No sooner had I inhaled a lungful of air than I swallowed twice the amount of seawater. This nightmare had not ended, nowhere near it. I was overcome with a sort of nausea in which my muscles were unable to move. I closed my eyes to block it all out. Strangely, I found myself drifting into an almost peaceful, dreamlike state. It was then that I heard a voice.

'Get a grip.'

I was completely unnerved by this voice in my head. My mind started racing. Perhaps this is what happened when you are close to death. No—I had been near death once before and this never happened. It's supposed to be peaceful: you drift towards a light, or float above yourself, or something like that. I didn't know. I just wanted the voice to go away, but it seemed to follow me. It now became familiar, very familiar.

'Pull yourself together, man.'

I realised it sounded like Pa.

'You heard me, Nicholas. Pull yourself together. You've come through worse than this.'

It was Pa—he was the only person to address me by my full name. To everyone else I was plain old Nick. This was the spur, hearing my dad's voice in my head. Sod the pain, forget the numbness in all your fingers, do something. You're your father's son, make him proud, get a grip.

I had to find help, and quickly. I shouted out, 'David, Matt, Gerry . . . It's Nick . . . Help! Get me out of here! I need help!'

Where the hell was everyone? My safety harness and life jacket were so tight round my chest that I began hyperventilating. I had to stop the panic, try to breathe normally. During a lull I managed to take a few deep breaths. Now that I had a little more control, I reached up and grabbed at the base of a broken stanchion on the deck of the boat. Another deep breath and I managed to raise myself slightly. It was then obvious that *Grimalkin* had been dismasted. With one numb, freezing hand gripped round the stanchion, I fought to untangle the snake-like lines that imprisoned me. Looking up at the oncoming walls of waves, I realised that if I judged the timing of the next upward surge I might be able to pull myself back aboard *Grimalkin*. I waited for the next wave to lift me, then, with my right hand still firmly gripping the stanchion, I grasped the starboard primary sheet winch and used it to yank my waterlogged body fully on board.

I lay slumped on the deck, breathless, panting, physically drained. Then the question began to race through my mind again: where were the others? My train of thought became a little clearer. David, our skipper, had been injured. Gerry had also been out of it. I vaguely recalled much shouting and screaming. In my muddled state of mind, it dawned on me that my crewmates, all of them, might have drowned. The last I could remember was receiving an almighty blow to the back of my head, then nothing. What had hit me? I didn't know. I desperately wanted to replay those last few seconds before I had lapsed into nothingness.

Suddenly I became overwhelmed with panic and started to shout again. 'David, Matt, Gerry . . . It's Nick . . . Where the hell are you?'

I kept shouting for what seemed like an age, but the names of my crewmates were simply taken away by the wind. I knew I had to get to the shelter of the cockpit. I tried to stand up by leaning into the gale, but I was immediately knocked forward by a massive gust. I felt a jarring pain in my chest as I hit the floor of the cockpit well, three feet below.

Grimalkin was still lurching heavily on the huge seas, crashing up and down. In the water I had been sheltered compared to this onslaught. I huddled back down into the relative safety of the cockpit and heaved much-needed air into my lungs. My legs dangled into the void of the storage well where the life raft was housed. As I stared down into this void, a cold fright came over me. The life raft had gone. It had gone! Wet and cold, I started to shake uncontrollably at the implication of this. Had the life raft been lost during the capsize? Or had the others panicked, then launched it? Yes, maybe they had gone for help. No, this wasn't possible. They would never have left me—injured, incapacitated—in these deadly conditions. They would have got me into the life raft somehow, taken me with them.

Not knowing what else to do, I stared down in disbelief. All the thoughts and fears I had experienced in the water replayed themselves in my head. I lifted my head above the cockpit. I had trouble keeping my eyes open in the spray, which was like horizontal rain, but I managed to scan the area around the boat. No orange canopy, no life raft. No sign of anything.

Images, confused and blurred, came into my brain and, slowly, my thoughts pieced themselves together. I had been in the cockpit with Matt, Mike, also David. Mike had been letting some flares off; he'd been crouching down and had been having difficulty with the parachute flares. Of course, yes, the flares, and the life raft. The last I remembered, the life raft had been securely tied and bolted to the floor, so it couldn't have been displaced during a capsize.

It was then that I took in the sight of a couple of blue safety harnesses, their safety hooks still attached to strongpoints. They'd been abandoned.

Then I saw two more—one of them looked as if it had been cut. What the hell was going on?

Had my crewmates abandoned me? No way, not David. He would never have left a crewmember on his beleaguered boat, dead or alive. A horrifying image suddenly flashed through my mind: our injured skipper being swept away from *Grimalkin* and then sucked under by a massive wave. Was that really what I had seen? I knew that he had been safely attached to the boat, like everyone else, but this vision of David being swept away felt powerfully real. I then had a blurred flashback of Gerry and me lying in the cockpit, tangled in ropes, while voices shouted around us. I must have had brief moments of consciousness after the blow to my head, for I now knew for certain that I had witnessed David's disappearance.

But where were the others? Where was the life raft? My life jacket had a yellow plastic whistle tucked under its collar. I blew it as hard as I could until I had no further breath. There was no reply. As I stared down into the empty well, dark thoughts of being abandoned passed through my mind. I began to recall remnants of an argument. I tried to piece it together. Should we leave on the life raft or stay and wait for rescue? I knew I had been against the life-raft option. But had they used it after David was swept away? They wouldn't have left me alone on *Grimalkin*, they couldn't have. But the cut harness line. Who had cut it, and why?

Nothing made sense; I began to doubt myself. I had to look for more signs, signs of life, signs of anything. I clawed my way to the side deck. The massive waves were still coming from all angles, all directions. I noticed something in the water alongside the boat. Something red—a mop of red hair. Hell, it was Gerry.

'Gerry! Gerry! Gerry!'

There was no reply. Gerry was floating there alongside the boat, supported by his life jacket and still attached to the boat by his harness. I inched my way across the deck and traced the line of his harness. I realised that he was clipped to the same strongpoint as me. How on earth had I missed him in the water? He must have been almost alongside me. Who cared now, there he was. But was he still alive? I had to get him back on board. I picked up a length of rope and then grabbed Gerry's harness lifeline to get him closer to me. I looped his line round the alloy genoa cleat, sited beneath the starboard primary winch. Then, by half kneeling, half crouching on the deck,and by leaning out over the side of the boat, I managed to thread the loop of rope through the straps of his harness lifeline. Gerry was absolutely waterlogged. He weighed a ton. Slowly, painfully, I started half pulling, half winching him aboard. My legs felt like lead, my head was throbbing, my eyes were salt-sore. I felt like giving up.

'No, you won't. Pull yourself together, man!'

God, I was talking to myself again, or was it Pa? Whoever it was, was helping me. As I yanked Gerry up towards the deck I was geed up by hearing what I thought was a moan. *He'd better not be dead, he had to be alive—Gerry had to be alive*. I was now talking to myself, shouting, encouraging. I needed to get the encouragement, the strength, from somewhere.

'Gerry's there, he's almost within reach. Get him aboard and he can help you with the boat—you can't do it on your own!'

A huge wave banged against *Grimalkin*'s port quarter. I watched as the rope slipped from the winch drum—Gerry was back in the water. My manic behaviour turned to rage.

'Come on, Gerry, help me! I'm doing my best here. I need your help!'

Once again I looped the line clockwise round the winch. I timed my pulling with the rhythm of the swells. Over my shoulder, the swells looked like green-tinged mountains. I was pitting myself against them, and they were against me; it was personal.

It took all of my strength to pull Gerry onto the deck. Once done, I fell back into the cockpit, shattered. My sense of achievement was soon dashed—a monster wave lifted *Grimalkin* and Gerry rolled into the cockpit on top of me. He was now pinning me down into the well, which was awash with seawater, only a few inches deep but enough to drown in. Gerry was so heavy I couldn't move. That's how we stayed for a while, me breathless, my crewmate lying face down on top of me. I felt no breath coming from Gerry's mouth which was pressed up against my face. His face was pale, and there was a massive abrasion across the left side of his forehead.

I could only take short breaths of air between the submerging of my nose and mouth in the water sloshing around in the cockpit. This was not really the way I wanted to die; to be found, pinned down, drowned, beneath my dead crewmate. I began to recite the Lord's Prayer. After this, 'Desiderata' came in my head, taught to me by my mother.

Go placidly amid the noise and haste,
And remember what peace there may be in silence.

'Desiderata', I recalled, means 'something to be desired'. Well, I, we, me and Gerry bloody desired something, and I was going to get it.

The struggle to get out from underneath Gerry was monumental. First I had to unclip his harness line and get my painful left leg out from under him. Then I squeezed the rest of myself out, using my fingers to gain purchase. Finally clear, I stood up shakily. Another huge wave knocked me off balance and I fell back, crashing into Gerry's chest. As I did so, I heard him moan, the same sort of moan I thought I'd heard when he was still in the water.

'Gerry, it's me, Nick. Can you hear me? Do something, anything; let me know you've heard me, for God's sake.'

Gerry remained still, lying contorted in the cockpit. I had somehow to get him flat, on his back. The only flattish surface that could take Gerry's full length was the side deck. I dragged him up and onto the starboard-side deck. Weakened by this manoeuvre, I waited a few moments for my head to clear. I then cleared Gerry's airways—his throat and mouth—with my fingers before I put my lips to his. They were far colder than mine. I gave him mouth-to-mouth. He stank of vomit and snot; his mouth was caked with the stuff—not nice but I didn't care. Every breath I took meant getting a buffeting from the gales. Somehow I combined this artificial respiration with pummelling his chest—relentlessly thumping his sternum. After what seemed like an age, Gerry coughed and spluttered and began to show signs of life. He vomited a great deal of water, but at last he breathed on his own.

Somehow I had revived my crewmate, but now what?

GERRY WAS STILL LYING on the starboard-side deck. I did not know where to place him to recover. Ideally he needed to be somewhere safe, somewhere dry. This was impossible, so I just knelt up in the cockpit, my head ducking the waves, to be near him.

Now that my crewmate was alive, no longer inanimate, no longer just a waterlogged body lying inert in the well of the boat, but someone who could work alongside me to get us out of this hellhole, I felt a lot better.

Gerry's position was precarious; his head was supported by the starboard genoa winch, his feet were tucked against the starboard spinnaker winch. The only thing keeping Gerry from rolling into the well or even over the side was the tension on his safety line, which I had tied off on the cleat, sited under the winch. He was moving quite weirdly, not in time with *Grimalkin*, for she was still crashing her way to nowhere.

Gerry's eyes were rolling. He was gurgling and moaning softly, trying to talk. I didn't really know what to do. I knew that I had to get him to a state of consciousness, get him to sit, get him to help me—but how? I knew what Gerry needed more than me; he needed medical help. He looked bruised and battered. He was suffering, he was shivering, his face was pale—no, not pale, ashen. The immersion in the cold sea had brought on hypothermia. This man, my crewmate, about whom I knew little but wanted to know more, was lapsing in and out of consciousness, trying to talk.

I started to think back a few years to some of my own most difficult, troubled times, the times when I had had to tap into my own reserves.

'Gerry, you can do this . . . You have to stay with me!' I shouted at him. I needed him, damn it.

I found myself telling him about the brain haemorrhage I had suffered eight years earlier, when I was fifteen years old. I told him about being on my back, bedridden, for months. I thought that if he could hear me this might motivate him; or, even better, it might annoy him back into a state of full consciousness.

'I counted the holes in the hospital ceiling tiles to keep myself sane,' I told him. Then I told him about my dreams of sailing again, and other dreams, and how I'd realised some—this bloody race was one of them. I told him about willing the fingers of my left hand to move again and about the pain of having to learn to walk once more. Compared to all that, this was easy, well perhaps not easy but at least here, on board, where we could move and breathe, we could—would—have a go. I had survived then, on the surgeon's table, and we, Gerry and I, would survive now on *Grimalkin*.

But Gerry had to recover. He had to help me repair the boat, pump it out. Stupidly, I thought of an inane question I really wanted to ask him: Why on earth had he bought a green Puffa jacket instead of a dark blue one, like the rest of the crew? I was getting angry; angry that I didn't have the full story of what had happened to me and Gerry. I was angry with myself and angry with Gerry for having been injured, although why I was angry, I was not quite sure. Yes, I was afraid, very afraid. Yes, I was cold, bitterly so, but I could cope with that. Physically, I was badly bruised and battered, but as I crouched in the cockpit looking at Gerry, I told myself that I was absolutely, utterly determined not to be beaten by myself, not today, not here, not alone.

Gerry was deadly pale. I felt for a pulse—there was none. I leaned low over Gerry's mouth, sheltering him from the gale with my back, and tried to feel his breath on my cheek. There was no sign of breath. Christ almighty, not again. I leaned over him to once more blow into his mouth. I saw his chest rise and fall, and blew again. I braced my arms, and with right hand over left I pushed hard down on his chest.

'Come on, Gerry!'

I pinched his nose to blow again. I did this for what seemed like aeons, but it must have been only minutes.

'You're not going to go, you bastard!' I yelled at him. 'You're not going anywhere. I want to ask you about your green Puffa . . . Please, Gerry.'

I shook his body, trying to encourage life back into him. I began to reassure him that help was on its way, even though I doubted that it was. I added that the others, Matt and David—'Remember David, Gerry? You know that our skipper would never leave us stranded'—would try their best. I felt like a con man trying to shoot a line, but Gerry might respond to it.

There was a look that Gerry gave me then. He revived and appeared to breathe for himself. He coughed, tried to say something. I leaned closer, my right ear close to his mouth. This was important, I knew it. Finally I deciphered a word—love. Christ, just say it, Gerry, please say it. Some more mumbles and I heard the name Margaret. Gerry took one further breath, deep as his water-filled lungs would allow. This time I heard the words of a man who knew he was dying, and it took all his effort to get them out.

'If ever you see Margaret again tell her I love her.'

Some more coughing, some inaudible stuttering, and that was it. I began to pummel his chest again. I tried in vain to thump some life back into him, but with no result. Gerry was gone. His eyes were red and open. I closed them, then kissed his forehead and said the Lord's Prayer. Then I said goodbye, sobbing selfishly, sobbing for myself. This sort of thing only happened in books, on the screen, in battle, not to me, not to Gerry. We were ordinary people. This couldn't happen. But it just had.

I had prayed, I had beseeched for help, for strength, and I'd got it, and somehow revived my crewmate. Now what? If I'd been shattered before, I was doubly so now. I clung on to Gerry and sobbed like a child. I was physically and emotionally shipwrecked. I slumped down into the cockpit and wept; I was sorry for Gerry and sorry for myself.

I began to think about the repercussions of Gerry's passing. If I got through this, if I saw Margaret again, what on earth was I going to say? Obviously, I would pass on what Gerry had asked me to, but what else could I possibly say? Impossible, I couldn't think that far ahead.

I remembered something that my godmother had given to me around the time of my confirmation more than ten years ago: an illustrated postcard with some lines on it. It was about a man who was walking along the beach with the Lord. I tried hard to piece together the words. I became obsessed, as if remembering it correctly might help to save my life. At first my thoughts were disjointed. Then the words began to assemble themselves in the right order. I recalled that the man became upset that in times of difficulty he could see only one set of footprints in the sand; he thought that during these times the Lord must have abandoned him. Eventually fluent, I cried the last couple of lines above the noise of the chaos around me:

'"Why, when I needed you most, have you not been there for me, Lord?"

'The Lord replied, "The years when you have seen only one set of footprints, my child, is when I carried you."'

I felt better for saying it, but only slightly. Words, however well said, are only words. Words could not save lives.

I poked my head above the cockpit coaming and looked astern. There were no footprints, no sand, there wasn't even a horizon or a sky, just cold grey nothingness. At that moment a wave swept me off my feet and threw me up in the air, past Gerry's body. I landed on my back, head first, onto the horizontal lip of the companionway, the entrance to *Grimalkin*'s cabin. It took me a while to recover, but when I did I swivelled my head and peered into the dark of the boat's interior. What a godawful mess.

Blood-tinged Red Roses

I lay there, staring into the depths of the dark cabin. Behind me the waves thumped violently into *Grimalkin*'s stern. Above me, thick black clouds hurled solid, ice-cold lumps of liquid at my face. This storm defied every meteorological term, defied every law of gravity; it quite simply defied everything I had been taught.

Through squinting, sore eyes, I caught a glimpse of another mountainous wave thundering towards *Grimalkin*. This wall of water must have been sixty or seventy feet high and as wide as Waterloo station. As the crest of the wave lifted the stern, I felt its power. *Grimalkin*'s angle steepened, she gathered momentum and I plunged down, pathetically snatching at sodden rope tails, mooring cleats, debris—everything slipped from my grasp. She was now almost vertical. A stanchion appeared—reaching out, I missed it by inches. I felt like I'd lost my footing on a crumbling cliff edge. Both prisoners of this wave, Gerry and I were flung round the cockpit—our limbs collided violently.

Grimalkin, now fully vertical, was on the brink of pitchpoling, exactly what Mike and I had spent most of the night trying to avoid. Her hull was swept up by an avalanche of high-speed madness. Her stern was above me, tumbling clockwise. She was cartwheeling, quick as a flash. Now her bow was in one wave, her stern in the next trough. Gerry and I hung in midair. The boat's stern overtook her bow and I felt myself corkscrew. With a thud I was slammed straight back into the cockpit on top of Gerry. Despite the pain, the choking and the vomiting, I thanked God that it was Gerry and not the sea that had broken my fall. I watched the floor of the cockpit slowly right itself and wondered just how this ballsy thirty-foot yacht had recovered yet again from these glacier-sized waves.

I clung on to the slippery sides of the cockpit. My life hung on the malicious whim of the next wave. As *Grimalkin* tumbled down yet another trough, Gerry's elbow walloped me, bang in the centre of my right cheek.

'Jesus Christ, Gerry . . . Back off!'

Gerry crashed into me time after time. There he was—a silent, lifeless shadow stalking me. I feared the unpredictable actions of his body, knowing that during a large swell I had no control over them. As I wondered how much more I could take, a thought went through my mind. It would be easy to unclip Gerry and let the sea do the rest. Lightning-quick flashes relayed information to me about the unlucky dead, about how they hindered a ship's progress, about corpses bringing bad luck.

But then I caught a view of Gerry's battered face. No way could I do that—no one could have done that to a crewmate. I dismissed the idea immediately. But, pursuing the idea in a more reasoned, rational manner, I thought maybe I could move his body into the cabin. I could drag him to the companionway entrance and then lower him down with a line. But then what would happen? I began to visualise Gerry being tossed about in the debris-filled cabin. Shuddering, I abandoned the idea—his body would be slashed to bits in no time and blood-red water would be left swishing around the bilges beneath. Gerry had to stay with me in the cockpit.

What should I do next? If *Grimalkin* rolled or capsized again, I would not survive, that I knew for sure. With no crewmates left and in my deteriorating physical condition, there was no point in trying to control the boat. This storm would beat me down—that, too, I knew for certain.

Only one option remained open to me—to risk going below into the cabin and see if anything was working down there. I needed to make contact with some kind of rescue.

I checked my harness tether, then grabbed the main-sheet traveller. I waited for a let-up in the violence around me.

'One . . . two . . . three . . . four . . .' I made it to ten, four, maybe five times, before the lull finally came.

Still anticipating the peaks and troughs, I clutched the bridge deck, the raised approach to *Grimalkin*'s cabin. My grip held firm. As I deliberated my next move, I heard a loud scraping noise from beneath the boat. What the hell was it? I warily scanned the area.

Finally, I saw the cause: the mast was still attached to the boat and was being dragged through the water. Bloody brilliant! On top of the mast was the three-foot whip antenna, and with that still attached there was a slim chance of the VHF working. As I ran my eyes over the length of the mast I saw that it was broken in what looked like two places. This was not good, but if there was no break in the coaxial cable and the aerial's connection, or in the wired terminal and the plug, it might still have power. My decision was made. I was going down there.

I glanced back down into the cabin. I noticed its smell for the first time: oily, acrid. I saw scum floating on the surface of the water, a surface that surged violently back and forth, up and down. Beneath me, I could feel the seas building. An image flashed into my mind—blood pumping from David Sheahan's gaping wound.

My resolve had weakened. I stared down into the depths of *Grimalkin*'s ravaged cabin.

'Go on, chicken . . . You can do it.'

Then a stream of voices, all my own, arguing.

'You can't risk your life down there.'

'You have to. How else are you going to survive?'

From nowhere, a monster wave reared its head. I was caught out, unprepared. I fought frantically for balance—none was possible. The wave knocked the legs from beneath me and tossed me about like a rag doll before smashing me face down into the cockpit—back on top of Gerry, back where I had started. At the last minute I had fluffed it.

Bodily battered, I could do nothing but stay slumped in the cockpit alongside Gerry. His face was next to mine. Poor Gerry; beyond prayer but still not at peace. More than his friendship I had needed his survival; instead I had experienced a death. I had heard the dying words of a friend. Death had been in my arms; I had tasted it. And I was likely to suffer a similar fate—with the difference that no one would hear my last words.

All the while, *Grimalkin* continued to buck and kick like an out-of-control bronco. I slumped further into the well, frozen, dispirited, waiting—waiting for what? I was so cold that I'd stopped shivering; my teeth had stopped chattering too. Although my brain was dulled, I knew well the symptoms and sequence of hypothermia. When the body begins using up all reserves, it stops chattering, stops shivering and begins shutting down. I began rocking in time, as far as I could, with the boat's violent, unpredictable motion.

Waves crashed onto *Grimalkin*'s decks; streams of water poured into the cockpit and joined the surging reservoir down below. I wanted peace now, with no pain. I had arrived at a point of oblivion. The noise around me began to grow silent; the smell drifting up from the cabin was replaced by something more familiar—the smell of nicotine and flowers. I closed my eyes and felt peaceful. I was going to a safer place, a place of refuge that offered comfort, warmth and security.

I was flat out on my hospital bed, at fifteen years of age. Ma was sitting on a chair beside me. Then that familiar tang of untipped cigarettes—Pa was coming. I tried to sit up, but I couldn't. Although weeks had passed I hadn't got used to being paralysed.

'Hello, old man, how are you today?'

Pa stood over me with a bunch of red roses in one hand and the stub of a Senior Service in the other.

'I thought these might cheer you up a bit. Here, take a smell.'

Pa leaned forward and held the red roses close to my face. For a moment I savoured their scent. As Pa pulled away, I felt something cold on my left arm. I stared down and saw that a droplet of water had fallen from the rose stems onto my skin. Pa and I exchanged a glance. Pa instinctively understood that I had experienced some kind of sensation, at last. He pressed the alarm button next to the bed.

'Nurse, Nurse! Please . . . Quick!'

Ma jumped to her feet. Pa kept calling until one, two, then three nurses ran to my bedside. Surrounded by so many concerned faces I became overwhelmed. A loud noise began to fill my ears, as loud as a turbine. I felt myself being pushed away—back into the mattress. Away from Ma, away from Pa. I wanted to stretch out my arms and hold on to them, but I was being sucked down into a murky, wet, freezing place. Their faces began to fade, then there was nothing. Moments passed before I was abruptly catapulted upwards, cracking my forehead on the lip of the cockpit lid.

This was a brutal awakening. I was drenched and freezing once again, but I had a greater recognition of myself, as if potent smelling salts had been wafted beneath my nose. I felt different. A new conviction engulfed me. That moment, eight years earlier, had given me a lifeline to recovery.

My parents were told back then that the left side of my body was paralysed and it was unlikely I would ever walk again. It was Pa who gave me this news. I clearly remember him and Ma sitting either side of my bed, desperately trying to retain some kind of composure. For myself I felt nothing, no reaction whatsoever. The thought of not being able to walk again was not something I would contemplate. I simply refused to accept it as an option. Maybe it was youthful naiveté or delayed shock, but it was the best reaction I could have had, because in the weeks that followed I was determined to prove them wrong. No walking? Worse still, no sailing? That's what I lived for. I'd rather have died than not sail again.

Back to the present on *Grimalkin*, the effect was equally inspirational. My teeth were beginning to chatter, my body was shivering again. Life was forcing its way back into my body. The turbine noises I had heard still rang in my ears—they were the same noises we had all heard circling above us before *Grimalkin*'s final capsize. I looked at Gerry, jumped up and started yelling with joy.

'It's back, Gerry, the Nimrod is back! They're coming to get us!'

With black clouds still low I could see nothing. Panic set in. I had to be sure the Nimrod could see me. The flares—I remembered they had all been used. But it was dark then, and we were in total pandemonium—one flare could have fallen aside, got trapped or wedged. I ploughed through the endless lines of sodden rope that surrounded me. I found nothing. I began wondering if there was an undischarged flare beneath Gerry. I forced my hands under his back but couldn't shift his dead weight.

'Come on, Gerry, *move*, for God's sake . . . Get the hell up.'

Gerry didn't move; the turbine noises were still above us. My desperation turned to anger. I locked my arms beneath his armpits and managed to roll him aside. No flares.

OK, so the flares were all gone. I needed another means of contact. What else could I do? I could risk going below, but time was against me and the Nimrod could be gone before I even got there.

Then I remembered the Callbuoy, a waterproof, removable transmitter that was stowed in the cockpit locker. How the hell had I not thought of it earlier? We hadn't used it last night because the main VHF set, in the cabin below, had been far more powerful. The Callbuoy had limited battery life and was only used as back-up in a last resort. Well, I was in that last-resort situation and back-up was exactly what I needed.

Down on my knees, I pulled open the cockpit locker—the Callbuoy wasn't in its stowage position. I scrambled through the locker's contents but could see nothing. It was bright orange so it would have stood out. Had the others taken the Callbuoy, my only other means of contact with the outside world? It made sense, if they had left on the life raft.

Head first now, I almost climbed inside the confined space—and there it was, under bilge water, tangled in the Morse gear and throttle cables. I grabbed it and extracted myself from the locker. I could still hear the Nimrod above, but how much longer would it stay there? I raised the aerial and deployed its earth over the side. The set crackled static. I began to shout into the transmitter.

'Mayday! Mayday! Over. Yacht *Grimalkin* dismasted—two crewmen, I repeat, two crewmen. Over.'

I waited for a response. None came.

'Mayday, mayday!'

I paused. One, two—deep breath—hands trembling.

'Yacht *Grimalkin*, sail number kilo, five, six, three, seven. Over.'

The noise of crackling static was beginning to fade out. I checked the earth line; it was OK. I checked its connection to the set; it was OK too. I checked the transmit button and again it looked OK. All this time the crackling noise was growing fainter. My right thumb ached from the pressure as

I tried in vain to reactivate the set. Then the crackling faded to silence. The Callbuoy was defunct, of no further use. I flung it into the waterlogged cockpit. Utterly distraught, I looked down at Gerry.

'What the hell are you doing there?' I yelled angrily. All the while, I could hear that damned Nimrod noise just above me. 'Help me, for God's sake. Jesus Christ Almighty, I can't do everything.'

Then I began to talk to him more calmly. 'Do you think we got through, Gerry?' Not thinking about it, I just carried on talking. 'It's still there, isn't it? You can still hear it, can't you?'

Instantly, Gerry was the greatest of sounding boards. It seemed right, somehow—not normal, but right. The clarity I gained from consulting with him was so reassuring. I certainly wasn't about to stop. I had to keep my mind active; any thoughts were better than none, any speech better than the wind-filled roar. I had a compulsion to risk going below once more and make that mayday call from the main VHF. I conferred with Gerry.

'You were down there last night . . . It was working then, wasn't it?'

All I could hear was that enticing Nimrod noise above me. My only means of contact with it, however slim, lay below deck. The decision was made. I waited for the next lull.

'Right, Gerry, you stay up where the Nimrod can see you. I'll go below.'

Standing upright was difficult. I stumbled across the cockpit and placed my hands firmly on each side of the boat's cabin entrance. Cautiously, I unclipped my harness and swung myself over the sill. With my legs dangling over the void, I saw the companionway ladder was wrenched from its mountings. As I lowered myself into *Grimalkin*'s cabin, my boots filled with seawater. It sounded like a fast-flowing but log-jammed river down here—wreckage was banging and crashing from side to side. Avoiding serious injury was going to be my biggest problem. By the time my boots touched the floor I was in water and debris above the knees.

I took a good look around. I'd never seen a boat so waterlogged. How the hell had she not sunk already? A small blue plastic bucket floated by and my instinct was to pick it up and start bailing. I had to stop myself—I had to keep focused on the job at hand.

Nothing looked familiar down here. The navigation table was off its hinges; the VHF had been wrenched off its bracket. My eyes quickly followed the cable to the handset; there it was, submerged. There was no hope of it working. Even so, I grabbed it. I pressed the switch. Nothing happened. I pressed again, over and over, till my thumb stiffened with cramp. The handset was completely useless. I smashed the handset against the bulkhead of the ravaged cabin and let out an almighty roar. I thought I could hear the screams of my crewmates in response—it was some job to convince myself that this was just my imagination.

Just beneath me I felt the seas shorten and steepen. *Grimalkin* tilted harshly, slamming down on her starboard side—sea forced its way through the shattered port light above me, filling my nose, mouth and ears. I stood there, trying to regain my senses, and then realised that I could no longer hear the jet engines.

I yelled up to Gerry: 'Is it still there?'

I pulled down my hood and strained to hear.

'Can you hear it?' I yelled. 'Come on, Gerry—pull your hood down! Open your ears and listen!'

With the noise of the boiling seas around me nothing was distinguishable. I had to get back on deck. Breathing hard, I dragged myself up through the companionway, snagging my trousers on the jagged, torn metal ladder. Freezing liquid shot into my oilskins up to the base of my spine.

As I jumped up into the cockpit an anger swelled up inside my head when I grasped that the noise of engines had disappeared entirely. The dead man sharing this cockpit with me inspired my wrath.

'What the hell are you doing? I told you to keep watch . . . Why the hell didn't you warn me the Nimrod was going?'

I shouted obscenity after obscenity at my deceased friend. Things I would never normally have dreamt of saying. I purged myself, purged that wrath, directly at Gerry. It was an expression—not an acceptance—of gut-wrenching loneliness. Was that my last hope of rescue gone?

Ceaseless waves were stacked up behind us, row upon row, as if awaiting their turns. I picked one out, choosing the most deformed monster from this cliff face of madness. I stared at it, enraged, waiting for it.

Grimalkin lifted sharply. The horizon was nearly vertical, but this time I made no effort to save myself. All instinct for survival had abandoned me. I stood in the cockpit with Gerry at my feet, taunting the wave to get me.

'Come on, you bastard, come on . . .'

The beast towered above me. Then a fleeting image—Pa, Ma, my family, my friends—my life, still unlived. My gut twisted, I stopped shouting. A rational, balanced, simple thought came into my head.

No, no . . . I don't want to die. Not yet.

The beast pounced, throwing Gerry and me upwards out of the cockpit. Eyes closed tight, I waited for my fate to be delivered. I landed, felt my legs being pulled through the icy water. Opening my eyes I saw I had been saved by the deck, but was being dragged towards the sea. Inches from my head, I spotted a winch drum—reached out and held on. This was it, life or death, right here, right now on the edge of this boat. As *Grimalkin* dragged herself upright again, shaking off gallons of water, I used every last ounce of strength to heave myself on board, into the cockpit and to safety. I clipped on, out of such senseless, self-inflicted danger.

This latest barrage left Gerry upside down in a posture only a tethered corpse could manage. I felt embarrassment at my verbal attack on him. None of this was his fault. I manhandled his body into a less ungainly position. I needed him now more than ever, just as I knew he needed me.

Overwhelmed by what lay ahead, I felt isolated and this feeling was compounded by Gerry's dumb presence. I had to get my sounding board back. We had to talk.

Dead or Alive?

I could see no real signs of change in the ferocity of the storm—the noise and the drenching went on and on. I needed a breather to gather my thoughts, regain some strength. My foremost worry was the amount of water we were carrying. I knew that just one more violent combination of wind and wave, together with the surging mass of water below, could lead to us sinking.

Maybe I could venture onto the deck to see how far the waterline had changed outside the boat?

On my knees, I grabbed a stanchion and slowly, cautiously, craned my head forwards into the gale. I couldn't see anything; the rain—the hail—bounced off the deck, creating a stinging, impenetrable obstacle. Glass-like lumps were hurled against my face. I reached out further and gripped the next stanchion—the guardrail wire painfully cut into my gut but I could just about see the water level. I quickly realised that what I could see was not the actual waterline. The spume created by the swells and the hailstones prevented this.

I stretched yet further. This was all getting gravely tricky. Holding on grimly, I gripped the next stanchion and looked over. My suspicions were confirmed. *Grimalkin*'s waterline was around two feet higher. She lay so low in the water that only a small portion of her exterior could be seen. I needed no further evidence to recognise that this boat could go down at any time. One rogue wave and we were gone. Utterly shocked, I loosened my grip and slipped as *Grimalkin* plunged down into a trough. For an instant I teetered on the brink of plunging head first over the side. Inches from tumbling overboard, I managed to grip the horizontal guardrail wires either side of my body. Heart pounding, on all fours, I retreated into the safety of the cockpit, once more thanking God and my harness for saving me.

I wanted to get back down in the cabin and start bailing, but the risks were immense. My primary worry was the free-floating floorboards, which could smash into me, breaking one or both of my legs, perhaps leaving me unable to get back on deck. Any injury at this point, no matter how small, would severely weaken my chances of survival.

It seemed that everything I attempted to do was thwarted by a barrier; every way I turned there was an obstruction. I knew, only too well, how all this stuff should work—Callbuoys and their like—but nothing wanted to work for me. *Grimalkin*'s once-inspiring hull was now just a sodden container for two sodden bodies.

'What the hell are we supposed to do now, Gerry?'

Glancing down at my watch I saw that it, too, was broken, and had stopped. Like so much else around me, my trusted timepiece had fallen victim to the battering. It was strange that I hadn't noticed earlier, but time, an integral part of any race, had become irrelevant—like the race itself. I remembered then that Gerry had a watch; of course he did, we all did. I took his wrist, gently pulling up his oilskin sleeve. Through the condensation I studied the face and realised that, like mine, his watch had stopped, the hands stuck at nine minutes past seven—probably around the time I had lost consciousness. I looked at Gerry's gnarled finger joints. They were blue in colour, squashed and slightly bloodied. At that moment I glimpsed an empty harness next to him, still clipped to its strongpoint. The sight of this abandoned harness left me feeling very uneasy.

'It just doesn't add up,' I murmured softly.

What exactly did take place at nine minutes past seven? What were the circumstances that led to Gerry and me being left alone in the Irish Sea during a storm of this magnitude?

Crouched in the weather-beaten cockpit with him, my head still swirling from the many blows I'd sustained, I began to picture the worst-possible scenario. Could Matt, Mike and Dave have been swept away from the boat to their deaths? It didn't make sense. What about the abandoned harnesses? Why had they taken them off? Even more bizarre, why was there a cut line? If they had gone overboard, I would have found one, perhaps two of them clipped on alongside the boat, like Gerry.

Even that last image I had of David being swept away confused me. How could he have been swept away while still clipped on to the boat? Unless, God forbid, it was his harness line that was cut. But who would have cut it, and why? All of my assumptions now led me to think that something else had occurred.

What if that last image I had of the huge wall of water had led to a B2 knockdown? There was strong evidence of this: the mast had broken, which was usual in a full 180-degree capsize. While this made sense, nothing I could bring to mind would explain the disappearance of my three remaining crewmates, the cut and abandoned harnesses and the missing life raft. Could the life raft have blown away while Matt, Dave and Mike were trying to transfer Gerry and me into it? I began to picture Gerry and me alongside the boat, in the water. But one of the crew would have seen us. And if so, why wouldn't they have pulled us out of the water? I began to remember the arguing, my own words strongly advocating that we stay on the boat. Perhaps my crewmates saw me as an inconvenience to their proposed course of action. Even this didn't really make sense—what of Gerry? Why didn't they take him? Maybe they saw us both as liabilities.

With my mind jumping from one scenario to another, my heart began to race and a new anger welled up inside me. What the hell had gone on? I knew for certain that David was dead, but what of the others? Where were my three crewmates?

The anger generated by the thought of Gerry and me being left behind turned to guilt as I considered the possibility of my three crewmates drowning. But I needed anger in order to survive; guilt would surely finish me off.

'No, damn it and damn them too.'

They were all damned as far as I was concerned. Damned by Gerry, too;

I was sure of it. I cursed all three of them. Expletives filled the wet air.

I felt motivated once more. I looked up—a palette of dark greys and blacks that was at once beautiful and evil. There was no sun. I guessed it was around eleven in the morning but I had no real idea. As I watched the formation above me, I noticed that occasionally, very occasionally, *Grimalkin*'s movement was less vehement. The weather, although still atrocious, appeared slightly less threatening. It was very subtle and I began to wonder if I was imagining it.

I noticed that the severed mast had a braking effect on *Grimalkin*, and realised that this may have prevented a total capsize in the hours Gerry and I had been alone. Gradually, after watching for a time—it could have been ten minutes, it could have been an hour—I gained confidence that there might be hope for us. We had hung on so far, as had *Grimalkin*. Even half-full of water, she had refused to give in. I felt now that she was protecting me and Gerry. She was awesome, bloody miraculous. I grabbed hold of Gerry.

'The weather is turning, Gerry, I'm sure of it.'

This confidence prompted me into thinking about my next move. I needed my medication and, Christ, I was thirsty, hungry. Hours and hours had passed since I had eaten or drunk anything. I knew that the body could go without food for days, but water was far more important. My mouth was salty-dry and needed hydrating. But still my most pressing worry was the water level inside the boat. Water, food, medication—all were irrelevant if the boat went down.

I was searching Gerry's face for a sign of what I should do, when a childhood memory flashed in front of my eyes. It was something Pa had said to me when I was nine. He was on his knees, weeding the back garden.

'If you're going through hell—keep going,' Pa said, borrowing from Churchill. He found some aspects of gardening a chore.

I knew if I was to survive this very real hell I had to keep going. That bucket floating among the debris of the cabin—I could and would bail the boat with that.

'Right, Gerry, I'm going below again. OK?'

There was work to be done.

I WAS IMMERSED in freezing water to well above my knees. I called up to Gerry. 'Jesus, you think it's cold up there . . . Try it down here, mate.'

My words were strangely muted in the cabin—probably because of all the water. Avoiding lethal debris—floating floorboards, shattered fittings and other items—proved difficult. I reached for a bunk pole and looped my safety harness round it. I kept it short for stability, but with enough length for me to reach out to about a three-foot range.

Odd noises came from both within and outside the cabin. It was hard to know what each noise meant. Powerful waves were still smashing into *Grimalkin*'s hull and the debris-filled water on the inside continued to surge back and forth. The reverberations made me feel nauseous, but if I was to progress in my task, I would have to adjust to this new environment.

First, I needed to establish the quickest means of escape. It was obvious: the companionway. My next task was to find the bucket—unsurprisingly it wasn't where I had last seen it. Treading cautiously, I rummaged through the mountains of debris. The boat lurched with an unexpected swell. A galley locker door swung open—J Cloths and a can of Bilgex floated out.

To my right, I spotted something blue wedged between the hanging locker and a shelf—the bucket. I reached out for it, but the floating floorboards trapped my feet and I fell, face first, into the freezing water. I gagged. Still gagging, I found the handle and yanked till the little blue bugger freed itself.

'Yes, yes, yes!' I whooped with joy. Something was going my way at last. 'I got it, Gerry, I got it . . . I got the frigging bucket!'

I now possessed an asset. I emptied its contents and tied it to the broken companionway ladder. My thoughts turned to the next priority—I was thirsty, so damn thirsty. I moved towards the sink pump, grabbed the handle and pushed. Nothing. I pushed again, this time with more force; what little liquid came out was salty and contaminated. Willing it to work, I gave it a couple more pumps but it jammed completely. This was pointless anyway. The main tanks had clearly ruptured.

I knew there were tanks of drinking water somewhere in the cabin. David had installed two extra five-gallon tanks specially for the race. They were more robust, so less likely to have punctured. I began to scour the debris around me. I was surprised I couldn't see them; they were too huge to miss. Then it struck me: if they hadn't been ruptured, would they be floating? No way, their weight wouldn't allow it. I got down on my hands and knees to dredge through the bilge. I noticed excrement floating on the surface. The toilet had been pumped dry, but the pipe had regurgitated its contents. I kept moving, keeping my mouth firmly closed. Water permeated my clothing. It was vile, fetid. I forced myself to stay down, trying not to think about what was seeping down the neck of my oilskin.

Agitated at my failure to find the tanks, I saw the reason staring right at me—the cabin entrance. The tanks had most likely been flung out of the boat during a knockdown, and were probably sitting on the bed of the Irish Sea. It was time to give up this pointless scavenge. I felt *Grimalkin*'s stern begin to lift, severely—I nonetheless managed to hold on to the bunk pole and regain my balance. As I waited for the boat to level herself, a can of pineapple chunks rolled down the water slide towards me. This was the most unexpected thing—a gift of liquid and food in one. The juice would slake my thirst and the chunks would quell the bile, stop the griping. It occurred to me I had no opener. Another hand and knee trawl through the cabin? No, that would be hopeless.

I was maddened. I also knew I was being sidetracked. The rising water level had to be tackled. My body could keep going without fluids for a while yet. I had to accept that my thirst was not immediately life-threatening, whereas *Grimalkin*'s foundering was.

I decided to scrap all thoughts of looking for my medication—there was no point. The Tupperware box in which it was sealed was long gone. Twenty-four hours must have passed since my last 30mg tablet; normally I'd have taken it twice daily. I knew that fitting or convulsing down here could lead to serious injury, to drowning. I reminded myself that so did every other option, and with that I prepared to bail.

With a piece of splintered wood, I scratched a mark on the forward bulkhead to give me the current water level. The boat's continuous seesaw movement made it impossible to determine the real level, but I had to have a reference point. I unhooked my bucket and started to bail. The most effective way was to throw the water up out of the companionway entrance and into the cockpit, which was self-draining. On occasion the motion of the boat allowed me to throw water right over the side. Getting into a rhythm was difficult at first. Apart from the continual swaying in the cabin, my clothing felt tight and cumbersome, heavy as lead from the immersions and constant drenching, but without it I would already be dead. Despite the restriction, something was telling me to keep going, and I settled into bailing with a will.

Having something to do lifted my spirits and my self-esteem. For the first time in hours I was no longer a passenger hanging on for grim death.

I felt elated, in control. This blue bucket was a joyous possession.

All too soon, I was out of breath. I was light-headed and confused. Without some kind of breather I risked passing out.

I sat on the edge of the cockpit taking deep, slow breaths. I carefully studied the sea. A monumental swell still ran, but I was sure that only every fifth or sixth wave was taller than its neighbours—rather than every second or third as it had been the last time I looked.

'Looks like it's eased off more. There might be some hope for us yet, hey, Gerry?'

Even so, this was still a dangerous place to be. I had to get bailing.

Back below I counted ten buckets out, then stopped for breath. I was slowing down. I tried to ignore the creeping exhaustion and plough on, pushing myself harder—until the pain of every intake of breath was cutting through my chest so sharply I had to stop.

I checked the marker. The water level was the same. But I managed to convince myself that while the water level may not have gone down, neither had it gone up. For the moment that was good enough for me.

Trying to get a rhythm back, I started singing 'Ten Green Bottles'.

'Come on, mate, join in!' I shouted.

Eventually I had to pause. My head was aching as badly as it did after a convulsion; a deep, nauseous, migraine-like headache that made my eyes throb. My weaker left hand was deadened. I knew I was wearing out fast but I was driven by a fear that if I stopped, everything would get worse. I splashed my head and lips with the cold water to refresh myself. The effect was the opposite. The murky water fouled my mouth with a taste so vile I gagged, over and over till I could barely stand, let alone bail.

To add to a worsening situation, *Grimalkin* lifted with a swell, my legs collapsed under me and I hit my head on the cooker.

Unclipped and dazed, I now drifted free through the cabin. A sock floated past me—I knew it was my skipper's. Overwhelmed, I retched again from the knowledge that unless there had been some kind of miracle, I would never see David again. I thought about David's wife, Gay, too young to be widowed. She was expecting a family holiday with her husband, not this. I sincerely hoped, prayed now, that Matt had survived. To lose a son as well as a husband would be too much for anybody to cope with.

I clambered onto the port quarter berth and slumped on my side. Water kept lapping against the soaking bunk but I didn't care. I had no energy.

I could not imagine ever being able to get back up again.

I kept my eyes open; I was afraid of falling asleep. I examined the effects of the storm on *Grimalkin*'s interior. The damage was beyond belief. Everything was precision-trashed.

My legs began to cramp, so I stretched out my back as far as my inflated life jacket allowed. I breathed deeply. While my body seemed to have stalled, my mind was off at double the speed, worrying, thinking, panicking about what to do next. Bail, rest or keep watch? My left arm and hand were painfully numb. I removed the glove of this hand and began touching my fingers in turn against my thumb—a coordination exercise I had learned in hospital. While I watched my bloodied, blistered hand trying to flex, I thought: I have to stay active. I have to keep my circulation going.

I wanted to talk to Gerry, tell him how important it was for me to keep active, but I said nothing; I just kept at my fingers, trying to flex them.

'Come on then, get on with it,' said a voice, not my own.

For a brief moment I thought it was Gerry. Then I realised it was Pa. No doubt whatsoever. He was back. I closed my eyes.

I saw my hand again. This time it looked different: smooth-palmed, if slightly wasted. It was a hand that hadn't been near salt water, a jib sheet or a winch for weeks. I tried to lift one finger, but the effort required was too much. Then there was another hand—longer, tanned, with slightly nicotine-stained fingers. It took my left hand and massaged it.

'Softly, softly, catchee monkey, Nicholas,' said Pa.

That's what he used to say to me when things became too much. Encouraged, I continued trying to move my hand. The movement began, little by little, to improve.

'Where there's a will there's a way, son.'

Pa again. My rhythm, my coordination was returning, and with it a resolve. With my head clearer, I knew that to maintain my stamina it was essential to bail and rest in equal measures. I needed to devise a system to match my physical capacity.

I decided to bail for one hour then rest for half an hour. I would have to guess the time by counting—maybe breaths, or bucketfuls of water. While lying there, mulling this over, I noticed something familiar drifting out from beneath the navigation table. Floating in the murk was a small brown plastic bottle.

'My medication . . . My bleedin' medication, Gerry!'

I pulled myself up and reached out for it. Got you! Trembling uncontrollably, I clicked off its white top to see nothing but a smidgen of white mush floating in the contaminated water. Nothing had survived this maelstrom intact. I began to panic again; finding this bottle was an all-too-vivid reminder that I was without medication and liable to fit at any time. I wished to God I had never set eyes on the damn thing. This was a setback; it just made it harder to maintain a positive frame of mind. As I stared into the floating debris, nauseated by the sight, I spotted something bobbing up and down just beneath the surface. A carton of longlife milk!

I cast aside the little brown bottle and grabbed the carton. Full and intact—it had somehow survived. Biting off the waxy corner, I put the carton to my sore, dry mouth and drank deep. Never before had I felt so much satisfaction from anything. I savoured every drop.

Drinking this nectar brought back to my mind a trip I had taken with Ma to see my brother Peter in Japan. We visited the water temple at Kyoto and drank cold, clear water from tin cups. I remembered Yuko, Peter's wife, telling me that to drink from this waterfall would assure me a long life. Now, more than ever, I hoped she was right. All too quickly the contents of the milk carton were gone.

Finding this milk had to be a sign. Everything that had happened had been a test of my will. Then this cardboard carton, filled with nectar, had floated in out of nowhere. Someone was on my side. What or who, I didn't know, I didn't care. But it lifted my spirits. The tide was turning; our luck was changing.

WITH MY ENERGY LEVELS back up, I wanted to get on with things. I fastened my harness, grabbed the blue bucket and began bailing and counting again—this time louder. As I got my rhythm back, I thought about those six weeks in Japan. Yuko had taught me how to count to ten, so I started to fill and empty the bucket in halting Japanese—*ichi, ni, san, yon, go, roku, nana, hachi, kyu, ju*.

I have no idea how long I carried on for—probably far less than my allotted hour—but long enough for me to get my confidence back. I rested on the port quarter berth, breathing deeply, regaining energy. Now that I was feeling more aware, the splashing water round my body and near my face irritated me. I decided to move up into the cockpit. Once up there and clipped in, I realised that this was probably a better place to rest. Although bitterly cold, I could scan the seas and skies for rescue, and talking to Gerry would keep me alert.

In the cockpit, though, I found it hard to relax. Doing nothing made me jittery—I forced myself to go below and back to work. Again, I got a good rhythm going. I was unable to judge if the water level was going down, but even so I felt compelled to continue. During this productive period my mind was uninterrupted by worries about anything else. My head was concentrated on keeping *Grimalkin* afloat.

After a while I could feel my right hand beginning to tremble. I was starting to lose control and most of the water was now coming straight back down on top of me. Something felt wrong. I was experiencing an overwhelming taste and smell. This felt like what is known to epileptics as an aura—early warning of an oncoming fit. I decided to take a breather by going back on deck and doing a scan of the sea and skies.

No sooner had I stuck my head up out of the cabin than I realised the drains of the cockpit had become blocked by debris and sludge and it was rapidly filling up with water. Damn this. All I had been doing for the last while was transferring water from one part of the boat to another. I clipped on in the cockpit and removed the blockage. The water began to drain. Then I noticed that Gerry had slipped and I had inadvertently been throwing water directly into his face. Poor Gerry.

'Sorry, mate, don't know what I'm at half the time here.' I propped him up in a more comfortable position, tightening his safety harness.

Standing up in the cockpit, I saw that the seas had moderated a little. I could swear that the hull was moving up and down less violently. Not much less, though—the waves were still around thirty feet high.

I scanned the greyness that should have been the horizon. No definition, nothing. It would have been encouraging to see anything at all, but it was still bleak out there. I stared into the abyss and began to will something to appear, a seal, porpoise, anything that might indicate we were near land. Seagulls know the weather better than any yachtsman and were most likely holed up under a hedge on the north Cornish coast. There was not one solitary living thing in the sky. This was a mournful place to be.

I was preparing to head back below when I did finally spot something in the distance. Whatever it was disappeared behind a curling wave. I took the whistle from my life jacket and waited for the wave to pass. Like a man-overboard drill, I kept my eyes focused on the spot where I was sure I had seen something. What I'd glimpsed could be a boat. The wave passed but nothing came into sight. Frustrated, I scanned the area rigorously. Still nothing. Determined to get a better view, I decided to get up on the cabin roof, the highest point now the mast was severed.

On my hands and knees, I pulled myself along, slowly, carefully. Unexpectedly, *Grimalkin*'s stern was lifted by a surging swell, leaving me hanging. My grip held firm, but I found myself looking down into the bottom of a trough thirty feet below. Terrified, I retreated, deciding that attempting this manoeuvre in these rolling, unpredictable seas was reckless. I was bound to fall in.

Back in the cockpit I waited, still watching. Was it an illusion, a trick of the light? A shiver went through me—my body was succumbing fast to the wind chill. Finally I concluded that I would be better off down below. At least, when I was bailing, my circulation was being boosted by the activity.

It was hard not to feel deflated. I looked at my scratched mark on the bulkhead—studying it closely, I thought levels were up rather than down. Small vortex-like whirlpools kept appearing all around me, adding to my confusion. With so much movement it was almost impossible to tell, but for the sake of my sanity I concluded that the water level must be the same. Starting to bail again, I became aware that my body felt more sluggish. With the water lapping up against my freezing shins and knees, I felt so very cold now. The wind may have been bitter up on deck but the water down here was colder.

I carried on bailing but found it impossible to be optimistic. The energising effects of the milk had diminished and the liquid had gone straight through me, filling my bladder. This was no place for niceties, so I let go. It was instant relief. I was wonderfully warm for a moment, then colder than before—smelly too. Filling a bucket with bilge water, I doused myself down. But the coldness shocked me and with this my left knee gave way and I head-butted the companionway. I heard the crunch of wood against bone. That was it—it was time for a break.

Too exhausted to climb up into the cockpit, I undid my harness and clambered onto my soaking bunk. I took short, sharp intakes of cold breath while clenching and unclenching my toes in my boots, trying to keep my circulation going. Afraid of falling asleep, I started to whistle. 'The Windmills of Your Mind'. The music just came into my head. Then I sang it—it felt good. I was no Noel Harrison but I sang my socks off until I was completely breathless.

Lying there, I began to hear eerie noises again, noises that only something afloat and waterlogged could make. To banish them, I allowed the music of my favourite album into my head: Pink Floyd's *Dark Side of the Moon*. I remembered every sound effect, from ticking clocks to cash registers, and I sang out the words.

More sound effects pounded through my head. I could hear the noise of helicopter rotors—another sound effect from this same album. My God, if only this joyous sound was real. Time passed. How much, I couldn't tell. Exhausted and somewhat light-headed, I finally dragged myself off the bunk to the companionway's entrance.

I looked into the cockpit. Gerry was still there, clipped on. I climbed into it, clipped myself on and looked around. It wasn't exactly a brand-new day, but I noticed the first patches of blue among the lighter clouds. What was the time? Where was the sun? I looked at the compasses. One was swinging drunkenly off its pivot; the other showed us pointing north or near on. With all this I guessed it was around 2 p.m. Although it was cold, the blueness of the sky, like my singing, had perked me up.

I propped Gerry up, then returned to the cycle of bailing and resting. I made concerted efforts to keep my brain alert. I shouted up to Gerry about Japan, about the traditional lodgings I'd stayed in while in Osaka with Ma. I told him about the next-door neighbour's minah bird, which had been trained to swear in English and Japanese. It had kept Ma awake, shouting at three in the morning, 'Bloody English' and 'Piss off, *gijan*.'

I reckoned I was boring Gerry with Japan so I began to sing again. I wanted music that meant something to me, so I allowed the Canadian melancholy of Joni Mitchell to fill my head. I belted out all of her classics. Singing helped the buckets of water out through the companionway opening. Some flew back in my face but I went on bailing. I had to do something to prevent me from giving up. Hopelessness was a place of no return.

As the afternoon wore on, the water level inside the hull was no lower, in fact it was undeniably higher. I felt like the Dutch boy with his finger in the dyke. My surroundings were becoming claustrophobic. It seemed as if *Grimalkin*'s interior was shrinking, the sides of her hull distorted as water continued flowing up and down her length. And the smell was overpowering. I was aware that the amount of time I was able to bail before needing to rest was shortening greatly. I wanted to lie down again but lying down mean more discomfort—resting in a wet, pitching stench.

I thought constantly about thirst. Dehydration was becoming my overriding fear. I became convinced that there had to be something else liquid or at least edible in this swirling mass. To hell with the bailing—I needed fluid. I hooked up the blue bucket and was back on my hands and knees, combing as far as my rope allowed, searching for sustenance. Less than a minute into my hunt I scooped up a silver tin—it had to be baked beans. I held the can in my shaking right hand. I'd been here before: a source of nutrition and energy, but no means of opening it. I tore off my gloves, gripped the can tightly in my numb fingers and began to whack it into the broken companionway ladder. Apart from a small dent, the only result was several cuts to my inflamed palms. I moved towards the cooker with the intention of smashing this damn tin open, but instead a huge wave pitched *Grimalkin* downwards, sweeping me off my feet as it went. I lost the can in the seething mess. I picked myself up, drenched after the fall, and slumped onto my soaked bunk.

What else could I do? The fruitless scavenging through sewage and bilge had left me so wrecked I couldn't imagine being able to move again. I looked at my hands. They were white and bloated; the swollen knuckles even looked like Gerry's. I saw how bloodied my palms were by the self-inflicted cuts. Christ, what was I doing to myself?

I stared blankly up at the headlining, praying for help, for dry clothing, for water, for food. I was distressed and upset, and my thoughts drifted from hunger and pain back to the same ongoing worry. Why had nobody come? The winds had calmed enough and the skies were getting clearer. Were they even looking? Had they given up the search? Then it struck me like a thunderbolt—maybe we had been presumed dead.

My legs began to stiffen with cramp and spasmodic pain, particularly the left one. I found it odd to feel pain in my left leg; I had to assume it was due to the injury I got while in the water. My left side was always more susceptible to cold, so maybe these freezing conditions were helping to bring the pain on. At least I was able to move the leg. I tried flexing it within the confined space of my bunk. Huffing and puffing like an old man, I was forced to stop. I had hit a brick wall. I could do nothing more physically, so I had to work mentally instead. I brought to mind my two main sailing mentors: Dick Langton and Eric Tabarly. It didn't help. Even thinking of Pa did nothing to inspire me, it just frightened me to think I might never see him again.

A sharp spasm pulsated through my leg again. I let out a pained screech.

I remembered a similar pain—self-induced. Pa and Ma had watched my right hand as it firmly gripped a beam. Then, pulling myself up and out of my wheelchair, I finally took my first step. My right hand began to tremble violently and I faltered, falling to the ground in a heap. But it didn't matter; after weeks of exercise, I had willed the wasted muscles to work again.

Back on the ward, I waited impatiently to tell Sister Sampson, a tough Scottish nurse, that I had at last taken my first steps. She wrote a quote into my autograph book beside the bed. I thought it was obscure, but cool: *Never measure the height of a mountain until you have reached the top. Then you will see how low it was.* – Dag Hammarskjöld.

As I endured the long road to recovery, I began to identify with its meaning. Now, on my bunk, I wondered exactly how high this mountain was. Just then, a rain squall pounded the deck above.

Hallelujah! As though answering my prayers, the heavens had opened, releasing cold, fresh, drinkable liquid. Untying my harness, I scrambled off my bunk, faster than I had at any time during that day. I grabbed each side of the companionway and pulled myself upwards. To my dismay the downpour stopped as suddenly as it had started. I tore off my gloves, clasped my palms together, held my face up to the heavens and caught the last few drops. It wasn't enough—my mouth was barely moistened. I scoured the deck for rainwater trapped in a crevice. Turning my glove inside out, I used its fleecy lining as a sponge and soaked up water from halyard bags, winch-handle pockets, anywhere I could see it. I got on all fours and licked rain from the deck until I was satisfied I had every drop.

It had to be well into the afternoon by now. I'd be lucky to see another shower, judging by the colours and layers of cloud. From the intensity of the light it wouldn't rain like that again until after dark. Then I spotted some liquid in the cockpit well, by Gerry's foot. On my knees, I scooped it up and quickly swallowed. I felt blessed with a second wind. Despite the freezing-cold conditions I was ready to bail once more. A primal need welled within me, an absolute yearning to survive.

I retreated below again in the renewed belief that somebody, somewhere was out there looking for *Grimalkin*. I began to bail again and finally got a momentum going. I felt warmth spread slowly through my legs. With warmth came determination. The water level was going to go down—it had to.

I bailed faster and faster. Head down, concentrating hard on the bucket and the rhythm of my breaths, counting the minutes, I became fixated. A one-man, time-and-motion bucket chain. A floorboard kept banging against the galley side, hindering my rhythm. I wedged it under the table.

In the midst of all this I heard an unfamiliar sound—but I had heard many unfamiliar sounds all day, none of which had been of any use to me. I decided it didn't warrant a look, so I carried on. I had to keep going. What chance had I of getting this water level down if I was distracted by every new noise I heard? Head down, I continued bailing as if someone had hypnotised me. I heard the noise again. Although it was close, I ignored it. Then, I stopped.

I finally distinguished this noise from all the others. There was something different about the sound—it was definitely not shipboard. Increasing in volume now, it sounded clearer, more urgent, like a midge getting closer. Christ, it was a piston engine, probably a spotter plane. I dropped the bucket and scrambled to get out of the cabin but fell flat on my face in the water—my harness was still attached to the bunk pole. I swallowed copious amounts of bilge water, but I didn't care. I could hear that spotter plane so close now that nothing else mattered. Desperate to get up there, I fumbled with my harness.

'Come on, Nick, for Christ's sake—Come on!!'

I lunged at the companionway. Out on deck I saw it not far off—it looked like a Cessna. Quick, my whistle. I started blowing it, at the same time waving my arms and jumping up and down. Then I stopped, horrified. The bloody thing had not even lowered its height or banked towards us. It just flew on, as if on autopilot. Maybe he didn't spot us in this early evening light? Maybe the pilot was in a sweeping search pattern. Yes, he'd return, lower his height, change direction and see us. *See us, for God's sake!*

'Look, man! Come down,' I implored the receding aircraft. But the plane flew on. I looked to Gerry for some kind of explanation. 'That pilot's blind, surely? He must be.'

I was distraught. So near yet so far. I shook a painful fist at him, at it.

'Look at your bloody radar screen . . . Open your eyes, man!'

I stood there open-mouthed, disbelieving. My heart pounded. The sight of this spotter plane receding into the horizon knocked me back. Eventually, accepting my chance had been lost, I stepped backwards and tripped over Gerry's harness. I felt a wrath rising—I swore at Gerry, berated him again and again. I tried not to but this was beyond my control. I was angry, furious with God. He'd created this mess. Why couldn't he get us out of it?

Still seething, I turned my rage on my missing crewmates. Vengefully I questioned them and all their actions. I accused them of abandoning Gerry and me—leaving us for dead. The belief gave me the justification I needed to judge and condemn all three of them. Where were they now? Bastards, three self-centred bastards. Wrath, I'd show them wrath.

Horizon to Horizon

I let myself fall headlong into the deepest part of the cockpit. My fall was broken by the webbing of a blue harness. My eyes focused on the label—'Made in England'. Seeing this harness, cast aside, brought my deepest fears to the surface. I felt like howling out loud.

Instead, I pulled myself up into a sitting position. I caught sight of my hunchbacked, swollen-faced crewmate. My God, Gerry looked awful. Remembering my outburst, I propped him up and apologised. Apologies to Gerry seemed to have become par for the course.

'Sorry, mate, don't know what came over me.'

I looked around. *Grimalkin* had slowed considerably since the last time I'd been up here, confirming my fears that her cabin was now more waterlogged. Peering over the side, I saw that she was at a slant, bows down in the water. Only the first four handwritten letters, '*Grim*', were discernible. She was becoming less stable. A wave slopped its way on board, over the deck and into the cockpit. I felt panicky, and my first thought was to continue bailing, though if I did I risked missing another flyover or sea rescue. But to stay up here in the cockpit with Gerry was to allow *Grimalkin* to settle even lower in the water and risk sinking. I was torn by indecision.

To attempt to process my thoughts in a more rational manner, I began taking slow, deep breaths. I felt my pulse slowing back to a reasonable pace. I tried to picture my parents and what they might be doing right now. I saw Pa in our garden, tending to his roses. I could hear him, in my head; he was shouting at our cat. 'Get off the roses, you black devil.'

Breathing more easily now, I turned my thoughts to Ma. A woman with strong faith, Ma was a regular churchgoer and spent much of her spare time singing in the choir, helping with fêtes and raising funds. I suddenly felt ashamed of myself for my torrent of abuse against God. If she had heard me, what would she have thought? Dear Ma, I couldn't stop feeling guilty. And as for my condemnation of my three missing crewmates, all three of whom could now be dead . . .

Calmer, I noticed that the cloud base seemed to have lifted a bit more. *Grimalkin* no longer thrust into and through the swells. Although still at heights of twenty-five to thirty feet, the waves were longer and slower. With less of a fight on her hands, *Grimalkin* rode them more comfortably, head into the direction of the decreasing wind. It seemed as if the air pressure was rising and the weather was going to improve a bit more.

I discussed our options with Gerry—bailing versus not bailing. I pointed out that each option carried with it a huge risk. Below, I could keep trying to attack the rising level of water. It would keep me active. But I was exhausted. Hour by hour, I had become progressively weaker, and the energy expended on bailing could be conserved for survival. Or I could stay here in the cockpit and keep watch, but *Grimalkin* might sink. Of course, this could just as easily happen with me down below. This dilemma was the worst I had ever faced.

The sun began to poke through the clouds. It was uplifting to see beams of sunlight glistening off the surface. Despite the swell, the better all-round visibility convinced me that we had more chance of being spotted than at any other point that day. With this heartening thought my decision was made. I armed myself with the foghorn and my whistle. I was fully prepared for being seen and for rescue. Along with occasional blowing and honking I stood up regularly. In between, I chatted away, trying to keep mentally active.

'Tuesday evenings, eh, Gerry? What would you normally be doing?'

Only a couple of Tuesdays ago I had gone to see Queen in Southampton. I told Gerry we sat next to Brian May's mum; she had told me that Brian had been classically trained. Freddie Mercury had worn a white, one-piece suit. We continued to talk about music: folk, rock, country and western. I was frustrated because I'd meant to ask Gerry what his favourite music was. So I chose a group for him. I thought Steely Dan were appropriate. This conversation lasted for ages.

Time dragged on; still nothing happened. I began to realise that jumping up and down, sounding the foghorn, waving arms and blowing my whistle was doing no good. It just made me more tired. With the increasing visibility, all I could see was empty seas. We were drifting off to God knows where. By now I was not only exhausted but also fed up with talking to Gerry, sick of the sound of my own voice. There's only so much you can say to someone who listens but doesn't respond.

If you don't care where you are, then you're not lost. I cared. I was lost. Staring at the empty sea, it was easy to visualise things: boats, ships, lifeboats, other forms of rescue darting out from behind the rolling swells. This was making me paranoid. I had to stop it.

But I was even more scared of stopping thinking in case I fell asleep. I needed a new device to keep me alert. I began picturing the lighthouses along Cornwall's southern coast and testing my knowledge on Gerry. I reeled them off, going east, up channel to Hurst Point and the Needles over and over, until I got bored with that. Then I began reciting my family's telephone numbers, including my brother's in Hong Kong. After telephone numbers, my family's birth dates. I'd always wondered why October was so popular. Then each sign of the zodiac rolled off my tongue. I recited the list again and again until I got it right. Then I went through them backwards. I tested Gerry, tested myself—same thing, but who cared? It kept me awake.

I felt myself stiffening, getting colder. I tried to whistle, but I had no spit. My thoughts were becoming darker again. I began to worry about all the noises *Grimalkin* was making. I tried to figure out which noises meant what. I flashed back to earlier in the day, when I had considered unclipping Gerry and letting him go. This filled me with mixed emotions: guilt that I had thought of it and relief that I hadn't done it.

I suddenly craved a cigarette. I checked the outside pockets of my oilskins and found some. They were pulp. I craved chewing gum, anything that would stop my jaw shivering, get the lingering taste of salt and bile out of my system. I thought about drinking my own urine, of which there was a seemingly endless supply. Where was it all coming from? It must have been my intake of salt water. I knew drinking urine could extend life by a day or so, but I also knew that urine was saline, which would only increase the speed of dehydration.

Desperate to rid myself of these revolting tastes, I sucked on the drawstrings of my hood, rolling the plastic toggles round my sore gums. Wet but salt. I spat them out.

To windward, the sun was beginning to make its slow descent. Was there anyone else out there with us in this empty sea? Probably not. Feeling abandoned and alone, even with Gerry by my side, I began to think about the darkness and the problems it would bring. The weather might worsen again. I panicked that the two of us, in *Grimalkin*, wouldn't last another night. I was at my lowest ebb.

I asked Gerry about his beliefs. I questioned my own faith, God, Jesus, Creation itself. Faith was a kind of insurance for me; it certainly wasn't blind. As I lay there next to Gerry, pondering faith and all its implications, I spotted something in the distance. A black dot; my imagination at work again, probably. I didn't react to it, just carried on mumbling to Gerry. The small dot on the horizon got bigger, too significant to ignore. Rubbing my eyes with gloved hands, I took a good look. Disbelieving, quivering, I told Gerry I was 99 per cent sure something was heading in our direction. I kept looking. It was getting closer. There was no mistaking it now. A very large commercial vessel was coming *Grimalkin*'s way.

'Bloody hell, Gerry, it's a frigging massive boat.'

I unclipped and climbed onto the deck to gain a higher vantage point, to make us as visible as possible. From up there I blew my whistle like a maniac and used what CO_2 was left in my foghorn to sound an alarm. I shouted frantically to Gerry that even if *Grimalkin* foundered right now, we would be rescued.

Then I stopped short—the vessel wasn't slowing down. It wasn't heading in our direction any more; its course had changed before even reaching us. It was steaming on, away from *Grimalkin*.

'What the hell's going on?' I yelled at Gerry.

Then it clicked. I could see the much larger boat, but they couldn't see us. With us floating so low in the water, without even a mast to spot, how would they? My instinct was to jump in and swim to the receding boat. But what if I didn't make it? What if, while I was out there swimming to the boat, *Grimalkin* went down, taking Gerry with her? What if I drowned? I'd miss my twenty-fourth birthday—only eight days away.

Tantalised, I hung on to the guardrail as the vessel passed its nearest point to us. As it ploughed on away from us, I looked at Gerry. If one boat had missed us, sailed right past, others would too. It was inevitable.

The dot on the horizon disappeared to nothing. Had we become invisible? Were we now in some make-believe world that nobody could see? Maybe we were both dead and already in hell.

THE SURFACE OF THE WATER in the cabin had risen. I wondered if *Grimalkin*'s name had now completely disappeared into the sea. If her name vanished, surely we would too.

Wasn't *Grimalkin* the name of a character in one of Shakespeare's plays? I looked back at Gerry.

'Do you know which play it is? Come on, mate, I bet you do.'

Chatting away here to Gerry, it occurred to me how little I knew about him. How weird was that? I had shared some of my most life-changing moments with this man and I had no idea what he even did for a living.

'What do you do, Gerry? How long have you been doing that for? Do you enjoy it?'

I couldn't stop bombarding my crewmate with inane questions.

'How do you get to work? Do you drive? You lucky bugger, at least you can drive if you want to. I've got to walk or cycle.'

I told Gerry how I nearly ran over a cat once. 'I was pissed . . . A pissed epileptic on a bike! Imagine that.'

Of course! A cat. That's who Grimalkin was—the witches' cat in *Macbeth*. I read that play in Mr Moseley's class in 4G. That thought reminded me of my old school song. I hadn't forgotten a word of it.

Hamble, our school, we have made thee
What thou art today.

I stopped mid-song and called over to Gerry. 'Come on, mate, join in.' I could feel a resentment building up against Gerry and his dumb presence. I was gunning for a row. 'You don't know the words, do you, Gerry? You don't know the frigging words.'

My thoughts and anxieties accelerated.

'What have you done to help our situation, eh? You haven't bailed, you haven't found food, water . . . Nothing. Not a bloody thing.'

I went berserk. Looking him straight in the face—Christ, it had turned a funny purple colour—I asked him why he had missed the spotter plane. I accused him of seeing lifeboats, helicopters, even other yachts while I was down bailing, trying to save the boat.

'You just couldn't be bothered to tell me, could you, Gerry?'

I stopped. A disturbing image flashed through my head. An image of my crewmates leaving on the life raft. Or maybe they hadn't left at all? With my dehydration-fuelled paranoia, I managed to convince myself that my crewmates were still on the boat, trapped up in the bows. I stood up, shakily.

'Come out, come out, wherever you are!'

There was no answer. I caught sight of Gerry's green Puffa jacket, poking out of the top of his oilskins. Green, that colour, that's what caused all our bad luck. This bloody jacket is what caused the storm. About to launch into yet another tirade, I hesitated—there was a warm, wet feeling on the right side of my mouth. I pulled my glove off and wiped my mouth, and was shocked to see blood smudged across my hand. I realised that the ranting had caused my cracked lips to split and bleed.

Christ, I needed to get a grip. I was the one at fault. Not Gerry.

Slowly, the heightened feelings of the last hour or so evaporated. Less alert, but calmer, I was able to reason better. I knew I had all the signs of dehydration and hypothermia: light-headedness, confusion, irritability. I didn't need a doctor to diagnose it.

There was no need to apologise to Gerry. I knew he understood. Scanning round *Grimalkin* I saw that the weather was no longer as evil. Over the last hour or two it had greatly improved. The wind had subsided and it was now quite bright. There was still a long steep swell—that hadn't changed. But the waves were slower, not as steep. Judging by the height of the sun it was late afternoon, early evening.

I looked out across the empty nothingness. Then I saw movement. Were my eyes deceiving me?

'Christ, there's something out there, Gerry. I'm sure of it. I saw it. It's about a mile away, swerving in and out of the swell.'

My heart rose at the sight of the white of a sail. This was a lone yacht—no doubt about it. I stood up on the cabin roof and shouted to Gerry. 'It's a yacht! I can't see any crew, but it's there all right.'

Who were they? Were they waiting for rescue or could they rescue us? Then an awful thought—maybe this lone yacht had already been abandoned. Maybe it was floating free, the crew already saved. As panic mounted, I remembered the white sail. Of course there was crew. Without a working crew how could the sail have been hoisted?

I put my whistle to my mouth and blew the hell out of it. I waved my arms, jumped about, yelled, then stopped. I had spotted a yacht again, but in an entirely different place. It was closer. I saw what looked like the name *Frayola*, and by the size of her rig I guessed this was a Class IV yacht. What was going on? Were there two boats out there? It wasn't possible for one yacht to have moved position so quickly. Was any of this real? Then, sure enough, two yachts came into view simultaneously, for the briefest of moments, before disappearing behind the swell. This was miraculous.

'Gerry, there's two of them . . . there's bloody two of them!'

One of the yachts emerged again. It was close enough for me to see its hull clearly. It had at least two people on board. They waved frantically. I managed to acknowledge them before they disappeared behind a swell. It seemed an age before I saw either yacht again. While waiting, I wondered: did either yacht have a VHF radio? Could we be transferred over to one of them? This would be tricky because of the swell. With no means of communication I waited as agonising minutes passed. Then I watched as a parachute flare was launched. That flare was for us. We'd been seen, acknowledged. Thank God. Rescue was on its way, and the launching of this flare told me it would be sooner rather than later.

I shook Gerry's hand. It was colder than it had ever been before. I started crying. We were going to be saved. I slumped back into the cockpit well and for the first time that day felt a vague sense of normality. These were real boats, real people. I felt elated, but impatient too. Why weren't things happening more quickly? I dreamed of seeing Ma and Pa, my brothers, my sister Cheryl. But I had to be patient and wait.

Out of nowhere, I turned to Gerry and announced, 'One day I'd like to get married and have a family, and settle down in the village.'

I continued talking to Gerry about my hopes for the future. Intermittently I stood up to get a sighting. Time was really beginning to drag now. Minutes seemed like hours. I felt faint, but I managed to keep looking, and finally I caught sight of one of the yachts. Relieved, I sat back down. I could feel my elation beginning to fade. I had this overwhelming feeling that we were in for another huge disappointment.

I needed to do something to help pass the time. I decided to clear up some of the mess in the cockpit—it looked awful. Christ, so did Gerry. I decided to deal with him first in case rescue came quicker than I thought. With my sodden glove I began to wipe the congealed blood from round the gash on his forehead.

'There's no need for Margaret to see you in this state, hey, mate?'

I had to shift him into a better position. I was dragging his six-foot-two frame upwards when an agonising pain shot from the pit of my belly, forcing me to drop him again. As he slid back down into his original position, I slumped back into mine. This was horrific—every breath I took was cut short by a knife-like pain. Lying back, completely knackered, I felt the pain gradually ease. That was the end of that idea. Gerry was staying as he was.

The sun was beginning to set. It must be at least 8 p.m. now. Had the yachts just let off a flare and moved on? Had rescue come by lifeboat? Were they having difficulty in finding us? We were so low in the water they probably couldn't see us and maybe they had presumed we'd sunk.

Once night fell, *Grimalkin*, without illumination or navigation lights, would remain undiscovered. I thought about securing a length of chain to a sail and chucking it over the side, allowing it to act as a sea anchor. But this would have required a physical effort I no longer possessed. I could never have done it.

Above me the skies had cleared further. The sun was luminous as it made its descent. It lit up the cabin and I could see what looked like the surface of hell boiling beneath us. I watched as water occasionally spat out over the bridge deck and into the cockpit well, filling it up. This was no optical illusion—the levels were rising. I was bucketless, having thrown it back into the cabin, and had not one ounce of energy left in my body. Retrieving the bucket, let alone using it, was an option no longer.

Gerry looked even more dead than before. I found talking to him more difficult now. I felt he had gone, not physically but certainly spiritually. I thought back to that conversation with him about my future, but now I thought about the possibility of no future whatsoever. I wanted to ask him what death was really like. I had been close to it once before but Gerry knew the reality.

I gazed at him, thinking about the inevitability of our drifting undiscovered in the darkness. I began to picture *Grimalkin* sinking into the depths of the Irish Sea. These thoughts gave me a sense of control. This was a reality to be faced up to. Put simply, when *Grimalkin* sank, what would I do?

I closed my eyes, then pictured myself and Gerry still clipped securely to *Grimalkin*. She was beginning to founder, and we were both being sucked downwards. I was struggling, my head bashing against the cockpit's sides. Gerry's head was cradled in my arms. I could smell death on him, it pervaded his lank hair and coarse stubble. Why was I clinging to him? Because I had to; there was no way I was going alone.

Grimalkin's deck canted steeply then plunged vertically under the surface and she began her final journey into the depths of the Irish Sea. I pictured myself, eyes smarting but open, looking around at *Grimalkin*. I saw her dragging Gerry and me by our safety harnesses ever downwards, bubbles of air surrounding us. I saw the surface of the water now twenty feet above us. As the last rays of light disappeared I wondered how long I should hold my breath for. I heard myself wanting to ask Gerry: How long before I die? He would know. Please God, make it quick. I didn't want to be alive when I hit the seabed.

I opened my eyes and found myself still above the surface, with Gerry three feet from me. I had scared myself almost to death. What was I doing? I had to get these scenarios out of my head. I saw the sun's top just above the horizon. The light was about to disappear. I tried to stand up to scan the seas one last time, before the light went but couldn't. Had I even seen the yachts at all?

My breathing had become quick and shallow. My brain seemed to be shutting down, along with other vital organs.

'I must not fall asleep, I must not fall asleep.'

But wouldn't it be better? Why not? My eyelids closed. I began to drift off. I thought of home, family, warm clean sheets. All was serene. I heard the strains of a wonderful symphonic tune. God, what was that tune? The beautiful tune changed into a pulsating beat, an unwanted mechanical sound effect—rock music. The last thing I wanted to hear now was Pink Floyd. I wanted it out of my head but its beat quickened: chop, chop, chop, increasing in intensity. I opened my eyes and looked up. I saw a blurred, light grey thing suspended in the sky, no more than a quarter of a mile away. Was this another trick? I couldn't cope with another knockback.

Then the downdraught from rotating rotors created swirling shapes on the surface of the heaving sea and I knew this was no delusion—it was the unmistakable metronome beat of a helicopter. Royal Naval help had arrived.

'Gerry, look, mate, look . . . It's a helicopter, it's a Sea King.' And in my bemused state I pointed to the sky and wept.

The navy-grey helicopter circled us. The noise was extraordinary. I could see the pilot clearly, and the winchman standing at the open door. A crewman waved down to me, to let me know he was coming. I'd been waiting for this moment all day but I felt unprepared, as if I had been caught off guard. What would the crew think? Gerry was lying in a precarious position; he was bloodied. I was bloodied. I realised, finally, that none of it mattered. We were being rescued; they'd understand.

Within moments the crewman was descending on a cable towards the cockpit, but with *Grimalkin* still rising and falling some twenty or thirty feet it became evident that his descent was going to be hindered. As he got lower he began to swing more violently, rotating on what must have been well over 100 feet of cable. His landing area was tiny. The pilot was trying to adjust height and pitch to suit the rise and fall of the yacht, but watching my rescuer struggle in the crosswind and with the downdraught, I panicked. What if he had to abort the landing? Perhaps I could help him—pull his legs over the pushpit. But this young man required no help from me. He was purposeful and strong. His boots hit the deck with some force. The light reflected off his visor so that I couldn't see his eyes. I was ecstatic to see someone else. I stared at him. He began shouting and gesticulating but I couldn't hear what he was trying to say. Finally I understood—he was going to lift Gerry first—Gerry's purgatory was over.

The crewman unclipped himself and asked if I was OK. I wanted to tell him everything—all that had happened to me and to Gerry, but I just nodded and said, 'Fine . . . Fine, thanks.'

This guy with all his gear had a huge physical presence and commanded instant respect. The very opposite of me—filthy, smelly and unkempt.

One glance and I felt sure he knew that Gerry was dead. I felt guilty that I hadn't been able to position my friend in a more dignified way. I began to murmur an apology, but the crewman was so busy doing his thing he didn't hear. He unclipped Gerry first, then turned him over onto his back, just as I had tried and failed to do. *Grimalkin* was still moving severely with the swell and he was forced to stop several times. Finally he managed to loop his heavy webbing strop under Gerry's armpits. I watched as he manipulated Gerry's stiff upper limbs into a position where he could be lifted off the boat. What a heart-wrenching sight, poor Gerry. I fell backwards and found myself sitting in the furthest corner of the cockpit. I wondered again if I was the only one of the crew left alive.

A thick shiny steel wire was being lowered towards the boat—it took several attempts before it was secured. I watched in awe as this young man managed to hold on to Gerry's fourteen-and-a-half-stone dead weight and secure the wire before attaching it to them both. This was it then. With a sharp cracking noise they were snatched off the deck.

The sadness I felt at watching Gerry leaving *Grimalkin* was overwhelming. Events were now overtaking me. With the constant downdraught, I was shivering violently. My teeth felt as if they might fall out of their sockets. I became uneasy. How long could the Sea King stay before having to return to base to refuel? What was its range?

Then the crewman reappeared. He was on his way down to me. I heard an almighty thump as he landed on the deck. He began to pull me to my feet. I reached up, trying to clutch the wire.

'Don't touch the safety wire—it's static,' he shouted.

What harm was a bit of static going to do me? But he was emphatic, impatient to get me off the boat.

'I have to get my gear.' As soon as I said it, I saw a look of sympathy, pity even. Christ, I felt pathetic.

Squeezing my arm gently he said, 'There's no time. She's going down. We have to get off the boat.'

These were his orders. I had to let him take control. Before I knew it, his strop was looped round me just as it had been with Gerry. Strapped to him now, I could see his face clearly. I wondered if he could smell me? He shouted for me to try to be still, then edged his way off the deck. The strop tightened round my chest; my armpits hurt like hell as I was lifted off the deck. I didn't care. I lay there, passive for the first time in hours. The view from this vantage point was amazing. The seas looked almost benign. Looking from horizon to horizon I saw the two boats. I was amazed at the clarity of the view of them and their waving crews. Not so long beforehand I had wondered if they were a figment of my imagination. There they had been all the time. I felt immense gratitude that they must have waited all those hours for our rescue.

About fifty feet up, looking straight down, I saw our abandoned boat and how ravaged she was. Her deck was strewn with wreckage. Damn, I had left her companionway open, with no washboards in place to keep the seas out. I wondered how long it would be before she foundered. Only a miracle could keep her afloat through the night.

The open door of the helicopter appeared in front of me and I was pulled in to safety. My legs wobbled as they guided me to a bench. There I sat, speechless. Gerry had been laid out behind a bulkhead and covered by a blanket. Someone placed ear defenders over my freezing ears. One of the crew signalled for me to deflate my life jacket. I was unnerved by this request. This life jacket had saved my life, time after time. Deflating it made me feel insecure. I felt I was outside what was going on. Everything around me looked alien. I saw a radar screen and my eyes followed its bright green indicator, tracking like a single clock hand round its black screen.

We were headed off somewhere—where, I had no idea. I wanted to ask questions about my crewmates and my family but apart from a few hand signals there was no conversation. The engine noise was too loud. The lack of communication made me suspicious. I could see the blanket that covered Gerry, but not Gerry himself. This was very distressing. I needed to talk to Gerry, to find out what he really wanted me to say to Margaret—were those few words enough? I wanted to feel for his pulse, just in case. This unfamiliar, noisy environment compounded the confusion I felt.

Then there it was—the coastline of England. This first sight of land gave me a great boost; my panic turned to elation as the land got bigger and the helicopter began to bank. This was like no other landfall I'd made before. From a side window I saw hedgerows, two tractors, a horse grazing. The boundaries of an airfield and then grey tarmac came into view. As we got lower I saw a large yellow H painted on the tarmac. There was a bump and then the sliding side door opened.

A military ambulance stood by. I tried to stand up but couldn't—my legs were like jelly. One of the crew gestured to me to stay seated. Gerry was laid onto a stretcher, then put into the ambulance. I watched as the ambulance drove away from us. Gerry and I were now separated; I hated that.

I was helped into a wheelchair on the tarmac. I saw the pilot, high up in his cab—he put his right thumb up. I wanted to thank him, thank everyone, but I couldn't. Everyone was smiling as though we were all long-lost friends. I was whisked away towards what looked like the entrance to a sick bay. Over the door was a sign that read: RNAS CULDROSE NAVAL BASE.

Once inside I was transferred from the wheelchair onto a trolley, where I was laid flat but with my head propped up. A bath was being filled. Christ, I craved water. As though she had read my thoughts, a nurse held a glass to my mouth. That first glassful didn't touch my throat. Despite the pain, I drank three, maybe four glasses before the nurse said, 'Enough.' I told her that I was epileptic and that I needed phenobarbitone as quickly as possible. She assured me that this would be arranged.

She then put some ointment on my lips and the naval doctors and the Wrens stripped me. There was no messing around. The room was hot. Briskly they rubbed me down with starched white towels. I wondered why when I was about to be plunged into a bath of steaming water. The nurse smiled at me and said, 'We have to get your circulation going.'

I nodded, too weary to question any more. They knew what they were doing. They immersed me in the huge bath full of water almost too hot to bear. This is standard practice for victims of hypothermia, to get the core body temperature up. I was asked questions about my condition and how I felt. I was hot but shivering at the same time. I asked a nurse if Ma and Pa had been contacted. She didn't know. I asked if anybody else had been brought here; nobody answered. Staring at my blue toes under the almost scalding water, I feared the worst. In sailing terms no news meant bad news.

A doctor came in, carrying a clipboard. He called me by my full name. I immediately asked if anyone else had been rescued from the yacht *Grimalkin*. He flicked through his clipboard—two or three pages.

'It's kilo five six three seven,' I said, willing him to find the names.

Without lifting his eyes he carried on. My gaze switched to the white tiles in front of me—this wait was killing me.

'Yes,' he said matter-of-factly. 'Three other men.'

I knew this must be Matt, Dave and Mike. 'And the fourth man? David Sheahan, the skipper. What of him?'

The doctor shook his head. 'Still missing, I'm afraid.'

Poor David; he was dead. Everyone in the room knew it. I could tell by the uneasy faces. I stared at the tiles, shocked but at the same time relieved; the others were alive, thank God, they had made it. I was going to ask how or where they had been recovered. I sank back into the bath. Not now. Something told me the implications would be too much to handle right now.

I was dressed in warmed pyjamas, then taken to a side room where I was helped into a preheated iron-framed bed. Lying in my bed, I was sure I saw, through the half-open door, Gerry, sitting in his bath, just as I had done, with a doctor beside him writing notes. I wanted to tell him that Gerry was dead and had been since early this morning. Poor Gerry, he looked as if he was just sleeping. And then the door was pushed shut.

That was the last time I saw Gerry.

MY DOOR OPENED. A trolley came in, pushed along by a smiling nurse. I smelt eggs—I'd forgotten how hungry I was. It had been over twenty-four hours since I'd last eaten. It felt more like a month. The nurse propped me up in bed and I ate scrambled egg piled high on buttered bread. My hand shook as I held the fork. I drank warm milk, lots of it. I felt better.

'My parents . . . Do they know? Has anybody—'

The nurse smiled reassuringly. 'Don't worry, Nick. Everything's been taken care of. Those who need to know, know.'

I drifted off, knowing I was safe. Sleep came easily but was disturbed by images of Gerry and David. In the morning I woke with a start. I thought I was fitting but realised I had been dreaming. In this dream I had seen Gerry mumbling through his abnormally coloured lips, repeating something over and over, something important. How could I forget? Those words were etched on my brain. Slowly, full awareness of my new surroundings registered.

Later that morning I was taken to Treliske Hospital in Truro. After being admitted I was visited by a journalist from the *Herald Tribune*. Although courteous and understanding, this man was a stranger and I wished he'd go away. At this point all I wanted was to see my family. The journalist left and later I was informed that Ma, Pa and my brother Simon were on their way. They had had to wait for news of where I was being transferred to before travelling. It was now early evening and it would be the following morning before I saw them.

I knew that in order for me to explain anything to my family, to officials, to my surviving crewmates, but mostly to myself, I would have to write it down—as it had happened, chronologically, watch by watch, knockdown by knockdown. What I needed now was paper and a pen. With a dozen sheets of paper before me, I wrote. I wrote motivated by guilt for not being able to save Gerry. I had to write it down to prove that I'd tried—a hard-copy proof for myself and for others.

So I began at Cowes, with the start—the weather, the crew, David, Gerry, Matt, the boat—all so fresh in my head. I wrote all of it down. This came easily, but the sequence of events just before I woke up in the water, that would have to wait. As far as I knew—I'd heard someone mention it the previous night—*Grimalkin* had gone down. Nine nonstop pages later, I'd run out of things I knew. I felt cleaner, as if by writing I'd washed. I put the sheaf of paper in the top drawer of my bedside table, to keep it safe until I knew what to do with it. I had a disturbed but less painful sleep that night.

The next day, Thursday, August 16, I was given a bed bath and then a shave by a kind young nurse. This same nurse soon had me sitting in a chair, but I ached so much that as soon as my bed was made up I had to lie on it. I soon found myself drifting off again.

Later that morning I heard more than one set of footsteps approaching—

instinctively I knew who it was. I opened my eyes and saw Ma, Pa and Simon walking towards me. Poor Ma, she looked so tiny as she stood there between Pa and Simon. There was a total loss of words so we just hugged. Ma wept, then so did I. It was such a relief to be in their presence. Later the young nurse brought in tea and biscuits and things slowly began to feel more normal. Ma told me our black cat, Tom, had gone missing for the whole time I had and only reappeared after they had received the phone call to say that I had been found safe. Pa reckoned Tom had been hiding from the storm but Ma was adamant it was a sign. I found myself talking but it was small talk. Eventually Pa looked me straight in the eye.

'What happened out there, son?'

I shrugged my shoulders. It was not so much reticence on my part as ignorance—I simply did not know. I quickly realised that my family knew far more than I did. They had heard radio broadcasts, spoken to race control, to Gay, to Margaret, and others too.

Pa told me that Matt, Mike and Dave had left *Grimalkin* on the life raft and been air-rescued at about 9.30 a.m. I went numb. Although Pa continued talking, I tuned out as the realisation dawned on me. At the time my three crewmates had been rescued, Gerry was still alive.

I was overcome with nausea. I told my family that that was enough. I knew now what I wanted to do with my notes from the previous night. I handed Pa the nine sheets of paper, asking him to read them later. He put them carefully in his coat pocket.

Later that day, Gerry's wife, Margaret, visited me. Even though I'd spent hours alone with this woman's husband, I was terrified. I do not recall much about her visit, only that we both, obviously, found it distressing, particularly when I passed on Gerry's last words. I'd been rehearsing them to ensure that what Gerry had told me came out right—exactly as he had said it to me on the boat. Margaret wiped her eyes; she looked drawn. I wanted to hug her but couldn't. I felt I was imposing on her grief. If she were someone I knew well, I could have. I wanted to know if she was taking Gerry home with her, but there was no way I could have asked her. Her grief was such that she asked no other questions of me. I had no idea at that time if she knew the circumstances under which we had been found. I did not know if she had seen or spoken to Matt, Dave or Mike; if she'd had an explanation from them of what had gone on. I knew nothing and did not ask. Margaret squeezed my hand and as she left I felt emptiness, and a slight sense of shame, wishing I could have said more to comfort her.

On Friday, August 17, I was released and the next day I was back in Hamble—it was so great to be home. I was still finding it difficult to talk about what had happened. So home was where I stayed. August 22 was my twenty-fourth birthday.

The day after my birthday I learned I had been the last survivor taken from the water during the Fastnet Race. That same day I received a newspaper article about Peter Harrison—a crewmember of Sea King 819. It was Peter Harrison who had come down on the wire to rescue me. He described how, after two hours of patrolling, the crew had spotted a dismasted white yacht with two motionless men in her cockpit. It was now just after 8.45 p.m. and getting dark so rescue was going to have to be executed quickly. Before he made his descent, he saw that one of the men was moving. He landed on the deck and this man, the younger of the two, had tears pouring down his cheeks and kept saying he had to get his clothes from the cabin. Peter then described how the other man, lying in the bottom of the cockpit, said nothing and it took a moment for him to realise that he was dead.

Strangely, I remembered the clothes but not the tears. It was surreal reading this, as though this article was about somebody else.

In another report I found out that the aircrew had been unaware there was anyone still alive on board *Grimalkin*, until they'd seen me in the cockpit. Their mission at that point was recovery, not rescue. The two yachts were not mentioned, so I can only surmise that while it was they who made the mayday call, they were unable to relay that there was a person alive on board. On reading this I felt all the luckier for being alive.

Aftermath

Early the following week I found to my delight that *Grimalkin* had not foundered after all. It seemed almost miraculous that she was not at the bottom of the Irish Sea. A Royal Navy helicopter crew had found her drifting not far from where Gerry and I had been lifted and had made her as watertight as possible. She was towed to a safe haven, but where, I did not know.

Fastnet 1979 was the biggest peacetime sea-and-air rescue operation that had ever taken place. There had been fifteen fatalities, twenty-four crews had abandoned ship, five yachts had sunk, 136 sailors had been rescued and only eighty-five of the 303 yachts managed to finish the race. Many different organisations were involved, including the Royal Navy, the Royal National Lifeboat Institution, the RAF, Her Majesty's Coastguard, and others. I heard that the Royal Western Yacht Club in Plymouth had been overwhelmed with enquiries about relatives and boats. There were no computerised switchboards in 1979, just a team doing its best to give out accurate information. Ma described it as being like the war, waiting for news to come in.

Pa and I were shocked to hear that the future of the race was in jeopardy. Despite all I had been through, I did not want to see Fastnet brought to an end. But people wanted answers. Inevitably most of the blame was put on the Royal Ocean Racing Club, who had organised the event. An inquiry was commissioned.

Over the weeks that followed, an intrigue was beginning to build around the events on *Grimalkin*. Why had we been left? National newspaper articles appeared, detailing our two separate rescues. After reading the press and my handwritten document, Pa wanted answers, my family and friends too. As I got better, so did I. But this was not proving easy.

Since my rescue, not one of my surviving crewmates had contacted me. Any information I had got so far was through word of mouth or in the press. I found myself asking people at my sailing club, and other people who had done the Fastnet that year, if they had heard anything. But nobody could add to what I had been able to deduce myself.

I felt it was inappropriate for me to make contact with my crewmates. But their seeming lack of concern nagged at me constantly. What had I done to them? Why didn't they have the guts to pick up the telephone? Matt, the only one I knew at all well, was grieving for his father, whose body was yet to be recovered; how could I call him?

In early September, Gay Sheahan telephoned and asked me to accompany Matt to locate *Grimalkin* in the Irish seaside town of Waterford. I was touched by her request. I hoped I could finally find out what had taken place on *Grimalkin* between the time I lost and then regained consciousness on that horrific morning of August 14.

Gay arranged for me to travel up to Camberley and stay overnight. I couldn't help but feel I was imposing on their grief but Gay was extremely kind. The next morning Matt and I caught the train to Fishguard to catch the ferry across the Irish Sea.

At first there was much uncomfortable small talk on both our parts. Then I pressed Matt. He told me his account of what had happened in the time that Gerry and I were unconscious. When *Grimalkin* had capsized, he'd been thrown clear of the boat and pinned just beneath the deck. From this position he was only able to grab the occasional lungful of air.

After a couple of minutes the boat started to right herself and Matt was flung back into the cockpit. The first thing he noticed was that the boat had been dismasted. Then he saw Gerry and me lying in the cockpit covered in rope and debris—unconscious or possibly dead. Dave and Mike were hanging on outside the boat so he had to help them back on board. It was then that he saw a body face-down in the water. The boat was drifting away from the body and he knew it was his dad, but there was nothing he could do. Hearing this from Matt was shocking. I really felt for him. But why had this happened? Why had David's harness not saved him?

Matt told me that his dad, who was unconscious, had got trapped underneath the capsized boat, and a crewmember had been forced to use his pocketknife to cut the line in order to bring him up for air. The crewmember then lost hold of David, who was washed away. This explained the cut line, and confirmed my image of David being washed away. Whoever had cut the line did it to save David's life, but in doing so there was always the risk that he would be washed away. This dilemma is not unheard of for crews caught in heavy storm conditions. Matt made it clear that he felt it was the right thing to do. Put in that position, any one of us would have cut the line to try to save David. He did not say who had cut the line, and I respected him for that, but I felt sure that it wasn't Matt himself.

Matt was faced with a decision—Dave and Mike wanted to leave the boat on the life raft. Gerry and I were in the cockpit buried under all sorts of debris. He told me they tried to move us, but couldn't. To the three of them—Matt, Mike and Dave—Gerry and I looked dead. He told me that it had not been an easy decision—the most difficult of his life—but what was he to do? Stay on a sinking boat alone with two crewmates he thought were dead? He made the decision to go. My three crewmates launched the life raft and after an hour or so of what he described as sheer hell, they were rescued by helicopter. My sympathy for Matt began to diminish. He sensed the change in me and closed down.

This latter part of the explanation was, to my mind, vague. It was also not exactly the one I wanted to hear. I wanted to hear that he, Dave and Mike had tried to resuscitate Gerry and me, that they'd checked our pulses, that they'd tried to give us mouth-to-mouth, that they'd tried to transfer us to the life raft. But it seemed that they had collectively decided to leave us.

I didn't quiz Matt further. I wanted to ask him why he, they, hadn't tried harder, but something prevented me from doing so. Maybe I was protecting him, a young man grieving for his father; maybe I was protecting myself from answers I could not bear to hear. I didn't go into any detail concerning the hours I spent alone with Gerry. Matt didn't ask—I didn't offer. But I thought it strange he didn't want to know. I wanted to pour my guts out but I couldn't. I felt that if I took things any further, our already strained companionship might turn into open animosity. So it was all small talk after that but with an underlying air of tension.

Near the quay in Waterford was *Grimalkin*. She was sitting on a trailer, looking out of place and sad. We climbed the ladder set against her stern and my first thought was: What a bloody awful mess.

Matt and I were both taken aback by what we saw and found. This was the one time on the trip when we felt at ease with each other: during our reunion with *Grimalkin*. Above deck, particularly in the cockpit, metres of ropes and lines were still strewn all around. Down below, the washing-machine action of *Grimalkin* during the storm was amply demonstrated when Matt discovered that one of her main batteries was wedged right up in the bows. It had travelled a distance of about twenty feet, taking a chunk of the boat with it on its way. The forces generated by the knockdowns and pitchpoles were tremendous—it was testimony to why we had all stayed above deck.

Grimalkin's port topsides were badly scratched and damaged. The starboard side of the coach roof was staved in, its cabin windows smashed, caused, obviously, by the final B2 capsize and subsequent dismasting. We were able to recover a few personal possessions, but almost everything aboard smelt of diesel oil or was damaged.

Nearing the end of our inspection I was very moved to hear Matt say how determined he was to get *Grimalkin* sailing again. He was sure that that was what David, his father, would have wanted.

During these days away from home, Matt and I didn't converse much. Apart from the chat we'd had on the train, talk of what had gone on was avoided. Finding and assessing *Grimalkin* were our objectives. We travelled back home and went our separate ways.

Several weeks passed, but David's body was not recovered. A memorial service for him was held at St Michael's Church in Yorktown, Camberley. The large church was packed and it was obvious that, well beyond his family, David would be sorely missed.

It was an emotional, dignified service. My heart went out to Gay and her young family. I didn't see either Dave or Mike there; I made a point of looking out for them but there was such a throng I could easily have missed them. I felt disappointed. At least Matt and I had talked, had a closure of sorts, even if an unsatisfactory one. On the journey back I became very upset. I found it almost unbearable that no one was going to add to the vague details I had been given by Matt earlier that month. I felt isolated by my crewmates. I wanted face-to-face answers, from all three of them, but there was nothing I could do. Pa assured me that an inquiry would examine all aspects of the disaster. For the moment I had to try to put it all to the back of my mind.

I did this by taking some positive action. I wrote many letters of thanks to those involved in the finding of *Grimalkin*, including a very personal letter of gratitude to Peter Harrison. It was not easy to trace the two yachts, however. I had seen '*Frayola*' written on the stern of the smaller one. I checked the official entry list and there was no yacht of this name, but there was a French-owned yacht *Fragola*. She was owned by a G.J.C. des Glenans, and had retired from the race. I felt sure that this boat had retired as a result of assisting *Grimalkin*.

I made every effort to find an address for Monsieur des Glenans and the home port of his yacht *Fragola*, but could find nothing. This being nearly thirty years ago, everything was by letter or word of mouth. While this search was proving fruitless, I did come across other information, including details about Gerry. He had been advised by his doctors not to sail on the Fastnet—I was reminded of Margaret's anxious face as she saw Gerry off. I found out that he was Irish; with that wild mop of red hair it made sense. Gerry had lived in London for nearly thirteen years and he ran an employment agency there. Saddest of all was that Gerry had married Margaret the previous year. They'd had only a year of married life together before he was cruelly taken from her. Reading this personal detail about Gerry was odd. Being with him during his final moments had left me with the feeling I knew him well. But the reality was I barely knew him at all.

For some time I experienced what would now be labelled post-traumatic stress, waking up in the middle of the night seeing images of Gerry and David. I also began experiencing more seizures. Ma would knock on my door to wake me for work and find me writhing, half asleep, in the middle of a fit.

I never found those two yachts I owe such a debt to. It is more than likely that the two boats were sold on and have new names. Although I never located them, just trying to helped me get back into the swing of things.

I wanted to know how the storm came about, why there was no warning, and how so many boats got caught up in the middle of it. I did a great deal of reading on the subject and was surprised to find that storms of similar ferocity had occurred before: in 1917, 1923, 1931, 1957 and 1975—all in the month of August. But the speed at which this force-10 storm swept across the Atlantic Ocean confounded forecasters.

Since the storm of 1979, technology has moved on apace. Depressions are tracked now in 'real time' from on board yachts, via sophisticated weather prediction and forecasting computer programs. But one thing we can be assured of is no matter how accurate weather predicting has become, Mother Nature can overturn it in an instant.

In October 1979 I received a questionnaire as part of the Fastnet Race Inquiry. Later that month one of the inquiry officials paid me a visit and put more questions to me. I felt better able to describe what had happened in this more personal way.

In late 1979 the official report was published. I went up to my bedroom to read the seventy-six-page document. When I came to the following paragraphs I knew immediately that this was what I had been looking for.

> The yacht rolled through 180° and remained upside down for a period of time estimated by various members of the crew to have been between two and five minutes. Two of the crew were thrown clear but remained attached by their harnesses. A third crewman extricated the skipper by cutting his safety harness, but after bringing him to the surface he lost his grasp on him and the skipper was washed out of reach. One of the three crewmen in the water climbed onto the upturned hull and the yacht then righted herself, dismasted.
>
> The three conscious survivors were able to climb back on board. They found that two crewmembers who had been trapped in the cockpit throughout the capsize were lying motionless in the bottom of the

cockpit and assumed they were dead. They launched the life raft and abandoned the yacht. They were unable to do anything about recovering the skipper and they were subsequently rescued by helicopter.

One of the unconscious casualties came to some time later, in the water alongside the hull. (It seems that the yacht may have capsized again while he was unconscious.) He was able to climb back on board and with the aid of a winch he pulled his semi-conscious companion into the boat. His companion was still alive and responded to resuscitation but died about three-quarters of an hour later. The one remaining survivor spent some 12 hours bailing the disabled yacht and keeping a lookout for rescue before being lifted off by helicopter.

ALTHOUGH MATT had given me his account of what had happened, it hadn't really sunk in until now. Everything that I pieced together on *Grimalkin* had indeed happened. As for our being left on the boat, much though I wanted to deny it, I could no longer do so: we had been abandoned. We had been left for dead—that was fact. But there was still something unaccounted for. If I had managed, on my own, to pull Gerry back on board and resuscitate him, why couldn't they have done the same for me and Gerry when the boat was upright with us in it?

The report was not easy reading and while I felt it was well put together and accurate, it did not tell the whole story of the storm or explain in detail the events that took place on *Grimalkin*. I didn't even know whether all three of my surviving crewmates had been interviewed. Looking back now I realise that each individual death, including Gerry's, should have had its own separate inquest. That way all the questions would have been answered.

As for safety precautions aboard *Grimalkin*, from my point of view there were no issues to account for. *Grimalkin* had qualified by sailing the required mileage; she was equipped with more safety equipment than the rules required. She had three radios, two for two-way communication (some boats had none). David Sheahan had provided the right tools for the job. We were simply not able to deal with the storm. The storm dealt with us.

Although the race fleet was spread out between Land's End and the Fastnet Rock, most of the helicopter activity was within a forty- to forty-five-mile radius around seventy miles northwest of Land's End. At 6 a.m. on August 14, *Grimalkin*'s reported position was thirty miles northwest of Land's End based on the previous evening's fix; she was described at this time as being capsized. An hour and a quarter later her position was reported a further thirty-five miles northwest, by whom I am not sure, possibly another boat. So there was some confusion over her exact position, which led to me and Gerry being left undiscovered for so long.

There were some questions that remained unanswered, but what could I do? Dwell on this for the rest of my days? Unlike my shipmate Gerry, I was alive, and I intended living my life to the full.

I HAVE BEEN ASKED many times how I managed to survive. I can link it to three things. The first is that at the age of fifteen, I survived a near-death experience: my brain haemorrhage. I had to relearn many basic skills, such as walking. I took things stage by stage. I set goals and targets for myself. I didn't waste any time. I retrained the fingers, the toes, the muscles of my body's left side, laid waste by paralysis. It took months; it was painful, but, young and determined, I managed. My ultimate goal was to be able to sail again. What I had to work hard on was dexterity. It has been proved that someone who has had a near-death experience is more likely to survive another one, and I can see that this was true for me.

My brain haemorrhage and subsequent operation left me with epilepsy. This is the second link. Fits, once considered a stigma, disabled me but I learned to cope with the love and support of my family. Some weaknesses are in fact strengths. These strengths, learned at a young age, helped me to survive on *Grimalkin*.

Gerry was the third, the most important link, in this chain of survival. I wish that I could have said this to Margaret, when I had the chance, twenty-five years ago. But at that time I was in such deep shock that I was unaware of exactly how big a part he had played. It is simply this: without that man, I would have perished. Even in death, he brought me life.

I BEGAN WRITING a book in September 2004, soon after meeting Sinéad. I found it hard so I stopped, feeling that maybe I was not yet ready for it. Sinéad and I kept in touch as she researched for the documentary. She often mailed me with questions and sometimes with information that she had found while researching. Although the events were never far from my thoughts, I had avoided thinking deeply about them. The process of being asked questions was invigorating, and it also forced me to face things I had blocked out for many years. At times I felt myself becoming angry, even bitter. The bitterness was mainly brought on by the action my three crewmates took in the early morning of Tuesday, August 14, 1979.

During Christmas 2004, my son Sam celebrated his seventeenth birthday. It was then the realisation hit me. I pictured Matt as the carefree young man I'd known at the age my son was turning now. Back in 1979, to me, Matt had been a man—self-assured and capable of decision. But he wasn't. He had been a teenager like my own son, still maturing. He has had to live with so much, including the knowledge that he would never spend another Christmas, another birthday with his father.

As the weeks went by I also began to think more about Mike and Dave. Despite my bitterness and anger towards them, I was beginning to see their situation in a different light. They had been young too, Dave not so much older than Sam. Survival in a force-10 storm is determined by each second that passes. Rash decisions are made when your life is in danger. They were quite simply terrified—I can see that clearly now. My crewmates had gone through a hell of their own, of this I was now convinced. And, apart from the horror of the storm, one of them has had to live with the consequences of cutting David's line. That day was no picnic for any of us. They were blameless, and I bear them no ill will.

IN JULY 2005, I had a call from Keith Grainger, one of the present owners of *Grimalkin*. Keith said he would be honoured if I came to visit the boat. Before I knew it, we had arranged a suitable date. My wife, Chris, took time off work and Sinéad flew over from Dublin.

On July 25 we drove to Weymouth, where *Grimalkin* was moored. I felt slightly detached. As we got closer, I began asking myself if I was doing the right thing.

We reached the marina. I couldn't see *Grimalkin* immediately. Then, there she was! Keith waved a hand and let us through the gate.

I could not go aboard straight away. Instead I paced up and down the pontoon alongside. I smoothed her topsides with the palm of my hand, rather like grooming a well-remembered thoroughbred mare, getting to know her again. This was the renewal of an old friendship.

Keith greeted us with gusto. It was quite a while since I had been welcomed aboard a boat in such a generous manner and with such a firm handshake. Then he left us to 'pop up to the shop' for a bottle of wine. It was such a gracious excuse, leaving the three of us alone with *Grimalkin* and me with my thoughts. I noticed that, apart from a few minor details, she was much as I remembered. Her hull was still white and her decks light blue. I moved into the cockpit: there were the same four winch-handle pockets but a lot cleaner. I lifted the cover to the cockpit well. There was no life raft. My heart missed a beat—and it all came flooding back: the noises, the braced knees, the effort to stay in one place long enough to breathe. All the moored yachts around me disappeared and I was back in the Irish Sea. I felt nausea, experienced a strange smell, almost an aura. Seeing how I was affected, Chris sat me down. I quickly came to my senses.

Sinéad sat alongside me, and I began to explain where everyone had been sitting, how high the waves had been. Things that had been difficult to convey before were easier to describe with us both on *Grimalkin*.

I climbed down the new companionway ladder. *Grimalkin* smelt the way she was meant to, that special odour of seasoned wood, fibreglass, salt and stowed sails combined, the smell of a yacht that has some stories to tell. Her bunks had been replaced. Her navigation table was to port, not to starboard as it had been. The thoroughbred racer/cruiser I had known and loved over twenty-five years ago was still a serious vessel. *Grimalkin* still turned heads.

We spent an hour or so with Keith, joined by his lovely wife and daughter. He told us that hardly a day passed when people didn't ask him about *Grimalkin* and what had happened to her in 1979. I recounted some of what had happened on the race—and I told Keith about what I had experienced after lifting the cockpit cover. He apologised, explaining that the life raft was being repaired.

But there was no need for him to apologise. This moment had been fated. It made me want to relive the hours I spent with Gerry on *Grimalkin*. Sinéad suggested I write down what I had seen exactly as I had described it to her on the boat. Two days after Sinéad's return home, I sent her what I had written and we decided to collaborate in turning my story into a book.

Recently, I met up with some of my old sailing friends from the past. Through them I learned more of the hearsay around the race. One piece of information was new to me. Apparently the crewmember who cut David's safety line had to cut his own first. It was the only way he could get to David. I have no reason to believe this is not true. To cut his own safety line was an act of great bravery. This crewmember had endangered his life in an attempt to save someone else's. It brought home to me all the more that the four of us—Matt, Mike, Dave and I—had experienced horrors that we have had to come to terms with. We all went through our own hell during and after this race.

I have never heard a version of what had happened from either Mike or Dave directly. It was never offered and I never asked. But what I do know is this. I have finally achieved what I had thought impossible for a quarter of a century—acceptance.

August 7, 2005

I wanted to do something I had not done since 1979—experience a Fastnet start. Sinéad and Chris came along too. A good friend of mine offered to take me out in his ex-Coastguard launch. My experience had never destroyed my love and respect for the sea and all things about it and I felt I was ready for this—more than ready. It was a bright day, warm and sunny, blowing around a force 3 or 4, conditions not unlike those at the start twenty-six years earlier. Sailing into Cowes Roads was very familiar: the chop, the atmosphere, the press boats. This was as I remembered it: Fastnet electric, truly uplifting—a race of such importance that it is now an integral part of any yachtsman's life. The race is tradition. Thank God it was not stopped.

Standing in the cockpit observing it all was not so different from when I stood, at seven years old, alongside Pa aboard *Snapdragon*. I swear I smelt the tobacco of a Senior Service cigarette waft by as a voice in my head said, *One hand for yourself, one for the boat, Nicholas*.

Later that day as we motored home I thought that maybe one day I would sail west out of the Solent again. Who knows? Never say never.

1
2
3
4
GROVES & CUTTRIE

LEFT FOR DEAD

Left page: 1 Sunday service with Ma, Pa and Simon. Pa's hand is resting on my shoulder. **2** All togged out in sailing gear for the beginning of the 1968 racing season. **3** Enjoying a break on one of my many boat deliveries (1978). **4** August 11, 1979: another Fastnet start at Cowes—this time I was finally taking part.
Right page: 5 This photo of *Grimalkin* was taken just one hour before our Fastnet 1979 start. While waiting, we put in some practice tacks as David carefully sussed out our Class V competition. **6** *Grimalkin* in Waterford in Ireland in September 1979. **7** The cockpit looking aft. This is the view I had while bailing. **8** This is me with my son Sam, shortly after his seventeenth birthday.

NO TIME FOR GOODBYE

Linwood Barclay

SPEED
25

If your family disappeared overnight, leaving you no indication where or why they'd left, how would you come to terms with it? What could possibly cause such a thing to happen?

Twenty-five years after her parents and brother disappeared, Cynthia Bigge is still wondering, still searching for answers. The truth, when she finds it, is far stranger than anything she could have imagined . . .

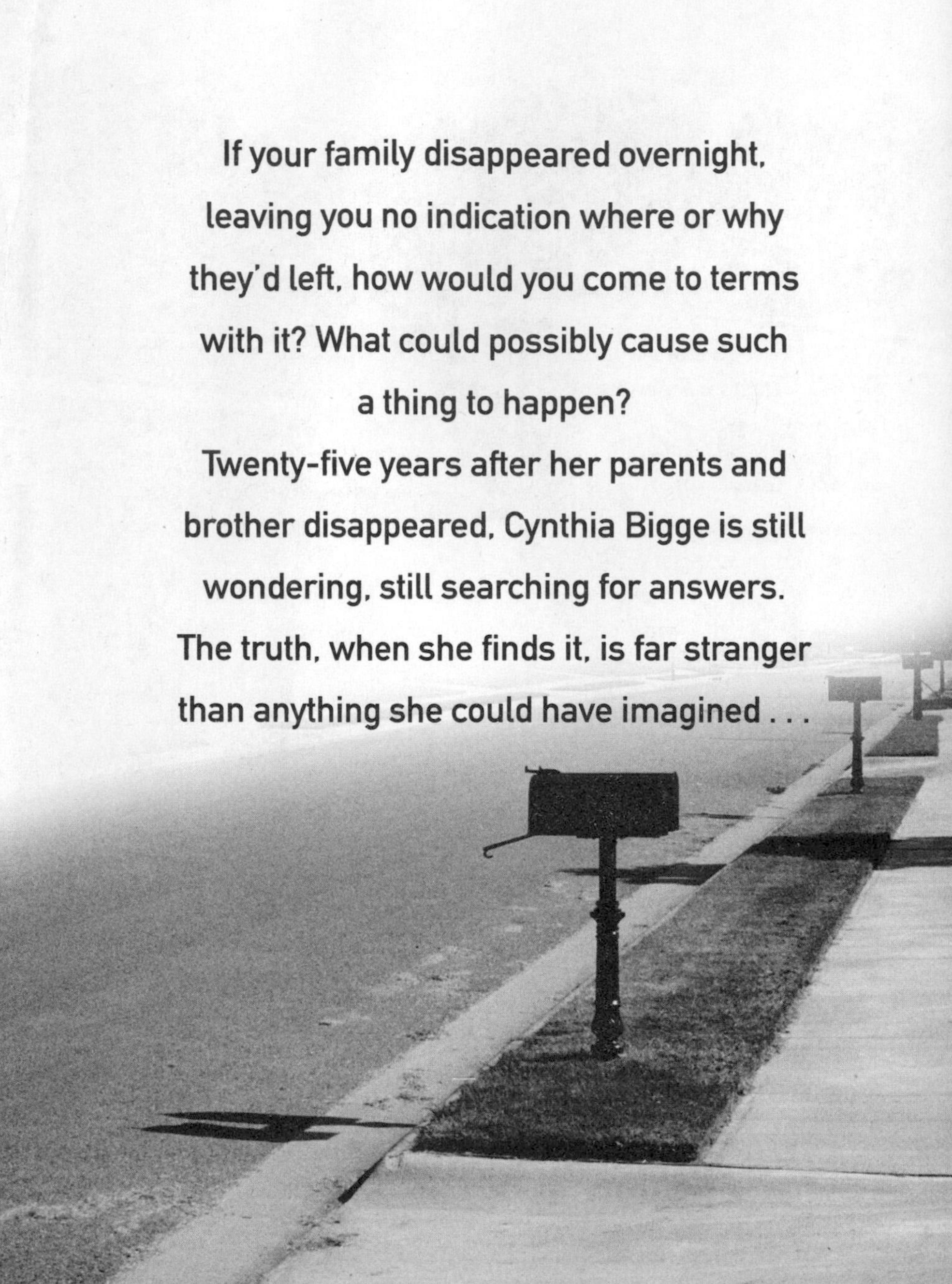

MAY 1983

When Cynthia woke up, it was so quiet in the house she thought it must be Saturday.

If only.

If there'd ever been a day that she needed to be a Saturday, to be anything but a school day, this was it. Her stomach was still doing the occasional somersault, her head was full of cement, and it took some effort to keep it from falling forward or onto her shoulders.

What was that in the wastepaper basket next to the bed? She couldn't even remember throwing up in the night, but if you were looking for evidence, there it was.

She had to deal with this first, before her parents came in. Cynthia got to her feet, wobbled a moment, grabbed the small plastic container with one hand and opened her bedroom door a crack with the other. There was no one in the hall, so she slipped past the open doors of her brother's and parents' bedrooms and into the bathroom, closing the door and locking it behind her.

She emptied the container into the toilet, rinsed it in the tub, took a bleary-eyed look at herself in the mirror. Not a pretty sight. She could barely remember what Vince had given her to try the night before, stuff he'd snuck out of his house. A couple of cans of Bud, some vodka, gin, an already opened bottle of red wine.

Something was niggling at her. Something about the bedrooms.

She splashed cold water on her face, dried off with a towel. Cynthia took a deep breath, tried to pull herself together, in case her mother was waiting for her on the other side of the door.

She wasn't.

Cynthia headed back to her room, feeling the broadloom under her toes. Along the way, she glanced into her brother Todd's room, then her parents'. The beds were made. Her mother didn't usually get round to making them until later in the morning—but here they were, looking as though they'd never been slept in.

Cynthia felt a wave of panic. Was she already late for school? Just how late was it?

She could see Todd's clock on his bedside table. Just ten before eight. Nearly half an hour before she usually left for her first class.

The house was still.

She could usually hear her parents down in the kitchen about this time. Even if they weren't speaking to each other, which was often the case, there'd be the faint sounds of the fridge opening and closing, a spatula scraping against a frying pan, the muffled rattling of dishes in the sink.

She went into her room and closed the door. *Pull it together*, she told herself. Show up for breakfast like nothing ever happened. Pretend there wasn't a screaming match the night before. Act like her father hadn't dragged her out of her much older boyfriend's car and taken her home.

Todd was usually banging around this time of the morning. In and out of the bathroom, shouting downstairs to his mother asking where his trousers were. She couldn't remember him saying anything about going in to school early, but why would he tell her anyway? She was a geeky ninth grader to him, although she was giving it her best shot to get into as much bad stuff as he was.

OK, so maybe Todd had to go to school early, but where were her mother and father?

Her dad, maybe he'd left on another business trip before the sun even came up. He was always heading off somewhere; you could never keep track. And her mother, maybe she'd driven Todd to school or something.

She got dressed. Jeans, a sweater. Put on her make-up, but not so much that her mother started making cracks about her going to 'tramp tryouts'.

When she got to the kitchen, she just stood there.

No cereal boxes out, no juice, no coffee in the coffeemaker. No plates in the sink. The kitchen looked exactly as it had after her mother had cleaned up from dinner the night before.

Cynthia glanced about for a note. Her mom was big about leaving notes when she had to go out. Even when she was angry. A long enough note to say 'On your own today', or 'Make yourself some eggs, have to drive Todd', or just 'Back later'.

There was no note.

Cynthia worked up the nerve to shout, 'Mom?' Her own voice suddenly sounded strange to her. When her mother didn't answer, she called out again. 'Dad?' Again, nothing.

This, she surmised, must be her punishment. She'd pissed off her parents, disappointed them, and now they were going to act like she didn't exist. OK, she could deal with that.

Cynthia didn't feel she could keep down any breakfast, so she grabbed the schoolbooks she needed and headed out of the door.

The *Journal Courier*, rolled up with a rubber band like a log, lay on the front step. Cynthia kicked it out of her way, not really thinking about it, and strode down the empty driveway—her father's Dodge and mother's Ford Escort were both gone—in the direction of Milford South High School. Maybe, if she could find her brother, she'd learn just what was going on, just how much trouble she might actually be in.

Plenty, she figured.

She'd missed curfew, an early one of eight o'clock. It was a school night, first of all, and then there'd been that call earlier in the evening from Mrs Asphodel about how if she didn't hand in her English assignments, she wasn't going to pass. She told her parents she was going to Pam's house to do homework.

When Cynthia wasn't home by eight fifteen, her mother phoned Pam's house. Not only was Cynthia not there, but Pam wasn't even home. That was when Cynthia's father grabbed the faded fedora hat he never went anywhere without, got in his Dodge, and started driving around the neighbourhood, looking for her. He suspected she might be with that Vince Fleming boy, the seventeen-year-old from the eleventh grade who drove around in a rusted red 1970 Mustang. Clayton and Patricia Bigge didn't much care for him. Tough kid, troubled family, bad influence.

It was just a fluke that her dad spotted the car at the far end of the parking lot of the Connecticut Post Mall, out on the Post Road, not far from the theatres. The Mustang was backed up to the kerb, and her father parked in front, blocking it in.

Good thing he hadn't shown up two minutes earlier, when they'd been making out, or when Vince was showing her his new switchblade—you pressed this little button, and zap! Six inches of steel suddenly appeared. Cynthia had tried holding it, had sliced the air in front of her and giggled.

Clayton Bigge marched over to the passenger door and yanked it open.

'Hey, pal, watch it!' Vince said.

'Don't "hey, pal" me,' her father said, taking Cynthia by the arm and ushering her back into his own car. 'You reek,' he told her.

She wished she could have died right then. She wouldn't look at him or say anything, not even when he started going on about how she was becoming nothing but trouble, that he didn't know what he'd done wrong, that he just wanted her to grow up and be happy, and blah blah blah, and even when he was pissed off, he still drove like he was taking his driver's test, never exceeding the speed limit, always using his turn signal; the guy was unbelievable.

When they pulled into the driveway, she was out of the car before he had it in park, throwing open the door to the house, striding in, trying not to weave, her mother standing there, not looking mad so much as worried, saying, 'Cynthia! Where were—'

She steamrollered past her, went up to her room. Her father shouted, 'You come down here! We got things to discuss!'

'I wish you were dead!' she screamed, and slammed her door.

That much came back to her as she walked to school. The rest of the evening was still a bit fuzzy. She remembered sitting down on her bed, feeling woozy. She decided to lie down, figuring she could sleep it off by the morning, a good ten hours away.

A lot could happen before morning.

At one point, drifting in and out of sleep, she thought she heard someone at her door. Like someone was hesitating just outside it.

Then, later, she thought she heard it again.

Did she get up to see who it was? Did she even try to get out of bed? She couldn't remember. And now she had almost reached her school.

The thing was, she felt remorseful. She'd broken nearly every household rule in a single night, starting with the lie about going to Pam's. She'd broken curfew. Gone parking with a boy. A seventeen-year-old boy. A boy they said had broken school windows the year before, had taken a joy-ride in a neighbour's car.

Her parents, they weren't all bad. Most of the time. Especially her mom. Her dad, even he wasn't too bad, when he was home.

First-period history was a write-off. Second-period math was even worse. She couldn't focus; her head still hurt. At lunch, Cynthia slipped out of the cafeteria, went to the school payphone, dialled home. She'd tell her mother she was sorry. Really, really sorry.

Cynthia gave up after fifteen rings, then thought maybe she'd dialled wrong. Tried again, no answer.

She was hanging out in front of the school with some friends when Vince Fleming drove by in his Mustang. 'Sorry about last night,' he said. 'Jeez, your dad's a prize.'

'Yeah, well,' Cynthia said.

'So what happened after you went home?' Vince asked. There was something in the way he asked, like he already knew. Cynthia shrugged and shook her head.

Vince asked, 'Where's your brother today? He home sick?'

Nobody'd seen Todd at school. Vince said he was going to ask him, quiet like, how much trouble Cynthia was in, whether she was grounded, because he was hoping she wanted to get together Friday night or Saturday.

Cynthia ran home. Didn't ask Vince for a ride, even though he was right there. Ran the whole way, thinking as she pumped her legs, *Please let her car be there. Please let her car be there.*

But when she rounded the corner to Hickory, and her two-storey house came into view, the yellow Escort, her mother's car, was not there. But she shouted out her mother's name anyway when she got inside. Then her brother's.

She started to tremble, then willed herself to stop. It made no sense. No matter how angry her parents might be at her, they wouldn't do this, would they? Just leave? Take off without telling her? And take Todd with them?

Cynthia felt stupid doing it, but she rang the bell at the Jamison house next door. She started blathering when Mrs Jamison opened the door. That when she woke up, no one was home, and then she went to school and Todd never showed up—

Mrs Jamison said, 'Whoa, everything's OK; your mother's probably out doing some shopping.' Mrs Jamison walked Cynthia back home. Together they looked upstairs and down and in the garage and out in the back yard.

'That sure is odd,' Mrs Jamison said. She didn't quite know what to think, so, somewhat reluctantly, she called the Milford police. They sent round an officer, who didn't seem all that concerned, at first. But soon there were more officers, and by evening there were cops all over the place.

'You're sure they never mentioned anything about going anyplace?' asked a man who was a detective, named Findley, or Finlay. 'You see, it doesn't look like your mom and dad and brother packed to go away or anything. Their clothes are still here.'

There were a lot of questions. When did she last see her parents? When had she gone to bed? Who was this boy she was with? She tried to tell the detective everything, even admitted she and her parents had had a fight, although she'd left out how bad it was, that she'd got drunk, told them she wished they were dead.

Why would her mom and dad and brother just disappear? Where would they go? Why wouldn't they have taken her with them?

Suddenly, in a frenzy, Cynthia began to tear the kitchen apart. Lifting up and tossing place mats, moving the toaster, looking under the chairs, peering down into the crack between the stove and the wall, tears streaming down her face.

'What is it?' the detective asked. 'What are you doing?'

'Where's the note?' Cynthia asked, her eyes pleading. 'There has to be a note. My mom never goes away without leaving a note.'

1

Cynthia stood in front of the two-storey house on Hickory. It wasn't as though she was seeing her childhood home for the first time in nearly twenty-five years. She still lived in Milford, Connecticut. She'd driven by here once in a while. She showed me the house once before we got married, a quick drive-by. 'There it is,' she said, and kept on going.

But it had certainly been a very long time since she'd stepped through that front door.

She was rooted to the sidewalk, seemingly unable to take even one step towards the place. I wanted to go to her side, walk her to the door. It was only a thirty-foot driveway, but it stretched a quarter of a century into the past. You could walk all day and never get there. I stayed where I was, on the other side of the street, looking at her back, at her short red hair. I had my orders.

Cynthia stood there, as though waiting for permission to approach. And then it came.

'OK, Mrs Archer? Start walking towards the house. Not too fast. Kind of hesitant, you know, like it's the first time you've gone inside since you were fourteen years old.'

Cynthia glanced over her shoulder at a woman in jeans and trainers, her ponytail pulled down and through the opening at the back of her baseball cap. She was one of three assistant producers on the *Deadline* show. 'This is the first time,' Cynthia said.

'Just look at the house and start walking up the drive,' Ponytail Girl said, 'thinking back to that time, twenty-five years ago, when it all happened, OK?'

Cynthia glanced across the street at me, made a face, then started up the driveway, slowly. As she mounted the steps to the door, reached out with her hand, I could just make out the trembling.

She had her hand on the knob, about to push the door open, when Ponytail Girl shouted, 'OK! Good! Hold it there!' Then, to her cameraman, 'OK, let's set up inside, get her coming in.'

'You're kidding me,' I said, loud enough for the crew—a half dozen or so, plus Paula Malloy, she of the gleaming teeth and Donna Karan suits, who was doing all the on-camera stuff and voice-overs—to hear.

Paula herself came over to see me.

'Mr Archer,' she said, 'is everything OK?'

'How can you do that to her?' I said. 'My wife's walking in there for the first time since her family vanished, and you basically yell "Cut"?'

'Terry, I'm sorry, we have to get the camera in position, and we want the look on Cynthia's face when she comes into the house after all these years to be genuine. We want this to be honest.'

That was a good one. That a reporter from the TV news/entertainment show—which, when it wasn't revisiting bizarre unsolved crimes from years past, was chasing after the latest drinking-and-driving celebrity—would play the honesty card.

'Sure,' I said tiredly, thinking of the bigger picture here, that maybe after all these years, some TV exposure might finally provide Cynthia with some answers. 'Sure, whatever.'

Paula showed some perfect teeth and went briskly back across the street, her high heels clicking along the pavement.

I'd been doing my best to stay out of the way since Cynthia and I'd arrived here. I'd arranged to get the day off from school. My principal and long-time friend, Rolly Carruthers, knew how important it was to Cynthia to do this show, and he'd arranged a substitute to take my English and creative-writing classes. Cynthia had taken the day off from Pamela's, the dress shop where she worked. We'd dropped off our eight-year-old daughter, Grace, at school along the way. The people who lived in the house now, a retired couple, had been paid off by the producers to clear out for the day so they could have the run of the place.

I followed two cameramen into the house, then got out of the way as they positioned themselves to catch Cynthia's expressions from different angles. They led her upstairs to her old bedroom. She looked numb. They wanted footage of her walking into it. The cameraman was waiting inside her bedroom, the door closed, to get a shot of Cynthia entering the room, ever so tentatively.

Paula Malloy got her make-up retouched and her blonde hair combed out. Then she and Cynthia went into the kitchen, cameras rolling. Paula asked, 'What must you have been thinking?' Cynthia appeared to be walking through a dream. 'You hadn't heard a sound in the house so far; you come down here into the kitchen and there's no sign of life at all.'

'I didn't know what was happening,' Cynthia said quietly. 'I thought everyone had left early. That my dad had gone to work, that my mother must have taken my brother to school. I thought they must be mad at me. I'd been out the night before with a boy my parents didn't approve of. I'd had something to drink.'

'We read in the police reports from the time, from the statements that you'd made, that you'd had an argument with your parents.'

'Yes,' Cynthia said. 'I said some awful things. About not being home when I promised, lying to them.'

'And where do you think they are, today, two and a half decades later?'

Cynthia shook her head sadly. 'It's all I ask myself. There's not a day goes by I don't wonder.'

'If you could say something to them, right now, what would it be?'

Cynthia, nonplussed, looked somewhat hopelessly into the camera. 'Why?'

Paula allowed for a dramatic pause, then asked, 'Why what, Cynthia?'

'Why,' she repeated, trying to compose herself, 'did you have to leave me? If you're able to, if you're alive, why haven't you got in touch? Why couldn't you have left just a simple note? Why couldn't you have at least said goodbye?'

I could feel the electricity among the crew, the producers. I knew what they were thinking. This was their money shot. This was going to be awesome TV. I hated them for exploiting Cynthia's misery, but I knew she was willing to be exploited if it meant someone watching would step forward with the key to unlock her past.

At the show's request, Cynthia had brought with her two dented cardboard shoeboxes of memories. Newspaper clippings, faded Polaroid photos, class pictures, all the bits and pieces that she'd managed to take from her house before she went to live with her aunt, her mother's sister, a woman named Tess Berman. They had Cynthia sit at the kitchen table, the boxes open in front of her, taking out one memory and then another.

'This is us,' she said, showing off a Polaroid, 'on a camping trip we took up in Vermont.' The camera zoomed in on a dishevelled-looking Todd and Cynthia standing on either side of their mother, a tent in the background. Cynthia looked about five.

'I don't have any pictures of my father,' she said mournfully. 'He always took the pictures of the rest of us, so now I just have to remember how he looked.'

She reached for a yellowed piece of newsprint. 'Here's a clipping from some things I found in my father's drawer.' The camera moved in again, scanned the square of newspaper. It was a grainy black-and-white picture of a school basketball team. 'Dad must have saved it because Todd was in it, although they left his name out of the caption. He was proud of us, Dad was. He liked to joke that we were the best family that he'd ever had.'

They interviewed my principal, Rolly Carruthers.

'It's a mystery,' he said. 'I knew Clayton Bigge. We went fishing together a couple of times. He was a good man. I can't imagine what happened to them.'

They interviewed Aunt Tess.

'I lost a sister, a brother-in-law, a nephew,' she said. 'But Cynthia, her loss was so much greater. She managed to beat the odds, to still turn out to be a great kid, a great person.'

Cynthia was stunned, when the segment aired a couple of weeks later, to see the detective who'd questioned her in her house after her neighbour, Mrs Jamison, had called the police. He was retired now, living in Arizona. At the bottom of the screen, it said: 'Retired detective Bartholomew

Finlay'. He'd led the initial investigation and finally moved it off his desk after a year because he wasn't getting anywhere.

'The thing that always nagged at me was,' he said, 'why'd she survive? Assuming, of course, that the rest of the family was dead. Why did she survive? There aren't that many possibilities.'

'What do you mean by that?' The voice of Paula Malloy.

'Figure it out,' Finlay said. 'That's all I'll say.'

When she saw that, Cynthia was furious. 'This again!' she shouted at the television. 'Implying I had something to do with it. I've heard these whispers for years.' But I had managed to calm her down, because the segment had been, on balance, pretty positive.

And so the programme ran. Cynthia waited by the phone the moment the show finished, figuring someone would see it, someone who knew something, and call the station immediately.

But there were no calls. Cynthia quickly became old news.

GRACE'S EYES were pleading, but her tone was stern.

'Dad,' she said. 'I'm. Eight. Years. Old.' *Where had she learned this?* I wondered. This technique of breaking down sentences into individual words for dramatic effect.

'Yes,' I said to my daughter. 'I'm aware.'

Her Cheerios were getting soggy and she hadn't touched her orange juice. 'The kids make fun of me,' she said.

I took a sip of my coffee. 'Your mom just wants to know that you get to school safely, that's all.'

Grace sighed and bowed her head defeatedly, a lock of her brown hair dropping in front of her brown eyes. 'But she doesn't have to walk me to school. Nobody's mom walks them to school unless they're in kindergarten.'

We'd been through this before, and I'd tried talking to Cynthia, suggested that maybe it was time for Grace to fly solo now that she was in third grade. There were plenty of other kids to walk with; it wasn't as though she'd be walking all by herself.

'Why can't you walk me instead?' Grace asked.

The rare times when I had walked Grace to school, I'd fallen behind the better part of a block. As far as anyone knew, I was just out for a stroll, not keeping an eye on Grace. And we never breathed a word of it to Cynthia.

'I can't,' I said. 'I have to be at my school by eight. Once in a while, when I get a first period spare, I can walk you.'

In fact, Cynthia had arranged her hours at Pamela's so that she'd be around each morning to make sure Grace was off to school safely. It had never been Cynthia's dream to work at a women's clothing store owned by her best friend from high school, but it allowed her to work part-time, which meant she could be home by the time school let out.

'Also, my telescope's broken,' Grace said.

'What do you mean, it's broken?'

'The thingies that hold the telescope part to the standy part are loose. I sort of fixed it, but it'll probably get loose again.'

'I'll have a look at it.'

'I have to keep a lookout for killer asteroids,' Grace said. 'I'm not going to be able to see them if my telescope is broken.'

'OK,' I said. 'I'll look at it.'

'What about Mom?' Grace asked. 'Does she have to walk with me?'

'I'll talk to her,' I said.

'Talk to who?' Cynthia said, walking into the kitchen.

Cynthia looked good this morning. Beautiful, in fact. She was a striking woman, and I never tired of her green eyes, high cheekbones, fiery red hair. People think she must work out, but I think it's anxiety that's helped her keep her figure. She burns off calories worrying. She doesn't jog, doesn't belong to a gym. Not that we could afford a gym membership anyway. Like I've mentioned, I'm a high-school English teacher, and Cynthia works in retail—even though she has a family studies degree and worked for a while doing social work—so we're not exactly rolling in dough.

We have this house, in a modest neighbourhood only a few blocks from where Cynthia grew up. Our cars are both ten years old, our vacations low-key. We borrow my uncle's cabin up near Montpelier for a week every summer, and three years ago, when Grace was five, we took a trip to Walt Disney World. But we have, I believe, a pretty good life, and we are, more or less, happy. Most days.

The nights, sometimes, can be hard.

'Grace's teacher,' I said.

'What do you want to talk to Grace's teacher for?' Cynthia asked.

'I was just saying, when it's one of those parent-teacher nights, I should go in and talk to her, to Mrs Enders,' I said.

'She's very nice,' Cynthia said.

'I have to go,' I said, taking another sip of coffee. As I got up from the table, Grace looked at me despairingly. I knew what she wanted from me. *Talk to her. Please talk to her.*

'Terry, you seen the spare key?' Cynthia asked.

'Hmm?' I said.

She pointed to the empty hook on the wall just inside the kitchen door that opened onto our small back yard. 'Where's the spare?' It was the one we used if we were taking a walk and didn't want to take a ring loaded with car remotes and workplace keys.

'I don't know. I might have left it next to the bed.' I sidled up next to Cynthia, smelt her hair as I walked past. 'See me off?' I said.

She followed me to the front door. 'Something going on?' she asked. 'Is Grace OK? She seems kind of quiet this morning.'

I shook my head. 'It's . . . you know. She is eight years old, Cyn. She needs to feel a bit more independent.'

Cynthia moved back a bit, bristling. 'That's what that was about. She wants you to talk to me, not her teacher.'

I smiled tiredly. 'She says the other kids are making fun of her.'

'She'll get over it. You know there are bad people out there.'

'I know, Cyn, I know.' I tried to keep the frustration out of my voice. 'But how long are you going to walk her? Till she's twelve? Fifteen? You going to walk her to high school?'

'I'll deal with that when it comes,' she said. She paused. 'I saw that car again.'

The car. There was always a car.

'I've seen it two times. A brown car.'

'What kind of car?'

'I don't know. An average car. With tinted windows. When it drives past me and Grace, it slows down a bit.'

'Cyn, it's probably just somebody who lives in the neighbourhood. People have to slow down. It's a school zone up there.'

'You've never taken these things as seriously as I do.' She waited a beat. 'And I suppose that's understandable, for you.'

I puffed out my cheeks, blew out some air. 'OK, look, we're not going to solve this now,' I said. 'I have to get going.'

'Sure,' Cynthia said, not looking at me.

I lifted her chin so that our eyes met. I said, 'I love you, you know.'

'I love you, too,' she said. 'I—I know I'm not easy to live with. I know it's hard on Grace. But lately, with that show, it's made it all so real for me again.'

'I know,' I said. 'I just want you to be able to live for the present, too. Not always fixate on the past.'

'Fixate?' she said. 'Don't patronise me. You think you know, but you don't. You can't ever know.'

There wasn't much I could say to that, because it was true. I leaned in and kissed her hair and went to work.

SHE WANTED to be comforting in what she had to say, but it was just as important to be firm.

'I can understand you might find the idea a bit unsettling, really, I do. I can see where you might be feeling a bit squeamish about the whole thing, but I've been here before, and I'm telling you, this is the only way. That's the way it is with family. You have to do what you have to do, even if it's difficult, even if it's painful. Of course what we have to do to them is going to be difficult, but you have to look at the bigger picture. It's a bit like when they said—you're probably not old enough to remember this—that you have to destroy a village to save it. It's something like that. Think of our family as a village. We have to do whatever it takes to save it.'

She liked the 'we' part. That they were a kind of team.

2

When she was first pointed out to me at the University of Connecticut, my friend Roger whispered, 'Archer, check it out. She's hot—she's got hair like a fire engine—but she's majorly screwed up.' Cynthia Bigge was sitting down in the second row of the lecture hall, taking notes on literature of the Holocaust, and Roger and I were up near the back.

'What do you mean?' I whispered back.

'OK, you remember that thing, a few years ago, there was this girl, her whole family disappeared, nobody ever saw them again?'

'No.' I didn't read the papers or watch the news at that time in my life. Like many teens, I was oblivious to current events.

'OK, so her parents, her brother, they all disappeared.'

I leaned in closer, whispered, 'So, what, they got killed?'

Roger shrugged. 'Who knows? That's what makes it so interesting.' He tipped his head in Cynthia's direction. 'Maybe she offed the bunch of them. She sticks to herself, doesn't hang out with anybody, doesn't go out to things. Pretty, though.'

It was the only course I shared with her. I was in the School of Education, preparing to become a teacher. I asked around, learned Cynthia was enrolled in the School of Family Studies at the Storrs campus.

I was sitting out front of the university bookstore, glancing at some lecture notes, when I sensed someone standing in front of me.

'Why're you asking around about me?' Cynthia said.

'Huh?' I said.

'Somebody said you were asking about me,' she repeated. 'You're Terrence Archer, right?'

I nodded. 'Terry,' I said.

'OK, so, why are you asking about me?'

I shrugged. 'I don't know. I just wondered whether—'

'You wondered whether I'm the one. Whose family disappeared. OK, I am. Now you can mind your own damned business.'

'My mom's hair is red,' I said, cutting her off. 'Not as red as yours. Sort of a blondy red, you know? But yours is really beautiful.' Cynthia blinked. 'So yeah, maybe I asked a couple of people about you, because I wondered if you were seeing anybody, and they said no, and now I guess I can see why.' I stood up and turned to go.

'I'm not,' Cynthia said.

I stopped. 'You're not what?'

'I'm not seeing anybody.' She swallowed.

We ended up having a coffee at a campus bar, and Cynthia told me that she lived with her aunt when she wasn't attending the university.

'Tess is pretty decent,' Cynthia said. 'She never got married or anything, didn't have any kids of her own, so my moving in, after the thing with my family, that kind of turned her world upside down, you know? But she was OK with it. I mean, what the hell was she going to do? And she was sort of going thorough a tragedy, too, her sister and brother-in-law and nephew just disappearing like that. I don't know how she's managed it, really, raising me, paying for my education.'

'I don't know how *you* handle it,' I said.

Cynthia took a sip of her coffee. 'Some days, I just want to kill myself, you know? And then I think, what if they showed up the day after?' She smiled. 'Wouldn't that be a kick in the head?'

Her smile drifted away as though carried off by a gentle breeze.

'The thing is,' she said, 'they could be dead, and they never had a chance to say goodbye to me. Or they could still be alive and couldn't be bothered.' She looked out of the window. 'I can't decide which is worse.'

WE STARTED HANGING OUT. We went to movies; we worked together in the library. She tried to interest me in playing tennis. It had never been my game, but I gave it my best shot. Cynthia was just a fair player but with a magnificent backhand.

As I got to know her, Cynthia told me more about her family, Clayton and Patricia and her older brother, Todd, whom she loved and hated, depending on the day.

She was a part of the Bigge family. It was, of course, a kind of constant joke, given that their extended family, at least on her father's side, was pretty much non-existent. Clayton Bigge's parents died when he was young; he had no brothers or sisters, no aunts or uncles to speak of.

'I'm it,' he liked to say. 'The whole family. There are no more.'

He wasn't much of a sentimentalist, either. No dusty family albums of previous generations to linger over, no snapshots of the past. There wasn't that much family on Patricia's side, either, but at least there was a history of it. Lots of pictures of her own parents and extended family and friends from her childhood. Her father died of polio when she was young, but her mother was still alive when she met Clayton. Thought he was charming, if a bit quiet.

Patricia had had a job in a drugstore in Milford, on North Broad Street, looking out on the town green. She stocked shelves, worked the cash register, helped the pharmacist. Clayton walked into the drugstore one day, looking for a Mars bar.

Patricia liked to say, if her husband hadn't been hit by a Mars bar craving that day in July 1967, as he passed through Milford on a sales trip, well, things would have turned out very differently.

It was a speedy courtship, and within a few weeks of getting married, she was pregnant with Todd. Clayton found them an affordable house on Hickory, a stone's throw from the beach and Long Island Sound. He had responsibility for a corridor that ran between New York and Chicago and up to Buffalo, selling industrial lubricants to machine shops along the way.

A couple of years after Todd was born, Cynthia arrived.

I was thinking about all this as I drove to Old Fairfield High School. Whenever I daydreamed, I found it was often about my wife's past, her upbringing, about the members of her family I never knew, would in all likelihood never be able to know.

I popped into the doughnut shop for a coffee and was carrying my take-out cup with me into the school, a satchel full of student essays slung over my shoulder, when I saw Roland Carruthers, the principal and my best friend here at this institution, in the hall.

'Rolly,' I said.

'Where's mine?' he said, nodding at the paper cup in my hand.

'If you'll take my period one class, I'll go back and get you one.'

'If I take your period one class, I'm going to need something stronger than coffee. They're savages.'

'What's happening with Jane Scavullo?' I asked. She was a student in my creative-writing class, a troubled kid with a messed-up family background who spent nearly as much time in the office as the secretaries. She also happened to write like an angel.

'I told her she's this close to a suspension,' Rolly said, holding his thumb and forefinger a quarter of an inch apart. Jane and another girl had got into a hair-pulling brawl out in front of the school a couple of days earlier. A boy thing, evidently.

'What'd she say to that?'

Rolly pretended to chew gum in an exaggerated fashion.

'OK,' I said.

'You like her,' he said.

'There's something there,' I said.

My friendship with Rolly was what you might call multilayered. He's a colleague and friend, but because he's a couple of decades older than I am, he's something of a father figure, too. I got to know him through Cynthia. He was an unofficial uncle to her. He had been a friend to her father, Clayton, before he went missing, and outside of her aunt Tess was about the only person she knew with any connection to her past. His retirement was imminent, and there were times when you could tell he was coasting, counting the days till he was out of there and down in Florida, living in his newly purchased mobile home someplace outside Bradenton.

'You around later?' I asked.

'Yeah, sure. Drop by after eleven.'

THERE WERE twenty-one bodies in the room as I walked into my first-period creative-writing class, about half of them sprawled across their desks as if during the night someone had surgically removed their spines. At the back of the room, seventeen-year-old Jane Scavullo was sitting so low at her desk I almost couldn't see the bandage on her chin.

'OK,' I said. 'I've marked your stories, and there's some good stuff here.' I riffled through the pile of papers in my satchel and pulled out one. 'Let me read a bit of this,' I said, holding out the paper. I could see Jane's head rise a notch. Maybe she recognised the lined paper.

'"Her father—at least the guy who'd been sleeping with her mother long enough to think he should be called that—takes a carton of eggs out of the fridge, breaks open two of them, one-handed, into a bowl. There's bacon already sizzling in a pan, and when she walks into the room, he tips his head, like he's telling her to sit down at the kitchen table. He asks how she likes her eggs, and she says she doesn't care because she doesn't know what else to say because no one's ever asked her before how she likes eggs. All her mom's ever made her that's even remotely egglike is an Eggo waffle out of a toaster. She figures whatever way this guy makes them, there's a pretty good chance they'll be better than a damn Eggo."' I stopped reading and looked up. 'Comments?'

A boy said, 'I like my eggs runny.'

A girl on the opposite side of the room said, 'I like it. You want to know what this guy is like. If he cares about her breakfast, maybe he's not a jerk.'

An hour later, as they filed out, I said, 'Jane.' She sidled over to my desk reluctantly. 'You pissed off?' I asked.

She shrugged.

'It was good. That's why I read it.'

Another shrug.

'You're a good writer,' I said. 'Some of your stuff, it reminds me a bit of Oates. You ever read Joyce Carol Oates?'

Jane shook her head.

'Try *Foxfire: Confessions of a Girl Gang*,' I said.

'We done?' she asked.

I nodded, and she headed out of the door.

I FOUND ROLLY in his office, sitting at his computer, staring at the monitor. He pointed at the screen. 'They want more testing. Pretty soon, we won't have any time to teach them anything. We'll just test them from the moment they get here to the moment they go home.'

'What's Jane Scavullo's story?' I asked.

'Jane Scavullo, yeah, shame about her,' he said. 'I don't even think we have a current address for her. The last one we have for her mother has to be a couple of years old, I think. Moved in with some new guy, brought her daughter along, too.'

'The fight aside,' I said, 'I think she's actually been a bit better the last few months. A little less surly. Maybe this new guy, maybe he's actually been an improvement.'

Rolly shrugged. 'How you doin' anyway?' he asked. 'You OK? You look off today.'

'Maybe a bit,' I said. 'Home stuff. Cyn's having a hard time giving Grace any kind of taste of freedom. I know why she does it. I mean, if I'd had the kind of life Cyn's had, maybe I'd hold on to things a bit tight, too, but I don't know. She says there's a car.'

'A car?'

'A brown car. It's been by a couple of times when she's been walking Grace to school.'

'Has anything happened?'

'No.'

'I should talk to her,' Rolly said. 'Time to hit the beach.' In the years after her family's disappearance, Rolly would occasionally take Cynthia off Tess's hands for a while. They'd get an ice cream, then stroll along the shore of Long Island Sound.

'That might be a good idea,' I said. 'I just wish this could end for Cyn, that she could get some sort of answers.' I paused. 'What do you think happened, Rolly? You knew Clayton. You went fishing with him. You had a handle on the type of person he was.'

'And Patricia.'

'They seem like the types to just walk out on their daughter?'

'No. My guess is, what I've always believed in my heart, is that they were murdered. You know, a serial killer or something.'

The police had never put much stock in that theory. 'If some kind of serial killer did come to their house, took them away and killed them, why not Cynthia? Why did he leave her behind?'

Rolly had no answer for me.

THE NEXT MORNING, as Grace picked at her toast and jam, I said, 'Guess who's walking you to school today?'

Her face lit up. 'You are? Really?'

'Yeah. I already told your mom. I don't have to be in first thing today, so it's OK.'

'Are you really going to walk with me, like, right next to me?'

I could hear Cynthia coming down the stairs, so I put an index finger to my lips, and Grace immediately went quiet.

'So, Pumpkin, your dad's walking you today,' she said. Pumpkin. It had been Cynthia's own mother's pet name for her. 'That OK with you?'

'Sure!'

Cynthia raised an eyebrow. 'I see. You don't like my company.'

'Mom,' said Grace.

Cynthia smiled. If she was actually offended, she showed no signs of it.

Switching gears, Grace asked, 'Where's my note?'

'What note?' her mother asked.

'About the trip,' she said. 'You were supposed to do a note.'

'Honey, you never said anything about any note for any trip,' Cynthia said. 'You can't spring things on us at the last minute.'

'What's it for?' I asked.

'We're supposed to visit the fire station today, and we can't go if we don't have a note giving us permission.'

'Don't worry about it,' I said. 'I'll bang off a note.'

I ran upstairs to what would be our third bedroom but was a combined sewing room and office. Tucked into the corner was a desk where Cynthia and I shared a computer. Also sitting on the desk was my old Royal typewriter from university days, which I still used for short notes since my handwriting is terrible.

I typed a note to Grace's teacher giving our daughter permission to leave school grounds to tour the fire station. I only hoped the fact that the 'e' key looked more like a 'c' didn't create any confusion.

I came back downstairs and handed Grace the note, and Cynthia ushered us out of the house.

'Mom seemed kind of happy today,' Grace said as we started off down the sidewalk.

'Of course she did,' I said. 'Mom's happy lots of times.' Grace gave me a look to suggest that I was not being totally honest here. 'Your mom has a lot on her mind these days. This hasn't been an easy time for her.'

'Because of the TV show,' she said. 'I don't see why you guys won't let me see it. You taped it, right?'

'Your mother doesn't want to upset you,' I said.

'One of my friends taped it,' Grace said quietly. 'I've sort of already seen it, you know. I went to her house at lunch.'

Even when they were eight, you couldn't keep a lid on things.

Grace looked at me. 'Did Mom like her brother? Todd?'

'Yes. She loved him. She had fights with him, just like lots of brothers and sisters do, but she loved him.' I paused. 'Maybe you should talk to her about it sometime, when everyone's having a good day.'

'Today's going to be good,' Grace said. 'I didn't see any asteroids last night, so we should be OK at least until tonight.'

'Good to know.'

'You should probably stop walking with me now,' Grace said. Up ahead, I saw some schoolkids about her age funnelling onto our street from side streets. The school was visible three blocks up.

'OK,' I said.

'Bye, Dad,' she said, and started putting on speed. I kept my eyes on her. She didn't glance back. She was running to catch up with friends.

That was when the brown car drove past.

It was an older American model, an Impala, I think, a bit of rust around the wheel wells, windows tinted. I stood and watched as it headed down the street, down to the last corner before the school, where Grace was chattering away with two of her friends.

The car stopped at the corner, a few yards away from Grace, and my heart was in my mouth for a moment.

And then one of the brown car's rear taillights started to flash; the car turned right and disappeared down the street.

Grace and her friends made it across the street and onto school property. To my amazement, she looked back and waved at me. I raised my hand in return.

So OK, there was a brown car. But no man had jumped out of it and run after our daughter, or anyone else's kid, either. It appeared to be some guy going to work.

I stood there another moment and felt a sadness wash over me. In Cynthia's world, everyone was plotting to take away your loved ones.

As I walked back in the direction of home, I tried to put myself into a better frame of mind, to shake off my gloominess. I went briskly up the driveway and, as I came through the front door, I called out, 'I'm baaaaaack.'

I heard a voice from the kitchen.

'In here,' Cynthia said. Her voice was subdued.

I stood in the doorway. She was sitting at the kitchen table, the phone in front of her. Her face seemed drained of colour.

'What?' I asked.

'There was a call,' Cynthia said quietly.

'Who from?'

'He didn't say who he was. All he said was he had a message.'

'What kind of message?'

'He said they forgive me.'

'What?'

'My family. He said they forgive me for what I did.'

I SAT DOWN next to Cynthia at the kitchen table. I put one hand over hers and could feel her shaking. 'OK,' I said, 'just try to remember what he said exactly.'

'I told you,' she said, clipping her words. 'The phone rang, and I said hello, and he said, "Is this Cynthia Bigge?" Which threw me, calling me by that name, but I said it was. And he said, "Your family, they forgive you."' She paused. '"For what you did." I didn't know what to say. I asked him what he was talking about.'

'Then what did he say?'

'He didn't say anything else. He just hung up.' A solitary tear ran down Cynthia's cheek as she looked into my face. 'What does he mean, they forgive me?'

'I don't know,' I said. 'It's probably some nut who saw the show.' I pulled the phone over closer to me. It had a small caller-ID display screen. 'Did you see where the call was coming from?'

'I looked and it didn't say, and then when he hung up, I tried to check the number.'

I pressed the button that displayed the call history. There was no record of a call in the last few minutes. 'It's not showing anything,' I said.

Cynthia leaned over the phone. 'I must have . . . what did I do? When I went to check where the call came from, I pressed this button to save it.'

'That's how you delete it,' I said. 'You deleted the call.'

'I was so flustered, I just didn't know what I was doing.'

I slipped an arm round Cynthia's shoulder. 'Just . . . don't worry about it. Too many people know about what happened to you. It can make you a target. You know what we should look into?'

'What?'

'An unlisted number. Then we wouldn't get calls like this.'

Cynthia shook her head. 'No, we're not doing that.'

'Why not?'

She swallowed. 'Because when they are ready to call, when my family finally decides to get in touch, they have to be able to reach me.'

THIS WAS THE DAY we met with Dr Naomi Kinzler after work. Cynthia had arranged to drop Grace off at a friend's house after school, and then we headed over. I'd been sceptical from the beginning whether there was anything a psychiatrist could accomplish, and after coming here for almost four months, I hadn't become any more convinced.

We'd been referred to Dr Kinzler by our family physician. He'd been trying, without success, to help Cynthia deal with her anxieties and felt it would be better for her to talk to someone—for us both to talk to someone—rather than her becoming dependent on a prescription.

Dr Kinzler had an office in a building in the east end of Bridgeport that had a view of the turnpike. She was short and plump, with grey hair pulled back and pinned into submission. She was pushing seventy, I guessed.

'So, what's new since our last session?' Dr Kinzler asked.

Before Cynthia could say anything, I said, 'Things are good. Things have been very good.'

'How's Grace?'

'Grace is good,' I said.

'Is she still checking the night skies?' Dr Kinzler asked. 'For meteors?'

I waved my hand dismissively. 'It's nothing.'

'How about her anxiety level overall? Would you say it's still somewhat heightened, or is it dissipating?'

'I think she's still anxious,' Cynthia said, glancing at me.

Dr Kinzler nodded thoughtfully. 'Why do you think that is?'

Cynthia knew where Dr Kinzler was going. She'd gone down this road before. 'You think it's rubbing off me.'

'What do you think?'

'We try not to talk about things in front of her,' Cynthia said.

I guess I made a noise, a snort or something, enough to get their attention. 'Grace knows a lot more than she lets on,' I said. 'She's seen the show.'

'What?' Cynthia said.

'She saw it at a friend's house.'

Cynthia bit her lower lip. 'She's not ready. She doesn't need to know these things about me. Not now. She needs to be protected.'

'That's one of the toughest things about being a parent,' Dr Kinzler said. 'Realising you can't protect your children from everything.'

Cynthia let that sink in a moment, then, 'There was a phone call.'

She gave Dr Kinzler the details, a near-verbatim account.

'The caller said that your family wants to forgive you. What do you think he meant by that?' asked Dr Kinzler.

'That's the part I keep thinking about,' Cynthia said. 'What's he saying they forgive me for? For not finding them? For not doing more to find out what happened to them?'

'There's part of you that still believes that it was somehow your responsibility,' Dr Kinzler said.

'Look,' I said, before Cynthia could respond. 'It was a crank call. All sorts of people saw that show. It shouldn't be a surprise that a few nutcases would come out of the woodwork.'

'Terry,' Dr Kinzler said, trying hard to be patient, 'of course it may have been a crank call, but what the caller said can trigger feelings in Cynthia just the same. What we're attempting to do here is help Cynthia deal with a traumatic incident in her childhood that's resonating to this day, not just for her own sake, but for the sake of the relationship the two of you share.'

'Our relationship is fine,' I said.

'He doesn't always believe me,' Cynthia blurted.

'What?'

'You don't always believe me,' she said again. 'I can tell. Like when I told you about the brown car. And when that man called this morning, when you couldn't find it in the call history, you wondered whether there'd even been a call.'

'I never said that,' I said.

'But I know you were thinking it,' Cynthia said, but there was no anger in her voice. She reached over and touched my arm. 'And honestly, I don't entirely blame you. If I were you, I'd be exasperated with me, too. Get over it, right? It happened a long time ago.'

'I've never said anything like that.'

'Well, I've said it to myself,' Cynthia said. 'Hundreds of times. And I wish I could. But sometimes, and I know this is going to sound crazy . . .'

Dr Kinzler and I were both very quiet.

'Sometimes, I hear them. I can hear them talking, my mother, my brother. Dad. I can hear them like they're right here in the room with me. Just talking.'

'What are they trying to say?' Dr Kinzler asked.

Cynthia took her hand off my arm. 'I don't know. It varies. Sometimes it's just talk. About what we're having for dinner, or what's on TV, nothing important. Other times, I think they're asking me to come and be with them so we can all be a family again.'

'What do you say?' Dr Kinzler asked.

'I tell them I want to go, but I can't.'

'Why?' I asked.

Cynthia looked into my eyes and smiled sadly. 'Because where they are, I might not be able to take you and Grace with me.'

'WHAT IF I SKIPPED all this other stuff and just did it right away?' he asked. 'Then I could come home.'

'No no no,' she said, almost in a scolding tone. She took a moment, tried to let the calm wash over her. 'I know you'd like to come back. There's nothing I'd like more. But we need to get these other things out of the way first. You mustn't be impatient.'

She could hear him sigh at the other end of the line. 'I don't want to screw it up,' he said.

'And you won't. You've always been a pleaser, you know. It's nice to have

at least one in the house.' Half a chuckle. 'You're a good boy, and I love you more than you'll ever know.'

'It's going to feel weird . . . doing it.'

'I know. But if you're patient, when the time comes, once the stage is set, it'll seem like the most natural thing in the world.'

'I suppose.' He didn't sound convinced.

'That's the thing you need to remember. What you're doing, it's all part of a grand cycle. That's what we're a part of. Have you seen her yet?'

'Yeah. It was strange. Part of me wanted to say hello, say to her, Hey, you won't believe who I am.'

3

The next weekend, we went up to see Cynthia's aunt, Tess, who lived in a small, modest house about halfway up to Derby. She was less than twenty minutes away, but we didn't get up to see her nearly as often as we should. So when there was a special occasion, like Thanksgiving or Christmas or, as was the case this particular weekend, her birthday, we made a point of getting together.

Tess was in her late sixties now, retired, getting by on Social Security and her pension. She gardened and pottered about, took the occasional bus trip like the one she took last fall up through Vermont and New Hampshire to look at the changing leaves, but she didn't have much of a social life.

And how Tess did love to see us. Especially Grace.

'I was going through some boxes of old books in the basement,' Tess said, flopping into her chair after we'd done the hug thing, 'and look what I came across.'

She leaned forward and handed Grace an oversized hardcover book, *Cosmos,* by Carl Sagan. Grace's eyes went wide, looking at the kaleidoscope of stars on the cover.

'Thank you!' Grace said, taking the book in her hands and nearly dropping it, not expecting it to be quite so heavy. 'Is there anything in here on asteroids?'

'Probably,' Tess said.

Grace ran down to the basement, where I knew she'd cuddle up on the couch in front of the TV, maybe wrap a blanket around herself while she leafed through the pages of the book.

'That was sweet,' Cynthia said, leaning over to kiss Tess.

'Didn't make any sense to throw the damn thing out,' Tess said. 'How are you, sweetheart?' she asked Cynthia. 'You look tired.'

'Oh, I'm fine,' Cynthia said. 'You? You look kind of beat today.'

'I'm OK, I guess,' Tess said, then, as if she'd just remembered something, 'Oh, I can't believe it. I meant to buy some ice cream for Grace.'

'That's OK,' Cynthia said. 'We thought we'd take you out for dinner anyway.'

'I don't know,' Tess said. 'I suppose I am a bit tired today. Why don't we have dinner here? I have some things. But I really wanted some ice cream.'

'I can go,' I said.

'I could use a couple of other things,' Tess said. 'Cynthia, maybe you should go; you know if we send him, he'll just get it all wrong.'

'I suppose,' Cynthia said.

Tess made up a list, handed it to Cynthia. I wandered into the kitchen as Cynthia went out of the door, glanced at the bulletin board next to the phone where Tess had pinned a picture of Grace taken at Disney World. I opened the freezer compartment of the refrigerator, looking for some ice to put in a glass of water. In the front was a container of chocolate ice cream.

'Hey, Tess,' I said, 'you've already got ice cream here.'

'Is that a fact,' she said from the living room.

I closed the freezer and took a seat on the couch by Tess. 'What's going on?' I asked.

'I've been to the doctor,' Tess said.

'What? What's wrong?'

'I'm dying, Terry.'

'What do you mean? What's wrong?'

'Don't worry. It's not going to happen overnight. I might have six months; I might have a year. You never really know. The upshot is, I can see the finish line. And I wanted to tell you first, because Cynthia, she's been going through a lot lately.'

We heard noises on the stairs. Grace emerged from the basement, lugging her new book with both hands. 'I'm hungry,' she said.

'There's some ice cream in the freezer,' I said. 'Chocolate.'

'Why don't you take the whole container downstairs,' Tess said. 'And a spoon.'

'For real?' Grace asked. This violated every rule of etiquette she knew.

'Go for it,' I said.

She ran into the kitchen, dragged a chair over to reach the freezer compartment, grabbed the ice cream and a spoon from the drawer, and ran back downstairs.

Tess's eyes were moist when I looked back at her.

I said, 'I think you should be the one to tell Cynthia.'

She reached out and held my hand. 'Oh, of course, I wouldn't make you do that. I just needed to tell you first, so when I tell Cynthia, you'll be ready to help her through it.' Tess squeezed my hand a little harder. 'There's something else,' she said.

The way she said it, it was like what she still had to tell me was bigger than the fact that she was dying.

'There are some things I need to tell, while I'm still able to, to get it off my chest. Thing is, I don't even know if it does Cynthia any service to know, because what I have to say only raises more questions than it answers. It may torment her more than help her.'

'Tess, what is it?'

'It's about the money,' she said.

'Money?'

Tess nodded tiredly. 'There was money. It would just show up.'

'Money from where?'

Her eyebrows went up. 'Well, that's the question, isn't it? Where was it coming from?'

I ran my hand over the top of my head. 'Just start at the beginning.'

Tess breathed in slowly. 'It wasn't going to be easy, raising Cynthia. But she was my niece, my sister's flesh and blood. I loved her like she was my own child, so when it happened, I took her in. She'd been a bit of a wild kid there, up until her folks up and vanished, and in some ways, that calmed her down. There was a part of her wanted to get herself together, in case her parents came back. She wanted them to be proud of her. So she decided to go to school, to college.'

'The University of Connecticut,' I said.

'That's right. I wondered how I was going to be able to afford it.'

'OK.'

'I found the first envelope in the car, on the passenger seat,' Tess said. 'It was just sitting there. I'd come out from work, got in, there was this white envelope on the seat next to me. It was pretty thick.'

I cocked my head to one side. 'Cash?'

'Just under five thousand dollars of it,' Tess said.

'An envelope full of cash? No explanation, no note, nothing?'

'Oh, there was a note.'

She got up from her chair and took a few steps over to an antique roll-top desk near the front door, opened the single drawer. Held together with a rubber band was a small stack of envelopes, maybe a dozen or more.

'They're all empty,' Tess said. 'But I always kept the envelopes just the same, even though there's nothing written on them, no return address, no postmark. But I thought, What if they've got fingerprints on them that might be useful some day?' Tess worked a piece of paper out from under the rubber band. 'This was the only note I ever got. With the first envelope.'

She handed me a standard-sized piece of typewriter paper, folded in thirds. I unfolded it. The message was printed in block letters. It read:

> THIS IS TO HELP YOU WITH CYNTHIA. FOR HER EDUCATION, FOR WHATEVER ELSE YOU NEED. THERE WILL BE MORE, BUT YOU MUST FOLLOW THESE RULES. NEVER TELL CYNTHIA ABOUT THIS MONEY. NEVER TELL ANYONE. NEVER TRY TO FIND OUT WHERE IT'S COMING FROM. NEVER.

That was it. I must have read it three times before I looked at Tess.

'I never told anyone,' Tess said. 'I never knew when, or where, it would show up. One time, I found it tucked into the *New Haven Register* on the front step one evening. Another time, I came out of the Post Mall; there was another one in the car.'

'You never saw anyone?'

'No. I think whoever left it was watching me, making sure I was far enough away for it to be safe. You want to know something? I always made sure, whenever I parked the car, to leave the window open a crack, just in case."

'How much, altogether?'

'Over about six years, forty-two thousand dollars.'

'Jesus.'

Tess reached out her hand. She wanted the note back. She folded it up, slipped it under the rubber band with the envelopes, and put everything back into the desk drawer.

'So nothing for how many years?' I asked.

'About fifteen, I guess. Nothing since Cynthia finished school.'

'So,' I said, 'who left it?'

'It's the forty-two-thousand-dollar question,' Tess said. 'It's all I've ever wondered, all these years. Her mother? Her father? Both of them?'

'Which would mean they were alive all those years, or at least one of them was. Maybe still alive even now. But if one or the other of them was able to do that, to watch you, to leave you money, why wouldn't they be able to get in touch?'

'You see what I mean?' Tess said. 'It just raises more questions than it answers. It doesn't mean they're alive. And it doesn't mean they're dead.'

'But it means something,' I said. 'After it stopped, when there wasn't any more coming, why didn't you tell the police?'

Tess's eyes grew weary. 'I was scared, Terry, and I was afraid of how much the truth, if we were able to find it, might hurt Cynthia.'

We heard a car pull into the driveway.

'It's up to you whether to tell Cynthia,' Tess said. 'About the envelopes, that is. The stuff about me, I'll tell her, soon enough.'

A car door opened, closed.

'I have to think about this,' I said. 'Thank you for telling me.'

The front door opened and Cynthia burst in with a couple of shopping bags at the same time Grace reappeared from the basement, holding the container of chocolate ice cream to her chest like it was a stuffed toy, her mouth smeared with chocolate. Cynthia eyed her curiously. I could see the wheels turning, that she was thinking she'd been sent on a fool's errand.

Tess said, 'Right after you left, we suddenly realised we had ice cream after all. But I still needed all those other things. It's my birthday. Let's have a party.'

CYNTHIA WAS SITTING up in bed, looking at a magazine, just turning the pages, not paying any real attention to them.

'I have some errands to run at the mall tomorrow,' she said, not taking her eyes from the pages. 'I've got to find Grace some new running shoes. You joining us?'

'Sure,' I said. 'We could grab some lunch there.'

'Tess seemed a bit preoccupied today. And I think she's starting to get a bit absent-minded. I mean, she already had ice cream.'

I took off my shirt. 'Oh well,' I said. 'That's not a big thing.'

Tess had held off telling Cynthia about her health problems. She would have wanted to spoil her birthday celebration. And while it was certainly up to Tess to decide when to break the news, it felt wrong to know this while my wife was kept in the dark. But an even greater burden was knowing, for the first time, about the money that had been sent anonymously to Tess over several years. Surely Cynthia was more entitled to know about it than I? But Tess had held back from telling because she thought Cynthia was fragile enough these days, and I couldn't disagree. And yet.

'You OK?' Cynthia asked.

'Yeah, good. Just kind of beat, that's all,' I said.

I KILLED SOME TIME in the bookstore while Cynthia and Grace looked at shoes. I had a book in my hand when Grace came running into the store. Cynthia trailed behind her, a shopping bag in hand.

'I'm starving,' Grace said, throwing her arms around me.

'You got some shoes?'

She took a step back and modelled for me, sticking out one foot and then the other. White sneakers with a pink swoosh.

I put the book back, and we took the escalator up to the food court level. Grace wanted McDonald's, so I gave her enough money to buy herself something while Cynthia and I went to a different counter to get soup and a sandwich. Cynthia kept glancing back over to the McDonald's, making sure she could see Grace. The mall was busy on this Sunday afternoon.

'She's got us a table,' Cynthia said. I scanned the court, spotted Grace at a table for four, waving her arm back and forth. She already had her Big Mac out of the box when we joined her.

'Eww,' she said when she saw my cream-of-broccoli soup. A kindly looking, fiftyish woman in a blue coat, sitting alone at the next table, glanced over and smiled.

I sat across from Cynthia, Grace to my right. I noticed that Cynthia kept looking over my shoulder. I turned round once, looked where she was looking, turned back. 'What?' I said.

'There's a man over there,' she said. I started to turn round, and she said, 'No, don't look.'

'What's so special about him?'

'He looks like Todd, like Todd would probably look today.'

OK, I thought. *We've been here before. Just be cool.* 'OK,' I said. 'Tell me what he looks like and I'll casually turn round and get a look at him.'

'He's got black hair; he's wearing a brown jacket. He's eating Chinese food. He looks like a younger version of my dad.'

I swivelled slowly on my chair, made like I was taking in the various food kiosks. I saw him, catching some sprouts with his tongue that were falling out of a half-eaten egg roll. Todd might look a bit like this guy. Slightly overweight, a doughy face, black hair, maybe six foot, although it was hard to tell with him sitting down.

I turned back. 'He looks like a million other people,' I said.

'I'm going to get a closer look,' Cynthia said. She was on her feet before I could protest.

'Where's Mommy going?'

'To the washroom,' I said.

'I'm going to have to go, too,' Grace said.

'She can take you after,' I said.

I watched as Cynthia took the long way round the food court, heading in the opposite direction from where the man sat. As she came up alongside him, she walked straight ahead, went to the McDonald's and joined the queue, glancing occasionally at the man she felt bore an amazing resemblance to her brother.

When she sat back down, she presented Grace with a small chocolate sundae in a plastic cup. Her hand was shaking as she put it on Grace's tray.

'Wow!' said Grace.

Cynthia looked at me and said, 'It's him. It's my brother.'

'Cyn, come on, it's not Todd.'

'I got a good look at him. It's him. I'm as sure that's my brother as I am that that's Grace sitting there.'

I felt my heart begin to pound. This could only get worse.

'I'm going to talk to him,' she said.

Bingo.

'You can't,' I said. 'Look, it doesn't make any sense that it's Todd. It's just some guy; he's got some passing resemblance to your brother.'

'He's leaving,' Cynthia said, a hint of panic in her voice.

I whirled around. The man was on his feet, wiping his mouth with a paper napkin and dropping it onto the paper plate. He started walking away.

'He's heading for the escalator.' She was on her feet.

I turned to Grace. 'You stay right here and do not move, you understand?' She nodded. The woman at the next table glanced over again, and I caught her eye. 'Excuse me,' I said, 'but would you mind keeping an eye on my daughter, just for a moment?'

She stared at me, unsure what to say.

'Just a couple of minutes,' I said, trying to reassure her, then got up, not giving her a chance to say no.

I went after Cynthia. I managed to spot the head of the man she was after, descending the escalator. The food court was so crowded it had slowed Cynthia down, and as she got onto the top step of the escalator there were half a dozen people between her and the man, and another half dozen between Cynthia and me. When the man got off at the bottom, he started walking briskly in the direction of the exit. When Cynthia hit the bottom, she broke into a run after the man.

'Todd!' she shouted.

She caught up to the man, grabbing him by the elbow. He turned round, startled by this out-of-breath, wild-eyed woman.

'Yes?' he said.

'Excuse me,' Cynthia said. 'But I think I know you.'

I was at her side now and the man looked at me.

'I don't think so,' the man said slowly.

'You're Todd,' Cynthia said.

'Todd?' He shook his head. 'I'm sorry, but I don't know—'

'I know who you are,' Cynthia said. 'I can see my father in you. In your eyes.'

'I'm sorry,' I said to the man. 'My wife thinks you look like her brother. She hasn't seen him in a very long time.'

Cynthia turned angrily on me. 'I'm not losing my mind,' she said. To the man, she said, 'OK, who are you, then? Tell me who you are.'

'Lady, I don't know what the hell your problem is, but keep me out of it, OK?'

Using as calm a voice as possible, I said to the man, 'My wife's family went missing many years ago. She hasn't seen her brother in years, and you, evidently, bear a resemblance. If you were to show me some ID, a driver's licence, something like that, it would put my wife's mind at ease.'

He studied my face a moment. Finally, he sighed and took his wallet from his back pocket, flipped it open and withdrew a plastic card. 'There,' he said, handing it to me. It was a New York State licence for Jeremy Sloan. An address up in Youngstown.

I handed it to Cynthia. 'Look at this.'

She took the licence tentatively between her thumb and index finger, examined it through the start of tears. Quietly, she handed the licence back to him.

'I'm very sorry,' she said. 'I'm—I'm so sorry.'

The man took the licence back, slid it into his wallet, shook his head disgustedly, and headed off.

'Come on, Cyn,' I said. 'Let's get Grace.'

'Grace?' she said. 'You left Grace?'

'She's with someone,' I said. 'It's OK.'

But she was running back across the main court, up the escalator. I was right behind her as we threaded our way back through the maze of busy tables to where we'd had our lunch.

Grace was not there.

The woman in the blue coat was not there.

'Where the hell . . .'

'Oh my God,' Cynthia said. *'You left her here alone?'*

'I'm telling you I left her with this woman; she was sitting right here.'

The woman had left her unfinished salad sitting on her tray, along with a paper cup half filled with Pepsi or Coke. It was like she'd left in a hurry.

Cynthia, standing in the middle of the crowded food court, started to shout our daughter's name. 'Grace?' she called. 'Grace?'

And then, behind me, a voice.

'Hi, Dad.' I whirled round. 'Why's Mom screaming?' Grace asked.

'Where the hell were you?' I asked. Cynthia had spotted us and was running over. 'What happened to that woman?'

'Her cell rang and she said she had to go,' Grace said matter-of-factly. 'And then I had to go to the bathroom. I told you I had to go to the bathroom. Don't everybody freak out.'

Cynthia grabbed Grace, held her close enough to smother her. If I'd been having qualms about keeping to myself the information about those secret payments to Tess, I was over them now. This family did not need any more chaos.

NO ONE SPOKE the whole way home.

When we got there, the message light on the phone was flashing. It was one of the producers from *Deadline.* Someone had got in touch with them. Someone who claimed to know what might have happened to Cynthia's parents and brother.

Cynthia phoned back immediately. 'Who is it?' Cynthia asked the producer. 'Is it my brother?'

No, it was this woman, the producer said, a clairvoyant or something. But very credible, as far as they could tell.

Cynthia hung up and said, 'Some psychic says she knows what happened.'

Terrific, I thought. A psychic. Absolutely terrific.

'I THINK WE SHOULD at least hear what she has to say,' Cynthia said.

It was that evening, and I was sitting at the kitchen table, marking papers, having a hard time concentrating.

Cynthia was standing at the sink, her back to me, loading the dishwasher. She said, 'We need to talk about this.'

'I don't see much to talk about,' I said.

Cynthia turned round. 'You're still pissed off with me. About today. About what happened at the mall.'

I didn't say anything. There was some truth to what she said. There were things I wanted to say but felt I could not. That I had had enough. That it was time for Cynthia to move on. That while she might have lost a family long ago, and that it was undeniably tragic, she had another family now.

'You think I like the idea of visiting a psychic? You think I don't know how desperate it looks? But what would you do? What if it was Grace?'

I looked at her. 'Don't even say that.'

'What if we lost her? What if she went missing? Suppose she'd been gone for months, for years? And then suppose you got a call, from someone who said she had a vision or something, that she'd seen Grace in a dream, that she knew where she was. Are you telling me you'd refuse to listen?'

I ground my teeth together and looked away.

'What if there was just one chance in a million that maybe this person knew something? What if she wasn't even psychic, but just thought she was, but had actually seen something, some clue? And what if finding out what that was actually led to finding her?'

I put my head in my hands.

WE HAD DINNER EARLY the next day to give us time to drive to the Fox affiliate in New Haven.

'They want me to bring one of the shoeboxes,' Cynthia said. 'She says she just needs to hold it, maybe hold some of the things inside, to pick up more vibrations or whatever about the past.'

'Do we even know who she is?' I asked.

'Keisha,' Cynthia said. 'Keisha Ceylon. I looked her up on the internet. She has a web page.'

'I'll just bet she does,' I said, and gave her a rueful smile.

'Be nice,' Cynthia said.

Later, when we were all in the car, backing out of the drive, Cynthia said, 'Hold it! I can't believe it. I forgot the shoebox.'

She had taken from the closet one of her boxes of family mementos and left it on the kitchen table so she wouldn't forget.

'I'll just be a second,' she said. I watched her unlock the house and run inside. She seemed to be in there for a while, longer than it would take to grab the shoebox, but then she reappeared, shoebox tucked under her arm. She locked up and got back in the car.

'What took so long?' I asked.

'I took an Advil,' she said. 'My head's pounding.'

At the station, we were met at reception by the ponytailed producer, who led us to the set. Paula Malloy was there, and she greeted Cynthia like an old friend, oozing charm. Standing next to Paula was a black woman, late forties, I guessed, dressed impeccably in a navy-blue suit.

'I'd like to introduce you to Keisha Ceylon,' Paula said.

'Pleased to meet you,' Keisha said, shaking hands with us. 'And this must be Grace,' she said, bending down to shake hands with our daughter.

'Hi,' Grace said.

'Is there someplace Grace could go?' I asked. 'Maybe, what do you call it, a green room?'

'Why is it green?' Grace asked as she was led away by some assistant to an assistant.

After they'd put some make-up on Cynthia and Keisha, the two of them were seated on the couch with the shoebox between them. Paula got herself into a chair opposite them, while a couple of cameras were wheeled into position. I retreated back into the darkness of the studio to watch.

Paula did a recap of the story they'd broadcast a few weeks earlier. Then she told her audience of a startling development in the case. A psychic had stepped forward, a woman who believed she could offer some insights into the disappearance of the Bigge family in 1983.

'I had seen your show,' said Keisha Ceylon. 'And of course I found it interesting. But I didn't think much about it after that. And then, a couple of weeks later, I was helping a client attempt to communicate with a lost relative, and I was not having the success I normally do, as though there were some kind of interference, like I was on one of those old party lines and someone is picking up the phone when you're trying to make a call.'

'Fascinating,' breathed Paula. Cynthia remained expressionless.

'And I heard this voice; she said to me, "Please get a message to my daughter." '

'Really? And did she say who she was?'

'She said her name was Patricia. She wanted me to reach her daughter, Cynthia.'

'Why?'

'I'm not entirely sure. I think she wanted me to contact her so that I could learn more. That's why I wanted you'—she smiled at Cynthia—'to bring some mementos, so that I could hold them, perhaps understand better what happened.'

Paula leaned in towards Cynthia. 'You brought some things, didn't you?'

'Yes,' Cynthia said. 'This is one of the shoeboxes I showed you before. Pictures, old clippings, just bits and pieces. I can show you what's inside—'

'That's not necessary,' said Keisha. 'If you would just give me the box . . .'

Cynthia let her take it, let her set it on her lap.

Keisha put a hand on each end of the box and closed her eyes. 'I feel so much energy coming from this,' she said, furrowing her brow. 'I sense . . . that you are about to receive a sign.'

'A sign?' said Cynthia. 'What kind of sign?'

'I'm not sure I can tell you more.' Keisha opened her eyes. 'I . . . I need you to turn the cameras off for a moment.'

'Huh?' said Paula. 'Fellas? Can we hold off for a second?'

'OK,' said one of the guys manning a camera.

'What's the problem, Keisha?' said Paula.

'I just wanted to get straight, before we go any further, how much I'm getting paid to do this,' Keisha said.

Here we go.

'Uh, Keisha,' said Paula, 'I think it was explained to you that while we would cover your expenses, we weren't paying you for your services in any sort of professional sense.'

'That wasn't my understanding,' Keisha said, getting a bit huffy.

I walked forward to the set, caught Cynthia's eye. 'Hon,' I said, tipping my head, the international 'Let's go' gesture.

She nodded resignedly, unclipped the microphone from her blouse and stood up.

'Where are you going?' Paula asked.

'We're outta here,' I said.

'What do you mean?' Keisha asked, outraged.

Cynthia said, 'I'm not going to be made a fool of any more.'

'A thousand dollars,' Keisha said. 'I'll tell you what your momma told me to tell you for a thousand dollars.'

Cynthia was rounding the couch. I reached out my hand for hers.

'OK, seven hundred!' Keisha said as we went to find our way to the green room.

'YOU WERE RIGHT,' Cynthia said on the drive home.

I shook my head. 'You were good, walking away like that. You should have seen the look on that so-called psychic's face when you took off your mike. It's like she was watching her meal ticket walk away.'

Cynthia's smile was caught in the glare of some oncoming headlights. Grace had fallen asleep in the back seat.

'What a waste of an evening,' Cynthia said.

'No,' I said. 'What you said was right. Even if there's only a one-in-a-million chance, you have to check it out. So we checked it out. And now we can cross it off and move on.'

We pulled into the drive. I opened the back door, unbuckled Grace, and carried her into the house, following Cynthia into the living room. She walked ahead of me, turned on the lights in the kitchen as I headed for the stairs to carry Grace up to bed.

'Terry,' Cynthia said. There was something in my wife's voice that said I should come into the kitchen immediately.

So I did.

Sitting in the centre of the kitchen table was a man's black hat. An old, worn, shiny-with-wear fedora.

4

Gently, I set Grace down on the couch in the living room, tucked a throw pillow under her head, and went back into the kitchen.

Cynthia was staring at the fedora, standing as far away from the table as possible, her eyes full of fear. 'He was here,' she said.

'Who was here?'

'My father. He was here.'

'Cynthia, someone was here and left that on the table, but your father?'

'It's his hat,' she said, more calmly than I might have expected.

I approached the table, then grabbed the hat with both hands, turning it over. It was an old hat, no question. The edges of the brim were worn, the lining darkened from years of sweat, the nap worn to the point of shiny in places.

'Look inside,' she said. 'My father, years ago, he lost a couple of hats, so he got a marker and he put a "c" on the inside of the band. For "Clayton".'

I ran my finger along the inside of the band, folding it back. I found it on the right-hand side, near the back. I turned the hat round so that Cynthia could see.

She took a breath. 'Oh my God.' I extended the hat towards her and she took it, holding it as though it were something from King Tut's tomb. 'It's him,' she said. 'He was right here, in this kitchen, in our house.'

'Cynthia,' I said, trying to keep my voice even, 'even if it is your father's hat—and if you say it is, I believe you—the fact that it's here doesn't mean that it was your father who left it.'

'He never went anywhere without it. He wore it everywhere. He was wearing that hat the last night I saw him. It wasn't left behind in the house. You know what this means, don't you?'

I waited.

'It means he's alive.' Cynthia put the hat back on the table. 'The police can take fingerprints.'

'Off that hat?' I said. 'I doubt it.'

'No,' Cynthia said. 'Off the knob.' She pointed to the front door. 'Or the table. Something. If they find his fingerprints in here, it'll prove he's alive.'

I wasn't so sure about that, but I agreed that calling the police was a good idea. Someone—if not Clayton Bigge, then somebody—had been in our house while we were out. I called 911.

There was a car at the house about ten minutes later. Two uniforms, a man and a woman. They checked for any obvious signs of entry, came up with nothing. Grace, of course, had woken up during all the excitement and was at the top of the stairs, peering through the banisters.

'Was anything stolen?' the woman cop asked.

'Uh, no, not as far as we can tell,' I said.

'Any damage done? Any vandalism of any kind?'

'No,' I said. 'Nothing of that sort.'

'You need to check for fingerprints,' Cynthia said.

'Ma'am,' the male cop said, 'I'm afraid there's no real evidence here that there's been a break-in. Everything seems in order.'

'But this hat was left here. That shows someone broke in.'

'So you're saying,' he said, 'someone broke into your house, just so they could leave that hat on your kitchen table?'

Cynthia nodded. I could imagine how this looked to the officers.

'There's no sign of the lock being messed with,' the man said. 'Maybe someone you've given a key to came in, left this here, thought it belonged to you. Simple as that.'

My eye went to the small, empty hook where we usually keep the extra key. The one Cynthia had noticed missing the other morning.

With that, they excused themselves. And in all likelihood, got back in their car and had a good laugh at our expense.

I thought about how Cynthia had forgotten to take her shoebox to the station for that disastrous meeting with the psychic. How she'd had to run back into the house, while Grace and I waited in the car.

She was in the house a long time, just to grab a box.

Not possible, I told myself. Surely not.

I POKED MY HEAD into Rolly Carruthers's office. 'Got a minute?'

Rolly looked at the stack of stuff on his desk. Reports, teacher evaluations, budget estimates. 'You had lunch?'

'No.'

'Let's go over to the Stonebridge.' He slipped on his sport jacket and told his secretary he'd be out of the school for a while.

His secretary insisted he speak to one of the superintendents, who was holding on the line, so he signalled to me that he would be just a couple of minutes. I stepped outside the office, right in the path of Jane Scavullo, who was bearing down the hall at high speed.

The handful of books she was carrying scattered across the hallway. 'Hell,' she said.

'Sorry,' I said, and knelt down to help her pick them up.

'It's OK,' she said, scrambling to get to the books before I did. But she wasn't quick enough. I already had *Foxfire*, the Joyce Carol Oates book I'd recommended to her, in my hand.

She snatched it away from me, tucked it in with the rest of her stuff. I said, 'How are you liking it?'

'It's good,' Jane said. 'Why'd you suggest I read it? You think I'm as bad as the girls in this story?'

'Those girls aren't all bad,' I said. 'And no, I don't think you're like them. But I thought you'd appreciate the writing.'

She snapped her gum. 'Can I ask you something?'

'Sure.'

'What do you care? About what I read, about my writing?'

'You think I'm a teacher just to get rich?'

She looked as though she was almost going to smile, and then caught herself. 'I gotta go,' she said, and did.

The lunch crowd had thinned by the time Rolly and I got to the Stonebridge. He ordered some coconut shrimp and a beer to start, and I settled on a large bowl of New England clam chowder with extra crackers, and coffee.

Rolly was talking about putting their house on the market soon, that they'd have a lot of money left over after they paid for the mobile home in Florida. There'd be money to put in the bank; they could invest it, take the odd trip. It's like he was already finished being a principal. He was someplace else.

'I got stuff on my mind,' I said. 'Cynthia's always thought of you like an uncle, you know? You looked out for her, after what happened. So I feel I can come to you when there's a problem.'

'Go on.'

'I'm starting to wonder whether Cynthia's losing it. It's not like it's any one thing. It's all these little things put together.'

I filled him in. The brown car. The anonymous phone call from someone saying her family had forgiven her, how she'd accidentally erased the call. Chasing the guy in the mall, thinking he was her brother. The hat in the middle of the table.

'What?' Rolly said. 'Clayton's *hat*?'

'Yeah,' I said. 'Evidently. I mean, I suppose she could have had it tucked away in a box all these years. But it did have this little marking inside, his first initial under the lining.'

Rolly thought about that. 'Why would she be making these things up?'

'I don't know. I just wish it would all end. Even if that meant we found out they had all died that night.'

'Closure,' Rolly said.

'I hate that word,' I said. 'But yeah, basically. The thing is, there's more. Cyn's in such a delicate frame of mind, there's stuff I'm not telling her.' Rolly raised an eyebrow. 'About Tess,' I said.

Rolly took a sip of his Sam Adams. 'What about Tess?'

'First of all, she's not well. She told me she's dying.'

'Ah, damn,' Rolly said. 'Cynthia'll be devastated. They're so close.'

'I know. And I think it has to be Tess who tells her. I can't do it.'

'What's the other thing?'

I hesitated. It seemed wrong to tell Rolly about the secret payments Tess had received before I told Cynthia, but that was one of the reasons why I was telling him—to get some guidance on how to break this to my wife.

'For a number of years, Tess was getting money.'

Rolly set down his beer. 'What do you mean, getting money?'

'Someone left money for her. Cash, in an envelope. A number of times, with a note that it was to help pay for Cynthia's education. It added up to more than forty thousand dollars.'

'Did she say who was it from?'

I shrugged. 'Tess has no idea, although she wonders whether the envelopes the money came in, the note, whether you could still get fingerprints off them after all these years, or DNA.'

'This is huge,' Rolly said. 'And Cynthia doesn't know anything about this?'

'No. But she's entitled to know.'

'Sure, of course she is. But suppose you do tell her. What then?' Rolly pressed his lips together and leaned forward over the table. 'I'd sit on it.'

I guess I was surprised. 'Really?'

'At least for the time being. It's only going to torment Cynthia. It'll make her think that, had she known about the money, maybe there was something she could have done.'

I thought about that. I thought he was right.

'And not only that,' he said. 'Just when Tess needs all the support and love she can get from Cynthia, when she's in poor health, Cynthia's going to be mad at her. She's going to feel betrayed. She's going to feel her aunt had no business keeping this information from her all these years.'

I nodded, but then stopped. 'But if I don't tell her, aren't I betraying her the same way she may feel Tess did?'

Rolly studied me and smiled. 'That's why I'm glad it's your decision instead of mine, my friend.'

WHEN I GOT HOME, Cynthia's car was in the drive, and there was a vehicle I didn't recognise parked at the kerb. A silver Toyota sedan.

I stepped in through the front door and saw Cynthia sitting on the couch in the living room across from a short, heavyset, nearly bald man with olive-coloured skin. They both got to their feet and Cynthia moved towards me.

'Hi, honey,' she said, forcing a smile.

'Hi, sweetheart.' I turned towards the man and extended a hand, which he took confidently in his and shook. 'Hello,' I said.

'Mr Archer,' he said, his voice deep and almost syrupy.

'This is Mr Abagnall,' Cynthia said. 'This is the private detective we're hiring to find out what happened to my family.'

'Denton Abagnall,' the detective said. 'Mrs Archer has filled me in on a lot of the particulars, but I wouldn't mind asking you a few questions as well.'

'Sure,' I said, holding a 'hang on just a second' finger up to him and turning to Cynthia to say, 'Can I talk to you a minute?'

She gave Abagnall an apologetic look. 'Would you excuse us?' He nodded. I steered her out of the front door and onto the top step.

'What the hell's going on?' I asked.

'I'm not going to sit around any more waiting for something to happen,' Cynthia said. 'I've decided to take charge of this situation.'

'What do you expect him to find out?' I asked. 'It's been twenty-five years.'

'Well, that hat didn't appear twenty-five years ago,' she said. 'And that phone call, that wasn't twenty-five years ago, either.'

I shook my head. I didn't know what to do.

'What's happening with you, Terry?' Cynthia asked. 'One of the reasons I married you is I knew you'd be a guy who was always there for me, who'd be in my corner. And for years, you've been that guy. But lately I'm getting this vibe that maybe you're tired of being that guy. That maybe you're not even sure you believe me all the time.'

'Cynthia, don't—'

'Maybe that's one of the reasons why I want to hire this man. Because he's not going to judge me. He's not going into this thinking I'm some sort of crackpot.'

'I never said I think you're a—'

'You don't have to,' Cynthia said. 'I can see it in your eyes.'

We looked at each other for a couple of seconds.

I pulled her close to me, whispered into her ear, 'I'm sorry. I'll always be that guy in your corner. I'll always be here for you.'

She put her arms round me and pressed her head into my chest. I had a pretty good feeling that we'd be throwing our money away. But even if Denton Abagnall didn't find out anything, maybe hiring him to try was exactly what Cynthia needed to do.

'We'll hire him,' I said. She hugged me a bit more tightly.

'If he doesn't find anything soon,' she said, 'we'll stop.'

'Let's go talk to him,' I said.

Abagnall had been sitting on the couch, looking through Cynthia's shoeboxes of mementos, and got up when we came in.

'I hope you don't mind,' he said. 'I was having a look at your things here. I'd like to spend some more time looking at them, provided you've reached a decision about whether you want my help.'

'We have,' I said. 'And we do. We'd like you to try to find out what happened to Cynthia's family.'

'I'm not going to give you any false hopes,' Abagnall said. He spoke slowly, deliberately. 'This is a very cold trail. I think you should have low expectations.'

Cynthia nodded solemnly.

'I don't see a lot here that jumps out at me,' he said, motioning to the shoeboxes. 'But I wouldn't mind hanging on to these, for a while, if you don't mind.'

'That's fine,' Cynthia said. 'Just so long as I get them back.'

Abagnall nodded. Inside his jacket, his cellphone rang. 'Excuse me one second.' He opened the phone, saw who was calling, answered it. 'Yes, love?' He listened, nodded. 'Oh, that sounds wonderful. With the shrimp?' He smiled. 'But not too spicy. OK. I'll see you in a bit.' He folded the phone and put it away. 'My wife,' he said. 'She gives me a call about this time to let me know what she's making for dinner.'

Cynthia and I exchanged glances.

'Now, Mrs Archer, do you have any photos of your father?'

'I'm afraid not,' she said.

'I'll check with the Department of Motor Vehicles,' he said. 'I don't know how far back their records go, but maybe they have a photo.' Abagnall folded his notebook shut and slipped it into his jacket, then handed each of us a business card. He gathered up the shoeboxes and got to his feet. 'I'll be in touch soon, let you know how I'm progressing.'

'I'll walk Mr Abagnall to his car,' I said.

Abagnall had his door open and was about to plop down into his seat when I said, 'You might want to talk to Cynthia's aunt Tess.'

'Yes?'

'She recently told me something, something she's not yet disclosed to Cynthia.' I told him about the anonymous donations of cash and gave him her address. 'I'll tell Tess to expect you.'

'Thank you,' he said. 'I'll report back to you folks in three days, sooner if I learn anything interesting.'

'MEN ARE WEAK—not you, of course—and they let you down, but just as often it's the women who'll really betray you,' she said.

'I know. You've said this before,' he said.

'Oh, I'm sorry.' Getting sarcastic. 'Am I boring you, sweetheart?'

'No, it's OK. Go ahead. You were saying. Women will betray you, too. I was listening.'

'That's right. Like that Tess. She stole from me.'

'Well . . . It's not like she spent it on herself. She did use it to—'

'Enough! It makes me crazy, the more I think about it. She should have found a way to tell me and make things right.'

And how would she have done that? he wondered. But he said nothing.

'Are you there?' she said.

'I'm still here.'

'Was there something you wanted to say?'

'Nothing. Just . . . Well, that would have been a bit tricky, don't you think?'

'I can't talk to you sometimes,' she said. 'Call me tomorrow. If I need some intelligent conversation in the meantime, I'll talk to the mirror.'

5

After Abagnall left, I called Tess from my cell to give her a heads-up.

'I'll help him any way I can,' Tess said. 'I think Cynthia's doing the right thing, having someone private look into this. If she's willing to take this kind of step, she's probably ready for me to tell her what I know.'

'We'll all get together again soon.'

'When the phone rang, I was actually thinking about calling you,' Tess said. She took a breath. 'Terry, I went for another test.'

I felt my legs going weak. 'What did they say?'

'I'm going to be OK,' she said. 'They said the other tests turned out to be wrong. This last one, it was definite.' She paused. 'Terry, I'm not dying.'

'Oh my God, Tess, that's such wonderful news. They're sure?'

'They're sure. But, Terry. Tell me you didn't tell Cynthia.'

'I never told her,' I said.

When I went inside, Cynthia spotted a tear running down my cheek. She reached up and brushed it away with her index finger.

'Terry,' she said, 'what? What's happened?'

I threw my arms round her. 'I'm just so happy,' I said.

She must have thought I was losing my mind.

FOR THE NEXT couple of days, Cynthia was more at ease than I had seen her for some time. After dinner one night, Grace vanished to watch something on the Discovery Channel about what Saturn's rings are really made of, and Cynthia and I plonked ourselves down at the kitchen table. I was writing down numbers on a note pad, adding them up, doing them another way.

'I'm thinking,' I said, looking at the numbers, 'that we could probably afford Mr Abagnall for two weeks instead of just one.'

Cynthia put her hand over the one I was writing with. 'I love you, you know.'

In the other room, someone on the TV said, 'Uranus,' and Grace giggled.

'Did I ever tell you the time,' Cynthia asked, 'when I ruined my mother's James Taylor cassette?'

'No.'

'I must have been eleven or twelve. Mom loved James Taylor. She said he could make her happy and he could make her sad. One day, Mom made me mad about something; there was something I wanted to wear to school that was in the dirty clothes pile, and I mouthed off because she hadn't done her job.'

'That must have gone over well.'

'No kidding. She said if she wasn't cleaning my clothes to my satisfaction, I knew where the washing machine was. So I popped open the cassette player she had in the kitchen, grabbed whatever tape was in there, and threw it on the floor. It busted open, the tape spilled out and the thing was ruined.'

I listened.

'I thought she'd kill me. But instead, she stopped what she was doing, went over, picked up the tape, had a look at which one it was, and said, "James Taylor. This is the one with 'Your Smiling Face' on it. That's my favourite. You know why I like that one?" she asks me. "Because it starts off how every time I see your face, I have to smile myself, because I love you." Anyway, something like that. And she said, "That's my favourite because every time I hear it, it makes me think of you, and how much I love you. And right about now, you need me to hear that song more than ever." '

Cynthia's eyes were wet. A single tear ran down her cheek and dropped onto the kitchen table.

'I love that song,' Cynthia said. 'And I miss her so much.'

LATER, SHE PHONED TESS. No special reason, just to talk. Afterwards, she came up to the bedroom and her red eyes suggested that she had been crying again.

Tess, she told me, had thought she was very ill, terminal even, but it had turned out to be OK. 'She said she didn't want to tell me, that she didn't want to *burden* me with it. Can you imagine?'

'That's so crazy,' I said.

She blew her nose. 'I can't imagine losing her.'

'I know. Neither can I.'

'She asked me to tell you to call her,' she said. 'She probably wants to tell you this herself. Don't tell her I already told you, OK? Please? I just couldn't keep it to myself, you know?'

'Sure,' I said.

I went downstairs and dialled Tess.

'I told her,' Tess said.

'I know,' I said. 'Thank you.'

'He was here. The detective. Mr Abagnall. He's a very nice man. I told him everything. About the money, the letter. I gave all of it to him. He was very interested.'

I nodded. 'I would think so. I think that was the best thing to do, giving him everything. If you think of anything else, you should give him a call.'

'That's what he asked me to do. He gave me his card. I'm looking at it right now; it's pinned to my board here by the phone, right next to that picture of Grace with Goofy.'

'OK,' I said.

'Give Cynthia a hug for me,' she said.

'I will. I love you, Tess,' I said, and hung up.

'She told you?' Cynthia asked when I got up to our bedroom. Now in her nightshirt, she lay on the bed, on top of the covers.

'She told me.' I leaned over, kissed her forehead. 'You try to get some sleep. I'll say good night to Grace.'

As usual, Grace's room was in total darkness so as to give her a better view of the stars through her telescope. 'Are we safe tonight?' I asked as I slipped in.

'Looks like it,' Grace said.

'That's good.'

'You wanna see?'

I squinted into the end, saw nothing but blackness with a few pinpricks of light. 'OK, what am I looking at?'

'Stars,' Grace said.

I turned and looked at her, grinning impishly in the dim light. 'Thank you, Carl Sagan,' I said. I got my eye back in position, went to adjust the scope a bit and it slipped partway off its stand.

'I told you,' she said. 'It's kind of a crappy stand.'

'OK, OK,' I said, and looked back into the scope, but the view had shifted, and what I was looking at now was a hugely magnified circle of the sidewalk in front of our house.

And a man, watching it.

His face, blurry and indistinct, filled the lens. I abandoned the telescope and went to the window. 'Who the hell is that?' I said, more to myself than Grace.

'Who?' she said. She got to the window in time to see the man run away.

'You stay right here,' I said to Grace, and bolted out of her room, went down the steps two at a time, and nearly flew out of the front door. I ran down to the end of the drive, looked up the street in the direction I'd seen the man run. A hundred feet ahead, red brake lights on a car parked at the kerb came on as someone turned the ignition, moved it from park to drive, and floored it. I was too far away to tell what kind of car it was before it turned the corner.

When I got back to the front door, Grace was standing there. 'I told you to stay in your room,' I said angrily.

'I just wanted to see—'

'Get to bed right now.'

She tore up the stairs lickety-split.

My heart was pounding and I needed a moment for it to settle down before I went upstairs. When I finally did, I found Cynthia, under the covers, fast asleep.

CYNTHIA HAD PHONED PAM and arranged to show up for work a bit late that morning. We had a locksmith coming at nine. If we hadn't already booked one, last night's incident surely would have tipped me in that direction.

I told Cynthia, over breakfast and before Grace came down to go to school, about the man on the sidewalk. I contemplated not doing so, but if someone was watching the house, we all needed to be on high alert.

'Did you get a good look at him?' Cynthia asked.

'No. I went to chase him down the street, but he got into a car and drove away.'

'Did you get a look at the car? Could it have been brown?'

'Cyn, I don't know. It was dark; the car was dark.'

'So it could have been brown. I'll bet it was the same person. The one who was driving past me and Grace on the way to school.'

AT SCHOOL, I found Rolly rinsing out a mug in the school staff room so he could pour himself some coffee. 'How's it going?' I asked.

Rolly shrugged. He seemed distracted. 'Same old. You?'

I let out a sigh. 'Someone was standing in the dark staring at our house last night, and when I tried to find out who it was, he ran away.' I got myself a coffee mug, filled it.

'What do you think he was doing there?' Rolly said.

I shrugged. 'I don't know, but they're putting dead bolts on the doors this morning and just in time, it seems.'

'That's pretty creepy,' Rolly said. He paused. 'I'm thinking of taking early retirement.'

So we were done talking about me. 'I thought you had to stay at least until the end of the school year?'

'It only means a few bucks less on my pension. I'm ready to move on, Terry. I gave the system forty years and now I want out.'

'You do look a bit tense today. Maybe you should go home.'

'I'm all right.' He looked like a smoker who desperately needed to light up. 'Millicent's already retired. There's nothing to stop me. None of us are getting any younger. You never know how much longer you've got. You're here one minute, gone the next.'

'Oh,' I said. 'That reminds me.'

'What?'

'About Tess. She's going to be OK. They did another test, turns out the initial diagnosis was wrong. She's not dying.'

'But,' Rolly said slowly, as if unable to take it all in, 'those doctors told her she was dying. And now, what, they say they were wrong?'

'You know,' I said, 'this is not what I'd call bad news.'

Rolly blinked. 'No, of course not. It's wonderful news. Better than getting good news and then getting bad, I suppose.' He glanced at his watch. 'Listen, I've got to go.'

So did I. My creative-writing class started in one minute.

'WOULD YOU LIKE some coffee?' Cynthia asked as Mr Abagnall came into our house late that afternoon. He had phoned to say he wanted to see us.

'Oh, I'd like that,' he said. 'I'd like that very much.'

He got settled on the couch, and Cynthia brought out coffee and cups and sugar and cream on a tray, and then she poured coffee into three cups.

Inside our heads, both Cynthia and I were screaming: *For God's sake, tell us what you know—we can't stand it another minute!*

Finally Abagnall got out his notebook. He opened it up, leafed through a few pages, then said, 'OK, here we are. Mrs Archer, what can you tell me about Vince Fleming?'

'Vince Fleming?'

'That's right. He was the boy you were with that night. When your father found you and brought you home. I've had a chance to go over the police files on this case, and this Vince Fleming fellow, he has a bit of chequered history, if you get my drift.'

'I'm afraid I didn't really keep in touch with him after that night,' Cynthia said.

'He's been in and out of trouble his whole life,' Abagnall said. 'And his father was no different. Anthony Fleming, he ran a rather significant criminal organisation back around that time.'

'My God,' Cynthia said. 'I had no idea. I mean, I knew Vince was a bit of a bad boy, but I had no idea what his father was involved in. Is his father still alive?'

'No. He was shot in 1992. Some aspiring hoodlums killed him in a deal that went very badly wrong.'

'You think Vince had something to do with my family disappearing?' Cynthia asked.

'I simply don't know. But he would have had reason to be angry. Your father had dragged you away from a date with him. That must have been humiliating, not just for you, but for him as well. And if he did have anything to do with your parents' disappearance, then he had a father with the means to help him cover his tracks.'

'But surely the police must have looked into this at the time?' I said. 'You can't be the first person this has occurred to.'

'You're right. The police looked into it. But they never came up with anything concrete. There were only some suspicions.'

We were all quiet for a moment. Then Cynthia said, 'He had a knife. In the car that night. He was showing it off to me. I can remember holding it . . .' Her voice trailed off, and her eyes were starting to roll up under her eyelids. 'I feel faint.'

I quickly slipped my arm round her. 'What can I get you?'

'I just, I just need to go . . . freshen up . . . for a minute,' she said. I watched worriedly as she made her way up the stairs.

Abagnall was watching, too, and when he heard the bathroom door close, he said quietly, 'This Vince Fleming, his father made a very good living from his illegal activities. If he felt some sense of responsibility for what his son did, it would have been financially possible for him to leave sums of cash for your wife's aunt to assist her in sending her niece to school.'

'You saw the letter,' I said. 'Tess showed it to you.'

'Yes. She gave it to me, in fact, in addition to the envelopes. I take it you still haven't told your wife about it?'

'Not yet. I think Tess is ready to, though. It might be worth seeing her tonight.'

'That's a good—' Inside his jacket, Abagnall's phone rang. 'A dinner report, no doubt,' he said, taking out the phone. But he scowled when he saw the number, tossed the phone back into his jacket, and said, 'They can leave a message.'

Cynthia was making her way back down the stairs.

'Mrs Archer, are you feeling all right?' Abagnall asked. She nodded and sat back down. He cleared his throat. 'Are you sure? Because I'd like to bring up another matter.'

Cynthia said, 'Yes. Please go ahead.'

'Well, when you were unable to produce a photograph of your father, I went in search of one, and that led me to check with the Department of Motor Vehicles. They weren't much help to me.'

'They didn't have his picture?' she asked.

'The thing is,' Abagnall said, 'they have no record of your father ever having a licence at all.'

'What do you mean?'

'There's no record of him, Mrs Archer. As far as the DMV is concerned, he never existed.'

'People go missing from computer files all the time,' Cynthia said.

Denton Abagnall nodded. 'The fact that Clayton Bigge didn't show up in the DMV files is not, in itself, particularly conclusive of anything. But then I checked past records for his Social Security number, and nothing came up there, either. It's hard to find any record of your father anywhere, Mrs Archer. We have no picture of him. There's no record of him with the IRS.'

'What are you saying?' she asked. 'Are you saying he was a spy or something? Some kind of secret agent?'

'Well, not necessarily. Nothing quite so exotic.' He took a sip of his coffee.

'Then what are your theories,' I asked.

'I could probably come up with half a dozen, based on what little I know at the moment.' he said. 'Was your father living under a name that was not his own? Was he escaping some strange past? A criminal one, perhaps? Did Vince Fleming bring harm to your family that evening? Was his father's criminal network somehow linked to something in your father's past that he'd been successfully covering up until that time?'

'We don't really know anything, do we?' Cynthia asked.

Abagnall leaned back into the couch cushions. 'What I know is that in a couple of days, the unanswered questions in this case seem to be expanding exponentially. I want to look further into this Vince Fleming character. Mrs Archer, what do you think? Could this young man have been capable of bringing harm to your family?'

She thought about that for a moment. 'After all this time, I guess I have to consider that anything is possible.'

'Yes, it's good to keep an open mind. Thank you for the coffee.'

Before leaving, Abagnall returned Cynthia's shoebox of mementos. Cynthia closed the door as he left, then turned to me and asked, 'Who was my father? Who the hell was my father?'

CYNTHIA WAS PREOCCUPIED all through dinner. Who wouldn't be, having learned only an hour earlier that the man she'd known her entire life as Clayton Bigge might not be Clayton Bigge at all?

'I think,' I said, 'that we should go visit Tess tonight. There's a lot to talk about. You should tell her what Mr Abagnall said.'

'Yeah,' said Grace. 'Let's see Aunt Tess.'

'I called earlier,' Cynthia said. 'I left her a message. She must be out doing something. She'll call us when she gets the message.'

I looked at the clock. It was nearly seven. 'Why don't we go for a drive, head up to her place? Maybe she'll be there by the time we arrive. There might be some things she might want to share with you.'

'What do you mean, she might have something to share with me?' Cynthia asked.

My mouth was dry. 'OK,' I said. 'Grace, your mother and I need some privacy here.'

'I haven't finished my dinner.'

'Take your plate with you and go watch some TV.'

She took her plate and left the room, a sour expression on her face.

To Cynthia, I said, 'Before she got those last test results, Tess thought she was dying.'

Cynthia was very still. 'You knew this.'

'Please. Just let me tell you this. You can get mad later.' I felt Cynthia's eyes go into me like icicles.

And so I told Cynthia. Everything. The anonymous note, the cash, how it would show up anywhere, any time. How it helped get her through school. How Tess kept this to herself all these years.

When I was done, she looked numb. She said something I didn't hear very often from her. 'I could use a drink,' she said.

I got down a bottle of Scotch from a shelf high in the pantry, poured her a small glass. She drank it down in one long gulp.

'All right,' she said. 'Let's go and see Tess.'

GRACE WASN'T HER USUAL chatty self on the way up. I think she was picking up the tension in the car and decided, wisely, to lay low.

When we pulled off the main road between Milford and Derby and drove down Tess's street, Cynthia pointed. 'Her car's home.'

We got to the door and I knocked. After a few seconds, I knocked again, only louder.

'Maybe she's round the back,' Cynthia said. 'Working on her garden.'

So we walked round the house, Grace, as usual, charging on ahead. Before we'd rounded the house, she was already running back, saying, 'She's not there.'

Cynthia rapped on the back door, which led directly into Tess's kitchen. There was still no answer.

'That's weird,' she said.

I crowded Cynthia on the back step and peered through the tiny window in the door. I thought I saw something on the floor of the kitchen, obscuring the tiles.

A person.

I grasped the knob, turned it slowly and pushed, testing to see whether the door was locked. It was not.

I stepped in, Cynthia looking over my shoulder.

Aunt Tess lay on the kitchen floor, face down, her head twisted at an odd angle, one arm stretched out ahead of her, the other hanging back.

'Oh my God,' Cynthia said. 'She's had a stroke or something!'

I didn't exactly have a medical degree, but there seemed to be an awful lot of blood on the floor for a stroke.

WHEN CYNTHIA HEARD our daughter running up behind us, preparing to leap into the kitchen, she turned, blocked her, and started moving her round to the front garden.

'What's wrong?' Grace shouted. 'Aunt Tess?'

I knelt next to Cynthia's aunt, tentatively touched her back. It felt very cold. 'Tess,' I whispered. There was so much blood pooled under her that I didn't want to turn her over. I shifted around, knelt even closer to the floor, to see her face. The sight of her open, unblinking eyes staring straight ahead left me chilled.

I stood. There were voices in my head, telling me not to touch anything. I dug out my cell and made the call.

'Yes, I'll wait here,' I told the 911 operator. 'I'm not going anywhere.'

But I did leave the house by the back door and walk round to the front, where I found Cynthia sitting, with Grace in her lap, in the front seat of our car. Cynthia looked at me, her eyes sending a question, and I answered by shaking my head back and forth a couple of times, very slowly.

'What is it?' she asked me. 'Do you think it was a heart attack?'

'No,' I said to Cynthia. 'It wasn't a heart attack.'

The police agreed.

There must have been ten cars there within the hour, including half a dozen cop cars, an ambulance, and a couple of TV news vans. Tess had been stabbed. Someone had taken one of her own kitchen knives and driven it into her.

The police had a lot of questions for me. Why had we come up? For a visit, I said.

Did I have any idea who might have done this? the detective asked.

'This might,' I said hesitantly, 'be related to something that happened to my wife twenty-five years ago.'

I told him as condensed a version as possible of Cynthia's story. About how there had been some strange developments of late, particularly since the TV item. And I told him that we had engaged a private detective to look into it.

He let me go and I went back out to find Cynthia. I found her where she'd been before, in the front of the car with Grace in her lap. When she saw me, Grace asked, 'Is Aunt Tess dead, Dad?'

'Yes, honey. She is.'

Grace's lip started trembling. Cynthia said, so evenly that I could tell she was actually holding back, 'You could have told me.'

'What?'

'You could have told me what you knew. What Tess had told you.' She paused. 'And then maybe this wouldn't have happened.'

'Cyn, I don't see how, I mean, there's no way to know—'

'That's right. There's no way to know. But I know this. If you'd told me sooner what Tess had told you, I'd have been up here talking to her about it, and if I'd been doing that, maybe we'd have figured something out, before someone had a chance to do this.'

'Cyn, I just don't—'

'What else haven't you told me, Terry? What other things are you holding back that I'm not able to handle?'

Grace started to cry and buried her face into Cynthia's chest.

'Nothing,' I said.

But there was one thing. Something I'd only just noticed.

I'd been brought back into the kitchen by the investigating officers, asked to describe all of my movements, where I'd stood, what I'd done, what I'd touched. As I was leaving the room, I happened to look at the small bulletin board next to the phone. There was the picture of Grace that I had taken on our trip to Disney World. What was it Tess had said on the phone to me? After Denton Abagnall had been out to visit her?

I'd said something along the lines of, 'If you think of anything else, you should give him a call.' And Tess had said, 'He gave me his card. It's pinned to my board by the phone, right next to that picture of Grace with Goofy.'

There was no card on the board now.

'YOU DON'T SAY,' she said. This was quite the development.

'Oh, it's true,' he said.

'That's quite the coinky-dink,' she said slyly. 'You being down there and all.'

'Yeah.'

'She had it coming, you know,' she said.

'I think it means we have to hold off for a couple of days on the next part.'

'Really?' she said. She was feeling impatient all of a sudden.

'There's going to be a funeral here tomorrow,' he said. 'So my sister, she's going to be pretty busy making all those arrangements, right? So maybe we should wait for that to be over.'

'I see your point. But there's something I'd like you to do for me.'

'Yes?' he said.

'Don't call her your sister.' She was very firm.

'Sorry. It's just, well, you know, she is—'

'I don't care,' she said.

'OK, Mom,' he said. 'I won't do it again.'

6

There weren't many people to call.

Patricia Bigge, Cynthia's mother, had been Tess's only sibling. Their own parents, of course, were long gone. And Tess had not kept up any of her friendships with the people at the office where she'd worked before retiring.

It wasn't as though we had to alert everyone to the funeral. Tess Berman's death had made the news. The word from the police was that they had no idea who had done this, no idea as to motive. And no suspects. There was no sign of forced entry. No signs of a struggle. It appeared that Tess's killer had struck quickly. Who had done this? Why? And where was Denton Abagnall's business card? Had Tess not pinned it to the board as she'd told me?

The next day, consumed with these and other questions, I found the card Abagnall had left with us and called his cellphone number.

The provider cut in immediately and invited me to leave a message, suggesting that Abagnall's phone was off.

So I tried his home number. A woman answered.

'Is Mr Abagnall there, please?'

'Who's calling?'

'Mrs Abagnall? This is Terry Archer.'

'Mr Archer!' she said, sounding a bit frantic. 'I was just going to call you! Have you heard from him?'

'Sorry?'

'Denton? Do you know where he is?'

'No, I don't.'

'This isn't like him at all. Sometimes, he has to work overnight, on surveillance, but he always gets in touch at some point.'

I had a bad feeling in the pit of my stomach. I said, 'He was at our house yesterday afternoon. He was bringing us up to date.'

'I know,' she said. 'I phoned him just after he left your place. That was the last I spoke to him.'

I thought about what I was going to say next before I said it, given that I'd developed a habit lately of keeping things from people out of fear I'd worry them needlessly. But that was a policy that didn't appear to be paying off. So I said, 'Mrs Abagnall, I don't want to alarm you, and I'm sure there's a perfectly good reason your husband hasn't got in touch with you, but I think you need to call the police.'

'Oh,' she said quietly.

'And you can call me if anything happens. Let me give you my home number, if you don't already have it, and my cell, too.'

After I hung up, Cynthia came into the kitchen. She was on her way back down to the funeral home.

'Cyn,' I said.

She didn't respond. She'd frozen me out. She was holding me, at least in part, responsible for Tess's death.

We were both home from work, of course. She'd taken off indefinitely from the dress shop, and I called the school to tell them that I'd be off for the next few days.

'I'm not going to keep anything from you from now on,' I told Cynthia. 'And something else has happened that you should know about. I just spoke with Denton Abagnall's wife. He's missing.'

She seemed to list a bit to one side, as if some of the air had been let out of her.

'What did she say?' Cynthia managed to ask.

I told her.

She put one hand up to the wall to steady herself and then said, 'I have to go to the funeral home, make some last-minute decisions.'

'Of course,' I said. 'Do you want me to come with you?'

'No,' she said, and left.

I WALKED OUT of the kitchen, and my eyes landed on the two shoeboxes on the coffee table that Abagnall had returned to us the day before. I picked them up, took them back into the kitchen and set them on the table. I started taking things out one at a time.

When Cynthia had cleared things out of her house as a teenager, she'd basically dumped the contents of drawers into these boxes, including those from the bedside tables of her parents. Like most small drawers they became a repository for things important and not: spare change, keys you no longer knew the use for, receipts, newspaper clippings, old pens.

Clayton Bigge wasn't much of a sentimentalist, but he saved the odd thing, like newspaper clippings. There was that one clipping of the basketball team Todd was part of, for example. But if it had anything to do with fishing, it was even more likely Clayton would hang on to it. Cynthia had told me that he read through the newspapers' sports sections for fishing tournament news, through the travel sections for stories about out-of-the-way lakes, where there were so many fish they practically jumped into the boat.

In the box, there were probably half a dozen such clippings. I unfolded each yellowed fragment, careful not to tear it, to make sure what it was.

There was something about one of them that caught my eye. It had been saved from the pages of the *Hartford Courant.* A piece about fly-fishing on the Housatonic River. Whoever had cut the clipping from the paper—Clayton, presumably—had been meticulous about it, taking the scissors carefully down the gutters between the first column of this story and the last of one that had been discarded. The story had been placed above some unseen ads, or other stories, that had been stacked like steps in the bottom left-hand corner.

That's why it seemed odd to me that a news story, unrelated to fly-fishing but tucked into the bottom-right leg of the story, remained. It was only a couple of inches long, this story. It said:

> Police still have no leads in the hit-and-run death of Connie Gormley, 27, from Sharon, whose body was found dumped into the ditch alongside US 7 Saturday morning. Investigators believe Gormley was walking alongside the highway near the Cornwall Bridge when she was struck by a southbound car late Friday night. Police say it appears that Gormley's body was moved into the ditch after it had been struck by the car.

Why, I wondered, had everything else around that article been so neatly trimmed away but this story left intact?

The date on the top of the newspaper page was October 15, 1982.

AFTER THE SERVICE, the funeral director took me, Cynthia and Grace in his Cadillac down to Milford Harbor, where he kept a small cabin cruiser. Rolly Carruthers and his wife, Millicent, followed, having offered to give Cynthia's boss, Pamela, a ride with them in their car, and the three of them joined our family on the boat.

Once we had left the sheltered harbour, we put out into Long Island Sound, only about a mile out front of the beach houses along East Broadway. The funeral director had brought along the urn containing Tess's ashes, which were to be scattered onto the Sound, as Tess had requested.

There wasn't a lot of conversation on the boat. Millicent put her arm round Cynthia and said, 'Tess couldn't have had a more beautiful day to see her final request carried out.'

Maybe, if Tess had actually died from an illness, there might have been some comfort in this, but when someone dies by violence, it's hard to find consolation anywhere.

'It is a beautiful day,' Rolly said, echoing his wife. He approached Cynthia, his eyes looking down at the deck. 'But I know that doesn't make any of this any easier to bear.'

He walked down to the stern to watch the boat's wake. I came up alongside him. 'Thanks for coming today,' I said. 'It means a lot to Cynthia.'

He looked surprised. 'You kidding? You know we've always been there for both of you.'

The boat slowed to a stop and the funeral director approached. 'Mr Archer? I think we're ready.'

We gathered tightly together on the deck as the urn was placed formally in Cynthia's hands. Holding it firmly, Cynthia moved to the side of the boat and upended the urn while Grace and I and Rolly and Millicent and Pam watched. The ashes fell out and settled on the water, dissolved and dispersed. In a few seconds, what physically remained of Tess was gone. Grace had brought a rose—her own idea—which she cast upon the water.

'Goodbye, Aunt Tess,' she said. 'Thank you for the book.'

Cynthia had said that morning that she wanted to say a few words, but when the time came, she didn't have the strength. And I could find no words that I thought were any more meaningful, or heartfelt, than Grace's simple farewell.

Coming back into the harbour, I saw a short black woman in a pair of jeans and tan leather jacket standing at the end of the dock. She was nearly as round as she was short, but she showed grace and agility as she grabbed on to the boat as it drew close and assisted in securing it. She said to me, 'Terrence Archer?'

I said yes.

She flashed me a badge that identified herself as Rona Wedmore, a police detective from Milford. 'I'd like to speak with you a moment,' she said, not asking.

Wedmore and I walked slowly along the dock.

'Is this about Tess?' I asked. 'Has there been an arrest?'

'No, sir, there has not,' she said. She spoke rapid-fire, the words coming at me like bullets. 'I'm here to ask you about Denton Abagnall.'

I underwent a bit of mental whiplash. 'Yes?'

'He's missing. Two days now,' she said.

'I spoke to his wife the morning after he'd been to our home.'

'You haven't seen him since then?'

'No.'

'Heard from him?' Ping, ping, ping.

'No,' I said. 'I can't help but think it might have something to do with the murder of my wife's aunt. He'd been to see her not long before her death. He'd left her a business card, which she told me was pinned to the bulletin board by the phone. But it wasn't there after she died.'

Wedmore wrote something down in her notebook. 'He was working for you?'

'Yes.'

'What do you think?'

'About?'

'What happened to him?' A glimpse of impatience.

I looked up at the cloudless blue sky. 'I hate to let my mind go there,' I said. 'But I think he's dead. I think he may even have got a phone call from his killer while he was in our home.'

'What time was that?'

'It was around five in the afternoon, something like that.'

'We got in touch with his cellphone provider, had them check all his incoming and outgoing calls. There was a call at five, made from a pay phone up in Derby.'

'My wife's aunt lived up that way,' I said.

'And then another call, from another pay phone, here in Milford, an hour later.' Wedmore leaned towards me aggressively. 'Who'd want to kill your wife's aunt and Abagnall?' she asked.

'Someone who's trying to make sure that the past stays in the past,' I said.

MILLICENT WANTED to take us all out for lunch, but Cynthia said she'd prefer to go straight home, and that was where I took her.

After Grace had gone upstairs to get back into some regular clothes, Cynthia said to me, 'I'm sorry. I don't blame you. For Tess. I was wrong to say what I said.'

'It's OK. I should have told you everything. Earlier.'

She looked at the floor.

'Can I ask you something?' I said, and she nodded. 'Why do you think your father would have saved a cutting about a hit-and-run accident?'

'What are you talking about?' she said.

The shoeboxes were still on the kitchen table, the clipping on top. I handed it to her and she read it.

'I can't believe I've never noticed this before,' Cynthia said.

'You thought your dad saved it because of the fly-fishing piece.'

Cynthia handed the cutting back to me.

'Every time I look through those boxes,' she said, 'I keep hoping I'll find something I've never noticed before. Some tiny clue. Like that one piece in a jigsaw puzzle, the one that helps you place all the others. What if that's it? What if that's the piece?'

'Do you think it is?' I asked.

She shook her head slowly. 'No.'

Neither did I.

But it didn't stop me from going upstairs and sitting in front of the computer and looking for information about the twenty-six-year-old hit-and-run accident.

I came up with nothing.

So then I started looking up Gormleys in that part of Connecticut, using the online phone listings, wrote down names and numbers, and started calling. When someone actually answered, I identified myself as Terrence Archer and said that I was trying to track down information about the death of Connie Gormley.

'Sorry, never heard of her,' said the person at the first number.

'Who?' said an elderly woman at the second. 'I never knew no Connie Gormley, but I have a niece goes by Constance Gormley, and she's a real-estate agent in Stratford.'

The third person I reached said, 'Oh God, Connie? It was so long ago.'

It turned out that I had managed to reach Howard Gormley, her sixty-five-year-old brother.

'Why would anyone want to know about that, after all these years?' he asked, his voice hoarse and tired.

'Honestly, Mr Gormley, I don't quite know what to tell you,' I said. 'My wife's family had some trouble a few months after your sister's accident, stuff that we've still been trying to sort out, and an article about Connie was found among some mementos.'

'That's kind of strange, isn't it?' Howard Gormley said.

'Yes, it is. If you wouldn't mind answering a few questions, it might clear things up, at least allow me to eliminate any connection between your family's tragedy and ours.'

'I suppose.'

'First of all, did they ever find out who ran your sister down?'

'Nope, never. Cops never found out a thing.'

'Did they ever have any leads?'

'Well, at first, they figured it was a hit-and-run, plain and simple. Maybe a drunk, or just a bad driver. But when they did the autopsy, they noticed something kind of funny.'

'What do you mean, funny?'

'What they told us was, a lot of what happened to Connie, the damage done to her from the car? That happened after she was already dead.'

'Your sister was already dead when the car hit her?'

'That's what I just said. And . . . this is hard to talk about, even after all this time. I don't like to say things that reflect badly on Connie, even after all these years, if you understand.'

'I do.'

'But they said, well, that she might have been with someone shortly before she got left in that ditch. My sister, she kind of got around, and they say she met up with someone that evening, most likely. And I've always wondered if that's who it was.'

I didn't know what to say.

'Connie and me was close. After all these years, I'm still angry and wish they'd find the bastard who did it.'

WHEN I WAS DONE talking to Howard Gormley, I just sat there at my desk for a while, staring off into space, trying to figure out if it meant anything.

Then, reflexively, as I often do, I hit the MAIL button on the computer keyboard to see if we had any messages. As usual, there were a bunch, most of them offering stock tips or solicitations from widows of wealthy Nigerian gold-mine owners.

But there was one email, from a Hotmail address that was nothing but numbers—05121983—with the words 'It won't be much longer' in the subject line. I clicked on it. The message was short. It read: 'Dear Cynthia: As per our earlier conversation, your family really does forgive you. But they can't ever stop asking themselves: Why?'

I must have read it five times, then went back up to the subject line. It wouldn't be much longer till what?

'HOW COULD SOMEONE get our email address?' I asked Cynthia. She was sitting in front of the computer, staring at the screen.

'My father,' she said. 'When he left the hat. He could have come up, got on the computer, figured out our email address.'

'Cyn,' I said cautiously, 'we still don't know who left that hat.'

I thought back to my briefly held suspicion that Cynthia could have placed the hat in the kitchen herself. And for an instant, no longer, I thought about how easy it would be to set up a Hotmail address and send an email to yourself.

'It's the same person,' Cynthia said. 'The person who phoned me is the same person who sent this email and the same person who snuck into our house and left the hat. My father's hat.'

That made sense to me. The part I was having trouble with was, who was that person? Was it the same person who'd murdered Tess? Was it the man I'd spotted watching our house?

'And he's still talking about forgiveness,' Cynthia said. 'That they forgive me. Why does he say that? And what does it mean, that it won't be much longer?'

I shook my head. 'And the address,' I said, pointing to the email box on the screen. 'Just a jumble of numbers.'

'That's not a jumble of numbers,' Cynthia said. 'It's a date. May 12, 1983. The night my family disappeared.'

'WE'RE NOT SAFE,' Cynthia said that night.

She was sitting up in bed, the covers pulled up to her waist. I happened to be looking out of the bedroom window, taking one last peek at the street before I got under the covers with her. This was a habit I'd developed in the last week.

'You're not safe. I'm not safe. Grace is not safe.'

I knew that very well. She did not need to remind me.

'My aunt has been murdered,' Cynthia said. 'The man we hired to find out what happened to my family is missing. Someone was in our house, Terry. If not my father, then somebody. Who left that hat, sat at our computer.'

I had nothing to say.

'Why do you think the DMV has no record of my father's licence?' she asked. 'Why's there no record of him with Social Security?'

'I don't know,' I said tiredly.

'Do you think Mr Abagnall found out something about Vince Fleming?'

'Look,' I said. 'It's been a long day. Let's try and get some sleep.'

'What *do* you think's going on?' Cynthia said. There was something almost accusatory in the way she asked the question, that suggested to me she still suspected I was holding something back.

'I don't know,' I snapped. 'It wasn't my damned family that vanished off the face of the earth.'

It stunned Cynthia into silence. I'd stunned myself. 'I'm sorry,' I said. 'I didn't mean that. It's just, this is taking a toll on all of us.'

'*My* problems are taking a toll on *you*,' Cynthia said.

'That's not it,' I said. 'Maybe, look, maybe we should go away for a while. The three of us. We'll pull Grace out of school. I can wangle a few days from Rolly—'

She threw the covers off her legs suddenly and got up. 'I'm going to sleep with Grace,' she said. 'I want to be sure she's OK. Somebody has to do something.'

ABOUT MIDAFTERNOON the next day, I was walking down the hall near the office when one of the secretaries charged out, saw me and stopped dead.

'I was just going to go looking for you,' she said. 'Phone call. I think it's your wife.'

'OK.'

'You can take it in the office.'

I followed her in and she pointed to the phone on her desk.

I grabbed the receiver, hit the button. 'Cynthia?'

'Terry, I—'

'Listen, I was going to call you. I'm sorry about last night. What I said.'

'Terry, something's happened,' Cynthia said, her voice low, almost breathless. 'I know where they are.'

'SOMETIMES, when you don't call when I'm expecting you to,' she said, 'I think I'm the one being driven crazy.'

'Sorry,' he said. 'But I've got good news. I think it's happening.'

'So you delivered it?'

'Yes.'

'But you need to stay a little longer to see what happens.'

'Oh, I know,' he said. 'There haven't been any more stories about Tess. I guess that means they haven't found out anything.'

'I guess we should just be grateful for whatever good fortune comes our way, shouldn't we?'

'And there was something else on the news, about this missing detective. The one my . . . you know . . . hired.'

'Do you think they'll find him?' she asked.

'Hard to say.'

'Well, we can't worry about that,' she said. 'You sound nervous.'

'I guess.'

'This is the hard part, the risky part, but when you add it all together, it's going to pay off. And when it's time, you can come back and get me.'

'I know. Won't he wonder where you are, why you're not going to see him?'

'He hardly gives me the time of day,' she said.

'You think he's ever really loved us?' he asked.

'The only one he's ever loved is her,' she said, making no attempt to hide her bitterness. 'And has she ever been there for him? Looked after him? Cleaned up after him? We're the ones who've been wronged here. We were

robbed of having a real family. What we're doing now, this is justice.'

'I know,' he said.

'What do you want me to make for you when you get home?'

'A carrot cake?'

'Of course. It's the least a mother can do.'

7

I phoned the police and left a message for Detective Rona Wedmore. I asked if she could meet me and Cynthia at our home. I said it was urgent. I left the school without explaining to anyone why, but they were, I guess, becoming accustomed to my erratic behaviour.

At home, Cynthia was standing in the doorway, an envelope in her hand. I came inside and she handed it to me. There was one word—'Cynthia'—printed on the front. No stamp. It had not gone through the mail.

I took the sheet of plain business paper out of the envelope. The back side of the sheet was a map, crudely drawn in pencil, some intersecting lines representing roads, a small town labelled 'Otis', a rough egg shape labelled 'quarry lake', and an 'X' in one corner.

I flipped the sheet over, and the moment I saw the typed message, I noticed something about it, something that jumped out at me, something that disturbed me very much.

But for the moment, I held my tongue and read what it said:

> Cynthia: It's time you knew where they were. Where they still ARE, most likely. There's an abandoned quarry a couple of hours north of where you live, just past the Connecticut border. It's like a lake, but not a real lake because it's where they took out gravel and stuff. It's real deep. See the map on the other side. Right down there, at the bottom of that lake, that's where you'll find your answer.

'That's where they are,' Cynthia whispered, pointing to the paper in my hand. 'They're in the water.' She took in a breath. 'So . . . they're dead.'

I reread the note, then looked at it again from a more technical point of view. It had been composed on a standard typewriter. Not on a computer. Not printed off.

'Where did you get this?' I asked her, trying to keep my voice controlled.

'It was in the mailbox. Someone left it there. The mailman didn't bring it. It doesn't have a stamp on it or anything.'

'No,' I said. 'Someone put it there.'

'We have to go up there,' she said. 'Today, now, we have to find out what's there, what's under the water.'

'The detective, Wedmore, she's coming. We'll talk to her about that. They'll have police divers. But there's something else I want to ask you about. It's about this note. Look at the typing—'

I heard a car stop out front, looked out of the window and saw Rona Wedmore striding up the driveway. I felt a sense of panic.

'Honey,' I said, 'is there anything else you want to tell me about this note? Before the police get here?'

'What are you talking about?' she said.

'Don't you see something odd about this?' I pointed to one of the words in the letter. 'Right here, at the beginning,' I said, pointing to 'time'. The horizontal line in the 'e' was faded, making it almost look like a 'c'.

'I don't know what you're talking about,' Cynthia said.

Wedmore was mounting the front step, fist ready to knock.

'I have to go upstairs for a moment,' I said. 'Answer that.'

I bolted up the stairs. I heard Wedmore knock, then Cynthia open the door. By then I was in the small room I use to mark papers. My old Royal typewriter sat on the desk, beside the computer.

It was obvious to me that the note Cynthia was showing to Detective Wedmore had been written on this typewriter. The faded 'e' was instantly recognisable. I knew that I had not typed that letter. That left only two other possibilities. The stranger who had entered our home had used my typewriter to write that note, or Cynthia had typed it herself.

It seemed unthinkable that Cynthia had done this. But what if . . . what if Cynthia had typed it up, and what happened if it turned out to be right?

'Terry!' Cynthia shouted. 'Detective Wedmore is here!'

I was breaking into a sweat. There had to be another explanation. Someone else had used our typewriter. Days ago. Planning ahead. That stranger who'd come into the house and left the hat.

'Terry!'

'Right there!' I acted on impulse. I opened the closet, picked up the typewriter and put it inside, on the floor.

As I came down the stairs, I saw that Wedmore was now with Cynthia in the living room. The letter was on the coffee table, open, Wedmore leaning over it, reading it.

'You can get divers, right?' Cynthia said. 'To go into the quarry, see what's there. They're down there. Their bodies are down there.'

Wedmore took a corner of the letter between two brilliant red-polished fingernails and turned it over. She stared at the map.

'Interesting,' Wedmore said, 'that it was done on a typewriter. Hardly anyone uses typewriters.'

I felt my heart in my mouth. And then Cynthia said something I couldn't believe I was hearing.

'We have a typewriter,' she said.

'You do?' Wedmore said.

'Terry still likes to use one, right, honey? For short notes, that kind of thing. He's had it since his college days.'

'Show it to me,' Wedmore said.

'It's upstairs,' Cynthia said. 'Come, I'll show you.'

'Cyn,' I said. 'It's a bit of a mess up there.'

'Let's go,' Wedmore said, moving up the stairs.

'First door on the left,' Cynthia said.

Wedmore disappeared into the room. 'I don't see it,' she said.

Cynthia was up the stairs before me, turned into the room, said, 'It's usually right there. Terry, isn't it usually right there?'

She was pointing to my desk as I came into the room.

'Uh,' I said, 'it was in my way, so I tucked it into the closet.'

I opened the closet door, knelt down. Wedmore was peering in, over my shoulder. I lifted it out, set it back on the desk.

'Don't touch it,' Wedmore said, and got her cellphone out of her jacket.

Cynthia looked at me with a puzzled expression. 'What's with you? What the hell is going on?'

I wanted to ask her the same thing.

RONA WEDMORE made several calls, most of them from the driveway, where we wouldn't be able to hear what she had to say. That left Cynthia and me in the house to mull over these latest developments.

Cynthia asked, 'Why did you hide the typewriter? That note, it was written on your typewriter, wasn't it?'

'Yes,' I said.

She studied me a moment. 'Did you write that note? Is that why you hid the typewriter?'

'Cyn, I hid it because I wondered whether *you'd* written it.'

Her eyes went wide in shock. 'Me?'

'I was doing it to protect you. I didn't want the police to know.'

Cynthia said nothing for a moment. 'So what are you saying? That I've always known my family were in this quarry?'

'Honest to God, Cyn,' I said, 'I don't know what to think any more. But the moment I saw that letter, I knew it had come from my typewriter. And I knew I hadn't written it. That left you, unless someone else came in here and wrote it on that typewriter.'

She looked right into my eyes, adopted a deadly serious expression. 'Do you think I killed my family?' she asked.

'No, I don't.'

'But it's crossed your mind, hasn't it?'

'No,' I said. 'But I have wondered, lately, whether the stress of what you've been through has made you think, or maybe even do things, in a way that's not been, I don't know, totally rational.'

Someone rapped on the wall outside the room and Detective Rona Wedmore walked in.

'It's a go,' she said. 'We're sending in divers.'

IT WAS SET UP for the following day. A police diving squad was to be on site at 10 a.m. Cynthia walked Grace to school and arranged for one of the neighbours arranged for one of the neighbours to meet her at the end of the day and take her back to her house in the event we weren't home in time.

I called the school again, got Rolly, said I would not be in.

'What now?' he asked.

I told him where we were off to, that divers were going into the quarry.

'God, my heart goes out to you guys,' he said. 'It never ends.'

I paused. 'Hey, this is kind of out of the blue, but does the name Connie Gormley mean anything to you?'

'Who?'

'She was killed a few months before Clayton and Patricia and Todd vanished. Looked like a hit-and-run but wasn't, exactly.'

'I don't know what you're talking about,' Rolly said. 'And what could that possibly have to do with Cynthia's family?' He almost sounded annoyed.

'I don't know that it does. I'm just asking. You knew Clayton. Did he ever mention anything about an accident or anything?'

'No. Not that I can remember. And I'm pretty sure I'd remember something like that.'

Cynthia and I hit the road shortly after that. It was more than a two-hour drive north. Before the police took away the anonymous letter in a plastic evidence bag, we copied the map onto another piece of paper so we'd know where we were going.

We headed east once we passed Otis, up to Lee and the Mass Turnpike. We were hunting for Fell's Quarry Road, but we didn't have to look that hard for it. There were two cars with Massachusetts state troopers marking the turnoff for us.

I put down the window and explained to an officer who we were, and he said Detective Wedmore was expecting us. He pointed up the road, told us to look for a narrow grassy lane about one mile up.

We drove in slowly. It wasn't much of a road, just gravel and dirt. We were driving uphill, thick trees on either side, and after about a quarter of a mile, the ground levelled off and the trees gave way to an open area that nearly took our breath away. We were looking out over what appeared to be a vast canyon. About four car lengths ahead of us the ground dropped away sharply.

There were two other vehicles already there, another state police car and an unmarked sedan that I recognised as Wedmore's. She was leaning up against the fender, talking to the officer from the other car. When she saw us, she approached.

'Don't get close,' she said to me through the open window. 'It's a hell of a drop.'

We got out of the car slowly.

'This way,' Wedmore said.

We took a few steps closer to the edge and now we could see the water. A mini-lake, maybe eight or nine acres in size, at the bottom of a chasm. The water was grey and lifeless.

'The map and the letter indicated that if we're to find anything,' Wedmore said, 'it'll be right down here.' She pointed straight down the cliff we were standing atop. I felt a brief wave of vertigo.

Down below, crossing the body of water, was a yellow inflatable boat. In the boat were three men, two dressed in black wet suits, wearing diving masks and with tanks on their backs. The men in wet suits dropped backward out of the boat and disappeared from view.

A cool wind blew over the top of the cliff. I moved closer to Cynthia and slipped my arm round her. To my relief, she did not push me away.

Wedmore had a radio that connected her to the man left in the boat. 'What's happening?' she asked.

'Not much so far,' a voice crackled through Wedmore's radio.

'OK.'

We stood and watched. Maybe for ten, fifteen minutes. Seemed like hours.

And then two heads emerged. The divers swam over to the boat, hung their arms over the edges for support, lifted up their masks, and removed from their mouths the gear that allowed them to breathe underwater. They were telling the man something.

We saw the man pick up his radio and Wedmore grabbed hers. 'Got something,' the radio crackled.

'What?' Wedmore asked.

'Car. Been there a long time. Half buried in silt.'

'Anything inside it?'

'They're not sure. We're going to have to get it out.'

'What kind of car?' Cynthia asked. 'What does it look like?'

Wedmore relayed the question.

'Looks sort of yellow,' the man said. 'A little compact car.'

Cynthia said, 'My mother's car. It was yellow. A Ford Escort. A small car.' She collapsed against me, held on to me. 'It's them,' she said. 'It's them.'

'NOTHING'S GOING to happen for a few hours,' Wedmore told us. 'They've got to figure out how to do this. Why don't you get some lunch? I'll call when it looks like something's about to happen.'

'No,' Cynthia said. 'We should stay.'

'Honey,' I said, 'there's nothing we can do now. Let's go and eat. We both need our strength.' To Wedmore, I added, 'Please keep us posted.'

We drove back down to the main road, where we found a diner. I ordered eggs and sausage. All Cynthia could manage was some toast.

'So whoever wrote that note,' Cynthia said, 'knew what he was talking about.'

'Yeah,' I said.

'But we don't even know if there's anyone in the car.'

'Let's wait and see,' I said.

We ended up waiting a couple of hours. I was on my fourth coffee when my cellphone rang. It was Wedmore.

'It's gone faster than we thought,' she said. 'It's out.'

THE YELLOW ESCORT was already sitting on the back of a flatbed truck by the time we arrived at the site. Cynthia was out of the car before I'd come to a full stop, running towards the truck, shouting, 'That's the car! My mother's car!'

Wedmore grabbed hold of her before she could get close.

'You can't go near it,' the detective told her. 'It's going to the lab.'

'What did they find,' Cynthia asked. 'Was there anything inside?'

'There appear to be the remains of two people,' Wedmore said. 'But as you can understand, after twenty-five years . . .'

One could only imagine.

'Two?' Cynthia said. 'Not three?'

'It's early yet,' Wedmore said. 'We have a lot of work before us.' She paused. 'We'd like to get a DNA sample from you.'

'Because?'

'If we're fortunate enough to be able to recover any DNA from . . . what we find in the car, we'll be able to compare it to yours.'

Cynthia looked at me, tears forming in her eyes. 'For twenty-five years I've waited for some answers, and now that I'm about to get some, I'm terrified.'

I held her. 'How long?' I asked Wedmore.

'A few days, maybe just a couple. You might as well go home. I'll have someone come by later today for the sample.'

Heading back seemed the only logical thing to do. As we turned to walk to our car, Wedmore called out, 'And you'll need to be available in the meantime. I'm going to have more questions.'

There was something ominous about the way she said it.

AS PROMISED, Rona Wedmore showed up to ask questions. There were things about this case she did not like. That was certainly something we all had in common.

She did confirm one thing I already knew. The letter that had directed us to the quarry had been written on my typewriter. Cynthia and I had both been requested to come down to headquarters and be fingerprinted. They compared our prints against those on the typewriter. They found a few of Cynthia's on the body of the machine. But the actual keys were covered with mine.

Of course, this didn't support our contention that someone had broken into our house and written the letter on my typewriter, someone who could have been wearing gloves and left no prints.

'And why would someone do that?' asked Wedmore, her hands made into fists and resting on her considerable hips.

That was a good question.

'And, whoever that someone was, he didn't try to hide that typewriter. Your husband's the one who did that.'

I asked her, 'Should we have a lawyer here when you're asking these questions?'

Wedmore pushed her tongue around the inside of her cheek. 'I suppose you'd have to ask yourself whether you believe you need one.'

'We're the victims here,' Cynthia said. 'My aunt has been murdered; you've found my mother's car in a lake. And you're talking to us like we're the criminals.' She shook her head in exasperation. 'It's like someone else has planned this all out, planned it to make it look like I'm going crazy or something. Don't you see? It's like someone wants you to think that maybe I'm losing it.'

That tongue moved from the inside of one cheek to the other. Finally, Wedmore said, 'Mrs Archer, have you ever thought about talking to someone? About this conspiracy that seems to be swirling around you?'

'I am seeing a psy—' Cynthia stopped herself.

Wedmore smiled. 'Well, there's a shocker.'

'I think we've had enough for now,' I said.

'I'm sure we'll be talking again,' Wedmore said.

VERY SOON, as it turned out. Right after they found the body of Denton Abagnall.

I was listening to the radio in our sewing room/study, not paying that much attention, really, but when the words 'private detective' came out of the speaker, I reached over and turned up the volume.

'Police found the man's car in a parking garage near the Stamford Town

Centre' the newsreader said. 'When the trunk was forced open, the body of Denton Abagnall, who was fifty-one years old, was found inside. He died of blunt trauma to the head.'

I told Cynthia what I'd heard on the radio.

Cynthia said nothing for a moment, then, 'I'm starting to feel numb, Terry. When's all of this going to stop? When are we going to get our normal lives back?'

'I know,' I said, putting my arms round her. 'I know.'

The thing was, Cynthia hadn't really had a normal life since she was fourteen years old.

WHEN RONA WEDMORE showed up again, she was direct and to the point. 'Where were you the night Denton Abagnall went missing? The night he left here, the last night anyone ever heard from him.'

'We went to visit Cynthia's aunt,' I said. 'She was dead. We called the police. We were with the police the entire evening. So I guess the police would be our alibi.'

For the first time, Wedmore appeared embarrassed and off her game. 'Of course,' she said. 'I should have realised that.'

'So,' Cynthia said coldly, 'I guess we're off the hook for that one.'

'Did they find any papers with Mr Abagnall?' I asked. 'A note, some empty envelopes?'

'Far as I know,' Wedmore said, 'there was nothing. Why?'

'Just wondering,' I said. 'You know, one of the last things Mr Abagnall told us was that he was going to be checking out Vince Fleming, who was with my wife the night her family disappeared. You know about Vince Fleming?'

'I know the name,' she said.

AND WEDMORE showed up again, the following day.

When I saw her walking up the drive, I said to Cynthia, 'Maybe she's tied us in to the Lindbergh kidnapping.'

I opened the door before she knocked.

'Yes?' I said. 'What now?'

'I have news,' Wedmore said. 'May I come in?' Her tone was less abrasive today. I didn't know whether that was good news or meant that she was setting us up for something.

I showed her into the living room and invited her to take a seat. Cynthia and I both sat down.

'First of all,' Wedmore said, 'you need to know I'm no scientist. But I understand the basic principles and will do my best to explain them to you.'

I looked at Cynthia. She nodded for Wedmore to continue.

'The chances of being able to extract any DNA from the remains in your mother's car were always slim, but not non-existent. As you might guess, the decay over the years had pretty much destroyed all the flesh on the bodies.' She cleared her throat.

'Anyway, we had bones, and we had teeth, so we attempted to get dental records for your family but struck out. Your father, from what we could tell, had no dentist, although the coroner determined pretty quickly, based on the bone structure of the two people in the car, neither was an adult male.'

Cynthia blinked. So her father's body was not one of the two in that car.

'But the thing was, even if we didn't have dental records, we still had teeth,' Wedmore said. 'Deep in the centre of the tooth, in the root, it's so protected in there, they can find nucleated cells and extract sufficient DNA to show a unique profile for each individual, including sex.'

'And?' Cynthia asked, holding her breath.

'It was a male and a female,' Wedmore said. 'The coroner's analysis, even before DNA testing, suggests a male in his mid-teens and a woman probably in her late thirties, maybe early forties. The forensic results suggest a mother-and-son relationship.'

'My mother,' Cynthia whispered. 'Todd.'

'Well, here's the thing,' Wedmore said. 'While we've more or less determined a relationship between the two deceased, we don't know beyond a shadow of a doubt that it is in fact Todd Bigge and Patricia Bigge. But, we do have your DNA sample, and once your sample is typed—and they're working on that now—they'll be able to determine the probability of any possible relationship you may have to the remains. But based on what we know now, the working assumption is that we've found your mother and your brother.'

Cynthia looked dizzy.

'But not,' Wedmore pointed out, 'your father. I'd like to ask you a few more questions about him, what he was like, what kind of person he was.'

'Why?' Cynthia asked. 'What are you implying?'

'I think we have to consider the possibility he murdered both of them.'

'HELLO?'

'It's me,' he said.

'I was just thinking about you,' she said. 'I haven't heard from you for a while. I hope everything's OK.'

'I wanted to wait to see what would happen,' he said. 'How much they might find out. There's been stuff on the news. They showed the car. On TV.'

'Oh my . . .'

'They had a picture of it being taken away from the quarry. And they had a story today, in the newspapers, about the DNA tests.'

'This is so exciting,' she said. 'I wish I was there with you. What did it say?'

'Well, I've got the paper right here. It said, "DNA tests indicate a genetic link between the two bodies in the car, that they are a mother and son." '

'Interesting.'

' "Forensic tests have yet to determine whether the bodies are genetically linked to Cynthia Archer. Police are operating on the assumption, however, that the recovered bodies are Patricia Bigge and Todd Bigge, missing for twenty-five years." '

'It's amazing what they can do these days, isn't it?'

'Yeah.'

'I mean, back then, when your father and I got rid of that car, who'd even heard of DNA tests? It boggles the mind, it does. You still feeling nervous?'

'A little, maybe.' He did sound subdued to her.

'I think you've done a wonderful job, lots to be proud of. Soon you'll be home, and you can take me back. I wouldn't want to miss this for the world. When the moment comes, I can't wait to see the expression on her face.'

8

'So, how are you dealing with this?' Dr Kinzler asked Cynthia. 'The apparent discovery of your mother and your brother.'

'I'm not sure,' Cynthia said. 'It's not relief.'

'No, I can see why it wouldn't be.'

'And the fact that my father was not there with them. This detective, Wedmore, she thinks maybe he killed them.'

'If that turns out to be true,' Dr Kinzler said, 'are you going to be able to deal with that?'

Cynthia bit her lip, looked at the blinds. 'I'm already having to come to terms with the idea that my father may have been something other than the man I knew,' she said. 'The fact that there's no record of him, no Social Security number, no driver's licence.' She paused. 'But the idea that he could have killed my mother and Todd, I can't believe it.'

'Of course,' Dr Kinzler said. Gently, she asked, 'Tell me more about your relationship with your father. If he was in a state of mind that led him to kill your mother and your brother, why wouldn't he have killed you, too?'

'I don't know. And I've told you, I don't believe he did it. My father wouldn't do something like that. You know why? Not just because he loved us. But because he was too weak.'

That caught my attention.

'He was a sweet man, but—this is hard to say about a parent—but he just wouldn't have had it in him to do something like that.'

I said, 'I don't see where any of this is getting us.'

'We know that your wife is deeply troubled by the questions raised by this discovery,' the psychiatrist said. Did she ever raise her voice? Did she ever get demonstrably pissed off? 'I'm trying to help her with that.' She turned to Cynthia. 'I don't think we should wait for two more weeks before your next appointment.'

'Sure,' Cynthia said, her voice soft and distant.

THERE WERE TEN CALLS on our answering machine when we got home, all from different media outlets. There was a long, impassioned message from Paula, from *Deadline*. She said Cynthia owed their viewers a chance to revisit this case.

I watched Cynthia hit the button to delete the message. Not flustered. No confusion. One quick motion with a steady index finger.

'Didn't have any trouble that time,' I said. God forgive me, it just slipped out.

'What?' she said, looking at me.

'Nothing,' I said.

'You're thinking about that morning. When I got the call. When I accidentally erased the call history. I told you what happened. I was shook up.'

'Of course you were.'

'You don't even believe I got that call, do you?'

'I didn't say that.'

Cynthia moved closer to me. 'How can I stay here under this roof if I can't be one hundred per cent certain that I have your support? I don't need you second-guessing everything I do.'

'I'm not doing that.'

'So say it. Tell me right now. Look me in the eye and tell me you believe in me, that you know I haven't had a hand in any of this.'

I swear I was going to say it. But my tenth-of-a-second hesitation was all it took for Cynthia to turn and walk away.

WHEN I WENT into Grace's room that night, she was already under the covers. She was wide awake.

'I thought you'd be looking for asteroids,' I said, sitting on the edge of the bed and touching the side of her head.

'I didn't bother,' she said so softly I almost couldn't hear.

'Are you not worried about asteroids any more?' I asked.

'No,' Grace said, turning her head into the pillow. 'They might still be coming, but it doesn't matter.'

'What do you mean by that, honey?'

'It didn't matter whether an asteroid was coming or not. Aunt Tess still died. People die all the time from all sorts of things. They get hit by cars. They can drown. And sometimes people kill them.'

'I know.'

'And Mom's acting like we're not safe. She thinks something's coming to get us, but it's not something from outer space.'

'We would never let anything happen to you,' I said. 'Your mother and I love you very much.'

Grace said nothing.

'I still think it would be worth checking just once,' I said, shifting off the bed and kneeling in front of the telescope. 'You mind if I have a look?' I asked.

'Knock yourself out,' Grace said.

'OK,' I said. I put my eye up to the lens, took hold of the telescope. 'Let's have a look here,' I said, and then the scope broke free of its stand, hit the floor, and rolled under Grace's desk.

'I told you, Dad,' she said. 'It's just a piece of junk.'

In the morning, when I got up, Cynthia and Grace were gone.

I didn't find it odd that Cynthia wasn't sharing our bed when I woke up. Even when we hadn't fought, she'd sometimes fallen asleep on Grace's bed and spent the entire night there.

I got up, pulled on my jeans, wandered into the bathroom, and splashed some water on my face. The towel bar is right next to the window that looks over the driveway. As I reached for a towel, there was something different about how the world beyond looked through the blinds. The cracks between the blinds are usually filled with white and silver, the colours of our two cars. But this time there was silver and asphalt. I prised apart the blinds. Cynthia's car was not in the driveway.

I padded down the hall and eased open the door to Grace's room. The covers were turned back, the bed empty.

I popped my head into the study, found it empty, went down to the kitchen. It looked as it had the night before. Everything cleaned up and put away. When I opened the front door, the morning newspaper was there waiting for me. It was hard, at that moment, not to shake the feeling that I was living out an episode from Cynthia's life.

But this time, unlike that morning twenty-five years ago, there was a note. It was folded and standing on its side, on the kitchen table. It read:

Terry:

I'm going away. I don't know where, or for how long. I just know I can't stay here another minute. I feel like I'm losing my mind, that no one believes me.

What's going to happen next? Who will break into our house? Who will be watching it from the street? Who will be next to die?

I don't want it to be Grace. So I'm taking her with me.

I want to look for my father, but I don't have any idea where to start. I believe he's alive. Maybe that's what Mr Abagnall discovered after he went to see Vince. I just don't know.

I won't have my cell on very often. But I'll check it once in a while for messages. Maybe, at some point, I'll feel like talking to you. Just not right now.

L, Cyn

I sat at the kitchen table and began to cry. I put my head in my hands and let it all come out.

I don't know quite how long I sat there, alone, at my kitchen table, letting the tears run down my cheeks. Long enough that there weren't any left, I guess. Once I'd exhausted the supply, I had no choice but to come up with another course of action.

I WENT BACK UPSTAIRS, finished dressing. I had to keep telling myself a few things. The first was that Cynthia and Grace were OK. It wasn't as though they'd been kidnapped or anything. And second, I couldn't imagine that Cynthia would let anything bad happen to Grace, no matter how upset she was. She loved Grace. But what was my daughter to think? Her mother getting her up in the middle of the night, making her pack a bag, sneaking out of the house together so her father wouldn't hear?

Cynthia had to have believed, in her heart, that this was the right thing to do, but it wasn't. It was wrong, and it was wrong to put Grace through something like this.

I went back into the kitchen, phoned Rolly at home. It was too early for him to have left for school yet. Millicent answered.

'Hi, Terry.'

'Millie, you haven't heard from Cynthia by any chance?'

'Cynthia? No. Terry, what's going on? Isn't Cynthia home?'

'She's gone. She took Grace with her.'

'Let me get Rolly.'

I heard her set the phone down, and a few seconds later Rolly said, 'Cynthia's gone?'

'Yeah. I don't know what to do.'

'Did you guys have a fight or something?'

'Yeah, kind of. And I think everything's just got to her. Look, if you hear from her, if you see her, let me know, OK?'

'I will,' Rolly said. 'And if you find her, call.'

And then a name popped into my head. Someone I'd never met, never spoken to, never even seen. But his name kept coming up.

Maybe it was time to have a chat with Vince Fleming.

IF I COULD HAVE brought myself to call Detective Wedmore, I could have asked her outright where I might find Vince Fleming and saved myself some time. But I didn't want to talk to Wedmore.

I went up to the computer and started doing some searches on Vince Fleming and Milford. There were a couple of news stories from the New

Haven paper over the last few years, one that detailed how he had been charged with assault. He owned a body shop in an industrial district somewhere in town, and there was a grainy photo of him going into a bar called Mike's.

Maybe I could try asking around for Vince Fleming at Mike's. Maybe there, I might find someone who could point me in the right direction.

I drove west on Bridgeport Avenue into the Milford neighbourhood of Devon. I'd been past Mike's a hundred times, a small brick building, its neon sign running vertically down the first storey, ending above the entrance. The front windows were decorated with signs advertising Schlitz and Coors and Budweiser.

I parked round the corner and walked back, not sure whether Mike's would even be open in the morning for business, but once inside I realised that, for many, it was never too early to drink.

There were about a dozen customers in the dimly lit bar, two perched on stools up at the counter having a conversation, the rest scattered about the tables. I approached the bar just down from the two guys and caught the attention of the heavyset man in a check shirt working behind it.

'Help ya?' he asked, a damp mug in one hand, a towel in the other. He worked the towel into the mug, twisted it around.

'I'm looking for a guy. I think he comes in here a lot.'

'We get a lot of people,' he said. 'Got a name?'

'Vince Fleming.'

The bartender had a pretty good poker face. Didn't flinch, raise an eyebrow. 'Fleming,' he said. 'Not sure. What sort of business you got with him?'

I smiled, trying to be polite. 'It's sort of a personal matter,' I said. 'Maybe if you could just tell me where he works.'

The bartender must have decided Fleming's place of business was pretty common knowledge, so he said, 'Dirksen Garage. Across the bridge over into Stratford.'

I went back outside and got in my car. Dirksen Garage was only a couple of miles away and I was there in under five minutes.

It was a cinder-block building with a paved front yard and a black tow truck out front. I parked and entered the garage through the business entrance. There was a young woman at the desk in front of me who asked what I wanted.

'I'm here to see Vince,' I said.

'Not in,' she said.

'It's important,' I said. 'My name's Terry Archer.'

'Like I said, Mr Fleming is not here right now,' the woman said. 'But I'll take a message.'

'The name,' I said again, 'is Terry Archer.' I gave her my home and cell numbers. 'I'd really like to talk to him.'

'Yeah, well, you and plenty of others,' she said.

So I left the Dirksen Garage. Stood out front in the sun, said to myself, What now?

All I really knew for sure was that I needed a coffee.

A red SUV bounced up and over the kerb and stopped abruptly in front of me. The back and front doors on the passenger side opened, and two slightly pot-bellied men in jean jackets and dirty T-shirts—one bald and the other with dirty-blond hair—jumped out.

'Get in,' Baldy said.

'Excuse me?' I said.

'You heard him,' said Blondie. 'Get in the car.'

They lunged forward together, each grabbing an arm. 'Hey,' I said as they dragged me towards the SUV's back door. 'You can't do this. Let go of me! You can't just grab people off the street!'

They heaved me in. I went sprawling onto the floor of the back seat. Blondie got in front; Baldy got in the back, rested his work-booted foot on my back to keep me there. As I was going down, I caught a glimpse of a third man behind the wheel.

'Look,' I said, 'you guys have made some kind of mistake.'

'Shut up,' Baldy said, looking at me.

We took a couple of turns, went over some railroad tracks, and then it felt as though the SUV was descending, as though we were heading towards the shore of Long Island Sound. Then the truck slowed, bounced up over a kerb and came to a stop.

'OK,' said Baldy, looking down at me, 'we're getting out and going up some stairs and into a house. I want you to be nice.'

Blondie and the driver were already out. Baldy opened his door, got out, and I pulled myself up first onto the back seat, then scooted over until I was out the side. We were parked in a driveway between two beach houses. I could see beach and, beyond that, the Sound.

Baldy motioned for me to climb up a set of open-back stairs that went up to the first floor. Blondie and the driver went ahead, then me, then Baldy.

At the top of the stairs, the driver held open a screen door and the rest of us walked in ahead of him. We entered a large room with sliding glass doors facing the water. There were some chairs and a couch just inside the door, a shelf weighed down with paperback novels, and a kitchen along the back wall.

A heavyset man with his back to me was standing at the stove, steadying a frying pan with one hand, holding a spatula in the other.

'Here he is,' Blondie said.

The man nodded without saying anything.

'We'll be down in the truck,' Baldy said, and motioned for Blondie and the driver to follow him out.

I stood in the centre of the room and stared at the man's back.

'You want some eggs?' he asked. 'It's no trouble. Fried, scrambled, over easy, whatever.'

'No, but thanks just the same,' I said.

'I get up a little later; sometimes it's nearly lunchtime before I make breakfast,' he said. He reached up into a cupboard and brought down a plate, transferred some scrambled eggs to it, added some sausages that had been sitting on a paper towel, then reached into a cutlery drawer for a fork and a steak knife. He turned round and walked over to the table, pulled out a chair, and sat down.

He was about my age, although he looked a bit worse for wear. His face was pockmarked, he had an inch-long scar above his right eye, and his once-black hair was now heavily peppered with grey. He was in a black T-shirt, tucked into some black jeans, and I could see the edge of a tattoo on his upper right arm. He motioned to the chair opposite him. I approached, cautiously, and sat down.

'Do I know you?' he asked, shoving some eggs into his mouth.

'No,' I said.

'But you're asking around for me.'

'Yes,' I said. 'It wasn't my intention to alarm you.'

The man I now knew to be Vince Fleming speared a sausage with his fork, held it in place, then picked up the steak knife and cut off a piece. He shoved it into his mouth. 'When people I don't know start asking around for me, that can be a cause for concern.'

'I guess I didn't fully appreciate that.'

'So who are you?'

'Terry Archer. You know my wife. Her name is Cynthia. You would have known her when she was Cynthia Bigge.'

He stopped in mid-chew. 'Oh. Man, that was a long time ago.'

'There have been some recent developments,' I said. 'I take it you remember what happened that night.'

'Yeah. Her whole family vanished.'

'That's right. They've just found the bodies of Cynthia's mother and brother, Todd.'

'Todd? I knew Todd.'

'You did?'

Vince Fleming shrugged. 'A bit. I mean, we went to the same school. He was an OK guy.'

'The police found them in Cynthia's mother's car at the bottom of a lake in a quarry, up in Massachusetts. And Cynthia's aunt was murdered. Someone stabbed her to death in her kitchen.'

'Is there some reason why you're telling me all this?'

'Cynthia's missing,' I said. 'She's . . . run off. With our daughter. We have a daughter named Grace. She's eight.'

'That's too bad.'

'I thought there was a chance Cynthia might have come looking for you. She's trying to find the answers to what happened that night, and it's possible you might have some of them. You were the last person to see Cynthia that night, other than her family. And you had a run-in with her father before he brought Cynthia home.'

I never saw it coming. Vince Fleming reached across the table with one hand, grabbed my right wrist with his left, yanked it across the table towards him, while his other hand grabbed the steak knife. He swung it down towards the table in a long, swift arc and the blade buried into the wood table between my middle and fourth finger.

I screamed. Vince's hand was a vice on my wrist, pinning it to the table.

'I don't like the sound of what you're suggesting,' he said, very quietly. 'I have a question for you. There's been a guy, another guy, asking around about me. You know anything about that?'

'What guy?' I said.

'In his fifties, short guy, might have been a private detective.'

'It could have been a man named Denton Abagnall,' I said. 'We hired him to try to find Cynthia's family. Or at least, what happened to them.'

'And that meant asking about me?'

I swallowed. 'He thought you were worth taking a look at.'

'Really? And what's he found out about me?'

'Nothing,' I said. 'I mean, if he did find out anything, we don't know what it was. He's dead. He was murdered, too. In a parking garage in Stamford.'

'Well,' said Vince, letting go of my wrist and working the knife out of the table, 'that's all very interesting.'

'So you haven't seen my wife?' I asked. 'She hasn't been by here, or your work, to talk to you?'

Very evenly, he said, 'No.' And he stared into my eyes, as though daring me to contradict him.

I held his gaze. 'I hope you're telling me the truth, Mr Fleming. Because I'll do anything to make sure she and my daughter get home safely.'

He got up from his chair and walked round to my side of the table, then he grabbed my hair in his fist, bent down and put his face into mine. 'Do you have any idea who you're talking to? Those guys who brought you here. They could—'

Outside, I heard footsteps on the stairs. I couldn't see the screen door, but I heard it swing open, and then a voice I thought I recognised said, 'Hey, Vince, you seen my mom, because—' Then, seeing Vince Fleming with a man's hair in his fist, she stopped talking.

'I'm kind of busy here,' he told her. 'And I don't know where your mother is. Try the mall.'

'Vince, what are you doing to my teacher?' the woman said.

Even with Vince's meaty fingers holding on to my scalp, I managed to turn my head far enough to see Jane Scavullo.

'Your teacher?' Vince said, not relaxing his grip. 'What teacher?'

'My creative-writing teacher,' Jane said. She approached. 'Hi, Mr Archer.'

'Hi, Jane,' I said.

Vince let go of my hair. 'Is this the guy you were talking about? Who likes your stories?'

Jane nodded. She was so relaxed, I had to assume she'd seen others getting this sort of treatment from Vince. The only thing different this time was that it was one of her teachers. 'Yeah. Why are you working him over?'

'Look, honey, I can't really get into this with you.'

'I'm trying to find my wife,' I said. 'She's with my daughter, and I'm very worried about them. I thought your fa—I thought Vince here might be able to help me.'

'He's not my father,' Jane said. 'He and my mom have been together for a while now. Remember that one story I wrote for you, about the guy making me eggs?'

I had to think. 'Yes,' I said. 'I do.'

'That was sort of based on Vince here. He's decent.' She smiled at the irony. 'Well, to me.' She walked up to Vince, got right in his face. 'You be nice to him. His is, like, the only class where I'm getting any decent grades. If he wants help finding his wife, why don't you help him find her?'

Vince walked her to the door. I couldn't hear what he was saying to her, but just before she went out, she said to me, 'See ya, Mr Archer.'

'Goodbye, Jane,' I said.

Vince walked back over to the table, much of the menace gone out of his posture, and sat back down at the table. He looked a bit sheepish and didn't say anything right away.

'She's a good kid,' I said.

Vince nodded. 'Yeah, she is. She's been needing some, whaddya call it, stability in her life. I never raised any kids, and sometimes, I kind of think of her like a daughter.'

'She seems to get on pretty good with you,' I said.

'She wraps me around her finger,' he said, and grinned. 'She's mentioned you. It's Mr Archer this, Mr Archer that. She says you've encouraged her about her writing.'

'She's pretty good.'

Vince pointed to the jammed bookshelves. 'I read a lot. I'm not what you'd call a very educated kind of guy, but when Jane said you thought she could be a writer, I found that kind of interesting.' Vince paused. 'Can I get you some coffee?'

'Thanks,' I said. 'That'd be good.'

He walked over to the counter, poured me a cup and came back to the table.

'May I be frank without having my hair pulled out?' I asked.

Slowly, Vince nodded, not taking his eyes off me.

'You were with Cynthia that night. Her father found the two of you and dragged her home. Less than twelve hours later, Cynthia wakes up and she's the only one left in her family. You are, presumably, one of the last people to see a member of her family, other than Cynthia herself, alive.' I paused. 'But I'm sure the police went over all this with you at the time.'

'Yeah.'

'What did you tell them?'

'I didn't tell them anything. That was one thing I learned from my old man, God rest his soul. Never answer questions from the cops.'

'But you might have been able to help them figure out what happened.'

'That wasn't my concern,' Vince said.

'But didn't it make the police suspect you had something to do with it?'

'Maybe. But they can't convict you on suspicion. They need evidence. And they didn't have any of that. Now, may I be frank with you without you pulling *my* hair out?' He grinned.

'I don't think you have much to worry about there,' I said.

'I felt bad about it. About not being able to help Cynthia because she was a very nice girl. And I wished I could do something for her, you know? But my dad said to me, he said, walk away from a chick like that. You don't need those kinds of problems. Cops are going to be looking at you already, with your background, with an old man like me involved in the shit I'm involved in, that's all we need, you messed up with a girl whose entire family probably got murdered.'

I chose my words carefully. 'Your father, he did OK. Am I right?'

'Money? Yeah. He did all right for himself.'

'Do you think your father might have thought you were responsible somehow and that he gave money to Cynthia's aunt, Tess Berman, anonymously, to help cover the costs of her schooling?'

'No.'

'Because,' I said, and I was debating with myself whether I should share this information, but sometimes you just go with your gut, 'someone did that.'

'Someone was giving her aunt money for school?' Vince asked.

'That's right.'

'And no one ever knew who?'

'That's right.'

'Well, that's weird,' Vince said. He leaned back in his chair, looked up at the ceiling a moment, came back forward and put his elbows on the table. 'I'll tell you something,' he said, 'but not if you're going to tell the cops.'

'OK.' My mouth felt dry.

'That night,' he said, 'after her old man found us in the car, took her home, I drove after them. I guess I was wondering just how much trouble she was in.'

I waited.

'I saw them pull into the driveway, go into the house together. I parked down the street, thinking maybe she'd leave again after her parents bawled her out. But that didn't happen. And after a while, this other car drove past me, going slow, like someone was trying to read the house numbers. When it got to the end of the street, it turned around and parked on the other side of the street, a couple of houses down from Cynthia's place.'

'Could you see who was in it? What kind of car was it?'

'It was an Ambassador or Rebel or something, I think. Blue, I think. Looked like one person in the car. It looked like it was a woman.'

'A woman was parked out front of the house. Watching it?'

'Seemed like it. And I remember they weren't Connecticut plates on the car. New York State, which were orange back then.'

'How long did the car stay there?'

'Well, not that long really. Mrs Bigge and Todd came out and got in the mother's car, this yellow Ford, and they drove off.'

'Just the two of them? The father wasn't with them?'

'Just Mom and Todd. As soon as they rounded the corner, this other car followed them. I sat there for another forty-five minutes or so, and suddenly the front door of the house opens, and the father, Clayton, he goes running out of the house. Gets in the car, backs out at like a hundred miles an hour, drives off fast as can be.'

I let that sink in.

'So everyone's gone except Cynthia. So I drive up, I knock on the door, figured I could talk to her. I banged on it half a dozen times, didn't get any answer, figured she was probably sleeping it off, right? So I went back home.' He shrugged.

'And you never told anyone this? You didn't tell the cops? You never told Cynthia?'

'No, I didn't tell her. And I didn't tell the cops. You think it would have made sense to tell them I was sitting outside the house that night?'

I gazed out of the window and into the Sound, as if the answers I'd been searching for, the answers Cynthia had been searching for, were always beyond the horizon, impossible to reach.

'And why are you telling me this now?' I asked Vince.

He ran his hand over his chin, squeezed his nose. 'I don't know. I'm guessing all these years have been hard on Cyn, am I right?'

'Yes,' I said. 'Very hard. Especially lately.'

'Hmmm,' Vince said. 'I wish there was something I could do to help.'

We were both startled at that moment when the door opened.

It was Jane. 'Well, Vince, are you going to help the poor bastard or not?'

'Where the hell were you?' he said. 'You been listening in this whole time?'

'It's a screen door,' Jane said. 'You don't want people to listen, maybe you better build yourself a little bank vault up here.'

'Damn,' he said.

'So are you going to help him?' she asked again. 'It's not like you're really busy or anything.'

Vince looked tiredly at me. 'So,' he said. 'Is there any way I could be of assistance to you?'

Jane was watching him with her arms folded across her chest.

I didn't know what to say. Not knowing what I was up against, I couldn't predict whether I needed the kinds of services someone like Vince Fleming offered. 'I don't know,' I said.

'Why don't I tag along for a while, see what develops?' he said.

'So you'll help him?' Jane said. Vince nodded. Then she left, and this time we could hear her going down the stairs.

Vince said, 'She scares the hell out of me.'

VINCE FLEMING offered to drive me back to my car in his own vehicle, an aggressive-looking Dodge Ram pick-up. My house was not far off the route back to the body shop, where I'd left my car. I asked Vince if he'd mind stopping there so I could check whether Cynthia had come home.

'Sure,' he said as we got into his truck.

I gave Vince directions to our street, pointed out the house up ahead. Once inside, I looked for any evidence that Cynthia might have returned, a note, anything.

She had not.

Vince wandered around the ground floor, looking at the pictures on the walls, the books we had on our shelves. His eyes landed on the open shoeboxes of mementos. 'The hell's this stuff?' he asked.

'It's Cynthia's. From her house when she was a kid.'

Vince sat on the couch, ran his hand through the stuff. 'Looks like a lot of useless crap to me,' he said.

'Yeah, well, so far that's exactly what it's been,' I said.

I tried phoning Cynthia's cell on the off chance that it might be on. I was about to hang up after the fourth ring when I heard Cynthia say, 'Hello?'

'Cyn?'

'Hi, Terry.'

'Are you OK? Where are you?'

'We're fine, Terry,' she said. There was a lot of background noise.

'Where are you?'

'In the car.'

'When are you coming back?' I asked.

'I don't know,' Cynthia said. 'I just need some time.'

'Tell her hi,' Vince shouted from the living room.

'Who's that?' Cynthia asked.

'Vince Fleming,' I said.

'What? What's he doing there?'

'It's kind of a long story. I'll tell you about it when you get back.' I hesitated. 'He told me a couple of other things, about that night, that he hadn't told anyone about before.'

'Like what?'

'Like he followed you and your dad back home that night, sat out front for a while, and he saw Todd and your mom leave; then later, your dad left. In a hurry. And there was another car out front for a while that left after your mom and Todd did.'

There was nothing but road noise coming through the phone.

'Cynthia?'

'I'm here. I don't know what it means.'

'Me neither.'

'Terry, I'm turning off the phone. I forgot to bring a charger and there's not much battery left.'

'Come home soon, Cyn. I love you.'

'Bye,' she said, and ended the call. I replaced the receiver and went into the living room.

Vince Fleming handed me a newspaper clipping, the one of Todd standing with fellow members of a basketball team.

'That looks like Todd in that one,' Vince said. 'Picture's goofy, though. I don't recognise anyone else in it. It's nobody from our school back then.'

I took it from him, although there wasn't much point. I didn't go to school with Todd or Cynthia and wouldn't know any of their classmates.

'And the name is wrong,' Vince said, pointing under the picture.

I shrugged. 'OK. So newspapers get names wrong.' I read the name where his should have been. The name was J. Sloan.

'Oh my God,' I said.

Vince looked at me. 'You wanna fill me in?'

'J. Sloan,' I said. 'Jeremy Sloan. The man in the food court. That was the name of this man Cynthia accused of being her brother.'

'What are you talking about?' Vince asked.

'A couple of weeks ago,' I said, 'Cynthia and Grace and I are at the mall, and Cynthia sees this guy; she's convinced he's Todd.'

'How did you get his name?'

'Cynthia goes right up to him, says that she knows he's her brother. It was a horrible scene. The guy denied it. So I said maybe if he showed Cynthia his driver's licence, if he could prove to her he wasn't who she thought she was, she'd leave him alone.'

'He did that?'

'Yeah. I saw the licence. His name was Jeremy Sloan.'

Vince took the clipping back. 'That's pretty damned curious, isn't it?'

'This doesn't make any sense,' I said. 'Why is Todd's picture in an old newspaper clipping with this different name?'

'You remember anything about the licence?'

'Just that it was New York,' I said.

'It's kind of a big state,' Vince said.

'I think it was Young something.'

Vince flipped the clipping over. There was text on the back. He was reading bits and pieces of stories, then looked up. 'You got a computer?'

I nodded.

'Fire it up,' Vince said. He followed me upstairs, stood over me as I pulled up a chair and turned the computer on. 'There's bits of a story here, involving Falkner Park and Niagara County. Throw all that into Google.'

I typed in the words, hit SEARCH. It didn't take long to figure it all out.

'There's a Falkner Park in Youngstown, New York, in Niagara County,' I said.

'Bingo,' Vince said. 'So this is most likely from some paper from that area.'

I turned round in my chair, looked up at him. 'Why is Todd in a picture in a paper from Youngstown, New York, listed as J. Sloan?'

'Maybe it's not a picture of Todd Bigge. Maybe it's a picture of J. Sloan.'

I gave that a second to sink in. 'What are you saying? That there are two people? One named Todd Bigge and one named J. Sloan—Jeremy Sloan—or is there one person with two names?'

'Hey,' said Vince, 'I'm just here because Jane asked me.'

I turned back to the computer, went to the White Pages website where you could look up phone numbers, entered in Jeremy Sloan for Youngstown, New York. The search came up empty but suggested I try the last name only. I tried the latter, and up came a handful of Sloans in the Youngstown area.

I pointed to the screen for Vince. 'There's a Clayton Sloan listed on Niagara View Drive.'

'Clayton? That was Cynthia's father's first name,' Vince said.

'Yeah,' I said. 'I'm going to give this number a call.'

'Whoa!' Vince said. 'You out of your mind?'

'What?'

'Look, if they've got caller ID, they'll know right away who it is. Now, maybe they know who you are and maybe they don't, but you don't want to be tipping your hand, do you?' He handed me his cellphone. 'Use this,' he said. 'They won't know who's calling.'

I took the phone and entered the number. One ring. Two rings. Three rings. Four rings. When it got to eight, I started to pull the phone away when I heard a voice.

'Hello?' It was a woman's voice. Older, I thought, sixties at least.

'Oh yes, hello,' I said. 'Is Jeremy there?' Even as I said it, I thought, *And what if he is? What am I going to say?*

'I'm afraid not,' the woman said. 'Who's calling?'

'Oh, that's OK,' I said. 'I can try again in a little while.'

'He's out of town,' the woman said. 'I can't say for sure when he'll be back.'

'Of course,' I said. 'He mentioned something to me about going to Connecticut.'

'He did? Are you sure?' She sounded quite perturbed.

'I could be wrong. Listen, I'll just catch him later; it's no big deal. Just a golf thing.'

'Golf? Jeremy doesn't play golf. Who is this?'

The call was spiralling out of control. Vince drew a finger across his throat. I folded the phone shut, ending the conversation. I handed it back to Vince, who slipped it into his jacket. 'Sounds like you got the right place,' he said. 'You might have played it a bit better, though.'

I ignored his criticism. 'So the Jeremy Sloan at the mall is very likely the Jeremy Sloan who lives in Youngstown, at a house where the phone is listed under the name Clayton Sloan. And Cynthia's father had kept a clipping in his drawer, of him with a basketball team.'

Neither of us said anything. We were both trying to get our heads around it. We went back downstairs to the kitchen.

'You got any ideas?' I asked Vince.

'Well, this Sloan guy is still out of town. Which means he may still be in the Milford area, probably in some local hotel.' He got the phone back out of his jacket, brought up a number from his contact list, hit one button. He waited a moment, then said, 'Hey, it's me. Something I need you to do.'

And then Vince told whoever was on the other end of the line to round up a couple of the other guys and start doing the rounds of the hotels in town.

'I want you to find out if there's a guy named Jeremy Sloan, from Youngstown, New York, staying at one of them. And if you find out he is, you let me know.' Vince put the phone back in his coat. 'If this guy is in town, they'll find him,' he said.

I took a seat at the kitchen table. Vince sat down opposite me.

He said, 'Do you have any idea what's going on?'

'I think I might be starting to,' I said. 'That woman who answered the phone. What if she's Jeremy Sloan's mother? And what if Jeremy really is my wife's brother?'

'Yeah?'

'What if I just spoke to my wife's mother?'

'Someone phoned here for you,' she said.

'Who?'

'He didn't say who it was. But he asked for you, and when I said you were away, he said he remembered you saying something about going to Connecticut.'

'What?'

'You shouldn't have told anyone where you were going!'

'I didn't!'

'Well, if you didn't, how would he know?'

'I don't know.'

'He said he knew you from golfing.'

'Golfing? I don't golf.'

'That's what I told him,' she said. 'I told him you don't golf.'

'You know what, Mom? It was probably just a wrong number or something. Don't be upset. Besides, I'm coming home.'

'You are?' Her whole tone changed.

'Yeah. If I get out of here soon, I'll be home late tonight.'

'You drive safely. I don't want you falling asleep at the wheel. You've never had the same kind of driving stamina your father had.'

'How is he?'

'I think, if we get things done this week, he'll last at least that long. I'll be glad when this is finally over. You know what it costs to take a taxi down to see him?'

'It won't matter soon, Mom.'

'It's about more than the money, you know,' she said. 'I've been thinking about how it'll be done. We're going to need some rope, you know. Or some of that tape. And I guess it makes sense to do the mother first. The little one'll be no trouble after that.'

9

Vince and I returned to his truck. He was going to drive me back to get my car, which was still parked near his body shop.

'So you know Jane has been having trouble at school,' he said.

'Yeah,' I said.

'She's a good kid, but she has a bit of a temper at times.'

'She needs to get a handle on that,' I said. 'You can't solve every problem by beating the crap out of someone.'

He chuckled softly to himself.

'Do you want her to have a life like yours?' I asked him. 'No offence intended.'

He slowed for a red light. 'No,' he said. 'But the odds are kind of stacked against her. I'm not the best role model. And her mother, she's bounced Jane around to so many homes, the kid's never had any stability.'

'You could send her to a good school,' I said. 'When she finishes high school, maybe send her to some place for journalism, or an English programme, where she could develop her talents.'

'You help me with that?' He glanced at me from the corner of his eye.

'Yeah,' I said. 'The thing is, will she listen?'

Vince shook his head tiredly. 'Yeah, well, that's the question.'

His cell rang.

'Yeah?' he said. He listened a moment, then said, 'Wait for me.' He put the phone away, said, 'They found him. He's registered at the HoJo's.'

Vince hit the gas and headed up to I-95. He barrelled up the on-ramp and, given that the Howard Johnson Hotel was the other side of town, he was doing eighty-five by the time he was merging with traffic.

We were to the other side of town in just a few minutes. Vince hung a right, then took another right into the HoJo parking lot. The SUV I'd ridden in earlier was parked just beyond the doors to the lobby, and when Blondie saw us, he ran over to Vince's window. Vince powered it down.

Blondie gave his boss a room number, said if you drove up the hill and round the back, it was one of the ones you could pull right up to. Vince headed up a winding driveway that went behind the complex. The road levelled out behind a row of rooms with doors that opened onto the kerb.

'Here it is,' Vince said, pulling the truck into a spot.

'I want to talk to him,' I said. 'Don't do anything crazy to him.'

Vince, already out of the truck, gave me a dismissive wave without looking back at me. He went up to a door, noticed that it was already open and rapped on it.

'Mr Sloan?' he said.

A few doors down, a cleaning lady looked in our direction.

'He gone,' the maid said. 'He just check out, a few minute ago.'

'How long ago?' Vince asked, taking a twenty out of his wallet and handing it to her.

She slipped it into the pocket of her uniform. 'Ten minutes?'

'What kind of car did he have?' I asked.

She shrugged. 'I don't know. Just a car. Brown. Dark window.'

'Thanks,' Vince said to her. He tipped his head in the direction of his pick-up, and we both got back in.

'What now?' I said. I had no idea.

Vince sat there a moment. 'I think you're going to Youngstown. It looks to me like that might be the only place where you'll find some answers.'

Vince reached across the car in my direction, opening the glove box. He grabbed a road map, unfolded it.

'OK, let's have a look here.' He scanned the map, looking into the upper left corner, then said, 'Here it is. North of Buffalo, just north of Lewiston. Youngstown. Tiny little place. Should take us eight hours maybe.'

'Us?'

Vince attempted, briefly, to fold the map back into its original form, then shoved it, a jagged-edged paper ball, at me. 'That'll be your job. You get that back together. I might even let you do some of the driving. But don't even think of touching the radio. That's definitely off-limits.'

IT WAS DARK when we got past Buffalo. We proceeded on to Niagara Falls, up the Robert Moses Parkway past Lewiston, where I noticed a hospital near the highway. Not far north of Lewiston, we took the exit for Youngstown.

We didn't have an exact address for Clayton Sloan. But Youngstown was a village, and we figured it wouldn't take that long for us to get our bearings. We came in on Lockport Street, then turned south on Main.

I spotted a bar and grill. 'They'll probably have a phone book,' I said.

'I could use a bite,' Vince said.

I was hungry, but I was also feeling pretty anxious. We were so close. 'Something quick,' I said, and Vince found a place to park round the corner. We walked back and went inside.

While Vince grabbed a chair at the counter and ordered some beer and chicken wings, I found a payphone but no phone book. The bartender handed me the one he kept under the counter when I asked. The listing for Clayton Sloan gave the address as 25 Niagara View Drive. Handing the book back, I asked the bartender how to get there.

'South on Main, half a mile.'

'Left or right?'

'Left. You go right, you're in the Niagara River, pal.'

I ripped the meat off a couple of wings and drank half a beer, but my stomach was full of butterflies. 'I can't take this any longer,' I said to Vince. 'Let's go.' He threw some bills on the counter and we were out of the door.

It wasn't any time at all before we spotted Niagara View.

Vince hung a left, trolled slowly down the street while I hunted for numbers. 'Twenty-one, twenty-three,' I said. 'There,' I said. 'Twenty-five.'

Vince drove a hundred yards further down the street before turning off the truck and killing the lights.

There was a car in the driveway at number 25. A silver Honda Accord, maybe five years old. No brown car. If Jeremy Sloan was headed home, it looked as though we'd got here before him.

The house was a sprawling single-storey, white siding, built in the sixties most likely. Well tended. A porch, two wooden recliners.

There was also a ramp. A wheelchair ramp, with a very slight grade, from the walkway to the porch. We walked up it and stood at the door together.

'How you wanna play this?' Vince said.

'What do you think?'

'Close to the vest,' Vince suggested.

There were still lights on in the house, and I thought I could detect the muted sounds of a television somewhere inside, so it didn't look as though I was going to wake anyone up. I raised my index finger to the doorbell, held it a moment.

'Showtime,' Vince said.

WE COULD HEAR some muffled movement in the house, and a moment later the door was opening, not wide, but haltingly. Once it was open a foot or so, I could see why. It was a woman in a wheelchair, moving back, then leaning forward to open the door a few more inches.

'Yes?' she said.

'Mrs Sloan?' I said.

I put her age at late sixties, early seventies. She was thin, but the way she moved her upper body did not suggest frailty. She gripped the wheels of her chair firmly, moved herself deftly around the open door and forward, effectively blocking our way into the house. She had a blanket folded over her lap that came down over her knees. Her silver hair was pinned back, not a stray hair out of place. Her piercing brown eyes were darting back and forth between her two unexpected visitors. Her features suggested that she might possibly have been, at one time, a striking woman, but there exuded from her now, perhaps from the strong set of her jaw, the way her lips pursed out, a sense of irritability, maybe even meanness.

I searched her for any hints of Cynthia but found none.

'Yes, I'm Mrs Sloan,' she said.

'I'm sorry to disturb you so late,' I said. 'Mrs Clayton Sloan?'

'Yes. I'm Enid Sloan,' she said. 'You're right. It's very late. What do you want?' There was an edge to her voice. She held her head up, thrust her chin forward, not just because we towered over her, but as a show of strength. She was trying to tell us she was a tough old broad, not to be messed with.

There was a TV on in another room on the ground floor and there was a comforting smell coming to us from further inside the house. I sniffed the air. 'Baking?' I said.

'Carrot cake,' she snapped. 'For my son. He's coming home.'

'Oh,' I said. 'That's who we've come by to see. Jeremy?'

'What do you want with Jeremy? Who are you people?'

'Maybe,' I said, 'if we could talk to your husband. Could we speak with Clayton?'

'He's not here,' Enid Sloan said. 'He's in the hospital.'

That took me by surprise. 'Oh,' I said. 'I'm sorry. Would that be the hospital we saw driving up here?'

'If you came by way of Lewiston,' she said. 'He's been there several weeks.'

'I hope it's nothing serious,' I said. 'With your husband.'

'My husband is dying,' Enid Sloan said. 'Got cancer all through him. It's only a matter of time now.' She hesitated, looked at me. 'You the one who phoned here? Asking for Jeremy?'

'I think we should continue this discussion inside,' Vince said, moving forward.

Enid Sloan held on to her wheels. 'I don't think so.'

'Well, I do,' Vince said, and put both hands on the arms of the chair and forced it back. Enid's grip was no match for Vince's force. He pushed her inside and I didn't see that I had much choice but to follow. I closed the front door behind me.

'Who the hell are you?' Enid spat at us.

'Mrs Sloan,' I said, 'my name is Terry Archer. My wife's name is Cynthia. Cynthia Bigge.'

She stared at me, her mouth half open. She was speechless.

'I take it that name means something to you,' I said. 'I have a question for you. And it might sound a bit crazy, but I'll have to ask you to be a bit patient here. Are you Patricia Bigge?'

And she laughed scornfully. 'I don't know what you're talking about,' she said.

'Then why the laugh?' I asked her. 'You seem to know these names I'm mentioning.'

'I'm calling the police,' Enid said, turning her chair. Vince came round behind it, went to grab for the handles, until I waved for him to stop.

'No,' I said. 'Maybe that would be a good idea. We could all wait here for Jeremy to return home and ask him some questions with the police here.'

'Why should I be afraid to have the police come?' she said.

'That's a good question. Could it have something to do with what happened twenty-five years ago? Or maybe with more recent events, in Connecticut? The death of Tess Berman, my wife's aunt? And a private detective named Denton Abagnall?'

'Get out,' she said.

'And about Jeremy,' I said. 'He's Cynthia's brother, isn't he?'

She glared at me, her eyes filled with hate. 'Don't you dare say that,' she said, her hands resting on the blanket.

'What about Clayton?' I asked her. 'Is Clayton Sloan actually Clayton Bigge? Are they one and the same person?'

'You can't do this,' Enid Sloan said. 'You can't barge into an old lady's house and hold her like this!'

'I need to go to the hospital,' I said to Vince. 'I want to see Clayton Sloan.'

'He's very sick,' Enid said. 'He can't be disturbed.'

'Maybe I can disturb him long enough to ask him a couple of questions.'

Vince said, 'If we leave, she's going to call Jeremy. Warn him that we're waiting here to talk to him. I could tie her up.'

I couldn't condone tying up an elderly disabled woman, no matter how unpleasant she seemed. 'What if you just stayed here?'

He nodded. 'That works. Enid and I can chat.' He leaned over so she could see his face. 'Won't that be fun?' He reached into his jacket, took out the keys to the truck and tossed them my way.

I grabbed them out of the air. 'What room is he in?' I asked her.

She glared at me. 'Third floor. Room 309.'

Before I left the house, Vince and I exchanged cellphone numbers. I got in his truc and once I'd found my way back to the highway, I headed south.

I took the first exit once I saw the blue 'H' in the distance, found my way to the hospital parking lot and entered by way of the emergency department. There were half a dozen people in the waiting room. I walked right through, past the admissions desk, where I saw a sign indicating that visiting hours had ended a couple of hours ago, at eight, and found an elevator to the third floor. If I could just make it to Clayton Sloan's room, I'd be OK.

The elevator doors parted onto the third-floor nurses' station. There was no one there. I stepped out, paused a moment, then moved on down the corridor, looking for door numbers. The corridor turned left and the first door I came to was 309. The door was partly ajar, the room in darkness.

It was a private room, one bed. A curtain obscured all but the foot of the bed. I took a few steps in and saw that there was a man in the bed, on his back, slightly raised, fast asleep. In his seventies, I guessed. He was emaciated-looking, with thinned hair.

I moved round to the far side of the bed, where the curtain gave me cover from the corridor. There was a chair near the head of the bed, and I sat down. I studied Clayton Sloan's face, searching for something there that I was unable to find when I looked at Enid Sloan's. Something about his nose, perhaps, a trace of cleft in his chin. I reached out and gently touched the man's exposed arm.

'Clayton,' I whispered, rubbing his leathery skin softly back and forth.

His eyes fluttered open. He saw me, blinked hard a couple of times, let his eyes adjust and focus. 'Wha . . .'

'Clayton Bigge?' I said.

That not only brought his eyes into focus but also made him turn his head more sharply. 'Who are you?' he whispered.

'Your son-in-law,' I said.

As HE SWALLOWED, I watched his Adam's apple bob along the length of his throat. 'My what?' he said.

'Your son-in-law,' I said. 'I'm Cynthia's husband.'

He took a deep breath through his nostrils, let the air out slowly. 'So,' he said. 'Am I supposed to know what you're talking about?'

'I think you do,' I said. 'You're Clayton Bigge.'

Another deep breath. Then, 'I'm Clayton Sloan.'

'I believe you are,' I said. 'But I think you're also Clayton Bigge, who was married to Patricia Bigge, who had a son named Todd and a daughter named Cynthia, and you lived in Milford, Connecticut, until one night in 1983, when something very terrible happened.'

He looked away from me and stared at the curtain. 'I'm dying,' he said.

'Then maybe it's time to get a few things off your chest,' I said.

Clayton turned to look at me again. 'Tell me your name.'

'Terry. Terry Archer.' I hesitated. 'What's your name?'

'Clayton,' he said. 'I've always been Clayton.' His eyes moved down. He stared at the folds in the hospital linen. 'Clayton Sloan, Clayton Bigge.' He paused. 'Depended where I was at the time.'

'Two families?' I said.

I was able to make out a nod. Remembered some of the things Cynthia told me about her father. On the road all the time. Back and forth across the country. Home for a few days, gone for a few.

Suddenly he brightened as a thought occurred to him. 'Cynthia,' he said to me. 'Is she here? Is she with you?'

'No,' I said. 'I don't . . . I don't know exactly where she is right now. She may be back home now, in Milford, for all I know. With our daughter. Grace.'

'Grace,' he said. 'My granddaughter.'

'Yes,' I whispered as a shadow went by in the hall. 'Your granddaughter.'

Clayton closed his eyes for a moment, as though in pain. 'My son,' he said. 'Where is my son?'

'Todd?' I said.

'No, no,' he said. 'Not Todd. Jeremy.'

'I think he may be on the way back from Milford.'

Clayton looked more alert. 'What was he doing in Milford?'

'I don't understand,' I said. 'Aren't Jeremy and Todd the same person?'

He looked at me. 'No.' He paused. 'Todd is dead.'

'When? When did Todd die?'

'That night,' Clayton said resignedly. 'With his mother.'

So it was them. In the car at the bottom of the quarry.

'Patricia and Todd,' I said. 'So they're both dead.'

Clayton's eyes closed again. 'You have to tell me what Jeremy is doing in Milford.'

'I'm not sure,' I said. 'But I think he's been watching us. Watching our family. I think he's been in our house. I can't say for sure, but I think he may have killed Cynthia's aunt Tess.'

'Oh my God,' Clayton said. 'Patricia's sister? She's dead?'

'She was stabbed to death,' I said. 'And a man we'd hired to try to find out some things, he's dead, too.'

'This can't be happening. She said he'd got a job. Out West.'

'What?'

'Enid. She said Jeremy got a job, in . . . in Seattle or someplace. An opportunity. Had to go out there. That he'd come back and see me soon.' He seemed to drift off a bit. 'Jeremy, he's . . . He can't help what he is. She made him what he is. He does whatever she tells him to do. She poisoned him against me from the day he was born. She says to me, "Hang on, just hang on a little longer." It's like, she doesn't care if I die. She just doesn't want me to die yet. She's been up to something. I've known it.'

'Why wouldn't she want you to know?'

'She must have seen it,' he whispered. 'Found it, something.'

'What? Seen what?'

'Dear God,' he said faintly. 'If Enid knows . . .'

'If Enid knows what? What are you talking about?'

'I'm dying. . . . She . . . she must have called the lawyer. I never intended for her to see the will before I died. . . My instructions were very specific.'

'Will? What will?'

'My will. I had it changed. When I die, my estate, everything will go to Cynthia. Enid and Jeremy, they'd be left with nothing, just what they deserve, just what she deserves.' He looked at me. 'You have no idea what she's capable of.'

'She's here. Enid is here; she's in Youngstown. It was Jeremy who went to Milford.'

'He'd do whatever she tells him to do. He has to. She's in a wheelchair. She won't be able to do it herself this time . . .'

'Do what herself?'

He ignored my question. 'So Jeremy's on his way back?'

'That's what Enid said. I think we beat him back here.'

' "We"? I thought you said Cynthia wasn't with you.'

'She's not. I came with a man named Vince Fleming.'

Clayton thought about the name. 'Vince Fleming,' he said quietly. 'The boy. The boy she was with that night.'

'That's right. He's been helping me. He's with Enid now. Making sure she doesn't call Jeremy, tell him that we're here.'

'But if Jeremy's already on his way back, he must have already done it.'

'Done what?'

'Is Cynthia OK?' He got a desperate look in his eyes. 'Is she alive?'

'Of course she's alive.'

'And your daughter? Grace? She's still alive?'

'What are you talking about? Yes, of course they're alive.'

'Because if something happens to Cynthia, everything goes to any children . . . It's all spelt out . . .'

I felt my whole body shiver. How many hours had it been since I'd talked to Cynthia? Did I really know, with any certainty, that she and Grace were alive now?

I got out my cellphone and punched in our home number.

'Please, please have gone home,' I said under my breath. The phone rang once, twice, a third time. On the fourth ring, it went to voice mail.

'Cynthia,' I said. 'You've got to call me immediatcly. It's an emergency.'

I ended the call and then tried her cell. It went to voice mail immediately. I left her pretty much the same message but added, 'You *must* call me.'

'Where is she?' Clayton asked.

'I don't know,' I said uneasily. I called another number.

A pickup, then throat clearing, then, 'Hello?' Sleepy.

'Rolly,' I said. 'It's Terry.'

'Yeah, yeah, OK,' Rolly said. 'You've found Cynthia?'

'No,' I said. 'But I've found someone else.'

'What?'

'Listen, I don't have time to explain, but I need you to find Cynthia. Go by the house, see if her car's there. Start calling hotels, anything you can think of.'

'Terry, what's going on? Who have you found?'

'Rolly, I've found her father.'

'I . . . I can't believe it,' he said. 'What's he told you? Has he told you what happened?'

'We're just getting started. I'll tell you all about it when I can. But you have to look for Cynthia. If you find her, she has to call me immediately.'

'Right. I'm on it. I'm getting dressed.'

'And Rolly,' I said, 'let me tell her. About her father. She's going to have a million questions.'

I ended the call.

'Clayton,' I said, 'why do you think they might be in danger?'

'Because of the will,' Clayton said. 'I'm leaving everything to Cynthia. It's the only way I know to make up for what I did. If she's dead, if your daughter's dead, then the money will revert back to Enid. There's no way Enid'll let Cynthia inherit. She'll kill both of them to make sure she gets the money.'

'But that's crazy,' I said. 'A double murder—that'd draw so much attention. Police would reopen the case; they'd start looking into what happened twenty-five years ago—'

I stopped myself.

A murder would attract attention. No doubt about it.

But a suicide. There wouldn't be much attention paid to something like that. Especially not when the woman committing suicide had been under so much strain in recent weeks. A woman who had called the police to investigate the appearance of a strange hat in her house. A woman who had called the police because she'd received a note telling her where she could find the bodies of her missing mother and brother. A note that had been composed on a typewriter in her own home. A woman like that who killed herself, well, it wasn't hard to figure out what that was about. It was about guilt. Guilt she must have lived with for a very long time.

A woman this overwhelmed with guilt, would it be any surprise if she took her daughter's life along with her own?

Could that be what was in the works?

'What?' Clayton asked me. 'What are you thinking?'

What if Jeremy had been spying on us for weeks, following Grace to school? Watching us at the mall? From the street out front of our house? Getting into our home one day when we were careless, then leaving with the spare house key so he could get in whenever he wanted. Leaving that hat. Learning our email address. Writing a note on my typewriter, leading Cynthia to the bodies of her mother and brother . . .

I gave my head a slight shake. It all seemed so diabolical.

'I need you to tell me everything,' I whispered to Clayton.

He took a deep breath. 'Take me to my daughter. Let me say goodbye to her. Take me to her and I'll tell you everything.'

'I can't take you out of here,' I said. 'If I take you out of here, you'll die.'

'I'm going to die anyway,' Clayton said. 'My clothes, they're in the closet over there. Get them.'

I started for the closet, then stopped. 'Even if I wanted to, they're not going to let you leave the hospital.'

Clayton waved me over closer to him, reached out and grabbed my arm. 'She's a monster,' he said. 'There's nothing she won't do to get what she wants. For years, I've lived in fear of her, did what she wanted, scared to death of what she might do next. But what do I have to fear any more? I've so little time left. Maybe, with what I have, I can save my Cynthia and Grace. There are no limits to what Enid might do.'

'She won't be doing anything now,' I said. 'Not with Vince watching her.'

Clayton squinted at me. 'Did you go to the house? Knock on the door?'

I nodded.

'And she answered it?'

I nodded again.

'Did she seem afraid?'

I shrugged. 'Not particularly.'

'Two men, coming to her door, and she's not afraid. Didn't that seem odd?'

Another shrug. 'Maybe, I suppose.'

Clayton said, 'You didn't look under the blanket, did you?'

10

I got out my cell again, called Vince's. 'Come on,' I said, feeling awash in anxiety.

'Is he there?' Clayton asked me, moving his legs over to the edge of the bed.

'No,' I said. 'I need to get back over there.'

'Give me a minute,' he said, inching his butt closer to the edge.

I went over to the closet, found socks and underwear, a pair of pants, a shirt, and a light jacket. 'You sure about this?' I said.

He nodded, gave me a weak smile. 'If there's a chance to see Cynthia, I'll find the strength.'

'What's going on in here?'

We both turned out heads to the door. A nurse was standing there, a slender black woman, mid-forties, a look of wonderment on her face.

'Mr Sloan, what on earth do you think you're doing?'

'Getting dressed,' he said. 'I'm checking out.'

'This is absolutely out of the question. Am I going to have to call your doctor in the middle of the night?'

'Do what you have to do,' he said to her.

'My first call's going to be to security,' she said, and sprinted from the room.

'I know this is a lot to ask,' I said, 'but you're going to have to hurry. I'll see if I can find a wheelchair.'

I went into the corridor, spotted a vacant chair and pushed it back to Clayton's room.

'Ready,' said Clayton. He'd not yet buttoned up his shirt, but his jacket was on. He looked like an aged homeless person.

I brought the chair up so Clayton could drop himself into it, then I spun him round and headed for the elevator.

Our nurse was at her station on the phone. 'Security! I said I needed you up here now!'

The elevator doors parted and I wheeled Clayton in, hit the button for the ground floor and watched the nurse glare at us until the doors slid shut.

'When the door opens,' I told Clayton calmly, 'I'm going to be pushing you out of here like a bat out of hell.'

He said nothing but wrapped his fingers around the arms of the chair, squeezed. I wished it had a seat belt.

The doors opened, and there was about fifty feet of hall separating me from the emergency room doors and the parking lot just beyond them. 'Hold on,' I whispered, and broke into a run.

The chair wasn't built for speed, but I pushed it to the point where the front wheels began to wobble.

Clayton hung on.

I was so pumped up on adrenaline, I didn't stop to think about what I was doing. I kept pushing Clayton, out into the parking lot, right up to the passenger door of the Dodge. I got out the keys, unlocked it with the remote, opened the door. The truck sat up high and I had to boost Clayton to get him into the passenger seat.

The truck tyres squealed as I tore out of the lot, heading back for the highway. Clayton, who was already looking exhausted, said, 'We have to go back to my house.'

'I know,' I said. 'I need to know why Vince isn't answering.'

'And there's something I have to get,' Clayton said. 'Before we go see Cynthia.'

'What?'

He waved a weakened hand at me. 'Later.'

'They're going to call the police,' I said. 'I've practically kidnapped a patient.'

I pushed the truck past ninety on the way north to Youngstown. I tried Vince again with my cell, still without success. I was nearing the end of my battery.

When the turnoff came, I was hugely relieved, figuring I was more vulnerable, more noticeable, on the expressway. I drove the truck down to Main, hung a left, went south a couple of miles, and turned down the road to the Sloan house. It looked peaceful enough as we drove up to it, a couple of lights on inside, the Honda Accord still parked out front. I drove the truck onto the back lawn where it couldn't be seen from the street, killed the lights and engine.

'Just go on,' Clayton said. 'See about your friend. I'll try to catch up with you.'

I leapt out, ran to the front and tried the main door.

It was unlocked.

'Vince!' I said, stepping into the front hall. I didn't immediately see Enid Sloan, or her chair, or Vince Fleming.

Not until I got to the kitchen.

Enid wasn't there and neither was her chair. But Vince lay on the floor, the back of his shirt red with blood.

'Vince,' I said, kneeling down next to him. I thought he was dead but he let out a soft moan. 'Oh God, man, you're still alive.'

'Terry,' he whispered, his right cheek pressed to the floor. 'She had a . . . she had a gun under the blanket.' His eyes were flirting with rolling up under his lids. There was blood coming out of his mouth.

'Don't talk,' I said. 'I'm going to call nine-one-one.'

I found the phone and punched in the three numbers. 'A man's been shot,' I said. I barked out the address, told the operator to hurry, ignored all her other questions and hung up.

'He came home,' Vince whispered when I knelt down next to him again. 'Jeremy . . . She met him at the door, didn't even let him come in . . .

said they had to go right then. She phoned him . . . after she shot me, said step on it.'

At the front door, I could hear Clayton shuffling his way into the house.

'It hurts . . .' Vince said. 'Damned little old lady.'

'You're going to be OK,' I said. 'Just hang in there, man.'

CLAYTON SAID, 'Enid never answers the door without a gun under her blanket. Certainly not when she's home alone.'

He'd managed to make it into the kitchen and was using the counter for support as he looked down at Vince Fleming.

'She can be easy to underestimate. An old woman in a wheelchair. No one ever really stands a chance against Enid.'

I had my mouth close to Vince's ear. 'We're going to have to take off. We have to go after Enid and Jeremy. They're going after my wife and my daughter.'

'Do what you gotta do,' Vince whispered.

I glanced up at a wall clock. It was 1.06 a.m.

'How much of a head start do you think they've got?' Clayton asked me.

'Whatever it is,' I said, 'it's too much.'

'OK,' Clayton said. 'There's one thing I have to take with me. I don't think I have the energy to go downstairs to get it.'

'Tell me what it is.'

'In the basement, you'll find a workbench. There's a toolbox sitting on top of it. There's a tray in the top you can lift out. I want what's taped to the bottom of the tray.'

The door to the basement was round the corner from the kitchen. I descended the wooden steps. Along the far wall was the workbench, the top of it littered with half-used tubes of caulking, scraps of sandpaper, tools not put away, and a dented red toolbox. I opened the lid. The tray was filled with rusty screws, broken jigsaw blades, screwdrivers. I raised the tray to see what was under it.

It was a standard letter-sized envelope, dirtied and stained, held in place by some yellowed strips of Scotch tape. I peeled the envelope off.

'You see it?' Clayton called down wheezily from the top of the stairs.

'Yeah,' I said. I picked up the sealed envelope, turned it over in my hands. There was nothing written on it.

'It's OK,' Clayton said. 'If you want to, you can look inside.'

I tore open the envelope at one end, gently pulled out a piece of paper. I read it. I felt as though my last breath was slipping away.

When I got to the top of the stairs, Clayton explained the circumstances surrounding what I'd found in the envelope and told me what he wanted me to do with it. 'You promise?' he said.

'I promise,' I said, slipping the envelope into my jacket.

I HAD ONE last conversation with Vince. 'The ambulance has to be here any time now,' I said. 'Are you going to make it?'

'Go save your wife and girl,' he said. 'Gun in the truck.'

I touched his forehead. 'You're going to make it.'

'Go,' he whispered.

To Clayton, I said, 'That Honda in the driveway. It runs?'

'Sure,' Clayton said. He pointed to a small decorative dish on a table near the front door. 'Should be a set of keys there,' he said.

'Give me a second,' I said.

I ran round to the back of the house and opened up the Dodge pick-up. In the bottom of the centre console unit, under a stack of maps, I found the gun.

Using Clayton's key, I unlocked the Honda, got into the driver's seat and put the gun in the glove compartment. I started up the car.

Clayton emerged from the house, took tentative steps towards me. I leapt out, ran to the other side of the car, got the passenger door open and helped him get inside.

'OK,' I said, getting back into the driver's seat. 'Let's go.'

I drove onto the road, turned right onto Main, heading north. 'Just made it,' Clayton said. An ambulance, followed closely by two police cars, lights flashing but sirens silent, sped south.

Once on the highway, I was tempted to floor it but was still worried about getting pulled over. I settled on a comfortable speed.

I waited until we were past Buffalo, heading due east to Albany. That was when I turned to Clayton and said, 'So let's hear it. All of it.'

'OK,' he said, and cleared his throat in preparation.

THE MARRIAGE WAS predicated on a lie.

The first marriage, Clayton explained. Well, the second one, too. He'd get to that one soon enough. It was a long drive back to Connecticut. Plenty of time to cover everything. But he talked about his marriage to Enid first. A girl he'd known in high school, in Tonawanda, a Buffalo suburb. They started dating and he could see that she was used to getting what she wanted. She used what she had to her advantage. She was attractive, possessed a terrific body, had a strong sexual appetite.

One night, teary eyed, she tells him she's late. 'Oh no,' Clayton Sloan says. He thinks first of his own parents, how ashamed they will be of him.

So there wasn't much else to do but get married. And right away.

A couple of months after that, she says she's not feeling well, says she's making an appointment to see her physician; Dr Gibbs was his name. She goes to the doctor alone, comes home, says she lost it. The baby's gone. Lots of tears. One day, Clayton's in the diner, sees Dr Gibbs, goes over to him and says, 'Enid, losing the baby and all, she'll still be able to have another one, right?'

And Dr Gibbs says, 'Huh?'

So now he has an idea what he's dealing with. A woman who'll say anything, tell any kind of lie, to get what she wants.

He should have left then. But Enid tells him she's so sorry, that she thought she was pregnant but was afraid to go to the doctor to have it confirmed, and then she turned out to be wrong. Clayton again worries about the shame he will bring on himself and his family by leaving Enid, starting divorce proceedings.

The longer he stays, the harder it is to leave. He learns quickly that what Enid wants, Enid gets. When she doesn't, there's hell to pay. Screaming fits, smashing things.

He gets a job in sales, supplying machine shops and factories. It's going to have him driving all over the country, a corridor running between Chicago and New York that skirts past Buffalo. He's going to be away a lot, his employer warns him. That's the clincher for Clayton. Time away from the harping and the screaming. He always dreads the drive home after a sales trip. The only thing that makes returning home worthwhile is seeing his Irish setter, Flynn. He always comes running out to greet Clayton's car, like he's been sitting on the porch from the moment he left, waiting for the second he returns.

Then Enid becomes pregnant. The real deal this time. A baby boy. Jeremy. How she loves that boy. Clayton loves him, too, but soon realises it's a competition. Enid wants the boy's love exclusively and begins, when

Jeremy is barely walking, her campaign to poison the father's relationship with his son.

Clayton wants out. Once, before leaving on one of his sales trips, he says he needs to talk to her.

'I'm not happy,' he says. 'I don't think this is working out.'

She doesn't cry. She doesn't ask what's wrong. What she does is, she gets up close to him, looks deep into his eyes. All she says is, 'You will *never* leave me.' And walks out of the room.

He thinks about that on his trip. We'll see about that, he tells himself. We'll just see.

When he returns, his dog does not run out to greet him. When he opens the garage door, there is Flynn, a rope round his neck, hanging from the rafters.

All Enid says to him is, 'Good thing it was just the dog.'

For all she loves Jeremy, she's willing to let Clayton believe the boy's at risk should he ever decide to leave her. Clayton Sloan resigns himself to this life of misery and humiliation.

He has to make a stop in Milford one time. On the prowl for some new clients, new businesses to supply. He goes into a drugstore to buy a candy bar and there is a woman behind the counter. Wearing a little name tag that says 'Patricia'.

She is beautiful. Reddish hair. She seems so nice. So genuine.

He takes a long time to buy that chocolate bar. Makes small talk about the weather, how he's on the road so much of the time. And then he says something before he's even aware he's said it. 'Would you like to have some lunch?'

Patricia smiles, says if he wants to come back in thirty minutes, she gets an hour off.

Patricia tells him over a tuna sandwich in a nearby coffee shop that she doesn't go to lunch with men she's just met, but there's something about him that intrigues her. He tells her his name is Clayton Bigge.

For the next few months, if his sales trips only take him as far south as Torrington, he drives the extra distance south to Milford to see Patricia. She adores him. She makes him feel important.

He considers the logistics. The company was rejigging the sales routes. He could get the one that ran between Hartford and Buffalo. Drop going to Chicago. That way, at each end of the run . . .

And there's the money question. But Clayton's doing well. He's already been taking extraordinary measures to conceal from Enid how much money he has tucked away. It might be enough, he thinks. Just enough for a second household.

How wonderful it will be, for at least half the time, to be happy.

Patricia says yes when he asks her to marry him.

He must deceive Patricia, but he tries to be good to her. At least when he is home. She gives him two children, Todd and Cynthia.

It is an astonishing juggling act. A family in Connecticut. A family in New York. Back and forth between the two.

When he's Clayton Bigge, he can't stop thinking about when he will have to return to being Clayton Sloan. And when he's Clayton Sloan, he can't stop thinking about hitting the road again so he can become Clayton Bigge.

Being Sloan is easier. At least that's his honest-to-God name. He doesn't have to worry so much about identification. His licence, his papers, they're legitimate.

But when he's Clayton Bigge, he's always on his guard. Doing the speed limit. Making sure there's money in the parking meter. He doesn't want anyone running a check on his licence plate. Every time he drives to Connecticut, he pulls off the road someplace secluded, takes off the New York plates, puts a stolen Connecticut plate on the back of the car in its place. Puts the New York plates back on when he goes to Youngstown. He has to always be thinking. Always uses cash. No paper trail.

Everything about his life is false. His first marriage is built on a lie told by Enid. His second marriage is founded on lies he's told to Patricia.

WE'D BEEN MAKING pretty good time. It was nearly four in the morning, and we were closing in on Albany. I thought that maybe it was time to let Rona Wedmore know what was going on. I dug around in the front pocket of my jeans and found the card she'd given me.

I entered Detective Rona Wedmore's cellphone number. She answered on the fourth ring.

'Wedmore,' she said. Trying very hard to sound awake and alert.

'It's Terry Archer,' I said.

'Mr Archer,' she said, already sounding more focused. 'What is it?'

'I'm going to tell you a few things very quickly. I'm on a dying cell. You need to be on the lookout for my wife. A man named Jeremy Sloan, and his mother, Enid Sloan, are heading to Connecticut from the Buffalo area. I think they intend to find Cynthia and kill her. Cynthia's father is alive. I'm bringing him back with me.'

'Where are you?'

'Along the New York Thruway. You know Vince Fleming, right?'

'Yes.'

'I left him in a house in Youngstown, north of Buffalo. He was trying to help me. He was shot by Enid Sloan.'

'This isn't making any sense,' Wedmore said. 'This Jeremy Sloan and his mother? What are they driving?'

'A brown . . .'

'Impala,' Clayton whispered. 'Chevy Impala.'

'A brown Chevy Impala,' I said. To Clayton, I said, 'Plate?' He shook his head. 'I don't have a plate number.'

'Are you coming back here?' Wedmore asked.

'Yes. In a few hours. Just look for her. Gotta go,' I said, then folded the phone shut and slipped it into my jacket.

'So,' I said, taking us back to where Clayton had left off. 'Were there moments? When you were happy?'

Clayton takes himself back again.

If there are moments of happiness, they only ever happen when he is Clayton Bigge. He loves being a father to Todd and Cynthia. As best he can tell, they love him in return, maybe even look up to him. They seem to respect him.

Sometimes, at night in bed, Patricia will say to him, 'You seem someplace else. You get this look, like you're not here. And you look sad.'

And he takes her in his arms, and he says to her, 'This is the only place I want to be.' It isn't a lie. He's never said anything more truthful. He doesn't like having that other life, the life he can't bear to return to, week after week, month after month, year after year.

Sometimes he'd wake up in the morning and wonder where he was today. Who he was today. He'd make mistakes.

Enid had written him out a grocery list once. A week later, Patricia was doing the laundry, comes into the kitchen with the list in her hand, says, 'What's this? I found it in your trouser pocket.'

Enid's shopping list.

Clayton's mind raced. He said, 'I found that in the cart the other day, must have been the last person's list. I thought it was kind of funny, so I saved it.'

There evidently was at least one time when he put a clipping from a Youngstown area newspaper, a picture of his son with the basketball team, into the wrong drawer. He clipped it because, no matter how hard Enid worked to turn Jeremy against him, he still loved the boy. He saw himself in Jeremy, just as he did in Todd. It was amazing how much Todd, as he grew up, looked like Jeremy at similar stages. To look at Jeremy and hate him was to hate Todd, and he couldn't possibly do that.

He made a mistake like that in Youngstown. A phone bill for the address in Milford. In Patricia's name. It caught Enid's attention.

But it wasn't like Enid to come straight out and ask what it was about. Enid would conduct her own little investigation first. Watch for other signs. Start collecting evidence. Build a case.

And when she thought she had enough, she decided to take a trip of her own the next time her husband Clayton went out of town. One day she drove to Milford, Connecticut. This was before she ended up in the wheelchair. When she was mobile.

'Which brings us,' Clayton said, 'to the night in question.'

THE FIRST PART of the story I knew from Cynthia. How Clayton found her in the car with Vince Fleming, brought her home.

'She was furious,' Clayton said. 'Told us she wished we were dead. Stormed up to her room, never heard another peep out of her. She was drunk.'

'I know,' I said, my hands on the wheel, driving on through the night.

'Just before I'd come back with Cynthia, Todd had been asking me or Patricia to take him out to get a sheet of Bristol board. He'd left some project to the very last minute, needed a sheet of this stuff for some presentation. It was already late, but Patricia remembered they sold it at the drugstore, the one that was open twenty-four hours, so she said she'd take him over to get it.'

He looked out of his window as we passed a tractor trailer.

'Todd and his mom were gone a long time. It had been about an hour. The drugstore wasn't that far. Then the phone rang. It was Enid. Calling from a pay phone. She said, "Guess who?"'

'Oh God,' I said.

'It was a call that, in some way, I'd always been expecting. But I couldn't have imagined what she'd done. She told me to meet her, in the Denny's parking lot. I flew out of the house, drove over to Denny's. She was sitting in her car. She couldn't get out.'

'Why?' I asked.

'She couldn't walk around covered in that much blood and not attract attention.'

I suddenly felt very cold.

'I ran over to her window. She rolled down the window, told me to get in. I got in, and then I could see what was all over her, that it was blood. I was screaming at her, "What the hell have you done?" But I already knew what it had to be.

'Enid had been parked out front of our house. She had the address from the phone bill. She was putting it all together. And then Patricia and Todd came out, drove off, and she followed them. By this point, she must have been blind with rage. She'd figured out that I had this whole other life, this other family.'

Just as Enid, in later years, kept a gun at hand in the case of an emergency, back then she kept a knife in the glove compartment. She reached in and got it, ran in the direction of the drugstore, hid round the corner, which was shrouded in darkness. It was a broad alleyway, used by delivery trucks.

Todd and Patricia emerged from the store. Enid emerged from the darkness. 'Help!' Enid said. 'My daughter! She's been hurt!'

Patricia ran over to meet her, Todd followed.

Enid led them a few steps into the alley, turned to Patricia and said, 'You wouldn't happen to be Clayton's wife, would you?'

She said yes. And then the knife came up and slashed her right across the throat. Enid didn't wait a second. While Todd was still trying to figure out what had happened, she was on him, slashing his throat as quickly as she'd slashed his mother's.

'She told you all this,' I said. 'Enid.'

'Many, many times,' Clayton said quietly. 'She loves to talk about it. Even now. She calls it reminiscing.'

'Then what?'

'That's when she found her way to a nearby phone booth, called me. I show up and find her in the car, and she tells me what she's done. "I've killed them," she says. "Your wife and your son. They're dead." '

'She doesn't know you also have a daughter,' I said quietly.

'I could tell, the way she was talking, that she had no idea that Cynthia was still in the house, that she even existed.'

'And you weren't about to tell her.'

'I was in shock, I think, but I had that much presence of mind. She started up her car, drove over to the alley, showed me their bodies. "You're going to have to help me," she said. "We have to get rid of them," she said.'

Clayton stopped for a moment, rode the next mile or so without saying a word.

'I could have put an end to things right there. I could have refused to help her. I could have gone to the police.'

'But you didn't.'

'She could tell what I was thinking. She said if I called the police, she'd tell them she was only helping me. That it was my idea. And so I helped her. God forgive me, I helped her. We put Patricia and Todd back into the car but left the driver's seat empty. I had an idea. About a place where we could put the car, with them inside. One time, heading back to Youngstown, I started driving around aimlessly, not wanting to go back, found this road that led to the top of the cliff that looked down into this abandoned gravel pit. There was this small lake. I stood there for quite a while, thought about throwing myself off the edge. But in the end, I continued on.'

He coughed.

'We had to leave one car in the lot. I drove Patricia's Escort, Enid following me in her car. Took a while, but I found that road to the quarry again, got the car up there, jammed a rock up against the accelerator with the car in neutral, reached in and put it in drive and jumped back, and the car went over the edge.'

He was winded, gave himself a few seconds to catch his breath.

'Then we had to drive back, pick up the other car. Then we turned round again, both of us, in the two cars, headed back to Youngstown. I didn't even have a chance to say goodbye to Cynthia, to leave her a note, anything. I just had to disappear.'

'When did Enid find out she'd missed one? That she hadn't totally wiped out your other family?'

'A few days later. She'd been watching the news, but the story wasn't covered much by the Buffalo stations or papers. I mean, it wasn't a murder.

There were no bodies. There wasn't even any blood in the alley by the drugstore. There was a rainstorm later that morning, washed everything away. But Enid went to the library and started checking out-of-state papers, and she spotted something. "Girl's Family Vanishes", I think the headline was. She came home. I'd never seen her so mad. Smashing dishes, throwing things. She was completely insane.'

'But she had to live with it,' I said.

'She wasn't going to at first. She started packing, to go to Connecticut, to finish Cynthia off. But I stopped her.'

'How did you manage that?'

'I made a pact with her. A promise. I told her I would never, ever, attempt to get in touch with my daughter, if she would just spare her life.'

'And she accepted that?'

'Grudgingly. But I think it always niggled at her, like an itch you can't reach. A job not done. But now, there's an urgency. Knowing about the will, knowing that if I die before she can kill Cynthia, she'll lose everything.'

'So what did you do? You just went on?'

'I stopped travelling. I got a different job, started up my own company. Enid made it very clear that I was not to travel any more. I've never set foot in Connecticut since that night.'

'Then how did you get the money to Tess?'

Clayton said nothing.

'It was from you, wasn't it?' I asked. 'You squirrelled some money away for Cynthia, kept Enid from finding out.'

'Enid got suspicious. Years later. So I told her, about sending money to Tess, to help with Cynthia's education. But I'd kept my word. I never got in touch with Cynthia.'

'So Enid, she's nursed a grudge against Tess all these years, too?'

'She despised Tess for getting money she believed belonged to her. The two women she hated most in the world, and she'd never met either one of them.'

'So,' I said, 'your story that you've never been back to Connecticut, even if you didn't actually see Cynthia, that's not true?'

'No,' he said. 'That's the truth.'

I thought about that as we continued to drive through the night. 'So if you didn't mail the money, and you didn't deliver it yourself, then you must have had someone do it for you?'

Clayton remained impassive. He closed his eyes, leaned his head back on the headrest, as though sleeping.

'I've one other question,' I said. 'Tell me about Connie Gormley.'

His eyes opened suddenly.

'I don't know that name,' he replied.

'Let me see if I can help,' I said. 'She was from Sharon; she was twenty-seven years old, and one night, twenty-six years ago, she was walking along the shoulder of the road near the Cornwall Bridge, when she was hit by a car. Except it wasn't a hit-and-run. She was likely dead beforehand and the accident was staged.'

Clayton looked out of his window so I couldn't see his face.

'You've admitted to a great many things tonight. A double life. Helping to cover up the murder of your wife and son. But you don't want to tell me about Connie Gormley or how you got money to Tess Berman to help pay for Cynthia's education.'

Clayton shook his head.

'Clayton, did you kill that woman?'

'No,' he said.

'Do you know who did?'

Clayton kept shaking his head, then finally spoke. 'Enough lives have been destroyed already. There's no sense in ruining any more. I don't have anything else to say about this.'

11

I didn't want to lose time stopping for breakfast, but I was also very much aware of Clayton's weakened condition. Once morning hit, and the car was filled with light, I saw how much worse he looked than when we'd fled the hospital.

'You look like you need something,' I said. We were going through Winsted, where Route 8 went from a winding, two-lane affair to four lanes. There were some fast-food joints in Winsted and I suggested we hit a drive-through window, get a McMuffin, something like that.

Clayton nodded wearily.

As we sat in the drive-through line, Clayton said, 'Tell me about her.'

'What?'

'Tell me about Cynthia. I haven't seen her in twenty-five years.'

I said, 'She's wonderful, the most wonderful thing that's ever happened to me. And as long as I've known her, she's been dealing with what you and Enid did to her. Think about it. You wake up one morning and your family is gone.' I gripped the wheel more tightly in anger. 'Do you have any idea? Do you? What was she supposed to think? Were you all dead? Or had the three of you decided to go off and have a new life somewhere else, a new life that didn't include her?'

Clayton was stunned. 'She thought that?'

'She thought a million things! She was abandoned! Don't you get it? So maybe she's alive today because you agreed to live out the rest of your life with a monster. Do you think that makes you some kind of a hero? You know what? You're no hero. If you'd been a man from the get-go, maybe none of this would ever have happened.'

Clayton put his face into his hands, leaned against the door.

'Let me ask you this,' I said, a kind of calm coming over me. 'What kind of man stays with a woman who's murdered his own son? Can someone like that even be called a man? If it'd been me, I think I'd have killed her myself.'

We were at the window. I handed the guy some cash, took a bag with a couple of Egg McMuffins and hash browns, plus two coffees. I pulled ahead into a parking slot, reached into the bag, and tossed a breakfast sandwich into Clayton's lap.

I NEEDED SOME AIR and to stretch my legs for two seconds. Plus, I wanted to call home again. I took my cell out of my jacket, opened it up and glanced at the screen. I had a message.

'Terry, hi, it's me.' Cynthia. 'Where are you? Something's happened. Something totally unbelievable. We were staying at this motel, and I asked if I could use the computer in the office? I checked my mail, and there was another message, from that address, with the date? You know. And this time, there was a phone number to call. I called, and, Terry, you're not going to believe what's happened. It's the most amazing thing. It's my brother. My brother Todd. He told me he was the man at the mall, the man I thought was my brother. I was right! It was Todd! Terry, I knew it!'

I was feeling dizzy. The message continued:

'Todd said he was so sorry, that at the mall he couldn't admit who he was, but that he can explain everything. It's like a dream. I'm finally going to see Todd again. I hope you understand. I just can't wait. I have to go now. Call me when you get this. Grace and I are heading up to Winsted to see him now. Terry, it's like a miracle has happened.'

Winsted?

We were *in* Winsted. And Cynthia and Grace were *coming* to Winsted? I checked to see how long ago she'd left the message. Nearly three hours.

I started doing the maths. There was a very good chance Cynthia and Grace were already in Winsted. They could have been here as long as an hour, I guessed.

Why here? Why lure her up to this part of the state?

I punched in the numbers for Cynthia's cellphone. I had to stop her. She was walking into a trap. With Grace along for the ride.

I put the phone to my ear. Nothing. My phone was dead.

If she'd come to Winsted, she might still be around.

Where would be an easy place to rendezvous? The McDonald's, where we were parked, certainly. It's the first big thing you see when you come off the highway coming north.

I ran back to the car, got in. 'What's happening?' Clayton asked.

'There was a message from Cynthia. Jeremy called her, said he was Todd, asked her to meet him. Right here, in Winsted.'

I backed the Honda out of the spot, whipped through the McDonald's lot, looking for Cynthia's car. When I couldn't find it there, I jumped out of the car with the engine running, ran over to the drive-through window.

'Hey, pal, you can't be there,' the man at the window said.

'In the last hour or so, did you see a woman in a white Toyota Corolla—she'd have had a small girl with her?'

'You kidding me?' the man said, handing a bag of food to a motorist. 'You know how many people go through here?'

'What about a man with an elderly woman?' I said. 'A brown car. She'd have been in a wheelchair. No, there might have been a wheelchair in the back seat. Folded up.'

'Oh yeah,' he said. 'Actually, that does kind of ring a bell, but it was a long time ago, maybe an hour. I remember seeing the chair.'

I ran back to the Honda, got in next to Clayton. 'Jeremy and Enid were here.' I squeezed the steering wheel, let go, squeezed again, banged it with my fist. My head was ready to explode.

'You know where we are, right?' Clayton asked.

'What? Of course I know where we are.'

'You know what we passed on the way down. North of here, few miles. I recognised the road when we went past it.'

The road to the Fell's Quarry.

'Don't you see?' Clayton said. 'You'd have to know how Enid thinks but it makes perfect sense. Cynthia, along with your daughter, she finally ends up in the place Enid believes she should have been all these years. Maybe people'll think Cynthia was distraught over what had happened, the death of her aunt. So she drives up there and goes right over the edge.'

'But that's crazy,' I said. 'That might have worked at one time but not now. Not with other people knowing what's going on. Us. Vince. It's insane.'

'Exactly,' Clayton said. 'That's Enid.'

I nearly rammed the car into a Beetle as I drove out of the lot, heading back in the direction we'd come from.

I HAD THE CAR going over ninety.

'The glove box,' I said to Clayton. 'Open it up.'

He reached forward with some effort, opened the compartment, revealing the gun I'd taken from Vince's truck. He took it out, inspected it briefly.

'Hang on to that till we get there,' I said. Clayton nodded.

'If she's there,' he said, 'if we're in time, what do you think Cynthia will say to me?' He paused. 'I have to tell her I'm sorry.'

I glanced over at him. I could tell, from his expression, no matter how late it would be in coming, his apology would be genuine.

He was a man who needed to apologise for his entire life.

'Maybe,' I said, 'you'll have a chance.'

Clayton, even in his condition, saw the road to the quarry before I did. It was unmarked and so narrow, it would have been easy to drive right past it.

'Give me the gun,' I said, as we rolled down the lane.

The road started its steep climb up; the trees began to open up. Then the road started levelling out into a small clearing and at the far end of it, parked facing the cliff edge, were the brown Impala on the right and Cynthia's old white Corolla on the left.

Standing between them, looking back at us, was Jeremy Sloan. He had something in his right hand.

When he raised it, I could see that it was a gun, and when the windshield of our Honda shattered, I knew that it was loaded.

I SLAMMED ON THE BRAKES and threw the car into park in one fluid motion, undid my seat belt, opened the door and dived out. I knew I was leaving Clayton to fend for himself but, at this point, I was thinking only of Cynthia and Grace. I hit the ground and rolled into some high grass, then fired wildly into the sky. I wanted Jeremy to know I had a gun, too. I looked around frantically for him, then saw his head poking out round the Impala's front bumper.

'Jeremy!' I shouted.

'Terry!' Cynthia. Screaming. Her voice was coming from her car.

'Daddy!' Grace.

'I'm here!' I shouted.

From inside the Impala, another voice. 'Kill him, Jeremy! Shoot him!' Enid, sitting in the front passenger seat. 'Do what your mother says.'

'Mom,' Jeremy said, 'I don't know . . . I've never killed anyone before.'

'Suck it up! You're about to kill those two.' I could make out the back of Enid's head, see her motioning to Cynthia's car.

'Yeah, but all I have to do is push the car over. This is *different*.'

Clayton had the passenger door of the Honda open and was slowly getting to his feet.

'Get back in the car, Dad,' Jeremy said.

'What?' Enid said. 'He's here?' She caught sight of him in the passenger door mirror. 'You stupid old coot! Who let you out of the hospital?'

Slowly he shuffled his way towards the Impala. When he got to the back of the car, he placed his hands on the boot, steadied himself. He appeared to be on the verge of collapse. 'Don't do this, Enid,' he wheezed.

Then Cynthia's voice: 'Dad?'

'Hello, sweetheart,' he said. He tried to smile. 'I can't tell you how sorry I am about all this.'

'Dad?' she said again. Incredulous.

'Son,' Clayton said to Jeremy, 'you have to put an end to this. Your mother, she's wrong to drag you into this, make you do all these bad things. Look at her.' He was telling Jeremy to look at Cynthia. 'That's your sister.

Your sister. And that little girl, she's your niece.'

'Dad,' said Jeremy, still crouched around the front of the Impala, 'why are you leaving everything to her? You don't even know her. How could you be so mean to me and Mom?'

Clayton sighed. 'It's not always about the two of you,' he said.

'Jeremy!' I called out. 'Get rid of the gun. Give it up.'

He rose up from his hiding spot in front of the Impala, fired. Dirt kicked up just to my right and I instinctively rolled left.

I heard fast-moving steps along the gravel. Jeremy was running, closing in on me. I stopped rolling, aimed up at the figure closing in on me, fired. But it went wide, and before I could shoot again, Jeremy kicked at the gun, the toe of his shoe slamming into the back of my right hand. The gun flew off into the grass.

His next kick caught me in the side, in my rib cage. The pain shot through me like a bolt of lightning. I couldn't catch my breath. Jeremy stood over me, looking down with contempt.

'Shoot him!' Enid said.

He still had the gun in his hand, but he just stood there with it. Clayton, still using the car boot to support himself, looked at me, his eyes filled with sadness.

'Are you not listening?' Enid screamed. 'Shoot him!'

'Momma,' he said, 'maybe it makes more sense to put him in the car. With the others.'

She thought about that. 'No,' she said. 'That doesn't work. They have to go into the lake without him. It's better that way.'

Clayton, using his hands, one over the other, was moving up along the side of the Impala. He still appeared on the verge of collapse. 'I . . . I think I'm going to pass out,' he said.

'You stupid bastard!' Enid shouted at him. 'You should have stayed in the hospital and died there.'

Jeremy was forced to choose between keeping an eye on me and running over to help his father. He decided to attempt both.

'You don't move,' he said, keeping the gun pointed in my direction as he backstepped over to the Impala. He opened the driver's door. 'Sit down,' Jeremy said, glancing from his father to me and back again. Clayton shuffled the extra couple of steps, then slowly dropped himself into the seat.

I'd managed to struggle to my feet now and was coming up alongside

Cynthia's car. She was in the driver's seat, Grace next to her. I couldn't quite tell from where I was standing, but they were sitting so rigidly, they had to be tied in somehow.

'Honey,' I said.

Cynthia's eyes were bloodshot, her cheeks streaked with dried tears. 'He said he was Todd,' she told me. 'He's not Todd.'

'I know,' I said. 'I know. But that is your father.'

Cynthia looked to her right at the man sitting in the front of the Impala, then back to me. 'No,' she said. 'He might look like him, but he's not my father. Not any more.'

Clayton, who had heard the exchange, let his head fall towards his chest in shame. Without looking at Cynthia, he said, 'You're entitled to feel that way. All I can tell you is how sorry I am, but I'm not so old and foolish as to think you'll forgive.'

'You get away from the car,' Jeremy warned me, coming round the front of Cynthia's Corolla, the gun pointed my way. 'You stand back over there.'

'How could you do it?' Enid said to Clayton. 'How could you leave everything to that bitch? I give up my whole life for you and this is the thanks I get.'

'Hey, Mom,' Jeremy said. He was standing by Cynthia's door. 'Shouldn't they be untied? Doesn't it have to look like my . . . you know . . . like she did it on her own?'

'You know what?' Enid said, ignoring Jeremy and turning her attention to Clayton. 'You never appreciated anything I did for you. You were an ungrateful bastard from the moment I first met you.' Enid shook her head disapprovingly.

'Mom?' Jeremy said again. He had one hand on Cynthia's door, the other still pointing the gun at me.

And then I heard a car starting.

It was the Impala.

'What the hell are you doing?' Enid screamed at Clayton, who was still sitting in the driver's seat. 'Turn that off!'

But Clayton wasn't paying any attention. He turned, calmly, to his left. He had a small smile on his face. He looked almost serene. The Impala was right alongside Cynthia's Corolla, and he nodded at his daughter and said, 'I never, ever stopped loving you, or ever stopped thinking about you, and your mother, and Todd.'

'Clayton!' Enid screamed.

And then Clayton looked at Grace, her eyes just visible above the door. 'I wish I could have got to know you, Grace, but I know without a doubt that with a mother like Cynthia, you are very, very special.' Then Clayton gave his attention to Enid. 'So long, you miserable old bitch,' he said, and dropped the car into gear and hit the gas.

The engine roared. The Impala bolted forward towards the edge.

'Momma!' Jeremy screamed, and ran round the front of Cynthia's car and into the path of the Impala, as if he thought he could stop it with his own body.

The car threw Jeremy up onto the hood, and that's where he was when the Impala, with Clayton at the wheel and Enid screaming in the seat next to him, shot out over the edge.

It was about two seconds before we heard the splash.

I HAD TO MOVE Clayton's Honda out of the way to make room to get out of there in Cynthia's Corolla. She got in the back so she could sit with her arms round Grace for the long drive back south to Milford.

I knew we should probably have called the police, waited there at the top of the quarry for them to arrive, but we thought the most important thing was to get Grace home, where she would feel the most safe, as quickly as possible. Clayton and Enid and Jeremy weren't going anywhere.

We didn't talk a lot on the drive back. I think Cynthia and I were on the same page—that we didn't want to go over what had happened in front of Grace. She just needed to get home.

But I did manage to get the rough details. Cynthia and Grace had driven to Winsted, met Jeremy at McDonald's. He had a surprise, he told them. He had brought along his mother. The inference being that he had brought along Patricia Bigge.

Cynthia, dumbstruck, was taken over to the Impala, and once she and Grace were in the car, Enid held her gun on Grace. Told Cynthia to drive the car to the quarry, or she'd kill Grace. Jeremy followed in Cynthia's car.

Once on the precipice, Cynthia and Grace were tied into the front seats in preparation for their trip over the side.

Then Clayton and I arrived.

Almost as briefly, I told Cynthia what I'd learned. About my trip to Youngstown. Finding her father in the hospital. What happened the night her family disappeared. Vince Fleming getting shot.

Something still wasn't quite right. I couldn't shake the memory of Jeremy standing over me, gun in hand, unable to pull the trigger. He certainly hadn't shown that kind of hesitation where Tess Berman was concerned. Or Denton Abagnall.

What was it that Jeremy had said to his mother? While he stood over me? 'I've never killed anyone before.'

Yeah, that was it.

A COUPLE OF HOURS later, we were home. As we made the turn into our street, I saw Rona Wedmore's car in front of our house, parked at the kerb. When she spotted our car, she got out. She was waiting for me by the car when I opened my door.

Her expression softened when she saw me wince as I slowly got out of the driver's seat. I hurt like hell.

'What happened to you?' she asked. 'You look awful.'

'That's pretty much how I feel,' I said, touching one of my wounds gingerly. 'I took a few kicks from Jeremy Sloan.'

'Where is he?' Wedmore asked.

I opened the back door of the car and, even though a couple of my ribs felt as though they were about to snap, took a sleeping Grace into my arms to carry her into the house.

Cynthia ran ahead to unlock the front door. Rona Wedmore was trailing us into the house.

'I can't carry her any more,' I said, the pain becoming excruciating.

'The couch,' Cynthia said.

I managed to set her down there gently, even though I felt I was going to drop her. Despite all the jostling and talking, she didn't wake up. Wedmore was still just watching, courteously giving us a moment. Once Cynthia had tucked a blanket round Grace, the three of us went to the kitchen.

'Where's Sloan?' Wedmore asked again.

'You're going to need to call in your divers again,' I said.

I told her pretty much all of it. How Vince had spotted what was wrong with that old newspaper clipping, how that had led us to Sloan and Youngstown, my finding Clayton Sloan in the hospital, Jeremy and Enid's abduction of Cynthia and Grace. The car going over the cliff and down into the quarry, taking Clayton and Enid and Jeremy along for the ride.

There was only one small part I'd left out, because I wasn't sure what it meant. Although I had an inkling.

'Well,' Rona Wedmore said, 'that's quite a story.'

'It is,' I said. 'If I were going to make something up, trust me, I'd have come up with something more believable.'

Wedmore nodded silently. Then, 'I'll make some calls, see about the divers, be back later this afternoon.'

Wedmore left, and Cynthia said she was heading upstairs to try to make herself look half respectable again. Wedmore's car had only been gone a minute when I heard another one pull into the drive. I opened the front door as Rolly, wearing a long jacket, reached the step.

'Terry!' he said.

I put a finger to my lips. 'Grace is sleeping,' I said. I motioned for him to follow me into the kitchen.

'So you found them?' he said. 'Cynthia, too?'

I nodded.

'And you found her father,' Rolly said. 'You found Clayton. That's amazing, that Clayton's still alive, after all these years.'

'Aren't you wondering about Patricia, too? Or Todd? Aren't you curious to know what happened to them?'

Rolly's eyes danced. 'Of course, yes, I am. I mean, I already know they were found in the car, in the quarry.'

'Yeah, that's true. But everything else, who killed them, I figure you must already know about that,' I said. 'Otherwise, you'd have asked.'

Rolly's look grew grim.

'Rolly,' I said, 'were you the one who delivered the money?'

'What?'

'The money. For Tess. To spend on Cynthia. It was you, wasn't it?'

He licked his lip nervously. 'What did Clayton tell you?'

'What do you think he told me?'

Rolly turned away from me. 'He's told you everything, hasn't he? The son of a bitch. He swore he'd never tell.' He shook his head in anger. 'I'm so close. So close to retirement. He's told you about Connie Gormley, hasn't he? About the accident?'

I didn't say anything.

'We were coming back from a fishing trip,' Rolly said. 'It was Clayton's idea to stop for a beer. We went into this bar, and this girl, she starts coming on to me, you know? She's had a few beers, and I ended up having a few more. I don't know what the hell happened. This Connie and I, we both slip out of the bar, end up out back of the bar in the back seat of her car.'

'How'd she end up going from that back seat to that ditch?'

'When we were done, and I was heading back to the bar, she asked me for fifty bucks. I told her if she was a hooker, she should have made that clear from the outset. She started scrapping with me by the car, and I guess I shoved back, a little too hard, and she tripped, and her head came down on the bumper, and that was it.'

'She was dead,' I said.

Rolly swallowed. 'People had seen us, right? In the bar? They might remember me and Clayton. I figured, if she got hit by a car instead, the police would think it was some sort of accident.'

I was shaking my head.

'Terry,' he said, 'if you'd been in that situation, you'd have been panicking, too. I got Clayton, told him what I'd done, and there was something in his face, like he felt he was as trapped by the situation as I was; he didn't want to be talking to any cops. I didn't know then, about the kind of life he was living, that he wasn't who he claimed to be. That he was living a double life. So we put her in the car, took her down the highway; then Clayton held her up at the side of the road, tossed her in front of the car as I drove past. Then we put her in the ditch.'

'My God,' I said.

'Isn't a night goes by I don't think about it, Terry. It was a horrible thing.' He shook his head again. 'Clayton swore he'd never tell. The son of a bitch.'

'He didn't,' I said. 'I tried to get him to, but he didn't give you up. But let me see if I can guess how the rest of this goes. One night, Clayton and Patricia and Todd, they disappear. Then one day a few years later, you get a call. It's Clayton. Quid pro quo time. He covered up for you, for killing Connie Gormley; now he wanted you to do something for him. Be a courier, basically. Deliver money. He'd send it to you. And then you'd slip it to Tess, drop it in her car, hide it in her newspaper, whatever.'

Rolly stared at me.

'Yeah,' he said. 'That's more or less what happened.'

'And then, like an idiot,' I said, 'I told you what Tess had revealed to me. About the money. About how she still had the envelopes and the letter.'

Now Rolly had nothing to say.

I came at him from another direction. 'Do you think a man who was prepared to murder two people to please his mother would lie to her about whether he'd ever killed anyone before?'

'What? What the hell are you talking about?' Rolly said.

'I'm kind of thinking out loud here. I'm talking about Jeremy Sloan. Clayton's son, from the other marriage, with the other woman, Enid. I figured Jeremy had killed Tess. And I figured he'd killed Abagnall. But now, I'm not so sure about that any more.'

Rolly swallowed.

'Did you go and see Tess after I told you what she had told me?' I asked. 'Were you afraid that maybe she'd figured it out? Were you worried that maybe the letters she still had, the envelopes, that maybe they might still carry some forensic evidence linking them to you? And that if that happened, then you'd be linked to Clayton and he wouldn't be obliged to keep your secret any longer?'

'I didn't want to kill her,' Rolly said. 'But I thought she was dying anyway. And then, later, after I'd done it, you told me how she wasn't dying after all.'

'Rolly . . .'

'She'd given the letter and the envelopes to the detective,' he said.

'And you took his business card from the bulletin board,' I said.

'I called him, arranged a meeting, in the parking garage.'

'You killed him and took his briefcase with the papers inside,' I said. I looked down at the floor. I felt a tremendous sadness. 'Rolly, you've been such a good friend for so many years. I don't know, maybe I'd be willing to keep my mouth shut about a horrible lapse in judgment more than twenty-five years ago. You probably never meant to kill Connie Gormley; it was just one of those things.'

He eyed me warily.

'But Tess. You killed my wife's aunt. Wonderful, sweet Tess. And you didn't stop with her. There's no way I can let that go.'

He reached into the pocket of the long coat and pulled out a gun. 'Go upstairs, Terry,' he said.

'You can't be serious,' I said.

'I've already bought my trailer,' he said. 'It's all set. I've picked out a boat. I deserve a decent retirement.'

He motioned me towards the stairs, followed me up them.

'What's going on?' Cynthia called from Grace's room.

I stepped into the room, followed by Rolly. Cynthia, over by Grace's desk, opened her mouth when she saw the gun, but no words came out.

'It was Rolly,' I said. 'He killed Tess. And Abagnall.'

'What? I don't believe it.'

'Ask him.'

'Shut up,' Rolly said.

Cynthia was flushed, her eyes wide. Too many shocks for one day. She lost it. She screamed and charged at him, but Rolly was ready, swinging the gun into her face, catching her across the cheek, knocking her to the floor by Grace's desk.

I thought I could take him at that moment, but he had the gun back on me. 'God, Terry, I hate to have to do this. I really do. Sit down. Sit on the bed there.'

He took a step forward, and I sat down on the edge of Grace's bed. Cynthia was still on the floor, blood running down towards her neck from the gash in her cheek.

'Toss me a pillow,' he said.

So that was the plan. Put a pillow over the muzzle of the gun, cut down on the noise. I glanced over at Cynthia. She had one hand just under Grace's desk. She looked at me and nodded ever so slightly. She was saying, *Trust me.*

I reached for a pillow at the top of Grace's bed. I tossed it to Rolly, but I made my throw just a bit short and he had to take half a step forward to catch it.

That's when Cynthia got to her feet. 'Sprung' would be a better word. She had something in her hand. Something long and black.

Grace's piece-of-crap telescope.

Cynthia first swung it back over her own shoulder, giving herself a chance to build up some speed; then she came at Rolly's head with her famous backhand, putting everything she had into it and a little bit more.

He turned, saw it coming, but he never had a chance to react. She caught him across the side of his skull and it didn't sound much like something you'd hear at a tennis match. It was more like the crack of a bat hitting a fastball. It was a home run.

Rolly Carruthers dropped like a stone. It was a wonder Cynthia didn't kill him.

12

'OK,' said Cynthia, 'so you know the deal?'

Grace nodded. She had her backpack ready. Her lunch was in there, her homework, even a cellphone. Cynthia had insisted and I'd put up no argument.

'So what do you do?'

'When I get to school, I call you.'

'That's right,' said Cynthia.

Grace smiled. That was fine with her. Being able to walk to school unescorted, even if she had to call home when she got there, made the deal pretty attractive to her.

We both gave her hugs goodbye, then we stood in the window watching her as long as we could, until she turned the corner.

Rolly was still recovering from one hell of a concussion. He was in the hospital. That made him easy to find when Rona Wedmore showed up to charge him with the murders of Tess Berman and Denton Abagnall. The Connie Gormley case had been reopened, too, but that one was going to be a bit trickier to prove.

I had to get my ribs all taped up, and the doctor says Cynthia will probably need plastic surgery on her cheek. As for emotional scars, well, who knows?

Vince Fleming was transferred from the hospital in Lewiston to the one here in Milford. He's going to be OK. I visited him the other day, and he said Jane better end up with straight As. I told him I was on it.

The phone rang. Cynthia had the receiver in her hand before the first ring finished. 'OK . . . OK,' she said. 'You're OK? No problems? OK . . . Bye.'

She hung up. 'Grace's OK,' she said.

'That's what I figured,' I said. 'You OK?'

Cynthia grabbed a tissue, dabbed at her eyes. 'Yeah. You want some coffee?'

'Sure,' I said. 'Pour us some. I have to get something.'

I went to the front hall closet, dug into the pocket of the jacket I'd been wearing that night when everything happened, and pulled out the envelope.

I came back into the kitchen, where Cynthia was sitting with her coffee.

She saw the envelope. 'What's that?'

I sat down, holding on to it.

'I was waiting for the right time and I think this is it,' I said.

Cynthia had the look you get when you're expecting bad news from your doctor.

'It's OK,' I said. 'Clayton, your father, he explained this to me, wanted me to explain it to you.'

'What?'

'That night, after you had that big fight with your parents and you went up to bed, I guess you kind of passed out. Anyway, your mom, Patricia, she felt bad. From what you've said, she didn't like it when things were bad between the two of you.'

'No, she didn't,' Cynthia whispered. 'She liked to smooth things over as soon as she could.'

'Well, I guess that was what she wanted to do, so she wrote you . . . a note. She put it out in front of your door, before she left to take Todd to the drugstore.'

Cynthia couldn't take her eyes off the envelope in my hands.

'Anyway, your father, he wasn't feeling quite so conciliatory, not yet. He was thinking it was too soon to smooth things over. So after your mother left, he went back upstairs and he took the note that she'd left for you and stuffed it into his pocket.'

Cynthia was frozen.

'But then, given what happened over the next few hours, it turned out to be more than just some note. It was your mom's last note to her daughter.' I paused. 'And so he saved it, just in case, some day, he'd be able to give it to you.'

I handed the envelope, already torn open at one end, across the table to Cynthia.

She slid the paper out of the envelope and opened it up.

I had already read it. So I knew Cynthia was reading the following:

Hi Pumpkin:

I'll probably be fast asleep when you get up and find this. I hope you haven't made yourself too sick. You did some pretty stupid things tonight. I guess that's what being a teenager is about.

I wish I could say these are the last stupid things you'll do, or that this is the last fight you'll have with me and your father, but that wouldn't be the truth. You'll do more stupid stuff and we'll have more fights. Sometimes you'll be wrong; sometimes maybe even we'll be wrong.

But here's the one thing you have to know. No matter what, I will always love you. There's nothing you could ever do that would make me stop. Because I'm in this for the long haul with you. And that's the truth.

And it's always going to be that way. Even when you're on your own, living your own life, even when you've got a husband and kids of your own (imagine that!), even when I'm nothing but dust, I'll always be watching you.

Some day, maybe you'll think you feel someone looking over your shoulder, and you'll look round and no one's there. That'll be me. Watching out for you, watching you make me so very, very proud. Your whole life, kiddo. I will always be with you.

Love,
Mom

I watched Cynthia as she read it to the end, and then I held her while she wept.

LINWOOD BARCLAY

Home: near Toronto, Ontario
Status: married with two adult children
Website: www.linwoodbarclay.com

RD: What was the starting point for this book?

LB: I was thinking about a true story of a family who awoke one day to find that their daughter had gone missing from their home in the middle of the night, and I thought: what if you reversed it? What if a young girl awoke to find all the members of her family gone, without a trace?

RD: And, after that, how did you proceed?

LB: Once you come up with a premise, you have to work out how it all happened. It's a bit like—this may be a bit of stretch—like coming up with a spectacular roof design first. Before you can get it up there, you need to build a solid foundation and supporting structure. Another answer: when I'm working out a plot's finer points, I leave the study and go cut the lawn. It's a great way to work out story problems.

RD: Are the characters based on anyone? I'm thinking particularly of Terry.

LB: My sensibilities about a lot of things probably come through in Terry, particularly since the book, all but the first chapter, is written in the first person. Most of the other characters are pure invention, and the true identities of any who *are* based on real people shall remain secret so as to protect, well, me!

RD: Where were you brought up and what was your upbringing like?

LB: I was born in Darien, Connecticut, but in 1959, when I was four, my parents moved to the suburbs of Toronto. Then, in the late 1960s, they bought a cottage in a resort/trailer park in the Kawarthas region of Ontario, and we moved up there. I wrote a book about it in 2000 called *Last Resort: Coming of Age in Cottage Country*.

RD: And where are you based now?

LB: We're half an hour from Toronto, which offers everything you could want from a city, and a couple of hours from beautiful vacation country. We have it all here, plus George W. Bush is not our president.

RD: Did you always want to write?

LB: Yes. I was filling entire school notebooks with stories by Grade 3. Of course, they were double-spaced and the handwriting was huge.

RD: You have three strands to your career: public speaking, filing a regular column for the *Toronto Star* and writing novels and humour books. How do you fit it all in?

LB: It's been a bit hectic. I've written six novels in the last five years on top of three columns a week for the *Toronto Star* and a busy speaking schedule. This coming year I'm going to ease up on speeches, and I'm taking a year's leave of absence from the *Star* so that I can focus on my next couple of books.

RD: Is there one thing you enjoy doing most, or do you like the variety?

LB: I do enjoy the variety. And the speaking is fun because it not only gets me out of the house but allows me to meet lots of interesting people from different backgrounds.

RD: How did you get into public speaking?

LB: In the mid 90s, my columns mocking our provincial premier-of-the-day here in Ontario, who was attacking hard-working teachers and gutting school budgets for political gain, sparked many invitations to speak to educational organisations. Word of the funny, self-deprecating stories I told in those speeches spread, and I ended up being asked to speak to all sorts of groups. I was even the featured speaker at a convention of folks who run parking lots. How many writers can say that? Who knew that parking-lot operators had an association and an annual convention?

RD: Where do you like to write?

LB: In my study at home, surrounded by books, my late father's beautiful paintings of 1950s-era cars—he was a commercial artist whose work appeared in *Life*, *Look*, *Saturday Evening Post*, etc., back in the 1950s before car advertisements turned to photography—and an assortment of toys such as trains, cars, sci-fi kitsch and replicas of spaceships from 1960s Gerry Anderson puppet shows.

RD: Do you have a routine?

LB: Nothing formal, but I'm in my study first thing in the morning. When I'm not on leave from the *Star*, my priority is the column. I'm reading through the papers, reading news online, looking for inspiration. When that's out of the way, I shift gears and work on a book, if I'm doing one at the time.

RD: What's the best thing about being a writer?

LB: You have no one to blame but yourself. Or maybe that's the worst thing!

RD: Do you have any unfulfilled ambitions?

LB: I think things are unfolding very nicely for me these days.

RD: You've been married for over twenty-five years. What would you say is the secret of a long and happy marriage?

LB: Maintaining a sense of humour, never taking your partner for granted, and resisting the temptation to lift the lid on stuff your wife is cooking to give it a stir.

THE OVERLOOK © Hieronymous, Inc 2007
Published by Orion

THE LAST TESTAMENT © Jonathan Freedland 2007
Published by HarperCollins

LEFT FOR DEAD © Nick Ward and Sinéad O'Brien 2007
Published by A & C Black

NO TIME FOR GOODBYE © Linwood Barclay 2007
Published by Orion

The right to be identified as authors has been asserted by the following in accordance with sections 77 and 78 of the Copyright, Designs and Patents Act, 1988: Michael Connelly, Jonathan Freedland, Nick Ward and Sinéad O'Brien, Linwood Barclay.

Illustrations, Photos and Acknowledgments:
Page 4–5: Michael Connelly © Mogjam Azimi; Sam Bourne © Krestine Havemann; Nick Ward © Simon Ward; Linwood Barclay © David Cooper.
The Overlook: 6–8: image: Narrinder Singh@velvet tamarind; page 144 © Mogjam Azimi; 145 Chuck Stewart/Redferns.
The Last Testament: 146–48: image: Glow images; page 326 © Krestine Havemann.
Left for Dead: 328–30: image: Richard Bennett Pictures; 436: 1: Miss Eileen Ramsay by kind permission. 2 and 3: Stanley Ward. 4: William Payne. 437: 5, 6 & 7: Nick Ward. 8: Chris Ward. Extract from the Fastnet Race Inquiry 1979 published by The Royal Yachting Association and the Royal Ocean Racing Club.
No Time for Goodbye: 438–40: image: Photonica; 574: © David Cooper.

Dustjacket spine: image: Richard Bennett Pictures.

Printed and bound by GGP Media GmbH, Pössneck, Germany

020-251 DJ0000-1